I0819854

the sound of his *Whisper*

Book One of the Pacific Coves Series

Eleni James

Selah Publishing Co.

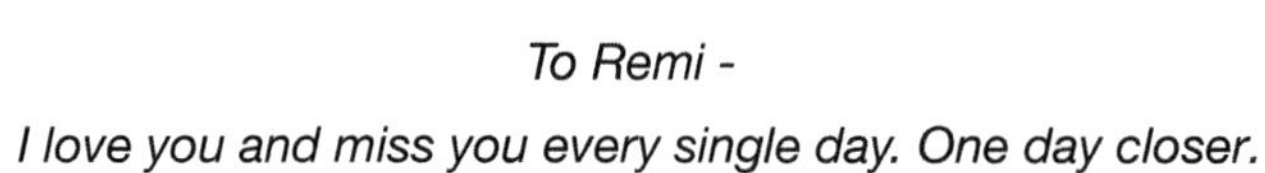

To Remi -

I love you and miss you every single day. One day closer.

Content Advisory:

This book has descriptive scenes of a miscarriage, the birth of the baby, and the grief that follows. It includes anxiety, depression, and dark thoughts.

If you, or someone you know, has lost a baby to miscarriage or stillbirth, my thoughts and prayers are with you. I too have lost three children during pregnancy, my last being born while I was 15 weeks pregnant. The pain is unimaginable. May all their memories be eternal.

If you, or someone you know, is struggling with suicidal thoughts or even struggling with harmful thoughts, please call 988.

Playlist

- Coastline by Hollow Coves (inspired the location)
    - Us by James Bay (Hello first night together <3)
    - All of Me by John Legend (I will forever love this scene)
    - Perfect by Ed Sheeran
    - Movement by Hozier (Shower Scene IFYKYK)
    - Falling Up by Dean Lewis
    - Happiest Year by Jaymes Young
    - Lose My Mind by Dean Lewis
    - Someone You Loved by Lewis Capaldi
    - Pray by JRY
    - Hold On by Chord Overstreet (oof...this song hits me)
    - Wild Love by James Bay
    - Betting On Us by Myles Smith
    - No Matter What by Jamie Miller
    - Don't Give Up on Me by Andy Grammer
    - Turning Page by Sleeping At Last
    - The Night We Met by Lord Huron
    - The Woods by Hollow Coves (chapter sixty-four)

- Last Man Standing by Livingston
- High, High, High by Camylio
- The Hardest Love by Dean Lewis
- Home by Myles Smith
- Work Song by Hozier

Chapter One

February

The meeting was dragging on, and all I could think about was getting out of here. Just thirty more minutes and I would be on my way to meet up with my two *new* friends, Natalie and Grey, for drinks at the new bar in town - Sapphire. It was their opening night.

I scribbled circles on my notes more and more, almost as if I couldn't find a place for them to end. Mr. Whitney, my boss and the CEO of Hope International was droning on about some legal hiccups we have encountered with a few of our placements. I let out a long sigh before setting my pen down. If I didn't stop now, my whole notepad would soon be covered in an unending geometric pattern. I checked my watch: twenty-nine minutes to go.

I usually considered myself a patient person, but today was different. My stomach was in knots, and I felt a restless weight pressing down on my chest. It was a mix of nervousness and excitement, though I couldn't pinpoint the reason behind it. Nothing significant had happened since I moved to the quiet coastal town of Pacific Coves three months ago.

Before leaving Seattle four months ago, I needed to wrap up my past. I sold my home, said goodbye to the few friends I had, and informed Diane, the Chief Administrative Officer at my parents' company, Caston, that I was interested in selling my share of the business. My parents had left half of Caston to me. Unfortunately, I needed to sever all ties and start fresh. I am now the communications director for Hope International, a small non-profit organization.

My phone buzzed loudly against the glass table, drawing everyone's attention. I glanced at it and then smiled sheepishly at the people around me.

"Sorry," I muttered, quickly grabbing my phone and silencing it. I placed it in my lap and looked back up to let everyone know I was still listening. After a few more minutes, as everyone seemed to forget about my phone going off, I glanced down to see who had texted me.

My heart nearly stopped. I couldn't tell if I felt excited or nauseous. It was Brooks Devonshire. I hadn't spoken to my ex-boyfriend since we broke up during my freshman year of college. Once, I had imagined marrying Brooks and starting a family with him, but life took unexpected turns that ultimately led to our breakup. My head spun as I tried to control my breathing, but I failed. Once again, everyone's eyes were on me.

"I'm sorry, Mr. Whitney," I said breathlessly. "I need to step out. I... I don't feel so well."

"Emily, go ahead and leave. We'll see you next week. Have a good weekend, and I hope you feel better." His voice was compassionate but clearly exasperated. I stood up, grabbing my computer, notes, and water bottle. In my rush, I nearly forgot my purse and quickly glanced around to find it. My breathing was still uneven as I hurried out of the conference room and into the large glass lobby of our coworking building.

"Are you okay, Miss Barlow?" a voice asked from my left.

"What?" I turned, confused. It was Audrey, my assistant. I nodded back at her for reassurance.

"Just fine," I lied.

"Have a good weekend," Audrey replied, nodding as she turned back the way she came.

My palm throbbed from gripping my phone tightly. I hadn't thought to read the text message yet. I scanned the beautiful, modern lobby for an open seat and went to the nearest one, nearly stumbling as I walked.

I hurriedly packed my laptop and notes into my bag and slid into the chair. Closing my eyes, I took another deep breath. What did Brooks want? Was it a mistake? I picked up my phone and, taking a deep breath, opened the message.

Brooks: Hey Emily, is this still your number?

Really? Is that it? Not, "Hi Emily, lost love of my life, I'm sorry"? My heart sank. I don't know what I expected, but it certainly wasn't this. I had been nursing a broken heart for years, hoping we could work things out. Now, he doesn't even know if this is my number.

I put my phone back in my lap and leaned my head into my palms. My stomach was still recovering from its recent gymnastic routine. *I could choose not to respond. I could wait a few days and torture him with my silence.* A small giggle escaped me at that thought. Who was I kidding, though? That wasn't me. I looked at my phone again, trying to decide if I could actually respond. I wanted to —I had a lot to say—but I couldn't. Not now.

I glanced at the time. Shoot, I needed to get going before the meeting ended, before everyone piled out of the conference room, noticing I was just sitting here. I stood quickly, grabbed my bag, and rushed out of the building to my car.

Once in the car, I called Natalie right away to complain about the text from Brooks. The phone trilled loudly over the speakers. I hesitated the moment she answered. I hadn't unpacked my previous relationships and past with her yet. Our friendship had only formed over the past few months. Still, this didn't seem like the right time to unload on her.

"Hey, Emily!" she answered, her excitement evident. Maybe that was why we got along. Everyone had always told me I used too many exclamation marks and was overly optimistic, so why didn't I feel that way right now?

"Hey. I just got out of work. Should I meet you there, or do you want me to pick you up?" I asked as I backed out of my parking spot.

"Eh, let's just meet there. You should ask Grey, though. I'm sure he would be happy to drive with you." She ended with a giggle, reminding me of those times in school when girls teased you over a crush while singing, "Sitting in a tree...k-i-s-s-i-n-g."

"Grey, Grey," I muttered to myself.

"Emily, come on! He's cute and totally in love with you. Everyone can see it." The tightening in my chest made me want to turn back home instead, but I was a big girl, right?

"I know," I groaned, feeling heat rush to my chest. "I just don't know if I have any feelings for him. I see him as just a friend, and it's..."

"Your choice, but he's pretty much the only hot, young, eligible bachelor in Pacific Coves, and he's rich," she interrupted. I could hear her smiling on the other end. I rolled my eyes but couldn't help grinning like an idiot. Grey was undeniably good-looking. His dark hair, bright blue eyes, and charming smile could take anyone's breath away.

"Okay, okay," I said, letting out a breath I hadn't realized I was holding. "I'll call him."

"See you there!" she responded excitedly before ending the call.

Natalie had become a great friend over the past three months. As I drove down Main Street, I called Grey. Workers were removing Valentine's Day decorations from the street lamps, and shop owners were wiping off the paint from their windows.

I never thought I would enjoy small-town life, but living here felt right. I could still hold onto a happy part of my childhood while leaving behind painful memories. Grey answered on the first ring.

"Hey, Emily!" His voice radiated warmth and assurance. He was just a friend, but there was something more.

"Hey! Want to ride together? I got off early, and Natalie said she'd meet us there!"

"I can drive. Would you prefer I pick you up, or should we meet at my place?"

"I'll come to you." I felt a confusing blend of emotions stir within me. We had undeniable chemistry, but I wasn't ready to jump into another relationship.

"Awesome! See you soon?" he asked enthusiastically.

"I'll be there in about ten minutes."

My hands gripped the steering wheel tightly. Grey was sweet, but my last relationship ended poorly because of Brooks. Why was he texting me anyway? I ran through several potential responses in my mind. Still, none seemed good enough to express everything I wanted and needed to say, probably because I wasn't sure of his motives. Then my thoughts shifted back to Grey. He was much less complicated. So what if things didn't work out with my last boyfriend, Parker? Grey was different—a fresh start in a new town with no connections to Brooks.

Grey Stanley is a complete sweetheart and a nerd beneath his hot, faux bad-boy exterior. He mentioned that very few people know the "real" him, and I suppose I'm one of those lucky few.

He's a few years older than me, born and raised in New Haven, Connecticut, and he's the only child of a senator. After earning his master's degree from Stanford, he landed a job as an app developer for a company in San Francisco. However, he loves Oregon and spends half the year in our little town of Pacific Coves. He's the constant talk of the town, and I find myself first in line to capture his heart — that is, if I want it at all.

As I guided my car into the parking lot, a sense of excitement filled me. Grey lived in the beautiful Austen Luxury Condos, a shining addition to our town. After taking a deep breath, I stepped out, ready for the moment. Just as I closed the door, I turned and found myself embraced by Grey's strong, welcoming presence.

"Hey," he chuckled, his arms catching me. *Oh crap*

"Oh, hey," I chuckled, a little embarrassed. "Didn't see you there."

I let my eyes rake over him, and heat spread through my core despite the platonic friendship I had hoped for with him. He wore a charcoal Tom Ford suit paired with a crisp white button-down. The top button was undone, revealing just enough of his tanned skin and a hint of chest hair. I inhaled sharply, filled with the scent of his Armani cologne.

He always looked and smelled incredible and had a way of taking my breath away. When I looked up into his iceberg-blue eyes, my earlier embarrassment faded away. He flashed me his warm, white smile, and Grey wrapped his muscular arm around my shoulders as we turned to walk into his building.

"C'mon," he said, pressing a kiss into my hair.

A small smile lifted on the corner of my mouth. But did I really just want a platonic relationship? One of the things that caught my attention was how unapologetically himself he is. While the other men sport Patagonia gear and drive 4Runners, Grey opts for tailored suits and designer clothes. That, along with his Audi sports car, is something I admire about him—his confidence, that is.

Grey released me from his arm to open the door to his condo. Once we stepped inside, the scent of sandalwood and vanilla enveloped me, prompting a deep breath of appreciation.

"Your house always smells so good," I said with a big grin. He chuckled as he glanced over at me.

"I just need to grab my keys. I forgot to bring them down with me," he replied.

He walked to his room, and I turned to take in the spacious, open area. His style was slightly edgier than mine, and I ran my hand along the back of his black leather couch.

The last time I was here, Grey and I watched a movie, and he was pretty clear about his intentions. By the end of the movie, his mouth was just inches from mine, inviting me to lean in for more. When he moved in for a kiss, I turned my cheek and bought myself some extra time. I rushed home that night, feeling a whirlwind of emotions, and had to reconsider my priorities.

I don't understand why I have this hang-up. Grey would probably ask me out tomorrow if I could stop overthinking things. But my mind is never quiet; it constantly reminds me that heartbreak is just a few steps away.

I glanced at a black-and-white photo hanging on the exposed brick wall, just above a row of vinyl records and a record player. The photo depicted a man playing piano on a New York City sidewalk. Grey loved music, movies, and cars—typical. For some reason, that annoyed me. He usually spent his weekends in San Francisco, attending clubs with pretty models, high society, and trust-fund friends. He drives Audis and races through town, knowing he can easily talk his way out of a ticket. I was attracted to his confidence but disliked his arrogant, flashy lifestyle.

Don't get me wrong, I had a trust fund and a large house, but I never felt the need to show off.

"Are you ready?" he asked, his eyes raking up and down my body. I had chosen a white sweater dress that stopped halfway down my thighs, paired with knee-high taupe boots and my camel coat for work today, knowing I would be heading to the club afterward.

"Yep," I nodded and turned toward the door, feeling a stirring low in my belly. His hand rested on my lower back, causing my heart to race. Was this a good thing or a bad thing? I still couldn't figure out why my body reacted to him this way, and right now, I was unwilling to investigate the reason. The door closed behind us, and before I knew it, we were in front of his black Audi.

The car roared to life, and my right hand gripped the seat as it jerked out of the garage and into traffic. I closed my eyes to shut out the dizzying blur of buildings rushing by. The sweet, heartbreaking voice of Dean Lewis—my new favorite indie artist—sang about lost love, temporarily distracting me from how he weaved in and out of traffic. When did he start listening to him? Grey typically preferred rock bands like the Rolling Stones and Red Hot Chili Peppers.

"Is it necessary to drive like this?" I groaned, trying not to sound rude.

"I can slow down." He glanced over and noticed my tight grip on the seat. His foot lifted off the pedal, and the car slowed to the actual speed limit.

"Is that better?" he asked.

I nodded, feeling the tension begin to leave my body.

"When did you start listening to Dean Lewis?" I asked, surprised.

"Uh, I don't. I just know you do."

Right. I returned to staring out the window.

My phone buzzed in my purse, and I quickly pulled it out to see if Natalie had beaten us there. It was another text from Brooks.

> Brooks: I'm sorry Emily. I just need to talk to you. Please call me.

"Great. He did know it was me," I muttered. I glanced over at Grey, who was looking at me curiously.

"Everything okay?" he asked.

"What? Yeah, of course. Why?" I hadn't meant for my response to come out so rushed.

He chuckled again. "Huh, well, it's just that your face looks like you've seen a ghost." Because I have, or at least I have, a text from one.

"Oh," I sputtered, releasing an exaggerated breath. "It's nothing. Just an old friend." It wasn't a lie. Brooks had been my friend before he was my boyfriend. Plus, a boyfriend—or ex—is still an old friend, right?

"From college?"

"Umm," I gulped. "Nope, from my childhood." My stomach twisted into a knot.

He turned his focus back to the road, so I guessed he wasn't going to press the issue. I turned back to my phone, realizing there was no avoiding him now. My heart raced as I typed out a message.

Emily: Out with friends. Call you later?

Brooks: ...

His response took forever, and before I knew it, we were pulling up to Sapphire.

Grey opened his door and stepped out. I looked back at my phone. Still no response. I sighed and tossed my phone into my purse just as Grey opened my door. I unbuckled my seatbelt and reached out, placing my hand in his as he helped me out of the car. He pulled me into his chest and wrapped his arms around me, hugging me. I allowed myself to forget everything momentarily and enjoyed being in his embrace. His scent was intoxicating, and a small ache in my heart urged me to let him in.

"C'mon," he whispered into my hair as he turned to lead me to the front doors.

The large blue doors opened as we walked inside. The room was dimly lit, with a huge dance floor at the center. A large glass chandelier hung above it, and small uplights softly illuminated the surrounding walls. The bar area was packed with people, and the frosted bar top was covered with cocktails.

"Wow," I gasped. Everything was so elegant and moody yet still fun. The room featured sapphire blue velvet furniture intermingled with soft gold metal accents. I spun around, taking it all in, and my gaze settled back on Grey, who was watching me. I giggled nervously; in this lighting, he was definitely more handsome than I had allowed myself to see.

"Hey!" Natalie exclaimed as she squeezed me from behind.

"Hey, Natalie!" I squealed in response.

"This place looks amazing. C'mon, Darrien saved us a spot," she said, pulling me along.

"Who's Darrien?" I asked.

"Oh, he's the manager. A friend of mine. That's how I knew about this place," she laughed as we made our way through the crowd.

Across the room, three sunken sitting areas opened up to the dance floor. Each area featured a couch wrapped around its edges, with a gold coffee table at the center. Sheer curtains were pulled to either side, ready to be closed for more privacy.

The club was loud, making it difficult to hear without shouting over the music. The DJ stood in the corner, a headset pulled up to one ear as he danced to the beat he was remixing.

We were in the middle of discussing our days when the waitress came by.

"Hi, can I get your drink order?" the waitress asked.

I glanced up at her. She was pretty and wore a form-fitting blue bodycon dress.

"Er, I'll take a glass of Pinot Grigio," I answered.

"What? No, come on, Emily. She will have a Lemon Drop, and I will start with a Cosmo." Natalie winked at me. I rolled my eyes. I wasn't a huge drinker, but Natalie knew it would take a few drinks to get me out on the dance floor. Plus, with her Type 1 diabetes, she would only have one drink tonight.

"I'll take a Gin and Tonic. Bombay with lime, please," Grey ordered. The waitress smiled flirtatiously back at him. Grey's hand slid onto my knee, and I could see the waitress's eyes widen in surprise.

"Okay, thanks, I'll be back," she said, turning red. Wow. Grey had recently become more affectionate, and selfishly, I didn't want to say no. I was still figuring out where I saw us in the future. For now, I liked the attention.

I looked at Grey's hand on my knee and then up at him. My skin tingled beneath his touch, and I found myself imagining his hands exploring me further. I sighed and tried to push the thought out of my mind. Not tonight.

"Was that necessary?" I chuckled, pulling his hand into mine.

"Emily," he purred, brushing my hair out of my face.

Our eyes met, and I felt an urge to kiss him. Before I could overthink it, his lips were pressed against mine. An instant scream of "no" erupted in my head, making it clear that this wasn't going to work, and I couldn't hurt him. I pulled back quickly, blushing.

Damn you, Brooks Devonshire. Give me my heart back. Would there be another man on this planet that could make me happier than Brooks?

"Sorry," he whispered.

"No, it's okay. I just don't know if I'm ready for a relationship. Sorry." I turned away from him, unable to meet his gaze. I knew my words would hurt him. Natalie watched me with curiosity, so I looked up and smiled softly at her.

Just then, my purse lit up as my phone buzzed. I reached down to pull it out and saw that it was a message from Brooks. His timing was impeccable, and I couldn't help but groan in annoyance.

> Brooks: I'm headed to bed. It's late here. Are you available for a quick call? If not, call me tomorrow. I'm in England, so the time difference is 8 hours.

My curiosity was getting the best of me.

"I'm sorry," I began, looking up at Natalie and then over to Grey. "I need to make a quick call." I stood up and hurried out the front door. I wasn't expecting the sun to be setting when I stepped outside. The two tall pillars flanking the doorway were illuminated with fire, and the bouncer was busy checking IDs as I slipped past him.

I found a quiet spot beside the building and called Brooks. My heart raced, and my stomach churned. I closed my eyes, trying to take a deep breath of the fresh coastal air. I hadn't heard his voice in so long.

"Hey, Em," he said, his voice rough and deep on the other end. The way my name rolled off his lips felt like it always belonged there.

"Hey, B," I whispered, feeling my heart leap into my throat. I shook my head, trying to get it together.

"Sorry to interrupt your evening. I just wanted to let you know I'm heading back to Seattle to step in at Caston. Can we meet up when I'm back in town? I need to talk to you about Caston."

"Uh, I live in Pacific Coves now."

"You do? Huh? I mean, I can come to you." His voice hitched up a pitch higher than usual.

"Yeah, sure. I have a guest house. Just let me know when." Shit. *Did I just invite him to stay?*

"Sounds good. I mean, probably not for another few weeks. I have to fly to Seattle to handle some things, but then I can head down." The tightness in my heart reminded me of how badly he had hurt me.

"Are you sure you need to come down? We can just do a Zoom call."

"Emily, I need to do this in person." There was a finality in his voice. He sounded so mature, older. I guess he was. We weren't high schoolers anymore.

"Fine. Yeah, sure, just let me know."

I brushed my foot against the concrete. Brooks was going to come and stay with me. *Well, this should be interesting.* I bit my lip and turned, staring into the sea of cars. It had been seven years since I had last seen him in person.

"Have you talked to Diane? I believe she was going to tell you that I was interested in selling my share?" I mumbled, hoping it would soften the blow.

"Yeah, she called. Emily, I don't think you should."

My anger momentarily flared up. When our parents agreed to leave us the company, I doubt they thought Brooks and I would end up in this situation.

"Brooks, I—" I paused, careful about how to phrase it without letting my anger make things worse. "I don't think it's a good idea for me to stay on. Besides, you'll be running it and will have full control. It's for the best."

"Emily, no." His voice cut through the air, sharp and unwavering, carrying an authority that made my heart race.

"I've made up my mind, Brooks. I'm done. I don't want this—not like this," I retorted with a mix of frustration and sadness, feeling a tight knot form in my stomach. How could he not understand that running a company together would be a recipe for disaster? The thought alone filled me with dread.

"Okay, can we talk about it in person when I get there?" he suggested, his tone softening slightly. There was a long, heavy pause between us as I stared at my surroundings, my emotions swirling. The bustling world around me felt distant; all I could really focus on was the ache in my chest and the tears that threatened to spill over. I missed him more than I could express.

"It's good to hear your voice," he said, finally breaking the silence, his familiar tone warming my heart.

"Yeah, same here." I quickly wiped away the tears on my cheeks, trying to regain my composure.

"Emily, I'm sorry. I didn't mean to make you cry," he said, his voice soft and sincere.

"I'm not crying," I protested, grimacing as I spoke, hoping he wouldn't see through my denial. Deep down, I knew he would. He knew me better than anyone else ever had.

"Emily. You are crying. I can hear it in your voice. I know you too well. Plus, you aren't a great liar," he pointed out, a hint of amusement mingled with his concern.

A soft chuckle escaped my lips despite myself, and I wiped away more tears, biting my lip to stifle the urge to break down completely. How did one conversation make everything feel so heavy?

"Emily," he pleaded, his voice filled with an urgency that made my heart ache even more.

I pulled the phone away, taking a deep breath to regain my composure. I hated how much I missed him. I hated feeling like half of my heart and soul were missing.

"Brooks," I responded, attempting to inject some lightness into the moment despite me feeling anything but.

"I'm sorry, Em. For everything. I miss you." His voice was soft, on the edge of breaking, and tears slowly traced their way down my face. I had waited years to hear him say those words, but now that he had finally said them, I couldn't shake the nagging thought that perhaps it was too little too late.

"I miss you too." My voice cracked as emotion threatened to overwhelm me.

"Sorry, Em," he repeated.

"Quit saying sorry," I sighed; I dabbed at my tears, hoping I wasn't smearing my makeup.

"I will never stop saying I'm sorry. I mean it. I messed up." The weight behind his words caused a sharp twinge of pain in my already shattered heart.

"It was a mutual decision, Brooks," I said more angrily than intended.

A long silence spread between us, broken only by the sound of my uneven breaths.

I could have chosen to wait for him to come home—could have held onto the hope that we would find our way back to each other. But anger simmered in me when he had broken his word that he was coming home. And yet, in the midst of that anger was love. I still loved him deeply despite everything we had been through and the time that had passed. All I truly wanted was for him to wrap his arms around me and whisper that everything would be okay. He had always been my person.

"Alright, I will text you once I know the dates. Hope you have a good night." I could feel him withdrawing from me. I hated it, but this was our life now. This is where that decision led us.

"Yeah, you too. See you." I smiled, trying to convey a genuine feeling.

When the call ended, I dropped my face into my palms. I missed him. Why now? Why did he have to call? I knew Brooks would eventually move back. He had a position waiting for him at Caston. I thought running away would make this easier, but I was clearly wrong.

After shedding a few more tears, I wiped my eyes and took a deep breath, pushing down all my emotions. I couldn't deal with this here, especially since Grey and Natalie were waiting for me.

Lifting my stamped hand as I passed the bouncer, I crossed the now-crowded dance floor.

"Sorry," I mumbled, dropping my phone into my bag before grabbing it again. I needed to escape to the bathroom immediately to fix my makeup.

"Hey, you okay?" Grey stood up, reaching out to me with concern.

"Yeah, I'm fine. I just need to go to the bathroom," I said, pulling away before he could get closer.

I dropped my bag on the counter and took in another deep breath.

God, I miss him. It had been four years since I had heard his voice. Four years since I decided to break up with the love of my life. Four years of regretting that decision. All the reasons I had at the time for breaking up with him now seemed inconsequential.

If I had known that even though I had spent the last two years in a relationship with my friend Parker, I would still have holes in my heart that could only be filled by Brooks, I would have waited for him. Try as I might to fight the memory, it consumed me.

The walk across campus to my dorm was chilly, but there was an exciting buzz in the air. Halloween was on Sunday, and with it being Friday, the parties were starting and would continue through tomorrow and Sunday. I had no interest in attending, even though various classmates invited me at least two dozen times. I couldn't understand why people thought I would go.

As a freshman and a self-proclaimed introvert, I was surprised by how I had made so many friends. Growing up in Bellevue and attending a private school my whole life, I hadn't formed many friendships outside of my classes and dance groups. I didn't need many friends, as I had Brooks and Connor. Brooks had been my neighbor for practically my entire life until three years ago. He's also my boyfriend and is currently in Texas trying to prove himself to the world. Instead of being together again, I am still here in Seattle, trying to hold on to the remaining pieces of my broken heart from everything that has happened over the past few years.

Connor was Brooks' friend, who later became my friend and eventually became a permanent third wheel, completing our little triad in fifth grade. Unfortunately, he wasn't here either. He decided to move to Portland and attend school in Vancouver. This left little old introverted me to fend for myself on campus. Thankfully, I had been paired with a socialite roommate who roamed our campus as if she were everyone's best friend.

The leaves had all fallen from the trees and were now dancing around my feet on a breeze. The chill in the air compelled me to tug my jacket closed. I wanted to get back to the dorms as soon as possible. Brooks was going to FaceTime me after training this evening, and we hadn't FaceTimed in two weeks.

Before moving to Texas, he lived abroad, and we would FaceTime no less than once a day. His new schedule disrupted our routine, leaving me increasingly lonely with each passing day. The delayed text exchanges and the two-minute phone calls to check in just weren't enough. Plus, I was still reeling from the hurt I felt after he dropped the "bomb" on me about not going to Princeton.

We had already been accepted and planned to live together for the first time. Before his sudden change of heart, I had believed that I would have a ring on my finger before we graduated college. Now, I was facing four more years without him—four years to grow and mature into adults and four terrifying years during which we could possibly drift apart.

The acid in my stomach and the ache in my heart reminded me that it was time to have the conversation with Brooks that I had been dreading. It wasn't supposed to be like this. We were meant to be that ridiculous couple on campus, planning a wedding and partying with a close group of friends, eventually returning to our apartment, safe in each other's arms.

Instead, he's not here. He didn't choose me. He decided to go off alone and "grow up" by joining the Air Force. He said he needed time. But I can't do time. I can't wait for a call telling me he's in love with someone else, he's moving to the other side of the world, or, even worse, a call that he didn't make it.

I hurried into the foyer of Elm Hall, my jaw dropping at the swarm of students dressed in various costumes, ranging from sexy pixies to murderous clowns. I focused on my loafers and gripped my leather bag tighter as I rushed up the stairs.

I reached my door without making any more awkward eye contact with the intimidating young adult crowd, and I slammed the door shut. Sliding down to the floor, I felt breathless and irritated at my anxiety that seemed to rush to the surface. The room around me felt like it was closing in. I wanted Brooks. I needed to feel his arms around me to steady my world. He always made everything better.

Before Brooks left, Halloween was one of our favorite times of the year. Every year, our parents let us stay up late watching Hocus Pocus and indulging in too much candy. For us, that meant three pieces each. Connor was always pleased when Brooks and I willingly handed over our candy haul. On our last Halloween together, Brooks and Connor dressed up as a peanut and a stick of butter while I was the jelly. The previous year, we had gone as Rock, Paper, Scissors.

Taking a steadying breath, I peeled myself off the floor and couldn't help but make a snide remark to myself about how pathetic I felt. I had never experienced anxiety until my first week on campus. Part of me wonders if it has to do with Brooks not being here. There was never a clear trigger—just the sudden tightness in my chest and the rapid breathing during my Literature class that caused me to rush *out the door five minutes before class ended. Now, these episodes occur at random times and seemingly without cause.*

↟ ↟ ↟

"Emily, can you skip this song? Ugh, I hate it." Another one?

I rolled my eyes and changed the track. I loved Iron & Wine, but Sara is more of a Taylor Swift and Lady Gaga girl.

She was standing at our door, finishing her makeup in the mirror that hung on the back. When I decided to switch colleges at the last minute to attend the University of Washington, I chose to live in the dorms. I could have opted for an off-campus apartment or even a single studio room, but I needed a friend. I didn't want any more reminders of being alone.

Sara, my roommate, wasn't shy at all. As a freshman, she carried the confidence of a senior. Her strawberry blonde hair hung just below her shoulders, her gorgeous mossy green eyes sparkled, and to my luck, she wore the same size as me. Since school began, people have asked if we are related. Maybe this is the closest I'll come to having a sister.

I was trying to study, knowing that Brooks would be calling later. The knot in my stomach and the wave of panic every time I thought about him wasn't helping. To say that I felt adrift and lost would be an understatement. I was going to break two hearts tonight. I just hope he forgives me one day and knows that I will always love him. That much I am sure of.

Brooks and I first said, "I love you," in seventh grade when our parents took us to Lake Tahoe. After a day at the lake, we were sunbathing on the deck. I had curled up beside him, and he whispered that he loved me. I said it back and truly meant it. From that day on, it felt like it was us against the world, just in a different way.

Our "I love yous" became more frequent, ingraining themselves in my very bones. I knew that most high school relationships didn't last, but I was convinced ours would. Now, though, with the constant pain in my chest, I understand that I need to break the promise we made after he left. We had vowed to always be there for each other, to always love each other, and to wait for one another—that was the last promise I made to him earlier this year.

"Come with me," Sara said, breaking me out of my reverie.

For the tenth time that day, I declined her invitation. She had been begging me to join her and Parker, a cute guy from our English Lit class, for the Halloween party at one of the fraternity houses. I looked down at my purple UW sweatshirt, having changed into it to get comfortable. Not happening.

"You can't sit in here and wait on him forever, you know? You're in college. You should be having fun and enjoying life. He's the one that chose to leave, not you."

I rolled my eyes again and dropped back onto my pillow.

"I know. It's just I haven't talked to him all week. This long-distance thing is getting to me." A single tear slipped out the corner of my eye and disappeared into my messy blonde hair.

"Well-" She puckered her lips and slid another layer of gloss across. "Text me if you change your mind." She adjusted her boobs so that her cleavage popped out of her already too-small, long sleeve midi shirt. After a quick air kiss, she slid her masquerade mask down and headed out the door. Again, I was left alone with my thoughts.

I glanced at my cell phone and realized he should have already called. It was almost ten in Texas. I quickly hit his icon, and the phone went straight to voicemail. Great. The acid in my stomach was navigating its way toward my throat, and the unshed tears I had been holding in all day were finally released. I stayed this way, curled up in my bed, until I woke up to my cell phone vibrating against my body.

I looked around the dark room, trying to orient myself. Sara was face-first on her bed, still dressed in the clothes she left for the party in. I was lying in a pile of paper and textbooks. I glanced back at the cell phone and realized it was 2 a.m. I quickly answered and whispered for him to hold on. I slipped out of bed, out into the halls of our building, and slid down onto the gray carpet.

I didn't even notice the shaking of my hands or the dryness of my throat as I brought the phone to my ear.

"Hey, B."

"Hey, Emily, what's going on?" Natalie asked, snapping me back to the present. Her arms were hooked over my shoulders, and her chin rested on her hand.

I looked up at her in the mirror and then back at myself. My eyes were red, and my tears had left trails in my makeup. I quickly grabbed my makeup bag out of my purse.

"Uh, I'm okay. Just had to deal with an old friend. It's nothing," I lied as I pulled out my compact.

"That doesn't seem like nothing." She stepped to my side and pressed her back against the counter to face me.

"It's a long story. Please, I don't want to talk about it right now," I pleaded, wiping away all signs of my tears.

"Okay." She hugged me tightly.

"I want to forget about it. Let's drink and dance," I huffed, trying to lift the mood.

"That's my girl," she teased.

Back at the table, Grey was sitting patiently by himself. I felt bad. Once again, Brooks was getting in the way. Grey's blue eyes met mine, and I smiled reassuringly, letting him know I was okay.

I grabbed my martini and chugged it. I was surprised by my own actions, but I didn't care—I didn't want to think about Brooks right now. I placed the glass back down and reached for Grey's hand, pulling him onto the dance floor. Natalie quickly joined us after downing a few sips of her drink.

I danced between them, letting everything fall away. The music changed everything, and I could finally fall into the fuzzy feeling. There would always be only Brooks.

More drinks arrived, and I continued twirling under the

chandelier. The crowd was turning into a blur the longer I danced. Before I knew it, shots were ordered, and I kept drinking. I wasn't ready to return to reality just yet. I wasn't ready to let go of this temporal bliss under this glowing chandelier.

↟ ↟ ↟

I inhaled deeply as I rolled over in bed, feeling the sheets tighten against me as I felt the wave of nausea hit me.

I sat up quickly, looking around. I was not at home. I barely made it before I was emptying the contents of my stomach into the toilet. I flushed and stood at the sink, turning on the cold water. The cool water felt good and helped with the waves of nausea and the awful headache that felt like it could split my head in half. *Ugh, why did I drink so much?*

A warm hand wrapped around my stomach and startled me. I spun to see Grey standing there. He wore low-rise jeans, and his bare stomach made my knees weak.

"How are you feeling?" he asked softly.

"Awful," I muttered, closing my eyes. *Damn, he's hot.*

"C'mon, I have some aspirin and juice for you."

"Juice. No juice," I whined, turning for the toilet again and puking more. Grey's hands softly pulled my hair from my face as I leaned over the toilet.

"You might have had a bit too much to drink," he whispered.

"I have never drunk like that," I sighed. The room was spinning. I wiped my mouth and stumbled backward, but Grey caught me before I fell.

"Okay, let's get you back to bed." He all but carried me back to the bed. Grey disappeared into the closet, returning with a shirt.

"Here, put this on."

I squeezed my head. *Ouch.* I didn't care about changing.

"Emily, c'mon. Let's get you changed. I will get you some aspirin."

"I don't need to change," I said sleepily.

"You do. You have some puke on your dress."

I looked down. *Gross.* Could this day get any worse?

The room spun again, and I fell back onto the bed. Grey's hand pulled me up again, sitting me on the edge.

"Okay," he whispered. "Can I help you?"

"I don't care," I muttered before realizing what I was agreeing to.

His hands were soft as he pulled my dress up over my head, exposing my bra.

"I like you," I said, placing my hand on his bare chest. My mind was foggy, and I could hear myself screaming to stop, but I was still a little too drunk to care.

He chuckled. "Okay, here we go."

He placed his clean white shirt over my head and laid me back on the pillow. I felt like I was on the edge of consciousness.

"Don't be like Brooks and disappear on me," I mumbled, sleepiness pulling me under.

↟ ↟ ↟

"Here," Grey handed me a plate of toast, but not before his eyes briskly skimmed down to my panties and legs.

"Thanks," I said, smiling up at him but swiftly sliding my legs forward to hide from him. "Sorry about last night. I have never done that." I could feel the heat on my cheeks as I blushed.

"Yeah, you keep saying that. Emily," he started looking away and then back to me. "Who is Brooks?"

"What?" I asked, almost choking on the toast.

"Brooks? You kept saying his name last night and rambling on about him coming to visit. Is that who called you and made you cry last night?" His eyes were soft on me, making me wish I could answer.

I swallowed the very dry toast down, feeling like it was stuck in my throat. "Uh." I glanced down, fidgeting with the next bite. "Yeah, he's kinda my ex. He's coming to talk to me when he's back in the States."

"Why were you crying?"

"It's complicated," I sighed.

"'Kay," he responded, rising from the couch. "I'm going to go shower."

I nodded, feeling guilty. He deserved an explanation.

"Grey," I started. He paused, turning to look at me. I wanted to tell him everything.

I love Brooks. I want us to work, but he has my heart, so we won't, and that's why I am so complicated. That's why you can't love me. I gave my heart to him, and he never gave it back. So please forgive me. You should probably hate me right now. That would be easier.

I wanted to get it out, but I couldn't, so I muttered, "Thank you."

Chapter Two

March - Present Day

Brooks was about to crash back into my life and I hadn't spent enough time considering how I'd feel about it. For the past few weeks, I had diligently tried to bury myself in work and use it as a distraction. The thought of him being so close for an entire week had my heart racing to dangerous levels, and it was impossible to ignore the flutter in my stomach.

I took a calming breath as I scanned the living room. Everything was ready—except for me. My eyes moved from the two-story stone fireplace on the far wall, across the length of the glass wall that led to the deck, to the oversized, plush sofa that could fit an entire family and more, and finally to the large potted tree in the corner. "Everything will be fine," I told myself.

My phone chimed in my pocket, signaling that a car had just gone through the gate. I checked my hair and makeup in the entryway mirror one last time as my stomach twisted into a tighter knot. I brushed my shaky hands through my blonde hair, internally battling whether I was excited to see him or still angry. Deep down, I accepted that I was, in fact, excited.

A firm knock on the door signaled he was here. My heart kicked up even faster, and I steadied myself before stepping forward to welcome him into my home and my life again.

"Hey!" I squealed as I threw myself into his arms, crashing into his body and holding him close, choosing to just embrace the moment. He stood at the base of the steps, and his familiar presence instantly made everything feel right—my whole world was brought back into alignment. My heart raced with joy, and a huge smile spread. I had missed him.

"Gorgeous house, Em," he chuckled, scooping me off the ground in one of his signature all-consuming hugs—the kind that made you feel loved deep in your soul.

At that moment, hearing his voice again, the world fell away. It felt as if time itself had been washed away. His firm, warm embrace was an anchor for my soul, and the scent of his amber cologne swirled in the space between us. The combination of Brooks and his cologne was intoxicating and utterly irresistible.

"Hey, B," I replied in a giddy, unfamiliar voice. As Brooks set me back on my feet, my heart fluttered. He had just returned from four years in the Air Force, two of which had been stationed in South Korea. I hadn't seen him since our sophomore year of high school almost eight years ago. The last time we were together, I was the love of his life, and he was mine. His eyes lingered on me as I stepped back, and I felt a warm blush spread across my cheeks.

It took a second to register the man in front of me. Double my size, muscular, manly. He was dressed in tight, dark jeans and a black shirt that fit his muscular build just right, with biceps bulging out of the sleeves. His blue eyes were brighter than I remembered, and he now had a short beard that seamlessly flowed with dark hair that was gelled into a perfect wave. *Holy cow.* Seeing him had my heart cartwheeling, and my muscles clenched somewhere low in my belly. The air crackled with unspoken words and a sense of possibility.

Meanwhile, my subconscious was warning me to protect my heart. He had broken it, *remember*? I tried to suppress my emotions. Of course, I didn't forget. Still, I couldn't help but feel comforted by his presence. He had always been my person, and during our time apart, I longed to be held by him again.

I let my emotions take control for a moment and stepped into his arms once more, resting against the warm, broad expanse of his chest. His arms wrapped around me, and for a few seconds, I allowed myself to believe he was still mine and that this was my home. However, his heavy sigh was enough to bring me back to reality. I quickly pulled away, letting my rational thoughts take over once again.

"So, how was your flight?" I asked, trying to break the ice before the inevitable awkwardness settled in. I hoped he couldn't sense the butterflies fluttering wildly in my stomach. I was at a loss for where to focus my gaze, so I forced myself to meet his eyes.

"Good. Long," he replied, a smile still lingering on his face as he looked down at me. His smile felt like a warm blanket, comforting and safe. I couldn't help but feel a rush of heat rise to my cheeks as my heart leaped into my throat. *How does he have this effect on me?* I shook my head, trying to gather my thoughts.

"How's the weather in South Korea?" I asked, my voice slightly higher than usual.

"Good. It's a little rainy. I was in the UK, though," he explained. "I had some business to take care of while I was there."

That's right. After departing South Korea, Brooks had flown to the UK to reconnect with an old friend in Suffolk. That was when he had texted me, asking if he could visit. We had our own matters to discuss, and I felt the weight of that thought pressing down on me.

"Oh, right, you mentioned that," I replied, my face flushing further. I took a deep breath in an attempt to calm my racing heart and gather my emotions, but all I could smell was his cologne—something rich and woody and entirely masculine, with undertones of amber that seemed to envelop me like a hug. It wrapped around me like a tether, pulling me toward him. I had to redirect the conversation quickly before I said or did something embarrassing.

"This is my house," I said, gesturing toward the front door. "You will officially be my first guest." I turned to walk back up the porch steps, feeling a mix of excitement and apprehension. "There's a detached guest house I like to call 'the studio,' which I use as my own private space. I promise you'll be comfortable up here." As I spoke, I couldn't help but glance back at him, curious about his reaction.

Brooks' warm, muscular hand grasped mine as he pulled me back down a step, drawing me into his sweet-smelling embrace and closer to his magnificent body.

"What does that mean?" His voice was soft but confused, and his face was just inches from mine. I could feel his warm breath on my cheek, igniting a wave of excitement throughout my soul, like it was happy to find its other half. His steel blue eyes gazed deeply into mine.

Still reeling from his closeness, he reached up and gently brushed a loose strand of hair behind my ear as if it were the most natural thing in the world. His fingers barely touched my cheek, but his touch was electric, leaving a warm trail on my skin.

I swallowed, possibly audibly, and noticed the same surprise on his face as a hint of red tinged his cheeks. He quickly pulled his hand back and tucked it safely into his pocket. My lip ached from the pinch of my teeth as I struggled to remember his question about the guest house.

"Oh, um, I live in the studio full-time right now. This place is just too big for me." Admitting that made me want to hide. What would he think? Here I was, owning this large home yet choosing not to live in it.

"Huh? Well, okay then. Mind if I see your house?"

"Sure," I mumbled. What else could I say? No?

"I'm sorry I missed your birthday. I was hoping to be here sooner but couldn't get away." His voice was gentle as he looked into my eyes; he meant it. His gaze studied me as we stood there. This was going to be more of a challenge than I had originally anticipated. I bit my lip, fighting back the urge to kiss him as I focused on the fullness of his lips. They were dark pink, full, and the kind of lips that made others jealous. He chuckled. Could he read my thoughts just by looking at my face?

"It's just this way," I replied, unsure how to respond. We hadn't talked like this in four years, ever since our long-distance breakup. Four birthdays had passed without each other. I released his hand and slowly turned toward the little path along the right side of the main house. I wrapped my arms around myself, feeling sidelined by the unexpected emotions and the desire coiling in my stomach.

We walked silently down the stone path. The waves were particularly loud today as they crashed against the rocks, spraying water into the air. The spray would land softly every few seconds, and another wave would hit, creating an almost predictable rhythm. As we walked, we kept glancing back and forth at each other. I wanted to look at him, to see who he had become during our time apart.

I remembered seeing a photo of him in the military. The Brooks I knew was always clean-shaven, but now he sported a short, neatly trimmed beard. His eyes were still a striking steel blue, contrasting with his thick brown hair. They looked different now—no longer the innocent eyes of a teenager, but eyes that held a story and had experienced both the good and the bad in the world.

His smile remained soft, and he was more handsome than I remembered. I had to remind myself to breathe normally; being near him made even the most basic functions feel challenging.

I focused back down the path, aware of his gaze studying me. Our eyes met again when I looked back up, and I let out an involuntary giggle—a nervous habit of mine. Pressing my lips shut, I noticed how tight his sleeves were around his now well-defined biceps.

Small, pointed tips of tattoos peeked out from his sleeve on one side while another display of images covered his other bicep. He walked confidently by my side, and my heart raced again. This feeling was becoming annoying. I needed to learn how to stay calm around him. He was no longer the tall, skinny soccer player I remembered; he was a grown man now.

I opened the tall metal and glass door and stepped inside, taking a deep, cleansing breath. I could feel the warmth of his body right behind me. As I glanced around the room, I was uncertain about the state I had left it in. The enormous glass wall at the back of the house revealed a sheet of gray clouds covering the baby-blue sky. However, as I looked around the living room, I was grateful I had tidied up.

"You can set your things here," I said, almost breathlessly. Brooks Devonshire was now standing in my home. So much for a clean slate and having no ties to him. I turned to face him as he gently placed his belongings by the door, taking in the room with a scanning gaze.

My Hollow Coves and Dean Lewis playlist was still playing softly throughout the house from earlier in the day. Most days, I left music playing unless I needed silence. It helped me feel less alone. I loved this space's mix of wood, concrete, and glass. I had filled it with soft lighting, a comfy white linen couch, and a live-edge coffee table. My bookcases overflowed with books, photos, and cute trinkets, many of which Brooks had gifted me over the years.

Brooks looked at me with a heat in his eyes that I didn't recognize. His gaze cascaded over my body before settling on my lips. My heart resumed its irregular beat once again. Slowly, he stepped closer, closing the gap between us until my back pressed against the wall and his warm body pressed against mine. A buzz of excitement flooded me from my toes to every hair on my head as he leaned in, pressing his soft, warm lips to mine. A warmth pooled in my belly as I arched my body further into his.

I had been angry at him. I had ached for him, longed for him, and now all I could think about was how amazing it felt to have his lips on mine. I missed him. I still loved him. Sure, I had kissed him before, but we were kids then. I had even kissed my ex, Parker, but it never felt like this. This was something entirely different. His powerful hands lifted me slightly up the wall as I reached up, wrapping my fingers into his hair and pulling him closer for a deeper kiss.

My lips parted as his tongue slipped in, greeting me with mint and longing. His tongue explored my mouth as if he were coming home after being gone for so long, seeking out differences before settling into the familiarity.

So many memories and emotions flooded through me. I recalled that first kiss when we played hide and seek with our friend, Connor. Brooks and I had been hiding together between the trees in our yard. Then, there was that moment before everything changed, and he left Seattle. His lips had felt strong and eager back then, just as they did now. But now, there was a charged energy between us, and my body responded like a hormonal teenager.

I couldn't make sense of all I was feeling: longing, lust, safety, wholeness, fear, and sadness. I was a mess. The only thing I felt sure of was that I was still madly in love with him—something I wasn't willing to admit until now.

A small moan escaped my lips, causing him to respond with a low growl of his own as his hips pinned me to the wall. I turned my face to catch my breath for fear I was going to pass out in his arms. His lips slowly moved along my neck, tracing it like he was memorizing the skin there. My whole body filled with a passion that I had never experienced. It was more intense, more real than anything.

The song switched, and the new beat broke whatever spell I was under. *What am I doing?* I released my grip on his hair and dropped my hands to my side, trying to regain some control of my body. Brooks pulled his lips away from my neck, settling his hands with mine as he took a deep, calming breath. His forehead rested on my temple, and my chest was heaving from the excitement.

"Sorry," he whispered, "I have really missed you." The warmth of his breath tickled my neck.

Hope surged in my heart.

I was sick and tired of missing him and rehashing our breakup every few months. I knew I was being reckless, but frankly, it didn't matter. I could tackle the hard questions later. I was a responsible twenty-four-year-old; I could have this moment. I turned my face to meet his again and pressed my lips to his, maybe a little too forcefully. I wasn't ready to return to reality. Not yet.

He was no longer mine, and we were both broken, shattered people walking around with half a heart. He still owned mine, and I still owned part of his, right? That had to mean something.

I opened the floodgates of my soul as I kissed him deeply, longing for our souls to reconnect and hoping that the seven years of distance would fade away. At that moment, time stood still, and I felt grateful. After what seemed like the best kiss of my life, I could sense that it was nearing its end. As the flutter in my heart slowed and the fire in my veins diminished, I pulled away, instantly reminded of the reality that we were no longer boyfriend and girlfriend. I felt embarrassed for acting so passionately, and I was sure I turned five shades of red. He chuckled, confirming my fear.

His warm body pulled away from mine, taking his warmth with it, and I physically felt the space between us.

"Wow," I laughed nervously. "I guess...I miss you too." I let the words trail off, utterly shocked that I had allowed them to escape my lips. I inhaled sharply, hoping to regain my composure since my mind felt blank.

"Are you sure about that?" He raised his eyebrows, honestly questioning whether I meant it.

"Yes!" Of course, I meant it. "Sorry, I'm not thinking clearly." Thoughts slowly trickled in, most revolving around the same questions: Why did he kiss me? What does this mean for us?

"I'm sorry if I crossed a line. I've thought about doing that since I knew I was coming here."

What? There was so much to unpack there, starting with what that kiss meant. I had to focus, though. Instead of responding, I nodded and flashed a quick smile.

"So, this is it," I said. Talking about my house would be a good distraction from our little moment of passion. "It's not much, but it's cozy."

"This is amazing, Em. How did you find this place? I mean, look at that view! I can't imagine what it's like at the main house."

"Yeah, it's pretty special. I had some help. My realtor managed to get a meeting with the original builder before it hit the market. He had to move before it was finished being built." I inhaled nervously. "I graduated a year early with my MBA and decided to leave Seattle. I love it here."

"I can see that. I'm glad you found something you love."

"Thanks," I murmured. "So, yeah, there's just one bedroom down the hall. It makes a nice guesthouse, but for now, it's mine." I laughed, finding it a bit ridiculous to own such a large estate and choose to live in the one-bedroom guesthouse.

Brooks remained silent as he looked around. I had a small fireplace in the corner that was still crackling, and piles of books were on the end tables, all half-read. He was slow and methodical, taking his time to absorb the details of my tiny home. The silence felt intense. My eyes couldn't help but watch him from across the room. I was drawn to his new physique—the muscles and tattoos driving me into a frenzy to explore him further, to get closer.

"I like your short hair," he said, still focused on a piece of artwork. I had visited a gallery show right after buying this estate and couldn't leave without it. The abstract layers of neutral whites and blues perfectly matched this ocean-side property. When Brooks turned his gaze to mine, I suddenly remembered my hair.

"Thanks! I just cut it after graduation. I needed a change, and it's much easier to manage now." My hair, which had been long since the last time he saw me, was now cut to just hover at my shoulders.

"So," I hesitated, "do you want me to show you the main house? You can sleep in whichever room you like."

Brooks chuckled softly, a hint of nervousness in his voice. "If it's alright with you," he said, clearing his throat. "Mind if I sleep on the couch?"

"Yes, but why? There's like eight beds up there." I didn't mean to agree, but it was too late now. He was going to torture me this week.

"Eight?" he murmured under his breath. "Well, I don't want to impose, but I'd prefer to stay with you. I just mean I came all the way here, and I don't know, staying up there alone would feel... distant?" His hands slipped into his pants pockets, momentarily distracting me.

I could feel warmth flooding my body and my heart beating loudly. Was he feeling what I was feeling?

"Okay, then," I whispered.

I walked over to the sofa, sat down, curling my legs beside me, and turned to face him. I couldn't take my eyes off him. He paced slowly back and forth, pretending to look at the art—I doubted it was that interesting.

What if there was nothing else to say? I was thankful his back was turned; it gave me time to take him in and process how my body reacted. It was strange to see him like this: mature, older, and definitely hotter. I wondered what he looked like without his shirt on. I gasped quietly at the thought.

Brooks sighed, turned towards me, and sat on the sofa before me, our knees almost brushing. I looked down at his dark blue jeans and felt an odd urge to place my hand on his knee. I couldn't. I shouldn't.

"How was the rest of college?" he asked simply, pulling me out of my strange urge to be near him—the urge to crawl into his lap and snuggle against his chest. His eyes met mine with a smile.

"Oh, er, good. Yeah. I mean, it was school," I responded with a huff of sexual tension.

"What degree did you graduate with? A Master's in Business Management?"

"Yes, along with a double minor in Communications and Advertising."

I felt an annoying ache inside. He should know this. We shouldn't be discussing my education; he should have been there.

"Wow, that's great. Did you live with Sara the whole time? You guys were on the dance team together, right?"

"Yep. We got a cute little house off campus our junior year. It was nice to be out of the dorms. I kept it for another year after she graduated. She's now working in Portland. And yes, we danced together all four years. I didn't dance in my fifth year just so I could focus."

"Yeah, I'm ready to live on my own. I've never—" he trailed off. Right. He went straight from the dorms at boarding school to the Air Force.

"How was the Air Force? What did you do there? How long were you in South Korea?" The twinge of anger I felt made me take a deep breath to catch his heady scent.

"I was in Osan for two years. It was nice. I was in Special Ops," he said, focusing on his hand resting on the top of the sofa near my shoulder.

"Did you learn the language?" I asked, trying not to lean into his hand.

"I picked up a bit, but not really."

"So why did you fly to Sussex afterward?" I began picking at a thread on my sweater.

"I was meeting with Michaelson to catch up and asked him to come work at Caston." Brooks's eyes drilled into me.

I involuntarily cringed, hoping he didn't notice. I wasn't ready to discuss work. I knew Brooks was here only to stop me from selling my portion of the company to him. Our parents had founded Caston together when Brooks and I were in second grade. After graduation, I had the opportunity to start working there but chose not to.

My mind raced with all the reasons why Brooks felt like a stranger sitting next to me. I wasn't ready to delve into that, so I took a breath and concentrated on the first part of what he had said.

"Michaelson. Wasn't he your roommate in school?" I asked, looking up at him with a forced smile.

"Yep. Same one." He pressed his lips together and nodded.

"How is he?" I swallowed, trying to maintain composure.

"He's good. Actually—"

Brooks continued speaking, but my mind drifted. *Why did he have to kiss me? But why did I want him to? Why did I kiss him back?*

This just complicates everything. What will happen when he leaves next week? Do we stay friends or revert to complete silence?

"Em?" he asked, placing his warm, heavy hand on my shoulder.

"Huh? Oh, sorry." I glanced at his hand as he quickly withdrew it.

I focused solely on the conversation ahead. It felt easy to be with him, surprisingly normal and comfortable after so much pain and time apart.

"Do you still dance?" he asked.

My stomach twisted. The answer wasn't simple. I had always danced; it was my way of expressing emotions and moving my body. However, I have felt blocked lately. Since I quit during my senior year, I hadn't been able to find my rhythm, and it wasn't for lack of trying.

"No. Maybe one day. I just started getting into indoor cycling, though. It's different, but it's a good workout."

He nodded, clearly not convinced. He knew me better than anyone.

"Is there a local studio where you can dance or teach?"

"They don't need any instructors, and well—" I paused, glancing outside and realizing it was late. "I'll find it again. I just need a reset. It will be okay." He didn't respond but brushed his hand across mine as if he understood what I meant. My broken heart shifted a bit closer to being whole. Talking, sitting, breathing—all of it felt better with him by my side; everything just... worked.

A comfortable silence fell between us as the sun set on the horizon. I wasn't sure if we had run out of things to say, but it didn't feel awkward. Then, he broke the silence.

"Emily, we need to get this out of the way." He shifted, placing his elbows on his knees and steepling his fingers.

I looked up, shaking my head, already knowing where this was headed. No. Not now.

"I don't want to talk about it, Brooks." Frustration and confusion were building inside me. Just hours ago, I was certain I would sell and live my life without him, free of any ties to him. Now, I wasn't so sure. Did I really believe I could escape that easily? That Brooks could stay at my house for an entire week, and things would remain unchanged? How naïve I had been. I stood up, hoping to calm my growing frustration.

"Fine, we don't have to talk about it tonight, but we need to address it eventually. I won't let you sell."

"Brooks, just stop," I demanded, tears filling my eyes. Did he not understand? This—us—it was too painful. I knew that when he left again, I would fall apart. I turned toward the fire, hiding my face in my hands.

"B, what are we doing? We could have done this over the phone." Did my voice sound as confused and broken as I felt? *Don't cry. Please don't cry. Hold it in.*

I heard Brooks rise from the couch and felt his warm arms wrap around me from behind. His voice was soft in my ear.

"I wanted to come see you. To apologize. I'm not here on business. Emily, I miss you. I still love you."

That was it. The tears finally brimmed, and my body broke into a full sob. It felt as if I had lost all control, with tears flowing freely and without restriction. Brooks turned me in his arms and pulled me close to his chest. He probably thought I was insane, but I needed to let these tears out; I had been holding them in for years.

After what felt like an eternity, I sensed the well of tears drying up. I pulled away from his chest to grab a tissue from the coffee table, hoping he wouldn't notice the snot draining from my nose.

"I'm sorry, Emily," he sighed.

"I'm sorry, too. This is hard." My voice broke.

His hand gently caressed my shoulder as I wiped away my tears. I focused on stabilizing my breathing before looking up at him. His eyes held a look of helplessness as they met mine. How could we go through this again? Everything felt so confusing when it came to him, and I wasn't ready to tackle the weight of those thoughts. I needed a distraction.

"I'm hungry. Are you hungry? I can order something in," I suggested. It felt odd to talk about food after my emotional outburst, but I risked breaking down again if I didn't.

"Sure, whatever you want," he replied. I could tell he wasn't ready to switch topics, yet he wouldn't bring it up again.

I glanced around the room for my phone, suddenly remembering that it had fallen from my hands when I had run out the door earlier.

"I need to go get my phone from the main house. Do you want to stay here or walk up with me?" I asked, wiping my eyes again.

"I'll go with you," he sighed.

He took my hand and interlaced his fingers with mine. I looked down at our hands. Why was he doing this to me? Didn't he realize the inevitable heartache he was causing? Still, I couldn't let go. I wanted to hold his hand; I wanted to feel his embrace. I squeezed his hand and stepped out into the darkness.

Chapter Three

The cool air outside brought a sort of clarity and calmness to my soul that I so desperately needed. I was seconds from combusting with jumbled thoughts and emotions warring for attention.

"Why do you choose to live in the studio instead of the main house?" he asked as we walked up the stone path, the solar lights illuminating our way. I looked into his eyes and felt the truth almost escape my lips. I was certain that Brooks would never make fun of me.

In return, I offered a simple truth: the house was big, and I was just one person. Maybe that was enough? Did he grasp the depth of my solitude? I was alone, drowning in the space that had initially felt welcoming.

Despite my love for the home, it felt overwhelmingly large and all too empty. That first week, I lay awake at night, my heart spiraling in despair over all the people I had lost. The crushing weight of being completely and utterly alone was unbearable.

As we climbed the steps to the front door, I reluctantly released his hand. I quickly punched in the code and pushed open the large wooden and glass door. My phone lay right next to the plant. As I bent down to grab it, I felt Brooks brush past me to stand in the entryway. I couldn't help but notice how his fingertips left a tender, burning sensation on my lower back, igniting something deep within me.

"Wow," he breathed, rocking back on his heels. I looked up and saw his eyes wandering around the room.

"Want a tour?" I asked with a playful laugh. Brooks looked back at me and nodded slightly.

"Well, this is the main level," I began. "There's a basement and an upstairs," I laughed, pointing to the stairs on our left that led to the next floor. "These stairs over here lead down." I pointed to the right as we stepped out of the entryway. "This," I said, facing the glass wall that extended the entire length of the living room, "was what sold me." The wall opened up to a sprawling deck that stretched toward the water, offering an unobstructed view of the horizon.

"This view is amazing, Em," he said, his voice almost a whisper laced with awe. An uncomfortable feeling stirred in my chest, something oddly close to regret, reminding me of the life we could have shared.

"This room," I began, leading him through the double doors on the right, "is one of my favorites." I watched his face in awe as he scanned the floor-to-ceiling bookcases. He stepped forward, running his hands along the two desks in the center of the room.

"This isn't even the best part," I added, attempting to infuse my voice with playfulness despite a tinge of nervousness that fluttered in my belly.

With a playful skip, I slid open the partition, revealing the expansive glass room beyond. Inside were furniture pieces in muted tones and soft textures, several lush green plants, and a baby grand piano in the corner. The moon peeked out from behind the clouds, occasionally causing the black ocean waves to glitter white.

A smile never left his face as he followed me, letting his gaze fall around the room.

"Okay, I have to agree with you. I mean, I haven't seen the rest of the house, but this is amazing," he said, taking a moment to soak in the beauty around him. He ran his fingers across the keys of the piano and looked back at me, curiosity in his eyes.

"Did you learn to play?" he asked.

I chuckled at the question and bit my bottom lip, shaking my head with a playful grin. "When would I have had the time to learn?" I replied, my voice laced with laughter. My cheeks flushed again as I said, "I have it hoping someone will play for me."

Brooks nodded a slight smile on his lips, and sat down on the bench. He began playing a beautiful piece that unfurled with a slow build. The notes filled the room, surrounding me with a wave of emotion. I closed my eyes, surrendering to the melody, feeling it as much as I could hear it.

I sank back on the plush ivory chaise closest to the piano and closed my eyes again. The song was taking a sad turn, each note touching on something broken within me. It had been far too long since I had heard him play. He had always been extraordinarily gifted and talented, playing so effortlessly, yet he would never acknowledge it. His parents enrolled him in lessons starting in kindergarten, but I never showed any interest. He had always been there to play for me.

After school, during middle school and high school, Brooks would find me buried in my schoolwork. Without having to ask, he would sit at the piano and serenade me, the notes intertwining with my thoughts. I had always told him the music helped me to concentrate, but deep down, I knew the real reason was that every note he played made my heart swell even more, deepening my love for him.

I opened my eyes when Brooks stopped playing and stood up from the bench. The song had finished on a lighter, more hopeful note, and I longed for more. When our eyes locked from across the room, a warm smile spread across his face, and I felt it settle comfortably in my chest. At that moment, I vowed to hold onto this memory, no matter what.

"Thank you. Come on, there's so much more to see." I reached for his hand and tugged him back into the living room. "Up or down?" I asked, closing the study doors behind me.

Brooks chuckled, amused by my sudden playfulness.

"Up?" he responded as if it were a question.

I smiled back at him as we climbed the floating wooden steps together. I pointed out the three guest rooms on the other side of the loft before we entered the master bedroom. We paused at the door, taking in the space. At the center of the room was a spacious oversized king bed with soft pillows and earthy linens. My heart raced with excitement at the thought of this intimate space being occupied by the both of us. It felt as if the room held its breath, waiting to see how he would react.

My hormonal body had me picturing him gloriously naked on it before I swallowed audibly, clenching my thighs and banishing those thoughts from my head. *What the hell is wrong with me?*

"Er, this is the bathroom," I said as I guided him to the right through the arched opening. "One of my favorite features is that the shower also doubles as a steam room."

"Emily, this is incredible. I love this house. You really did well," he replied, planting himself in the opening and leaning against the wall with his hands tucked into his jeans.

A small smile formed on my lips.

"The closet is just through those doors— that's it!" My voice rose slightly with excitement. I was hoping he loved it as much as I did.

Brooks scanned the room, absorbing every detail. The tub was spacious enough for two people—just the right size for both of us. Ugh. I tried to clear my mind again, but a small laugh escaped me before I could stop it. Taking a deep breath, I fought to suppress the smile creeping in due to these inappropriate thoughts. I turned and walked back to the bedroom, with Brooks following closely behind. He crossed the room and opened the door to the small deck outside.

"Nice view," he said, turning back to face me.

I nodded.

"Okay, we still have the basement," I stated. I needed to get out of this room immediately before my mind kept undressing him in this bedroom draped in moonlight.

We descended both sets of stairs and stepped into the basement den. Brooks placed his hands on either side of my shoulders, and it took all my energy not to melt under his touch.

"This is unbelievable," he said.

The back wall of the house was made entirely of glass and pivoted open to reveal an infinity pool, which was steaming against the cool air. To the right, there was a hot tub and an outdoor kitchen. Just inside the glass wall, there was a bar, a ping-pong table, and a shuffleboard table. Straight ahead was a large TV in front of an oversized plush couch.

"There's a bathroom and three more bedrooms just down the hall to the left, and that hallway by the TV leads to another bedroom and a gym. There's an infrared sauna in there, too. Feel free to use everything while you are here." One day, this home would be filled with family and friends, and laughter would echo through here. For now, it was just me.

"I can see why you don't live up here," he chuckled, still trying to process the room. He raked a hand through his hair and wandered around.

"I'm going to order us some food." I pulled out my phone and opened the app to order gyros. "Is lamb okay?" I asked. There was no answer. I looked up to find Brooks standing outside by the pool with his hands in his pockets, his shoulders slightly hunched. I couldn't help but wonder what he was thinking. I crossed the room and pushed the glass door open behind him.

"Is lamb okay?" I repeated.

He turned to face me, and a storm of emotions brewed in his eyes —possibly sorrow.

"Yeah," he muttered, turning back to the waves.

I closed the glass door and sat down on the barstool to complete the order. Twenty-five minutes.

Glancing back outside, I noticed Brooks was still standing there, unmoved. I watched him for a moment, lost in thought. We had so much history together, but that couldn't erase the painful void between us.

Images of Grey flashed through my mind. It had only been a few weeks since Grey and I had kissed, and every day since had been awkward. I had told him I needed time to think, and I was waiting to see how things would unfold with Brooks. Could we finally say our goodbyes and move on? Would the pain lessen now? Could I ever love someone as much as I loved—correction—love Brooks?

I knew Grey could make me happy if I could figure out how to let go of Brooks. I sighed in resignation, knowing I had an entire week with Brooks before deciding what to say to Grey. We hadn't talked since that night at Sapphire. We had both been dancing around our unspoken feelings and the lack of progress in our relationship.

I stood up and walked outside to meet Brooks by the pool.

"Ready to head back?" I asked softly, looking up at him with curiosity.

"Yeah," he replied, pulling his hand out of his pocket and reaching for mine.

My fingers unconsciously wrapped around his as if my soul knew exactly where it belonged and to whom it belonged. I bit my lip, fighting back another smile. I felt like a schoolgirl with her first crush. I rolled my eyes, then focused on him. What was he thinking? And why did this make me so happy? I should be angry with him. We stepped off the deck, down the stairs, and back onto the path leading to my little studio.

"So, do you still sail?" Brooks asked as we sat back down on the sofa.

"Eh, not really, no. I went a few times in college but sold my boat before graduation. I would like to sail again; I just wasn't sure where I would end up, and the boat was old and needed repairs. Maybe one day." I really did miss sailing. "What about you?"

"Not since I went with you. I want to get back out there or even buy a yacht. I miss the water."

"A yacht, huh? Mr. Fancy Pants over here," I teased, slapping my hand on his knee.

Brooks laughed. "Says the girl with an eight-bedroom oceanside estate. Plus, I'm pretty sure we make the same income." Right. Our trust funds kicked in after graduation.

I rolled my eyes and sat back, pulling my hand away. "Guess you're right." Just then, there was a knock on the door. Brooks rushed over to answer it, grabbing the food and tipping the driver.

He sat beside me, and I watched him, feeling slightly overwhelmed by his gorgeous figure. His black shirt and denim look was undeniably sexy. I pulled my lips in, grinning to myself.

"You know, you've done that a lot tonight," he chuckled, still focused on the food.

"Done what?" I asked.

"Hidden your laughter, hidden your smile. Why?" He tilted his head, studying me for a moment before returning to sorting our dinner.

"It's nothing." I shrugged it off, mortified that he had even noticed.

"Tell me," he said playfully, bumping shoulders with me.

"Not a chance," I giggled, opening the gyro he handed me.

He shook his head and grinned, pulling the wrapper down on his food. Everything felt so... right. We had always interacted this way—teasing, laughing, and being completely comfortable with each other. Well, I suppose I wasn't comfortable enough to share the truth just now.

We sat silently while eating, and I thought back to the last time Brooks and I had gone sailing together. We had spent much of our childhood on the water, but the summer before sophomore year, my dad had dedicated time to refreshing our sailing skills before buying us our own boat.

It had been the perfect day. The sun was bright, the air was warm, and Brooks and I couldn't keep our hands to ourselves. We laughed and kept sneaking kisses whenever my parents weren't looking. I was pretty sure they were fully aware of our actions, though. I couldn't help but blush when I thought back to that day.

"What are you thinking about?" he asked, clearing his throat.

I looked up and found Brooks' eyes on me.

"Oh—" my face flushed in embarrassment. "Uh, our last sailing trip."

"Yeah," he chuckled, taking another bite.

"No, wait—tell me. What about it?" I playfully pulled his food away.

He looked at me, laughing and almost choking on his bite. I couldn't help but smile. After swallowing, he took a quick sip of his drink before answering.

"What part of that day made you smile?" he asked, reclaiming his food.

I blushed again.

"Right. That's what I thought." The smug smirk he offered up had my whole body igniting. That was the first day Brooks and I explored each other's bodies with our hands. We had never done anything together, but we had pushed the boundaries to second base that day.

"Get your head out of the gutter," I teased, though I felt my cheeks heat from embarrassment. Well, the memory was there now. Brooks' hands had slid up my shirt and untied my bathing suit top playfully. I hadn't stopped him. He kissed me as his hands moved to my boobs. This was all after sailing. Our parents were outside grilling, and Brooks and I were supposed to clean up for dinner.

We had both agreed to wait until we were married to have sex, but that night, we had come dangerously close. I shook my head, trying to ignore the memory. I cleared my throat and looked back up at Brooks, who was watching me again.

"Stop," I groaned, though I ended up laughing. The tension in the air was thick, making it almost hard to breathe.

I stood up and cleared the trash, taking it to the kitchen because I needed something to do. It was almost ten o'clock already. How was that possible? I needed to get to bed, but my thoughts were still swirling. As I returned to my room, I quickly searched for extra blankets and a pillow. Brooks was pacing the living room with his hands in his pockets.

"Here," I murmured as I handed him the bedding. "Are you sure you want to stay on the couch? The beds upstairs are considerably more comfortable."

He glanced at me, a hint of color rising to his cheeks. "I know," he admitted, his voice barely above a whisper. Did he just blush?

Our hands barely brushed as we exchanged the bedding, and my heart raced at the contact, a mix of exhilaration, desire, and nervousness flooding me. He cleared his throat, his gaze falling to my lips before bouncing back to my eyes.

"I want to be here with you," he said sincerely. "I could have stayed in a hotel room."

I nodded, flustered by his words. "Okay," I replied bashfully. "Well, goodnight." I turned abruptly, fighting the urge to stay with him.

"Goodnight, Emily," he replied softly, his voice distant as I stepped into my bedroom and closed the door. My heart still raced at the thought of him just a few feet away.

I hastily changed into my blue silk pajama set. I brushed my hair and teeth, working as robotically as possible to ward off the increasing desire settling between my thighs. *No, don't even think about it!* I inhaled deeply. I could hear the lamp click off in the distance. *See, he's in bed.* Then, there was a knock on the door.

"Emily?" Brooks peeked his head in.

"Huh?" I gasped, trying to collect my thoughts. His eyes scanned me from head to toe, and I suddenly felt self-conscious, as if he had x-ray vision and could see my naked body.

"Can I use the bathroom?" He held up his toothbrush.

Oh right. I had completely forgotten that I ditched him out there and that he would need access to the bathroom. I chuckled nervously and motioned toward the bathroom door, unable to find the words.

"Thanks," he said, crossing the room and shutting the door behind him. I could hardly contain the heat flooding through me, so I sat on my bed and picked up the nearest book. I could read. I should read. Reading was one of my favorite pastimes. I noticed the book I had grabbed from the stack on my nightstand was *The Giver* by Lois Lowry.

I tried to focus my attention on the words, but my mind was elsewhere, fixated on the bathroom door. I muttered to myself for a few minutes before realizing I hadn't understood anything I had just read. A small giggle escaped my lips just as the bathroom door slid open.

"Thanks, Em." He wasn't wearing his shirt, and his athletic pants sat incredibly low on his hips. My eyes slowly scanned his body, taking in his impressive transformation. He was fit—his rock-solid stomach gave off the perfect Abercrombie model vibe. His chest was fuller, and his biceps and shoulders were noticeably larger. Every inch of him deserved recognition for his hard work. *How and when did he become so hot?* A fine sheen of sweat broke out on my brow, and my fingers ached to trace the deep valleys of the 'v' that dipped into his pants.

He chuckled as I looked up into his deep blue eyes, which sparkled with delight and perhaps something a little darker, a little heavier.

"Nice bod," I giggled. I realized he had caught me staring. Did I really just say "nice bod"? That sounded so lame.

Brooks smirked again.

"Goodnight, Emily." His voice was husky and deep as he walked to my door, shutting it softly behind him. Oh gosh, this was going to be a hell of a week. I fell back onto my pillow, trying to hold back laughter from embarrassment. Rolling over, I turned off the light. Time for sleep. "Nice bod"? Seriously?

My mind and body were not ready for sleep, though. Instead, my thoughts kept returning to Brooks. The silence was deafening, and all I could think about was his lips pressed against mine earlier. The way his muscles rippled and stretched under his tattoos, and what it would feel like to have him pressed into my naked body.

Ugh. I rolled over, burying my face in the pillow. I wanted to scream. This was completely insane. I tossed and turned for what felt like forever. Focus on the waves, I told myself, trying to visualize them coming in and being pulled back out. But then my thoughts drifted back to Brooks and the way he had pressed his body against mine.

"Ugh," I silently screamed in frustration. Morning could not come soon enough.

I glanced at the clock. 12:34. Great. Annoyed, I sat up. I needed some water. Maybe I should go sleep in the main house. I slid out of bed quietly, hoping not to wake him.

The house was quiet, and I tried to walk as softly as possible to the kitchen. I was so focused on the couch that I bumped into the wall as I tried to turn the corner. A small groan escaped my lips before I could stop it. I reached for the cabinet that held the glasses and opened it, wincing at the creak.

Of course, this would be the one night. I grabbed a glass and turned to make sure I hadn't woken Brooks. I gasped, startled, clutching the cup in one hand and the counter in the other.

"Oh God. Sorry, did I wake you?" I asked breathlessly, my heart hammering in my chest.

He was standing at the other end of the island, looking all hot and playful in the dark. His brown hair was messy, like he'd been obsessively running his hands through it. A trait he picked up in middle school when he started to experience anxiety.

"No." He smiled softly. "Just struggling to sleep," he admitted. I exhaled deeply and bit down on my lip to suppress the deep need in my stomach.

"You never have trouble sleeping." I paused, confused. Also, why would I know that? I haven't spent a night with him in six years. I rolled my eyes, more to myself, turning to the water pitcher with embarrassment. Every nerve ending in my body was awake, and my muscles were restricted.

"Yeah, I know," he chuckled behind me.

The tension in the room was almost unbearable. I took a deep breath, focusing only on the water pouring into the cup. Every small, shallow breath worked against the emotions flooding my body.

"Mind if I grab a glass?" His voice was soft in my ear as one hand slid down my arm and the other reached around me into the cabinet. My arm was on fire.

"Yep," I inhaled breathlessly. The air was charged, and I could feel every single one of his movements, the heat from his body behind me, and each shaky breath he took.

I huffed nervously as I sipped my water. Brooks wrapped his arms around each side of me, filling up his glass. I almost choked on my water. All the hair on my body stood on end, fully attuned to him. I could barely concentrate. My whole body was filled with nervous giggles, only a small, soft one escaping my mouth as I pulled my lips tight.

"What's so funny?" he asked, whispering into my ear as he finished, pulling away from me. My shoulder rose involuntarily to my ear. I giggled again, turning to face him. We both sipped our water with our eyes fixated on each other. I set my cup down with a shaky hand. I cleared my throat and looked back up at Brooks.

I couldn't deny how my body hummed with possibility. I loved him, and now here he was, standing in the dark, looking like desire embodied.

"Good night," I whispered. *Go to bed. Don't do it.*

"Good night, Emily." I wanted to walk away, back down the hall, but my feet wouldn't move under me. It was as if they were glued there. I could feel the blood rushing to my cheeks, and my whole body filled with heat. We were like two magnets, drawn to each other, and the pull was too strong to ignore or fight.

Brooks' mouth turned up amused. I had never been more hot and bothered than I was now with Brooks standing here in my dark kitchen half-dressed.

"Screw it," I groaned, closing the distance between us and pressing my lips to his soft, warm ones. This was a battle I wanted to lose. My arms wrapped tightly around his neck while he set his glass down. Once his hands were free, he moved them to my waist, lifting and spinning to place me on the counter. My muscles tensed. This was all so new, so intimidating. I let my legs open so he could step between them.

My hands gripped his bare back while I focused on the pressure of his lips against mine. I could feel the pain from our heartbreak being poured into the intensity of our kiss. His hands were tight on my waist, inside my shirt. His tongue barely brushed my lip, driving me wild. My subconscious reared its unwelcome voice with a loud *Slow down.*

I released my grasp on his neck and leaned back, trying to catch my breath. His lips worked down the side of my neck to my collarbone. An embarrassingly loud moan escaped my lips, only encouraging him. My breath hitched when he sucked in, leaving a small mark on my chest. Easy enough to hide, but did he seriously just give me a hickey?

"Brooks," I started trying to catch my breath. His lips pulled away from me, and my whole body began to calm down. I chuckled in nervousness as his eyes met mine.

"Sorry," he said. His lips were wet and swollen, and I wanted nothing more than to feel them on me.

"Don't be." I ached for him in a way I had never allowed myself to before. I needed his lips on my neck, his heavy breath in my ear, and his firm grip digging into my hips, causing my stomach to flutter. I needed him to keep going.

He began to step back away from the counter, but my feet wrapped around his legs, pulling him in tighter.

"Don't go," I whispered.

His eyes softened as he caressed the side of my cheek before brushing a chunk of hair back behind my ear. I leaned into his hand. I longed for this connection with him, and it was finally here. It was better than I could have ever dreamed. My eyes closed softly, and I inhaled for some clarity.

I wanted him - all of him. I exhaled again, feeling the weight of what I was about to do. I had waited for him. I wanted him to be my first, and this might be my only opportunity, so I slid off the counter.

"C'mon," I whispered, pulling his hand along with me.

"Emily, no. It's okay." He halted.

"Brooks." I nodded in reassurance. He hesitated, searching my face to see if I wasn't ready, but he must have seen how sure I was because he followed, grabbing his wallet on the way.

Once back in my room, I flipped the side lamp on to see him. He was a sight to take in. Everything in my body was awake. Parts that had lay dormant my whole life were suddenly there, ready and needy. I wanted a minute, though. I wanted to see what this gorgeous man that my heart ached for looked like.

I walked around him, slowly tracing my fingers around the deep curve of his hips, up his broad, solid chest, across the valley of his collarbone, down his toned arm.

"What are these tattoos?" I ran my fingers over the lines of black ink.

"From the Air Force." His breathing was staggered, and his voice barely a whisper. I could feel his body tensing under the slow trace of my fingers. The American flag wrapped tightly around a cross with some triangular symbols below I didn't understand. I continued around to his back, where a small scar was just below his right shoulder blade. I exhaled nervously but continued my fingers to his other bicep.

"And this one?" I looked up at him. His eyes were closed.

"For our parents." It was a busy image with clouds, a clock, a hydrangea, a sailing mast, and some pearls. Both tattoos were black and white and really beautiful.

"Will you tell me about them sometime?" I asked, my voice barely more than a whisper.

"Yes."

I continued down his arm, brushing the tips of his fingers with mine as I returned to stand in front of him again. He exhaled a staggered breath, opening his eyes to meet mine. A soft smile tugged at the corner of his lips. His hands moved up to my neck as he brushed both sides of my cheeks with his thumbs.

I inhaled, breathing in once again that intoxicating scent that still lingered on his wrist. I could feel the nervousness in both of us and his hesitation to move forward. His hands brushed along the tops of my shoulders, brushing the strap of my nightshirt down my arm. He looked at me inquisitively as if asking permission to proceed. *Yes.*

"Go slow," I responded breathily, brushing the other strap loose, allowing the shirt to fall free to my waist. I had never been more nervous, and I had never been more thankful for my generous C cup. His gaze darkened at the site of them.

"God, you are so breathtaking." His voice was soft as his fingers tilted my chin up so his eyes communicated with mine. The sound of his whisper drew me in, reminding me that I trusted him. I sighed as he brushed his hands softly around my collarbone and down to my breasts. His fingers brushed lightly over the soft peaks of my breast.

Electricity and desire warmed me. His hands continued down my sides to the waistband of my shorts before following the same pattern as me. He, too, was slow, methodical, careful. There was a slow building of trust and intimacy. He felt safe.

As he stood in front of me once again, I knew I would need to be the one to walk us forward. He wasn't going to push anything tonight, and I was thankful he was willing to go at my pace. I pushed my shorts and shirt to the floor and leaned back on the bed in nothing but my underwear. His eyes softly raked down my whole body, and his eyes darkened.

"Breathe, Emily." His voice was soft and encouraging. I hadn't realized I had even stopped breathing.

I wasn't sure if I wanted him to say something, so I resolved to just sit in the awkward silence. He took a step forward, softly brushing his hands along my thighs.

"Are you sure?" he asked quietly.

"Yeah." I nodded. He hooked his thumbs into his pants and pushed them to the floor, exposing his black boxer briefs. He looked as if he stepped out of a Calvin Klein magazine. I blushed more than I ever had before. He was gorgeous and nearly naked, with a large bulge under the tight black material. He leaned over me, placing his swollen lips back on mine. Laying back, I pulled him with me until his heavy body was pressed into mine.

"Are you sure?" This was my out. My chance to protect myself. I knew there was a high likelihood that he would walk out of my house at the end of the week, and we would once again become strangers or, at best, acquaintances. Still, I wanted this more than anything. My one chance to be with him.

"I'm sure," I whispered nervously. His fingers were soft as they wrapped into the band of my underwear. I could barely breathe between my nerves and the raging desire that consumed me.

Should I have shut off the light? He began to pull my panties down. I lifted my butt into the air, allowing them to slide free. I pressed my legs closed, scolding myself that I definitely should have shut off the light. I closed my eyes, unsure of what came next.

"Are you okay?" he asked, brushing his hands up my thighs from my knees.

"Yep," I giggled. "Just nervous."

"I will go slow. Look at me." His voice was both reassuring and demanding.

I opened my eyes to meet his cobalt ones. His smile was soft, reassuring. He kept his eyes locked with mine as I allowed my legs to softly open with his hand. He crawled back up on the bed to lie beside me after dropping his underwear to the floor beside mine. My eyes must have conveyed my worry about his length, and my heart was racing, and my mind was clouded. I struggled to breathe at regular intervals.

"It's okay," he whispered, locking his mouth on mine.

"I trust you," I whispered back.

His hand brushed past my thigh as he gripped in between my legs. I shuddered against his touch and moaned quietly, my eyes still locked with his.

"Have you never been touched?" he asked curiously.

"No." I smiled bashfully.

His lips turned up as he caressed me, carefully building up my desire and my trust until I was soaked. His middle finger slipped inside of me, and I gasped.

"Oh my god," I moaned, embarrassed. The stretch burned, but it also felt amazing.

I could feel the warmth on my cheeks again. He set a slow pace, stretching me and preparing me. Brooks huffed as he added another finger. I began to twist in anticipation and could no longer keep my eyes open. I moaned softly as his fingers moved in and out, and his thumb pressed in circles.

All the sexual desires I had always suppressed were now coming to the surface more potent than ever, like a need that had always been left unfulfilled. Brooks' lips were soft on my shoulder. I moaned again. His fingers slid out slowly, and my eyes shot open. My heart continued to race as my eyes once again locked on his.

"Please, go slow. I'm so nervous." He nodded before rolling over on top of me.

"Are you okay?" His voice was husky and full of need.

"Yeah." I gulped again.

"It might hurt a little, okay?"

I nodded. He tore the wrapper of a condom and rolled it down while I watched.

Sara had mentioned it briefly when she lost her virginity during our junior year of college. Still, the idea of pain and pleasure was hard to grasp. Brooks softly pushed my legs open further. His hands moved slowly up and down my thighs as I worked to steady my breathing.

My eyes locked with his as his warm body pressed me further into the bed. His lips locked onto mine, and I felt the tip of him slowly push into me as he notched himself at my entrance. The newness of this feeling and the vital need for more had me gasping as he entered me slowly. Inch by inch. Pain and pleasure. My body curled around him until he was settled.

"Are you okay?" he whispered breathlessly in my ear.

"Yeah, it feels...kind of good," I replied. I didn't lie - entirely. The pinching sensation was masked by how good it felt to be full of him.

"Relax, baby." He paused, allowing me to breathe and relax.

"I'm okay," I sighed.

"Okay." He slid further into me, pulling out a shallow whimper.

"One more breath, Em. It's okay," he groaned into my lips.

I focused on relaxing with another inhale and exhale. I felt him push further into me and fill me in a way I didn't know was possible. I wanted to cry, not because of the pain but because I wanted him forever. I wanted to stay here forever, connected like this.

He was slow and careful as he slid in and out. I opened my eyes to look at him, only to find him studying me.

"I love you," I whispered, reaching up to cup his cheek. A single tear slid down the side of my face into my hair.

"I love you, Emily." We stayed like that for a few minutes. Just a slow rhythm, adjusting to each other, relearning each other, discovering new things about each other. I needed more. More of everything. Desire curled in my belly, wanting to burst out of me. I moaned, bringing his eyes to me, and his lips twisted into a confident smile.

"This feels good and -" I couldn't finish that sentence.

"Huh." His smile was a little devious. *Huh what?* He thrust his hips into mine, deeper, faster. I moaned loudly. *Yes.* He pulled out quickly, hissing and breathing heavily.

"What did I do?" I sat up.

"Nothing," he chuckled, reaching for me. "I just need to slow down, or I'm going to come, and then it's game over."

"Really? What does that mean?"

He smiled, shaking his head. His chest was heaving, and his body glistened. He looked like the child of Thor.

"You'll see." He groaned before returning to me, sliding in with more intensity this time. His mouth moved to my breast as he cupped the other, massaging gently before twisting my peaked nipple in between his fingers. The sensation alone had every nerve ending in my body warming, forcing me to an edge I wanted to fall from.

I moaned louder, embracing every embarrassing moment as his thrusts became quicker and his mouth intensified on my breast. I gripped the sheets, needing to ground myself, unable to contain the fire that filled every inch of my being. Every inch of me shook, and I could feel myself gripping around him. My hips raised, and I cried out as my vision darkened. My legs trembled, clenching him tighter. The all-consuming joy and fire kept me pulled under until I could feel the light returning and my lungs searching for air.

"There we go," he chuckled, pulling away from my breast with a loud pop.

I couldn't breathe as I lay back in the sheets, trying to regain my intake of oxygen. I curled my head into the sheets, longing to melt into a pool. Brooks' hands moved to my shoulders, and with a few more thrusts, he pulled out, wrapping his hand around himself.

His body stiffened as he moaned my name like it was the last word he'd ever say. It was all so fascinating to watch, and I realized what he was doing. My inner self did a victory dance. It felt good to make him feel pleasure.

After cleaning up in the bathroom, he returned to the bed beside me, where I was still trying to calm my racing heart.

"Are you okay?" he asked, lying on the pillow beside me. I rolled over on my stomach to look at him.

"More than okay." I drew my bottom lip in between my teeth, a little embarrassed.

"You are amazing." He brushed the hair from my eyes before I laid my head on his chest and curled into his side, my leg draped over his.

"Why did you wait, Em? I mean, I am glad you did, but -"

"I was waiting for you," I responded in no louder than a whisper. "I don't understand what you meant earlier when you slowed down." I traced the contours of his stomach muscles, eager to change the topic.

"If I didn't stop for a second, I would have come. I wanted you to come first."

"Is that what happened?" I laughed.

"Yes." His hand was drawing circles into my cold back.

"But I thought," I paused. Probably a dumb question. Why did I not know any of this? This was so embarrassing. I hated that my mom wasn't around to talk to me.

"Thought what?" he asked, pulling the blankets around us. I settled into the warmth of his body like it was completely natural to curl up with Brooks naked.

"No, it's dumb, never mind," I said into his chest. I hated feeling like this. I hated not knowing anything about sex. While everyone in college was enjoying their sex life, I kept locked up in my dorm, pushing away all thoughts of sex whenever Parker tried to touch me. I wasn't ready for that kind of intimacy with him.

"It's not dumb. What? You thought that girls don't come?" he asked, his voice amused.

"Yep, that's it." *He said it, not me.* He chuckled, tossing my head.

"They do if their partner is good and willing to encourage them." I could feel the heat in my cheeks. How is it possible to be a college graduate and have no clue about the world of sex.? *I wasn't that sheltered, was I?*

"Do you want your clothes?" he asked, brushing his fingers through my hair.

"No, not yet." I blushed, sitting up on my arm to see him. His face was calm and beautiful.

"I love you," he whispered.

My heart leaped, but my stomach tensed. *He loves me.* I need to get used to hearing that again, but if I am going to be honest with myself, it scares the crap out of me. I wasn't sure where we stood and where we were going.

Hell, it had been less than twenty-four hours before he had come waltzing back into my life. I leaned over to kiss him, parting his lips with my tongue. His mouth tasted like salt and mint. We stayed locked in our kiss as the exhaustion began to set in.

I pulled away and nuzzled him again before rolling over to shut off the lamp. I pulled my panties off the ground and slid them on. Brooks pulled the covers up over us and curled around my back. I could feel his warm breath on my neck. Tomorrow, we will talk. Tomorrow, we could deal with the fallout. Tomorrow was coming. I closed my eyes and dreamt of him.

Chapter Four

The morning light filtered into the room as I squinted, trying to focus my eyes. Had it all been a dream? I sat up quickly, realizing I was completely naked, aside from my black thong which left nothing to the imagination. Beside me, Brooks was asleep looking so peaceful, so at ease. I couldn't tear my eyes away from him. His long dark lashes sat against his skin and his dark hair was a mess. Images of last night danced through my mind. Me running my hands through his hair while I cried out his name. *Oh my God.* I had sex with Brooks.

Panic set in while my thoughts ran desperate hoping he didn't hate me when he decided to leave. I glanced at the clock. 10:03. I sat there pondering whether I should go for a run or just make coffee. I was still really sore from last night so coffee it was.

I giggled softly, turning to look at Brooks. Last night was amazing, better than I could have imagined. I could still feel his body pressed into mine and him inside of me. I could remember that feeling when I had reached my climax. The smell of sex and sweat that had pooled up and dried on my body now surrounded my senses.

"I need to shower," I muttered while turning my feet off the bed.

Brooks' hands wrapped around my waist as he pulled me back to the pillow and turned me to face him as I squealed.

"No, stay," he mumbled, his eyes still closed.

"Brooks, I need to shower," I whined.

"No." He inhaled deeply and opened his eyes, squinting, trying to focus on me. I watched his face lift with a full grin. My heart swelled with how his blue eyes admired me. His hands tightened around me as he pulled me into his chest. The smell of sex, salt, and Brooks was an even headier combo. My whole body responded with intense desire. I wanted him, but was it okay to want him? I knew laying here with him had changed the course of everything.

"You're driving me wild," I whispered into his chest.

"Oh, Em, you have no idea," he responded. I pulled my head back to meet his eyes. I blushed suddenly, embarrassed to be lying here naked, pressed against him.

"Why are you blushing?" he asked.

"Because," I whispered, smiling, too embarrassed to say it out loud.

"Because why?" His teeth raked his bottom lip. Memories of those lips all over me last night played in my head. I wanted to feel them again, to taste them, to feel their warmth and power.

"Because I'm naked against your naked, insanely hot body."

He chuckled, his hand squeezing my hip.

"Emily, you have a beautiful body. You don't need to be embarrassed." I rolled my eyes. Brooks had always made me feel safe and beautiful.

Growing up, I expected the awkward pre-teen phase to drive us apart, but he made sure I knew he thought I was beautiful every day, zits and all.

"Can I ask you something?" My fingers were tracing the valley of his chest.

"Anything." He swallowed audibly as he trembled under my touch.

"Last night, out by the pool. You were sad?"

He exhaled, sliding his hand up my back to rest on my shoulder.

"You always said you wanted a house by the ocean. Once upon a time, I thought I would be the one to give it to you."

I nodded acknowledging the gaping hole in my chest from years of him no longer belonging to me.

"Tell me about your tattoos." My eyes glanced to his left shoulder which had the one for our parents.

"Each item represents our parents. The clock, my dad. Always on time, very punctual. The mast, your dad. That man lived and breathed sailing."

I sighed as my eyes began filling with tears.

"The pearls, your mom of course. She loved that pearl necklace."

"I still have it," I whispered, running my fingers across the inky pearls.

"The flower is for my mom. She always smelled like flowers to me."

"She did." Heavy, slow tears hit the sheets.

"Don't cry, baby." His thumb brushed the tears away. I ignored the way he said baby. It felt like something you said to your girlfriend, not your hookup. I wasn't ready to ask the hard questions yet.

"Your other one?"

"It's just the Air Force symbol. I don't know, it was something I got before being stationed overseas with my team."

"I think it's beautiful." My eyes met his before dropping to his beautiful, parted lips. My heart skipped and right on cue his lips met mine. They were soft, careful. Not like last night. No, these lips were settled, peaceful, and perfect.

I would have stayed locked in his arms with our mouths moving in sync except the gathering moisture between my thighs and the need to feel him again had me moving. Involuntarily, my hips rocked forward tapping his. A small moan escaped from my mouth into his. Somehow, now with my body being completely ravaged and spent with Brooks at the helm, I only craved him more.

He smiled against my skin as his mouth moved to my breast, sucking it while his hand reached up grasping my other one.

"Your body is so responsive to me," he praised around my nipple. "It's like you were made for me."

"Oh," I moaned as his hand released my breast and moved in between my legs. His fingers were soft as he traced them down my slit and carefully slipped them in and out. My panties were soaked and annoyingly in the way.

"Are you sore today?" he asked, his mouth returning to mine. I gasped in pain and at the intensity of the pleasure.

"Umm..." I bit my lip. "Kind of."

His fingers slid out immediately and he rolled over to his back.

"No. Please don't stop." I giggled, embarrassed.

"I don't want to hurt you." He turned his head to look at me.

"I will tell you if you hurt me."

"Emily, you have to tell me. What hurts, what feels good, what doesn't." His voice was breathless. "I want to make you feel incredible things, but until I learn, you have to communicate with me."

I nodded, unable to respond. His words had a way of both making my heart melt and sending a fiery need coursing through me.

He looked at me inquisitively, slowly removed my panties, one leg at a time, and returned his fingers, all while maintaining eye contact. I gasped and my legs shook as his fingers slid inside of me.

I moaned into my palm while staring into his eyes. My legs rocked back and forth, my back arched off the bed as I tilted my pelvis, receiving more of his fingers. It's like my body acted on instinct. I couldn't prevent the automatic reactions my body had with his hands on me. He grinned back, pleased. I moaned his name, unable to keep my focus. His fingers were magic. Just then, I felt him against my hip. He was ready to go.

"I want you," I gasped, still trying to find my breath.

"I don't have any condoms, Em."

"I don't care." A little voice in my head reminded me I should care but why start listening now? Without hesitation, he pulled back his hand before rolling over on top of me. He moved inch by inch into me. Another gasp escaped my mouth and a loud moan from his. I expected him to put up more of a fight, but then again, it was *us*.

"Damn," he groaned. "I've never done this, Em. I've -" he stopped talking.

His hands moved to rest on my breasts while he palmed them. I couldn't keep my eyes open. I focused on the pleasure and pressure that consumed me. He thrusted in and out with more intensity, moving his hand down to my swollen bud, his thumb swirling in quick circles sending me to my climax once again. I gasped for my breath, and with another thrust, I felt his body tighten over mine. The free fall of my climax was painted in beautiful colors, but I wanted him with me.

"Don't," I panted. I didn't want him to pull out. I didn't care. I wanted him inside of me to stay like this for as long as possible. With another thrust, he fell to his hands over me.

"Emily." He was out of breath and his face twisted in something like remorse or disapproval. As he pulled out of me, I winced. My body was ravaged and ached both good and bad. Emotionally, I wanted him buried in me still, the emptiness I felt was a stark contrast to moments ago. He fell to the bed beside me and kissed my shoulder. "Emily, I wasn't wearing protection. Are you on birth control?"

"No," I muttered, suddenly embarrassed for not thinking of that beforehand. But now that I have Brooks, I don't want anything separating us again.

"Shit. We have to be careful, Em."

I rolled over, looking at him.

"I know. I just wanted you. All of you." He shook his head, still trying to catch his breath. I was surprised by my honesty with him and could feel the heat of embarrassment creeping up my neck. I don't know if it's the high from intimacy or my familiarity with him, but had I had a second to think, I don't know if I would have been so open.

"I need to get some condoms. I am not getting you pregnant."

I nodded, taking in what he just said. There would be more of this. Will he want to keep having sex after he leaves?

↟ ↟ ↟

As I waited for the warm water, the bathroom door slid open.

"Do you have a tub?" Brooks asked.

"Just the ones at the main house." I looked back at him, confused.

"You should soak in the tub, Emily. It will help."

I half smiled but could feel the panic rising in my chest. How did he know so much about this? I mean, I guess I didn't expect him to wait like I had. Still, it irked me on some level. I wanted to be his first and clearly, I was far from it. This man was no beginner. He was experienced in the art of pleasure. My face turned back to the shower. It was so clear now. He knew exactly what he was doing. Deep down I already knew the truth. Everything clicked into place shattering my high.

"Emily? What's wrong?" he asked, running his hands up and down my arms. I should have known my thoughts were like an open book written on my face.

"Nothing, I'm fine," I lied. *Don't be stupid. Keep your damn mouth shut. Don't ruin this.*

"Emily?" His hands were soft on my shoulders. I needed him to stop touching me. I couldn't focus with his hands on me.

"How do you know so much about this, Brooks?" I snapped, still focusing on the shower door.

He sighed and dropped his arms. I turned to face him just as he rolled his eyes.

"How many girls, Brooks?"

"Emily, it doesn't matter."

"How many girls?" I could feel the tears now falling with anger and shame.

"Can we not do this? It's not a lot, okay." *Great. Avoidance.* I was a fool. Just another girl. I don't know what made me think this was special for him like it was for me.

"How many is not a lot?" I whispered. Did I really want to know?

"Emily, please stop. I will tell you if you want to know, but not right now, okay? Please. Let me take care of you and then we can talk."

I turned angrily and stepped into the shower turning to face him. I could take care of myself. Thank you very much.

"I can take care of myself, just like I always have. Let me remind you since you seem to have forgotten, but you just got here. You haven't been here." I slammed the shower door.

The hot water burned as it hit my skin, but not as much as the shame and guilt from my sudden outburst. The glass door opened and Brooks stepped in. I closed my eyes and stepped back into the water, letting it fall over my face as I fought back more tears. Brooks wrapped his arms around me, pulling my head to his chest. I wanted to fight and scream, but I broke and I cried softly into his chest instead.

"I'm sorry," he whispered into my soaked hair.

I didn't want to respond. I was tired of him saying I'm sorry. We made a mess of this, and now it's complicated. As we stood in silence, I thought about the number of girls who had experienced this level of intimacy with him. It hurt to think about. He was mine, or was, but I guess I let him go. That was on me. I didn't plan on him ever returning to me, so why did I care how many girls? I guess I didn't. I just wanted him and I wanted him to stay.

Brooks was my first for everything up to this point. He was the beginning of all of it. When we broke up, I had never considered losing that level of intimacy with him. I never considered I wouldn't be his first. Who thinks about their first love having sex with someone else?

Still, standing here with him, knowing there were other girls in the mix, hurt. On some level, I felt betrayed.

His hand reached up, pulling the bottle of soap down. I couldn't pull away from him. I stayed wrapped up in his chest because I was too scared to pull away and see what would happen next. He turned with me out of the water, still holding me, and I felt the cold, smooth soap stream down my back. The scent of jasmine and vanilla filled the air.

His hand was warm and gentle as he massaged the soap into my back, my shoulders down and back up. My breathing slowed to match his, and my whole body relaxed. I mustered the courage to finally pull away, looking up at him.

"I don't really care. I'm sorry. It's none of my business," I whispered, too tired to fight.

"A few," he responded, matter-of-factly.

"What?" I gasped.

"I have slept with a few girls, okay?" His hands were still massaging soap into my back.

My eyes closed as I tried to comprehend how, in three years, he had managed to sleep with a few girls. He wasn't that person. I sat down on the bench and gasped, closing my eyes. *Two? Three? Seven? How many are a few?*

"Emily." Brooks was kneeling in front of me.

"Please, just give me a minute," I snapped. I stood quickly and rinsed off before stepping out and wrapping the towel around me. I rushed to my closet across the room, leaving Brooks in the shower. I hurried to get dressed in my workout clothes, nervous he would get out of the shower before I could escape. I dropped my towel on the bed and raced outside up to the main house.

I paced back and forth, fighting back the tears. It didn't matter, but it did. Didn't it? My heart and brain were at war with each other. My mind switched to Grey. I had denied him. Why? Maybe I should have slept with him. Or Parker. Either one. I didn't though because I loved Brooks. The more I thought, the angrier I got. Was I just another number for Brooks?

I didn't actually believe that, but how stupid could I be? I knew him, deep down, I knew the *real* him. I reached the front steps of the main house and fell to the ground, gripped with emotion, and sobbed. I wanted so badly to go back to yesterday. Or even back to February when Brooks had first texted me so I could tell him it wasn't a good idea. This wasn't a good idea. Here I was, feeling even more broken than the last time. This is what they mean when they say sex complicates things.

His hands slid across my back as he kneeled on the ground in front of me. My body ached for him, to be held by him, but my mind was a wreck. His warm hand was calming and once again, I found myself at the mercy of my body's reaction to him.

"Emily, hey." His voice was soft.

"Leave me alone right now, please," I sobbed.

"I can't do that, Em,"

"Why did you do it? Why are you here? To get what you wanted before you head back to Seattle? It's not okay, Brooks." My body shook with the storm of emotions.

"Emily, let's talk, please," he pleaded.

"Talk about what?" I cried.

"Us, this. I didn't come here to leave you again. C'mon, please." He held out his hand. Through my soaking-wet hair and tear-stained eyes, I looked at his pleading eyes. The same eyes that I looked at when we greeted each other at the door each morning before school. The same eyes that worried over me whenever I was sick or crying. The same eyes that shined when he first told me he loved me.

"Okay." I hated this void between us and I wanted to hear him out. Hopefully, he would have a good excuse because I couldn't stay here on these steps all morning crying.

Out on the main deck, Brooks started the fireplace and wrapped a blanket around me while I dabbed at my eyes.

"Emily," he cleared his throat. "I..." he paused again. I looked up, confused to see the pain in his eyes. His hands reached for mine and our fingers interlaced. My anger and hurt were subsiding, but now I felt confused, scared, and unwilling to rush this. The crashing of the waves in the distance mimicked our souls being bruised and beaten.

"Emily," he began again. "I love you. I always have and never stopped." I inhaled, possibly with too much force, causing his eyes to meet mine.

"Those other girls, they meant nothing. It was different. I have never had sex like that. I have never made love to anyone before. You are different. I love you. I came here to apologize. I just want you back in my life. I was just so angry, hurt, lost. I was trying to fill the void. I know how messed up that sounds, but it's the truth."

"Brooks, I -" I started.

"No, wait please," he interrupted. "I know I can't just march back into your life and expect you to come running back into my arms. I don't know enough about your life. I don't even know if you have a boyfriend. I mean, I assume you don't." He almost laughed the last part out.

"No," I whispered, fighting back an amused smile.

"I will do whatever it takes, but I can't live without you. I tried, but it didn't work. I understand if you don't feel the same, but please know, I came here to see you, that is all. I never imagined sleeping with you. I mean, it was amazing, but all I want is you. Sex or no sex, just you."

Guilt consumed me. It wasn't fair how I was treating him. He had been nothing but gentle and kind, and I acted like an ass. Every word that poured out of him was like a soothing, healing balm, gluing and taping the broken pieces of my heart back together. It terrified me more than anything.

He said he loved me and I believed him. It still didn't change the fact I felt hurt over the number of girls, but I would need to accept that. I crawled into his lap, wrapping the blanket around us both. My lips crashed down on his and I felt a sigh escape.

I needed us to be okay. I couldn't do more anger and pain, I had lived with that for too long. It might have been selfish, or sweeping it under the rug, but for now, I needed to feel like we were moving forward. My heart was beating differently. Taped for now but at least it was healing.

"Emily," he started, pulling away to look at me. His hand cupped my cheek tenderly.

"Brooks." How could there be so much pain and love between us?

"Can we try this?" In a millisecond, the wind was knocked out of me.

"Try what?" My voice was almost a whisper.

"Can we try us? Being together again? We can take it slow."

I nodded. "Yes." Tears brimmed my eyes. Brooks' hands gripped my hips while his lips softly kissed me again. This is all I wanted - us.

↟ ↟ ↟

I looked at the omelet on my plate. Even though I was famished, my stomach was swirling alongside my emotions.

"What's wrong, Em?" Brooks asked, keeping his voice low.

I looked up. "Long distance again?"

"It will be different this time." The tape on my broken heart slipped - just a little.

"Brooks, it's a four-hour drive. How will this work?" I slipped my hand over his on my thigh and curled my fingers around. I needed to touch him, to make sure he was real and still here.

"We can take turns. I can work remotely and come stay here, and you can come stay with me." He was so confident this would work.

"Brooks, I have a job. I can't just pick up and leave."

"I can spend every other week here. I don't know. Emily, we will figure it out." He sounded exasperated.

I nodded, even though I couldn't imagine a way that this was going to work. I guess I would just have to wait and see. I picked at my breakfast for a moment and realized I didn't want to spend the morning all gloomy. I inhaled and turned.

"I am going to throw you a party on Friday. I want you to meet my friends," I beamed.

Chapter Five

The week had passed too quickly, and I was still trying to catch my breath. Everyone was going to be here any minute and Mrs. Hall, my house manager, and the catering team were up at the house, ready to welcome them in.

Brooks and I had a busy week hiking, eating ice cream on the pier, and a beach day, and we spent the rest of the time catching up and kissing. There was a lot of kissing. My lips were in a permanent state of swollen and my mouth had been thoroughly memorized by him. The week had been playful, handsy, and fun, but there was no sex which was a great thing.

I think we both felt the need to slow down and reconnect without all the sex that could have happened. It was surprising how easily we fell back together. Deep down I knew I was still holding my breath, waiting for him to leave even though he has promised every single day this time will be different.

The shower turned off and the sound of the shower door opening and closing sent a shiver down my spine. We might not have been having sex, but I still wanted him. I was just finishing my makeup when Brooks stepped into the room dripping wet. The trails of water and the white towel wrapped around him made the ache between my legs even more pronounced.

"See something you like?" He grinned.

I rolled my eyes and went back to my mascara ignoring the way my body hummed, begging for him to touch me.

Brooks dressed in a pair of navy slacks and a white button-down, rolling the sleeves to his elbows. I had seen him in all states of dress this week and each time I had decided it was my favorite.

"You know I leave in the morning?" He frowned, strapping his watch on.

"Mm-hmm." I nodded. I had been avoiding this day. Tomorrow would be the first day of long distance and the second attempt at making us work. I glanced down at my shoes. *Do not cry.* "I won't miss having to share my shower," I teased.

Brooks chuckled. "I see how it is." He crossed his arms across his chest, leaning against the door. He was so sexy even when he wasn't trying. "Don't worry. I will miss you enough for the both of us."

I shot him a big, knowing grin.

We walked into my house to a room full of guests that had all arrived on time. New people in town were a rarity so I chalked it up to interest. Knowing we would be pulled in different directions, I wrapped my arm around his and clung to him. He pressed a soft kiss to my head in response.

Natalie was the first to approach with her eyes scanning us like she was trying to solve a puzzle. I still hadn't told her about Brooks and now my stomach was in knots over it. Not because she would say something negative, but because she was my friend. My only real friend I've made since moving. She deserved more from me.

Natalie's long chocolate-colored hair was pulled up in a flirty pony and she wore a slim-fitting mauve cocktail dress that looked great with sparkling green eyes.

She kissed my cheek first.

"Who's this cutie?" she asked, eyeing Brooks. He responded before I did, introducing himself.

"I'm Natalie Spencer, one of Emily's friends."

I chuckled, watching her take him in. *Yeah, I know the feeling.* "Brooks just got out of the Air Force and is heading back to Seattle tomorrow. He spent the week here visiting."

Natalie tilted her head, glancing back and forth between Brooks and me, then down at our interlaced fingers and how I clung to his arm with my other hand. She must have been putting the puzzle together from our night out a few months ago and me mumbling about Brooks at Sapphire.

She excused herself for another drink and promised to catch up later. We were intercepted before we could reach the couples I'd been dying to introduce Brooks to.

The single ladies from my spin class were openly admiring Brooks which made me annoyingly jealous. Brooks must have noticed because his hand dropped, wrapping around my waist and tugging me closer as we approached.

"These are my friends from spin class. Ladies, Brooks, my boy... friend. He just returned home from the military." I looked up to meet his eyes. He smiled softly showing his approval of the title.

"I'm Nayla, welcome home soldier." Nayla wasn't shy at the young age of nineteen. She was attractive with her honey-blonde hair, hazel eyes, and pouty lips, and she knew it.

"Nayla is traveling the States right now. She's taking the time to travel the Pacific coast, trying to find a place to settle," I said, filling in the gap.

"Oh, very cool." Brooks nodded.

"Any suggestions?" She eyed him flirtatiously. Irritation flared through me like a meteor in the night sky, quick, hot, and a little scary.

"Ah," Brooks turned to look at me. I shrugged. "I mean here is great, or Seattle. That's where Em and I grew up."

Nayla's eyes turned to me.

"You grew up in Seattle?" she asked, shocked.

"Yeah. Brooks and I own a company in Seattle that our parents started. We grew up together," I responded feeling a little possessive. Brooks grinned. I had just said we owned Caston. Guess I really was keeping it.

"So like brother and sister?" The smile she gave us made my temper flare.

Brooks stepped in to correct her.

"What company?" Jaymi, my instructor, asked.

"Caston. We own several hotel chains and investments. We are also about to start a few acquisitions expanding into the tech industry." He somehow made talking about work sexy.

After a few more questions fired off at random, Brooks and I excused ourselves to go chat with my realtor-turned-friend, Leah, and her husband. She gave me a huge hug and gushed over my interior design which I had done myself. I found that I loved it, but as a hobby. I would leave the business side of it to the professionals.

When I introduced Brooks as my boyfriend she almost asked about Grey but held back. I hadn't told Brooks about him. Not that I was hiding it, but there wasn't much there anyway and our week had been so busy it never came up.

She introduced her husband, Peter, to Brooks. He was a high-school teacher and her complete opposite. Leah loved high fashion, she was bright and bubbly, and Peter was quiet, dressed in khakis and a cardigan.

Others joined the conversation. My stylist, Aleksandr, and Michaela and Josiah, a couple who had moved to PC last year, were last-minute invites. And Natalie had made her way back to me.

The conversation with this group flowed much easier, and it was pleasing how easily everyone accepted Brooks. The men were especially interested in his time in South Korea.

I took in the room around me and noticed Grey walking through the door. *Shit.* I needed to talk to him before he talked to anyone else. I had let Natalie and Leah do the inviting since I was still new even though I had met almost everyone in town by now. Call it naivety but I didn't stop to think they'd invite Grey.

"I'll be right back," I muttered softly to Brooks before crossing the room to the entry.

"There's my girl." Grey grinned, reaching out for me. Guilt sunk into my stomach like a ten-pound rock. I quickly hugged him asking if we could talk privately upstairs. He must have thought I was ready to take the next step because he only grinned bigger.

I led him upstairs to the loft, away from everyone, giving myself the time to scramble together my thoughts.

His eyes raked my body in the dim light of the loft and I hated myself even more. This was not how I planned on having this conversation.

Chapter Six

"Want to sit or stand? You seem nervous?" Grey asked, holding me by the elbow before I turned to take a few steps across the loft, away from him.

"Umm, standing is fine," I breathed out, trying to hide my nervousness. He looked great in his gray slacks and black button-down shirt that fit just tight enough to show off his build.

"You okay?" His arms crossed over his chest.

"Er, no, not really. Okay, first..." The last time I had this conversation with a guy, my ex, Parker, it didn't go so well. I was a people pleaser. It's just who I was and breaking up with someone, even though Grey and I weren't actually a thing, felt like pure torture. "Please understand that I never expected this, and this conversation was going to happen eventually, but I need you to listen to everything first. Please."

"Okay?" He tilted his head as if trying to break inside my brain and read my thoughts. It was now or never.

"Well, Brooks, my ex, you asked about him a while back from the night at Sapphire. Brooks and I grew up together and our parents were best friends. Our parents co-owned a large company that was handed over to Brooks and me -" I paused, trying to breathe. Was I even making sense? "Umm, well, Brooks and I now own the company and he was in the Air Force in South Korea and just got back. I wanted to sell, but we decided that I shouldn't."

"Emily, what are you talking about?" he interrupted.

"Please," I begged. "Just listen."

"I am listening." His voice was calm, almost soothing.

"Okay, so Brooks came to visit. I thought he was here to talk about the company. He's stepping in as CEO. I haven't seen him since high school, we dated long-distance, and the last time we had talked was when we broke up our freshman year of college. We had kinda dated from middle school until then. Anyway, it was messy and the long-distance thing was awful. So at Sapphire, I was upset because it was the first time I had heard from him in four years." I was rambling a million miles a minute, a trait of mine whenever I got nervous.

Grey was pacing the loft slowly, listening, but I could sense he was still waiting for the story to get somewhere.

"So this week, Brooks and I kinda reconnected, and we want to give it another shot." I exhaled my last breath and inhaled sharply, holding it all in, waiting for it all to sink in.

"What?" Grey turned, looking at me, confused and hurt.

"I know I said we would talk when he left, but I didn't expect this to happen. I am so sorry," I mumbled.

Why did this have to be so difficult? I never wanted this to happen. A single tear escaped as I hugged myself tighter, waiting for Grey to say something. I wasn't sad about Brooks and I being together, but I hated hurting someone, especially him. He had been nothing but sweet, caring, and patient with me. He was one of the first friends I had made here and I knew that going forward, that wasn't going to be a possibility.

"Hey, Em, everything okay?" Brooks asked, walking up behind me. I spun, looking first at Brooks and then back to Grey as his eyes widened looking at Brooks.

"Yeah, I'm okay. Just talking," I responded, quickly wiping away the tear. Brooks wrapped his arms around my waist and reached his hand out to shake Grey's. His body pressed into mine from behind. I knew he was claiming me, but I couldn't be mad. I had wanted to do the same downstairs.

"Brooks Devonshire." He reached out, shaking Grey's hand.

"Grey Stanley." Grey's whole demeanor changed, finally realizing that we were over before we started.

"Hey B, could you give us another minute? I'll come find you." I asked politely, hoping he would be okay leaving me up here in the dark with a handsome man.

"Yeah, sure. See you in a few." He kissed my cheek before nodding to Grey. "Nice to meet you," he said and turned down the stairs.

We waited in silence, looking at each other, waiting for Brooks to step off the last step.

"I'm truly sorry, Grey. I honestly should have told you from the start. It's just that I never stopped loving him. I had a boyfriend in college after Brooks, but we broke up after graduation because I didn't share the same feelings. Then I met you and I wanted to make it work, but my heart wasn't available, even if I wanted it to be. I thought once Brooks left, I would finally have some closure, and maybe I'd be able to move on. I was counting on it, actually. You have been so sweet to me and I didn't want to hurt you."

"I know," he nodded. "I wish it would have worked out for us. I should have spent more time with you." Another punch to the heart.

"You did nothing wrong. Promise. It's me. I just belong to him." I wanted him to understand. He was truly amazing. Of course, it was easier to admit it now that I knew we didn't have a future.

"I'm sorry." I hugged him tight. His arms wrapped around me and his head rested on top of mine.

"I know. You know, I wish I was the one."

We stood there in silence for a moment, knowing the second we let go that was it for us. I exhaled and released my arms to gaze up at him. He reached out and brushed a single tear away.

"No tears, Emily. I'm happy for you, as long as you're happy."

Grey and I rejoined the party and to my surprise, he and Brooks hit it off instantly. For the remainder of the evening, they stayed in conversation, Peter and Josiah sometimes joining in.

I sat back and watched chatting with the ladies and I felt settled for the first time in a week. We could do this. We were more mature, we both knew what we wanted, and he was making an effort to make friends. I just needed to trust him.

As the night went on and the room emptied of friends, I found myself needing Brooks and his full attention. I felt the clock like a timer in my head counting down until he was gone again.

↟ ↟ ↟

"Emily, slow down," he chuckled. "Baby, I thought you wanted to take things slow?" I arched my body into him, pulling him in for another kiss. I pushed his hand between my thighs.

"Please," I begged. "I know what I said. I changed my mind." He pulled away studying my eyes and he must have seen the heat and desperation because I was ready to argue my case but then his mouth was on me and I forgot everything I was going to say.

His mouth demanded control as he kissed me mindless as his hands roamed my body, leaving no place untouched. He pressed his erection into my belly before lifting me and carrying me to the couch.

I dipped my head, deepening our kiss, and I worked to unbuckle his belt and pants. With his help we both stripped each other, never breaking our mouths for more than a moment. If this was our last night together for a while, then I wanted to make it memorable.

After rolling on a condom, he filled me and pulled me against his body. It wasn't enough. God, it would never be enough. I wanted him closer. As we moved together, hot tears streamed down my face. I loved him. I was in love with him. I needed him more than my next breath and he was leaving.

He didn't ask if I was okay or why I was crying. He just held me, bringing the first wave of my orgasm, and then another. For hours, that's how we stayed, wrapped around each other, conveying promises through our touch and kisses. And when I finally drifted off to sleep, he spoke just before I was lost to darkness.

"I love you, Emily."

Chapter Seven

Brooks was playing with a strand of my hair when I finally woke up. The sun was still low on the horizon and the room still dark.

"It's too early," I groaned, completely exhausted. The handful of orgasms last night definitely played a factor leaving me completely sated.

"My car will be here in a few hours and I want to spend as much time with you as I can before I leave," he whispered into my shoulder.

"Don't remind me." I didn't want him to leave. It felt safe having him around. If he left, what would happen? I felt torn. Part of me felt consumed with a familiar anxiousness and the other part was completely confident we would figure it out. We had to, we had made it this far. Plus, we had both barely survived our first breakup. Another one might do us both in.

I rolled over, trying to adjust my eyes to his.

"Good morning, beautiful," he said, brushing my blonde hair from my face.

I was still attempting to keep my eyes open. I exhaled and planted my lips on his. His lips caressed mine softly. In our time apart, I had forgotten how good kissing him felt. The way our mouths moved together had always been our connection to each other, reminding us we still belonged to one another. It was a powerful connection I had longed for, and neither Parker nor Grey even came close.

I kissed him softly, trying to savor it, remember it. I could do this. One week. How silly. I had spent six years away from him and now a week seemed like a monumental feat.

"Wanna go for a run and grab breakfast with me?" he inquired against my mouth.

"Yes. No." I smiled, running my hands down his chest.

"C'mon Em. I need food." He pulled me in close for a deep kiss and then he released me, rolling out of bed.

↟ ↟ ↟

The chilly air pricked at my skin while puffs of white breath clouded my face. The sun was still low in the east and the ocean was dark, only catching small glimmers of sunlight. Clouds were rolling in from the ocean most likely bringing rain with them.

We ran in silence, listening to the roar of the ocean and the cry of the gulls just waking up for the day. The leaves rustled in the light breeze. It was so peaceful.

The coffee bar was one of the few businesses open at this time of day. As we neared the modern concrete building, the big, white glowing letters appeared. Lulu's Coffee Bar.

"Good morning, Emily." The young blonde high school barista waved, making me blush. Jack was always the first to say hi to me whenever I came in. He worked the early shift before school trying to save for college. He was going to WSU in the fall.

"Hey, Jack." I waved back.

"Another one of your admirers?" Brooks teased in my ear.

I gave Brooks an eye roll, ignoring him.

"Emily!" Kelsey, another one of the baristas grinned and waved at me as she made her way over.

"Hi, Kelsey."

"Hi, I'm Kelsey." She reached her hand out to shake Brooks'.

"Brooks Devonshire."

"Oh gosh, sorry, this is my boyfriend, Brooks," I replied.

"Did I hear boyfriend?" Vasyl, the owner of Lulu's, rounded the corner.

"Hi, Vasyl," I chuckled.

"Emily, my dear, come give me a hug." His arms opened wide with his thick accent and generous smile that could make you feel like you were someone special.

As he rounded the corner I slipped into his arms. His daughter was about the same age as me, and according to him, looked like me. Though I had only seen her in photos, I couldn't see the resemblance. Her name is Lucy, Lulu is his nickname for her. Unfortunately, she still lives in Chicago and decided not to move when her dad came out here two years ago for a fresh start after an ugly divorce.

"Vasyl, this is Brooks Devonshire, my boyfriend," I said, pulling out of his coffee and pastry-scented embrace.

"Dochka, I didn't know you had a boyfriend," he responded, shocked.

"Long story." I returned to Brooks' side, wrapping my arms around his waist.

"Nice to meet you, Brooks. I am Vasyl. I'm the owner. Please, order. Do not let us keep you. Come back and talk soon."

"We will." I waved to both Vasyl and Kelsey as they returned to their original spots behind the counter.

"I will take a London Fog and a blueberry scone warm please," I looked back at Jack who had been patiently waiting.

"Good choice, Emily. And for you, sir?"

"Coffee, dark roast, with a bit of cream. I'll take the quiche." Brooks' eyes were still on the menu.

"That will be $24.70."

Brooks handed his card to Jack, who was studying him. I tried not to laugh. Jack was always so friendly to me when I was in here, and I knew he had a little high school crush on me. Jack handed the card back, and Brooks turned wrapping his arm around my shoulder as we made our way to a table.

"So," he started, pulling the chair out for me. "Grey?"

I shook my head. I should have known this was coming before he left town. "It's nothing. Promise."

"Tell me, Em." He pulled his chair out gracefully and took a seat in the beautiful leather wingback chair across from me.

"Well, we met shortly after I moved here. We started hanging out a lot. His feelings were deeper than mine." I shrugged.

"Did anything happen between you two?" He was tracing mindless patterns into the faux granite table between us.

"He kissed me once. That day you texted me and we talked. I was out with him and Natalie. I didn't feel the same. I got too drunk." My voice got quiet.

Brooks waited patiently, studying me, waiting for the rest of the story.

"Er, I passed out. I woke up in his bed. He was on the couch. Nothing happened. We talked about giving it a go, but I wanted to see how things would play out with you. I was still very much in love with you and yeah." I shrugged again. I could feel the pink heat on my cheeks and the embarrassment in my stomach.

"So, last night?" he prompted.

"Last night, I told him you and I were back together. He was sad, I think, but he genuinely wanted to meet you." I was still shocked at how easily he had accepted Brooks being back in my life.

Brooks groaned, sitting back in his seat and looking out the window.

"What?"

"I'm leaving town and leaving you here with a decent-looking guy who's in love with you. Oh, and a barista who can't keep his eyes off you. What am I going to do with you?" His voice was full of amusement allowing me to smile back at him.

"In love with me? No. And Jack is just a kid, he doesn't like me." I shook my head and looked out the window thinking of all the ways my relationship with Grey had played out.

"Emily." His eyes softened. He was probably right. I refused to see it. I didn't want to. Brooks had nothing to worry about, though.

I shook my head. "Don't worry. I waited half a decade for you, Mr. Devonshire. I am not leaving you now."

"Your London Fog and a dark roast coffee with cream. Food will be right out," Jack said, setting our cups down in front of us.

"Thanks, Jack." Brooks nodded.

Brooks' lips curled up in a smile. I guess that response was good enough for now. We sipped our warm drinks and ate slowly as the sunlight filled the room. More of the town's early risers and younger generation swept in and out ready for another day.

After breakfast, we walked hand in hand back to the house, talking about Caston and what Brooks' new role would be. He would be completing his master's degree online while figuring out how to expand the company into the tech world. His excitement about Caston and plans for the company were hypnotic.

Once upon a time, I had envisioned us running the company together. We would share the top floor office, and one day, our kids would run around just like Brooks and I had done when we were young.

Even with us back together, the image in my mind looked different. I wouldn't sell, but I loved my job at Hope and couldn't imagine giving it up. Plus, I had just left the city and bought a house. I didn't want to return to Seattle. One of the many things Brooks and I would need to work out I guess.

"What is *dochka*?" His face turned up like he was trying to say the word correctly.

I swallowed before I could spew my tea.

"It means daughter in Ukrainian. Vasyl is from Ukraine and

moved to the States to start a family. He lived in Chicago, but his wife, Kateryna, I guess she left him a few years back, bringing him here. He doesn't talk about what happened but he has two daughters. Sofiya, who is traveling the world as a photographer and is a little older than us, and Lucy, who this place is named after, is in Chicago finishing her degree in biotech. He's very proud of her."

"I like it here. I like that they all know who you are. I can see that you are really happy." A lump in my throat formed.

"I am happy here. Even happier now that you are here. It feels complete. I feel like I can breathe again and look forward to a future again." I picked at my scone now wondering if I had divulged too much.

"Em, look at me." He reached for my hand.

My eyes met his gorgeous deep blue ones.

"I feel the same way. We'll make this work okay? I can't live without you. I mean that." His voice was calm, reassuring. I never thought that we could be here again. I never thought I could feel this again yet here I was soaking in every promise of his.

I blew out a breath I didn't know I was holding in.

"I know. I love you."

"Love you." He grabbed my hand and squeezed.

↟ ↟ ↟

We walked into the studio and back into the room. Brooks worked his way around the room, gathering his things and packing them into his bag.

"Are you sure you have to go?" I whined, plopping down onto my messy bed.

"It's six days, Em. I will be back Friday night, okay?"

I pouted. I didn't want him to leave. Why couldn't he just stay here? He could move in.

"Brooks," I started. He looked up, his eyes meeting mine. "When you come back, bring stuff to leave here. This can be your home too," I said, but it sounded more like a plea.

He looked at me inquisitively.

"You want me to move in with you before I have even unpacked into my place?" He chuckled a bit.

"Why not?" I drew in a shallow breath. My stomach twisted in knots waiting to hear his answer.

He stopped what he was doing and crossed the room to hug me, enveloping me in his scent and warmth, melting away all the tension and fear.

"What happened to taking it slow?" He kissed the side of my head.

"I don't know. Maybe slow isn't right. For us, I mean. We already know each other and—" I could hear the hopeful hesitancy in my voice.

"Okay," he interrupted.

"Okay?"

"Okay, I will move in with you." He pulled away to continue packing.

I jumped a single, small leap in excitement off my bed.

"Really?"

"Yes, Emily. I will just leave the basics there." He chuckled, returning to fill the bag with the stack of clean shirts I had washed and folded on my dresser.

"Is it too late to break the lease?" I asked.

"Er, probably. I mean, I guess I can see if Michaelson is still looking for a place. He was planning on moving soon, anyway."

"Yes. Do that." I all but cut him off with excitement.

Brooks chuckled again, zipping up his leather bag.

"A week ago we were strangers, Emily, and now you've invited me into your bed and to share your home." He turned, pulling me back into his arms.

Okay, maybe things were moving a little fast, but it wasn't like this was all new. I mean, this was the original plan. We were just going about it a little differently now.

"I want you here. I want us, Brooks," I pleaded. I hoped he would understand and not feel overwhelmed. I wasn't feeling the least bit nervous. If anything, I felt like I was finally being true to myself.

In the past, I had tried not to let my thoughts drift to Brooks very often so I couldn't imagine this whirlwind finally happening, but it just felt right. I just wanted to be with him every second of the day.

"I know, Em. Me too. Whatever it takes to make you happy and trust me again." He kissed the top of my hair before releasing me.

Those worlds crushed me.

"I do trust you."

Chapter Eight

The car door closed and Brooks blew one last kiss as the driver pulled out of my driveway. I waved and then turned back to the main house. I had so much to do before work on Monday morning. Plus, if I wanted Brooks to move in, I would need to clear some space in the closet.

Mrs. Hall was finishing wiping the counters when I walked in. She was a widow in her fifties who had never remarried and often spent her days off with her grandson while her daughter, a single mom, worked as an insurance agent. Grief had aged her and her once strawberry-blonde hair was now almost all silver.

"Oh, hey!" I smiled, standing beside her.

"Ms. Barlow. How was your visit with Mr. Devonshire? He seems nice." Her lips pursed together hiding her approving smile.

"Yes. It was great. I wanted to let you know, Mr. Devonshire is moving in next weekend. I don't know what he is bringing, but I will keep you updated. Do you think you could help me move some of my gowns and winter clothes up here into the master closet? I want to make sure he has room down in the studio."

"Yes, of course. Please, just let me know what he would like stocked in the fridge and what dishes he likes."

"Of course. Thanks, Mrs. Hall. Oh, and about Brooks," I paused. It didn't matter what she thought, but I still felt I owed her an explanation. "Eh, he's kinda my ex or was. We had plans to get married one day, but some things happened. Anyway, we are going to work on it."

"Well, I'm very happy for you." She nodded politely before returning to the counter.

"Also, are you okay?" I asked. "I mean, you just seemed a little tired this week. If you need some time off, you can just tell me."

"Ms. Barlow, thank you, but I'm alright. I just had to watch Braxton this week while my daughter was out of town for training."

"What?" My heart ached. I wished I had known. "You can always bring him here or take the day off. Please, if anything like this happens again, I am happy to be accommodating. We can have someone come and watch him here if you want."

"No, Ms. Barlow, thank you. I will be okay. He is enrolled in daycare. I'm just not as young as I used to be, so watching a toddler in the evenings is exhausting."

I nodded. "Okay. Well, I hope you get some rest."

With that, I grabbed my phone and clicked the phone icon for Natalie. She would want all the details and a large part of me needed to gush about Brooks being back. My head was dizzy, and my body was exhausted and deliciously sore, but I couldn't help but feel the buzz of excitement in my bones. My broken heart was healing. The phone rang once before an excited "Hello" came over the speaker.

"Hey, Natalie! Brooks just left. Can you come over?"

"Great, see you soon."

I ran back down to the studio to grab my water bottle. When I stepped into my room I saw a wrinkled envelope sitting on my pillow. My heart cartwheeled in my chest as I reached for it. The envelope looked old and worn. Across the front, my name was scribbled out in Brooks' neat handwriting.

Clutching the letter in my hand, I went to sit on the small porch that overlooked the beach. Sadly, the sound of the surf below did nothing to calm the feeling of anxiousness that was winding its way around my heart. My fingers traced the letters back and forth multiple times.

I knew I was avoiding opening it, but I wasn't sure if I was prepared to read what was inside. After a few more minutes of delay, I slid my finger through the top and revealed the notebook paper inside. With another calming breath, I pulled it out.

My dearest Emily,

I am sitting at the airport right now about to head to Osan, South Korea where I will be stationed for the next two years. There's a part of me that is excited to see this new country and have this adventure. But there's a bigger part of me that realizes I have messed up big time. I once promised you I would come home, that I would return for you. I broke that promise. I am so sorry for that. Sorry isn't a big enough word to fully cover how I feel. I could write a ten page letter about how sorry I am but I am not sure I could convey the depth of my regret.

I know I don't deserve you, and I know I don't deserve a chance to give you an explanation, but I need to. If this letter ever finds you, I hope it's because we worked things out and not because you had another person to bury. God, I hope not. Anyway, when I was in the last month of my senior year, all the guys were preparing for grand adventures around the world, some of them had job offers, and some were headed to college. I was preparing to head home to you.

Instead, on the first day of finals, there was a man in the halls dressed in his United States Marine Corps t-shirt. He was there to visit his younger brother. As I walked past him, I thanked him for his service. I had no plans to stop and chat, but that simple interaction turned into one of the most important conversations of my life.

He told me about his decision to join the Corp and how it was the one thing that so far had helped him find his place in the world. Before then, he felt lost, and he didn't know what he was doing with his life. I envied him. After finals that week, I was still thinking about what he told me. I did some research on the different branches of the armed forces, and I could feel the shift in my veins. I needed to do this. It was like an instant pull I couldn't ignore.

I know that still doesn't explain why - I am getting there.

After I was sent to boarding school, I hit rock bottom. Looking back now, I was probably borderline clinically depressed. I lost everyone Em. I showed up for our phone calls because it was the only thing that kept me going. During my time there, I forgot who I was. I had become a different version of myself, defined by circumstances, in a different country away from everything, and everyone I ever loved.

I knew I couldn't come home and be who you needed me to be. I didn't even know who I was and I had nothing to offer you. You deserve the best of me. You deserve everything and more, and I was nothing. I was a broken kid.

When you said you weren't going to Princeton, I knew I was causing you more damage than intended. It just reinforced what I was already feeling. I wasn't good for you.

I could have spent the whole time loving you. I never stopped, but that is all I could have given you. I had nothing else to give. So please, as hurt and angry as you are, please understand. I only left to be better for you. I want to give you everything, and more, and I hope that one day you will let me. I pray to God that He lets me find my way back to you. I pray that you don't give up on me, and selfishly, I pray that you wait for me to come home to you.

I can't live my life without you. You are the best part about me. You are more important to me than the air I breathe. Almost every memory I have includes you. You are in me, in my heart, in my bones, all of me.

If you are reading this, and I have died, I want you to know that I loved you every second until my last breath, and

I am so sorry for everything, and for leaving you here.

If you are reading this and by God's grace you have given me another chance, I promise you this.

I promise to always love you more than the day before. I promise to always put your happiness above my own. I know what life is like without you, and I can't fucking breathe without you. (Sorry for cursing, but it's true) I promise to fight for you. I promise to cherish every second of my life with you. I promise to try my hardest to make you happy and give you the life you deserve. I promise to give all of myself to you, every day of forever.

Please forgive me.

I love you always.

Brooks.

I don't remember when the tears started, but by the time I allowed myself to come back to the present, I was covered in snot and hot tears. I set the letter down and leaned into my hands to sob. I was feeling so many things at once I couldn't get a hold of my emotions. He carried this letter for two years. *What if he had died?* My stomach turned sour, and I had to remind myself he didn't. But the thought of losing him now terrified me even more.

Panic seized my chest and I needed to hear his voice. I don't even consciously remember calling him, but he answered on the first ring.

"Hey, sweetie." His voice was cheerful and so unlike every emotion I was drowning in.

I couldn't even respond at first. Instead, I just sobbed into the phone. I wished he was here.

"You read my letter?" His voice cracked.

"Brooks..." I cried. "I love you so much. I forgive you. Thank you for coming home. Thank you for loving me." I pulled the phone away to blow my nose.

"I meant every word." His voice was soft, tender.

I was nodding, even though he couldn't see me. We just sat quietly, letting my breathing slow, and the tears dry up.

"I have to go. Natalie will be here soon. Call me later?" I whispered.

"Of course. I love you so much, baby." My heart ached for him to be close. I needed to feel his arms pull me into his lap and hold me.

"I know." Another tear escaped. "I love you more."

We both chuckled, both a little watery.

"Not a chance, but I am willing to continue fighting for the top spot for the rest of our lives."

"Okay. Forever." I was nodding to myself again, and my heart felt like it was going to come out of my chest. "Please drive safe. I need you to stick around," I laughed through more tears.

"I will, or my driver will." He assured me.

"Okay, chat later."

"Bye, sweetie." My heart leaped into my throat again. How was it possible that in such a short time, we had come this far?

"Bye, love."

↟ ↟ ↟

Natalie arrived with lunch and lattes shortly after I cleaned up my makeup, and safely stowed his letter in my jewelry box. I didn't realize how badly I needed both food and coffee. Our run this morning was a little early, and I was already bonking after my cry fest.

"Deck?" I asked removing a very large cup of hot coffee from her hands.

"Yes!" she squealed.

I slid the large glass door open, allowing the now warm air to settle my nerves. I sat down on the couch, nearest the glass railing, and pulled a pillow to my chest.

"Okay, so please do share. What's the deal with you and Brooks? Also, you seem to have a type," she started.

"Okay. Jumping right in, huh? Also, a type?"

"The handsome, dark hair, blue eyes, clearly wealthy vibe." She motioned with her hands like she was painting a picture.

I rolled my eyes. *A type?*

"What do you want to know?" I grinned.

"Everything." She took a long sip of her coffee.

"Everything?"

"Duh. I mean, a week ago, I was thinking Grey might finally have a chance, and then I found out you have a boyfriend. Please share." Her voice was filled with anticipation.

I laughed. She was right. This past week had flown by and everything just happened so fast I hadn't even had time to process it all.

"Hmm..." I smiled. "Well, it's a long story but the short version - I've been in love with him for as long as I can remember. A few years back, he had just finished up boarding school in Europe. The kind where you live there year-round. Anyway, the plan was for him to come home after graduation and we would go to college together. He graduated from boarding school with a bachelor's degree completed so he would be getting his master's, but things changed. He joined the Air Force instead. We broke up a few months later. It was brutal and it broke both of us.

"A few months ago, right after I moved here, Brooks got an early release. He stepped into his father's role at our parent's company, and I thought I was ready to sell my share to him. I wasn't interested in running the business alongside him. It hurt too much. He reached out and asked if he could come visit. That was the night we went to Sapphire, hence my drunkenness." I paused, taking a long sip of coffee.

"We texted a bit before he came. Neither of us had fully recovered from our breakup." I shrugged to hide the well of emotions at the surface. This was the first time I had shared this with anyone. "When he showed up, I don't know, we are both still in love, and he wanted to stick around and make it work."

"Wow, Emily, that's a lot. I can't believe you never told me about this. So long distance?" she asked, bringing the panini to her mouth. It looked amazing and I wished I could be the one asking questions so I could chew through an explanation.

"No. He's moving here. I mean, I guess we will be living together. He has a place in Seattle he was going to move into, but I think he said he was going to see if his friend would take over the lease. I mean, this was never the plan, but..." I blushed.

"But..don't stop now," Natalie teased.

"I don't know...I mean I just feel like I can't breathe unless he's near me. It's overwhelming and amazing. I know it's so fast but I just want him around me like every second of the day." I huffed. "I'm sure I sound like a lunatic."

"No, I don't think so." She waved like it was a foregone conclusion. "So tell me..." she paused, her eyebrows dancing. "Did you guys um..."

"Well, he kissed me like right when he got here, and then one thing led to another." My voice trailed off all sing-songy.

"Oh, my god Emily! That's a big deal." She was beaming. "So, is he good in bed?"

"Natalie!" We both laughed. Not that I had any other experiences to compare it to, but it was more than I could have imagined. The memories dancing through my mind cause my cheeks to burn red.

"What? He's hot, Emily. I hope he's good in bed." She took another bite.

"Okay, yes. We can't seem to keep our hands off each other. It's nice. It wasn't like this before. I mean, we were in high school and things were simple then." I reached for my panini. She had stopped by the PC Cafe. They played off the name and not only was it a cute little cafe with amazing food and coffee, but they had free wi-fi and a few workstations for people to work at.

"Do you think things will work out between you two then?" she asked around a mouthful.

"I don't know. I mean, I hope so. I think the breakup was kind of a wake-up call. He had the chance to move on and he didn't, well not emotionally. He came back, and now he says he is committed to making this work." I could feel the band wrapped around my chest. *We will make it work. We will.* If I had to make it my life's mission I would.

"Have you guys talked about marriage or anything?" she asked, slowly looking up at me like she knew she was crossing a line.

"We did in the past. We always talked about the future together and would dream up where we would live, what our kids would look like...it was just something we both wanted."

"And now?" Her big green eyes studied me.

"And now we are taking things slow ... ish," I laughed. Nothing about what we were doing was slow. "I don't know, I want to marry him, but I don't want to just throw it out there right now, ya know? I think secretly, deep down, I'm still hoping to see a ring on my finger and to change my last name. In high school, I would always practice writing my name - Emily Devonshire."

I smiled softly at the idea. I dreamed of it for many years, and now it seemed like a possibility once again.

Natalie chuckled and looked down, picking at her nails.

"This is really fast, Emily. I know you guys have history, but have you thought everything through?"

"No, not really," I muttered. "I just don't want to keep waiting. That's all I've been doing since he left. I think at this point I am kind of in this weird state of giving it my all, or nothing. If I fall flat on my face, then I know for sure we weren't meant to be. I just can't dance around it anymore. I need to know for sure. It's why I couldn't move forward with Grey. Why my last relationship didn't work. I was waiting for him."

She nodded and looked out to the roaring ocean. Her brown hair floated with the wind before her green eyes returned to mine.

"Does Brooks have a brother?" she joked.

"No, unfortunately, but -" I bounced my eyebrows. *Maybe Michaelson.* He's cute. Or was the last time I saw him on FaceTime.

"But what?" she prodded taking another bite.

"Brooks' friend I just told you about. He's cute, and he's British." I groaned very unladylike, taking my first bite of the delicious food in my hands. The bread was perfectly toasted and the melted cheese tasted like heaven mixed with the warm tomato and turkey.

"How cute?" Natalie laughed.

I held up a finger while I swallowed the taste of heaven before taking another long, generous gulp of coffee.

"Not as cute as Brooks, but close," I assured. This was nice. Nice to laugh and smile and have a girlfriend. Even when I was younger, I had never had girlfriends. Brooks and Connor were really the only two people I'd consider friends. Sure I had my dance friends and girls in class, but they were just acquaintances.

Natalie and I talked for a good long while about the week and my feelings for Brooks over the years. She was the first person to know everything aside from Brooks. I wanted her to be my friend which meant I needed to open up and let her in.

Since I had moved to PC, I learned about her family, where she went to high school, why she chose nursing, and her type one diabetes. She opened up about living with type one and what that meant. I did a lot of research after that hoping to learn more so I could make the right food choices and lifestyle choices to help her.

"So, why boarding school?" she asked before taking another sip of her latte.

"Er, another long story. It was after our parents died." I took another bite, delaying my response to further explain the bomb I just dropped. Aside from Sara and Parker, nobody since high school had known about what happened. I didn't want to talk about them.

"Oh, Emily, I am so sorry. I had no idea." Her eyes looked like a Disney character's all round and full of tears. I swallowed down the bite of food and the lump in my throat.

"Yeah, it was hard, we don't usually talk about it. We were in high school. I think that's why the breakup with Brooks was so hard. He was all I had left. So, choosing to go enlist just hurt because I didn't have anyone, and he was joining the military and it felt selfish. I dunno." I sighed and looked out at the shoreline. Waves were rhythmically crashing into the rocks, sending a spray into the air each time. My stomach tensed with talking about them but it was time she knew it all.

"So, his parents died too?" she asked, her eyes still focused on me.

"Yeah, they were all in an accident." I glanced at her, and then back out to the ocean. The endless horizon of varying shades of blue was mesmerizing. "It was raining and there was a drunk driver. It was a head-on collision. They said it was instant and they didn't feel anything."

"Gosh, Em, I'm so sorry." Silence stretched between us for a minute before I swallowed down the fear and sadness that consumed me every time I thought about them.

"Well, enough about that," I huffed and smiled back at her. I hadn't talked about my parents much. Another reason I had left Seattle. The memories were a lot to deal with. "So how's work?"

↟ ↟ ↟

It was late when Natalie left. I walked back to my little studio feeling oddly exhausted, and so full of gratitude. What a week.

I laid down on my bed, too tired to fully undress. I missed Brooks already. His warm body next to mine had become a source of comfort. It felt so empty in my room without him. The room hadn't changed over the past week but somehow, it felt smaller, lonelier.

The white sheets were crinkled, the closet door half open, and the beige curtain pulled to the side from him opening and closing the window all week. They were all visible signs he had been here. Even my pillows smelled like him.

I checked my phone again. Nothing. I bit my lip while

contemplating whether to call. Surely he was back in Seattle already. It had been seven hours since he left.

My mind got the best of me, immediately going to a worst-case scenario. Was it because I talked about the accident today? Or the letter he left? Either way, I just needed to hear his voice to know he was alive and well.

He didn't tease me for calling. Instead, he listened to my fears openly accepting them and reassuring me. He asked me to come to Seattle for a date which I hesitantly agreed on. It's not that I didn't want to go on a date with him, but Seattle had become a place of loss and depression for me.

I would need to get over it or work through it because if I was staying with Caston, I would need to attend board meetings at the very least. After saying I love you too many times to count like a lovesick teenager I got off the phone.

Telling Brooks I love him was easy. It was all I felt all these years, I had only repressed the feeling because I had never considered a future with him. I glanced at my closet to the box that held my journal.

I rolled off the bed and pulled the box down. My journal was sitting on top, right next to my favorite stuffed animal, moonbeam. He was a jellyfish stuffed animal Brooks got years ago from our trip to the aquarium.

I rubbed my finger along the plush taupe face of the animal and was thrown back to Brooks bouncing the animal along my face. Our laughs and giggles filled the hotel room while beams of golden light from the setting sun filled the room.

I sat down to write, not quite ready for bed.

Well, Mom,

It's been a while since I last wrote to you. I have so much to tell you but first, I miss you. I told

Natalie about you today. She might be my best friend. She's different than Sara, she's softer. You'd like her a lot. It's nice to have someone to confide in who doesn't judge and doesn't push.

Brooks is back. I know, how and why right? Well, it's finally happening. He's stepping in at Caston and the big news is I'm not selling!! We talked about it this past week. He came to stay with me - I'll get to that in a minute. He convinced me. It's our company now and since I don't hate him, I guess I don't see a reason to sell! He was going to put up a good fight if I tried. I hope that you guys are happy wherever you are. I hope you know how much I miss you and want to make you proud. I hope this makes you proud.

Okay, so, now about Brooks staying. He's out of the military and he came here, to Pacific Coves, my new home, to see me, to say sorry. When he showed up, I was expecting anything and everything but what happened. I wish I could sit with you and tell you how much I still love him!! If anything, that love has only grown these years apart. Does that mean he's the one?! I can finally breathe when he's around. He makes me smile, he makes me feel safe. We had a few arguments this week. Mostly my fault, I know, my anger. I need to get better at controlling it. We went hiking and I gave him the cold shoulder. It wasn't intentional but I got scared at how deeply I was feeling for him. Brooks still has that unending patience with me.

I thought it would be scary to have him in my life again, but it isn't. After the hike, we sat on the ground next to the car and worked it out. He understood. He was feeling the same. We agreed to be honest with each other and to communicate everything - the good and the bad. Please don't be angry. I'm an adult capable of making my own decisions, but I slept with him. It was amazing. It felt right. You guys always wanted us to get married, and things got a little messy after you died, but we are finding our way back to each other. Mama, I love him, like a lot. Honestly, it scares me more than anything. Not because I'm scared to love him, but because I'm scared to lose him again.

In a single week, he tore down every wall I built over the past few years. Well, who am I kidding? They were down within a few hours. They're all gone, and I can't go through that heartbreak again. How do I trust him? I want to. I do, but not like I should. I can feel it. Like I am holding my breath, terrified inside. What if I say something or do something, and he leaves? What if after all this time the excitement fades, we realize we are too different? We were just kids when we fell in love, and we aren't kids anymore. I just hope that it's enough. I know love isn't enough. I remember that conversation you and Carrie had with me about love being a choice, a daily choice. I haven't forgotten.

I wish you were here, I wish you both were. I need my moms to help me navigate this intense, unending, forever love I feel for him. How can I love someone so much that it hurts? I feel insane. I feel like I want to cry when he's gone. I just want to be a part of everything he does, and vice versa. I want him to be a part of me. In a non creepy way, I wish I could just climb inside of him and stay forever surrounded by his warmth, safety, and love. Oh boy! That sounds creepy. Lol.

Well, I guess that's it for now. He left for Seattle today. I asked him to move in with me!!! I couldn't face long distance again. The distrust and growing apart-the separate lives. It really messed with us last time, and since we are already on unsteady ground, I didn't want to risk it. He's moving in this weekend. It's fast, I know, but it feels right. Without the judgment of others, I know I would marry him tomorrow if he asked.

Okay, that's it this time. I won't wait two years to write to you again. I love you, mama. Send my love.

xEmily Claire

Chapter Nine

I woke up early Thursday morning with a text from Brooks telling me he loved me and was looking forward to tonight. I couldn't wait for tonight either. My nerves were all over the place in anticipation of seeing Brooks again. It's funny how after spending years apart, a week felt painful. The weather outside was tumultuous, with a huge storm system blowing in so instead of my morning run, I settled on cycling.

I raced over to the basement den where my indoor home cycling studio was. I loved cycling. It beat running on a treadmill, at least. I clipped my shoes in and started pedaling to the beat of Waka Waka by Shakira.

My breathing raced the stronger the tension got on the pedals. My thighs were already burning, but my mind couldn't stray too far from the thought of Brooks' hands on me. His warm lips. I was a worried mess thinking about shaving, finding something to wear, and wondering if he was driving down or what the plan was.

When he told me he would handle all of it, I was happy to release all control to him, but now I needed answers I didn't have. It brought out my anxiety about our relationship. I trusted him, but if I asked or pushed for answers over tonight, would it create a divide?

My thoughts were exhausting. I was so excited to be with him again, but I never stressed like this before.

Sweat was dripping down my back, and beading up in my hairline. Energy flowed through me without restraint. I kept up the pace until it was time for me to shower and pack.

Mrs. Hall had already cleared the closet space this week, and all my warmer items were now upstairs. I glanced out to the pool where the rain was thrashing against the deck and the waves were scary today.

I ran up to the master, turning the water on hot in the shower. As I undressed, I allowed myself to momentarily think about my home.

Would Brooks and I stay together? Would we move into this home? Would we get married and have kids? I looked over at the king-size bed that had never been slept in. It was a shame. It was so beautiful and inviting.

The dark seafoam green linen duvet with the white eucalyptus sheets and enormous amounts of pillows looked warm and cozy, especially with the crazy storm outside. I didn't have time to dwell so I stepped into the steaming shower.

↟ ↟ ↟

"Ms. Barlow?"

"Yes, Audrey?" I asked, looking up at her. She was wearing a navy dress which looked amazing against her mocha skin and ebony-wavy hair. Audrey was in her last semester of a communications degree online. When I started at Hope, they had offered to hire an assistant for Kate and me. I pulled her resume out of the stack of applicants. She started the next week.

"Mr. Kavinsky is asking about the gala next month. He wants to know if anything is finalized and if not, when can he expect to see something?" She was leaning against the glass wall of my office.

"Yeah, I saw his email. I haven't responded yet, but I will today before I leave. I haven't finalized the venue, but I talked to Kate, and she has all the sponsors nailed down. I think we are just waiting on some logos for the banners and print materials. Could you follow up with her?" I asked, shuffling through a stack of papers in front of my MacBook.

"Yes. Also, I have a package that just arrived for you." She stepped forward, and it was only then that I saw the large box in her arms.

Audrey set down a white gift box decorated with an oversized dark green bow. I lifted the paper card off the top.

A car will be at your place at 5. Wear this tonight. Love you.

Warmth flowed through my body thinking about the fact that Brooks had gone out of his way to buy me a dress. All my worries from earlier ceased immediately. This was the man I wanted to spend forever with. The least I could do was trust him with a date.

"Do you need anything else? I can run out and grab lunch, or the break room has some Italian they catered today."

"I'm good, Audrey. Thanks. I'll go get something here in a few. Also, don't forget to follow up with Kate. Let me know what she says." I locked eyes with her, and she nodded.

"Sure thing." She turned, and my eyes were back on the box. I carefully cut the tape. Brooks used to buy me presents all the time growing up. As I lifted the lid, a black dress was lying tucked into the white tissue. It was magnificent.

I measured the dress up to me to find that it was the perfect length. The gown was floor-length with a thigh-high slit. The crushed velvet was soft. I also loved the one-shoulder with a long sleeve. I decided to pair my Jimmy Choo heels with it for tonight.

I shot Natalie a photo along with a text.

Emily: Brooks bought me a dress for tonight and surprised me with it at work. Is it appropriate to ask him to marry me? Asking for a friend of course. Lol

Natalie: Girl!!! No way. Gosh, he's so dreamy. I think it may be too soon but what do I know? I'm still single and have no prospects.

Emily: I'm going to hook you up with Michaelson. But also…I shaved like 3 times in the past 24.

Natalie: I'm jealous of your new sex life. The last time I had sex was a one-night stand with some guy I knew from college. Ugh, it was awful. Send me pics when you put the dress on. Gotta go. Luv ya.

I giggled and responded with three white hearts. Before sending Brooks another text telling him I loved him over and over again.

↟ ↟ ↟

The dress was a perfect fit. I glanced in the mirror one last time. My mom's pearl necklace was so beautiful, it reminded me of her. Growing up, she would always wear it on date nights with my dad, or any fancy event they went to. My fingers touched each of the pearls and I found myself wishing I could remember the scent of my mom.

As a little girl, I would climb onto her lap and play with these pearls. I remember thinking how pretty she was, and how good she always smelled. I wanted to grow up to be just like her.

My phone buzzed, alerting me that a car just came through the gate.

I grabbed my purse and weekender and slipped out the door. I shivered against the cold air the storm had brought. Thankfully, the rain has stopped, *for now*. I pulled my coat tighter around me. As I reached the driveway, an older gentleman was standing at the back of the black SUV.

"Good evening, Ms. Barlow. I will take your bag," he said, reaching out for the weekender in my hand.

"Good evening." All of this felt so surreal. Brooks and I were no strangers to money and fancy things, but aside from my house and car, I wasn't one to spend. I guess I never had a reason to. I climbed into the back, and the driver closed the door.

"What is your name?" I asked when he climbed into the driver's seat.

"Ryan, ma'am." He sounded so formal.

"Ryan, do you know how traffic is and what time our ETA is?" I asked, clipping my belt in.

"Mr. Devonshire has asked me to keep your destination a secret." He pulled the car forward and back down my long driveway.

"Of course he has," I muttered to myself. I sat back, smiling. I pulled my phone from my bag and texted Brooks.

Emily: The suspense is killing me. Where are we going?

Brooks: Good! See you soon.

I chuckled. I should have known he would do something like this. The town was quiet tonight, and it was dark as we passed through. It was strange. Just a few weeks ago, I would have been home reading, or if I had any plans, I would have been with Natalie or Grey. As the town's lights faded, I realized we were pulling into an airstrip.

Once out on the tarmac, a jet was waiting all lit up. Its lights were bright against the dark, stormy sky. As the headlights danced across the plane, I saw Brooks. My heart raced ready to be with the man who owned it.

He's here! A whole swarm of butterflies took flight. As Ryan pulled the car to a park alongside the jet, Brooks opened my door. He was so handsome. His beard had been shaved down shorter, revealing more of his perfect pink lips. He was dressed in black slacks with a navy jacket over a white shirt and black bowtie. His brown hair was perfectly gelled in a classic quiff. His broad shoulders and build made his clothes fit in all the right areas.

"Hi, beautiful." He smiled, reaching out his hand. I squealed and launched into his arms, burying my face in his neck and breathing him in. How had I gone seven years without him? Immediately, all fear and hesitation about our future settled around me and there was just peace. If I wasn't so excited about our date, I might have cried.

"Where are we going?" I implored sliding back down to the ground unable to keep my eyes off him as we neared the stairs to the plane.

"You'll see," he whispered back. "That dress looks amazing on you."

"My boyfriend has great taste," I replied playfully. I wanted to kiss him, but not here out in the storm, not in front of all these strangers. I couldn't help but notice the way his bespoke suit hugged him, accentuating his butt in the tight material. Of course, my thoughts drifted to later when I could explore him with my hands.

I turned to look back at the car. "Thanks, Ryan!"

"Have a great evening, Ms. Barlow."

I climbed the stairs into the jet, feeling like I could burst with joy and excitement. It had been years since I had flown. Inside the cabin, four cream leather chairs faced each other and just behind them there was a small sofa with a TV stand. I turned to look at Brooks, who was watching me.

I couldn't help but lean in for a kiss. His warm lips met mine with a gentle force, his minty breath cooling my mouth. The slamming of a compartment outside brought our kiss to a premature end. A shy smile crossed my face.

I sat down in the nearest chair on the left, Brooks sat in the chair in front of me.

"So, how do you like it?" He looked around the cabin gleefully.

"Like what?" I laughed.

"The jet?" A wry smile crossed his face.

"Wait, it's yours?" I gasped, confused.

"Of course. I figured we would need a quicker way to travel back and forth to Seattle. Driving just takes too long." His voice was confident like it wasn't a big deal he purchased a jet because he needed to get to work. Because I asked him to move in with me. Because I refused to move to Seattle. Because he was trying to prove to me, he would do anything for me.

I looked around, taking it all in. It was gorgeous, but was this necessary? Did I ask too much of him by expecting him to move to PC knowing full well that work was in Seattle?

"What?" he asked, confused, watching my expression.

"I'm sorry. I didn't think about the pressure I put on you expecting you to move away from Seattle." Guilt sank into my stomach like a heavy weight. The smarter choice would have been to move to Seattle with him. I could work remotely for Hope if I needed to. He can't work remotely as CEO.

"Hey Em, no. I want to live with you, and PC is great. Plus, the company needed a jet for travel anyway. This will make it easier."

I didn't believe him, so instead I shook my head.

"Okay," I whispered, my mind still trying to process everything. The pilot stepped into the cabin and before I knew it, the jet was lifting into the air. Takeoff still scared me, that much didn't change. Brooks grabbed my hands before I had even processed the uneasy feeling. I looked up into his blue eyes and melted.

"Thank you," I whispered.

"Still scared, huh?"

I chuckled. "Does it ever go away?"

"Maybe, if you fly more."

I rolled my eyes. Of course, that was the answer. "Are you going to tell me where we are going yet?"

He laughed. "Emily, Seattle."

"So we are spending the weekend at your place?"

"Yes."

I rolled my eyes again. I wouldn't get anything out of him.

"How long is the flight?"

"Less than an hour." He looked at me puzzled.

I bit my lip, concentrating on the plane reaching altitude. *Finally,* I released my hands from Brooks and sat back against the cool leather. We were going to Seattle. A few months ago, I packed up my family's home and sold it. It had been sitting vacant while I was in college. Upon returning, I realized I couldn't stay. I needed to move on, to get out of the city, to leave the past behind.

I was happy when a young family purchased it. Brooks and I had so much fun growing up there. Our houses sat adjacent to each other at the end of an empty, single-lane, road, backing up into the trees in Bellevue. Both estates housed pools and theater rooms. Mine had a tennis court, while Brooks had an indoor golf simulator. Together, we shared an oversized worn-down swing set, and our favorite, a treehouse. We never needed to leave and had the best of everything. Our parents loved spoiling us.

We were only minutes from Puget Sound and Brooks' home backed up to Lake Washington. Our families loved spending the weekend on the water.

On the last day in the house, I spent time in every room. Taking in the smell of the fireplace in my dad's office. Though it hadn't been lit for years, the firewood smell never left. It was soaked into the dark mahogany floors and built-ins. I sat there remembering how Brooks and I had played hide and seek in every small cabinet we could fit into. The sofa in the living room was the same one that Brooks and I were asleep on when we heard the news about our parents. Each room, and each piece of furniture, had memories attached to them. Most of them were good, but the empty home only made the ache in my chest unbearable.

I could have stayed for college, but I wanted my own place, out of the memories. Plus, I always felt sad when the couple who purchased Brooks' home stepped outside.

The new family who purchased mine would enjoy the home,

though. Plenty of room to grow, to play. The pool and patio were perfect for hosting large groups of people. I hoped their daughter would enjoy the window seat in my room just as much as I did. I would sit there journaling to the sound of the rain against the window, looking for Brooks to be done with his homework or watching the endless hours he spent outside with a soccer ball. *Wonderful memories.*

"We are almost there. You okay? You're awfully quiet." His voice called me back to the present.

"Yeah," I whispered. "Last time I was in Seattle, I had just sold my house." I didn't need to say anything else. He would understand.

"It's strange being back." His hand brushed through his hair.

"I was happy to sell it. It was time."

He nodded softly, studying my face. He reached out for my leg and his warm, strong hand slid up my thigh into the slit. I sighed deeply and returned a coy smile, all sad memories forgotten and in their place a need to be fully connected with him. I longed to feel the deep, satisfying connection with him, but couldn't get past how nervous I still felt.

"We are beginning our descent into Seattle Boeing Airfield," the pilot announced.

Brooks sat back, his thumb brushing up to his lip. His eyes never left mine, and I could feel the weight of the evening setting in. Once dinner was over, we would be in his penthouse and free to explore each other once again.

Chapter Ten

The black Mercedes pulled up to a black-clad restaurant with vast glass windows. The rock was lit up in front where the valet and host stand sat under a canopy. A large gray wall lit up the black letters reading Canlis. I couldn't fight the smile. This was one of Seattle's most prestigious places with gorgeous views of the docks and Lake Union. The waitlist to get in was usually pretty long, and reservations were required months in advance.

"How did you get us a reservation?" I gasped.

"I know some people." He grinned, taking my hand in his.

I rolled my eyes. "Know some people," I mocked, making him chuckle.

As we walked through the restaurant, I couldn't help but glance around at the beautiful architecture and the large beams on the ceiling. As we crossed the room to the stairs along the back wall, I noticed people kept glancing over at me, causing me to worry something was wrong with the dress. I tugged the dress down further and shifted the top.

"You look perfect, Em. Don't," Brooks whispered in my ear. I relaxed my hands, sliding them down the soft, crushed velvet. I had been gifted with a decent bust size despite my weight only coming in at 120. Any top, no matter how high or low, always left me feeling nervous like I was about to pop out of it. A size small didn't exactly fit a full C cup size. I focused on the warmth of Brooks' warm hand on my back instead.

Upstairs, we were guided into a smaller, more private room overlooking the lake. The city lights twinkled in the night sky off in the distance. Seattle had one of the prettiest skylines, and it was even more beautiful from up here. Brooks pulled the chair out for me at the small table in the corner of the room, before pulling his own out beside me.

"We'd like to start with a bottle of the Château Beau-Séjour Bécot 2016 Premier Grand Cru Classé. Thanks," Brooks said before the server even had a chance to introduce herself. She nodded, clearly impressed, and left out the same door we had just come through.

My eyes met his. They reflected the same overwhelmed feeling that was consuming me. Desire. Playfulness. The need for more.

"You look hungry, Ms. Barlow." I snorted. *Hungry?* I guess that's one way to describe it.

I cleared my throat.

"It's been a long, boring week, Mr. Devonshire." My voice was huskier than usual, bringing a blush to my cheeks.

His eyes heated in understanding.

The waitress returned with the wine bottle and a corkscrew. Brooks nodded in approval as the waitress began uncorking. I waited, somewhat amused at how intrusive her presence seemed to be.

At last, the cork popped free, popping the tension in the air at the same time, and she filled his glass for a taste test. He nodded in approval letting her fill our glasses before stepping away.

"Well," I huffed, trying to regain some composure. Brooks laughed through his teeth. "You know your wine," I said.

His face broke out in a full grin while he played with the stem of his glass.

"I lived in Europe and spent a lot of time with Michaelson's family." He said it like he was just stating facts. "Are you going to make it through dinner, Emily?" he chuckled. *Probably not.*

This wasn't like me. Just over two weeks ago I was a virgin and had never even made it to second base. Now I could barely stand to sit two feet from the man that consumed every thought. The man that made me want to beg and cry out his name, the one who made me feel so alive, and so desired, I wasn't sure if I should cry.

I cleared my throat hoping to find my voice.

"As long as it doesn't take too long," I whispered, my voice laced with need.

He grunted in approval, shifting in his chair. His eyes were watching me, as I fought against the burning desire building between my thighs. I was in for an uncomfortable evening, especially since it would be a while before I found a release. One I knew Brooks was sure to provide.

"You are enjoying this, aren't you?" I asked, biting my lip for dramatic effect.

Brooks leaned closer, sliding his hand once again up the slit in my dress to my inner thigh, careful to hover ever so slightly, without actually touching my lace panties. A slow moan escaped. I bit my lip, fighting the feeling to rip his clothes off.

I laughed nervously. "Please say something. Change the subject," I plead. I glanced around the room. The mixture of dark woods, the light artwork, and the fireplace made it feel intimate. That and the ten-foot-tall windows overlooking Lake Union.

"What would you like me to say?"

"Tell me about work." I inhaled a deep, heady breath of him and smiled.

He laughed reluctantly before scraping his teeth across his bottom lip, and eyeing me like he was mentally undressing me. I swallowed a generous amount of wine.

"Stop," I giggled.

"Oh, I'm just preparing you for tonight." He steepled his fingers, relaxing back against his chair.

"Work, remember." My voice was stern. More stern than I meant it to sound. Thankfully, Brooks complied.

"Diane and Paul have me flying to Vancouver in a few weeks to meet some developers. I've been introduced to everyone and it's been a week of long meetings getting caught up. I'm ready to hit the ground running now that I'm stepping in full-time.

"Michaelson will be here next week, and we are looking at an acquisition of a small tech startup, Paradigm Wallet. They are creating a new system using blockchain technology to revolutionize online payments using crypto wallets. So no more cards, no more stolen bank account numbers. They're hoping to expand to be able to use Apple Wallet and other payment systems as well. So, if you're in line at a grocery store, you can tap and go."

Yep, that worked. I don't know much about tech companies, but it sounds interesting.

"So, why Paradigm...wallet? I mean, is that even a thing at this point? I thought most people were still hesitant about using crypto. I mean, I don't even know anything about that whole world, so why would they develop a technology that the user base is already really small?"

The waitress returned.

"Are you ready to order?"

"Emily?" Brooks gestured. I didn't look at the menu. I was a little distracted. I glanced quickly at the menu. Thankfully, it's easy. Pick three.

"I will do the Artichoke, Halibut, and Strawberry, please." I handed her my menu.

"Venison, Coulotte, Smoked Cacou. Thanks."

The waitress disappeared again. Brooks sighed, placing his hand on mine. I looked up, confused.

"Dance with me," he whispered.

"What here?" In the middle of the restaurant?

"Emily, nobody is watching." He's right. I placed my hand in his and stood up. His other hand rested just above my bottom and pulled me close. I gasped at the intensity with which he pulled me into him. I rested my hand on his shoulder and laid my head against his sturdy chest. His heart was beating rather rapidly.

"I love you," he whispered into my hair. My body shuddered at the puff of air that touched my neck. I pulled back so that I could look into his deep blue eyes.

"I love you," I whispered back. His eyes softened with his smile. I closed my eyes, inhaling the scent of his beautiful concoction. I could drown in this smell. His lips pressed gently against my forehead and I melted. How could I love someone so much? How did I survive without him? Without his touch?

Our bodies swayed back and forth to the soft music, and I almost forgot that we were in the middle of a restaurant. In his arms I felt safe, I felt whole. I lost track of time, lost in the music, lost in his embrace. His lips found mine, next his tongue.

Once more I melted, overwhelmed with love for my man. Our tongues danced, and embraced, as our bodies slowed. My back arched into his weight and intensity. My hands gripped the lapels of his coat as I pulled myself up into him more. I wanted him. The once burning, passionate desire had faded and in its place, a desire of love and connection flowed through me.

That was until I heard the sound of footsteps on the steps outside the room and reluctantly pulled away, feeling a little dizzy. His eyes met mine and he smiled. I mirrored it back before returning to my seat, giggling at the close call.

↟ ↟ ↟

The elevator doors closed and without hesitation, our bodies turned towards each other. Our lips embraced while his strong hands pulled me into him. Sixteen floors to go. Hopefully, nobody would stop the elevator.

When the doors opened, Brooks tapped his key card, opening the door to his penthouse. My eyes darted around the room, almost forgetting about the desire consuming me. The far wall was all windows expanding the length of the room. Soft gray tufted furniture sat around a light wooden oval coffee table next to an expansive fireplace. The floor and ceiling both housed the same light wood and the kitchen island, just to the left, a marble waterfall countertop over a navy cabinet, welcoming you into the kitchen.

"Wow, B," I stepped away from him, taking it all in.

He chuckled behind me. I would resume momentarily.

"I almost feel bad you're leaving this place," I teased, running my hand along the floor-to-ceiling artwork in the entry.

"Almost?" he chuckled.

I looked back at him finding his eyes bright and filled with amusement.

"Almost." I nodded, smiling.

His hand caressed my cheek before sliding into my hair, exposing my neck. Involuntarily, my head fell back in ecstasy. His lips softened on my neck.

"Now," he whispered. My body shuddered with delight as his hot breath danced on my neck. "Can I help you out of this dress?"

He could rip it off if he wanted. I kicked off my shoes and lifted my arms resting them on my head as Brooks knelt in front of me. I had to work to control my breathing. Brooks on his knees in front of me did funny things to my insides and he was moving at a glacial pace. His fingers trailed along my inner thighs leaving heat and desire as they slid inch by inch up my dress along my legs, his mouth occasionally pausing to kiss as he worked his way up to my inner thigh.

"Brooks," I moaned.

"Be patient, love."

How could I be patient? I could barely stand. My legs were turning to jello with every passing second. His fingers gently grasped the hem of my lace thong and began gently pulling it down. My body nearly convulsed and I grabbed his head to stabilize myself, but he took it as an invitation and moved his mouth into me. I moaned loudly, this time unable and unwilling to quiet the desire consuming me. His tongue was warm and soft, teasing me and pleasuring me in a way I had never experienced.

"Please," I begged, pulling him up to my mouth, my tongue tangling with his, tasting my arousal on his tongue, as I worked quickly to undress him. His hands pulled up on my dress, causing a brief, yet agonizing, separation of our mouths, just long enough for my dress to slide up over my head, exposing my black strapless bra.

His shirt fell to the floor alongside my dress. I burned, needing to release the explosive passion within.

"Brooks," I moaned into his mouth. The taste of wine and chocolate still lingered on his tongue. His arms lifted me to straddle his waist, while he carried me to his bedroom. I didn't have time to take it all in. I wanted him and he was still wearing his pants. His body pressed into mine as we frantically crawled back on the bed.

"Give me...two seconds," he whispered breathlessly, pulling his mouth from mine.

My back arched, yearning for him. He stood up, slid out of his pants, slipped on a condom, and crawled back in between my trembling legs. His hands softly traced up my side to my bra and to the back, to release the clasp.

"I want you Emily..." he panted. "But I want you to come first." His voice was laced with need.

"Brooks, please," I moaned.

My bra was thrown off the bed as he bit down on my nipple. A shock of pain and desire caused a loud gasp to fall from my mouth. His fingers plunged into me in the next moment. I could hardly take it anymore and almost climaxed with just his touch.

"B," I cried out. His mouth moved back to mine, removing his hands, and with a hard thrust, he penetrated deep inside of me, causing me to curl around him. My body stretched and accepted him in full.

"You're so ready for me," he groaned into my hair. Those words felt deep and so satisfying, pushing me to my peak.

"Come on, Emily, release." He thrust forward again, and I fell. His words were my undoing. I fell into an earth-shattering orgasm, wave after wave, knocking me under. I wasn't sure I could ever recover.

"That's my girl." My body clenched around his length. I was shocked at how pleased I felt when he talked to me like this. With my shoulders pinned to the bed under his heavy hands, he thrust faster and deeper.

We were a tangle of limbs of breathy kisses, finding new ways to please each other and connect. Our bodies moved together like they'd always known each other. I accepted whatever he gave and when I pushed him to the bed, he let me take control.

"Baby, I'm going to come and I need you to come with me." His voice was strained. I rolled my hips forward, grinding on him and pulling me closer to another release. His mouth dropped to my nipple and with a gentle tug, the edges of my vision began to blur.

"Okay," I whispered, as I surrendered once again. He found his own release, our bodies clinging to each other as we rode out every single wave together.

Eventually, his eyes cleared, and our breathing slowed. I fell against his chest and stayed there, unwilling to end the connection I felt.

"That was." I was unable to form coherent sentences. *Amazing. Hot. Satisfying.* I also had a newfound appreciation for his experience and confidence. The words "That's my girl" lingered in my ear causing me to blush.

"Give me a few minutes and we can go for round two."

Chapter Eleven

Waking up in an unfamiliar space was puzzling when I opened my eyes, unsure of what time it was. As I searched the bed for Brooks, I heard him typing away in the other room. Curiosity got the best of me as I crawled out of the silky gray sheets and tugged on one of Brooks' undershirts that was draped across a chair. I brought the soft fabric to my nose and inhaled his scent which instantly calmed me.

It was pitch black outside, with only the city lights gleaming through the fog. The glass along the bedroom wall slightly reflected the room. I looked around at the bedroom and its minimalist decor. Brooks and I at least shared this in common. A large fig tree sat in the corner and the tufted gray headboard matched the same furniture in the living room. The dimly lit clock on the nightstand read 2:36. Just seeing the time made me yawn.

As I crossed the vast living room, I could see Brooks on the couch with his back to me and the computer open on his lap. I slid my hands down his shoulders to his chest causing him to startle a little at my touch.

"Em, what are you doing awake?"

"I could ask you the same thing." He was wearing joggers and blue light glasses, his chest bare. Something about the glasses and the dimly lit room had heat pooling in my belly. I should have been completely exhausted from the two rounds earlier, but just seeing him had my whole body waking up.

His arms reached up behind him, pulling me down to him until our mouths collided. I could taste the lingering notes of his peppermint toothpaste.

"Mmm," I moaned. I reluctantly broke away and walked around the sofa sitting next to him, curling my legs up beside me. His warm arm draped across me. He was always warm, my own little heater.

"You should go to bed," he whispered, kissing the top of my head that was now resting against his bicep.

"I will go when you go." My eyes glanced at the computer screen. Caston documents. Something to do with our Kildaire hotel chain and financial reports. I closed my eyes. I didn't care. Another yawn had me curling further into him.

"Okay," he replied, closing the lid on his laptop. He stood up, and I shifted to the pillow on the other side. I was too tired to move and barely conscious. "C'mon, Em." His arms came around me as he scooped me up and curled me into his chest.

"You look good in this shirt," he said. I buried my face into his shoulder. That was about as much energy as I could give. Once I felt the sheets pull up over me and Brooks curl up behind me, pulling me to his chest, I was out once again.

↟ ↟ ↟

Images of the night of the accident tortured me. It was inescapable and unrelenting. I wanted to scream, to cry. Why did I have to relive this? Brooks descended the stairs and this time, I chased after him. "No!" I yelled. The faster I took the steps, the longer the staircase became. I was frantic. Please don't go. Mr. Mason smiled maliciously, pushing against Brooks' back and moving him toward the door. "Please, no, Brooks!"

"Emily!" Brooks shook me awake. It took a moment for me to open my eyes to come back to reality. My heart pounded in my chest. I closed my eyes again and inhaled deeply, attempting to calm my racing heart. *It was just a dream. You are okay. He is okay.* I rolled over, shoving my face into the pillows. I wanted to cry. The amount of times I relived the same dream was exhausting.

"You're still having nightmares?" Brooks' voice was laced with concern. I rolled over to face him, opened my eyes, and met his. The room was bright and his eyes shone a brighter blue. They were always shifting shades based on cloud cover. I studied them, almost getting lost in them. A few weeks ago, I wasn't sure I would ever get this opportunity again. Grateful wasn't a big enough word to describe how I felt.

My eyes welled with tears at the sight of him and my heart ached for all the years he wasn't here. I inhaled, pushing down every emotion before remembering he asked me a question.

"Yeah. It's been like a year since the last one though." I sighed against the thousand-thread count pillowcase.

He frowned, brushing my hair out of my face.

"I'm okay, promise." I pulled closer, placing my head on his chest. His hand rubbed soft circles along my back. He let out a sigh. The tension from the nightmares released with his touch and the steady beat of his chest.

"What time is it?" I asked through my yawn. I had never been so tired but so completely alive. My body was ravaged, my mind a scrambled mess - in all the right ways - and yet, I felt almost invincible with him at my side.

"Almost eight." *Eight?*

"Oh, crap." I sat up, my eyes searching the room for my bag.

"Em, hey, what's wrong?"

"I still have to work today. I have a conference call at 8:30 with the executives to discuss the gala. Where's my bag, B?"

"It's probably in the entryway. Ryan was supposed to drop it off while we were at dinner."

"Wait. Ryan? The driver?"

"Yeah, Em, he's my driver. No car yet, remember?"

You buy a plane before a car, really? Was he insane?

"Okay, I need to shower. Can you grab my bag for me and point me towards the bathroom?"

He chuckled, wrapping his hands around my waist and pulling me back. My greedy body clenched with expectation.

"Not yet." He bit my shoulder. Of course, my body reacted with a quick pulse between my thighs.

"Brooks, I have to get to work." I moaned and reluctantly wiggled free of the sheets. I looked back at the half-naked, gorgeous man. His eyes were on me and full of desire. I still felt exhausted from the lack of sleep and two am wake-up. I giggled, leaving the room to fetch my bag since he was preoccupied.

The water was warm and soothing after such an intense night. I scrubbed my face, wiping yesterday's makeup off. My subconscious yelled at me again. *Slow down.* All of this felt fast, but so normal. It was confusing and exhausting, but also better than I could have ever imagined. So of course, I chose to just ignore it.

Cold hands grasped my waist, shocking me and causing me to gasp.

"Brooks," I giggled. His chin rested on my shoulder. I couldn't see as I rinsed the soap off my face. Once clean, I spun in his arms. He pulled me into his naked body.

"I do have to get to work, you know," I reminded him, spitting water from my mouth.

"One minute."

"Nice try." I kissed him swiftly before my body decided it was in charge of making decisions. It was my only chance to escape and get to work on time. I pushed the glass door open and stepped out into the ice-cold air.

"You're mean, baby," he groaned.

I laughed, wrapping the towel around me and another around my hair.

"Some of us actually have a boss." I turned back, smiling at him. He was under the water and his need was fully evident. With one more promising glance, I left the bathroom.

↟ ↟ ↟

I clicked the Zoom link. I was already a minute late and this was my meeting. All of our executives were waiting to hear about the Gala. It was going to be our biggest fundraising event of the year and we desperately needed the donations. *Great.* My makeup was rushed and my hair was damp, but thankfully I had a barrette in my bag and could pull it back.

"Good morning, Mr. K, Mr. Whitney, Mrs. James," I said, sounding winded.

"Emily." Mr. Whitney nodded.

"Morning, Emily." Audrey's face popped up in a box.

"Okay, so today we are just doing a quick overview of the gala. Audrey, were you able to get anything back about the sponsors from Kate?" I asked.

"No, not yet. She will be in the office on Monday," she replied. *Crap!*

"Okay, well, let's talk about the venue. With our sponsors and guests, we have it narrowed down to three locations."

"Three? I thought two?" Mr. Kavinsky interrupted. He was not a morning person even though he had five kids at home. Dark circles under his eyes interrupted his too-pale skin.

"Well, Sapphire is an option. We could rent it out if we wanted to keep it local. The other options are the country club in Southport or the Seaside Bed and Breakfast that hosted the gala during the first one. They have that fantastic outdoor venue."

"What about the weather?" Mr. Whitney chimed in.

"Well, they don't have an indoor option. Honestly, I am leaning towards the Southport Country Club, if we are okay with the distance. I have already talked with their event planner, Stephanie, and they could handle the whole thing. Sapphire is another option, and I know the manager. I just don't know if throwing a charity ball in a nightclub is the vibe we are going for."

"Yes, I think Southport is good. Mrs. James?" Mr. Kavinsky asked.

"Is it within the budget?" Mrs. James asked.

"Yes, Audrey and I worked on this last week." I screen-shared the financial projection analysis sheet. The sheet was colorful and detailed, I had spent hours on it. Brooks walked past the front of my computer causing my eyes to focus on him. Looks like he traded his joggers for chinos, but still hadn't found a shirt. I bit into my lip, admiring his body. *How is he mine?*

"You better pay attention, Ms. Barlow," he whispered, smiling. I blushed and returned my eyes to the screen. The rest of the meeting was a blur as we talked about financials and the image the gala was going to create in the community. I closed my laptop in relief once the meeting was over and dropped my head into my arms. *God, I am so tired.*

A cup slid across the table. I looked first at it and then up to Brooks.

"You're a lifesaver. Thank you." I said, desperately reaching for the steaming cup.

I sipped the warm coffee. It was rare that I drank coffee. I mostly enjoyed tea, but when I was overly tired, coffee was the only thing that could keep me awake. Brooks sat down on the table in front of me and I let my eyes rake his bare stomach.

"Are you missing your shirt, Mr. Devonshire?" I laughed, thinking about the black shirt on the bathroom floor. I should probably go clean up the clothes scattered around the house.

"I just like the way you look at me when I am not wearing one. You blush and bite your lip a lot more," he teased. I grinned and walked around the table. He was leaning back on his hands. I knelt down and kissed his stomach trailing down the hard lines of his hips, visible from his low-hanging pants. His abs tensed under my mouth, and he groaned, sending shivers down my spine.

"It's a nice bod," I giggled, rephrasing my line from the first night together. I stood up between his thighs. He rolled his eyes as he pulled me in for a hug.

"How much longer do you have to work?" he asked through his teeth as he began tickling my side. I squealed and twisted in his arms.

"Stop," I begged breathlessly.

"Not a chance," he laughed, before releasing me. I enjoyed being tickled even though it was a form of torture. Brooks tickled me all the time growing up.

"I asked, how much longer?" His voice was soft. I looked up into his eyes and melted.

"I have a few emails. Why?"

"I want to take you to breakfast."

"Okay, Mr. Devonshire." I flung my arms around his neck. "Let's go. Emails can wait." He leapt forward, pressing his lips into mine. A small giggle escaped my mouth.

Chapter Twelve

I sat back on the sofa while the fireplace roared to life next to me after hitting the remote start. Brooks sat at the other end, working on emails and reviewing the documents from early this morning. I had three emails waiting for my attention. The one from Audrey was a summary of this morning's meeting. The second one caught my eye.

Subject: KGW - Gala Interview

Good Afternoon Ms. Barlow,

This is Harper Thompson, from KGW in Portland. We would love to do an interview with you about the work that Hope is doing for the local community, and the communities across the nation. We heard from one of our producers about your Gala event this summer and would love to come and do the interview there.

> We look forward to hearing back from you.
>
> Harper Thompson - Executive Producer

I held my breath and forwarded the email to our director and he responded almost instantly telling me I should take it. I loved the work Hope International did, but being a face for the company was something that had my insides twisting.

I wasn't shy, but something about being the spokesperson felt like more responsibility than I was prepared for. He was offering for my career to grow though, so I pulled up my big-girl panties and scheduled the interview with Harper.

A few hours later, I reached a stopping point and pushed my laptop off my lap. I crawled across the couch to Brooks' lap, pushing his laptop out of the way. His hands brushed my hair back over my shoulders sending a shiver down my spine. My head fell to the side, leaning into his hand.

"Thank you," I whispered.

"For what?" He chuckled, bringing his lips to my jaw as he tilted my head to the side, igniting my core.

"Coming back. Calling me." He pulled back.

When our eyes met, I pulled him in for a hug. His eyes conveyed the depth of his pain and apology.

"Em, all I wanted was you. The whole time. My life isn't whole without you," he admitted, pulling me toward his chest.

I rested my lips on his, allowing myself to feel a sense of peace. We held our locked lips, unwilling to move. Brooks' hands slid down my back with pressure. I smiled, releasing his lips, and pulled back. The fact that he was here now made everything better.

"Em, why don't you come to Caston?" I rolled my eyes ignoring the instant excuses swirling in my head prepared for a fight. *Because I love my job. Because I feel unqualified to run Caston.*

"I love my job, Brooks. Plus, you don't need me there. I will just be a distraction." I tried to free myself from his embrace, suddenly feeling uncomfortable.

He shook his head, gripping my hips tighter. A small smile formed on his mouth while he stared deeply into my eyes.

"I want you there. There is always plenty of work to do and I was thinking, you could help us expand into new markets. You're smart and people like you. You are a natural leader. During my interview with Seattle Times, they had a lot of questions about if, and when, you would be stepping in. Lucky for you," He gripped my butt, getting a little yelp out of me. "I told them you were busy trying to save kids but they would be the second to know. After me, of course."

I chuckled at his ridiculous response, but it was probably better than one I would have given. When I graduated, The Times had reached out to me, asking if I was stepping in, and my only response was no comment. I basically went into hiding after that. My current silence must have been enough though, because he pulled me back to his chest and whispered, "Just think about it." I nodded.

My body rose and fell with his breathing as his arms wrapped around my back like a weighted blanket. My body relaxed against his, inhaling his sweet, familiar scent. Just the smell of him mixed with hints of the cedarwood soap from our shower earlier was enough to make me putty in his arms.

"Let's go on a walk out at South Beach Trail," he said.

"B, I need to finish working." His face fell and I gave in. "Give me like thirty minutes."

↟ ↟ ↟

The elevator doors closed and I felt trapped. Brooks had been unusually quiet since earlier. *What could be wrong? What did I do?* I rested my back on the wall and looked up at him. The silence was killing me.

"B? What's wrong?" I asked. My stomach was in knots and my obsessive inner monologue had me questioning my worst fears.

He was staring off into the distance and his hands were gripped tight around the rail.

"Nothing." His voice was curt. *Liar.*

"Brooks, I feel like I did or said something to upset you, and I don't know what it is." His blue eyes were cold when he looked at me. *Shit.*

"Emily, I don't understand why you won't work at Caston. Our parents left us this company. It provides us with this lifestyle. You could pick your hours, I just don't understand." The words pierced me, possibly deeper than he meant them too.

Irritation grew within me and I was suddenly unsure of everything that had happened over the last two weeks. Would Caston come between us?

"Brooks, I have told you. I love my job. I..." I paused. My mind was racing with all the reasons I decided to move, why I decided to work at Hope, and why I decided to move on.

"I want something of my own okay? At least for now. So much of my life was consumed by you. Every inch of my house, college, work. I just needed to do something that was for me. I love working at Hope. I don't care about the money, B. I want to do work that matters, and Hope is doing things that matter. Matching kids with forever homes and giving them a place in this world is so rewarding. Caston is...well...Caston. We build hotel chains and invest in real estate, and tech companies now. Who is that serving? How is that making a difference? I mean, I just want to do something that I can wake up every day and know I am making a difference. That in some small way, the world is a better place because of it."

That was the truth of it. I couldn't get behind Caston because the work didn't matter to me like Hope did. I could make an actual difference at Hope. The elevator doors opened into the garage where

Ryan was waiting with the black SUV. *Ridiculous. He needs to buy a car.*

Ryan opened the door for me and I slid across the back seat. The tension between Brooks and I only seemed to build. The air was thick with unsaid words and unstable ground. He crawled in next to me, his bottom lip pulled into his teeth and his hair wild from his hands running through it.

I stared out at the other cars in the garage and a single tear fell on my cheek. I wiped it away quickly. I wanted Brooks to make everything better, yet this was something we needed to work through. I wasn't going to budge just because he showed up again. I owed it to myself to keep him and work separate. At least for now. Ryan slid into the driver's seat and the car jerked forward.

"Okay." His voice was soft as he broke the silence. I turned to look at him, his hand slid over mine on the seat, clasping it tightly. His eyes turned up to mine. The irritation in his eyes was gone.

"I want you to be happy. Stay where you are, but maybe you can help Caston find meaningful work, too. Maybe it's time the company did more than write checks to charities, and made a real impact. I want you to love the work you do, but I also want you at my side at Caston." His body was tense and I could see the war in his eyes.

"I will think about it," I said with as much hope as I could.

He nodded and turned to look out the window as the car pulled out of the garage and into the bright light. It was something to at least consider.

My stomach was still in knots from our disagreement. He sat there withdrawn, staring out the window, but at least his hand was still wrapped around mine, offering me a little lifeline of stability.

↟ ↟ ↟

The clouds and fog had lifted by the time we reached Loop Trail. I looked at the water, it was a grayish blue today and calm. The rocks and earth crunched beneath our feet as we walked down the trail toward the water.

Bainbridge Island was a dark, moody blue land mass in the distance. The silence between Brooks and I was deafening and it made me uneasy.

I didn't know what to say to make him break out of this mood. I took a moment and thought about the fact that he might be feeling the same thing I was, putting us both at an impasse. I paused and he stopped, turning to face me. His face was unreadable as he studied my hesitation.

I grabbed a hold of his raincoat and pulled myself up to his lips. His arms wrapped around me, pulling me in. I let my lips rest on his for a moment before I pulled away.

"I hate this, B. I hate fighting and not talking." Still on my toes, my forehead rested on his chin. His arms tightened around me.

"I know," he agreed. "Please forgive me for getting upset." *Always.* I forgive him for everything he has done and will do.

"I forgive you. I'm sorry if I hurt you. I didn't mean to."

His arms released me, and I stepped back to look up at him.

"I just want you with me all the time, and it's not fair to ask you to quit your job. You did nothing wrong." He sighed, tucking his hands into his pant pockets. His dark brown hair was beautiful in this light.

"I know."

↟ ↟ ↟

It was raining when we got back to his condo and somewhere behind the clouds, the moon was already replacing the sun that had hidden behind cloud cover most of the day. Brooks set the bag of our Chinese takeout on the counter and started pulling out the small white boxes of food. I curled up against his arm, which was pressed firmly against the counter.

"Your hands are like ice," he chuckled. I slid my hands into his shirt, warming them against his unusually warm skin.

"Geeze, Em." He jerked away, and I giggled. He chuckled, turning to face me, and lifting me up to set me up on the countertop. I giggled again, placing my hands on his shoulders and sliding my hands down into the neck hole.

A smirk crossed his face, all traces of our earlier disagreement erased. "What am I going to do with you?"

Warm me up. Give in? "You are going to be my personal heater, Mr. Devonshire."

His face lit with amusement before planting a chaste kiss.

"Okay, chicken or beef?" he asked.

"Both." I pulled my hands from his neck and unwrapped one of the wooden chopsticks from its paper wrapper. My feet wrapped around his legs so he couldn't go anywhere while he grabbed the box of beef and broccoli and unfolded the top. I was feeling quite playful, and it was much needed after all the tension from this afternoon.

I grabbed a piece of beef, raising it to his mouth. The corner of his mouth turned up as he bit down and pulled it off the sticks. Heat raced through my body that had nothing to do with the room temperature or his warm body against mine. After a bite for myself, I playfully raised a piece of the broccoli to his mouth before pulling it back last minute to my mouth. He sighed with a playful smile.

"Too slow," I laughed around a mouthful. His eyes melted into mine as I finished chewing.

"What?" I giggled at his intensity.

"I love you." I grabbed another piece of beef and lifted it to his mouth. The sauce brushed the side of his mouth on the way in.

"Oh," I giggled. "I'll get that," I whispered as he chewed. My lips met the side of his as my tongue slid across the sauce, wiping his face clean.

My body begged for more, dampening my inner thighs. *Is Chinese food an aphrodisiac?* Brooks swallowed, his eyes going from playful to smoldering. His hands yanked on my hips, pulling me closer to the edge of the counter.

"Tell me what you want." His blue eyes locked with mine and incinerated my panties.

"I want you, Brooks. I want you to show me you're sorry." I was nervous about being so vulnerable but we had agreed to be honest. Plus, he had a way of making me feel safe to say these things and making me feel sexy. My lips met his, as my hands worked to pull his shirt up. We momentarily pulled away to work his shirt free. His body was warm as I pulled myself back into him.

Brooks moved his hands to my thighs, and up into my dress. He gripped me tightly, pulling me off the counter and into him. My legs instinctively wrapped around him as he carried me to the living room floor. The fire was raging behind the glass, just like the hormones piping through my veins as I lost myself in him. The shag carpet felt like heaven as Brooks laid me out before him, my knees trembling with need, and my dress bunched around my chest.

Brooks released my mouth, inching his way down my body, nipping and sucking to my inner thigh. I moaned, ready for him. He was so good at building anticipation and driving me wild in the process.

His lips were soft on my thigh, and his tongue left a moist trail as he worked his way up. Brooks tugged my panties off, tossing them to the side as his lips crushed back into mine. I pulled his body into mine, sinking my nails into his back. His tongue hungrily moved with mine.

Heat consumed me and my need came in the form of low whimpers and soft moans. His hips had me pinned while his erection ground into me.

"Please," I whimpered, "I need you." Brooks pulled back just enough so I could work at his belt and button. His erection sprung free, already dripping precum onto my belly.

"You're still dressed, Ms. Barlow. Let me help you out of this cute dress." He stood, dropping his pants, looking like the gods themselves had sculpted him. I was a panting mess as his hands pulled up on my dress. His hands made quick work of releasing my bra. My nipples were already hard pebbles but as the air brushed against them, a shiver ran down my spine.

"Baby, you're so beautiful," he whispered, moving so he could pull one of my perky nipples into his mouth while his fingers tugged on the other.

"I like it when you call me baby," I moaned, dropping my head back.

I lifted my hands, freeing the bra and tossing it to the couch with my dress. Brooks moved over me, settling between my thighs. My hips lifted to meet him and he groaned.

"What else do you like?" His mouth embraced mine, and my needy body exclaimed I was ready for him. His lips moved to my neck in a tortuous, slow descent.

"What are you waiting for?" I gasped as he bit down.

"Patience," he growled, against my tender skin.

I should have known by now, this was part of the thrill. He enjoyed and teased every inch of my body. His lips grazed softly over my collarbone a moment before the slow assault of bites and licks on his way down to my core. *Oh my, yes.* I gasped, bursting with pleasure as he used his tongue to sweep my slit. My hand reached down, holding him in place while my hips thrust up, grinding against his face. His mouth broke free just long enough for him to find my sensitive bud.

"I can't..." I cried, my vision blurred with another languid stroke of his tongue. His fingers gripped my hips, holding me still until I melted into submission as his tongue continued its gentle assault. His fingers found my sweet spot, sending a warm, powerful orgasm through my body.

"Brooks," I cried out. My vision went dark as his mouth brought me to a place somewhere between heaven and hell. Wave after wave of my orgasm rolled through me and all I could do was lay there and take it.

"I am so sorry, baby. I will support you no matter what." His breath tickled me while his fingers found new depths. Ripples of another orgasm edged closer.

"I know," I moaned, gripping the rug like it was a lifeline.

"Show me you know." His voice was low and I was peaking again, just as he hummed against me. I don't even remember begging, but somewhere in the distance, I could hear his encouragement. Still reeling from my release, his mouth was back on my neck.

"Don't...hold...back," I panted. His face turned up like he'd just been granted keys to the kingdom. His thrust into me wasn't like last time, it was rough and needy and the feeling was singular - pleasure.

"God, you feel so warm and tight," he groaned. I was so sensitive to every movement I was clamping down around him. "Don't," he barked. "Relax, Em."

I nodded, relaxing, allowing him deeper. With one hand, Brooks pinned my wrists above my head while his other hand groped my breast.

"I love your tits," he panted.

"Keep going, keep talking like that," I panted, digging my heels into him while my hips met him thrust for thrust. It wasn't enough. I needed more. I wanted him deeper than my body would allow.

"Your body is so greedy. I love it. I'm going to come, and you are going to come with me, understand?" His whisper tickled along my neck. "Turn over."

I nodded and rolled before he thrust back into me without warning, shooting me forward. He pulled my back to his front in a kneeling position, using his hands to grip my breasts. Blurry flashes of the firelit room around us made me feel cozy and cherished.

"You better be ready." He bit into my neck.

"Yes," I cried, as I exploded around him in the most intense orgasm yet. Together, we worked, pulling each other's orgasms until we were both a heaping pile of sweat and sex gasping for air on the rug.

When my pulse finally returned to normal, I found the energy to move on top of him, pushing him into the rug this time. I laid flat against him, my hair splayed out across my back while he played with it.

"I will never get enough of this. Of you," I replied. His face relaxed into a small smile and his eyes softened. His hand clasped mine and he pulled it up to his mouth, planting a small kiss on it.

"I love you, Emily. I always have, and always will." I nodded. We lay quietly on the floor; the fire crackling just above us. I wanted this - forever. I wanted him.

"I didn't use a condom, Em," Brooks said softly. "That's twice now. I need you to get on birth control."

"Yeah, I know. I don't know if I want to start birth control yet if that's okay with you. We just need to be more careful."

"Okay," he sighed. "I want babies, just not right now and I doubt you want them right now."

"Okay," I said, planting a kiss on his chest. He was right. We were playing with fire. I still had ten days before my cycle started. Even though my app said my fertile window was closed, I knew I was being stupid. "I will make an appointment."

He kissed my head.

"Do you think," I paused, sliding off of him so that I was curled into his side. *Would we be married had you not gone to the Air Force?*

"What?" he asked. His eyes were closed and the light from the fire danced across his face.

"No, never mind."

"C'mon, what?" he asked, now very curious. One eye opened to look at me.

"Do you think that if everything hadn't happened, we would be married?" I don't know why I even bothered asking. Was I ready for his response? I think I just needed hope for a future that we had planned so many years ago.

"Probably." He let out a little chuckle. I rolled over to my stomach to look up at him. My heart gripped with how soft his eyes were.

"Did you know my mom, and yours, gave me the "talk" like halfway through freshman year?" I bit my lip in amusement at the memory. "They gently, and very lovingly, reminded me that you would still love me even if we waited until we were married. They were so sure we would get married after high school."

Brooks' mouth turned up.

"Yeah, my dad had the same conversation." He laughed. "I think my dad was probably a little more worried about you getting pregnant, not necessarily about us having sex."

I let out an involuntary laugh.

"Did he think we were already having sex?"

"No, I don't think so. But I think they were all trying to navigate our relationship as our hormones were kicking in." He tucked his free hand behind his head.

"Did you ever wish that we did?" I asked, playing with a piece of the rug.

Brooks chuckled. "Of course." He rolled his eyes, moving his hand down his face and back to his chest.

I bit my lip, concentrating on the idea of us being teenagers, and having this kind of intimacy.

"You didn't?" His voice was confused.

"A few times. Do you remember that one night up at the cabin? Our parents left us to go to dinner with those friends."

"Uh, yeah."

"It pretty much took everything I had to not give in." I smiled at the memory.

"I remember. You got up and left the room." His eyes were closed again and I couldn't stop staring at the inky eyelashes that were so beautiful as they gently sat on his cheek.

"If I had stayed, I would have given in."

Brooks laughed again.

I leaned down and kissed his bare chest. *You have no idea how close.*

"It was worth the wait," I whispered.

Chapter Thirteen

After Brooks moved in with me, it felt like the weeks were flying by leaving both of us feeling a little off-center as we navigated our new life together. The guilt I felt about dragging him away from Seattle was beginning to ease as he found a new routine of working half the week in Seattle and half the week home.

Before Brooks had come back to me, my routine was very busy. I would spend my mornings in a spin class before heading to work. I rarely worked from home, and if I did, I would plan a night out with friends, usually Natalie and Grey were my go-to buddies. Now with Brooks here, I hadn't seen them since the party a few weeks ago.

I had even started working from home more, usually leaving in the afternoons to be home early. While working remotely, Brooks used the study to take most of his meetings. Life together was new and exciting.

The aching feeling was all but gone, and the fear that he would leave again was dissipating with every passing day. Living together brought its challenges that we both agreed to laugh through, and work toward a happy medium. Like the fact that he was so anal about clothes immediately being put away once Mrs. Hall put them in our room. We agreed that we would do it together in the evening before bed. He hated the fact that I had half-read books all around the house, leaving little room for anything else on all the end tables. Begrudgingly, I put them all on the shelf where they belonged except for the current book I was actively reading.

He liked to sleep with the windows open, which meant I needed to stay glued to him all night to keep warm, but of course, he didn't mind. I was still working on making sure he felt at home, which he promised would come with time because, and I quote, "I was his home now." Of course, I melted, and because I was on my cycle, I turned into a sobbing mess on the floor. He made up for it by buying me three different flavors of ice cream and promised to watch Outlander with me.

"How about a run before work?" Brooks was just waking up beside me. I had been awake for a while and was sitting up in bed creating a shopping list for Mrs. Hall.

"A run?" His eyes squinted open up at me. "I thought you had spin today?"

"I do, but I was thinking I could skip it. It would be nice to do something together. Plus, I'm craving an iced chai from Lift. I haven't been there in a while."

"Or..." He pulled the sheets up over us with one hand and the other pulled me into him making me giggle. "We could just stay in bed today." His hands were colder than usual as he slid them up my silky nightgown.

"Nope, no, none of that. Let's go." I slid out of bed. I pushed the closet doors open with flair. The closet was overcrowded now, but I didn't care. It made me happy to have his things here. I pulled open the bottom drawer and grabbed the black LuluLemon leggings and matching sports bra.

"B, let's go," I called from the closet. He was probably still wrapped up in the sheets.

"Alright, alright, I am up," he groaned. I could hear him rustling in the sheets. I rolled my eyes and chuckled to myself.

↟ ↟ ↟

A warm salty breeze swept through the streets of Pacific Coves while we ran. The sun was already above the horizon and casting a golden glow on the surrounding forest. My ponytail swayed back and forth across my back. I hadn't noticed how long it was getting already. Maybe it was time for another haircut. I looked over at Brooks who seemed to be lost deep in thought.

He looked like he was taking an easy stroll, clearly, my pace was a little too slow for him. Lift was only three miles from our house, but I maintained my pace. Brooks and I used to stop here in high school to grab an iced coffee, before heading down to the beach. Our driver, Mr. Michaelson would bring us down here when our parents were staying in Portland on work trips. As we rounded the last row of trees, Lift came into view.

It was a little standalone cabin on the edge of town. The cabin backed into a group of trees, leaving only the front of the building exposed. Orders were taken from a walk-up window and guests sat at one of the many faded iron tables on the sprawling wood deck.

"That was a good run," I said on an inhale, looking over at Brooks. I could feel the beads of sweat on my brow that were about to drip and my back was soaked.

"Easy peasy," he teased, leaning in for a kiss.

"Eww, you're all sweaty," I whined teasingly, pushing his face away.

"So are you my love," he laughed, slapping my butt playfully.

"Hey, Jenny, I'll take an iced chai with some cream please!" Jenny had been the owner here since Brooks and I were kids. She was a single mom and worked hard to provide for her daughter, who was probably in high school now.

"Make that two," Brooks chimed in from behind me. We turned

away from the window and sat down at one of the smaller, more private tables near the edge of the deck that tucked into the tall pine trees.

"Do you remember that summer we came here almost every day?" A soft breeze cooled my skin as we sat, reminding me of summers here.

"Of course. That was the summer before freshman year. You were convinced she made the best frappuccinos."

"She did. Even Mr. Michaels agreed. I loved that summer. It was so nice to get out of Portland and away from the busyness of everyone."

"Em, I hate to break it to you, but Mr. Michaels only agreed with you because it was his job." My face scrunched, but he was probably right.

That summer our parents had rented a house in Portland because of all the meetings they had for the boutique hotel they wanted to build in Portland. The first few weeks of summer, Brooks and I had spent every day in the pool, or riding bikes, but we grew tired of the same routine. One of the investors suggested Pacific Coves for hiking and beach days. Our parents brought Mr. Michaels on full-time for Brooks and me to get around.

Of course some days we spent around Portland but there were too many tourists. When Mr. Michaels finally drove us out here, Brooks and I hiked one of the trails that led down to the beach. It was magical, winding through the forest, along a stream, and eventually reaching a sandy beach with massive rocks just beyond the break.

Pacific Coves quickly became *our* spot. Connor's parents even let him come down for a week to spend the summer days with us.

We rode bikes along the boardwalk and through downtown, we played in the water, and there were even several evenings our parents let us stay out and we had a bonfire on the beach. Mr. Michaels put up with a lot from us. That was also the summer I realized I wanted to marry Brooks.

"Here's your chai," Jenny yelled out the window.

I snapped back to reality and saw Brooks rise from the table to go get the drinks. I stood up to follow him so we could start the walk home before work started.

"So, I need to fly back to Seattle on Monday, and then I have that meeting in Vancouver and another with some developers. Do you want to come with me? It will be a two-week trip."

Two weeks? "B, I can't do that. I have work and since when is it two weeks? I thought you were going to be in Canada for a few days?"

"Sorry, Em. We're just trying to get as much done as we can while I'm in town. Also, Forbes found out I've stepped in, so they are running an article. You should be there. The meetings with the developers will only be four days." He pulled me closer and continued, "I want you to come. Would your boss mind that much if you work remotely?"

I'm sure Mr. Whitney wouldn't care about me working remotely, but with the Gala coming up I needed to be available for last-minute meetings and I had planned on making the trip out to the Country Club with Kate and Audrey. There was still so much to do and we only had a few weeks before the event.

"B, I can't. I just have too much to do. Plus, I'm pretty sure my passport is expired." I took another big sip of my chai.

"Okay," he sighed. "Michaelson can come with me." Why did I always feel so guilty telling him no?

We walked in silence sipping our chai ignoring the tension between us. As we walked I thought about working at Caston. I could start a new department, or work alongside our current team to look at giving back to the local Seattle community, or even across Washington and helping serve the lower-income community. Or could we partner with a non-profit in other low-income countries and provide housing?

Something to think about at least, and I would need to have an idea and the support of the board before I switched. But did I even want to switch? Or did I just want it because Brooks wants me to want it? I could still support Hope even if I didn't work there.

A black Audi rolled up beside us and the window rolled down.

"Hey, Emily, Brooks," Grey said, sliding his aviators down.

"Hey." I smiled, pausing my walk. I glanced over at Brooks who seemed surprised to see Grey as he was just pulled from his thoughts.

"Are you doing anything for Natalie's birthday? I was thinking we could get a group together and go back to Sapphire. She seemed to enjoy it last time."

I had spaced that her birthday was next week, but Brooks would be gone.

"Thanks for the reminder. Yeah, let's get a group together. I can call Sapphire, and see if Darrien can get us one of those rooms again. Maybe next Friday night?" Brooks finally snapped out of it and rested his free hand on my back.

"Emily, we should talk about it first." *What was there to talk about?* I looked at Brooks confused, taking note of his smoldering eyes, and clenched fists. My stomach turned sour. I looked back to Grey, who seemed to have the same reaction to Brooks as I did.

"Well, let me know. I'll see you guys later." Grey nodded.

"Yeah, bye." I waved, stepping away from the car. Grey rolled up the window and the loud music inside the car resumed. He pulled away slowly and then sped off. I looked back to Brooks confused.

"What is your deal? What do we need to talk about?" I snapped.

"Emily, the last time you went there, you passed out drunk and woke up in his bed. I just don't know how comfortable I am with you going out like that again." He wasn't wrong, and what he was saying wasn't unreasonable, but things were different. I was different. Nothing about last time was even remotely the same as now. I rolled my eyes, feeling anger creeping up inside of me as I stormed past him trying to put some distance between us before I said anything I would regret.

"Em, c'mon, I'm sorry. Let's talk about it," he called out from behind me.

"Just give me a minute, Brooks." *Did he not trust me? Also, who was he to say what I could and couldn't do? It isn't my fault he's leaving town for so long.* The more I thought the more frustration consumed me. Not just at him, but at myself. I knew I was overreacting, but I was so frustrated with him, Seattle, and Caston, and always feeling guilty for saying no, and it all melted into one big irritation.

Brooks took a hint, and stayed back, giving me the time to think. I dropped my empty cup in one of the trash cans at the trailhead by my house, before running up the driveway. I needed to shower and get to work, and I would still need to deal with Brooks. I kept running until I met the little path to head down to the studio. I looked back expecting Brooks to be on my tail, but he was nowhere to be seen.

Guilt consumed me, so I turned back and walked the driveway back to the gate. Brooks was just turning into the driveway when I got there.

My arms flew around him and I stood tall, planting a kiss on his lips. They tasted like Chai and salt. His arms pulled me in, lifting me slightly off the ground.

"I'm sorry. I shouldn't have reacted like that. I'm just dealing with a lot of emotions right now," I whispered, dropping my forehead to his chin.

"I forgive you. Please forgive me for not explaining better, and being so rude and blunt." He released me, letting me slide down until my feet hit the soil.

I stepped back and turned to walk with him up the driveway, my arm linked through his. The tall maple trees rustled with the breeze. The sun peeked through the trees down onto the damp earth floor, speckling it with golden irregular spots and the ocean roared loud just ahead.

"Emily, I just worry about you, that's all. I know I shouldn't be, but I don't exactly have any confidence leaving you in the hands of Grey."

"That won't happen again. The last time was different. I didn't know where we stood, you had just told me you were coming back, Grey kissed me." I probably shouldn't have brought that up.

"Exactly," he huffed.

"He knows we are together. Plus, I won't drink like last time. It will be just a few drinks with some friends, maybe some dancing, and then I will come home okay?"

We neared the concrete driveway that led up to the house.

"How about this? How about I send Ryan down, and he can drive you, that way you aren't driving after drinking. Plus, I know you will make it home okay."

"That's a bit much don't you think? You do know I survived without you for seven years. I think I can manage getting home on my own. Unless..." Unless he didn't trust me and wanted Ryan to keep an eye on me.

"Brooks, do you not trust me?" I stopped walking and turned. My ponytail whipped me across the face, with the sharp turn of my head.

"What? No. Of course, I trust you. I just don't want anything to happen, okay? Sure, maybe it's a little over-protective."

"You think?" I retorted, interrupting him.

"Em, please. I just care about your safety. You can go, and have fun, Ryan will be there in case anything happens, and I know he will get you home safely."

"Fine, Ryan can come babysit me." I pushed the door open to the studio and kicked off my shoes into the basket next to the door.

"Not babysit, drive...and protect," he replied, closing the door. I groaned in resistance.

"My turn." I paused halfway down the hall. "I feel guilty every time I tell you no."

"Em, you can tell me no. Please don't feel guilty. I'm sorry if I made you feel like that." He was toeing off his shoes and placing them gently in the basket, unlike me.

"You didn't, but I just don't want anything to come between us, and ruin this." I dragged my hands down my face.

"Emily. You need to be honest and you need to be able to say no.

I'm not going anywhere. Fights and disagreements will happen." He was bringing my head to his chest now.

"Okay, well, I'm also mad about Seattle. I know I shouldn't be, I just didn't realize you were going to be gone for so long."

"I should have told you when I was planning it. I will make sure to communicate better."

"Okay," I sighed.

I finished back down the hallway, feeling a weight lifting off my shoulders. Communication was key to making us work, and I was thankful that he was willing to sit with me in these hard moments.

As the steam billowed out above the shower, I undressed, my thoughts already distracted by my meeting with Kate and Audrey at nine. We needed to go over our list of sponsors and make sure all communications were coherent.

The water soothed my aching muscles and tension from the fight with Brooks. The scent of my shampoo had my mind drifting to Natalie. She had purchased this soap from our favorite salon in town that focused on sustainability and clean products. The eucalyptus felt cool against my scalp as I rubbed it in.

The sound of the shower door opening and closing had me smiling. *I knew he couldn't resist.* Warm hands rested on my hips while his lips brushed along my cheek.

"Brooks, I have to get to work and you're distracting me." I chuckled when his hands softly ran up the length of my sides. What was meant to be a warm caress felt more like a tickle.

"I'm aware," he whispered into the hollow of my neck. His body pressed against mine, sending all my warmth south. I didn't have time for distractions. I rinsed the shampoo with Brooks still pressing his erection into my belly while I focused on the task at hand. I managed to run my conditioner through my hair but just as I was about to start on the body soap, his hand reached the bottle first.

"Let me," he said. His voice was husky and low causing every nerve ending to hum in excitement.

I ignored the needy pulses between my thighs as the silky soap was massaged onto every inch of my body. I made a mental note about the fact that I was able to stand here and not beg.

With a tug on my shoulders, I spun to face him again. Soapy hands massaged my breasts while I fought the urge to giggle. Brooks was focusing a little too much on his hands and running his thumbs over my now pebbled nipples. I inhaled sharply and held it, hoping to tamp down the rush of arousal.

I was buzzing by the time he bent down on his knees, his hands continuing to soap up my thighs while his hot breath hovered over my slit. *Meeting. Sponsors. No time.* Just as I felt myself gaining ground, Brooks stood, smashing his lips into mine. A little moan escaped before I could swallow it down. A moment later, he had me pinned against the wall under the water, letting all the suds bubble around our feet.

"Fine. Make it fast," I said into his mouth. There wasn't a second of hesitation before I was lifted from the ground and accepted his full length. The power and intensity had me arching and rocking further into him.

"Brooks," I cried.

"I know, baby," he grunted. I was so close to my climax and he knew how to play my body. Small nips and tugs on my neck had me exploding around him. Wave after wave of pleasure rocked through me as he picked up pace.

He pulled out so fast that I gasped, still reeling from the loss of fullness. Something warm settled in my chest. The connection Brooks and I had with each other left me breathless and needy for more. *So much more.*

"How do you do that?" I chuckled, coming down from my high.

"It's not just me, Em. It's us. Together. I don't know." I knew I had spent too much time in the shower already but I wasn't ready to leave just yet. I filled my hands with soap and started massaging it onto his chest.

"My turn," I said, running my palms along the valleys of muscle. He took a deep breath, relaxing under my touch. I worked my way around his body, memorizing the curves and valleys, the dime-sized scar on his hip from when he fell on a rock in the fifth grade, and how his tattoos wrapped around his biceps. I especially loved the dimples that sat just above his butt.

I would never be able to tell him or show him enough just how deeply I loved him and was grateful for his return. My hands rested on his shoulders as I planted a soft kiss on his soapy back.

"Finished," I said. He turned to face me and pulled me under the water with him while my head rested on his chest.

"I want to marry you and have babies with you, Emily. I love you," he whispered into my ear. I melted into him, letting the words soak in.

I looked up, squinting at the water spray. I didn't know how to respond. Was this some kind of proposal?

"I want to marry you too." I stood tall, finding his lips with mine. His tongue reached out brushing my top lip. "I love you, so much, but we really need to get to work, and if I stay," I inhaled. I wanted more of him.

"If you stay, what?" His eyes darkened, drawing me in. I pulled back, released my arms, and pushed open the glass. *Time for work.*

I was gathering my things when Brooks stepped out from the hall. "Hey, I have a few meetings this morning, but do you want to grab lunch?" His hand brushed across mine.

"I would love to normally, but I'm meeting Leah for lunch. She wants to talk about you." I bit my lip fighting the grin that was threatening to take over my face. After the party, I had several messages from my friends asking to meet for coffee or lunch. They were all interested in learning more about my boyfriend.

"Mm...I see." His eyes were cheerful and relaxed. He bent forward and whispered, "Tell her all the good parts."

I giggled when his breath tickled my neck. "And what are those parts exactly?"

"I'll leave that up to you to decide," he teased.

"Okay, Mr. Devonshire. Well, I need to go. I love you."

His hand brushed my hair back. "I love you more, Ms. Barlow."

I smiled. "Not a chance." I kissed him, my whole body instantly melting into him. The kiss lingered, I wasn't ready to pull away just yet and wanted to see how long he would stay locked onto me.

He grinned. "I thought you needed to go?"

I laughed. "Okay, going."

Chapter Fourteen

The next evening, the Isaacs came over for dinner at the main house. It was a chance for Brooks and I to get to know a couple together, instead of them already being all my friends. Erik and Monica had just moved back to Pacific Coves.

Erik had grown up here but moved to Arizona for college, where he met Monica at ASU. The two of them decided to move back to Oregon and settle down. Brooks had met Erik at the gym and had mentioned having them over and I agreed. I was excited to get to know her.

"Wow, you have an amazing house," Monica stated as I led her and Erik out to the deck where Brooks was grilling. It was warm out tonight and there weren't any clouds in the sky. The sun was beginning to set, casting pastel shades of pink, purple, and yellow across the sky.

"Hey man," Erik said, walking over to Brooks. Monica and I laughed.

"Looks like a bromance is brewing."

"So tell me, what do you do?" I asked, guiding Monica over to the couch. She was beautiful. Her light mocha skin with her long wavy chocolate hair made her hazel eyes pop.

"Er, I own a little boutique downtown called Covet. I know the name is cringe." She paused, making a disapproving face. "I didn't pick the name, but since it was established before I got here, and already had a customer base, I decided to keep it."

"Oh, is that the one over by the farmer's market?"

"Yep, that's the one. I love it, it keeps me busy."

I was absolutely in love with that store. It carried beautiful closet staples on one side while the other half looked like it belonged to a boutique in downtown Hollywood, with its dramatic prints and upscale gowns.

"And what does Erik do?" I asked, feeling a little more at ease.

"Oh, he's a project manager for a small fin-tech company based out of Phoenix."

"So, he works remotely?"

"Yep." No wonder they hit it off so well.

"What about you?" she asked.

"Brooks and I own a company in Seattle. We do a lot in real estate and own a hotel chain, Kildaire, that we are currently expanding into Europe. Well, and a few boutique standalones. Brooks also wants to start looking at the tech industry more." Why hadn't I mentioned Hope?

"Wow, so you both work together or how does that work?"

"No, I actually work for a small non-profit in town called Hope. We match children in need with a family. It's not an adoption agency, we operate a little differently. We take cases, usually failed foster placements, and sometimes orphans, that struggle to be adopted, and we match them with waiting families around the U.S. Since we aren't an agency, we aren't working with just a single set of clients, we can find matches using adoption and fostering agencies, and their list of waiting families. It's really great."

"Yeah? That's amazing. My cousin fostered for a little while and she said it was really hard."

"Our goal is to make placements that make sense for the kiddos, and the families based on the stage of life, needs, financial situation, and a few other boxes. It's a lot like the current system, but our team just handles specific cases based on severity. It allows us to be more in-depth and careful with placements. The children we place are almost always adopted. I think maybe three kiddos weren't, but that was before I started working there, and I think it was pretty early on in the company."

"Not to sound rude, but how does one become CEO fresh out of college?"

"Our parents left us the company. The board is helping train and teach him. The previous CEO is training him personally until he retires. They've known us our whole lives so..."

"Okay. That's amazing. So, I guess I'm confused. Do you own Caston too? Or just Brooks?"

"No, we both do." I shrugged. *Yeah, confusing.* "Our parents started the company together. When they passed, they left it to us. Brooks and I just graduated, well, I did. He technically finished his degree in high school. Long story. Anyway, he's stepping in as CEO and I don't know my path yet."

Monica nodded, and then a curious look crossed her face.

"Okay, last question. Sorry." She laughed. "How did he finish his degree in high school? I've never heard of that before." I laughed when a look of genuine shock crossed her face. Brooks and Eric both turned to see us. I dropped my eyes back to her fierce hazel eyes.

"He went to boarding school in the UK. The school was insane. So, yeah, he graduated with a Bachelor's in business admin with a concentration in corporate finance. He is working on his MBA right now online."

Monica shook her head. "Wow, what? That's insane. Is that even possible?"

"I know. It was rough on him and he was finishing high school and college at the same time. He didn't get summer breaks and he was always in school. The school systems and timelines vary greatly in Europe." I shrugged.

I don't know how he did it. By the time Brooks was sent there, he was already a year behind. He left our sophomore year, so he only had three years to take the required classes for a four-year degree, while finishing the required high school credits. Thankfully, most of the credits doubled for both.

I had always felt bad. In high school, I struggled just with a normal high school schedule. Brooks was always in class or doing homework. His only downtime was playing soccer for the school team, or when he was sleeping. It wasn't fair. He was forced to grow up quickly, quicker than me.

The conversation with Monica and Erik flowed easily for the rest of the evening. It was fun to laugh while they shared stories about their life in Arizona and their crazy romance story. It was worthy of a Hallmark movie. He was preparing to propose to someone else when they met, and she was in a serious relationship with a different guy.

They accidentally fell in love, and their exes ended up dating. It was like divine intervention made a couple swap. It was fun to also see a different side to Brooks. He came alive hosting. He opened up a lot, and there was just a confidence about him that was comforting.

"Well, that was fun," I yawned, closing the door behind them.

"I enjoyed tonight." Brooks pulled me into him. "Ready for bed?" he whispered, kissing my forehead. His phone buzzed in his pocket.

"Yeah, it's late." I was tired. I had been awake since six.

Brooks shut off the lights and pulled me out the front door, closing it behind us. I stumbled off one of the rock steps leading down the path. Brooks chuckled and pulled me in closer to his side, while he read his text.

His grip loosened on me. "Emily?" He growled.

I looked up at him confused. His voice was so laced with anger and tension radiated off him in waves.

"What's wrong?" I asked, feeling a chill run through me.

"What the fuck?" The panic hit me like a truck and I flinched at his words. Brooks never cussed - or at least never in front of me.

"Watch your mouth," I yelled. "What did I do? What is wrong?"

His mouth pursed, and his eyes were smoldering as he stepped away from me and marched into the studio alone. *Great,* what now?

I dragged myself into the studio reluctantly. My mind was racing with all the possibilities that could have set him off. When I closed the door, Brooks was pacing the living room, fuming mad. My muscles seized and fear gripped my belly.

"Emily..." he started, clearly trying to not raise his voice. His voice was strong and stern. "What did you text Connor?"

Connor? Why is he so angry about Connor? Connor had been his best friend, aside from me, from fifth grade on. They played soccer together every year until Brooks left for England. He only lived a few blocks away while we were growing up and was pretty much our permanent third wheel. A position which he gladly accepted.

It had always just been the three of us. After Brooks left though, Connor became more like a brother to me, but he never mentioned talking to Brooks. I had always thought it was weird but didn't push.

"What? I just texted him that we were living together. Why? I didn't even know you talked to him anymore." I was so confused and his anger only made me angry. My subconscious was telling me to calm down but did I ever listen to it?

"Emily. God. Could you just for once keep shit to yourself."

His words were like a punch to the stomach. *Fine.* "What the hell is wrong with you?" I yelled. I was angry and hurt now.

"Fuck." He threw his cell to the couch. Nothing about this made any sense. After Brooks left for boarding school, Connor never mentioned staying in contact with Brooks so nothing about Brooks' current reaction was making any sense. Connor and I had stayed in touch through college and he was always there for me when I needed someone I could talk to that would truly understand.

"Are you going to tell me what I did that was so wrong, or are you going to stand there fuming?" My sassy voice was not going to make this any easier, but I didn't care.

His eyes turned to me with a glare I had never seen. *Shit.* This was so out of character for him.

"Did you ever stop to think that maybe I wasn't ready to talk to Connor about us? It's none of his goddamn business, Emily. You just had to go and stir the pot didn't you?"

"What are you talking about?" I yelled. I felt like I was going to pull my hair out. "Connor and I have been friends this whole time. He's never mentioned you. How was I supposed to know you two even talked anymore? What did he say? Why are you acting like such an asshole?"

"Fuck off," he sneered before snatching his phone from the couch and disappearing into the room.

I was too angry to pay attention to the fear that pulsed through me. My stomach was sour, making me nauseous, but the adrenaline kept it at bay. "Asshole," I yelled back.

I turned back for the door and made sure to slam it on my way out. Like the self-righteous person I was, I marched straight into the main house and slammed that door too, for good measure. I was shaking by the time I reached the couch. I hated fighting with him.

I screamed at the top of my lungs needing a release. I hated yelling but at this moment, it felt good to raise my voice. My mind was racing a thousand thoughts a minute trying to replay my text with Connor and Brooks' reaction. What could Connor have said that would set him off like that?

"Ugh," I groaned, dropping to the cushions. After a few minutes of trembling and trying to control my breathing, I remembered how exhausted I was. I was still too angry and shaken up to go find Brooks, so instead I climbed the stairs to the master. For the first time, this bedroom would get some attention. I pulled back the duvet, leaving all the pillows in place, and crawled in to cry myself to sleep.

Chapter Fifteen

I was lying in a pool of tears when Brooks pulled the sheets back and crawled in behind me. I was still too hurt, too angry, to turn around and face him, but my body instantly relaxed into him. A small part of me was relieved he was here. My body relaxed more as he wrapped his arms around me and pulled me back to his chest.

"I'm so sorry, Emily. I shouldn't have yelled at you. I shouldn't have cussed you out. I'm unbelievably sorry." His voice was full of remorse, tearing down my walls while my heart beat in a small pitter-patter.

Even if I had already forgiven him, my heart hurt. We had agreed on communication and instead, he blew up over something I didn't even understand.

"Brooks, I don't understand. Connor is my friend. What happened?" His body tensed behind me as he sucked in a sharp gasp of air.

"Connor and I got in a huge fight when I was still in training in Texas."

"What?" I turned to face him. "He never told me. I didn't even know he went to see you."

"He called me out for acting like an ass. It was after we broke up, and let's just say it wasn't well received."

"What happened?" I was clinging to Brooks' shirt now, and wrapping my leg over his, hoping he wouldn't run from my questions.

"I will tell you some other time. It's a way longer conversation that will only lead to more questions. For now, please know how incredibly sorry I am." I could see the battle in his eyes as he fought back his anger toward whatever had set him off. Brooks had always been the peacemaker growing up so seeing him so worked up was startling.

"What did Connor text you?" I asked again. There was no way I could drop it when he had such a visceral reaction.

Brooks pulled me into his chest tighter, my body going limp with exhaustion while the trace smell of his cologne enveloped me like a hug to my soul. I was so tired but being wrapped in his embrace, my defenses fell and I melted into him.

"He reminded me that I don't deserve you. He said I would just fuck it up again. He said I should leave you alone. Only after sending me a photo of myself that I didn't appreciate, let alone know he had. Like it was a form of blackmail or something."

My breath caught in my throat and my body seized. *Why would Connor say that? What photo?*

"Did you respond?" I asked, my voice no louder than a faint whisper.

"Not yet. I will. When I calm down."

"I'm sorry. I didn't know. I was just trying to share the good news."

"Don't be. I'm the one who is at fault. I overreacted. I was being an asshole. That was completely unacceptable, and I promise I will never yell at you like that again. You are amazing, kind-hearted, and such a great friend. I'm happy that you and Connor stayed friends and I'm sorry I treated you like that. Please forgive me. I will do anything to make it right."

"Brooks, I will always forgive you. I told you, I want to make this work, I want you. All of you. The good, the bad, the ugly," I paused for a yawn. "All of you. Next time, please just talk to me first. We can handle it together."

"I can do that. I'm sorry baby. I won't make that mistake again." He kissed the top of my head. I was now angry with Connor, but I would have to worry about that tomorrow. If he thought he was doing me a favor he was wrong.

"Don't make promises you can't keep, B."

"It's a promise I intend to keep."

I yawned again and nestled deeper into his warm chest.

"Go to sleep, baby. We can talk about this tomorrow."

I nodded and let sleep pull me under.

↟ ↟ ↟

A cool breeze tossed my hair as we walked down the pier to the small ice cream shop located at the end.

"I haven't been here since junior year." My stomach was still in knots from our fight last night. We hadn't talked about it yet and all morning there was tension between us.

"You came back?" His eyebrows raised in curiosity.

"Yes. I was almost done with school and was feeling lonely. I think that was around the time you were doing finals. Anyway, Mr. Michaels suggested it, and Ms. Hutchins thought it would be a great idea. She actually came down with us."

It was an unusually warm day for mid-May and Mr. Michaels drove with the windows down, a very rare thing. Ms. Hutchins sat in the backseat with me, and they both sang along to the voice of Lady Gaga on the radio. They were trying hard to cheer me up, it was sweet. It was working. With prom coming up, all I could think about was Brooks and my mom and Carrie taking me dress shopping. Seeing all the other girls in school sharing photos of their prom dresses and bragging about their dates and plans had me burying myself in self-pity.

I didn't want to be the girl who lost her parents and boyfriend, but I was, and because of that, everyone whispered around me and danced around me like I was going to detonate at any moment.

When Mr. Michaels asked if I wanted to get out of town, I jumped at the opportunity. They picked me up the next day after lunch, letting me skip the rest of my classes, and we drove to Pacific Coves.

"Oh, Ms. Hutchins...I haven't thought about her in a long time." Brooks laughed, shaking his head. "I was always in trouble with her."

"Well, probably because you were constantly distracting me from my homework and were always running through the house." I giggled at the memories of her snapping at him or grumbling about something he did.

"It was nice to have her around while finishing school though. I don't know what would have happened if she wasn't there to care for me." I sighed, it was painful to remember and think about. The Devonshires were the first option for guardianship but since they too had passed, the responsibility fell to Ms. Hutchins, my nanny/housekeeper turned pseudo-mother. "She's living in Southern California now. I think she met someone online."

"Online? I didn't even know she knew what online was," Brooks teased.

That was a hard season of life but I couldn't help but feel grateful it was all over and Brooks was here.

"Em, I have to leave at six tomorrow." His voice was soft like he was trying to soften the blow.

"I know," I sighed. "Two weeks." I groaned, looking out to the waves rolling in. Him being gone for three to four days of the week wasn't awful, but knowing he would be gone for fifteen made my head swim.

It would be the longest we've been apart since he came back to me and I could only hope it would go by quickly.

"You can always come with me, or join me at any time if you change your mind." He pressed his lips into a line, sliding his hands into his pockets.

"Yeah, yeah." I rolled my eyes. "I will be fine..ish. Just hurry home." I paused, looking up at him. We had reached the end of the pier and the wind was whipping my hair around my face. Brooks smiled, brushing it out of the way before his lips brushed mine.

"I love you," he whispered. "I'll come home soon."

↟ ↟ ↟

I woke up naturally reaching over for Brooks to find the bed space still cold and empty. He had only been gone for five days and already I was missing him with a physical ache in my chest. I wanted more than anything to feel his body heat on my back while he woke up, placing soft, open-mouthed kisses along my shoulder.

It didn't help that the past five days we had been missing each other. I was either in the shower when he called or he was in a meeting when I did. I just wanted to hear his voice.

The phone trilled in my ear as I sat up pulling the sheets with me. *Please pick up.*

"Good morning, beautiful," Brooks answered. He sounded winded.

"Hey, love." Just hearing his voice made me smile and some of my tension dissipated.

"Did you sleep okay?"

"Er, not really. I miss you." I glanced at the pile of laundry on the floor by the bathroom and knew if Brooks were here, I wouldn't be in this dumb mental pattern.

"Yeah, same." His voice was distracted. "Em, I'm sorry sweetie, but I need to go. I am walking into the coffee shop now to meet with Jerry from Xpansion. Call you later?"

My heart sank again and I could feel the tears flooding my eyes.

"Yeah, sure," I sighed, fighting back the tears.

"Em, hey," he said. "Okay, what's going on?"

"Nothing. It's okay. I'm good." I wasn't though. It was to the point that I contemplated renewing my passport and having a rush put on it, but he'd be back in Seattle before I could get it.

"No, you aren't. Emily, you aren't great at lying, remember? Tell me what's going on? Please."

A single tear brimmed, splashing down onto my cheek. I rolled to the edge of the bed, running my feet back and forth on the rug below.

"I miss you. That's all. I'll be okay."

"I'm coming home soon, okay? We need to get your passport updated so you can come with me next time." *Next time. Right.* Brooks was going to be traveling more now that he had plans of expanding the company.

"Yeah. Don't worry about me. I'll be okay. Call me later." I mustered the positivity I needed to assure him I was okay.

After saying our goodbyes, the phone clicked on the other end. Why was I so emotional? Then I remembered I was starting my period today or tomorrow. I wiped the tears from my eyes and stood up needing to get myself out of this funk.

It was warm outside so I figured it would be great to get some vitamin D, and just work out by the pool today. I grabbed my tea and laptop, then headed up the steps to the lower deck. I plopped down on one of the chaise lounges near the edge of the pool, my favorite spot.

Emily: I miss you, let's hang out this afternoon.

Natalie: I can't - I'm sorry. I'm working right up until we leave.

Emily: :(

Natalie: Everything okay?

Emily: Yes. No. Brooks and I got into a big fight the other day over nothing. Or I feel like it's nothing. I dunno. I need to find out what's going on. Let's chat tomorrow. I don't want to spoil tonight.

Natalie: Kk

I groaned, annoyed at my haywire emotions, and opened my laptop. I would welcome any distractions today.

Brooks and I briefly talked about Connor before he left, but there was still something there he wasn't telling me. I decided that I would rather wait for him to share when he was ready. In the meantime, I needed to deal with Connor.

Emily: What the hell did you say to Brooks? He flipped out. You never told me that you still talked to him. He said you guys had a fight in Texas?

Connor: What do you mean he flipped out? Are you okay? What happened?

Of course, he's avoiding my question.

Emily: I'm fine. Of course, I'm fine. Brooks just got upset. Why didn't you answer me?

Connor: You need to ask him. I gotta go.

Emily: Connor what the hell is going on? Ugh. Fine. But you will tell me. Let's grab coffee soon. What are you doing next week?

He never texted me back which only fueled my anger towards

him. Why were they both evading what happened? What could be such a big deal that neither of them wanted to talk about it?

↟ ↟ ↟

It was already noon when my phone buzzed under me. *Finally!*

"Hey, B!" I answered in a cheerful voice.

"Hey, baby. Sorry that the meeting ran long. You sound better?"

"Yeah. Sorry about this morning. I hate waking up to an empty bed, plus I started my period this morning. Anyway, I decided to work from home today out by the pool. It's a gorgeous day." I felt guilty but I didn't want to mention my short conversation with Connor. When Brooks got home, we would need to work this out.

"That sounds nice. It's cold and rainy here."

"Yuck. That sucks."

"So, good news. We are rearranging the schedule for next week, and I should be home on Wednesday." My heart leaped. *Yes!*

"Thank you. How was your meeting?" I tried not to sound too excited.

"It was good. The investors said yes. They want to move forward with Kildaire opening up next spring in Germany and Scotland."

"That's awesome! Is that what you're meeting with the developers for?"

"No. The developers are looking at an additional location in LA."

"Whew. Sounds busy. What about Paradigm? Where are you with that?"

"We have another meeting set for next week, then the purchase will happen here in a few weeks."

"Wow." I would be lying if I didn't feel a bit jealous about all the excitement that was happening at Caston.

"It's busy, but we've been taking off. It's great for the company but there is a lot to do." I could hear the hinting in his voice. Honestly, it was starting to sound more appealing. Especially if I could travel with him. I needed to change the conversation.

"Have you looked at cars yet?"

Brooks chuckled. "Emily, I haven't had a second to breathe, let alone car shop. Let's just do that next week."

"Sounds good. Hey B, just wanted to remind you tonight I have Natalie's party."

"I remember. Ryan texted me this morning. He will be there at eight and I told him he could stay again, hope that's okay."

"Yes, of course. Do you think he would be okay with picking up Natalie too?"

"Yeah, I don't see why not. He gets paid by the hour. Pick up whoever you need, just promise me you will call me when you get home, and please don't drink too much. I know, I sound controlling, but I just want you to be safe and make clear decisions."

My body tensed at his words. I knew rationally what he was saying made sense, but I couldn't help but feel there was an underlying issue he was still holding onto.

"Brooks, do you seriously not trust me to make wise decisions? It was one time."

"I trust you, Emily, but I also am not there to protect you if anything does happen. Just be safe okay?"

"I will be. Promise." *I will be on my best behavior.*

"I miss you," he sighed. "Wish I was there with you tonight."

"I know. I miss you."

"Okay. Well, call me before bed, no matter how late, okay? I just want to make sure you get in bed safely."

I chuckled. "Yeah, I will. Love you."

"Love you too."

I hung up the phone and sat back, closing my eyes to the bright sun. The warm, salty air was soothing, and the gulls circling above the crashing waves were crying out. It was peaceful. I had the time to finally think about the past few weeks. Everything was happening so quickly, but I was sure of two things. Brooks was home, for good. Two, we both wanted this to work and last. I had forgiven him of everything, and we were both just biding our time.

His "*I love you*" lingered in my ear. I could never grow tired of hearing it. I could never grow tired of his touch, his kiss, the way he made my heart race. I could never tire of his kindness and compassion, the way his breath felt on my skin, or the comfort and safety he brought. I loved him irrevocably and could only hope one day, I would be able to bind myself to him forever.

Chapter Sixteen

I turned, checking my dress in the mirror. It was almost eight, and Ryan would be here soon if he wasn't already. Monica had picked this dress out for me and I was obsessed. The short dress was a blue sapphire color that was playful, yet elegant, and sparkled with every move I made. The high-necked dress featured balloon sleeves and a silver button closure at the neck above the open-back.

My silver Jimmy Choos and diamond drop earrings paired perfectly. I slipped my mom's stacked diamond band onto my ring finger loving how it completed the look. I glanced back in the mirror, tweaking a loose curl, and reapplying another coat of my lipstick before FaceTiming Brooks.

"Hey baby, you look mighty fine."

"Hey, B," I smiled teasingly. "Thought I would show you my outfit so you can regret leaving me," I told him, with a sly smile on my face. A chuckle erupted from him. I flipped the camera to the mirror so he could see my whole body while I turned back and forth.

"Damn, Em." He cleared his throat. "A little short. Every guy in the room is going to have eyes on you." Good thing I only wanted his eyes.

"Miss me yet?" I teased.

He sighed, chuckling. "You are torturing me, Ms. Barlow. Not kind. I do wish I was there."

"Oh yeah? Why?"

He laughed even harder now. I wanted to hear him say what he wanted to do to me. I flipped the camera back to my face. "Tell me."

"I would like to do a lot of things to you, Emily. All of them include making you scream my name like you do every time." He flashed a teasing smile and winked.

"Really?" I responded a little breathless. I could feel my arousal and knew I was torturing him too.

"We will need to find another use for that dress when I get home." His eyes were smoldering and even through the phone I felt the heat of his gaze.

"Mm-hmm," I purred. "Gotta go," I whispered.

He groaned, throwing his head back into the pillows on his bed. "Thanks for that, Em."

"You're welcome." I giggled.

He rolled his eyes. "Love you. Have fun tonight. And remember, if Grey or any other guy touches you, I will knock them out."

"I know. Don't worry."

I blew a kiss and hit end after telling him I loved him. Before marching toward the door, I snapped a quick selfie and texted it to Brooks.

Emily: Dream of me!

He sent back a fire emoji and then reminded me I was supposed to call him when I got home. I slipped my phone into my purse after double-tapping a heart back.

↟ ↟ ↟

Ryan pulled up in front of Sapphire after we picked up both

Natalie and Grey. It felt so surreal to be back here with the two of them knowing my life was so different from the last time we were here. The fire pillars were already lit, and it looked like it was going to be a busy night. Ryan stepped out of the car, opening my door.

"Thank you, Ryan," I said with a smile, stepping out. I wished more than anything Brooks was here with me.

"Ms. Barlow, Mr. Devonshire has asked me to keep an eye on you inside. I will be off to the side if you need anything, and we can leave anytime you feel like it," he said.

"Thanks, Ryan." I waved while walking to meet up with Natalie and Grey. As much as I complained to Brooks about Ryan coming, I couldn't shake the warm feeling that settled in my chest knowing I was being taken care of.

I wrapped my arm in Natalie's. "Ready?" I squealed.

I had invited several of her co-workers, a few of our friends from spin class, and a couple of other friendly faces that we occasionally hung out with. The air was much cooler from earlier, so I huddled close to her, shivering. Grey was on my right and I could feel his eyes on me. We hadn't had much time to work out what went down between us and I knew it wasn't as simple as telling him no. He had tried for three months to get me to date him.

The bouncer marked our hands and we stepped into the noisy room. The dance floor was full of people, and the DJ was dancing up on his stand. Darrien, the manager we met our first time at Sapphire, greeted us just as we passed the full row of barstools.

"Happy birthday, Natalie!" he hugged her.

"Thank you," she squealed.

"Great to see you again, Emily, and Grey. I have the room reserved, and I think there are already a few people in there."

"Thank you!" I yelled out over the music.

We crossed the dance floor into the sunken room, where several of her friends were already sitting with their drinks. Natalie let my arm go and ran down the steps to hug them.

"Want anything to drink?" Grey whispered in my ear. My body

tingled, and my shoulder rose to my ear, annoyed at how my body responded to him. I put some distance between us before telling him I'd just wait for the server. I excused myself and settled in next to Leah who was with her husband in the corner of the sofa.

After ordering a glass of white wine, I caught up with them and told them about Brooks being in Vancouver. Peter promised to catch up with him when he was back in town.

Natalie tugged on my wrist, pulling me out to the dance floor while I gripped my almost empty glass of wine.

"I want to dance, let's go," she yelled over the music and I was happy to comply. We stepped out onto the dance floor, finding a place in the crowd. The music was poppy tonight, perfect for fun dancing. Our hips swayed to the music, and our arms rocked back and forth above our heads. For just a little while, I decided to let loose and act my age despite my heart being a few hundred miles away.

Chapter Seventeen

The sound of the car door closing outside came through the open windows. I was up in the main house reading about how to be in mature relationships, stretched out on the couch. I had taken the day off to be home when Brooks got home. My heart raced with the knowledge he was finally here while my body ached to hold him. My book thunked to the floor behind me as I ran for the door. I reached out for the knob when the door flew open, and Brooks stepped in.

"Hey!" he exclaimed, clearly shocked at my appearance.

"Hi," I flung my arms around him. He chuckled in my ear, dropping his bag to the ground.

"Miss me?" His hands lifted me, so I could lock my ankles behind him as I buried myself in his familiar scent while clinging to him like a needy child. He didn't seem to mind.

When I asked how he knew I was up here instead of in the studio, he reminded me I had the music playing as Hozier belted out about love and identity.

"God, I missed you," he whispered. Brooks' hands dropped to my thighs, lifting me higher. My heart found a slow, calming rhythm now that I was back in the safety of his arms. My lips locked onto his, sending a wave of peace crashing through me and I was happy to drown in it.

The taste of his minty, cool breath had me wanting more. My tongue reached out, teasing his lip. With me still wrapped around him, he stepped down into the living room while his kiss playfully devoured me. He gracefully laid me back onto the couch, allowing his body to sink between my thighs. The warmth and weight of his body felt like a weighted blanket. My body melted into him as I ran my fingers through his hair.

He had only been gone for less than two weeks, but it felt like an eternity. Being in his arms, I felt complete, whole. The stress and anxiety of travel and distance melted away with every breath, every caress of his tongue. Each time he returned to me, it mended me, piece by piece.

His hair was rougher than usual, most likely a result of the hotel shampoo I could smell wafting through the air between us. He moaned as my fingers brushed through his hair.

"I need to shower," he whispered in my ear before rising to his feet, taking my hand with him. "I'll be back," he said, releasing my hand.

"I can help with that." I was nearly begging, sliding off the couch behind him. He turned into me and grabbed me, pulling my butt in closer. His eyes heated as his gaze dropped to my lips. He smirked before bending down and throwing me up and over his shoulder.

"Let's go, Ms. Barlow."

↟ ↟ ↟

I reached into the oversized glass shower turning on both shower heads letting cold water cascade down on my arm from above. Brooks' body pressed against me from behind, pinning me to the glass, and heating my core. I was already panting, and he hadn't even touched me yet. A jolt of hot desire raced down my spine, and through my body, already begging to be released. My breathing hitched, as his arms wrapped around me, releasing the single button on my lace top, while his mouth moved along my neck.

"Mmm...this feels so good," I said breathlessly. My head fell back against his already bare chest, as my back arched in anticipation. His fingers tickled my hips in a soft caress as he lifted my shirt, palming my breasts along the way.

As my shirt pooled at my feet, his hands moved back to my breasts, cupping them and tugging on my pebbled nipples through the thin lace fabric. His heavy breath on my neck, and erection pressed into my back, had me wanting to drop to my knees. His hands unclasped my bra, allowing it to fall free to the floor, alongside my shirt.

His hands softly traced my shoulders, and down my back, to my skirt. His fingers lifted the elastic band away from my hips and down my thighs. I could feel his breath on every inch of my body, as he knelt down. Soft kisses wrapped around my thighs, leaving a hot trail. My legs were becoming more unstable by the second. His fingers dipped into the waistband of my panties, pulling them down in one swoop.

His groan against my hip snapped my thoughts back to the present ache between my thighs and made deep muscles clench causing my breathing to become more staggered. I could feel his smile on my behind. My body had always been so responsive to him and that wasn't ever changing. I was one thrust, or lick, away from combustion.

With one tug on my hips, I spun so that I was facing him. I fell back into the glass with a loud gasp escaping my mouth. His hands pulled my hips back to him, and his lips pressed softly to my lower stomach, and my core - every touch, every tingle, creating a new connection between us. My legs felt shaky as his lips moved along my hip and to my inner thigh, his tongue barely brushing the skin, leaving a trail of fire behind.

"I want you," I panted. His tender assault would cause me to collapse at any moment, I was sure of it. His kiss strengthened against my thigh, causing me to moan and arch my hips greedily toward his face. My hands grasped his face, pulling him up from the ground, allowing our lips to crash into each other. We were both panting heavily into each other's mouth, kissing between each breath. Our movements were frantic as we worked together to get him undressed, never leaving each other's mouth.

"I missed you, baby," he admitted while keeping his lips on mine.

Brooks reached past me, pulling the door open on the steaming shower. My hands pulled at Brooks' back, bringing him with me as I stepped into the hot, steaming water. I continued backward until I felt the cool glass wall that overlooked the forest on my back. The water trickled down both of our faces, filling our mouths with water between each gasp for air.

I moaned when two of his fingers slipped inside of me, hooking into the soft pad. I gasped, and moaned, tilting my hips up to him in pleasure. My other hand was still draped over his shoulder, pulling him closer.

"You're always so wet for me," he groaned.

"Always," I gasped. I was seconds from a climax, heat already spreading from the base of my spine.

"No, not yet," he growled.

He pulled his fingers out, leaving me on the edge. My mouth fell open in protest as a small laugh escaped through his smile. In a sexy as hell, act of love, he dropped to his knees again, his eyes never leaving mine.

"Just a quick taste," he groaned, burying his face into the apex of my thighs. His right hand pressed me further into the wall, stabilizing me when my knees buckled at the first swipe of his tongue. His left hand drifted up the back of my left leg, eventually lifting it over his shoulder. I was spread wide open for him. I had never felt so wanted, and so sexy, being this vulnerable in the light of day.

With gentle licks, sucks, and the brush of his beard, I was a heaping mess and more than ready for him. Warmth was spreading through my whole body faster than a wildfire. His left hand rested on my thigh, while his fingers found the sweet soft spot.

"Brooks...I...can't.." I was collapsing as I surrendered to the most mind-blowing fall yet. It was warm and right, and I felt like I was soaring. It was absolutely beautiful, and breathtaking, and I loved that only Brooks could take me there. When the edges of my vision returned, Brooks was still lapping me up like I was his favorite treat, all while holding me in place. I hadn't noticed my hands moving to his hair, but there they were gripping his hair, and holding him in place.

"Sorry," I panted, releasing my grip. He chuckled in return, and stood, pressing his lips into my neck.

His hands gripped my thighs as he pulled me up the glass wall, turning so that our tangled bodies were pressed against the tiled wall. He thrusted deeply into me with a power as if he was taking possession of my soul.

"Relax, baby," he whispered into my ear. On his command, I exhaled and allowed the rest of him to fill me. It was beautiful, and fulfilling in every way, making tears prick the back of my eyes. I clawed his back, trying to get closer, needing to feel him so deeply within me in every way.

With my body wrapped around his, and him buried within me, silent tears fell from my eyes, onto his shoulders, mixing with the water. We stayed there, not speaking, just breathing, and connecting.

"I love you...so much. It's so overwhelming," I whispered, my breaking voice giving me away.

He leaned back just enough to kiss away a tear streaming down my face.

"I love you, Emily. So damn much. I missed you. I don't know how I lasted all these years without you, but I feel like I need you more than the air in my lungs."

I nodded, another tear trailing down my face. His thumb wiped it away, as his mouth found mine. With slow kisses that promised forever, he rocked his hips, back and forth again, this time *gently* connecting our souls.

Just as my body relaxed, and melted further into him, he surprised me with a deep, powerful thrust that had my body clamping down around him.

"Forever. That's what I want, Em." I could feel his racing heart vibrating against my chest. My own doing the same as I gasped for air. I quivered around him with another climax already building with the promise of another blissful release.

"Yes, forever." I gasped for air. "Come...with me..." I begged, pulling his head closer to my neck. I shattered around him as the first hot spurt of him poured into me.

"Mine, forever," he promised as my body trembled against his. His penetration was deep and ecstasy was consuming me. When the trembles subsided, he kissed me as he guided my legs to the floor, careful to ensure I didn't slide to the floor in a puddle.

I glanced up at him. "You possess every part of me," I slurred, feeling drunk off him. His eyes focused on me, heavy with exhaustion from his release, but his adoration for me was clearly visible. The water was dripping off his face as his nose nuzzled into mine.

I closed my eyes feeling so relaxed that all I wanted to do was sleep tucked into his side. He kissed me again, before pulling away, and stepping under the raining shower head.

I used my remaining energy to push off the wall and grab the soap. I lathered it into my hands and began to soap Brooks up. The soap was like silk as I brushed my hands down his shoulders, his chest, past his stomach, and to his hips as he hummed in enjoyment.

"My turn," he whispered, grabbing the soap, and returning the same soapy touch, down and around my overstimulated body. It was slow, and we enjoyed the warmth and touch of each other under the falling water. The longer we stayed in the water, the more we talked about our time apart, and catching up with all the in-between moments.

Before the water bill ran any higher, Brooks had me bent over the wooden bench, claiming one last orgasm until I literally collapsed into his arm before he brought me down to the floor with him.

"I.can't.move," I chuckled. My body had never taken such a glorious beating. All the running, all the cycling, all the years of dance, could not have prepared me for this. The only thing that drove me to move was the guilt of how much water was being wasted while we lay breathless on the ground. Brooks had branded every inch of my body, and soul. Even my DNA had his name written on it.

I slapped the controls for the water, immediately stopping the waste, and turned to see Brooks, perfectly content with his head resting on his hands. He promised me forever.

Chapter Eighteen

By the time we stepped out into the air-conditioned bathroom, I resembled a prune. I gasped, shocked at the wave of cold air that hit me, causing goosebumps to pebble my skin from head to toe.

"Why?" I groaned at the universe, or to myself. Brooks laughed, tossing a towel around me before wrapping one around his waist.

The doorbell rang through the house.

"I'll get it." Brooks released his hands from my arms and grabbed his pants off the floor. He hopped into them with precision as he raced out the bathroom door. He threw the towel around his neck like a milk-maids yoke and disappeared out of sight.

I searched the floor for my underwear, finding them piled up nicely with the rest of my clothing. I pulled them up under my towel, hearing the front door open downstairs. Thanks to the warm water and post-orgasm high, I was so relaxed I couldn't wait to curl back up on the couch with Brooks as my heater. I pulled my skirt off the floor and dropped my towel.

Brooks reappeared with a confused look as I was buttoning my top. My hair dripped down on my shirt, soaking through to my bra.

My eyes cascaded down his bare chest letting my gaze take every toned inch of him in. He looked sexy, dripping wet, with his boxer briefs peeking out the top of his low-rise jeans.

"Hello, Mr. Devonshire." I playfully traced my tongue along my bottom lip. His lips curled up in a half-fake smile that never touched his eyes. A chill crept up my spine that was unrelated to the room's temperature.

"Em, there is a guy at the door asking for you. He said his name is Parker Jones." I choked on my spit as I inhaled too quickly.

What is Parker doing here? What does he want? "Er, I'll handle it." I stormed from the bathroom, feeling flustered as I passed Brooks. I was tempted to take the stairs two at a time, and I would have if I knew I wouldn't break an ankle.

I held my breath as I opened the door and saw Parker Jones standing on my porch. His whiskey eyes were soft and lifted to mine as he looked up at me.

"Hey," he said in a sweet voice, the same one that used to make me smile. Except now, it just made my stomach plummet. Parker and I had not ended on good terms.

"Parker, what are you doing here? How did you get my address?" The words tumbled out of my mouth in a less-than-eloquent manner.

"Sara." He paused. "I need to talk to you. Please, Emily. Just for a minute."

I wanted to close my eyes and wish him away. *What could he possibly want?* The last time we talked was during our breakup last year after my graduation. We had dated our senior and my fifth year, but his attachments were always much deeper than mine. He asked me to move in with him when I graduated, but I couldn't. I didn't love him.

I sighed. "Sure, come on in." I pushed the door open, seeing no way out of this. Parker stepped inside, glancing around the room and then back to me.

"So..." he started. "Who's he?" His voice was thick with jealousy, and he clearly noticed my wet hair matching Brooks' wet, half-naked body when he had answered the door.

"Er..." I rocked back, glancing down at my feet. "That...is Brooks," I mumbled in a half-breathless tone, trying to ease the words out. I could sense Brooks behind me. It was a new thing that my body seemed to sense him before I could see him.

Brooks stepped off the last step, and Parker and I turned to face him. *Good, he's dressed and here.* I didn't want to be in this situation; it was too bad the ground refused to open up and swallow me whole. Brooks had already dealt with Grey, and now here was Parker.

Was there some old karma coming back for its vengeance? Boys didn't usually flock around me and claim their love, but now that Brooks had returned, I couldn't help but feel like I needed to search my brain for any other guy I had ever talked to who might come strolling down the driveway to profess their love.

"Brooks Devonshire." Brooks' eyes were strong and determined, reaching his hand out to shake Parker's while his left hand slipped across my lower back, pulling me in front of him. *Subtle.*

I fought back a smile, remembering his comments about not being jealous. Still, I rewarded him with my behind softly sliding across his groin. His fingers dipped into my hips further.

"Parker, Emily's ex." Brooks' hand possessively gripped me tighter while his body tensed. *Damn it.*

I glanced back and forth between Brooks and Parker, trying to read their expressions. Neither of them budged on confidence. *Okay then.*

I wouldn't have known Brooks was upset if it wasn't for the slight set of his jaw.

"Yeah, so, er, Parker and I dated for a short time in college," I expressed in an overly smooth tone.

"Two years, Emily," Parker spat. He turned to look at Brooks. "I was there to pick up the pieces after you broke her." I couldn't help but wince.

"Parker," I scolded. Brooks paused momentarily, his hand clenching the back of my shirt ever so slightly that I almost missed it.

"It's okay, Em. Well, I guess I should thank you." Brooks smiled politely. "I'm sure Emily needed you, and I'm glad she had someone to care for her." A smile pulled at the corners of my mouth.

That was the thing about being fully and honestly in love with someone; you just always wanted what was best for them, even if it hurt you in the process. A slight twinge of more healing beat in my heart.

I turned back to Parker, finding my voice. "So, er, what do you want, Parker?" I asked, gesturing him into the living room. I gripped Brooks' hand tightly as we made our way to the sofa behind Parker.

I looked up at Brooks and mouthed, "I'm sorry." I couldn't believe this was happening. Brooks nodded and kissed the top of my head.

Parker sat at the opposite end of the oversized couch from us while I sat down next to Brooks, leaving no room between us, not even for a paperclip.

"Well," Parker started. "I didn't plan on this going this way," he said, gesturing to Brooks. "I came to tell you I am still in love with you and I want you back. You didn't give me a chance to change your mind. I was willing to wait, to take things slower, I just want you back in my life, Emily." He didn't even seem phased by the fact he just admitted that in front of Brooks. Instead, his voice was even and certain, as his eyes drilled into mine.

Right. Typical. He still doesn't understand and clearly never did.

"Parker, I have told you several times I was still in love with Brooks and still am." My voice was pleading. "I don't understand how I can say the same thing repeatedly, and you don't get it. I would have never stopped loving him. I don't feel the same way you do."

Brooks sighed at my side before standing up and turning to face me. "I think I'll leave you two to talk. I'll be in the study." His hands slowly slid away from mine as he walked away and out of the room, leaving Parker and me in this tragic turmoil.

"When did you two get back together?" Parker asked quietly, looking down at the rug.

"About two months ago," I responded. The swing of emotions this past hour left me feeling like I should crawl into bed and not wake up for a week. I ran my sweaty palms back and forth across the linen fabric of the sofa.

"Huh, never saw that coming." My eyes shot up, and I stared at him. He lifted his eyes just in time to meet mine.

"Never saw what? Parker, we haven't talked in almost a year. Did you think I was just going to sit around regretting my decision? I told you I didn't feel the same way. I am sorry I hurt you, but I could never love you like I do him. It wouldn't be fair to either of us." This was ridiculous. He was insane. Parker and I's relationship had always been more of a close friendship than anything.

"Emily, he left you. He didn't choose you. How can you accept him back so easily, but scoff when I show up at your door?" he asked, clearly frustrated while his fingers tapped a steady rhythm on his knee. "He was gone. He broke you. Don't you remember? Because I do. I remember listening to you cry night after night and watching you disappear inside of yourself. I remember you basically becoming invisible. It took months for me to convince you to just live. I was there. I made you happy, I know I did."

He was right, but it could never replace the feelings I had for Brooks.

"It was a mutual decision to break up. And yes, I remember all of it. I lived it Parker," I argued back.

Parker and I sat silently, trying to see who would break the tension first. My blue eyes were probably burning with the hottest shades of fury. *How dare he bring that up!* After another minute of our staredown, my vision cleared, and I could see the hurt buried beneath those beautiful eyes that once held so much love and patience for me.

"Parker, I love him. Nothing can change that. I have always loved him, and I always will. Why can't you understand that? This isn't some childish crush, sixteen years of life together doesn't just disappear overnight." My voice broke, giving way to the tears that brimmed.

"That's just what you tell yourself, Emily. He wouldn't have left you like that if he loved you. I was there to pick you up, not him." Parker's voice slowed as he started to accept the situation.

"I'm just going to go," he said, standing up to head for the door. I felt gutted. I hated hurting him again and now this was the second time I was watching him leave after breaking his heart.

"Okay," I replied, following him to the door.

Parker reached out, opening the door in front of him.

"I'm sorry, Parker. I truly hope you find someone who can love you back. Someone worthy of all of that love." Parker turned, his face only inches from mine. He paused, searching my eyes before moving down to my lips. I breathed in slowly, stepping back and putting a few more inches between us. I knew that he was about two seconds from making a huge mistake. I shook my head softly. I didn't want Parker to hurt anymore.

"Yeah," he said, putting his earbuds back in his ears. "I hope he's worth it." He turned his back to me, walking down the driveway to his black Volvo sitting just beyond the garage.

Goodbye, Parker. I lingered at the door a moment before closing it softly.

Brooks' hands slid up my shoulders, his chin resting against my temple.

"I'm sorry, Em," he whispered. I turned to face him feeling the blow of all that just transpired.

"You're sorry?" What did he have to be sorry about? "I should have told you about him." I gripped his shirt and buried my face into his chest.

"Emily, stop. No. You didn't need to. You were free to do as you pleased. I am glad he was there for you." His voice was soft and tender.

I inhaled the scent of his cologne and the rosemary soap from the shower. Another tear escaped, and I swiftly wiped it away. Those memories were painful and dark. After Brooks and I broke up, I struggled. I didn't want to live anymore. With our parents gone and then him, I had nothing left.

October was the month when I knew. Deep down I knew. I could feel Brooks pulling further and further away from me. Or maybe I was the one pulling away. Either way, just two days before Halloween while everyone was partying, dressed in the craziest costumes they could get away with, I was locked up in my dorm waiting for Brooks to call. He was training at joint base Lackland in San Antonio to become Special Ops. It had been almost two weeks since we talked and I was nervous about our call. My stomach was in knots the whole week. When he did finally call later that night, he was drunk. Something in me snapped. I had been sitting in my dorm waiting for him to call and he had been out drinking with his buddies.

I knew right then that we were in two different worlds. I sank to the floor when I heard his voice. Full of regret and possibly feeling the same thing as me.

The last conversation we had was still so clear in my head.

"I'm sorry, Emily."

"This isn't working," I whispered back, tears streaming constantly down my cheeks.

"I know. I love you."

"I love you too, B, always."

We were both silent, too scared of what came next. After what felt like an hour, he sighed heavily into the phone.

"I will always love you. Please don't forget that."

I nodded and broke into a sob. "Me too."

"See you, Em."

I didn't respond. I just stared at my screen, my thumb hovering over the red end call button. This was it—the end of us. Slowly, my finger tapped the button, and every part of me shattered. All the oxygen was gone and wouldn't return. My heart would never beat the same.

November rolled around and while everyone was preparing for Thanksgiving, winter finals, and the upcoming holiday break, I was barely living. I had no one to return home to, nothing to look forward to. I was numb and lost in the raging ocean of depression. Sara had been worrying about me for weeks, I had spent every free moment in bed crying or drowning out the noise with Netflix. She had called Parker, he had become a close friend of ours from our English Lit class, and he had spent his whole winter break locked up in our dorm room with me, watching TV, sitting in silence, reading, making sure I ate, whatever it took to keep me alive.

The worst part about all of it was that I couldn't even drop out of school. There was nothing to return to and nowhere to go. Parker sat with me in the dark when I needed him to and pulled me back into the light. He found a way to make me smile and laugh. I began leaving the dorms for small social gatherings, and one day, I looked up, and a whole year had passed. He had stayed by my side through all of it.

It was at the end of our junior year, Sara and I were moving into a house down the street from campus. Parker was helping us unpack when he kissed me. I didn't stop him, I had been glad to actually feel something, to know he cared about me and loved me, even though I was broken.

That summer, Parker and I visited his family in Tennessee. We stayed out late, kissed under the fireworks on the Fourth, and genuinely got to know each other. When we returned home for school, Parker and I had become an official item and I felt the fog lifting from my life. Parker saved me.

In my fifth year, it became clear that my feelings were not as deep as his. I tried, I really did, I wanted to love him. It became a huge void in our relationship. After my graduation, Parker had asked me to move in, hoping it would fix us, but I couldn't. In a moment of clarity, I knew that it was over for us and this was as far as I could ever go with him. I was still tethered to Brooks and unavailable for anything more.

Brooks held me, not saying anything; I think we both felt the wreckage that had been left in Parker's wake. I pulled back to look him in the eyes knowing he had heard everything. To think our breakup had not affected him was naive.

We hadn't really had a chance to talk about what that period of time looked like for us, I think we were both avoiding it in some ways. The breakup was a mutual decision and there wasn't one responsible party, but I think we both felt it was best to leave the past in the past, or at least that was the goal until Parker dropped in.

"I'm sorry," I muttered. How could I explain how I felt, how this was the opposite of what I wanted? Brooks brushed his thumb down my jaw softly.

"C'mon, let's get something to eat."

"I'm not that hungry, B." I stepped back, laying against the cool door.

"Well, I need to eat and I think you should too. This afternoon was a lot and you need to eat something." He was reaching for the hem of my skirt with a smile.

I shook the tingles off as the memory played through my mind. A small smile formed across my mouth.

"Yeah, that's what I thought." Brooks laughed, kissing my forehead. "C'mon."

He took my hand, leading me to the kitchen. It was like the dark cloud was lifting and Brooks and I were safe, together, and home. I sat down at the island watching Brooks search the fridge for food.

"How about tacos?" I asked. I wasn't in the mood for cooking and I was pretty positive he wasn't either.

"Sounds great," he said, looking back at me as the fridge doors closed.

I sighed. "Well, that wasn't the homecoming I had planned," I huffed as we walked down the hall to the garage.

"I mean, that shower was pretty great." His lips curled into a megawatt smile. I followed him to the car knowing we needed to finally talk and finish healing ourselves.

Chapter Nineteen

The breeze was soft on the pier tonight, blowing just strong enough to keep the air from feeling stagnant. Brooks interlaced our fingers as we walked in silence toward the taco shop. It was a quiet night; the only sounds were that of our shoes on the boards, distant conversation from the family further ahead than us, and the soft roar of the ocean.

I contemplated life at Caston. I could do a lot of good if I was willing to try. That would mean leaving Hope and focusing all my efforts on our company, I was sure they would all be delighted to have me there.

When our dads were running the business, our moms played supportive roles at the company wherever they could, and that also meant supporting what our dads were doing and their vision. It was a beautiful example to Brooks and me of how we could work together and bring strength to Caston, especially since it had been missing since our parents passed.

The board was supportive of my decision not to step into an official role after graduation, but I knew they were all a little disappointed. Growing up, the employees were like a second family to us. But could I really leave Hope, and if so, when would be the right time? I felt bad. The gala was just over a week away, so would it be wrong to give my notice now?

The man behind the counter, Lane, was an old surfer who settled down here years ago and decided to open a taco stand. He made it his personal goal to know everyone's name, or at least learn it if they were citizens of our little town.

"Welcome back, Emily. It's nice to see you again." He smiled, leaning over the bright blue counter. The paper fish garland swayed just above his head. His long, sandy brown hair was pulled back into a small bun. He had natural beach waves, which made all the women jealous.

"Hey, Lane, this is my boyfriend, Brooks. He just moved here," I said, leaning over into Brooks' bicep. After introductions were made, we placed our order and wandered to the railing to wait.

"Let's go to Portland tomorrow," Brooks started, looking over at me as we leaned over the wooden railing of the pier, watching the white cap of the waves over the dark ocean.

"Yeah, sure, what for?" The wood was splintering from the constant weather and salty air, digging into my skin.

"Car shopping," his voice lifted. "The BMW dealership has the car I want, just arrived Sunday on the truck."

"What car?" I responded, pulling away from the ledge and rubbing my hand across the indents the grains of wood had left.

"The IX M60."

We took our tacos to the sand below, eating silently before I asked Brooks if he thought Michaelson might be interested in Natalie. Brooks said he wasn't ready to settle down, but we would see. I wanted my friend to find someone.

"Em, I don't mean this to come off as rude, but are there any other admirers or past lovers I should expect to show up at our door?" *Ouch.*

"No," I muttered, feeling ashamed. "B, I really am sorry."

He looked at me and smiled softly before returning his eyes to the waves ahead.

"The night we broke up, well, morning, I lost it. If I'm being honest, I didn't want to break up, but I knew you did and didn't want to make it harder on you. I could feel you drifting away from me in ways I didn't expect in the weeks leading up to it. I called Connor. I didn't know who else to call. I mean, Michaelson had only known us apart. Connor flew to Texas, where I was just finishing up training." He paused.

Warm tears were already racing down my cheeks silently. *Why did he not tell me? Why did he not fight for me?* My nails made crescents in my palm while I fought for control over my emotions.

"I was broken, Emily, for a long time. I put everything into work and partied hard, just to try to drown out the pain." He looked over at me. "I just want you to know, and believe me, when I say there was and is no one else for me. It was always you, and will always be you."

I nodded. "I'm sorry I broke up with you," I whispered between tears.

"Hey baby, don't cry. I just needed to tell you that because I heard what Parker said today." His thumb wiped a tear away. My silent tears became more of a sob as I wrapped my arms around him, burying my face into his neck. The tears were, in a way, healing that fractured, dark part of my soul that I kept hidden, even from myself. As the tears began to dry up, I felt like it was my turn.

"I didn't want to break up either." My voice trembled. "I just couldn't breathe with you gone, and I was scared. I was scared you would move on, you would cheat on me, and you would begin to live your life without me. I was angry with you, so angry, for enlisting. I felt like you had ripped away everything." I moved so that I was now sitting between his thighs, facing him.

"It was hard being on campus with all the couples. I felt like everywhere I went, there they were. I would talk about you, and everyone would give me this look. I could never tell if it was pity that you were gone, or a disbelief that you were even real.

"Whenever I would go out, I felt alone even though I was surrounded by people. I could never embrace the fun, or the friends, or the circumstance, because I wanted you there with me, to experience it with me. I was becoming more depressed by the day, and Sara and Parker kept dragging me to more parties, thinking it would help, but it was just making it so much worse." I paused to look up at him. "I'm sorry."

He mirrored the same shattered feeling I had, and I knew. There was nothing we could do to change the past but we could accept it, and move forward together. He turned me, pulling me back into his chest. His breathing staggered like he was fighting back tears. We sat in silence, letting the sound of the waves and the humid, salty air wash over us like a balm for our broken and battered souls.

The roar of the ocean, the light breeze, and the dark of the night made Brooks' heavy arm around me feel secure. No matter what happened to get us to this point, I know for a fact, I would do it all again if I meant I got to sit here with him. The only thing left that was digging at me was the fight with Connor.

"B?" My voice was barely audible above the soft roar. I kept my eyes on the foaming water.

"Yeah, baby?"

"Tell me what happened with Connor. Please?"

I could feel his whole body tense under me. He inhaled deeply and then began dragging his thumb up and down my spine. *That bad?*

I looked up at him. His eyes were pained, and his eyebrows pulled together in a v shape. "What's wrong, Brooks?"

Brooks released me, and draped his hands over his knees, keeping focus on the ocean.

"Brooks, now you are scaring me. What happened?"

"Emily, I just haven't told you everything about after our breakup, and it has been eating me alive. I just don't want to lose you." I was fighting back waves of panic and nausea.

"Hey, nothing you say will change how I feel about you." There was nothing, *right?*

"I don't think that's true," he said. "I was angry after we broke up. I was angry about our parents, you, and almost everything in life. When I wasn't working, I was drinking and partying a lot, trying to drown out everything." He paused, staring down at his feet.

Yes, and? I could tell he was in mental anguish. I moved, wrapping my arms around him. *Nothing will change the way I feel.*

"Emily, I am so sorry. I...I was sleeping around, I was always getting drunk. I wasn't recognizable." He dropped his head into his hands. "I didn't think I would ever get you back." His voice was almost a whisper now.

"Hey," I whispered, hugging him tighter. "Hey, Brooks, it's okay. I understand. Why are you beating yourself up over this?" Brooks turned to hug me.

"Connor came to visit. I was such a mess. I was drunk and had girls all over me while he sat in the corner. After a while, he got up and confronted me. He reminded me I would never get you back by acting like that. We got into a huge argument. Said some things we both regret. We threw some punches." I gasped audibly, causing him to pause and look at me. Brooks and Connor had never fought physically. Sure, they both got upset and needed to calm down, but throwing punches? I placed my hand back on him, encouraging him to continue.

"I don't know. He was right. I didn't deserve you. There are a lot of apologies I need to give out. Starting with him. I hated myself so much."

"Unconditional love means unconditional, B. This doesn't change anything," I assured him. I laid my head on his shoulder while we sat there in each other's embrace for a minute.

"Please, say something," he whispered.

"Brooks, I love you. I never stopped loving you. When you came back and we decided to stay together, I knew you had a life without me. Whatever that looked like, I didn't care. Okay, well, maybe for a few minutes, I cared." A small smile tugged at his lips.

"I don't care what you did or who you did it with. I love you. I want you. Nothing will ever change that. Now, I hope you can work it out with Connor. You guys are better together. He was your best friend." The knot in my chest didn't lessen though. I just sat there with a thousand questions looming that I was too scared to ask.

He exhaled a sigh of relief, and we continued our gaze out into the dark ocean.

↟ ↟ ↟

Brooks stepped into the bedroom carrying his suitcase down from yesterday. I pulled the blankets up around me. I was too comfy to think about getting out of bed this early.

"You're up early," I groaned.

"Yeah, sorry, love. I thought I would get a jump start on some contracts. I also...never mind. I will tell you later." He sat on the edge of the bed, leaning in closer to kiss me.

"I slept so deep last night," I sighed. "I didn't sleep well when you were away."

"Same. I'm sorry, but I need to review these contracts before we leave. See you in a bit." He planted a kiss on my forehead, taking his warmth with him.

"Okay." I yawned before closing my eyes again. I sighed and rolled over, burying myself deeper into the warmth and comfiness of the pillows and blankets.

The sun was high in the sky by the time I woke again. I reached for my phone. *Five texts?*

Sara: Hey Emily, I'm so sorry about Parker!

Sara: I had no idea he would just show up.

Sara: I thought he was mailing you something.

Sara: Please call me.

Sara: Are you mad?

Ha. No, not at you. I needed to get up and move and should probably let her off the hook. I dressed quickly and ran up to the study. Brooks was pacing in the study on the phone with someone and was upset. His hair was already a mess from his hands, and his shoulders were hunched. His soft, deep blue eyes were sharp and cold sending a chill down my spine.

"Running to Lulu's, I will be back," I whispered.

Brooks nodded and then pulled the phone down.

"Grab me a large dark roast, please." He sighed, some of the tension leaving his shoulders. I nodded and began backing out of the door, before thinking better of it. I crossed the room in under five strides and snuggled into his side. His arm wrapped around me, and I felt a fraction of his stress leaving his body.

"Not good enough. Figure it out. We have three days to lock this down," Brooks barked into the phone. I flinched a little, but Brooks only squeezed me tighter. Just as I was about to go, he kissed me on the top of my head. Even if he was in bossy CEO mode, that one gesture had me melting into his side. I snuggled back into his side for another second before reaching up on my toes to kiss his cheek. That earned me a smile.

With that, I left his side and closed the door. *Yikes.* Seeing him angry again brought back our fight about Connor.

I backed out of the garage and clicked on Sara's number. The phone trilled loudly over the speakers.

"Hey, Sara."

Chapter Twenty

"Ready to go?" Brooks' head popped out through the glass door. I was out on the deck, enjoying the sun.

"Yes. Let me just send this text." I finished the last sentence and hit send. *Perfect.*

The phone call with Sara this morning lasted the length of my drive. When she told me she still talked to Parker, a flash of betrayal reared its ugly head, but then I remembered she was friends with him, too. She profusely apologized, and when I told her about Brooks' response, she told me we had to get coffee.

Sara liked Brooks as much as she did a screaming toddler, which was to say, not at all. It didn't matter how much I told her about our relationship and what he was really like; she had made up her mind. Now, she was being forced to reconsider, and that would take a very long coffee date and maybe some shopping to smooth it all out.

We were all set to meet in Tillamook next week. We had stumbled across a coffee shop when we were touring a creamery, and she fell in love with their Miami Whammy, a mocha with coconut and almond. Now that I lived two hours from Vancouver, we met there as a halfway point.

I grabbed my phone and laptop and returned to the living room, where Brooks was waiting for me. *Oh, boy.* My heart fluttered as I set my computer on the coffee table, unable to remove my eyes from him. My teeth pinched my inner lip as I surveyed my very handsome boyfriend.

Brooks wasn't one for dressing casually unless he was doing something active. His outfit of choice most days included a button-up and chinos. Not today, though. He had traded out his everyday outfit for a pair of faded, ripped skinny jeans, cognac boots, and a black button-up that was form-fitting enough that his build was visible. I swallowed noisier than usual.

"Wow," I purred, raising my brows at him.

"What?" he looked down at his clothes.

"Mr. Devonshire." I bit my lip and raked my eyes up and down, shaking my head as I walked across the room toward him. "My, my, you take my breath away."

Brooks chuckled. "In skinny jeans?"

I shrugged. *Yes.*

His eyes rolled as he reached for the garage door. I could feel a small dose of heat running through me.

"Let's go before I get more distracted."

We arrived in Portland in good time. The drive had given us time to talk about Connor. Brooks had been meaning to reach out to him to apologize for their fight, which I still didn't fully understand. This was so unlike either of them that it made me want to cry, to help fix them. For now, I would just let them both simmer out.

"Are you sure you want a BMW?" I teased as we pulled into the dealership.

"Yeah. You'll see," he chuckled confidently.

We weren't at the dealership for more than ten minutes before Brooks was behind the wheel of a charcoal-colored SUV. He was beaming ear to ear as the salesman worked through all the specs. I had to admit that it was a nice car, and I loved the luxury touches and trim line that BMW offered. I could see the sparkle in Brooks' eyes and knew he was buying the car.

"Race you home?" He winked as we walked out of the building. I was still processing how amazing he was at handling the negotiations. It was exciting to see him operate like that. His car was being pulled around to the front, the stickers and papers had all been removed.

I laughed, knowing he would win. Still, I wanted to join in on the fun.

"Sure." I grazed my lip, looking up at him through my lashes. "What do I get if I win?"

Brooks pushed his body into mine, pinning me against my car. *Okay*.

His lips brushed my ear. "A couple of orgasms and a bubble bath." My laugh came out filled with lust. He was speaking to my body, which piqued my interest immediately.

With a dry mouth, I asked, "And if you win?"

He looked mischievous before gracefully leaning in again, letting his tongue caress my ear.

"Same." His whisper was hot in my ear. The delicious clench of muscles low in my stomach stood at attention. My body sang, and with a small moan, I replied, "Yes, please," like I was answering a question. He inhaled deeply as he pulled away from me and turned to get into his car. If he wanted me to drive quickly, he sure knew how to get what he wanted.

"See you at home." He smiled back with a wolfish grin.

↟ ↟ ↟

Once outside Portland city limits, Brooks gunned it, pulling ahead of me. I giggled, pushing the pedal down. I glanced in my rear-view mirror to check for cops. My heart raced as we weaved back and forth through the light traffic. If it had been any heavier, there would be no way I could do this, I was too much of a chicken.

We pulled into the driveway in record time. Brooks had, of

course, beat me back to the city limits and slowed down until I caught him. He pulled in on the opposite side of the garage ahead of me, and I couldn't help but smile when I saw his car there.

"Fast, huh?" He grinned.

I rolled my eyes. "Yes, you're crazy." Adrenaline was still pulsing through my body, and the two-hour drive had not settled the deep-seated desire.

Brooks wrapped his arms around me, pulling me in for an aggressive kiss. I moaned, feeling the weight of his warm body against mine. My perky nipples pressed into his chest. I could feel his heart racing as I leaned back onto my car so that I was pinned between the two. The adrenaline brought a fresh rush of desire that seemed to consume me quicker than usual like a light being flipped on; it was instant. Brooks' hand slipped up my white cotton sundress to my panties.

"You are soaked, Emily. Should we take care of that?"

Soaked? Only Brooks could make the word soaked sound sexy. I would have laughed if I wasn't so turned on.

I nodded, feeling a little breathless, shifting my hips up to grind against his growing erection.

He chuckled, picking me up and carrying me inside. His lips were firm against mine as his hands gripped my butt with intensity. He sat me on the edge of the island and pulled my hips to the edge, settling in between my knees.

"Lean back, baby." His voice was thick with arousal, and I could have come right then and there.

I was already trembling with the expectancy of the multiple orgasms he had promised me. Just seeing him between my legs, his broad shoulders holding them open, made the constant pulsing between my legs grow stronger with each passing second.

I took a sharp inhale as his lips grazed my inner thigh, working their way up in a slow assault. I dropped my head back and stabilized myself on my elbows. My body was already responding with familiarity with what was to come. *Me.*

Oh.
My.

↟ ↟ ↟

It had been a while since I had seen Brooks. I shut off the TV and looked around. *Where is he?* I ran upstairs, thinking he had to be in the study. He was out on the deck, pacing as he talked on the phone with someone. This time, he was smiling. *That's good.* I slid open the glass, his eyes met with mine.

"Yeah, sounds great. Thank you." He hung up the phone. He stepped forward, grabbed my face between his palms, and kissed me deeply.

"We are going somewhere for the weekend. We leave tomorrow once you get off work," he said against my lips.

I pulled back. "Where are we going?"

"You'll see." His nose brushed against mine. Excitement filled every corner of my body. Going away with Brooks for a weekend would mean I would get his undivided attention.

Chapter Twenty-One

I sat at my desk, tapping my fingers on the frosted glass while my leg bounced up and down nervously. Brooks planned to pick me up for our "surprise trip" in fifteen minutes. I sensed his nervousness this morning, but I couldn't determine if it was due to the trip or the call he was on with Michaelson. Something was happening at Caston, but he hadn't shared any details yet.

The gala was all set for next weekend, our sponsors were happy with the promotions, Harper's interview was set, and all the vendors were ready. The event was going to be featured in the Seattle Times. I felt pleased that I could go out with a bang. Now, I just needed to actually talk to Brooks about my decision before I put in my notice. I had decided this was the right switch, and I was ready to explore the new work I would bring to Caston.

Sure, maybe I had had a sudden change of heart, but something in me felt settled the moment I decided to go ahead with it. This job was temporary, and my future always belonged to Caston, even if I had been too stubborn to see it.

I rechecked my phone. I was expecting to see something from

Natalie since she had been packing for the mystery trip at my house today.

The last *surprise* trip was weeks ago when Brooks took me on our official first date in Seattle. I was busy thinking about how his body was pressed into mine while we swayed to the music. His hand softly rested on my lower back, and the way he held me made me feel like the whole world could have burned down, and I would have been okay. A knock on the glass door pulled me from my reverie.

"Emily?" My boss, with his heavy build, was crowding the doorway. His wrinkles were deep, and his glasses bowed out around the roundness of his cheery face.

"Hi, Mr. Whitney." Dread filled my stomach. I needed to be able to walk out of here in a few minutes, and I could only hope I wasn't about to be pulled into a last-minute meeting.

"I just wanted to tell you I hope you have a wonderful trip. I will see you next Tuesday."

Tuesday? How did he know about this weekend?

"Wait, Tuesday?"

"Yes, Brooks called, saying you needed Monday off." Of course, he did. I was beginning to sweat with anticipation—that feeling of anxious excitement that leaves you feeling cold and sweaty.

My phone buzzed on the glass.

B<3: Here, gorgeous. See you outside.

Outside, Brooks was leaning against his new car, tantalizing and confident. My heart somersaulted at his mere presence. He was comforting, gorgeous, and all mine.

"Good afternoon, my love. Are you ready?" His arm swung around my shoulder, pulling me in for a quick kiss.

"Yes." I blushed as he opened the passenger door for me.

He was quiet in the car but kept glancing over. His fingers interlaced with mine, and he brought my fingers up to his lips and kissed them softly.

We headed south out of town, and I remembered Ryan had driven this way to the regional airport.

"Are we flying?" I asked excitedly.

Brooks just smiled with his eyebrows raised, keeping his eyes on the road. I laughed.

"Okay, so secretive," I teased.

We pulled out onto the tarmac, where the jet awaited us. Tate, Brooks' pilot, was waiting next to the stairs. Brooks pulled into a private parking spot near the plane.

"Ready?" He looked over at me with delight in his eyes, releasing the clip on his seatbelt. I shook my head in disbelief. *How? Where?* So many questions. I stepped out of his car into the warm air while Brooks opened the back where our bags were stored. Two weekender bags and his work satchel.

After loading, I fastened my lap belt and settled in, considering all the possible destinations. It would have to be within the US since I didn't have my passport. Well, if Brooks wasn't going to tell me where we were going, I would find out soon enough when Tate announced it over the speaker. Brooks grabbed a glass of champagne from the stewardess.

"Emily, this is Deborah, our new stewardess. She will be assisting on some of the longer flights."

"Nice to meet you, Deborah," I said, taking the glass from her. Deborah was middle-aged, and her brown hair showed hints of gray in her slicked-back chignon. She reminded me of our chef, Ms. Allen, who we had growing up. I looked over to Brooks, who had a self-satisfied smile.

As expected, Tate announced our departure for the Sonoma County Regional Airport minutes after the cabin door closed.

"Really? Sonoma?" I asked gleefully. He nodded.

"Of course, I wanted a weekend away with you."

The flight was only an hour and a half, and we touched down just before six. A car was waiting for us as the cabin doors opened. The crew helped unload our luggage and wished us a fantastic weekend. It was silly, but somehow, being here made me feel like an adult, taking an adult vacation. Brooks and I climbed into the back of the Mercedes van.

"Hotel, please," Brooks told the driver. He settled into the captain's chair beside me. The interior of the van was much fancier than I was expecting. The white leather captain's chairs faced each other. A TV hung just above the seats across from us. Dark blinds over the windows and the lighting above us were dim, creating a moody atmosphere. *Who knew a Sprinter could be so sexy?*

"Yes, sir." The driver was an older gentleman with gray hair. His tone of voice and manner told me he had been in the business a long time. The door closed beside Brooks.

"So," Brooks took my hand, kissing it. "We can change and then go down to dinner. There's an amazing restaurant in the hotel."

"Okay." I could feel the ridiculous smile on my face. I honestly didn't care what we did or where we went; I was just overjoyed to be here with him. Brooks grabbed a remote, and the blinds lifted so that we could enjoy the scenery.

↟ ↟ ↟

The car turned into what appeared to be a private drive, winding through lush rows of grapevines. At the end of the road stood a modern building crafted of rock and glass. The circular pull-in showcased two elegant fountains that glimmered in the evening light.

"Wow," I breathed in awe as the driver stopped in front of what looked like the lobby and stepped out to open the door for us.

I let my gaze fall to the vineyard, captivated by the spectacular view. The setting sun dipped lower in the sky, bathing the landscape in a warm golden hue that spilled over the hills. Brooks intertwined his fingers with mine and an undeniable send of romance enveloped us alongside the sweet scent of grapes.

After checking into our rooms, we received a map that would

guide us to The Guesthouse, which was nestled among towering oak trees and overlooked the valley and vineyard.

I felt a surge of excitement as I ran toward the double wooden doors. Brooks opened the large door, revealing an outdoor courtyard with a breathtaking view of Mount St. Helena and the Alexander Valley that stretched out before us. I paused for a moment, trying to absorb it all, and then felt Brooks wrap his arm around me from behind as I leaned against him.

"Like it?" His lips grazed my ear, making me grin. Whoever said romance was dead lied because this place was possibly the most magical, most romantic place I'd ever been. The valley was filled with golden rays, a subtle breeze brushed along the leaves, and the air was fragrant with soil and something sweet and aromatic.

"This is amazing. Thank you." Three small water features bubbled quietly to our right. After standing there for too long, Brooks showed me around, weaving in and out of the three bedrooms, asking which one I wanted.

Though the other two were absolutely stunning, I chose the one with the largest tub. Each room had floor-to-ceiling windows, soft furnishings against light wood, and private balconies.

After settling in, we planned to head to dinner before it was too late. I opened my bag, concerned with what Natalie had packed. I first pulled out a brand-new lingerie set with tags dangling from it. I chuckled and searched until I found a garment bag for a few dresses.

"Got everything you need?" Brooks rounded the corner from the bathroom. He wore his new Proper Cloth navy suit with a blue and white gingham button-up shirt under a matching navy coat and tie. My eyes bounced up and down, taking in the whole picture. My breath was stolen from my lungs until Brooks tucked his hands in his pants pockets and smirked.

I rolled my eyes as he chuckled, closing the distance between us with a look of hunger in his eyes.

"What did you tell Natalie to pack?" I asked, trying to remain focused.

"Clothing...and things." He shrugged. My bare breasts were front and center while I stood there in nothing but my black lace panties.

"Well, that's not cryptic," I teased, pulling my blue Sapphire dress up while Brooks groaned dramatically. He helped with the back buttons and held my hand while I slid into my heels.

"You look gorgeous," Brooks whispered into my ear as his hand plunged down the low back of my dress, sending goosebumps up my spine. A sultry smile crossed my face as I looked at him in the mirror. The slow movement of his hand brushing across my lower back fogged my mind.

"So do you," I whispered back as his hand continued south, gasping as his fingers brushed between my thighs. He pulled his hand back with a large sigh.

"This dress should be illegal. I might have to tear it off of you later."

I chuckled. "Hey, I like this dress." He looked at me in the mirror and let his yearning eyes do the talking.

"Yeah, me too."

Chapter Twenty-Two

I swam across the hot tub and slid onto Brooks' lap.

"How is your evening so far, my love?" he asked, pulling me closer until our chests were pressed together.

"The best." I dragged my nose up his jawline, leaning in close. My lips brushed his softly as my arms draped over him, hugging him with tenderness.

After returning from dinner, I had expected Brooks to quite literally rip the dress off of me. Instead, he did something unexpected. He unbuttoned the neck and kissed my cheek before telling me to meet him in the hot tub. I groaned but happily obliged with unholy thoughts of what may follow.

We were both more than content to be in this serene valley, secluded with only each other for company. All the distractions of home and work were gone, and for the first time, I felt like we were just two kids again, with no care in the world and entirely in love. We held each other in blissful silence, listening to the sounds of nature enveloped in the warmth of the water.

Before going to bed, Brooks stripped my bottoms off and bent me over the side of the hot tub. He delivered two mind-blowing orgasms that left me completely exhausted and sated.

Memories of his mouth, hands, warm body, and water splashing around us gave me plenty to dream about. Thankfully, the guesthouse was far enough removed from the other suites that the canopy surrounding us swallowed my moans and screams.

↟ ↟ ↟

Morning light filtered through the soft linen curtains early. The clock read 5:54 and Brooks was still asleep next to me. He always looked so young when he slept, his inky lashes against his light skin and his hair a complete mess. He reminded me so much of the boy I grew up with.

I slipped out of the sheets quietly, hoping to not disturb him. I wrapped the white robe around my satin nightgown, another great choice from Natalie, and slipped outside onto the patio.

It was chilly out, but the bright sun promised to chase away the gray darkness in the valley while birds danced in the sky, singing their morning song. I laid my head back on the armchair.

"I miss you, Mama, I wish you were here. I wish you all were," I whispered. I thought back to my mom's smile, my dad's embrace, Carrie's encouraging and sweet voice, and James' hand tossing my hair playfully as he rubbed my head and felt a tug on my heart. They were the best parents anyone could ask for.

I inhaled the sweet morning dew, enjoying the still, quiet morning and the gratitude that consumed me.

Brooks slid open the glass door quietly with two mugs of steaming liquid in his hand. I had been sitting outside for a solid hour and was thoroughly chilled.

"Good morning, baby." He looked as if he was still half asleep.

"Morning. How did you sleep?"

"Great, wish it was more."

"Yeah, but it's so calming out here. Come sit."

Brooks' weight shifted me as he sat down on the sofa next to me. "Here, tea."

I grabbed the steaming mug from his hand and laid my head on his shoulder. *Time to tell him the good news.*

"B?"

"Yeah?"

"I might be out of work for a minute." My voice was soft, not hinting at anything.

"What?" he asked, sitting up and looking at me. I couldn't fight back my smile.

"I just mean, I am putting in my two weeks on Tuesday, and until Diane can find me an office-"

Brooks' lips slammed into mine. He grinned and kissed me again.

"Baby, I love you so much. Thank you." My heart leaped into my throat.

"Yeah, yeah. It's not just about you, though. I can't let you have all the fun," I teased.

"I don't care. I just want you with me all the time; I want you to be happy, though."

I rolled over, straddling him. "I am happy. More than happy."

His lips met mine with intensity again, almost spilling my tea.

I giggled. "Love you." My free hand reached up, cupping his cheek. His eyes softened as they lightened into a grayish blue, deepening their gaze into mine.

"I love you," He paused. "How about breakfast? I'll place an order."

↟ ↟ ↟

After breakfast, Brooks had me wear my summer dress and flats Natalie had packed. I was so anxious to find out where we were going, but I knew he had kept this part a secret. All I knew was that I would be in the spa later today, and all I needed was him by my side.

The drive out of the resort was just as beautiful as the day prior, reassuring me that I hadn't dreamt it. Brooks was fiddling with his buttons, and then rerolled his sleeves. He was unusually silent in the seat next to me. His breathing was shallow, and the way he bit into his cheek told me he was nervous. That, and the fact that his hand had brushed through his hair no less than five times already, leaving a ruffled but sexy mess in its wake.

I pursed my lips, considering all the reasons for his silence and anxiousness, but there were too many unknown variables. I huffed in resignation and returned my eyes to the passing vineyard. Brooks finally broke the silence as we left the town of Healdsburg.

"Just about twenty more minutes," he said calmly as I laced my fingers absentmindedly with his. I looked at him, studying and taking in his more relaxed state.

"It's pretty here," he started.

"Yeah, it really is. Such a cool culture, too."

Brooks chuckled. "Very different from Seattle."

"I like Seattle too, well, mostly. I just don't want to live there anymore. I will happily visit often, though."

"You know, if you are traveling with me for work, you will be there every few weeks."

I shook my head. "No work talk."

"Right, sorry. You look beautiful, by the way. I like that color on you."

I glanced down at the soft pink linen dress. I didn't own a lot of pink; my closet was mostly full of neutral pieces. It was a nice color, though. "Thank you. You seem tense. Are you okay?"

"Yep, sorry, just thinking about a lot. I will try to be more present."

"Stop saying sorry. You can just say you have a lot on your mind."

"Sor-" We both laughed. *He really needs to work on that.*

The car was winding through the countryside until we arrived at the Armstrong Redwoods State Natural Area. I stepped out into the forest, twirling under the canopy of bark and distant greenery.

"Wow, these are tall."

Brooks chuckled as I continued to twirl. "Em, you are going to make yourself dizzy."

"I'll be fine," I sang out playfully. "These are so cool. I can't believe we have lived so close our whole lives, and we've never been to the Redwoods. Or at least I haven't. Have you?"

"Nope, first time." He grabbed my hand.

We continued our walk deeper into the forest, observing the insanely tall trees. It seemed unlikely that a tree could continue to grow like that, especially since it started as a little seed. It was as if we had walked out of a fairytale into a mystical land of giants. The forest smelled aromatic and was buzzing with life.

"Mmm...I want to bottle this smell." I inhaled. "Thanks for bringing me here. This is fun, and I was definitely surprised. I was not expecting to see Redwoods in Sonoma."

Brooks chuckled and looked down at his feet. "Yeah, pretty cool."

"What?"

"Nothing." He shrugged with a sly smile.

I giggled. "I will figure it out, you know."

His grin widened, "I'm fully planning on it."

↟ ↟ ↟

We had spent almost an hour in the forest before returning to the car. I couldn't stop thinking about what Brooks could possibly be hiding. When we were in middle school, my parents decided to surprise me with a trip to Atlantis in the Bahamas. Brooks could hardly keep his mouth shut. He had been acting weird for weeks, and as we got closer, he became antsier and nervous. He was acting like that again.

The car wove through the valleys opposite from where we came. I glanced over at Brooks, who seemed to be clinging to the door and watching out the window. The car pulled off a little dirt road until we reached a clearing where a helicopter awaited.

"Oh my God." I laughed. "We get to ride in it?"

Brooks was beaming. "It's the best way to see Sonoma and Napa. C'mon." He took my hand as we slid out of the open door. Brooks held my hand as we navigated the small trail to where the helicopter was.

"Good morning, Mr. Devonshire. Let's get you guys in, and we can get going." The pilot slid the door open. Brooks lifted me into the helicopter, and I sat down in one of the bucket seats. Brooks climbed in behind me and helped me fasten the seatbelt with the headset. I felt so official. He sat down next to me and buckled.

"Can you hear me?" he asked, smiling over at me.

"Mm-hmm." I was too giddy to talk. He was full of surprises this weekend. The pilot climbed into the front and cleared us for take off.

Chapter Twenty-Three

I clung to Brooks' hand as we lifted higher into the sky. He chuckled quietly, gripping tighter and caressing my thumb with his.

"Don't worry, love." I wasn't worried, I just didn't like the butterflies in my stomach when they were associated with takeoff and the change of altitude. The once giant trees now seemed small beneath us as we floated through the valley. I relaxed, trying to soak it all in. Sonoma was beautiful, but from up here, there were no words.

The pilot floated in and out of different valleys and over vineyards, naming each one and a fun fact about the family or company that owned it or which wine they were best known for. He pointed at landmarks and towns. My favorite part was flying out over the coast and the view as we came back in again. The vast blue ocean met by rolling hills of green was absolutely stunning.

Brooks' voice came through the headset as the helicopter descended into the valley.

"See this vineyard right up here. This is Donum Estate. They have several sculptures throughout the property. It's really an amazing place. That's where we are landing." Brooks was beaming.

"How did you plan all this?" By lunchtime, I would need an ice pack for my cheeks.

He smirked back before we both glanced out the window to the estate below and the rows of grapevines with the occasional sculpture dotting the landscape. As we landed with a quiet thud, Brooks slid off my headset. The blades were slowing down already, but the sudden noise was startling.

The door slid open, and Brooks hopped out, then turned back to help me down. Two women greeted us with a glass of their summer white. It was chilled to perfection and awakened my taste buds in the best way.

"Welcome to Donum Estate," the tall brunette said. She was wearing a white, chic pantsuit that fit her amazing curves.

"Thank you," I said with a grin. My cheeks had never hurt more, but I couldn't figure out how to mold my face into any other emotion.

"We have lunch for you and our favorite wine and cheese pairings whenever you are ready. For now, feel free to enjoy the grounds, and we will see you there soon."

Brooks and I thanked them before heading down one of the trails in the waiting UTV.

"I am just lost for words," I said breathlessly. "Brooks, this is just amazing. I don't know what to say other than thank you."

"I'm glad you are enjoying it." He brought my hand to his mouth and softly kissed my knuckles making my heart swell.

The side-by-side was definitely a quick way to get around the vineyard. We came up on a giant mirrored heart sculpture that reminded me a lot of the Chicago bean. We parked the UTV and got out to admire the large sculpture closer.

Brooks and I paused, looking at our reflection. We both laughed at the distorted image. Brooks turned me and kissed me like the world was on fire, like this was his last kiss and I could feel him trembling. When he pulled away, he got down on one knee. I gasped. *Oh my god, he's proposing*. It all made sense now. *Yes. Yes.*

Brooks pulled a wooden box from his pants and lifted his

trembling hand to display the ring inside while his other hand took mine.

"Emily Claire Barlow, for almost twenty years, you have been my best friend, cheerleader, confidant, my whole heart and soul." His voice broke as hot tears streamed down my face.

"I have loved you from the first moment I saw you. You were dancing in the rain, spinning with your teddy bear, and I just knew I had to meet you." He chuckled. "I have experienced my highest highs and lowest lows with you, and through it all, you were my beacon, guiding me, grounding me. I have known life without you, and I never want that again. I want to spend every second of forever with you, choosing you each day. Loving you and putting your needs above my own. Will you please do me the honor of becoming my wife?"

My heart was pounding so loud in my ears as I nodded eagerly, my whole body warming at his declaration of love. Laying all worries of our past, present, and future to rest, I made the final step toward him.

"Yes, yes, yes. I want to spend forever with you," I rasped. I had apparently lost my voice.

Brooks launched from his kneeling position, lifting me up to swing me around. I laughed, feeling slightly delirious from all my joy and happiness.

"I love you. God, I love you," I squealed. He set me back on my feet and pulled the ring from the box. I hadn't really had a chance to look at it until now. It was breathtaking. The three-carat oval diamond sat perched above a dainty gold band. It was simple, elegant, and so very perfect. Brooks' shaky hands slid the ring on. *Perfect fit too.*

"It's so beautiful," I sniffled, twisting it back and forth on my finger. The sun caught it just right, scattering rainbows onto the ground and our clothes. I couldn't take my eyes off the ring with the realization that I would finally get to change my last name to his. I smiled softly before reaching over to cup his face into my palms.

"I love you so much. More than you will ever know," I whispered before kissing him.

It was surreal as we finally withdrew from our moment of joyful rapture and rejoined our surroundings. Everything around us seemed more full of life, brighter, and substantial. The view from our little haven next to the oversized mirrored heart sculpture was magnificent. The rolling hills of beige soil against the continuous rows of green grapevines were incredible.

I rested my head against Brooks' bicep and wrapped my arms around his. I exhaled, finally coming down from my extreme exultation and reached my left hand out in front of me again to look at the ring.

Brooks took my hand in his and kissed my head softly. I felt like melting into him. This proposal was better than anything I could have dreamed. Excitement and hope for our future filled every inch of me, chasing away any concern or doubt.

I had finally started to believe he was truly here to stay, and this had solidified every thought and worry that he would disappear again. My childhood self was dancing and screaming, my teenage self was crying, and my broken college-age self was healing.

For so long, all I have ever wanted was to be his. Sure, dating him I was in a way, but marrying him was the closest way to becoming one with him, and that's all I really wanted. For our souls to be one and never parted again.

"I will have to tell you the story about this ring, but for now, let's return. They're waiting for us."

↟ ↟ ↟

When we returned to the house, the staff were waiting for us with large, hopeful smiles. The white modern building was picturesque. A large palm tree sat along the concrete path leading up to the opened French doors. We were greeted with a fresh glass of wine and led to an open-air dining space. The wooden table was set with various cheeses, a tray for each of us, and four glasses of wine alongside a beautiful lavender bouquet. To the side sat plates of what appeared to be a steak salad.

I hadn't thought about food all day, and now I was hungrier than I realized. Our guide walked us through each of the pairings and the different wines, explaining how they were made. After he left us to our meal, we ate our salads while looking out at the serene lawn and towering fountains.

It was almost one by the time we walked back to the helicopter to take us back to the resort for our massages. The sun was high in the sky, scorching the earth beneath us. While I wanted to stay and see more of the estate, I was ready to escape the heat and return to the resort with my fiancé.

Brooks once again lifted me into the helicopter and helped with my headset. He was such a natural at this, and I wished for a moment I could have seen him in action when he was in the Air Force.

"Ready to go?" He smiled delightfully.

"Yes, and no. This place is amazing. Thank you, B."

"We can always come back."

"Maybe a future anniversary trip." I smiled. *We will have a lifetime of them.*

"Sounds great."

The chopper lifted into the air, and once again, we were soaring over the rolling hills of grapevines below. The ride lasted only a few minutes before we landed at the Healdsburg airport.

Chapter Twenty-Four

We returned to the guesthouse late afternoon after the most relaxing massage and facial. As we entered our room, the bed was covered in white and pink rose petals in the shape of a heart with an oversized white box in the center. A big tag read, **Congrats!!**

"What is this?" I giggled. Brooks leaned back against the wall, crossing his arms and feet at the ankles as he smiled in delight.

"Another gift?" I rolled my eyes teasingly. I slid open the box to find a tray of various desserts, all mini sample sizes. There were two cookies in the shape of rings, a strawberry cake of some kind, tiramisu, and several others.

"Now this, I didn't plan," he said, walking to me. "This was our friends. I only asked for this." He lifted a bottle of champagne from the ice bucket. "Well, and the roses."

"Really? Who sent this?"

"Michaelson or Natalie, I presume. They are the only two I told. The staff mentioned it to me earlier. It was a surprise for me as well."

I glanced back at the box of treats. How did we end up with such amazing friends and all of this?

"We can get into that tonight." He kissed my cheek before disappearing outside, pulling his buzzing phone from his pocket.

"Do you want to go for a swim?" I called out to Brooks, who was outside in the courtyard.

"Sure, can you give me like five?"

"Yeah." I pulled my bag from the closet and shuffled through it to find another swimsuit. The one from last night was still damp, hanging in the shower.

Sure enough, the garment bag had a new white swimsuit with a note pinned to it. I opened the small envelope that had clear instructions for it to be opened Saturday evening.

For the bride-to-be

I pulled on the swimsuit while my phone rang. I peeked out at Brooks, who was still on the phone with someone, and he seemed happy.

"Hey, Emily!"

"Natalie! You are amazing. Thank you so much for packing, for the new swimsuit, and, I presume, for the desserts."

"Of course. I love you! Have you tried the lingerie yet?" I chuckled and spent a few minutes cleaning up our room as I talked to her and told her all the details of the day. She kept cooing and awwing at every little detail. When I asked if we could meet for coffee, she chuckled.

"I'll check my schedule because your fiancé refused to show me the ring ahead of time. Now, get off the phone and go enjoy him."

"I like the sound of that." I felt like a teenager again, giddy with excitement. "To quote Jane Bennet, "Can you die of happiness?" because I feel overwhelmed with it."

"Well, I'm glad you are happy. I know this has been a long time coming. He is a great guy and genuinely loves you. I'll talk to you later. 'Kay?"

"Yeah, bye."

↟ ↟ ↟

"Wow, that suit is amazing on you," Brooks' voice exclaimed excitedly. "Mmm, you look so beautiful." His arms wrapped around me, and his touch was ticklish on my sides, causing me to close up in his arms. Brooks playfully nipped my neck as he slid off the one-shouldered silver sequined strap.

"Stop," I giggled breathlessly. "C'mon, get changed."

"I like this," he teased, sliding his fingers across the bare skin in the hip peephole. I twisted, pulling away from his lightning touch.

"Okay." He planted one more kiss on my shoulder before disappearing into the bathroom.

"Who were you on the phone with?" I asked, unpacking the rest of my bag into the closet.

"Michaelson," he said, kissing my cheek as he passed me to head back to the room.

"Really? Work? Also, did he have any part in the desserts?" I closed the drawers in the wooden cabinets.

"He did. Seems he and Natalie worked together. And no, not for work. He's traveling this weekend for personal reasons. He was bouncing ideas off me." Brooks rounded the corner.

"Oh, is he flying back to the UK?" I pulled out my pink leather and rope Jimmy Choo wedges, sliding them on as I plopped down on the bed.

"No. He's not on speaking terms with his parents right now." Brooks pulled a t-shirt over his head.

"Why? I thought he was close with them?"

"Yeah. I don't know the full story. He's pretty private, but he just disagreed with his sisters, and it sounds like his parents took sides."

"Huh." It was interesting that people could hold onto grudges with their parents. I would give anything to speak to mine again. I would love to argue and fight with them because it would mean they were around to fight with. I grabbed my sunglasses off the table and pulled the door open. *Some people just don't know what they have until it's gone.*

↟ ↟ ↟

When we arrived, the pool was crowded, but we were able to find a spot at the end of the row of loungers. I glanced around, noticing the grill just set beyond the chairs, Hudson Springs. The smell of burgers and fries wafted over to us, making my tummy rumble.

After applying sunscreen on each other playfully, we waded into the pool, where the water was temperate, perfect for a warm spring day like today. I floated over to Brooks, wrapping my body around his.

"Thank you for today, *fiancé*." I nuzzled his nose before planting a kiss on his warm lips. He smiled against my lips, breaking our kiss.

"I like the sound of that."

"How did you plan all of this? Everything is amazing. It's like a dream, honestly."

Brooks' eyes softened with his smile as he looked deeply into mine.

"I've been working on it for a bit, and I may have had some help from a certain friend of yours."

"Natalie?"

"Yeah. There was a lot to coordinate, and she was a huge help."

"She's pretty great. So, how long have you been planning this?"

Brooks chuckled. "February."

"February? We weren't even back together then."

"Yes, I am fully aware. I actually bought your ring while I was still in England." The thought that he had been wandering the streets back in February without knowing if I would accept him back and forgive him made my heart somersault. I already knew he missed me, but to think about him feeling the same loss and the need to be together again made me feel warm and wanted.

Even after years of separation, fate, or whatever you want to call it, brought us together again. We were made for each other. Our connection couldn't be severed. I was his, and he was mine.

I lifted my hand out of the water to admire my ring again. "I really love it."

"I found it in a small jewelry store run by an elderly man. It was storming outside, and I happened to pass by the shop. For some reason, I wanted to go in and check it out. I honestly had no thoughts of proposing to you until I was there. Each ring was custom-designed by him. I saw this one," he said, grabbing my hand to look at the ring himself, "and I knew. I knew at that moment I had to do whatever it took to win you back. I didn't know if you were already dating someone. Diane had told me she didn't think you were, but she didn't know for certain. I was willing to take the risk. I don't know how else to describe it other than I felt like the ring was meant for you like you were made for me."

I planted my lips on his again and slid my hand up his neck, threading my fingers through his hair. "Maybe," I breathed heavily into his mouth. "We just go back to the room now?" I needed him deep inside me. I needed to be closer to him than I already was, wrapped around him.

Brooks inhaled sharply. "We have been here for two minutes."

"Well, I have some other ideas for fun." My voice was husky and full of need as I ground my hips further into him. His eyes darkened, and his grip tightened on me.

"Well then, how can I say no?" We released and grabbed our towels and headed for the golf cart.

Chapter Twenty-Five

My back slammed against the outdoor shower wall. The intensity was exhilarating. Brooks' lips were pressed into my neck while his teeth softly grazed the skin. Desire coursed through my body like an untamed wildfire. Brooks' hands worked on freeing my swim top, which was more like a soaked sports bra clinging to my skin.

"I'll help," I panted, pulling the top over my head. His mouth moved to my breasts, biting down with intensity, sending my hips thrust forward off the wall.

"You are driving me wild, B." The water was warm as it continued to fall on us. Brooks took my breast into his mouth while his free hand massaged the other like I was his favorite plaything. His hips had me pinned to the wall with his swollen head waiting just out of reach.

I moaned again, louder than the first time, as I twisted under his mouth. He finally released my breast, tugging my bottoms to the side, unable to wait another second. I needed him to fill me just as much as he needed to be in me.

I wrapped my arms around his neck as he lifted me up, pressing me further into the wall. I gasped in both pleasure and pain at the sudden fullness as he slammed into me, my body stretching to accommodate him and molding perfectly around him.

"B," I gasped out. His lips returned to my neck, marking me as his as if I could be anything more. The simple act alone sent a pulse of heat down my spine. I had always thought hickeys were tacky, but somehow, in this moment, I wanted my body covered in them, his mouth marking *his* territory.

"Come on, baby, give it to me," he groaned. His words were all I needed to push me over the edge.

Every muscle in my body went stiff as I rode my orgasm out, crying out his name over and over until my voice faded to just rasps. Power and heat flowed relentlessly through me. I gasped, trying to regain my breath while his hips thrust quicker before he released into me.

Warm liquid pulsed into me, instantly reminding me that I needed to get on birth control. I had missed my appointment when Brooks came home early last week. Something I refused to bring up at this exact moment. I had been tracking ovulation like a hawk, so I knew I still had a few days until my "window."

"Wow," I gasped as he released his hold on me. He chuckled and tilted my chin, kissing me. The watery kiss was passionate. His tongue was wrestling with mine like we were finally tethered, and our souls knew it. They belonged to each other, and there was safety and comfort in it.

Round two was much slower, more intimate, pausing to adore every inch of each other and commit every moment to memory.

↟ ↟ ↟

Brooks and I sat on the lounge chairs overlooking the vineyard, wrapped in robes. "So, what are we doing tomorrow?" I asked, dropping my head back into the cushion.

Brooks' playful smile said it all. "Another surprise?"

Brooks chuckled. "Don't worry, you will enjoy it."

I huffed in false annoyance. "I love all of them, but can't I know just one?" I whined.

"Uh, there will be food involved."

"Wow, what a hint," I said playfully, throwing a fry at him.

"You want to start that?" he teased.

I threw more fries at him before launching from my seat. Brooks was fast behind me, grabbing me off the ground as I squealed. He tickled my sides as I twisted and turned in his firm grip.

"Okay, okay," I breathed out in laughter.

"You are going to pay for that," he chuckled. Brooks carried me over to the hot tub and dropped me in. The once fluffy robe now weighed heavy against me, soaked. As I breached the water, I couldn't stop laughing. Brooks was sitting on the edge, fully dry, smiling down at me. I wiped the water from my eyes and untied the robe, pulling it off and handing it to Brooks.

"Here," I laughed. Water poured out of it as he lifted it to throw it over the railing. The water was warm and mixed with the warm air, but it wasn't all that appealing. As Brooks sat back on the edge, I tugged on his wrist, surprising him by pulling him into the water.

"You didn't think you would remain dry, did you?" I laughed again.

"I guess not, no." His breath was muffled as he wiped the water off his face.

I draped my arms around him. "Do you remember that summer our parents took us to that lake up in Michigan or something?"

"It was the Ozarks in Missouri." He grinned, holding me close. "My parents got into a fight over something and I remember my mom crying to yours. Why?"

"Well, that wasn't the memory I was thinking of." I chuckled nervously. *Not even close.*

"That was the lake you pushed me in fully clothed, and it was freezing. I had a hard time swimming from the shock of it. You jumped in to help me." Brooks nodded.

"Right. I felt so bad. My dad scolded me for it, too. Didn't you get sick?"

"Yep," I chuckled. *Like really sick.* "But you also cared for me the rest of the trip and promised never to push me in again."

"Oh right, sorry."

"No, no," I chuckled. "You are forgiven. You can push me in anytime, as long as you're willing to come in after me."

Brooks rolled his eyes. We both laughed in unison. "I love you, fiancé," I whispered into his lips teasingly.

"Love you, Em," he whispered back, pressing his lips to mine.

"I want some of those cookies." I smiled, pulling away slightly.

Brooks paused, thinking of something and smiling.

"What?" I asked.

"C'mon, I have an idea." He jumped out of the hot tub and reached for my hand. We ran back to our room, and the air-conditioned room hit us like a frozen wave.

Brooks grabbed some towels from the bathroom and tossed one to me. My bra was soaking wet, so I pulled it off before pulling my underwear down my thighs.

"Do you trust me?" His voice was soft. I looked up at him.

"What?" My insides were liquid, and my tummy clenched excitedly.

"Do you trust me?" His boxer briefs were tight against his erection.

"Is that a question?" A smirk tugged at my lips.

"Come here." He took my hand in his.

The tips of his fingers slowly traced up my arms, causing my whole body to tingle.

"B? What are you doing?" I exhaled, melting into his touch.

He gently guided me to the bed, pushing me back onto it. As tired as I was, I could never get my fill of him, like my body was at his command, I could feel the moisture gathering at the apex of my thighs. Brooks climbed up, settling between them.

He grabbed the box of treats, and my eyes followed him

curiously. He pulled a finger full of frosting out and wiped it on my nipple. I shuddered against his touch while liquid hot lava raced to my toes as desire pooled in my belly. His finger returned with another batch of frosting for my other nipple. My breathing was erratic as his mouth hovered just above my nipple. I closed my eyes at the sensation.

"Are you okay?" he asked.

"Perfect," I hummed. "And very, very turned on." I couldn't help but feel the urge to giggle while focused on the pulsing between my thighs. My breast entered his mouth softly as he slowly licked the frosting off. I was burning with desire now, my hips lifting off the bed to meet his. I gasped as his mouth left my breast and took in the other. The same gratifying sensation pulsed through me. His mouth released once again as his body hovered over me. My eyes lifted and met his.

"Want me to stop?"

"No." I smiled, embarrassed. "I like it."

Brooks grinned, pleased. He reached into the box for more frosting and slowly traced a thin trail on my inner thigh. *Oh god.* My hands fisted the sheets in anticipation. His breath warmed my skin as his tongue softly licked the frosting off, leaving a euphoric trail in its wake.

My body arched as his mouth worked higher and closer.

His beard scratched against the skin of my thighs when he sucked my clit into his mouth, making my thighs close around his face. With one of his hands, he gently pushed my thigh away, reminding me to open up. His tongue was magic as he alternated between licking and sucking my swollen bud. My whole body was quivering, and I was ready to explode. I wanted him in me. I wanted him to be in me when I came.

"You okay?" he asked breathlessly when I tugged on his chin.

"Great," I panted, "I just want you in me." He crawled up to me between my legs and leaned over me to kiss me. The sweet taste of the frosting mixed with my arousal lingered on his tongue. His hand cupped me as two fingers slipped between my folds, making me moan. His mouth rested on my neck, caressing the area with his tongue. I was wild with desire.

"Brooks, I want you. Need you."

"I know," he whispered. "Come first. You're so wet. I want you to say my name like always, baby."

I nodded, dipping my finger into the box and grabbing a finger full of frosting. I traced his chest with the frosting while trying to concentrate on something other than his magic fingers. I slipped my finger into his mouth, and he gently bit the pad. For some reason, that was enough.

His bite pushed me into a free fall as I moaned out his name in ecstasy. Bright shades of color and warmth surged through and around me. I searched for my breath as I came back down to earth. He had become an expert at my body. He knew exactly what to do, where to touch, just how much pressure. It made me feel loved, safe and wanted. Somehow, it was like he was mapping new routes of my body each time.

"There we go," he whispered into my ear before pulling his fingers out. I sat up, running my tongue over the frosting still lingering on his chest, his erection prodding me in my belly. I returned my mouth to him once his chest had been thoroughly licked clean.

"Turn over," he demanded against my lips.

I rolled to my stomach, still feeling the daze associated with my high. He pulled out a condom, rolling it down his length. Disappointment crowded my chest, but I was brought back when he lifted me to my knees and shoved into me, sending me forward to the headboard. I gasped again, followed by a wild moan.

"Damn, baby," he moaned. "You feel so tight. Now, you need to understand that I can't keep filling you if you aren't going to get on birth control. I know you missed your appointment." *Shit.*

I arched my back and bucked against him hard, causing him to fall back on his heels as I backed down onto him, lost in a new sensation.

"I have another one scheduled. I'm sorry." I panted, my head dropping back to rest on his shoulder. My hand cupped his neck, bringing his mouth to mine.

"You're so warm and tight. I hate this condom, Em," he whispered into my lips as his hand moved to my swollen bud. Our bodies lifted and fell, moving in sync and chasing each other to the brink.

His free hand wrapped across my chest as he thrust into me harder, and waves of pleasure crashed over us both as he twitched inside of me. Together, we fell into the abyss, connected deep inside. In one swift move, we were on our sides, tangled and nothing but a pile of sweat, limbs, and euphoria.

"How does it get any better than that?" I asked, still trying to slow my breathing and avoiding the elephant in the room - namely, birth control.

"Pretty sure it doesn't," he replied breathlessly. "Well, only if I wasn't wearing this damn condom that kept me from feeling all of you." He slid it off and tossed it into the trash can.

I rolled over, wrapping my naked body around him. "I love you, Brooks Devonshire, and I promise I will be on birth control ASAP because I happen to hate them too."

"I love you, future Mrs. Devonshire, and you better," he teased, pulling my bottom lip between his teeth.

I smiled, beaming with joy and love for my man. I pulled my lip free.

"You can just keep calling me that."

He laughed.

"Okay, I am going to go clean up," I mumbled.

"Want a bath?"

"Yeah." I kissed him before rolling off the bed and running for the bathroom.

Chapter Twenty-Six

We sat in the tub, brimming with bubbles and hot water. The scent of the bergamot bath oil sat heavy in the air alongside the fresh buzz of *forever*. Brooks squeezed the sponge out on my back, so I leaned forward to hug my knees and pulled my hair around. The sun was finally beginning to set, sending that same golden glow through the valley outside the window. It was magical, indescribable.

More water cascaded down my back, causing my muscles to relax under the warmth. Brooks' arms wrapped around me, pulling me back into his chest, and I exhaled, laying my head back on his shoulder and his hands interlaced with mine.

"What is one thing that really scares you?" I asked.

He inhaled deeply, then exhaled. "Losing you." I rolled my eyes and flipped over to look at him, water trickling over the edge of the tub on the floor.

"Besides that. I think we both have that fear, so it doesn't count."

"Failing."

"Failing at what?" I looked up inquisitively at him before returning my back to his front.

"Running Caston. Not living up to the title of CEO and being a grand disappointment. My father left some big shoes to live up to, and I just don't know if I can fill them. Why do I deserve this position? There are a million others more qualified than I am."

His honesty ripped at my insides, my own insecurities running just as deep. He played with our fingers while I fought the negative voice in my head that said I couldn't do it.

When we were eighteen, we found out about our trust funds and that our parents had left us the company. Their hope was that we would run it together. I remember being so weighed down with grief, fear, and confusion at the time —grief because they weren't there and fear because I knew absolutely nothing about running a multibillion-dollar hotel empire.

I was confused that they had left us the company but somehow didn't change the will for a secondary guardianship. They were always traveling together. They should have been more prepared for that. Still, the weight of owning Caston weighed heavy on my shoulders. I had made a promise I would do everything I could to continue their legacy. Unfortunately, that didn't pan out like it should have. I had been avoiding Caston like the plague, but having Brooks back in my life was the ground-breaking cure that reassured me that I could do anything with him by my side - just as I intended.

"Hmm. Well, I think you will do great. Sure, others may be more qualified, and you will probably make some mistakes along the way, but I know you. You will fight for Caston. You're the right person for this job, even if you can't see it yet. It's your legacy, and the fact that you want to live up to it means you will exceed everyone's expectations, including your own, and our parents'. You're amazing. Inspiring. A true leader and supportive teacher. You face it all head-on and don't back down. Brooks, you're stronger than you know."

He smiled softly against my temple. "What about you?"

"Umm," I chuckled. *A million and one things.* "Disappointing everyone, upsetting them, disappointing myself. I don't know. I just think I try so hard to keep everyone happy. Sometimes, I wonder if it makes a difference or not. I'm scared about what Mr. Whitney will say when I put in my two weeks. What if I start at Caston, and nobody wants me there? I don't want to cause you any trouble or stress. What if I look back in ten years and wish I had done things differently? Will the work I do at Caston matter? Will it make a difference, or just be a small splash in the ocean?"

"Hmm." He dropped my hand and rested his chin on my shoulder. "Everyone loves you, Emily; they always have. I don't think you could disappoint anyone. They'll be sad to lose you but happy for you. With Caston, you will find your place there. And I know you will make a difference. You won't settle for anything less."

"I wish I could believe you."

"You will. I promise. Plus, I will be there to support you and help you however I can."

I nodded. *I know.*

"Okay, one irrational fear?" I laughed, trying to lighten the mood.

"Hmm..." He looked out the window thoughtfully. "Tripping over those large grates." He barked out a laugh that made my lips tilt up as I watched him over my shoulder.

"What?"

"You know those large grates in the ground? I don't know why. I always think my shoe will get stuck or something. It's dumb, I know, but I avoid them at all costs."

I couldn't help but chuckle. It was a little irrational but precisely what I asked for. Now, I had a mental image of Brooks walking down a Seattle sidewalk and his Oxfords getting stuck in the grate. It was very dramatic.

"You aren't J-Lo," I chuckled.

"Your turn," he teased, tickling my sides.

"Okay, okay," I giggled. "Sorry. No grates got it." I inhaled deeply, filling my lungs with the delicious scent of the oil. "Spiders in the bed that will bite me at night, falling off something high and falling to my death, getting trapped in a riptide and drowning, hitting someone with my car." I couldn't fight back my smile and laughter. They were all so ridiculous.

"Hold on. Let's start with hitting someone with your car?" He chuckled.

"Yeah, like looking at something on the road and not seeing someone who decided to cross the road, or if my car swerves and there happens to be someone on a bike or something."

Brooks hummed before talking again. "Okay. Spiders in your bed? Do I need to start checking the sheets before bedtime?"

I giggled. "Sure." I paused. "No. Of course not. Unless we go somewhere exotic and there are large spiders. Like South America or Australia. Did you know that almost all the deadliest animals and spiders are in your homeland?"

"I did know that." He smiled. "Lighter subject. Where do you want to go for a honeymoon?"

I couldn't fight back the large, ridiculous smile that crossed my face. I used to have a journal that I kept with all the places we would visit, or our parents did visit, as potential honeymoon locations. I guess I didn't care as long as there was a warm beach because I already had everything I needed - Brooks.

"Mm...somewhere warm, maybe tropical, on a beach with lots of sun and no spiders."

"So, no trips to Iceland or Patagonia? There's no deadly spiders there."

"No!" I giggled.

"Why? We can stay in one of those ice hotels. It might be romantic."

"No!" I splashed him. "Plus, I am pretty sure those are in Norway, not Iceland. Iceland doesn't have ice, remember?"

"Fine. Norway? I want to see the fjords, and we can go whale watching and freeze to death on the boat. Then, return to our ice hotel and make love on a bed of freezing cold ice. Doesn't it sound so romantic and icey?"

"Haha. No, thank you. That's where we go if you don't want to have sex. I will be so bundled up like Randy in A Christmas Story."

Brooks snorted. "That's an image."

"Seriously though, where do you want to go?"

"Everywhere. I want to take you everywhere. So, I don't care where we go for the honeymoon. That will just be the first of many trips."

"Okay." I smiled before turning back around and laying my head back on his chest. I yawned, and Brooks' arms wrapped around me again, tightly wrapping me in warmth.

"One more question -" he started. "Where do you see us in ten years? What do you want, Em?"

He lifted his hand from the water and let the water drip down onto my neck.

"Hmm...I want a few kids, I want to travel, and I want to make a home with you. Wherever that is. We don't have to stay in Pacific Coves if you don't want to. Oh, and I want a dog or two. What about you?"

"I want to have a whole soccer team of babies with you and a big backyard to chase the kids around. The dogs can chase them when we're exhausted. At night, we can lay on a deck with blankets and cocoa, look at the stars, and tell them stories. I want to make all your dreams come true."

"You are my dream come true," I whispered back.

Chapter Twenty-Seven

There was a loud knock on the door, jolting Brooks and me awake. He groaned as he rolled over to check the clock.

"Damn," he grumbled as he rolled off the bed, pulling on some shorts he had on the floor. I closed my eyes, feeling sleep pull me back under as I turned away from him, yanking a pillow over my head.

"Em, baby." His gruff voice was an audible reminder of the lack of sleep from waking up at 3 a.m. for another round of orgasms.

"No, I want to sleep. Come back to bed. They can come back later." I slapped the sheets where he should be.

Brooks laughed sleepily. "No, they can't. C'mon." He pulled the sheet off of me and smacked my butt. *Ugh, fine, I am awake.*

"Who's here?" I groaned.

Brooks handed me my dress. "Get dressed and meet me out there."

"Ugh, fine, but I do so in protest."

He laughed through a yawn as he walked out of the room. I blinked several times, trying to fight the urge to go back to sleep. Seriously, who was here? I could hear Brooks from the courtyard, and curiosity got the better of me. I pulled the dress over my head, forgoing my bra.

I gasped when I saw the light markings across my breasts and sides that Brooks had left in his wake of sucking and nibbling last night. A warmth spread through me at the sight of them, a mixture of arousal and embarrassment flushing through my cheeks at how much I enjoyed seeing my body marked by him. At least I could hide them, well, maybe not the one on my neck. Thank God for makeup. I wrapped a cardigan around myself and went to meet Brooks and our unnamed guest.

"Oh my god!" I shrieked, jumping into Natalie's arms. "What, how?"

I looked over at Brooks and Michaelson and then back to Natalie.

"Last day here. I thought you'd like to enjoy it with some friends." Brooks' face softened as he took in my squealing delight.

"Let me see the ring," Natalie demanded, yanking my hand up.

"Dang, Brooks, you did good."

Brooks and Michaelson laughed in unison. This was the first time meeting Michaelson in person. I've spent years knowing him through Zoom and FaceTime, but I still found comfort in his familiar face.

He congratulated me, pulling me in for a side hug, which should have been awkward, but it wasn't. He felt like an old friend, and I squeezed him back.

He was tall like Brooks but had sandy blonde hair and light green eyes that almost looked clear. His handsome face was chiseled, and his body was slim, but I could tell he was fit.

When we finished with a round of hugs, we pointed to their rooms. Now, it all made sense why Brooks would have rented the GuestHouse. We agreed to meet for breakfast before heading back to our room to get dressed.

"You aren't upset they're here?" Brooks asked as the door shut.

"No! Are you kidding?"

"Okay. I debated on whether to invite them or not. I didn't want to intrude on our weekend, but I also know you love your friends, and you wanted Natalie and Michaelson to get to know each other." His lips pulled up into a ridiculous grin, and he gave me a playful wink.

"Ooh, Brooks Devonshire. Are you playing matchmaker now?" My eyebrows bounced twice as I smashed my body into his that was leaning against the door.

"No." He smiled. "But I do think a girlfriend might be good for him."

I giggled. "So, what do I dress for today?" I rolled my eyes playfully.

"A cooking class." He kissed me on the temple, lifting off the door as he brushed past me to the bathroom.

"B, are you serious?" I asked, my voice laced with excitement.

"Yes. Natalie and Michaelson are joining us. After that, we are headed to a winery. We can come back and change before dinner tonight," he called from the bathroom, which I followed him into.

I threw my arms around his neck, inching up on my tiptoes to kiss him. He lifted me up onto the cold counter, but the temperature change had no effect due to the burning inside of me. My fingers knotted in his hair, and I could feel the deep and needy hints of arousal crackling in the air between us.

"Didn't we say we would meet them in thirty?" I laughed, reluctantly pulling away.

He groaned as he peeled himself off of me, unlacing my fingers from his messy hair. "Fine." He chuckled, shaking his head.

I should have been exhausted and overstimulated from hours of mouths, hands, and bodies colliding. Still, he made my head spin, and my whole body was practically vibrating, crazy for his touch, especially when he's turned on - it's a sensual touch that makes me weak in the knees.

I searched the closet through the dresses that Natalie packed for me and pulled out my white summer maxi dress. It paired perfectly with the leather sandals she packed. I quickly slid the soft material up my body, fixing the delicate straps on my shoulders, and threw on a light layer of makeup. I had just finished with the last curl when Brooks reappeared from the deck.

I nibbled on my bottom lip, teasingly eyeing him up and down. He looked dashing in his copper trousers and white button-down shirt, just a button lower than usual, showing off his chest. His new leather loafers finished the stylish, polished look perfectly.

He smirked, watching my eyes as he crossed the room to me. I inhaled, breathing in his cologne. My thoughts went blank, and I was suddenly delirious with need again. I needed to get my libido in check, or we were never going to survive the day without getting caught in a compromising position.

His face was hovering, just inches from mine. His thumb brushed over my lip, pulling it free from my teeth. I wanted to kiss him and tear off his clothes - get lost in all things Brooks, but we had two minutes before we were supposed to be in the courtyard. I gulped while my heart raced, and his hand brushed my cheek.

"You okay there?" he asked softly, with hints of amusement in his voice. He knew exactly what he was doing to me. I shook my head and looked away, trying to clear my thoughts.

Sensing my weakness, his lips crashed down on mine as he pushed me back against the wall. My back arched into him. My hands brushed along his neatly groomed beard.

Stop on the count of three. His hands were strong, and his fingers dug into my hips just to the point of pain. *Three.* His tongue brushed my bottom lip again. *Two.* His hand slid down my back and began lifting my dress. *One.* His fingers brushed my panties, sending goosebumps up my thighs. My whole body shuddered. *Half.* Brooks groaned softly in my ear as he pulled his hand away.

"Time to go."

"No." I grabbed his hand, pulling him back to my aching core. "They can wait. I cannot." He nodded as he lifted my dress once more.

"What do you want Emily?" He pulled my panties to the side as he brushed his thumb down my slit.

"I want you." I trembled with need. His lips moved to my collarbone as I worked to unbutton his pants.

"They're waiting on us," he breathed into my neck.

"Make it quick," I replied, breaking him free from his pants. In a swift movement, he lifted me off the ground and back up onto the counter. My shaky hands held my dress out of the way, pushing my panties to the side as I watched him thrust into me with a force that had me seeing stars as my body stretched around his.

He pounded into me fast and hard, setting a new, torturous pace. There was no hiding the loud moans that escaped my mouth, and I didn't even try as my hips met his, silently begging for more.

"Babe, shhh." He fought back a sexy grin and cupped his warm hand over my mouth. I was so close to peaking that when his length swelled with his own release building inside of me, my body shuddered and tightened around him, sending him over the blissful edge.

"Fuck, I'm sorry," he groaned as he pulled out of me, releasing his grip on my thighs. My body missed him the moment he was gone, still begging for its own release.

He yanked me back to him and used his fingers to finish the job. Within minutes, I screamed into his neck, earning a cocky smile from him.

"You didn't think I would leave you unsatisfied, did you?"

"No. I don't know. Maybe?"

"Never." He kissed my forehead and turned to the sink to clean up. "I'm not complaining, but what has gotten into you lately?" He shot me a sexy grin.

"I don't know," I said, still trying to regain a steady breath. "Maybe it's this place. Or you." I fixed my hair and lipstick in the mirror before turning to Brooks to wipe the pink smudges from his lips and neck.

"Now, I'm ready." I smiled with satisfied relief.

He nodded and grinned, grabbing my hand.

"What am I going to do with you?" He laughed, pulling me back across the room to meet our guests.

Chapter Twenty-Eight

When we pulled up to the winery, it was early afternoon. We had just finished our cooking class and were anxious to sit and relax in the perfect Sonoma weather.

There was a reason this winery was rated one of the best. They practiced sustainability and biodynamic farming, something I felt our society needed to do more of. I wanted to support any business that chose the environment over easy. Brooks' fingers wrapped in mine as we walked to the main house where we met our tour guide.

Our host drove us around the vineyard in a cart, explaining their farming practices in depth. These included allowing animals to roam the vineyards and naturally fertilizing the soil. We even got to see one of their Highland cows, which was my favorite part. We stopped by their wine cave before concluding the tour with a private tasting in their parlor.

After our tour, we found a sectional under a large oak tree that provided just enough shade to keep the heat from becoming overbearing.

"So, have you thought about when you want the wedding?" Natalie whispered as if it was a huge secret.

I laughed. "No, not yet. It's only been a day." *A day that has felt like heaven.*

"Yes, but you said you have had all this planned forever." Images of my fourteen-year-old self surrounded by bridal magazines, scissors, glue, and my journal danced through my head. I had it all planned out. A beach wedding, a silk and organza mermaid gown made by Galia Lahav, pink peonies and navy chrysanthemums, and an arch of eucalyptus and white floral vines would overlook the Puget Sound. Back then, aside from Connor, I didn't know who would act as our bridal party, but I knew I wanted at least five bridesmaids and a maid of honor.

"True, but that was years ago, and in recent years, I wasn't exactly planning my dream wedding." As in, after Brooks and I broke up, I tossed said journal into a bonfire and cried my eyes out.

"Maybe this fall? I don't want to be that couple that waits a whole year - or worse, longer. There isn't really anywhere in Pacific Coves that I would want to have it, so maybe somewhere outside of Seattle. There's this breathtaking venue on Bainbridge called IslandWood. It's in the middle of the woods, and there is a wide, open grass area where you can have the ceremony. There's a suspension bridge, I mean, it's all just so dreamy. I definitely do not want a hotel wedding."

"Well, we can start venue shopping when you get home. I'm happy to help however I can."

"Thank you." I smiled and leaned over, resting my head on Brooks' shoulder. His hand had been resting on my thigh, but he was deep in conversation about work with Michaelson.

"No work talk, remember?" I whispered.

Brooks paused his ramblings. "Okay, sorry."

"Michaelson, tell me, what have you been up to these past few years?"

"Er," he chuckled. "Not much, honestly. I got my MBA at Oxford, started working for a small tech startup, took a few trips here and there - Japan, Barcelona, met up with Brooks in Byron Bay, when he had leave."

"Really?" I turned to look at Brooks. His eyes rolled to Michaelson with an unreadable expression.

"It was two years ago. We were still broken up, obviously. We just went to surf and..." he started.

"And?" I asked, amused.

He croaked out a nervous chuckle. "And to party."

I gave him an overexaggerated eye-roll.

"The surfing was great. The parties, not so much." Brooks sighed.

I looked back to Michaelson for clarification.

"He drank too much," Michaelson added. "No, but really, I haven't done much. I moved back to Suffolk for a bit, then Brooks offered me the position in Seattle." Michaelson's parents came from a long line of wealthy English families, and he was expected to stay in England. But I've heard he had never been much of a rule follower.

We spent the afternoon discussing how Brooks and Michaelson met in boarding school and some fun stories about them getting into trouble. Natalie and Michaelson took over the conversation while Brooks and I sat back, letting them get to know each other.

"Where are you from? What's your story?" he asked.

"Oh, I'm from Bend. I grew up in a normal, middle-class suburbia neighborhood. My mom is a realtor, and my dad works in sales. Baby sister, Aubry, still lives in Bend. I moved to Portland to attend nursing school at OHSU. I went to Pacific Coves during my senior year with some girlfriends and fell in love with the town. After school, I applied to the local hospital, which had an opening in pediatrics, which was my focus. I got accepted. So, now I have been in PC for a little over a year. That's pretty much it."

Michaelson looked intrigued by her story, listening intently. "Do you ever come up to Seattle?"

"No, not really. I went a few times as a kid, but I guess I can hitch a ride up with these two and make the trip a lot quicker."

Michaelson smiled ever so slightly before turning to Brooks to talk more about a soccer match.

I stood up and grabbed Natalie's hand. "Let's get another glass." Once free of hearing range, "So, Michaelson."

Natalie laughed nervously. "He's cute, and that accent is swoon-worthy."

Swoon-worthy? I couldn't help but laugh. "What did you guys talk about on the plane?"

"Not much, actually. We did a quick introduction when I boarded, but he was deep in work or something on the computer. He just mentioned he worked with Brooks."

"Yeah, he's his Chief of Staff." I placed my drink on the counter. "Could we grab another glass of your house white?"

"How is he single?" She pursed her lips, pondering the thought.

"Brooks said he's not one for serious relationships, but -"

"Great," she interrupted, sighing deeply.

"But, Brooks thinks that could change. Especially now that we are engaged. Most of our friends are married or coupled, so maybe it will influence him to settle down?"

"We will see, but I won't hold my breath."

↟ ↟ ↟

I rolled over, stretching, and opened my eyes. The sun was lower in the sky. I glanced at the clock: 7:14 p.m.

"Shoot." I jumped out of bed. *Ouch.* My head was pounding. After returning to the hotel, I felt a little tipsy and needed to lie down. I guess I overslept.

There was a bottle of water on my nightstand, along with a bagel. I drank a few sips and took a few bites of the now-cold bagel. A piece of bread had never tasted so good.

I pulled the blanket up and wrapped it around me before snatching the bagel and bottled water to head out to the courtyard. I could hear them talking, but I couldn't see where their voices were coming from. I rounded the corner by the hot tub and knew I was headed in the right direction as their voices got louder. I continued around the deck to the backside, where they sat around the outdoor fireplace.

"Hey babe, how are you feeling?" Brooks stood up, coming to my side.

"Fine. I am so sorry that I slept so long."

"No, it's okay."

"What about dinner?"

"Depends on how you feel? We can go out, or we can just order something from Hazel."

"I don't want to keep you guys trapped here."

"Are you kidding? I am just fine with sitting here all night," Natalie said.

"Same." Michaelson nodded.

"Okay, can we just do Hazel Hill then?"

"Yes. I can place the order. What do you want?

"The chicken and a side of the asparagus."

"Okay." Brooks pulled out his phone and turned to Natalie and Michaelson while I curled into a chair beside the sofa. Michaelson and Natalie were sitting on the couch, and I wasn't about to separate them. Brooks pulled up the menu for them, and they both gave Brooks their orders. Brooks stepped away to call it in.

"Remind me to never drink again," I whined while taking another sip of water.

"I didn't even think about the heat, plus the wine. Sorry." Natalie smiled apologetically.

"It's not your fault. You aren't my babysitter. Just remind me to not drink at all," I laughed before wincing slightly.

"Deal."

"How are you feeling?" Michaelson asked.

"Okay. Much better than earlier. My head was spinning when we got back. How are your rooms?"

"Great. Yeah, this place is epic." Michaelson nodded before looking out over the valley.

The conversation flowed so easily between us that it was like we had all been friends for years. Hearing about Natalie's and Michaelson's childhood stories and reliving mine and Brooks' was comfortable and fun. Throughout the evening, we all learned that we collectively wanted to visit Greece. By the time the food arrived, my energy had returned, and all signs of my drunkenness had disappeared. I was so thankful to finally be free to enjoy our last night here in this little slice of paradise.

Chapter Twenty-Nine

"We should play a game." Natalie smiled playfully. *Uh-oh, I know that look.* She squirmed in her chair with delight.

"Ha. What game?" I asked, curious.

"Never Have I Ever, Charades, Hide & Seek." She laughed, ticking them off with her fingers.

"Not Never Have I Ever," Michaelson chimed in. He shut that idea down faster than the cops raiding a spring break party. *Not that I would know.*

"I agree." I nodded. Nothing good ever came from that game. The one time I played, I found myself wishing the floor had swallowed me up. Being a virgin through college and an introverted book nerd had not served me well at that moment.

"We don't have what we need for Charades, do we?" Brooks asked.

"How about Hide & Seek?" I chimed in. I was feeling playful. Besides, how often did you get a chance to play kid games?

"Hide & Seek, really?" Brooks looked at me and rolled his eyes playfully. Hide & Seek had been our favorite game growing up, especially when playing with Connor.

"Hey, it will be fun," Natalie said, not understanding how Brooks and I played. Initially, it was an excuse to find a hidden corner, steal kisses, and feel each other up.

"I'm down." Michaelson stood up. "Not it, though," he chuckled, his voice booming into the dark night.

"Not it," I smirked.

"Not it," Natalie and Brooks said almost in unison, but Natalie said it first.

"Ah, gotta be faster than that," she teased.

Brooks shook his head and laughed. "Okay. So, ground rules?"

"No leaving the house," I suggested. I was so excited to get started that I bounced on my feet.

"Count to fifty. Outside of the courtyard doors," Michaelson stated.

"Good one," Natalie said.

"Anything else?" Brooks asked.

"No. Go count," I said, nudging his shoulder.

Brooks sighed playfully as he stood up and walked out to the courtyard. We all waited until the door closed and then made a break for it, running in opposite directions.

I knew I would need to hide well. Brooks and I always played so often growing up that he knew all my favorite hiding places, and I was always the first one he would find. Looking back now, I think there may have been more to that. Like, somehow, he sensed where I was.

I ran towards Natalie's room as quietly as possible while she and Michaelson disappeared in different rooms. Once inside, I snuck out onto her deck, which had a small sofa. I decided to roll under it, making myself as small as possible while I closed my eyes and counted back from ten.

The air was charged with electricity from excitement and

anticipation. I knew if Brooks walked out onto the deck, he could find me just by how heavy I was breathing. The door opening and closing in the distance alerted me to him finally being done counting and now on the hunt.

It wasn't long before I heard a scream, followed by laughter. The door to Natalie's room opened noisily, signaling Brooks was coming. I stifled a laugh into my arm, picturing him yanking back curtains and pillows with a gleeful smile.

The glass door opened, and my eyes shot open. My heart was racing so loud in my ears, and my body was on full alert, waiting for him. I wanted him to find me. I wanted to reach out and say I'm here, but I didn't. Instead, I pulled myself into a smaller ball.

When the weight shifted the cushions above me, I almost laughed out loud. He had found me, of course he had. There was like a homing beacon on me, and he knew it called out to him, only him.

"I know you're under there, Emily," he chuckled, sitting back against the cushions.

"How do you do that?" I grumbled as I rolled out from under him. His warm hands reached out, cupping my face. I stood, allowing him to pull me into his lap.

"You'll never know," he smirked. His chest brushed against my nipples, causing them to pebble, before he planted a soft kiss on my lips. I rocked my hips forward while he palmed my breast through my shirt.

"For old time's sake," he said against my lips. "Time to go find Michaelson." Following Brooks out of her room, I found a seat next to Natalie on the edge of the concrete hot tub that sat along the edge of the courtyard.

"Where's Michaelson?" I asked.

"Look behind me," Natalie giggled. I turned to see Michaelson hiding in the hot tub, his face barely above the water. He shot me a quick grin.

"Oh," I snickered, turning back to Natalie. She nudged me playfully with her shoulder, heat spreading across her face. So much was said in our little glance. I could hear Brooks still hunting in Michaelson's room.

"Where were you?" she asked, trying to change the subject away from their flirtatious smiles.

"Under the sofa on your deck. You?"

"In your tub with a white towel draped over me." She rolled her own eyes knowingly.

"Really?" I teased. "That's an awful spot."

Brooks returned to the courtyard, looking slightly flustered than when I left him. I looked down, trying not to give away Michaelson's hiding spot. He would know with just one look at me. Brooks approached us, and Natalie and I ever so softly moved in closer to each other. I flung my arm around her shoulder, resting my head on her shoulder.

"Where is he?" he asked, amused.

"I don't have the slightest idea," Natalie fibbed without hesitation or giggling. Brooks looked over at me, but I couldn't meet his eyes and lie, so I just shrugged.

"Really, Michaelson? The hot tub?" Brooks asked, running a hand through his hair. A fit of laughter erupted out of Natalie and I. I didn't realize how badly I needed to let it out. Michaelson stood up out of the water, the moonlight glistening off his soaking wet body, his shirt clinging to what I could only imagine, *not that I was,* a great set of abs. Natalie's eyes raked over him appreciatively before turning to me, cheeks pink and eyes wide.

"One more round?" Natalie asked, anxious to change the subject.

"Sure. Let me change," Michaelson said as he stepped out of the water.

Brooks sat beside me. "Ridiculous. He's committed, though. I will give him that."

"Do you think we could order s'mores?" I asked Brooks.

"Doubt it," he replied, tucking a strand of hair behind my ear.

"Please." I gave him puppy dog eyes, my hands praying at my chest.

"Emily," he chuckled. "I don't think they have anything in the shop."

"Well, send our driver to go? He's on for another hour, right?" I batted my eyes for dramatic flare, to which Brooks only rolled his.

"Fine," he said, kissing my cheek before standing up to talk to the driver.

"Wow." Natalie shook her head. "That was next level."

"I hardly ever ask for things, and since he's paid by the hour anyway, I'm sure he won't mind the extra tip to go run a quick errand for us." Natalie rolled her eyes.

"Where's Brooks?" Michaelson asked, appearing in dry clothes.

"Paying the driver to bring Emily s'mores," Natalie teased.

"Great idea." Michaelson grinned, shaking out his hair. *See, he understands.* Natalie just rolled her eyes *again.* Brooks returned a moment later and clapped his hands, ready for another round.

"Natalie, you're up," Michaelson declared, pointing a finger gun at her and shooting.

When Natalie was outside the courtyard, Brooks and I took off toward our room, wrestling in the doorway to see who would get in first. I squealed when his arms wrapped around me, picking me up and turning so he could back into the room first.

"Hey, I was here first," I cackled, pulling on his arm as he set me down.

"I was here first." He laughed, pulling away from me. When he slid behind the sofa in our room, I snickered and skipped to the bedroom. Brooks was in too easy of a hiding spot. I looked around the room, deciding to wrap myself up in the floor-to-ceiling curtains behind the cream chaise.

With little warning, Natalie opened our room door and passed by Brooks. *Lame.* Hearing her footsteps padding through the bedroom, I held my breath. She was opening and closing the cabinets and sighed when she came up empty. On her way out, I heard her say, "Found you." She was talking to Brooks, not me.

"Yeah, yeah," Brooks said. Sneaking a peek out of the curtains, I saw him standing up from behind the coffee table, using the end table for support. Under his weight, it bobbled just enough that he thought the lamp would go flying, but he caught it just in time.

"You can go join Michaelson. I already found him." She grinned.

They both exited the room. I was so happy because I had never won before. I stood in the silence, hoping she would reappear so that I could rub my victory in her face—okay, maybe in Brooks' face. I was ready to give myself up, but their voices could be heard outside in the courtyard. The door opened again.

"Emily, I know you are in here. You win," she said, sounding both amused and exasperated. Pleased, I popped out from behind the curtain.

"Boo!" I exclaimed.

"What? No way," she sighed playfully. "Good one."

"Where was Michaelson?" I asked, leaving the room with her.

"Cheating," she grumbled. "He was hanging onto the railing off the deck of his room."

"Eh, it's borderline. I mean, he was still on the railing, right?" I asked. It was definitely a spot I would have loved.

Without responding, she shook her head, accepting defeat.

"Finally," Michaelson yelled out like he'd been waiting forever.

"Heard you were cheating?" I quipped.

"Yeah, yeah, doesn't count." His hand waved to the air in disagreement.

"Just teasing, I believe you." I made my way over to Brooks' lap and sat down. His arms wrapped around my waist, pulling me into his chest. I melted into him, feeling like I was returning home after being gone all day.

"Are the s'mores here?" I asked.

"No, probably any minute, though. There's a store just ten minutes away, and it's already been twenty." Brooks was burying his nose in the crook of my neck.

"Thank you," I whispered into his cheek, taking in his singular, masculine scent - his smell. He exhaled, turning his lips to mine. When I pulled his bottom lip between my teeth, he groaned.

"Ahem." Michaelson cleared his throat. "Yeah, none of that."

I pulled away from Brooks, blushing. Brooks punched Michaelson's arm before turning to face me again.

"Love you," he whispered before planting another kiss. "Okay, so tomorrow we have a late checkout. Do you guys want to go to the pool before we leave, or we can do whatever. I think they have bikes for rent. There's archery, bocce ball, and pickleball." Brooks asked.

"The pool sounds nice. What time does the plane get here?" Natalie asked, taking a seat on the ground in front of us.

"They'll be on standby whenever we are ready to leave."

"I have some emails to tend to in the morning, but I can just work at the pool," Michaelson offered.

"Yeah, the pool sounds nice," I said, grinning at Brooks and wiggling my eyebrows. Any time spent with Brooks without a shirt is an afternoon well spent. Even if I would have to keep my hands to myself and my libido in check.

↟ ↟ ↟

It was late by the time we gathered around the fire pit to finally indulge in my late-night craving for s'mores. The yellow chairs were comfy, and the warmth from the fire was lulling me to sleep despite the rush of sugar into my system.

Natalie had a campfire playlist playing in the background to complete the mood, but I couldn't stifle the yawn that fell from my lips. I pulled the blanket around me tighter, feeling the heaviness of sleep. I didn't want this weekend to end; it was too perfect and special. So, instead of going to bed, I pushed through, fighting against exhaustion.

I invited them both to the gala, and Natalie and I made plans to go shopping for a dress for her. Michaelson told us about his sisters and the upcoming wedding, which was published in the newspaper as Wedding of the Year.

I had no idea what it would have been like to grow up with our parents around and at weddings. They died just as they started including us on more trips and bringing us around for work events. Would Brooks and I have had a *Wedding of the Year?* I wasn't even sure that's what I wanted anymore.

As the conversation died down, we relaxed comfortably in each other's presence, just listening to the music and watching the flames dance around inside the glass. The evening chill was beginning to set in, and I was finally ready to crawl into bed. Now that it was settled that Natalie and Michaelson would have another opportunity to be together, I felt like it was mission accomplished. I yawned once again.

"Time for bed?" Brooks asked, turning to me.

"Yeah, I cannot stop yawning." He stood, pulling me from my chair.

"Goodnight," I said, stifling another yawn.

"Night, guys." Michaelson half-waved.

"Good night," Natalie said with a sleepy smile.

A short time later, I was draped over Brooks' chest, listening to the sound of his heart against my ear while voices of laughter trickled in from the patio door.

"Sounds like they're hitting it off," Brooks whispered, brushing hair off my shoulder as he traced circles into my back.

"Yeah, I think they're a great match. They're both good-humored and playful. She's stable, while he's adventurous, and they can help each other."

"Did you have a good weekend?"

I looked up, resting my chin on the backs of my hands.

"Are you kidding? This was the best weekend of my life. I can never say thank you enough. It was really amazing."

"Good. I'm glad you liked it." His hands pulled the sheets up higher over my back, and I turned, resting my cheek on his bare chest. The rising and falling of his chest kept me from falling asleep, but I didn't want to move. After a few minutes, Brooks' breathing changed, and I could tell he was asleep.

I rolled back over on the pillow, tucking myself into his side, and closed my eyes. Just when I was about to fall asleep, my phone rang. I was ready to ignore it, but Brooks woke up and reached for it before I could say no. I felt him instantly tense under me.

"Why is Connor calling you?"

Chapter Thirty

"So, how are you settling into Seattle? How's Caston?" I asked, splashing my feet against the water.

"It's good. I like Seattle. Caston is also great. Brooks and I have a lot of ideas of how to expand into tech, so that will be fun." Michaelson stared off into the water. I couldn't read his expression with his dark aviators on.

"Brooks said things aren't going very well with your parents? How are you doing with that?"

"No, things aren't great between us. I mean, we will work through it. We just had a disagreement about my sister. She was being pushy, which is fairly typical, but I'm not a kid she can boss around anymore."

"I have always wondered what it would be like to have a sibling. Brooks is probably the closest thing I've had to a sibling, except we've always had a crush on each other, so that changed the dynamic."

Michaelson laughed. "I would say it's pretty different." He paused for a moment before speaking again. "He doesn't talk about his parents much. What were they like?"

"Amazing. I loved them almost as much as my own parents. It

was like getting to have two sets. They were all so special. Brooks' mom will always be one of my favorite people, and I look up to her so much. She was always so kind and gentle. She was always the first one to drop whatever she was doing to give us a hug or offer to take us somewhere. She was so selfless, always helping others." I swallowed and forced back the lump in my throat.

"My mom was too - don't get me wrong, it was just that Carrie was very affectionate, and my mother wasn't. I think physical touch was her love language, as is mine. My mom's was more of a 'shower you with gifts' type of mother. She was always spoiling us, but she was also a lot tougher on us. His dad, James, was the life of the party. No matter where we were or what we were doing - he had a booming voice that was always cheerful and positive. His joy of life was so contagious."

I could feel Michaelson's attention on me as he nodded along in understanding as I continued. "Whenever I was in a bad mood, he would crack jokes, mess my hair up, or do anything to get me to crack a grin. I could never not laugh, he won every time. James had a way of making everyone feel like they belonged."

A tall brunette squealed from the other end of the pool, breaking my trance. A man about our age lifted her off her feet and jumped into the water with her in his arms.

"And your dad?" he urged me, drawing me back into our conversation. I gave him a tight smile and continued.

"My dad was always grilling or planning our next vacation. He was adventurous but also really sensible. He would wear this dumb apron with a six-pack drawn on it. Our parents were hilarious and best friends - always joined at the hip. We literally did everything together. Aside from sleeping in separate houses at night, it was rare to see us apart.

"Even at meal times, like breakfast, it would be chaotic. Brooks would run in, our housekeeper would yell at him for running, and he would jump up on the barstool next to me. Carrie and James would come in, always laughing about something. My parents would still be half awake, searching for coffee. It was great.

"We almost always had breakfast at my house and dinner at his unless we were going out." I didn't realize I had started crying until a tear splashed down on my thigh. I missed the chaos, the loud home, their laughs, and the busyness of life - our parents gave us a spectacular life.

"Do you miss them?" he asked, his voice steady.

"I do." I exhaled. "Thanks for being there for Brooks in school. I can't imagine what he went through. I mean, I lost him and our parents, but I got to stay in school. I stayed in my home. He lost everything and everyone."

"Not everyone. He still had you. Trust me, you were his lifeline."

"Well, still, thank you. I know you brought a lot of life back to him."

"He was, and still is, a great friend. I think it was mutually beneficial. I was dying in that place until Brooks showed up. It was pure luck that we got put in the same dorm. I mean, at first, I was a little angry. I had the room to myself until he showed up halfway through the semester. I thought he would be like everyone else. All stuck up, too prideful to even be human. I was thankful when I realized he was the opposite. It was even better that he played soccer so we could join the team together."

"Do you still play?"

"Nah. Maybe one day I can find an adult league, but it doesn't seem likely in Seattle."

Brooks splashed water on both of us.

"What are you two doing? Get in the water." He laughed, splashing us again. I was thankful for his playfulness. Even though Connor calling had nothing to do with Brooks, it still took a while for both of us to fall asleep. Connor had only called because he had a bit too much to drink and wanted to check in and finally apologize.

Before I could say something smart, Michaelson launched off the edge, pulling Brooks down under the water. I chuckled, jumping in to join them. Natalie swam over to me as we watched them wrestling in the water.

"They're crazy!" she gasped. "I got five on Michaelson that he takes Brooks down."

"Deal. Brooks is way stronger. Look at those muscles." I watched the water slide down his biceps, making my heart flutter. "Actually, don't look," I teased, covering her eyes. She laughed, splashing water at me. "Sorry, my eyes were on the other hottie." She giggled between splashes, trying to move away from me.

"Other hottie, huh?" I grinned. "Hey Michaelson, Natalie just called you hot." Natalie pulled me under the water just as I got the last word out. When we both resurfaced, I saw the guys were done wrestling, their attention on us. I couldn't stop laughing and almost swallowed water.

"Way to throw it out there," she groaned under her breath, turning five shades of red.

"I'm just helping you out." I blew a playful kiss at her and then looked over to Brooks, who was laughing and shaking his head, purely amused.

I brushed my wet hair out of my eyes and tried to wipe my sunglasses clean, unsuccessfully. The saltwater clung to the shades like a film. When I saw Natalie's nervous look, I instantly felt guilty.

"Sorry, Natalie," I said.

"It's fine. Hopefully he doesn't hide from me now," she said nervously.

"Doubt it."

Brooks and Michaelson wadded over to us. With Brooks just inches away, I closed the distance between us, wrapping around him and burying my tongue in his mouth. It was quick and short-lived since I promised to be on my best behavior while those lips were pleasuring me this morning.

"I like seeing you so happy," I murmured softly into his ear.

His mouth met mine again, locking our lips together while his tongue slid along mine.

"Really, guys?" Michaelson scoffed. I rolled my eyes, pulling away slightly.

"Hey, you're the one crashing my engagement weekend," I teased.

"Wanna grab some food at the grill before we go? We still need to shower and change before checkout," Brooks said, turning to the three of us.

"Is it time already?" I pouted.

"Unfortunately. Back to reality, we go."

"Ugh, okay. Let's go." I playfully groaned as I turned to climb out of the water, smiling to myself as I felt Brooks' gaze on me the entire way.

↟ ↟ ↟

"Hi, Tate," I smiled as I ascended the jet's stairs.

"Ms. Barlow, congratulations," he said with a nod.

"Thank you!" I smiled back.

I sat down in my usual seat beside Brooks. Natalie sat across from me and Michaelson across from Brooks.

"It's almost depressing having to leave this place," I confessed to Natalie.

"I know. It's so magical here. We will have to come back."

"Yeah," I agreed solemnly.

The door closed loudly behind Natalie.

"Wow, that was quick." I looked at Brooks, confused. Usually, it took a while before the door closed, and we were ready for takeoff.

"I think there's a storm at home," he said, pulling out his phone.

As we settled in for the flight, I let my eyes wander outside. Memories of golden sunsets in the valley, Brooks on his knee in the middle of the vineyard, and the helicopter ride had me turning into a pile of weepy emotions.

"Flight time to Pacific Coves Regional Airport is one hour and twenty-seven minutes. Weather in Pacific Coves is a chilly fifty-eight degrees, and raining. Wind speed is sitting around twenty miles an hour. Please buckle up, and we will get you there safely," Tate's voice said over the speakers.

"How is it so cold there and so warm here?" Natalie asked, looking out at the glow of the setting sun. I rested my head back against the seat and looked over to Brooks. He smiled softly and reached out to take my hand. The plane jolted forward.

"Ready?" Brooks asked. *Time to quit my job.*

Chapter Thirty-One

The sound of rain hitting the windows woke me up earlier than usual. Glancing at my phone, I let out a small groan - 5:17. *Ugh.* I rolled back over to Brooks and tucked myself into his side. He was still fast asleep. We had been home for a few days, trying to get back into work mode but failing. Days back at the office away from Brooks, I felt like I was missing an essential limb, only confirming that I had made the right decision to leave my job at Hope.

The weight of my ring made me smile in the dark as I replayed Brooks down on his knee, nervous and excited, pouring out his heart and soul to me. It was an image that would forever be a part of me, one I would treasure until the day I died. It was a moment when the stars aligned, making me feel invincible, being loved by a man like Brooks.

When sleep evaded me, I slipped out of bed and headed for the living room, closing the door softly behind me.

After settling on the sofa with a fresh cup of tea, I decided to try and sneak in some work. I would have to create a new position from scratch and get the board's approval.

The Director of Philanthropy and Corporate Communications title seemed a fitting description for the role I wanted to fill. But as quickly as the questions came to me, so did the answers. I broke out the details of the whys and hows, along with the importance of the role, sent it to Brooks to review, and then moved on to wedding planning because my mind was still in vacation mode.

I opened the photos from my iCloud and saved the one of Brooks and me from the vineyard. I was holding out my ring, and Brooks and I were kissing. I set it as my desktop background, wanting to bask in the ooey-gooey emotions the picture brought me.

"I should look for wedding planners," I muttered to myself. Google gave me a short list of available planners in my area. Most of them were in Portland or Seattle.

"Well, I need to go to Seattle anyway, so..." I had multiple tabs open for venues, wedding planners, TheKnot - you name it. Soon enough, my head spun with a thousand ideas and a mile-long to-do list.

I opened another tab and searched for venues in various parts of Oregon. I knew I already loved the one in Seattle, but was there anything closer? I didn't want all of our guests to have to travel.

"Hey, Em," Brooks called from the bedroom. I jumped from my spot on the sofa and ran back to the room.

"Hey, you okay?" I asked.

"Yeah. Just wasn't sure if you went for a run or something." He was still groggy and half asleep.

"No. Just wedding planning." I crawled over to him and kissed him.

"It's too early in the morning for that. Come back to bed."

"B, I tried. I can't."

"Come here." He pulled me to his chest. His breathing was still staggered, and his lips were pursed like he was fighting against the pull of a dream. I pulled the blankets up and settled in. He was warm, making my cold skin tingle.

"You're freezing," he grumbled when my frozen feet touched his calves. He pinned my feet between him, warming them up.

"Can we get married soon? I'm tired of waiting." His voice was sleepy, and his eyes were still closed.

"If I can find a venue and plan it, maybe this fall," I offered.

"That's so far away," he complained, making me snort. *We just got engaged.*

"Hey, what's going on with you?" I asked into his neck.

"I'm just tired." He exhaled.

"Then go back to sleep."

"I can't. I had a bad dream."

↟ ↟ ↟

I must have finally dozed off because I woke up to Brooks sliding out from under me. My eyes shot open, confused.

"Morning, love." Brooks smiled, leaning back in for a kiss. "Sorry, I didn't mean to wake you."

"It's okay, I need to get up."

"Please remind me of the timeline for today."

"Um," I sat up, trying to shake the sleepiness away. "Natalie and I have a hair appointment at one. The car will be here at four. The gala starts at six."

"So, Michaelson and I need to be ready by four?"

"Yep. What are you guys doing today?"

"I don't know. I was thinking about heading into Southport for the boat show."

I huffed, crossing my arms over my chest like a petulant child. *I want to go.* "Just don't buy one without me," I grumbled playfully.

He grinned his high-wattage, panty-melting smile. "No promises."

I rolled my eyes and laughed. There was probably a 50/50 chance he would buy one.

"Want to go grab breakfast this morning? You could invite Natalie."

"Yeah, sure. Is Michaelson up?"

"I'll find out." Brooks sat up beside me and grabbed his phone to text him while I grabbed mine to text Natalie.

"Where do you want to go?"

I looked out the window. It was a beautiful spring day now that the rain had stopped. "Uh, how about Ilona & Chambers?"

"Ilona and Chambers?"

"Yeah, it's a cafe downtown. They have good crepes."

Brooks laughed. "Okay. Ilona and Chambers, it is."

↟ ↟ ↟

Brooks' hand was tracing circles on my thigh under the table. He always seemed to be touching me in some way lately, like we could never be close enough. I appreciated the small gesture of letting me know he loved me. Everyone was looking down at their menus, but I couldn't help but notice how Michaelson and Natalie seemed to be sitting awfully close in the booth across from us. I pretended to be interested in the menu even though I knew what I wanted. *Ooh-kay, she has to spill.*

"What can we get started for you?" the waitress asked.

"Ladies first." Michaelson gestured toward Natalie.

I noticed how the young redhead blushed as she took both men in. Her eyes quickly glanced back to her notepad when she glanced my way.

We went around the table listing off our breakfast orders before she took the menus and left in a hurry. I leaned into Brooks' side, lifting a brow in curiosity as Natalie and Michaelson whispered to each other. She seemed awfully playful, with the grin playing on her lips as he nudged her with his shoulder.

"Look at them," I whispered.

"Mm-hmm. I know. Don't push, though, Em." Brooks kept his eyes on me and interlocked our fingers.

"I won't." I nudged his shoulder with mine, mocking Michaelson's flirty gesture.

Natalie caught my eyes on her, and she sat up straighter and smirked. *Caught ya.*

Breakfast was delicious. I practically inhaled my Nutella Crepes and raspberries, deciding against the limoncello pancakes I thought about ordering. Still, they were everything I had hoped for. Brooks had ordered an omelet, which I stole a few bites of as well. The melted feta and avocado on top melted in my mouth, causing me to groan.

Brooks' hand squeezed my inner thigh, and I nearly choked. The fire behind his eyes, followed by a low rumble that reverberated through me, told me everything I needed to know. I couldn't help playing with him for the rest of the meal as I let my lips linger on my fork a little too long and then licked my lips clean.

Behind his calm exterior, as he made small talk with Natalie and Michaelson, he was blazing with carnal desire. With only a few bites to go, he took matters into his own hands and ran a finger over my panties, pressing his thumb over my clit. My eyes widened, and I coughed, attempting to cover my gasp, as I felt a deep shade of red creep up my neck.

"Two can play the game, baby," he whispered into my ear, sending a fresh flame of need through me. The sound that escaped was something between a whimper and a groan.

When the check came, Brooks dropped a handful of cash and chucked his keys at Michaelson, who chuckled knowingly and dragged me out into the fresh air. To my surprise, an Uber was waiting for us. His mission was clear—beat Natalie and Michaelson home.

↟ ↟ ↟

Natalie and I climbed into my car to head to our hair appointment. My legs were still shaky from how hard Brooks buried himself in me. It was playful, fast, and deep as he devoured every inch of me. The lingering electricity of our connection sent a fresh wave of desire through me. These days, it seemed I was insatiable, and he was more than willing to deliver.

"So, how did it go at work this week? Did you give them your notice?" Natalie asked, breaking me from my thoughts of Brooks whispering dirty things in my ear.

I clicked the seatbelt in and swallowed. "Um, yeah. It was okay. It was hard, but they were all really understanding."

Mr. Whitney genuinely seemed sad to see me go, while Mr. Kavinsky encouraged me that I was making the right move. Audrey and Kate had spent a whole hour in my office with a tub of ice cream for themselves while they begged me not to leave and told me the office would be so quiet and boring without me.

"So, when do you officially start at Caston?"

I backed out of the garage and waved to Brooks, who leaned against the door frame with a sated smile. It took everything I had not to let that smile do funny things to me. Natalie was either clueless or pretending not to notice.

"I don't know yet, actually. My last day with Hope is June 10th. There was no reason for me to come in those last two days. Enough about me, though; please spill. Michaelson?"

She blushed, her face saying it all. "Yeah, yeah." She rolled her eyes, acting nonchalant. "Well, after you guys went to bed, we just stayed up talking. We talked about some hard things, some fun things, and everything in between. We talked about my diabetes and our families. I don't know, it got really flirty and...well, we almost kissed."

"Almost?" I cut her off.

"Almost. After that night, he has been texting me non-stop. I don't know, though. He's in Seattle, and I'm here." Her shoulders slumped forward.

"True, but how do you feel about him?"

"I mean, I like him. He's cute and sweet." Her smile was shy, and I could see the hesitancy and fear in them. It made me wonder who had put it there.

"Well, I don't know him enough to say anything, but I think you guys look great together. You can definitely come with us to Seattle whenever we go up. I mean, if it does go somewhere, would you ever consider moving to Seattle?"

"Possibly. I'm not against it. It's still early, but they have an amazing pediatric hospital up there. I just don't know if I can transfer."

"Well, Michaelson does make a lot of money, I'm sure he wouldn't mind."

"Emily! C'mon. I'm not that person. I don't care about the money, and I'm more like you in wanting to pave my own way. I want to work. I love my job."

"Just saying. You would have options," I teased. She laughed before turning to look out the window. "Told you he was cute."

Her reflection in the window showed a big smile across her face.

We were almost to the salon when I decided to ask the burning question that had been eating at me. Natalie and I had become fast friends, and so far, we've trusted each other with hard secrets.

"Natalie," I paused. "Did you have a serious boyfriend before?"

She looked at me, her eyes guarded, but then she relaxed. "No, not really."

"Can I ask why you're scared then? I see it in your eyes."

She sighed, leaning against the window. "I was manipulated and almost raped."

Chapter Thirty-Two

"What?" I gulped. Tears were already pricking the backs of my eyes.

"I'm okay now. It was a while ago."

We sat in the salon's parking lot, its towering brick facade shading us from the afternoon sun. I wasn't sure if she was done talking about it, and I didn't want to push, so I sat there, stunned, trying to be a stable friend.

She looked down at her nails and started picking at them before breaking the silence. "It was my junior year of high school. I had just found out about my diabetes. I mean, my life was kind of falling apart. There was a young nurse who always helped me when I came in for visits. During my hospital stay," she gulped, and I could see that she was fighting back tears. I reached across the console, wrapping her hands in mine. A single tear brimmed, streaking down her cheek.

"He was twenty-two, fresh out of med school and doing rotations. I was young and naive. My parents weren't always around, so I was often alone that week. He umm...." her voice was shaky, but she continued after a deep breath. "He flirted with me a lot, which made me feel special and important, and then he gave me his number. He had started following me on social media. I liked him a lot and trusted him more than I should have been in hindsight. When I was discharged, we texted, and he asked if I wanted to hang out. I was still out of school, and my parents were at work."

I could sense where the story was going, and I was trying really hard not to let my emotions get in the way. I squeezed her hand for reassurance. My beautiful friend was a fighter.

"Anyway, I invited him over. He brought coffee and pastries. We spent a good portion of the day on the couch making out. It felt good, but I knew deep down it was wrong. He was out of college, and I was sixteen. Anyway, we snuck around for a few months. He always pushed the boundaries, and I told him I wasn't ready. He made me feel bad about it, telling me it seemed like he loved me more than I did him. I don't know," she frowned.

"I was so desperate to feel accepted and alive...normal." She gave a slight shrug. "Anyway, like two months later, he invited me to his apartment. I told my parents I was going to hang out with a friend. They used to hover a lot, but they actually let me go. When I arrived, he was just wearing his jeans, no shirt. He handed me a mocktail, and we decided to watch a movie. I should have known."

Her fists clenched, making me release them. There was a fierce look in her eye.

"He slipped something into my drink. I was feeling so fuzzy and warm, but I think somewhere inside, there was a gut feeling, an alarm going off inside of me. I told him I needed to go to the bathroom. He tried to follow me, but I played along and told him I needed a minute. I was being a tease. Inside the bathroom, I fumbled with my phone. My vision was already blurring. I sent a quick text to my parents and Aubry with an SOS and the address. I flushed the toilet after slipping my phone into my back pocket. The door opened, and that's when everything went black."

I don't know how long we were sitting there, but I felt like I was suffocating in the car. The air around us was thick, and hot tears were streaming down my face. I had heard about date rape drugs in college, but I had never experienced them. All I could picture was a sixteen-year-old, vulnerable girl, scared in an unknown apartment with a manipulative boy who took advantage of her in a time of weakness.

"Anyway, my parents called the police on their way over. The police broke down the door, and I was unconscious on his bed. I still had my panties on, but all my clothes were on the floor." Natalie looked down at her nails again. "He was arrested. The police had me take a rape test. My parents didn't even ground me. I was in counseling for a while. So yeah," she looked up at me now. "That's why it's so hard to trust people. I know not everyone is Sam freaking Houton, but it just takes some time."

"Can I hug you?" I asked, wiping away tears and snot.

"Of course," she chuckled through her tears.

I leaned across the console, hugging her tighter than I had hugged a friend.

"I'm so sorry. Thank you for telling me," I said into the crook of her neck.

"Thanks, Em. Now," she inhaled sharply, pulling away from me with a smile. "Let's get inside."

↟ ↟ ↟

"Emily!" Natalie gasped as I returned from the closet to the master bath, where we were getting ready.

"Do you like it?" I smiled, twirling my pink satin evening gown. It was a Monique Lhuillier, all flirty yet classy. It also fit perfectly, even with my lack of curves and big boobs.

"I love it. You are absolutely gorgeous. I mean, that slit is a little daring, but Brooks won't let go of you tonight, so it won't matter." She laughed.

"Okay, your turn," I said, shoving her into my closet. We had been keeping things light all afternoon after her story. My heart broke for my friend, and I could only hope that I wasn't pushing Michaelson toward her when she wasn't ready for him.

"Knock, knock." Brooks' voice was at the bedroom door.

"Hey babe, you can come in."

I smiled as he entered the bathroom in his black tux. My eyes glided over him while my stomach did a somersault.

"Wow." I stood from the vanity to greet him.

"Em, baby," he inhaled sharply. "You look amazing." He took my hand and twirled me.

If there was one thing I would never grow tired of, it was having him admire me like I was the prettiest girl in the room.

"Thank you, you too," I whispered, wrapping my arms around him.

"You look amazing, too, Natalie," he said over my shoulder.

"Thanks, Brooks," she replied. "Not too bad yourself."

"Is the car here?" I pulled away from him.

"Yeah," he whispered, still holding tight onto my hips. His eyes were bright, full of admiration and excitement. I had always wondered what going to prom with him would have been like. To get all dressed up like this and attend a dance. This gala was our chance at that, I guess.

Natalie walked out of the front door first, toward the car where Michaelson was waiting. A large smile crossed his face when he saw her. Her dress was a mermaid fit with a black lace bodice, long sleeves, and a plunging neckline. The skirt was silk tulle that fanned out behind her. I insisted on paying for it since she was tagging along to my event. After a quippy argument, she finally conceded. But only after I snapped a photo and sent it to Michaelson. He responded with a flame emoji and the heart eyes emoji, making her blush crimson.

"Wow, Natalie," he paused, "you look beautiful." He held out his arm for her to take it.

↟ ↟ ↟

"Miss Barlow, may I have this dance?" Brooks whispered into my ear as his hands slid around my waist from behind. Warmth, safety, and excitement settled in my bones.

"I don't know, Mr. Devonshire. My dance card is awfully full. I will have to see if I can squeeze you in," I quipped, tossing a playful smile over my shoulder.

He chuckled. "Have they not seen this rock? I'm pretty sure it says that you are taken, Miss Barlow. Maybe I should have bought a bigger one." His breath was heavy on my neck, sending tingles down to my toes. I sucked in a sharp breath of air in an attempt to calm myself.

"No, it's perfect," I whispered, settling back into his embrace.

Our hips swayed back and forth with the music, but I couldn't help but relax and spin to face him. I took him in under these soft lights. His beard was thicker than when he first came to visit. His eyes were softer, more cheerful. His hair had grown out on top and now swooped back, perfectly coiffed.

His lips were still the same—soft, warm, and plushy. I leaned in for a kiss, and his tongue softly traced my lips before parting them to move into my mouth. He lifted my hand between us, clasping it tightly against his chest. My other arm was draped over his shoulder as we swayed to the music.

I would never find the right words, or even enough words, to tell him how madly in love with him I was. I would never get enough of us. He and I shared this feeling, this closeness, this irrevocable love, and our inconceivable connection. Our kiss deepened as time passed around us. The music ended, but I wasn't ready to pull away just yet. I wanted to savor every second wrapped in his arms like this. Everything faded. We were wrapped in love and solace, hope and dreams. I was his, and he was mine.

When Brooks pulled away, I was jolted back to reality, and the next song had already begun. A smile played on his lips, and he pushed me back onto the dance floor from where we had drifted.

Three songs later, we were back to swaying to Make You Feel My Love by Adele. My head rested on his shoulder.

"I love you," I whispered.

He pressed his lips to my forehead for a long kiss. "Love you too, Em. Always."

"Hey guys," Natalie said excitedly as she approached us. Her hand was linked in Michaelson's. Brooks and I hid our amusement, but I couldn't help but feel more protective of her now.

"Hey! Where have you been?" I asked.

"We were just, er, talking." She smiled, blushing. *Talking? Right.* Michaelson's hair wasn't as tamed as it was when we had left, and if I wasn't mistaken, his lips were also a rosier shade. Natalie's guilty smile and flushed complexion confirmed everything I suspected.

"Well, if Michaelson won't ask you..." Brooks looked over to Michaelson and then back to Natalie. "May I have this dance?"

Natalie giggled and then looked over to me to make sure it was okay. I nodded, loving how he treated people, especially his friends.

"In that case," Michaelson spoke up. "Emily?" I smiled and grabbed his hand as he twirled me back into the crowd. I was thankful it was a fast, playful song. Michaelson was actually really good at dancing, and we both seemed to have a playful side. We broke apart to dance wildly to the music, which was completely opposite to the style of music.

We looked like we belonged at a concert, jumping and twirling to some rock band, not Marvin Gaye. The band seemed to take notice and quickened the pace before switching the music to something more upbeat. Brooks and Natalie made their way over to us and broke apart, joining in our playful dance.

↟ ↟ ↟

June brought warm weather and longer summer nights. I was finishing up my time at Hope. At the same time, Brooks left with Michaelson early Monday morning for Seattle for meetings and a last-minute fundraiser that I didn't want to attend. There would be too many questions about Caston and our engagement.

We had already done an exclusive interview with Forbes to discuss our engagement, plans for Caston, and our parents.

Natalie stayed the weekend at our place while Michaelson was in town. They seemed to be getting along great, and we even caught them snuggling up to each other on the couch. She was at work today, and I was alone at home finishing my day out on the deck, enjoying the view that sold me the house.

This morning, I emailed Diane Anderson, our Chief Administrative Officer, about my ideas for Caston and when I wanted to start. Of course, she responded with a lot more than her approval of my ideas. Her email was full of excitement for me starting the following week.

I would work part-time while we figured out my new position, which I was completely okay with. I had a wedding to plan. She also sent along her congratulations on our engagement.

I had been working all week with Audrey on the ins and outs of my job. She knew most of it. She was the perfect person for this position. She was sad I was leaving, but she, too, showed unending support for my move to Caston. She was also overly excited about my engagement and made me promise to invite her to the wedding.

I closed my laptop and shoved it off my lap to the seat beside me. Brooks would be home tomorrow and I really wanted to finish the study. Brooks has never complained about the decor, but I thought it was only fair if he at least had one space that was truly his.

After he left Monday, I had the wild idea to make the study more of a man cave. I hired a painter to change the mood of the room with dark charcoal and navy walls. I replaced the lighter furniture with several leather pieces and changed the decor to dark, simple, Asian-inspired pieces. I even found an older, tattered American flag that I hung above his new desk. A brand new Chesterfield sat at the center of the room with a live-edge driftwood coffee table.

I pulled some of the books out of the shelving and replaced a section of the bookcase with a minibar full of new whiskey, scotch, and gins. I ordered a new chair, which just arrived and that I still needed to put together. My nerves were getting the best of me, leaving me with a stomach in free fall and a buzz that made me feel like I needed to run. I prayed he liked it.

↟ ↟ ↟

"Hey, baby," he sighed, pulling me closer and relaxing.

"Hi, love." I pressed my lips into his. His tongue grazed my bottom lip, causing me to smile and pull away. I was too excited to get distracted from showing him the new study. "C'mon, I have a surprise for you." I spun, pulling him out of the entry.

"What?" he chuckled. I pushed the doors open and walked into the new study. His eyes danced around the room, and a huge smile appeared.

"How?" he chuckled excitedly.

"Well, since this is your home, too, I thought you needed a space that was just yours."

He rolled his eyes, turning his gaze to me. "Em, you didn't have to."

"I know, but I wanted to." He smiled softly and pulled me closer for another quick kiss.

"This is amazing. Thank you." His lips turned up against mine. He pulled away again to take it all in. He first went to the mini bar and turned to me with a large grin. "How did you know what I like?"

"I feel insulted." I dramatically grabbed my chest before laughing. "I called Michaelson. He said the Macallan and Balvenie were a must. He said you liked Hendricks over Bombay, but I grabbed both just in case."

He shook his head gleefully and moved across the room to the sideboard below his framed Air Force photos, his ribbons, and a custom Air Force symbol wall piece. His fingers clung to the blue iron Air Force piece and then to the flag.

He sighed and turned to face me. He was quiet. The look in his eyes was unreadable, and I worried that maybe I had crossed a line.

"Thank you," he whispered. I melted, seeing the genuine smile on his face. I didn't realize how much it would mean to him to show my support for his service. We never talked about it because it was a painful period in our relationship, and I had always blamed his time in the military as the reason for our breakup. Truth is, I couldn't be more proud of him. I was grateful he was willing to leave the comfort of home and money to join the military.

Growing up in the PNW, there wasn't a lot of support for our troops, like towns in the Midwest. If anything, more people found reasons to hate our government and military. That wasn't how our parents had raised us, though. We were raised with an appreciation for our troops and their sacrifices. Brooks wasn't born in the States. He was born in Perth, Australia, but his parents had moved here when he was a baby, so this country is all he's known. His parents were grateful to live in America.

"I've never told you this," I started as I slid into the leather sofa. "But I wasn't angry with you the day you signed."

Brooks looked at me, confused.

"Okay, maybe I was mad at your decision, but I was really proud of you." Tears began to well up in my eyes. "I knew what that would mean; I knew the sacrifices you were making, and honestly, I fell even more in love with you. I was just already in so much pain from the distance that I let my anger get in the way of telling you. I was proud of you, Brooks. Still am."

He nodded before coming to kneel in front of me. I could see the tears building behind his own eyes. He laid his head on my lap and wrapped his arms around my back. My fingers brushed through his hair. He didn't need to respond with words. I could feel the rising and falling of his chest against my legs as he fought against the tears. I looked up at the space on the wall dedicated to his service and smiled. *I am really proud of you.*

↟ ↟ ↟

We enjoyed dinner out on the deck, talking about work when Brooks cleared his throat.

"I didn't bring this up before," he paused, looking past me. "Something is going on at Caston. I don't know what yet, but something isn't right."

My heart lurched itself into my throat. "What do you mean?"

"Something is off. I can feel it, but I'm just now digging into it. I'm not experienced with running a multibillion-dollar corporation, but the money doesn't make sense. I can't talk to Paul about it because, as the CFO, he should have noticed. Rebecca and Ethan are also too high up. I don't know what to do." He ran his hand through his hair.

"Well, how do you know?"

"Paul had me going through our finances with him and reviewing the documents for the past few months. I didn't say anything then, but I need to take more time to analyze it. Odd transactions, missing invoices, complaints from vendors about never getting paid. There are a lot of expenses that just don't add up. Just don't say anything to anyone, okay? This stays between us and Michaelson only because I have him pulling invoices and documents for me."

"Okay," I shuddered. The idea that someone was stealing from our company, our parent's company, made me sick. Most of the executive team had been around since before our parents died and were family to us.

Ethan, our COO, was my dad's golfing partner when James couldn't make it. Rebecca, our CIO, was brought on just a month before the accident, but the little I knew of her was that she was a sweet, down-to-earth mom who also happened to be kick-ass at her job.

I stared back out at the ocean as Brooks took his last bite.

"Dance with me?" Brooks asked, pulling me from my thoughts. Etta James's crooning voice was playing over the speakers.

"Okay." I set my empty plate on his and took his hand. He led us out of the sitting area to the open space behind the sofa. His warm hands pulled me into his chest as he swayed.

"I like dancing with you," I said, letting his warmth envelop me.

I got nothing in response but a low hum. We stayed wrapped together, listening to Etta James and the slow roar of the ocean slapping against the rocks.

Chapter Thirty-Three

"Hey, babe. I'm home," I yelled as I opened the front door to our little studio. It was Saturday, so I knew he wasn't working, but I heard no reply. I left the studio and headed up to the main house, assuming he was probably in his study.

When I walked in through the door, I found him in the kitchen with music playing. Brooks appeared with a glass of wine.

"Hey, love." He smiled, handing me the glass and planting a big kiss on my cheek.

"What's this?" I smiled back, loving how my heart pitter-pattered at the mere sight of him.

"I'm making dinner tonight, and then we are headed down to the water to watch the sunset." A ridiculous grin crossed my face.

"Really? Thank you. Do you need help?" My heart swelled and felt like it was trying to break free of my chest.

Brooks shook his head and returned to the stove with me trailing behind. I inhaled the smell of the chicken and pasta. He was a natural, bouncing around the kitchen entirely in the zone. Honestly, it was sexy.

"How was your day?" I asked as I slid my hand down his arm. He smiled at me over his shoulder. My hand wrapped around his waist as I leaned through his arm, sticking my finger in the sauce to taste it.

"Hey, now. Hands off until I am done." He laughed, swatting my hand away. "It was good. Just went to the gym and got some work done. How was your day with the girls?"

I took a sip of my wine and sat down on the barstool. Natalie had tried to keep her lips sealed about Michaelson the majority of the time until I prodded. Leah dominated the conversation about how she and Peter had been in a massive fight about his parents continually asking for grandbabies. Monica supplied us with all the fresh gossip in town.

"It was great. Natalie and Michaelson seem to be doing well. I guess they've been FaceTiming quite a bit."

"Really? Huh. I hope he doesn't break her heart."

"Yeah, me too." I sipped my wine again, eyeing Brooks, who hummed to the music while he drained the pasta. "You look sexy in the kitchen, you know," I said with a grin. Brooks smirked, still mouthing the words to the song as he tossed the pasta in the bowl with the chicken.

The music changed, and he began humming the new tune and singing along with All of Me by John Legend. I rested my chin on my fist and tried not to giggle. He walked over to me with his face only inches away from mine and continued singing, gesturing with his hands, then pressed his lips to my hair.

I laughed now, pushing his face away. Brooks pulled my wine glass out of my hand and set it on the counter, pulling me out of the barstool into his arms.

We were swaying to the music, Brooks singing the lyrics to me, directly to my soul. Word by word, etching promises into the fabric of *us*. I was melting as tears pricked the back of my eyes. We were as I always pictured we would be, as I'd hoped.

He stopped swaying, noticing my tears, and paused, lifting my chin. His voice turned to a whisper while he continued to sing. Whispering lyrics about giving all of himself to me had me wanting to wrap myself around him and cry into his neck. I knew the song well, but having my fiancé sing it was a completely different experience.

I melted further into him. A sense of peace flooded me as we swayed, body to body, knowing with my whole heart that Brooks Devonshire was my beginning, middle, and end, and I wouldn't have it any other way.

The music continued to play as our lips finally met, locking onto each other. Our bodies continued to sway with the rhythm. We kissed slowly, enjoying only this moment and letting all the hurt from the past and fear of the future fade away.

When we finally separated, he began to hum again, swaying with me in his arms. The music changed again, and Brooks released his grasp. I wiped my drying tears, stepping back, my eyes still locked with his.

"God, I love you so dang much," I cooed. Brooks leaned in for another peck.

"I love you, Em." He took a deep breath, breathing me in. His thumbs swiped away the tears. "Okay, dinner," he reminded himself and pulled away, returning to the stove.

↟ ↟ ↟

Outside, the air was warm even though the sun was starting to fall on the horizon. I laid out a big picnic blanket with a few throw pillows and brought a basket of all the necessities down. While I unloaded the basket of silverware and napkins, Brooks sat down with the two pasta bowls.

"This is nice," I said, resting my chin on his shoulder.

"Yeah," he agreed, turning to kiss me. I sighed as I reached for my bowl. We sat in silence, listening to the rushing sound of the waves as the sky turned bright pink and orange. I practically inhaled my dinner, not realizing how hungry I actually was. I had skipped lunch today.

"So, I was thinking," I started as I set my empty bowl down.

"Uh-oh," Brooks teased.

"Shut up." I giggled, pushing his shoulder away from me. "Anyway," I exaggerated. "I was thinking we should hire a wedding planner in Portland. I don't think I want the wedding to be in Seattle. I don't want most of our guests to worry about traveling. But, anyone we invite from work can just come down on the jet."

"Yeah, sounds good." He swallowed his last bite. "When do you want to have the wedding?"

"I am still thinking about fall, or maybe August? I don't know. I'm not in a hurry, but I have waited long enough to marry you, so best to get on with it," I laughed.

Brooks leaned back on his elbows and gazed up at me.

"We could just run away to Vegas," he offered, sounding completely serious, but I could see the slight twitch of his mouth as he fought back a laugh. I looked down at him and lifted my brow before he burst into laughter. "Just kidding, Em. I know you want a real wedding. I do, too. I just want to marry you." He kissed my thigh.

My lips curled into a smile while I began to think about the most ridiculous wedding ceremonies to test him. "What about elephants or saying our vows while skydiving? Ooh, we can get married underwater. I heard it's a new thing." I couldn't fight back my own laughter. I never could make a joke without laughing before the end of it.

Brooks laughed as he rolled over on top of me, tickling me as I screeched, falling back onto the pillows.

"Underwater, huh?" he asked teasingly. His eyes deepened into mine. He leaned in for a kiss, but I shoved his face away with my sandy hand. My laughter dropped into a full belly laugh. His face had a sandy imprint on it.

"Okay," he said as he smiled, lifting off of me. I rolled over and tried to run, but he grabbed me from behind. "You're going to pay for that," he warned as he pulled me into the water.

I couldn't help but squeal as the waves crashed into me, Brooks still holding onto me. After another wave, he let go of me and dropped me into the water. When I resurfaced, I erupted into laughter again, wiping my wet hair out of my eyes. I reached for Brooks, wiping the sand off his cheek.

He was grinning ear to ear when another wave hit us, knocking me into him and pushing us under the water and into the sand. When the wave pulled back, he grabbed my face and kissed me as another wave slammed into us, pulling us apart.

The sun dropped below the horizon, changing the sky to a dark gray. Brooks grabbed my hand and pulled me out of the water. Our clothes were heavy against our bodies when we reached the picnic blanket. Brooks chuckled, looking over at me as we gathered the blanket and dishes.

"You still want an underwater wedding?"

"I think I might have changed my mind," I said, wiping water and sand from my face. My hair was stuck to my face, and the saltwater had me chafing against my bra and cotton sundress.

"C'mon, race you to the house." He grabbed the dishes and pillows and ran toward the house.

I gathered up the blanket and remaining pillows and followed behind him, one thing on my mind.

Chapter Thirty-Four

My dreams were relentless and kept pulling me in deeper and deeper. Subconsciously, I knew it was time to get up, but I couldn't fight the urge to stay and see how the dream played out. Brooks and I were walking in a city, and the weather was so warm that it was almost suffocating. It definitely was not Seattle or Portland. The air felt thick, like when you open the dryer halfway through the cycle, and you're hit with hot, humid air. We continued walking and laughing until we reached a park filled with families and screaming kids.

Why are we here? It wasn't until Brooks stopped walking and bent down that I noticed he had been pushing a stroller. As he stood up, a beautiful brown-haired little boy who looked just like Brooks was in his arms, reaching for me. I reached for the baby, who snuggled into me. I knew this baby. He was mine.

I looked back to Brooks, who was smiling. The little boy pushed away from me, and naturally, it was like I knew what he wanted. I set him on the ground, and he ran toward the playground. Brooks followed him, pretending to chase him. The little boy squealed and giggled as Brooks caught him, tickling him.

Hot tears streamed down my face. My heart felt like it would burst as I watched them playfully wrestling in the grass. I felt the urge to yell, "Be careful," but as I did, I was jolted awake into my empty bedroom. I looked around, confused, as a tear slid down my face. My heart pounded as I tried to separate the dream from reality. It felt so real that I wanted to cry, but I couldn't figure out why.

Brooks would be home today from his short trip back to Seattle. I reached over for my phone: 8:52. *Crap!* I sat up quickly and wiped my eyes, still fighting the urge to curl into a ball and sob. My meeting with our C-level was at nine-thirty, and I needed to pull myself together.

↟ ↟ ↟

The Zoom link was easy to find in my email, and I joined the meeting just in time. Diane was already waiting, along with three others: Ethan, our COO; Thomas, our Vice President; Rebecca, our CIO; and Carol, our head of HR.

"Hi, Emily. How are you?"

"Yeah, good," I replied breathlessly as I sat on the couch.

"So, let's talk about your visit. I thought we could do a quick run-through of what meetings we want you to attend and what meetings we've set up for you to pitch your ideas to the team. First, though, let me see the ring," Diane said.

I laughed as I lifted my finger to the camera. I had known Diane since middle school. My parents hired her shortly after I finished fifth grade; she has worked at Caston ever since. She felt like an extended family member.

"Emily, that's beautiful. He did so good. Wow. Okay, so let's get started. We have you guys flying in on Monday..."

The executives were excited to have me join them and expressed their willingness to help Brooks and me.

I stifled another yawn as the meeting came to an end. I wasn't usually this tired by mid-morning. My sleep quality without Brooks was never as good as it was with him by my side. Or maybe it was the odd dream from this morning. The sun's warm rays shone through the window, brightening the room.

I should run and get some vitamin D. That will help with my energy level. It didn't sound as enjoyable as it would on a typical day. Still, reluctantly, I slipped on my running shoes and headed outside, determined to turn the day around.

Thirty minutes later, I slowed my run to a walk as I entered the long driveway. My legs were so heavy, a clear sign that I was not up for a run. I still couldn't shake the feeling from my dream this morning. I checked my watch. Brooks would be landing in two hours, and that reminder comforted me.

I pulled my phone out as I walked up the driveway, which suddenly felt forever long. I groaned, ready to be off my feet. I could feel the urge to cry again. Confused by my emotional state, I clicked on Brooks' phone icon, and thankfully, he answered on the first ring.

"Hey, love. About to leave work. What's up?"

"I don't know. Just needed to hear your voice," I sniffled into the phone.

"Are you okay?" he asked, sounding concerned.

"Yeah. Just in a weird mood today. I'm just feeling emotional."

"Well, we can curl up on the couch later, watch something, or maybe go down to the pier for ice cream. Whatever you want."

"Yeah, we'll see, I've been so tired today. Are you headed to the airport?"

"Yep. Just need to swing by Michaelson's and grab my bag."

"Will you still be home at one?" I asked.

"Should be. Why?"

"I don't know. Just my emotions talking. Ignore me," I sighed.

He chuckled. "Okay. Well, I will see you soon, okay?"

"Yeah, love you. Fly safe."

"Love you."

The phone clicked, and I dropped it to my side as I continued toward the house. I kicked off my shoes before making my way to the fridge. "Smoothie, smoothie," I mumbled while pulling out the ingredients. On second thought, the chicken pasta from the weekend was still in the fridge.

I pulled it out with the yogurt and ate it while the smoothie swirled in the blender. I yawned while taking another bite of the pasta. When the blender stopped, I poured my smoothie into a cup and wandered outside to the deck.

The sun was warm, and a nice breeze was blowing in from the ocean. I lay back on the sofa and closed my eyes, enjoying the serenity around me. The sound of the waves calmed me as my thoughts drifted to Brooks.

I still wasn't sure how fate had managed to bring us back together. I could feel the tears running down the side of my temples. I allowed my emotions to flood me, and I was suddenly sobbing over nothing. I hugged the pillow and cried myself into a good nap.

"Hey, Em," Brooks whispered, brushing my hair back.

I groaned as I lifted out of my warm nap. I sat up and looked around, finding Brooks kneeling before me. My hair was stuck to the sides of my face where the tears from earlier had dried.

"Baby, hey, are you okay?"

I started crying again. His arms wrapped around me, pulling me into his shoulder. He smelled like home. I hated him leaving and that Pacific Coves was too far from Seattle to be a small commute.

"Hey, hey. Shhh. Why are you crying?"

"I don't know. I missed you. I'm glad you're home," I hiccuped.

Brooks chuckled. "Love, I was gone for two nights."

I nodded into his chest. I knew it was ridiculous, but I missed him. "I just miss you and love you so much." I looked up at him as he wiped my tears with his thumbs.

Confusion swept across his face. "I love you, too." I huffed, trying to regain control of my emotions. My smoothie was now a melted cup of mush, sitting on the table's edge. For some reason, that got me crying again and made me feel ridiculous, but I really wanted that smoothie. Brooks sat in silence with me as I sobbed, soaking his clean shirt with my tears and snot. Once I cried long enough for us both to start to question my sanity, I sat up, determined to stop crying and welcome home my fiance the proper way.

"I'm okay. Sorry." I exhaled, wiping away my tears. Brooks looked at me and then down at his shirt.

"What's going on?"

"I don't know." I did know, though. That dream was getting to me.

"Em?"

"It's nothing. It was just a dream."

"About our parents?"

"No," I mumbled, placing my hand on his thigh. I sat up quickly and launched forward for his lips, needing to feel close to him. He slowly wrapped his arms around me in confusion as I kissed him frantically, trying to drown out all the waves of emotions. His arms rested on my lower back as he kissed me lightly before pulling away.

"Hey, what was your dream?"

I rolled my eyes, annoyed he wouldn't drop it, but also because I couldn't get over it.

"It was about a baby. I think it was our baby. I don't know. I am just really confused. It felt so real." I shook my head in confusion, trying to clear the fog from my brain.

"So why are you crying?"

"I don't know," I whined. I could feel the tears brimming again. "Because I love him." They splashed down onto my cheeks.

Brooks chuckled, confused. "Emily, you're crying because you love our baby from your dream?"

I inhaled. *Yep. I've gone crazy.* I nodded.

"I know it sounds ridiculous, but I don't know. I just want to return to my dream, hug and tell him I love him. I didn't get to in my dream."

"Well, I'm sure you will have plenty of chances to tell our baby that you love him or her. Do you want kids right away?"he asked curiously.

"No, I don't think so. I don't know. I mean, I guess I have been so caught up in us that I haven't even thought about kids. I know we talked about them jokingly in school, but -" I trailed off.

"I want babies with you, sweetie. You just say when, and we will try, okay?"

I nodded, wiping away the last tear that halted on my cheekbone. "What changed?" I sniffled.

"You agreeing to spend forever with me, and me realizing it doesn't matter when. Now or ten years from now, I just want to have them with you." More hot tears raced down my cheeks while I melted inside.

"C'mon, let's go inside. I will clean up the mess in the kitchen, and you can find something for us to watch. We can just order dinner, okay?"

"Sorry, I must have been distracted. I guess I was really looking forward to my smoothie." I burst into laughter as I lifted my cup off the table. Brooks chuckled.

"It's okay. I got it. Go find us something to watch."

"Okay." I put the cup down and turned back to him, planting my lips into his. Now, I just needed to get my emotions under control and decide when I wanted to start trying for a baby. I didn't want one right away, *did I?*

Chapter Thirty-Five

We stood on the step in the living room, surrounded by our friends. Even Michaelson had driven down to be here. We had told everyone we were just throwing a party but didn't say why. I was standing beside Brooks who was chatting to Michaelson about something probably sports-related. Natalie stood beside me, and I couldn't stop fidgeting with my white sequined dress.

"Stop, Emily," she whispered, swatting my hand.

"It's itchy," I complained. It wasn't just the dress, though. The whole room was hot and uncomfortable, and my stomach was doing some crazy dance routine that had me struggling to calm the waves of nausea.

She chuckled. "You look amazing. You are glowing. Just stop messing with the dress. Also, Grey just walked in. Did you invite him?"

"Yes," I whispered annoyedly. "Brooks said it was fine. He's my friend."

"You invited your almost-ex to your engagement party?" We were whisper shouting at each other now.

"Almost-ex is not a title."

Natalie rolled her eyes as she slapped my hand away from the hemline I was picking at and nodded to Brooks.

Brooks cleared his throat. "Can I have everyone's attention?" he called out in a loud voice. The room grew quiet as everyone turned to face us. I looked over at Brooks and sighed in relief, thankful we were getting on with the show, before I picked my entire dress apart.

He glanced down at me and smiled before returning his gaze to the crowd of friends.

"We are engaged!" he said with excitement. Our friends started to clap and cheer. Brooks continued as the crowd grew quiet again, "She said yes to forever with me. Not many of you know our story, so I will make it quick and give you the cliff notes." A few people chuckled.

"I met Emily when I was four years old. We had just moved to the neighborhood, and it was a typical Seattle day - raining." The crowd chuckled again quietly. "Emily lived in the house next to ours at the end of the street. I was looking out the window in my new room when I saw her. There she was, just this little girl in a pink dress with a teddy bear wrapped in her arms, dancing in the rain. I instantly loved her." Brooks squeezed my hand and continued.

"We became fast friends and spent everyday together at school and after. Our parents eventually became friends and business partners, which made it that much easier to spend every single moment with her. We both attended the same private school, so from waking up to sleep, we were always together. My love for her grew daily, and we navigated all stages of life together. We learned to rely on each other.

"We would come to PC for ice cream at Evie's or head down to Harbor Point Beach. Our parents always traveled for work together, so Emily and I only had each other. You could have guessed we were siblings if we didn't love each other romantically." The crowd chuckled again. Warmth settled across my chest. Hearing his version of our childhood made it more magical.

"Our sophomore year of high school," he paused, looking down at me and took a deep breath. The warmth was gone, replaced with the cold reminder of our grief. "Our parents were coming home from a trip and were in a fatal car accident. In a matter of hours, our lives were ripped apart. Emily stayed home with her nanny and other staff members, and I was sent to boarding school in Europe.

"My parents hadn't updated their will, and therefore, I was under the guardianship of my uncle. He never intended to have kids and didn't know the first thing about raising a teenage boy, so he had me sent away. Emily and I spoke every day." His voice was a little rough as he tried to retell the story. I squeezed his hand and rested my head on his bicep.

"After high school, I had originally planned to move home, but I was an angry teenager. When I was released from my uncle's grasp, I felt like I needed to burn off some anger and, quite frankly, grow up. I enlisted in the Air Force and spent the next four years traveling across the world. Emily was left at home in Seattle, and our plans to go to college together were taken away. About seven months into my service, we split. The time away was hard enough, and I had just extended it four years." My heart squeezed at the pain in his voice and the reminder of the agony I felt not having him by my side.

"About six months ago, I was done with my service and ready to come home. I was ready to step in at our company and run it alongside Emily until I realized she wanted to sell so she didn't have to put up with me." A few light-hearted chuckles came from the crowd, bringing more oxygen back into the room.

"I came here to see her and to apologize. I hadn't seen her in seven years. I initially blamed my reason for visiting on work, but really, I needed to apologize in person and try to win her back. I still loved her and realized in our time away that she was the one, the only one." A few tears escaped my eyes. Brooks looked at me and offered a smile of gratitude.

"It had been a long time since I held her close, and returning to her arms felt like coming home. I couldn't be happier that she has agreed to be my wife, and I am so thankful I get to wake up next to her every day." Brooks leaned over and kissed me. I wanted to hold it longer, but he pulled away.

"So, a toast to the most beautiful, amazing, selfless, funniest, and kindest best friend and future wife a man could wish for. To Emily." He raised his glass and returned to my lips to finish the kiss. My whole body melted into him.

The crowd around me clapped and clinked glasses before sipping on the champagne. I could feel all the attention warm on my cheeks. I looked back at Natalie's smiling and teary-eyed face and quickly scanned the crowd. The women were still wiping tears from their eyes as I snuggled into Brooks' side.

Everything seemed to mute as I relaxed into his chest. It was almost as if I was breathing out a sigh of relief that I had been holding in all these years. I had never shared our story with anyone aside from Natalie and Sara. I hadn't been ready to share it, but now, with Brooks, I was prepared to move forward. Ready to write the next chapter of our lives.

"I knew it!" Sara screeched into my ear.

I turned and hugged the familiar voice. "You're here!"

"Of course. Congrats. Finally!"

I laughed. "Thank you."

"Let me see the ring," she squealed. I lifted my hand, my three-carat diamond twinkling.

She took my hand. "Why do I feel like I will do this all night?"

"Because everyone loves pretty rings," she replied.

I turned to Brooks, gesturing back to my friend. "This is Sara, my college roommate."

"Yeah, I know who she is." He reached around to give her a quick hug.

"Nice to finally meet you in person." She blushed, pulling away from him. I pressed my lips into a firm line to keep from giggling.

"Yeah, same," he responded.

Peter and Leah walked up. "Congrats, man." Peter threw his arm over Brooks, slapping his back.

"I'll let you go. Come find me later," Sara whispered before stepping away so we could greet the rest of our guests waiting for us.

↟ ↟ ↟

The party dwindled as the moon settled over the ocean and the cool nightly breeze rolled in. Brooks had been caught up in a conversation with some of the men from town out on the deck.

"Congrats, Emily." I would recognize that husky voice anywhere. I turned to see Grey standing a few feet behind me.

"Hey, thanks for coming." I reached over to hug him stiffly.

"I'm happy for you. It sounds like you guys have a lot of history together, and I'm glad it worked out. There's definitely no way I could have competed with that."

I laughed nervously. He wasn't wrong, but I decided not to comment on it. My stomach turned, and I was instantly fighting back the vomit rising in my throat. I had been nauseous all day, and now it was ready to leave my body. I smiled awkwardly at Grey, trying to think of a way to excuse myself without sounding like I was running from him.

"Well, I'm actually headed out. Good seeing you. Congrats again," he said before kissing my cheek and heading for the door.

A group of ladies made their way over to me before I could escape; I really needed to lie down. I looked around the room for Brooks or Natalie. Even Sara would be helpful.

"So let us see the ring," Jaymi cooed. I held out my hand for what felt like the hundredth time.

"Wow. How big is that rock?" one of the girls from my cycling class asked, her voice coming out louder than the crowd in the room.

I blushed, pulling my hand back to my side.

"How's class been? I haven't been in a few weeks," I asked, rapidly changing the subject.

"It's been so good. We definitely miss you," Penny, another girl from class, said.

"Hey, did you catch Winter's class last week?" Jaymi's voice faded into the distance as I focused on the queasiness of my stomach.

Brooks' arms wrapped around me from behind, instantly comforting me and holding back the vomit that was about to explode from me. I sighed, melting into his warm embrace, and closed my eyes, resting my head on his chest.

"You ready to go? You don't look well." My heart swelled with his attentiveness. It was almost like he always had a beacon on me, sometimes knowing what I needed before I did. I nodded slowly. I turned back to the girls, who all looked at us with envy.

"Excuse us, ladies," Brooks said as he guided me out of the group, out of the house, and down to our studio.

"I just need to sleep," I groaned as I crawled into bed.

"Okay," he replied before he kissed my head, running his hand along my side. "I'm going to have to buy more shirts at this rate if you're sleeping in them every night."

I smiled. "I mostly wear the ones you take off. They smell like you."

He chuckled. "I like them better on you anyway. Can I get you anything?"

I stretched out my arms, finding his hands and wrapping mine up in them.

"No, I'm okay. You should go back to the party. I'll be okay. Give my apologies."

"Sure," he whispered before standing up and planting a kiss on my temple. He paused at the door. "I love you, future Mrs. Devonshire."

I couldn't help but smile. "I love you too, B."

"Be back soon. Text me if you need me."

I nodded, closed my eyes, and pulled the duvet and extra blankets under my chin. The lights dimmed overhead, and I heard him place a glass on the nightstand before he left the house again.

A moment later, I was racing for the bathroom. I emptied my stomach into the toilet, my thoughts racing about the food and drinks I consumed today.

↟ ↟ ↟

The movie credits rolled when Brooks stood up from the couch to stretch.

"I need more coffee. Can I grab you something? I think you should eat, Em."

I agreed to toast as I reached for the remote, ready to search for a new movie. I stretched my arms and neck and glanced out to the pool where a storm was brewing. I turned back to the TV and scrolled through my saved list.

When the next movie ended, I had forgotten all about my stomach. I was lying against Brooks' chest, completely smitten with the movie and in love with the soundtrack of the romance we had just watched.

Brooks left to take our dishes upstairs and make me some eggs, leaving me alone to rest. I grabbed the remote and shut off the TV. I was exhausted and just needed a few minutes to close my eyes. I laid back on the pillow and curled into the large, plush blanket. My stomach decided to twirl again, leaving me running for the bathroom.

As soon as I reached the toilet, everything came up and kept coming. I thought I was going to die of suffocation since I couldn't catch my breath between violent heaves. Once I felt a break, I moved to the sink and rinsed my mouth. I slid down to my knees and draped my arm over the bowl, thankful the next round of churning in my stomach was just that. Whatever this was, I was ready for it to be over. I just wanted to eat and sleep in peace.

Don't die in this pathetic state. The obituary will read: died on the bathroom floor with head in the toilet. She suffocated from puking. I don't know why, but whenever I got sick, which was rare, I always thought about Brooks' mom, Carrie. She would be the first to bring over a basket of all the things that would make me feel better. Movies, sprite, ginger ale, saltine crackers, peppermint tea, gum, and almost always, a new stuffed animal.

When I graduated from high school, my room had about twenty stuffed animals from her, just from my sick days. I donated all but one to the local shelter. I kept my jellyfish, though. I don't know why, but that one was my favorite.

We were at the Monterey Bay Aquarium when I puked all over the floor of the Kelp Forest exhibit. My parents rushed me back to the hotel even though we hadn't made our way out to the Open Sea area to see the jellyfish. I ensured that before we left, they would let Brooks complete the tour without me so he could take pictures of all the animals I missed.

When Brooks returned to the hotel, he slid into bed with me to show me all the pictures. I laughed when I saw the one with him in front of the jellyfish tank. They were like black shadows with long, creepy tentacles against the glowing blue water. He had already picked out an animal for me, a jellyfish, and had it in the photo, pretending to suck his head in. The long tentacles on the stuffed animal wrapped around his face and down his shoulders. He had the craziest face.

Brooks handed me the jellyfish and then attacked my face with it. We were only nine. Of course, Carrie came in right at that exact moment and tried to kick him out for attacking me. I came to his defense and pleaded with her to let him stay. She agreed that as long as we promised to relax and watch a movie, he could stay until I felt better.

"Em?" Brooks knocked on the bathroom door as he entered. I groaned, unable to move. "C'mon," he said as he lifted me up off the floor and pulled me to my feet.

"I guess I'm not feeling better," I sighed.

"Maybe you should try to eat."

"Ugh, okay." I turned for the sink to rinse out my mouth again. "I hate puking."

"I know. C'mon, let's get you to the couch."

I picked at the plate of scrambled eggs, unwilling to lift any to my mouth. I could hardly breathe in the smell of them without wanting to puke. It hit me like a ton of bricks. *How could I not see it?* I searched frantically for my phone.

"Hey, you okay?" Brooks asked, sitting up to my side.

"I need my phone."

"It's right here," he said as he handed it to me. *Please no. Please no. Please be wrong. This can't be happening. It's too soon.*

I hastily opened my period app. 10 Days Late. Would You Like To Record?

Chapter Thirty-Six

Panic set in as the room spun, and my stomach somersaulted for a whole new reason. My chest heaved with short gasps as I stood quickly, needing to brace myself against the side of the couch. I had rescheduled my appointment again to get on birth control for next week. The air in the room was heavy and my thoughts became jumbled from lack of oxygen.

"Emily? What's wrong? Are you going to be sick?"

"Mm-hmm," I hummed. *Just wait. Don't panic. Take a test.* I could be late because of stress. I've never been late though. But maybe this time, it's different. Maybe I have the stomach flu, and it's caused my cycle to be late. Is that a thing,? I couldn't be pregnant. My thoughts were everywhere all at once.

I tried to calm my racing heart and take a long, staggered breath as I sat back on the couch. I chanced a sideways glance towards Brooks, who was watching me. My only thoughts were on how and where to buy a test.

"Sweetie, are you okay?"

"Fine," I lied, still feeling stunned. Brooks stared back at me, looking skeptical, but I gave him a tight smile and then faced forward, pulling the blanket over me.

"Do you want to watch another movie?"

"Yeah, sure." I curled up onto his chest so he couldn't see my face. I wanted to cry. I wanted to scream. Of course, I wanted babies, but *after* my wedding. I groaned inwardly as the weight of my choices crashed in on me.

"What do you want to watch?"

"Anything. Just pick something," I mumbled.

Brooks clicked play on some random rom-com I had saved in my list. Just a few days ago, I longed to hold my dream baby, and now I was sitting here with the reality that soon, I would be. I closed my eyes and focused on calming my breathing. As the movie played, I reminded myself to focus on what I could control. At this point, there was nothing I could do until a test confirmed what I already suspected - I was pregnant.

↟ ↟ ↟

It was Wednesday morning, and three days had passed since I realized I was more than a few days late for my cycle. The sun was barely cresting the horizon when I slid out of bed. I still hadn't explained to Brooks why I was acting so strange. I wanted to wait until I was sure. There was no need for us both to be a nervous wreck.

I slid into the bathroom, trying not to wake Brooks, quietly unwrapped the foil wrapper, and took out the test. I had hidden it in a pile of towels on the shelf, knowing today would be the day. Part of me felt terrible hiding something like this from him, but the other part of me had to do this alone. I needed to be sure.

Slipping away to the pharmacy had been a task in itself. Brooks was happy to go for me, but I assured him I was okay and just needed to get out of the house.

As I sat down with the test, I noticed my hands were shaking. This wasn't how I pictured this going.

Brooks only proposed a month ago, and now suddenly, I just wanted more time—more time to be young and in love. I wasn't ready to be a mom.

I closed my eyes and peed on the stick. When I finished, I washed my hands while the timer flashed on the screen of my digital test. My heart galloped, and nausea had me leaning over the sink just in case. *Please, please.* I closed my eyes and exhaled. "Okay. If it's positive, so what. You are having a baby! If it's negative, whew, it's time for birth control," I said to myself. Great, now I'm losing my mind too.

I peeked at the test through my fingers as if that would help shield me from the truth I already knew. **POSITIVE.** I slid down the wall to the floor, holding the test. "It's going to be okay. He will be okay," I whispered to myself as a stream of fresh tears streaked down my face. I could try to convince myself I was fine, but my body trembled with fear, knowing I was anything but.

"Em?" Brooks called out, startling me from my pity party. I sighed and stood up, sliding the door open, unable to leave the bathroom. "Are you feeling okay, sweetie?" It was time to come clean.

I dropped my hand to my side, ensuring the test was visible to him. I had a lump in my throat, and my mouth was so dry. Brooks' looked at me confused, down to the test, and back up to me. With an attempt at a calming breath, I crossed the room and crawled back into bed beside him. More tears welled in my eyes, but I still couldn't find the words as I slid the test into his hands.

Brooks accepted it quietly, sitting up, and stared at the screen for half a second.

"Oh my God, Emily! We're going to have a baby?" I couldn't read the expression on his face as he sat there, analyzing the test.

"I'm sorry. I am so sorry. My appointment is next week and -" Brooks' lips slammed into mine, cutting me off.

"It's okay, baby. We will figure it out," he assured me, his lips still pressed into mine. His hands were soft on my face, and his kiss was so reassuring. I half smiled when he pulled away. His arms wrapped around me, pulling me in closer.

"Are we really having a baby?" he asked on a whisper. I nodded as he pulled away. "Em, you're pregnant! No stomach bug. Just a baby. Our baby. This is great news."

"Is it?" I cried as the tears flowed freely from my eyes. "B, we just got engaged. This wasn't supposed to happen. You said you didn't want to get me pregnant." Brooks wrapped his hands in mine.

"Shh, hey. I love you. Em, c'mon. Babies happen when you have sex. We have a lot of sex. It was bound to happen. I told you I was okay having babies with you. I want this baby." He planted a long, hard kiss on my shoulder while more tears trailed my cheeks.

My soft tears turned into a sob as the reality hit, we were going to be parents.

"Hey, Em, sweetie, it's going to be okay. I'm so happy. We are going to have a baby." His voice was so encouraging. He planted his lips on mine again even though I had snot running down my face. I smiled through my tears, his happiness melting my fears away.

"We're having a baby," I whispered.

I laid back on my pillow, trying to process the news. Brooks lifted his shirt that I was wearing to expose my stomach and pressed a soft kiss to it.

"Hi, little one," he whispered. My heart squeezed with adoration and love. This baby was going to have the best dad. Brooks' head rested on my pelvic bone as his hands rested on my sides. I began to feel an ounce of excitement as I ran my fingers through Brooks' hair.

"I'm going to call Dr. Williams and see if she can get me anything for this nausea."

"Good idea." He smiled, lifting his head from my stomach, then planted another soft kiss on my stomach before crawling up to plant one on my lips. "We're going to have a baby. It's going to be okay, sweetie. We will figure it out together." I nodded back, feeling our lives instantly changing. I turned and glanced at the clock to see if I could call now.

I hit the phone icon, unsure of what I would say.

"Women's Care, how can I assist you?" A friendly voice came over the speaker.

"Hi, my name is Emily Barlow. I am a fairly new patient of Dr. Williams. I just found out I am pregnant, and I have been really sick for a few days. Is there anything I could take?"

"Okay, Emily. Let's see here. Is everything still the same? Insurance, phone number, address?"

We went through all of my information and made an appointment while I logged into my app. I kept it open in front of me and changed the setting to pregnant. A few fireworks popped across the screen, celebrating my pregnancy.

Congratulations! Your baby is due February 21st. Baby is the size of a sweet pea.

A little green pea with a smile danced across the screen. I clicked on the calendar. May 25th was the last time that I had logged having sex with Brooks. The day Parker showed up was the day of the most incredible orgasms of my life.

Brooks was sitting beside me on his phone. He must have felt my eyes on him because he turned to face me.

"Well," I started, swallowing back more tears. "Our baby is due in February and is the size of a sweet pea, and we became parents because of shower sex."

Brooks nodded, processing my brain dump. "Okay. We will take it one day at a time, okay?" His hand wrapped gently around my neck, pulling my forehead to his lips.

↟ ↟ ↟

The week passed in slow motion. Most of it had been spent running back and forth to the bathroom or laying in bed, burying my head into the pillows. Tonight was the first night I didn't feel like I was dying. I missed spending time with Brooks instead of in this stupid bed or bathroom. We weren't even parents yet, and I felt distant from him.

The fire pit crackled while we lay out by the pool. Brooks' head was in my lap, and his hands were playing with the hem of my shirt while I dragged my fingers through his hair. He hadn't stopped kissing my stomach since I told him the news. He would kiss my stomach and whisper "Hello" or "I love you" anytime he got the chance. I couldn't help but fall in love with him more because of his constant attention and love for our child.

"Hi, baby. I'm your dad. I'm pretty excited to meet you. Please stop making your mommy sick."

"The baby can't even hear you yet," I giggled.

"I know, but as soon as he or she can, I want them to hear my voice. I want them to know I love them." I smiled softly before letting out a low groan. "What's wrong?" Brooks asked, sitting up.

"Nothing, I'm okay. Just the nausea. It's so insane. I just need a break. I'm so tired."

"We are going tomorrow, baby. Just a few more hours." I nodded at my fiancé, who now had his eyes glued to me.

"I'm okay, promise."

This time, he laid his head back down on my chest while I stared into the fire. I just had to hold on until tomorrow.

Chapter Thirty-Seven

I curled up on the cold bathroom floor, exhausted from puking all night and needing to shower before my appointment with Dr. Williams.

I slid my phone across the floor to check the time: 7:29 a.m. There were only two hours and thirty-one minutes until my appointment. And then relief—at least I hoped. As I turned on the shower, running the water on hot, Brooks startled me.

He knew I had been spending more nights on the bathroom floor than I cared to admit, and I saw the sympathy in his eyes as he helped me undress. Every bit of energy was completely stolen from me.

I sat on the bench as the warm water rained over me. I felt so miserable. It had been days since I was able to keep anything down. Brooks had purchased some prenatal vitamins for me yesterday, but I threw them up immediately.

How were you supposed to take prenatals, which apparently a baby needs, when morning sickness kicks your ass? As steam closed in around me, Brooks reappeared outside of the glass shower door. He had been hovering a lot because he was worried about me - and the baby.

Brooks opened the shower door, revealing that he was already dressed and ready for the day. He looked so handsome and so *mine*. He was wearing navy slacks and a white button-down. His hair was swept nicely to the side. He reached in, shutting off the water.

"C'mon," he said, pulling me up from the bench and wrapping a towel around me. I wanted to cry. He had been caring and supportive and needed a break as much as I did.

He helped me to the bed, sliding a bowl beside me as he went to the closet to get clothes.

"I'm sorry," I whispered when he returned with a pair of joggers and a tank. He also brought my favorite comfy bra and panties set.

"Nothing to be sorry about," he said, kissing my soaking wet head. "Let's get you dressed."

He sat down on the bed beside me, softly rubbing one hand down my back.

"I can reschedule my meeting with Michaelson this afternoon. We need to get you better."

"Okay," I mumbled. I was feeling sick again. Reading my thoughts, Brooks grabbed the bowl sitting on my other side. He gently held my hair back, softly brushing my leg with his other hand.

How much more can I possibly puke? There was nothing left in my system. Now I was just dry heaving into the bowl.

Inside, I was crumbling. I had never been this sick. I laid my head on Brooks' lap, exhausted. I knew he was feeling helpless. *Have babies*, they said. *It will be great*, they said. They left out death by morning sickness. Also, why is it called morning sickness? Pretty sure it lasts all day and all night. It's more like an unending sickness. They should just rename it. Why not pregnancy sickness or baby sickness? At least there's no misleading timeline in the name.

↟ ↟ ↟

Brooks opened the door to the doctor's office. As if I didn't have enough going on with the nausea, I was nervous. I had no women in my life who could tell me what to expect from this first appointment. Would there be an ultrasound? Do we get to hear the baby's heartbeat? Would I be judged for being unmarried? Maybe my engagement ring could pass as a wedding ring.

I stepped inside, feeling the full weight of what was happening. *I am pregnant. I am having a baby. This is a good thing. Brooks is happy. I am happy...I think. I love my baby.* The empty reception area was cold even though it was almost July, but I tugged the sleeves of my sweater down over the heels of my palms.

The small office was adjacent to the local hospital. It was an older brick building that had been repainted to look more modern. Inside, soft music played over the speakers, and a water wall featured just behind the check-in desk.

"Hi, we are here to see Dr. Williams," Brooks said nervously. I clung to my puke bag, hoping I wouldn't begin dry heaving again.

"Okay, go ahead and have a seat, and we will be right with you." Brooks' hand slipped to my lower back as he guided me to the chairs.

As awful as I felt, I couldn't miss the fact that the waiting room was peaceful. The chairs were soft and comfortable, with pillows for support. A coffee table sat in front of us covered in outdated versions of People magazine and Cosmo. Brochures sat on the end table with information about midwives, breastfeeding, what to expect, and hospital tours. My heart melted when I saw Brooks grab a few and stuff them in his pocket.

There was nobody else in the room except for Brooks and I. We sat quietly, his hand wrapped around mine while his leg bounced up and down nervously. Time seemed to pass excruciatingly slowly as the clock's hands slowly ticked by.

A nurse came through a side door, greeting me and leading us back to our room.

The nurse, whose name tag read Linda, had kind eyes. She was an older lady with laugh lines, and her hair had streaks of gray that she no longer cared to hide. I wondered if she was a grandma. I bet she was, and probably a great one, too.

Brooks and I didn't know our grandparents. My mom's parents cut her out of their life after she married my dad, and my dad's parents both died around the time I was born. Brooks' grandparents were still alive until he was about six. He doesn't remember them, but before they moved to the States, his grandparents were very active in his life.

James' biological parents were probably still alive, but he had grown up in the foster care system. He didn't keep in contact with any of his family. So after our parents died, we had nobody except for each other. Our child would also grow up without grandparents, aunts, and uncles. The cycle would continue. I gripped my stomach. *I'm sorry, baby.*

She motioned us down the hall to an open door. "The nurse will be in momentarily," she said before disappearing down the hall.

Brooks helped me to the table, *or is it a chair?* He stood next to me. I watched as his eyes glanced around the room. Darting first to the 3D model of a woman's pelvic bones and then to another model of a woman's uterus and cervix with a form of birth control tucked up inside what appeared to be the vagina. I squeezed his hand in reassurance. He smiled down at me briefly before glancing up at the nurse.

"Hi, Emily!" The door closed behind her. "I am Carly, Dr. William's nurse. I am just going to get some vitals on you really quick."

She hadn't even wrapped the blood pressure monitor around my arm before Dr. Williams walked through the door.

"Hi, Emily. Nice to see you again." She smiled, looking first at me and then over to Brooks. "I hear you aren't feeling so well?" *That's an understatement.*

"No, not really," I chuckled weakly.

"She hasn't been able to keep anything down for a few days and can't usually stray too far from a toilet or bowl," Brooks said.

"Okay. You must be Dad?" she asked with a reassuring grin,

reaching to shake his hand. Her soft New Zealand accent stood out more than it had the first time I met her.

"Yes, ma'am. Brooks Devonshire."

"Okay, Brooks, well, she will be just fine. I know it's hard to see her like this, but we are going to get her some fluids and some medicine and get her back to where she needs to be, okay?"

Brooks exhaled and sat back on a chair. "Okay."

↟ ↟ ↟

Brooks was beaming like a proud dad as we walked back to the car, ultrasound photos in hand. Between my bloodwork, ultrasound, and the very lovely banana bag of fluids they pumped me full of, we had spent the better part of the day here.

Dr. Williams sent me home with some nausea pills to take until my second trimester starts. Hopefully, by then, my morning or pregnancy sickness, which I am now choosing to appropriately name, will subside.

She also wants me back in two weeks to check my vitals, especially if I keep throwing up as often as I am. In some rare cases of pregnancy, apparently, women can develop what is called Hyperemesis Gravidarum. The jury is still out on whether that's what I have. I'm hoping not.

Brooks closed the car door and hit start. The car did its fancy little jingle as I laid the seat back, feeling like it was the first time I could breathe or rest since I began puking the night of our engagement party. After a few silent moments of bliss and no nausea, I realized the car was still parked. I opened my eyes to find Brooks still studying the stack of black-and-white photos.

I closed my eyes again and smiled to myself. Why did I ever think for a moment that he would be upset? Of course, he wouldn't. He's Brooks. Stable, strong, optimistic, kind, and overly-loving, if that's a thing. I thought back to the ultrasound. It was nothing like the movies. I didn't get a cute wand placed on my stomach.

Instead, I was informed that early on, you get a long, thin wand shoved up inside. Brooks, of course, couldn't stop fighting a chuckle while I was being prodded. That was until the blurry image of a tadpole-like baby appeared on the screen. Then, his mood switched to pure amazement. He squeezed my hand and grinned at the screen, soaking in everything the technician told us. Our baby has a strong heartbeat and loves to wiggle around already.

"Boy or girl?" he asked.

"What?" I opened my eyes to see him looking at me.

"What do you think? Is the baby a boy or a girl?"

It's a boy. I had already dreamed of him. He's beautiful and looks just like Brooks, but I didn't want to jinx it, so I responded, "Girl."

Chapter Thirty-Eight

"Em," Brooks started. "How would you feel about moving upstairs into the main house? We will be more comfortable and not have to walk up and down every day. Besides, we need room for the baby." I had just woken up, happy that the nausea meds had been working. I sat up beside him, pulling the blanket with me.

He hesitated to ask, but I didn't know why. As long as I wasn't alone, I was never against moving up there. I looked around the bedroom we had called ours the past few months.

We wouldn't need to move much, but I would want to hire a few movers to help with the few boxes, and I would want the mattress switched out in the master. I liked this one. The light filtered through the room, causing a beam of light and dust to dance through it.

"Okay," I responded.

"Okay?"

"After the wedding."

"The wedding?" he asked curiously.

"I want to do the wedding soon. I don't want to wait. Just a small, private wedding. Maybe a few friends." I'd been mulling it over the last few weeks, and while I originally thought I wanted a big ceremony, the circumstances changed drastically. Now, I just wanted to be married to my best friend with a few friends by our side. The where and when didn't matter so much anymore as long as, in the end, he was mine.

"Are you sure? You've always wanted a big wedding. I remember all the drawings and play sets you had as a little girl. Just because you're pregnant doesn't mean you have to give up that dream." I smiled to myself, knowing he knew me so well. He always has, and that is just one of the many reasons I love him.

Growing up, my closet was full of Barbie and doll play sets, and I used to make them get married. Brooks would play Ken. He would even dress up with me. My closet was also full of princess dresses that I would prance around the house in. I would pretend to marry Brooks and try to kiss him, but he would always run from me.

"Do you remember I used to make you marry me?"

Brooks rolled his eyes and laughed. "Yeah, I do. I was being tortured. I just wanted to play outside, but you always wanted me to play pretend."

"You never let me kiss you."

He shrugged. "Girl cooties." He had barely finished talking before his lips were on mine. His kiss was slow, fully exploring my mouth like it was his first time.

"Mmm," I moaned, melting into him as his hands fumbled with my pajama top. I missed him. I missed being close and connected, but my body was already being ravaged. "Sorry, B, I can't," I sighed despite wanting him in every way possible.

"I know," he whispered, pulling away. "It's okay. But you can kiss me for the rest of your life, and I will let you."

I nodded. "Sounds good. Now, back to the wedding. I don't think I care as much as I used to." I looked down and placed my hand over my stomach. "You, me, our baby. This is all that matters. Plus, I want to do it before I start to show. I don't want our wedding pictures to become a spectacle."

He smiled softly as if he wanted to say something but didn't.

"I'll go make you some toast." He stood up, planting a kiss on the top of my head. When he returned, I had acted like an ass, taking his excitement about me being on my feet as a judgment. Before I could apologize, he left the room, needing to be in a meeting.

↟ ↟ ↟

Brooks was in the study, pacing back and forth on the phone, so I sat on the sofa and rested against one of the pillows. His eyes softened when he looked at me, but I could tell he was stressed about something. He was pulling at the collar of his dress shirt and unbuttoning the top button. I felt awful for how I had treated him earlier.

I pulled my legs up underneath me as I watched photos slide across his screen. Most were of us, but a few were from his time in Osan. Several images were of Brooks with guys I had never met, a few of him in uniform, and one of him and Michaelson on their surfboards waiting for a wave.

"Almost done," he whispered, pulling the phone from his face. I nodded. I would wait here all day if I had to.

I could hear the staff enter through the front door. Brooks had brought on a few more people to help since I was down, and he spent all his free time caring for me. Aside from Mrs. Hall, who was still managing the groceries and shopping, we brought on Mr. Kincaid, our new chef, who came three times a week, and Mrs. Renata handled the cleaning and laundry.

I was thankful they had been brought on, but it made me miss the old staff we had growing up. They were all in Seattle and getting older, so it didn't make sense to reach out, though I am sure they would have made it work if we had asked.

"Okay, call me as soon as you hear anything." Brooks put the phone down and sat beside me.

"I'm sorry. You didn't deserve that." I leaned over, placing my head against his bicep. His hand moved to my thigh.

"You're okay. I forgive you. I truly am happy to see you feeling better."

"I know," I sighed. Emotions were flooding my body, and I felt the urge to cry. I always had the damn urge to cry. I also hated being sick. Brooks held a kiss to the top of my head.

"I miss you," I cried.

"I know, baby. I miss you too. We will get through this." He pulled me into his lap, and I curled up in his warmth. I wiped away a few tears still trailing down my face. "How about," he paused, lifting my chin to meet his eyes, "we have dinner on the deck tonight. No phones, no work - just you and me."

"That sounds perfect," I sighed. "This is hard. I want you in so many ways, but I feel like my body is betraying me."

He chuckled. "I'll be waiting whenever you're ready."

He placed me back on the sofa and crossed the room to his desk. He adjusted himself before leaning over the chair. Even if I wasn't feeling good, I could still look at him and feel desire. Chinos and a nice tucked shirt with rolled sleeves were his outfits of choice most days. Until recently, he always wore a lovely amber cologne, but now it was unbearable for me. As I watched him move about the room, returning to work, I admired him, and for the first time in weeks, I felt a warmth flooding my lower half.

↟ ↟ ↟

"So, I found this little glass chapel just south of us. It kind of looks like an oversized greenhouse, but it's used for private events. I was thinking -" I paused for suspense. "We could have the wedding there?"

"Whatever you want, I don't care. I just want to marry you."

My heart sank. I promised I would try to do better and not get frustrated so easily. I hated that anger was my biggest vice, especially when I was tired and hormonal, which was every day now. My legs were draped across his lap, and the fire was roaring beside us. I took a few calming breaths before responding.

"Brooks, I want you to care. Even if it's just a little. I know I said I didn't care this morning, but I do. I still want a beautiful wedding, just smaller than I originally wanted before I was pregnant."

"Forgive me." He squeezed my leg reassuringly. "I do care. Will you show me pictures?"

I nodded and looked for my phone. *Oh, right.* "No phones, remember?"

Brooks rolled his eyes and laughed. "Right. Okay, what else do we need to do for the wedding?"

"We need a planner, photographer, florist, er, a bunch of stuff."

My words trailed off, and my thoughts drifted away as I became distracted by Brooks, who was looking at me with those eyes—the ones that said a lot more than what he was saying. I leaned forward and straddled him, surprising us both. Unlike before pregnancy, my whole body vibrated with need as warmth spread through my veins. This was different. It was more like a slow burn, but at least I felt something other than nauseous.

"Kiss me," I whispered.

He didn't need any more of an invitation. His mouth was immediately against mine, and his hands were all over me, somehow trying to pull me in closer than I already was. His kiss was passionate, slow, and careful. It was interesting to experience all these different sides of him. How moods, or time, changes the way someone holds you and kisses you. Right now, I could feel his apprehension. I could feel he wanted me but was too scared to approach the topic.

Dr. Williams had told us it was okay to resume sexual activity once I started to feel better, and there would be no harm to the baby. According to several blogs, I felt like the odd one out. Most bloggers talked about not wanting their spouse to touch them. I didn't feel that way. Even sleeping on the bathroom floor, I craved his closeness. Something about us, how we were connected, and how his child grew within me made it feel like he was literally my other half. It was cold, painful, and lonely when we weren't experiencing some sort of physical connection.

"What are you doing?" he whispered against my lips.

"Unbuttoning your pants. I want you."

"Em, stop. It's okay."

"Brooks, Dr. Williams said the baby would be fine. Please, I know you want this as much as I do. It will be okay." He gave me a look of reluctance as I tugged on the button of his pants loose and gave him a seductive smile. His eyes darkened with need as he gave in. His hands were quick to help me free him before he moved my panties to the side.

"Just go slow," I whispered as I guided him to my entrance and took in his length in one slick movement. It took a moment for my body to adjust to his size after weeks apart and for him to fill me. He groaned euphorically.

"I've missed you," he said into the hollow of my neck as our bodies rocked slowly. It wasn't just the sex. It was our bodies molding together, the closeness, the love that had me already racing toward my climax.

"I know, me too." *Finally*, the connection we needed, to be one again, with him buried deep within me. I needed him more than my next breath, and as I clawed at him, trying to get closer, I realized that this was as close as I'd ever get.

↟ ↟ ↟

Brooks had shut off all the lights so we could go to the studio. Now, knowing that we were moving up to the big house, the walk felt old and tedious. I let my thoughts wander back to earlier today, to his office and remembered how tense he was. I had forgotten to ask him about it.

"Brooks, earlier today, you were upset on the phone when I came to the study. Why?"

He sighed and ran a hand through his hair. "I guess some invoices didn't get paid for the remodel in LA. I don't know how that happened. I need to talk to Paul and see who is responsible for the remodel budget."

"Do you think this has to do with the other invoices?"

"I don't know. I promise you, I will get to the bottom of it. There's a big mess, and I just feel like I'm drowning a bit right now trying to learn the ropes, expand the company, and look into years of paperwork."

I felt a wave of guilt wash over me. "I'm sorry if I've added to it."

He leaned in, planting a kiss on my head. "No, baby. You are exactly who I need you to be."

I nodded, pushing the door open to the studio. On Monday, I would see if there was any way I could help him. After all, it was my company, too.

Chapter Thirty-Nine

"I think it's just up here," I said as we walked along the boardwalk in Southport, a little coastal town just north of Pacific Coves. We had just finished brunch at a local cafe and were going dress shopping today. Last week, I asked Natalie to be my maid of honor and Sara to be my bridesmaid. Natalie had cried and hugged me, and Sara shrugged like it was a no-brainer.

When we were looking for dress shops, I had found a custom boutique in Southport, so here we were, ready to find a gown that would fit my slowly growing body—not that I was showing at all.

The smell of brine was thick in the air today, and the lapping of water around the hull of the boats pulled into their slips along the harbor comforted me like a familiar lullaby. I could never live too far from the water. It was as much a part of me as my own heartbeat.

"How are you feeling?" Natalie asked.

"Good, actually. The medicine is helping. I'm really thankful to be feeling more like myself. Dr. Williams was scared it might have been HG, but since I'm not puking anymore, at least I don't with the meds. She thinks I just had bad "pregnancy sickness" and ended up dehydrated, which obviously makes everything worse."

"Yes, staying hydrated is important."

The bell jingled above us as Natalie pushed the door open.

"Hello, my dears. Welcome in. What can I help you with?"

An elderly lady approached us. Her hair was long and silver, the top half pulled into a knot. She wore a black chiffon blouse that pulled together around the neck into a big, black bow. Just below the bow were three rows of pearls. Her face and hands were covered in deep wrinkles, and the way she smiled brought warmth to my whole being.

"Well, she is getting married in a few weeks, and we need to find her a dress," Natalie responded.

My eyes scanned the room. It was so unique for a dress shop. Most other shops were decorated with mirrors, light carpets, and soft white furnishings. This felt more like someone's personal closet in an upscale New York penthouse. The dark wood floors were covered with Persian rugs and dark green velvet couches that sat back to back, creating a line through the center of the room.

The outer edges were stacked with shelves broken up by mannequins and small racks that could only fit one or two dresses. Each section was styled around the gown being displayed. The mannequin was dressed in the displayed wedding gown, and the shelves nearby held shoes, veil options, and purses. The racks held alternate-style dresses similar to the mannequin.

The room was rather dark in place of the bright white walls and lights, with charcoal walls and a stained wood beam ceiling. Strings of pearls, lace, and tulle draped the ceilings across the beams and around the lights in an unorganized pattern.

As I took it all in, I felt the gaping hole in my chest. I wished my mom and Carrie were here. They should be here. They should be taking me dress shopping, helping plan my wedding, decorating a nursery, and completely overjoyed that they have a grandbaby on the way. Instead, I'm here with my best friend because they can't be.

"Emily?" Natalie's voice interrupted my thoughts.

"Huh? What? Sorry." I wiped away a tear that dared to breach.

"What size are you, dear?" A tape measure was draped around the older lady's neck like a shawl.

"Um, well, normally like a 2, but I don't know now." I could feel more tears in my eyes. *Now that I am pregnant.*

"I have just the dress," she said with a clap of her hands before leaving us and disappearing into the back.

I wiped my eyes again. These hormones were making me weepy.

"Hey, what's wrong?" Natalie's voice was soft and comforting.

"I miss my mom and Carrie. I had always dreamed of the day they would take me dress shopping. I know they would have loved this. They would be simultaneously planning my wedding and the nursery. I would probably have a completed nursery by now, and our baby would have way more clothes than he or she could ever wear." I laughed through my tears at the thought.

"I wish I could have met them. They sound like they were the best."

"They were. It's weird to constantly feel like I am doing fine, and then, out of nowhere, I am grieving them all over again. Like life is fine, and then their absence is everywhere. I don't know. It's hard. I think I'm also just really angry right now because I didn't just lose one set of parents. I lost them both." I looked down at my hands, toying with the hem of my shirt.

"That would be extremely difficult. I know I can't do or say anything to make it better, but I am here for you, and I will try my best to fill in some of those gaps. Your baby is going to be so loved, I promise."

The elderly lady returned with a large white bag and a knowing smile.

"Sɐwˈðaðɨ," she whispered under her breath. "I have been holding onto this dress for one day when just the right young woman walked through this door," she started. She hung it on a hook from the ceiling and unzipped the bag.

Both Natalie and I gasped. *Holy cow, I love it. It's perfect.*

"Now, my dear, let's get you dressed and ensure it fits."

↟ ↟ ↟

I pranced through the front door, excited to share that I had said yes to a dress. The large white bag was taller than me.

"I found my dress!" I exclaimed, closing the door behind me. Brooks popped his head out from the study with a huge smile. "There was this little shop along the pier in Southport that just called to me. We went inside, and this old lady designed and customized each gown. She rushed to the back and returned with this one. It was a perfect fit. It was like it was made just for me."

Brooks chuckled, grabbing my hips and leaning in for a quick kiss. His eyes moved to the bag.

"Can I help carry it?"

"No peeking!" I warned, giving him a playful glare.

"Promise." He took the bag from me. "Did you have fun?" He turned, and I followed him upstairs.

"I did! Also, I met with Evie today, our wedding planner. She is going to help book the venue and gather a list of photographers and other vendors we will need. I was thinking, what if we just did a small reception here?"

Brooks sighed, laying the dress down on the bed.

"Hey, what's wrong?" I wrapped my hands around his bicep.

"I'm good. I was just thinking about how much I wish our parents were here. Our mothers would have loved to take you shopping. They probably would have fought over who would pay for it." He chuckled. "I'm sure you miss them. I know I do."

"I actually had a little breakdown in the dress shop earlier. I miss them a lot." I sighed, pressing my forehead to his chest. Brooks wrapped a sturdy arm around me, comforting us both as our bodies relaxed against one another.

"Have you talked to Connor yet?"

"No, I haven't." He pulled away, running a hand through his chocolate locks before settling against the wall.

"Well, call him up. He's still living in Portland. Go see him, or invite him here. Brooks, he was your best friend and always has been."

"Wrong. You, my love, are my best friend and always have been."

I rolled my eyes. "That was a little cheesy. Just call him. I'm sure he would be glad to hear from you."

"Okay. Also, Michaelson has agreed to be my best man, so Natalie should be happy."

"Sara and Connor?"

"Stop playing matchmaker with our friends, Em." His laughter trailed after him as he headed back downstairs.

"What? I just want them all to be married and happy so we can all just stay friends forever," I called after him.

↟ ↟ ↟

Dear Mama,

Today I found my dress. I wish you were here. The old lady at the shop had saved this dress, and I felt like it was meant for me. I don't know how to explain it. It's so beautiful, and I know you and Carrie would have cried when you saw it. When I came out of the dressing room, Natalie had tears in her eyes, and the older lady, Mrs. Abel, had this look about her as if she were watching her granddaughter or something. At least, that is what I envisioned a look from a grandma to look like. She told me that she custom-made the gown from a dream she had.

The bodice is lace with a glittery material. It's not a lot of sparkles, but just enough to catch the light. It has long sleeves that are almost sheer, but the lace is laid out like vines wrapping around my arm, and the back plunges to the bra line and is completely open. The rest of the gown is soft pink and white. The underskirt is a soft pink but light enough that it almost makes you second guess if it's pink or white. It's shimmery and hidden beneath several silk tulle or silk chiffon layers. I don't know the difference. The train isn't very long, but just long enough to make me feel like a princess. Instead of a veil, I chose a custom crown she had made for this dress. It has the same lace pattern as the dress and ties together with a silk ribbon in the back. I am thinking about getting extensions for the wedding. I want my hair longer with curls.

I asked Natalie to be my maid of honor. She said yes. Sara will be a bridesmaid. At first, I felt guilty because I had known Sara longer, but my relationship with her was different from that with Natalie. Natalie is more like me. She's calmer and understanding. Sara is still Sara. Wild, carefree, fun. I, of course, had to be all cheesy when I asked them and had cute gift boxes made with different gifts. They loved it. I decided on a sea foam green for their dresses. I initially thought about champagne or even blush pink, but since my dress has pink in it, I think the green will fit better.

Brooks asked Michaelson to be his best man. He also said yes. Now, he's waiting to ask Connor. I don't know why. I feel like what happened between them is old news, but I am trying to not step in and make both of them play nice.

Anyway, I think the guys should wear gray tweed suits with a matching seafoam tie, and Brooks can match his tie with my dress. I might have to have one custom-made.

Wedding planning has been fun, but we both really miss you guys. It's so hard to keep moving forward with significant milestones, knowing you will never experience them with us.

Oh, also, baby is good. The medicine that Dr. Williams gave me is working. I am finally starting to feel excited about being a mom. I still think it's a boy, but Brooks believes it's a girl because of how sick I have been. He keeps wanting to try different wives' tales tricks to find out. No matter what, I am sticking with a boy. We are moving our stuff to the main house soon, which will be nice. I can't wait to start setting up the nursery and not having to walk up and down every day. I was thinking of doing the nursery ocean-themed, like sailboats, whales, and jellyfish, but I feel that's really boyish. What if Brooks is correct, and it's a girl? Then I considered woodland-themed with murals of trees and bunnies, but that also seemed like a lot. I could just do neutral and stick with plants and textiles. I feel overwhelmed thinking about it. Another thing that I wish you were here to help with.

I forgot to tell you about the venue! I was so excited when I found it. Brooks likes it, too. It's called the Glasshouse. It's twenty minutes south of us, and it's like an oversized greenhouse. There are large window panes that overlook the forest outside. There's a beautiful chandelier above the aisle and cobblestone floors. They've only had one wedding there before, so we are trying to work out the details. I am considering having an arbor at the front with ferns, blush pink peonies, and maybe some white hydrangeas. We can probably fit like twenty to thirty people, which is plenty. We rented gold and white chairs for the space. Also, we can have real candles. I want the aisle lined with them.

Mama...so much of this is coming together, and I am so happy but so nervous. Will I be a good wife? Will I be a good mom? How do I handle tough times? Who do I cry to when we start to fight and need guidance? You had Carrie, and Daddy had James. Brooks and I only have each other and our friends, but it's different. Is it okay to confide in them? I am terrified it won't work out and that I'll mess it up somehow. I am so scared he will leave me, and then I will be a single mom.

I just keep trying my hardest, and I keep trying to apologize quickly. I love him so much it hurts. I can't imagine life without him. And I love our baby. What if I just suck at being a mom? I don't know anything about babies. I think about life with a newborn, and I want to hide. All these irrational fears flood my mind. Like, what if the baby chokes while sleeping, and I don't hear it? Or what if I drop him or her? What if they open the door at night, wander out *to the ocean, and get swept away, and we never find them? See what I mean by irrational? It's nonstop, so I have been avoiding the topic as much as*

"Hey, Em, what are you doing in here?" I looked up to see Brooks pushing the door aside.

"Just journaling."

"It's a little dark. Do you want the lamp on?"

"Sure." I hadn't noticed how dark the glass room had become. There was a massive storm outside that was pressing against the windows. "Did you talk to Connor?"

"I did. We are going to meet for coffee tomorrow here in PC. He was wondering if you would be up for company after?"

"Duh! I miss him too."

Brooks chuckled, but it seemed forced.

"You want to head down and get ready for bed?"

"Yeah, just give me one second." I looked back down at my letter.

I can.

Love, Emily

"All done."

Chapter Forty

With the movers here, our entire staff worked today to rearrange everything. Boxes from Brooks' childhood home were being brought over from storage, and we agreed it was finally time to sort through them and decide what to keep and what to donate. I was in the kitchen preparing some tea when Brooks walked through the front door with Connor.

"Connie!" I yelled, running for my friend, throwing my arms around him. Nothing had changed. He still had the wavy, blonde, boyish surfer look.

"Hey, Millie!" He swung me around and set me back down.

The three of us chuckled at the nickname. Connor was the only person who had ever called me Millie, and only because he thought he needed to have a special nickname for me.

"I'm really happy you both worked things out. I could never picture either of you with anyone else. Plus, Brooks has been planning a proposal since high school."

"Really?" I asked, glancing at Brooks before turning my attention back to Connor, who wore an award-winning smile on his face. It only made me miss him more. With Connor here, everything felt complete. He had always been an essential part of the bond between Brooks and me, and this was the first time in seven years that the three of us were together in the same space.

Seeing them both standing close together, I felt grateful that they had managed to resolve whatever had caused their previous conflict. It was as if nothing had ever happened between them.

"Really," Brooks said, wrapping his arm around my waist, bringing me back to the present.

"Wow, Em, this place is nice," Connor whistled, nudging me with his hip. It was meant to be playful, but he nudged my stomach. Brooks inhaled sharply at my side. Brooks glanced back and forth between us nervously, but I could tell he was waiting to see if I would say something.

"The original builders had to relocate out of state, so they planned to put the house on the market once the construction was completed. My realtor caught wind of it before that happened, and we went under contract the very same day. I just had to have it."

"You always talked about wanting a beach house," Connor said as he stepped down into the living room.

"Well, come on in. Do you want anything to drink? Soda, water, tea, beer?"

"Water is good. Could I use your restroom first?"

"Yep. Down the hall, just to the right." Once Connor disappeared, Brooks dipped his head, bringing his forehead to mine.

"How are you feeling? You okay?" Brooks asked. He looked softer as if a heavy weight had been lifted from his shoulders. I guess it had. Brooks had his best friend back.

"Perfectly fine." I planted a kiss on his lips before resting my head on his shoulder and inhaling him. He wasn't wearing any cologne today, just his masculine scent that I loved so very much. "How'd it go?" I asked quietly.

"He said yes." A huge grin spread across his face.

"See. Nothing to worry about." His hand lifted to cup the back of my head as he kissed the top.

"I didn't say anything about...you know."

"We can tell him," I whispered. "I think it's only fair that everyone in the wedding party understands the rush."

"Well," Connor cleared his throat. "I can see that nothing has changed," he said, then chuckled. Brooks and I pulled away from each other, laughing.

"Always a third wheel, Connor," I teased, returning to the stove to shut off the water.

"Ouch," he mockingly complained, grabbing his heart.

"I have a friend, you know." I winked at him.

"No. No more matchmaking, Emily." Connor grimaced, shaking his head.

I rolled my eyes. "Fine. Your loss." Brooks looked at me expectantly.

"So, Connor, umm, guess what?" Butterflies fluttered in my stomach as I looked at my friend. Despite the disagreement between him and Brooks, Connor has always been our best friend. He felt more like a brother than just a friend in many ways. As I gazed at him, my heart softened; he was a part of our little family. He would always be our Connor, no matter how much time has passed.

"What?" he asked, looking between Brooks and me.

My hands moved to my stomach. "You're going to be an uncle. I'm pregnant." I smiled, watching his face turn up with the biggest grin. Connor has always been one of those people who just loves life and finds joy in everything. He's always cracking a joke or finding a sliver of hope.

"What?" His hands moved to his wavy blonde hair as he glanced back and forth between Brooks and me excitedly. "Oh, shit! Congrats, Mom and Dad. That's amazing." *Mom and Dad!* Hearing those words out loud made my heart leap into my throat.

"I don't want to be a big, pregnant bride or a nursing one," I chuckled.

"Can I teach my cute little niece or nephew to surf? I mean, I'm practically the cool one of the family." We all laughed, smiling at each other while silently reflecting on the memories we shared and the newest chapter that was soon to come. A blanket of happiness and belonging swept over me, and even with the lingering tug at my heartstrings when I thought of our parents not being here for this, I couldn't deny that I was surrounded by family.

"Duh." I leaned in for another hug.

↟ ↟ ↟

It was late when we crawled into bed. I couldn't stop yawning. Brooks was lying next to me on his stomach, watching me as I rubbed my flat tummy, admiring the life that was growing in me. I still wasn't showing, which I was both sad about and really happy about. I didn't want my body to change too much until after the wedding. Then, I would gladly sport the pregnant lady look.

I shouldn't care, but the idea of being judged by everyone for the rest of our lives when they realized I was pregnant before our wedding made my heart sink. I didn't want them to assume Brooks and I were only getting married because a baby was on the way, which was far from true.

"You're beautiful," Brooks muttered into the pillowcase.

I looked over at him and then back to my stomach with a small smile tugging at the corner of my lips. How was it possible to love someone so much without meeting them? I knew that the love I felt for my baby was the same kind of unending love I felt for Brooks and my parents, but possibly even more. I knew no matter what, I would protect my baby and love this baby for the rest of my life. How was I going to wait until February?

"Did you know that our baby is the size of a kumquat?"

"A what?" Brooks looked at me like I was insane.

I laughed. "A kumquat."

"What is a kumquat?"

"Like a baby orange, but it's sweeter."

"I don't think I've ever had a kumquat. Maybe I should go to the grocery store."

"I doubt you'll find one. I don't think they're popular."

"Okay," he chuckled, grabbing his phone from the pillow. "I need to see what this thing looks like."

I giggled, looking back at my stomach. *My little kumquat baby.*

↟ ↟ ↟

The next morning, I wandered down into the basement where all the boxes from storage had been staged. The basement was towering with boxes of all shapes and sizes. I moved through the room, looking at the labels. It felt weird knowing these boxes contained a home that was all but my own. The boxes were all marked with big black labels.

Brooks' Room. Books. Carrie's Jewelry and Personal.

I pulled the top box down to get to Carrie's stuff.

"Em, you shouldn't be lifting boxes. Let me help you," Brooks scolded, taking the box from me.

"It's fine. I will only lift light ones."

He rolled his eyes. "Where do you want this one?"

"The bar top?"

"'Kay." He carried the box out to the kitchenette. "I thought you wanted to wait until we returned from Seattle?"

"I do. This box is your mom's stuff. Do you mind if I look?"

"Em, you know I don't. I'm sure she would have left it all to you anyway."

I nodded. He was right. I was like a daughter to his parents, just as they were like a second family to me.

"I'm going to go upstairs and grab my cell. I'll be back." He disappeared upstairs, leaving me alone with my thoughts.

I opened the box to find a large velvet jewelry box, a few smaller necklace boxes, some books, her sunglasses, a candle that I knew she usually kept on her nightstand, and a picture frame containing a photo of Brooks with his parents from their vacation in Hawaii. Brooks looked about twelve in the picture, with his parents leaning over his shoulders. They all appeared so happy.

As my fingertips grazed over the items, I pulled the frame close to my chest and sighed, setting it aside. A single tear slipped down my cheek. Maybe this wasn't a good idea; it all hurt so much. I glanced at the various items I had taken out of the box, absorbing the moment. Carrie would have never thought twice about me going through these things, yet it felt so personal and private. I had even struggled to sort through my mom's belongings.

There's no preparation for handling personal belongings when a loved one dies. Their jewelry, notebooks, wallets, and clothes are all left to their loved ones to sort through. All the while, we suffer and laugh as we wade through the memories attached to the belongings. I reached back in and pulled out the stack of books.

What was she reading? I rotated through the books and noticed a journal among the stack. I set the journal next to the photo but a small envelope fell out as I did. I looked down to the floor where the envelope was. *My Dearest Emily* was scripted out across the front. *What?* I gulped, reaching down for the envelope. My heart was racing. Why was there a letter to me?

I sat on the floor, resting against the cabinets. I closed my eyes as more tears splashed down my cheek. I carefully pulled the letter out.

Chapter Forty-One

August 25, 2017

Dear Emily,

If you are reading this, it is your wedding day to Brooks. I can now officially call you my daughter, though I have considered you one for a long time. I am writing this letter as you both begin your sophomore year, and I have no doubt that you will officially be family. I see the way you two look at each other. Nothing beats love like that. I am so proud of you both.

My sweet Emily, from the day we moved in across the street, Brooks has always been in love with you. Constantly peering from his bedroom window to catch a glimpse of you. After school, even from a young age, he would always come home and tell me all about his day, most of which has to do with you. Not much has changed in the years that have passed because you still seem to be the reason why he comes home each day with a smile on his face. I pray that you two will never let go of this love. That it will carry you through life and one day into your children. Oh, how I cannot wait to meet my Grandchildren.

I hope you know how much James and I love you. I hope you know that you have always been the daughter we never had. You have brought so much joy to our family. You are my special girl, Emily. I want you to know you will always have a home with us. My arms are open and here for you. When you and Brooks fight, I promise to listen and love you and give you the best advice I can. I am here for you when parenting is so much more complicated than you thought, and the exhaustion has you doubled over. I will be there with coffee and food and to care for the babies so you can rest. I will be here, my sweet girl, for whatever you need.

Thank you for loving my son, for your constant smile, and for your unending love for our family. We cannot wait to celebrate, hug you, and finally call you our daughter.

With all of my love,

Carrie.

Y*ou aren't here, though.* A steady flow of hot tears poured out of me as I sobbed. My shoulders shook with each sob as the grief took over. Years of keeping my emotions tucked away have turned my pain into a dark void of agony that has managed to work itself free from reading a letter.

These were her words. These were meant for her to share with me on my wedding day. She should be here. They should all be here. Uncontrolled whimpers fell from my lips, and my chest ached as the letter slipped from my fingers. I buried my face in my hands and continued to ugly cry.

I knew I shouldn't have held this in so long, that I needed to release it in a healthy way, but it just seemed easier to pretend everything was fine - to focus on what we had instead of what we had lost. Because we've lost so much. But no, my messy box of emotions was spilling out, and there was no stopping it.

"Em?" Brooks asked worriedly. "Hey, it's okay, baby." Brooks dropped to his knees next to me, pulling me into his shoulder. "Shh... it's okay."

"She had no idea that she would never be the one to deliver the letter. She won't get to see our wedding. She won't get to meet our baby..." I continued to sob.

Brooks sighed, running his hand along my arm as he held me. He held me for a long time until my sobs quieted and my tears dried, and the only thing I was left with was a pounding head and an aching heart.

"What letter?" he asked after a few minutes.

I pulled my face away from his tear-soaked shirt, my vision still blurry from my tears, but I didn't miss the pain etched on Brooks' familiar features. He swiped a thumb under each eye and pressed his forehead to mine as I sniffled, still struggling to gain my composure.

"Can you grab the box of tissues off the table?" I asked, almost inaudibly, even to my own ears.

Silently, he pulled away, leaving me feeling cold, but he was back in a beat, bringing the whole box of tissues with him. I wiped my eyes and blew my nose before I grabbed the letter and handed it to him. His brows furrowed, his own questions seemingly forgotten for a moment.

"She wrote it two weeks before the accident," I began, but another sob escaped, and I buried my head into his shoulder.

"C'mon, let's get you up off the floor." Brooks' arms cradled me effortlessly as he carried me to the sofa. My chest heaved as I fought back more sobs, as I rested against Brooks' chest when he sat beside me, tugging me closer.

"She loved you, baby." Brooks' voice was solemn and laced with his own pain.

"I miss her so much," I whispered, fighting against the feeling that I would break into two. I curled myself into a ball, reassuring I would remain whole.

I was curled up next to Brooks on our sofa, waiting for our parents to return from their work trip from Ontario, Canada. My eyes felt too heavy to keep open, and Brooks was already asleep. He had an early start with soccer practice that morning. His arm was wrapped around me, pulling me close to his chest, while another arm rested above him.

The movie "Before I Fall" played softly in the background, where Samantha was stuck reliving her car crash over and over. Outside, I could hear the rain pounding against the windows. The soothing sound of the rain, combined with the gentle rise and fall of Brooks' chest, finally lulled me into sleep until there was nothing but darkness.

Mr. Gordon's hand shook me awake. "Miss Emily." Brooks and I both groaned, waking up with another shake. The TV was still on, though the movie had ended. Mr. Gordon didn't usually wake us up; our parents were always the ones who did.

"I'm so sorry," he said gravely, his eyes moist with tears. I looked at him, confused. I had never known Mr. Gordon as a soft man. He was so professional. Yet there he was, tears streaming down his cheeks. "There has been an accident."

My world was spinning before I had finished comprehending what he was saying. In the movie? Sleep tugged at my eyes, but somewhere inside, I felt the truth like a blow to my stomach.

"What kind of accident?" I asked, my voice no more than a whisper. Mr. Michaels appeared with our coats. Brooks took them both in his hands as he lifted me from the couch.

“C’mon, Emily.”

“We’re so sorry,” Mr. Gordon muttered as we put the coats on. I still couldn’t find the ability to speak. Am I dreaming? Am I dreaming this because of the movie? Please tell me I’m dreaming. Wake up. Wake up. *I clenched my arms around my stomach.* This isn’t real. *It was real, though. As real as the rain that landed on my face as I stepped out into the cold night.*

The ride to the hospital felt like an eternity. Every second wasn’t fast enough to get to them and too fast for the reality they weren’t there. I couldn’t stop crying even though nobody had told us anything. Still, deep down, I knew. I could see it in everyone’s eyes. I could feel it in the air. They were gone. Brooks sat quietly, wiping several tears of his own as he looked out the window into the dark night while the rain slapped the window. His arm was holding my body as I trembled against him.

When we finally reached the hospital, one of the hospital administrators met us at the door. Mr. Michaels and Mr. Gordon stayed with us as we were led into a room of doctors and hospital staff. I glanced around the room, confused. “Where are they?” I sobbed hysterically.

“I am so sorry, Miss Barlow. Your parents, they didn’t make it.”

“What about mine?” Brooks’ voice broke from behind me.

“I’m so sorry. They were already gone when paramedics arrived on the scene. It was a head-on collision. An intoxicated driver crossed through the median and hit them head-on. We believe it was instant.”

She seemed so matter-of-fact it was almost startling. As if this news isn’t going to alter every day of our life from this day forward. As if two teenagers lose their parents every day. As if knowing the simple facts would make this earth-shattering discovery somehow hurt less. I stumbled back, falling into Brooks while she continued talking, though her voice was miles away.

“They’re gone?” I cried, my stomach was in free fall, and my heart was shattered, laying in pieces at my feet. I wanted to see them before...

before they were cold. I already knew that this was all I would get, but having it confirmed was worse.

I slid to the floor, taking Brooks with me. His grip on my shoulders tightened like I was supporting him, too. He hugged me from behind, and we both cried while the adults talked in the background, their voices muffled in the distance. It's just us now. *When people described being numb, I never understood until now.* They're gone.

Too soon, Mr. Michaels helped us up from the floor. "We will take you home until your uncle arrives, Brooks."

"My uncle?" he asked, wiping away his tears. "I haven't seen him since I was a kid. Why do I have to wait for him?"

"Unfortunately, your parents haven't updated their will in a long time. He is listed as your sole guardian. He will fly in Saturday morning to take you back to New York. I'm so very sorry," replied Mr. Gordon.

New York? No, that's not right. That can't be right. That's on the other side of the country. *"New York?" I asked, confused. Mr. Gordon nodded. The pain in his eyes confirmed my worst fear.*

"You can't leave. I can't lose you too." I threw my arms around Brooks, and he stumbled back and caught me. His palm brushed over my hair, attempting to comfort me in his own time of need. My body went limp against his as the exhaustion took over.

"Emily, I can carry you," Mr. Micaehls offered.

"No, it's okay," I whimpered, standing to bury myself into Brooks again. This can't be right. He has to stay. I can't breathe. I can't breathe. *I began to hyperventilate. "I can't breathe," I sobbed, pulling my face out of his jacket. A nurse behind us grabbed my arm.*

"Deep breaths, sweetie. Slow, deep breaths." My heart was pounding, and I couldn't catch my breath. The room seemed to be getting smaller. It was like someone was sitting on my chest. Everything inside of me was in full-on panic mode. I gripped Brooks' coat tighter, closing my eyes as I focused on breathing.

"That's right. Slow. In and out." In and out. In and out. "Okay, just keep practicing that breathing, okay? You aren't going to die. Just

slow, deep breaths." The nurse nodded at Mr. Michaels, who guided us back to the car. In and out. In and out.

Just two hours ago, everything felt right in the world. Brooks and I were lying on the couch, cuddled up together, eagerly awaiting our parents' return. Brooks was the captain of our school soccer team, and I was in my seventh year of dance, with a recital coming up in a few weeks. We both had good grades, a lot of friends, and we spent every single day together. Now, it is all gone.

The world felt dark, and tomorrow loomed ahead like a giant demon I wasn't ready to confront. I couldn't face it. In and out...they are gone...in and out... he's leaving...in and out...I can't do this.

Chapter Forty-Two

The world seemed to move in slow motion as we pulled into the driveway. Brooks' house was dark, with only the exterior lights casting a soft glow against the rock facade. Our little corner of paradise at the end of the street felt darker than ever. It no longer resembled the perfect, safe bubble we once lived in. Instead, it had become a place devoid of life, joy, light, and laughter. Our homes used to be sanctuaries filled with love.

Now, these dark, empty houses bore no resemblance to what we had just left behind. It was as if the homes themselves understood that things had changed irrevocably during our absence, transforming the atmosphere into something lonely and melancholic.

We didn't ask for permission; we simply climbed into my bed together and cried. I had never felt more exhausted, but sleep wouldn't come. Part of me wished I could drift off and dream the last few hours away. My eyes burned, my head felt like it was going to split in two, and my stomach was in knots with no relief in sight. When would the pain end? Never. That was the answer—never. I could never get over this. And how was I supposed to let go of the very person who was keeping me afloat in just a few short days?

The tears kept flowing, softer than before, providing my body with some mercy from the uncontrollable sobs at the hospital that had left me with aching muscles and a broken heart. Brooks and I lay together in a continuous pool of tears. It felt like a metaphor for the drowning sensation we both experienced.

The rest of the week was a blur. It was like I was watching life pass me by on fast-forward. People were coming and going, flowers filled every space of our homes, and Brooks and I sat in a daze, unable to break out of our trance.

On the day of the funeral, the staff had picked out black outfits for us. I looked at the slim black dress, noticing how dark it was, how empty and devoid of life it was. Wearing black clothing didn't feel like my parents. Black isn't a happy color. I wondered who first decided to wear the painful, gloomy, dreadful color to a funeral. We talk about remembering life, but black reminds you they're gone, that there is a hole in your life. If I had had any energy to care, I would have found something else to wear, but I was moving on auto-pilot then.

We buried them at Lake View Cemetery in Seattle. So many friends of our family were there, and they all came one by one to offer their condolences, but after just a few, I shut down, sitting in the front row, no longer having the energy to stand or shake people's hands. Brooks stood in front of me, quietly being a presence for both families while I stared blankly off into space. I know you are so sorry for my loss. Me too.

The crowd followed us back to my house, but I was in no mood to sit in a room of adults who looked at us with pity and sorrow. I knew they all meant well, but it was suffocating, and unless one of them could change Brooks being taken away from me, well, I could care less about saving face. As if Brooks could read my mind, he followed me to my room, where we both changed into pajamas, crawled back into my bed, and turned on a movie.

We didn't move for the rest of the day, not even for dinner when Ms. Hutchins brought it in. Neither of us was hungry. Tomorrow was Saturday, and Brooks was leaving. In the brief moments when I wasn't sulking in self-pity or zoning out while staring at the TV, I kept thinking that if I could have frozen time, I would have, even with the unbearable ache in my chest. If my grip had been tight enough, they would never have been able to separate us. Unfortunately, that wasn't the case. Morning arrived.

When Ms. Hutchins came in to get us ready, my tears had soaked his shirt, and his breathing was uneven.

"Emily, Brooks, time to wake up," she whispered, shaking us lightly.

I looked at her and shook my head.

"No, he can't go. We have to do something. Please. Just ask his uncle," I begged.

"Emily, sweetie, he has to go. We've asked."

I looked back at Brooks, who was just opening his eyes. Dark circles surrounded his bloodshot eyes. It wasn't fair. Everything I had ever heard about E.W. Mason was that he was not a kind man. He was wealthy and had never married or had kids. He barely spoke to Carrie. She was pretty much the exact opposite of him. E.W. refused any sort of personal or intimate relationships. They were seen as a "roadblock" to his success. He didn't even come to his own sister's funeral. What kind of name was E.W. anyway?

"Brooks, the staff are at your place already packing. They are waiting for you. They will pack whatever you want to take. Your uncle's plane should be here in a few hours. As much as I hate doing this, you both need to get up and ready. We don't want to leave Brooks without clothes and his belongings, do we? You know his uncle is not going to wait around."

I sighed. She was right. I rolled off the bed on Brooks' side, never letting go of his hand until Ms. Hutchins shoved me into the bathroom with a fresh set of clothes.

"Ms. Hutchins," I began to cry softly. The hole in my chest, the big, ugly hole, was somehow widening, beginning to consume every part of me. "I can't do this. I don't know how to do this without him. Please."

"Emily," her voice was tender. "I wish I could help. I wish more

than anything I could stop him from leaving, but I can't. Mr. Mason has already made up his mind. There was no remorse in his voice. We offered to keep Brooks here and raise him. He would hear nothing of it." She swatted away a stray tear of her own.

"Then can we move? I just can't stay here without him. I can't."

"No, Emily. You can and you will. One day at a time."

They didn't understand. There was nothing left.

↟ ↟ ↟

Brooks and I sat silently on his bed as the staff around us packed his clothes, books, and all other belongings. Brooks grabbed a photo of us off his nightstand.

"I love you, Emily. I will always love you. I will come home as soon as possible, and we can get married. I promise."

Everything hurt as I laid my head on his shoulder. "I love you," I whispered through silent tears.

There was an obnoxious knock at the door, one that only an impatient and thoughtless man could contrive.

"I can't." I clung to Brooks.

"Emily, you have to. Please. For me. I promise I will come home for you." His voice was cracking as tears raced down his hollow cheeks. Mr. Mason rounded the top of the stairs and stepped into Brooks' room.

"Time to go, Brooks. You're not ready yet?" His voice was cold and unwavering. He gave me a once-over and motioned to the door. "Let's go, Brooks. Let her go."

Brooks stood, taking the photo of us with him. I watched him take each step with hesitancy as he descended the staircase. His eyes danced around the wall, taking in all the happy family photos. This was his home, and it had only ever been filled with the happiest of memories, and now, he was losing this, too.

Brooks turned to look at me at the base of the stairs. His eyes were heavy with tears, and I saw a lifetime of hopes and dreams shattered staring back at me.

"Bye," he whispered. Heavy, quiet tears splashed on my cheeks. I had to do this for him.

"Bye," I replied.

In the months that followed, I remained on autopilot. I woke up feeling more tired than the day before, I ate a few bites of food when it was placed in front of me, and I slept as much as possible. The only moments of reprieve were the rare moments when school managed to pique my interest and when I was on the phone with Brooks.

Connor tried to help, but even he was a source of pain. Another reminder of the missing member of our triad. After Mr. Mason took Brooks to New York, he was only there for a week before he was sent to live at Brighton's Boys College in England.

He was now an eight-hour time difference away, making it difficult to connect. It was as if the universe was trying to keep us apart. But I wouldn't let that happen. I would make it. We would make it. So, I repeated that mantra to myself several times a day until I started to believe it. He would come home.

After several weeks of watching me dwindle away, Ms. Hutchins, who became my primary caregiver alongside Mr. Michaels and Mr. Gordon, agreed it was time that I start therapy.

Initially, I was reluctant, but eventually, I found the key to the dam. Once lifted, it all broke free from me, raging and thrashing. By senior year, I felt as stable as a new foal could be on day three of their young life. There wasn't another word for it. Just stable. I was no longer teetering on the edge of something dark but wasn't happy or healthy either.

Brooks and I settled into a new routine and found ways to stay connected. He loved sending me gifts; they always showed up when I needed them. I even received a teddy bear in a tophat when I was sick with the flu. I finally let Connor in, and he even asked Brooks if he could take me to the prom so I wouldn't miss it. Of course, Brooks had agreed, but I would hear nothing of it, no matter how much they tried to convince me. I knew friends went with friends all the time, but again, I just existed. I was stable.

By the end of senior year, I looked forward to Brooks returning home. It had been a week since I had talked to him. He was doing finals and wrapping up classes. It was June, and I was sitting out by the Sound when Brooks called. He normally FaceTimed me, so it was weird that he was calling. I should have known then that something was wrong.

"Emily." I could hear the regret in his voice.

"Hey, B. What's wrong?"

"Please, don't be mad. Please, don't hate me."

Chapter Forty-Three

"I'm not coming home yet." My heart stuttered to a stop.

"What do you mean you're not coming home, Brooks?" My voice was shaky, and my hand struggled to hold the phone still.

"Em, I," he paused. "I joined the Air Force."

Big, heavy tears fell before he finished the sentence, and the air was sucked out of my lungs. Had I heard him wrong? A long beat passed as he left me to my thoughts, putting two and two together. Anger sped through my veins, replacing my shock and confusion.

"You lied to me. You promised you would come home. You're a liar."

"Emily, please. I know I said I would come home, and I will. I just have to do this. I know you don't understand, but I can't come home right now. This is my path." There was desperation in his voice. I knew he didn't want to stay away, but he was choosing this. He knew, and he didn't tell me.

"You lied." My voice broke as my anger subsided, and the loss and pain crept back in. "You promised."

"Please, forgive me. I know I promised, and I still mean it. I am coming home, just not for a few more years."

I gasped, feeling the hole in my chest break open again. "A few years? I...I" The same panicky feeling crept in, and I gasped for air. Brooks was going to be gone for a few more years. Did he not love me anymore? Was I in this alone?

"Em, c'mon, breathe. Remember, in and out. Deep breaths, Em."

I couldn't breathe in or out, though - I couldn't breathe at all. He knew this would break me. He knew I couldn't do this alone. I needed him.

"I can't do this." I gasped for air. "Please, don't do this. Just come home first. Please, please, please."

"Em, I can't. I have to be in Texas in a few weeks." He sounded as broken as I felt.

"You can come home tomorrow. Please."

"I wish I could."

My heart pounded in my ears as we sat in silence, and I tried to focus on one breath at a time - without Brooks. I couldn't fathom four more years without him.

"You promised we would get married. I can marry you and come with you. Please."

"Emily, I can't be the husband you need right now. I just need some time. I love you and want to marry you, but I have to do this first."

"I don't know how to -" I trailed off, unable to finish my sentence.

"You don't know how to what?"

"I don't know how to keep going. You said two years."

"I know, and I'm sorry." His voice was shaky, and I could hear the tears in his voice. "Please understand I have to do this. I am just asking for more time."

More time? Could I give him more time? It was Brooks, after all. One day at a time. That's what Dr. Jordan said. One day at a time.

"Four years, Brooks? Do you promise?" I couldn't believe I was actually considering this. Brooks hummed, sounding surprised on the other end, but I continued. "You better promise me and not break this promise. I won't live without you. If you die, I will die. I won't

survive us not making it, Brooks. We're supposed to be in this together."

"I know, Em. I know. We will be, I promise," he pleaded.

"I can't hold on much longer. Please come home. For one day. Please."

"I promise you with my life, Emily Claire Barlow, I will come home to you. Four years is all I'm asking."

As we lay in bed that night, my head rested against Brooks' side. We were both emotionally exhausted, reflecting on everything we had and lost. I was certain nobody could separate us this time, and Brooks wasn't going anywhere. I could hear his erratic breathing matching the rhythm of my own.

"Why Brighton?" I asked, breaking the silence. "Why couldn't he have sent you home to us?" Without skipping a beat or asking how I even came to ask that question in bed all these years later, Brooks simply answered as if we were both there, reliving it all.

"I don't know, Em. He had some connection there and thought it would be better if I grew up there."

"It wasn't fair. You lost everything. We lost everything, even each other. He didn't have to send you away."

"I know. I didn't lose everything, though. I still had you."

"No, you lost me too," I reminded him quietly.

"Almost, but thankfully not forever. I love you, and I'm sorry. I will say I am sorry for the rest of my life."

"B, I said I forgive you, and I do. Just don't ever leave again." I nuzzled into his embrace, needing to be as close as possible to him, hoping his warmth would reassure the worries in the back of my mind.

"I'm not going anywhere. I promise. It's okay to sleep, I promise. I will still be holding you when you wake up."

I sighed. "I know." It just didn't feel that way. The memories were a little too raw.

↟ ↟ ↟

The first week of August filled me with panic as the wedding date approached quickly. The past few weeks had gone by in a blur, filled with wedding planning, getting the bridesmaids fitted for their dresses, starting at Caston, and attending my eleven-week ultrasound and checkup. Dr. Williams informed me that I could begin tapering off my medications and only use them as needed.

During my first week at Caston, Brooks was in Seattle, which was slightly inconvenient, but I wasn't ready to travel just yet. I was still uncertain about how I would respond to being off my medication. I met with our executive team and decided it would be best to establish a new department dedicated to corporate philanthropy.

Diane and I conducted interviews to find my new assistant, who would temporarily fill in while I was on maternity leave. I needed someone I could trust with my vision. We found my perfect match, Mina Issa. She graduated with her MBA while I graduated from high school, but I wanted someone older than me to rely on.

Mina had worked for a year at Google before moving to Seattle, where she served as a finance officer for a local non-profit. She was excited about the change; her previous job hadn't been a good fit, and I was pleased to have someone with her experience on board. Last week, we held interviews for my new team and hired five new members, men and women of different ages, all with backgrounds in various charity-focused professions.

After all this time, I couldn't shake the feeling that working at Caston was exactly where I belonged. I was excited to focus on philanthropy while supporting the company in any way I could.

Brooks had been working with the team in Los Angeles all week on the new Kildaire Hotel in Santa Monica. He didn't need to be there, but he had been struggling with self-doubt about his ability to run a company of this size. Michaelson decided to accompany him, for which I was thankful. I woke up to his text saying his flight home was this afternoon and that he couldn't wait to see me. The message included a bunch of heart and googly-eye emojis.

I settled into my spot at the kitchen island with a notepad, MacBook, and a steaming cup of tea when I heard a knock at the door. I hadn't received any notification about a car coming up the driveway and wasn't expecting anyone. I grabbed my phone and headed to the door, checking the camera. A girl whom I didn't recognize stood there.

Another loud clap of thunder sent chills down my spine as I yanked the door open. The girl at the door had a baby strapped to her chest in one of those carriers. Her rain jacket was zipped up around both her and the baby. She pulled down her hood, revealing long brunette hair pulled into a high braided ponytail falling down her side. Her big brown eyes looked sad and tired behind black-rimmed glasses. The baby in her arms was crying, and she bounced gently while shushing to calm her.

"Can I help you?" I asked. I searched around for a car and saw none.

"Does Brooks Devonshire live here?" she asked, shuddering from the cold.

"Yes, come in." I pulled the door open. *What was she doing out here in the rain with a baby, and how did she know Brooks?* I had so many questions.

"Umm, he isn't here right now," I started as I closed the door behind us. Her eyes wandered around the room before settling again on me. "He should be home later, though."

"I'm sorry to intrude. It's just that I really need to talk to Brooks. I have been trying to track him down for a few weeks. I was sent to an address in Bellevue and then was given this address by a couple across the street. They said that you might know how to find him."

"Umm..." I stopped, puzzled. She must have gone to Brooks's childhood home and then to mine. It seemed odd that the couple who purchased my home would think I knew anything about Brooks since I never mentioned him, but then again, everyone on our street knew that Brooks and I had always been close.

The baby was wailing now, and I could see the exhaustion in the girl's eyes. Her wet, loose strands were clinging to her face.

"You can use the bathroom to dry off if you want. Then we can talk?" I asked. She nodded and removed a tiny baby dressed in a pink shirt and cream leggings from the carrier. The baby was chubby and had dark brown hair like her mom. It wasn't until she placed the baby on her hip that I noticed how blue her eyes were. I shook off the familiar feeling and led her down the hall on the other side of the kitchen to the bathroom. It wasn't until I was closing the door that I heard her say, "Shh... it's okay, Brooklyn. We will be okay."

Fear gripped my stomach and chest as I made my way back to the couch. A blue-eyed baby named Brooklyn showed up on our doorstep with a young mom looking for Brooks. I tried to calm my thoughts. Babies have blue eyes all the time. Just because they're looking for Brooks doesn't mean this is his baby. He would have told me. He never said anything about a serious girlfriend. My mind was racing, keeping me so preoccupied that I didn't notice them returning to the living room where I was pacing.

"Thank you." Her voice was soft and weighed down with sadness. I looked up to see her standing near the counter with her baby on her hip.

"Can I get you water or tea or coffee?" I asked, moving to the kitchen.

"Coffee would be great," she responded, pulling out a barstool.

"Sure." I was opening cabinets with less grace than usual. I wanted to call Brooks, but he was on his flight back home. Plus, I didn't even know who she was. In all the shock and chaos, I hadn't even thought to ask her name.

I flipped on the coffee maker and turned to see her with baby Brooklyn on her lap.

"Umm...so..." I gestured for the door. "How did you get here?

How do you know Brooks?" I started, still completely anxious. I was twisting the ring on my finger over and over.

"Well, it's a long story. I'm Cailey. Cailey Langston, this is my daughter Brooklyn. She's named after Brooks."

I nodded and sucked in a sharp, dizzying breath before turning back to the coffee.

Brooks had been pretty shelled up about his time in the Air Force. I had asked so many questions, but he always gave vague, short answers, some probably because he was on the Special Ops team. I had always chalked it up to him not wanting to talk about it, but was this why? Was Cailey his ex-girlfriend? Or was she one of the "few"? The biggest burning question was whose baby was that.

I poured the coffee into the mug and turned back to Cailey and Brooklyn. I slid the mug over along with a sugar bowl and a steamed cup of cream and pulled my shaky hands back before she noticed.

"She isn't his," Cailey started.

I looked up at her. "What?" I gulped.

"Brooklyn. She isn't Brooks' baby. I can see it on your face." She smiled weakly.

"I'm sorry, I just -" I blew out a long breath I had been holding and placed my cold palm on my forehead.

"Are you Emily?" she asked, sipping her now cream-filled coffee.

I nodded.

"Brooks talked about you non-stop. He's crazy about you. Which I am assuming you know since you live here with him and have that big rock on your finger." I looked down at my hand, which was rubbing across my stomach.

"The wedding is in a few weeks." I smiled, feeling at least some of the tension leave my body.

"He will be a great dad." She smiled more brightly and laughed, looking down at the little girl steadying herself against her mom's shoulders. Cailey had her arm draped around her daughter, who was standing on her lap.

"I don't know who her dad is. I know that sounds terrible, but please don't judge me. It's another long story. I know Brooks because he's my friend. We met when he was in San Antonio. I worked at the bar he used to come into with his friends." She paused, smiling at her daughter.

"I got to know Brooks first. We hung out a lot and went out a few times before I realized he had more than just a crush on his ex. We stayed friends, though, and then he introduced me to his friend Cliff. It was an on-and-off thing until they left for Osan. I went to visit them once. They paid for my ticket shortly after they got there. Cliff decided he wanted to be in a real relationship." She made quotes with her fingers.

I was pacing the room again. So she was an "ex" date of Brooks'. Did they sleep together?

"Can I ask," I swallowed down the bile rising up my throat and looked down at the ring on my finger. "What are you doing here?"

Chapter Forty-Four

Her face turned down, and she took another long drink of coffee. "Cliff died. Brooks never showed up for the funeral, which is really unlike him. They were so close." She set her cup down and then looked back at me. "Brooks and Cliff had made a promise to each other before they left for Osan. If anything had ever happened to Brooks, Cliff was to deliver a letter to you, and Brooks' belongings, and Cliff was supposed to look after you." She wiped away a stray tear.

"And Brooks promised the same to Cliff?" I finished for her.

She nodded. "I know it sounds stupid, and he doesn't owe me anything, but he's kinda all I have now. He and Brooklyn. I can't go home. I lost my apartment when I had her because I couldn't pay the bills. I couldn't afford daycare. My parents wanted nothing to do with me because having a baby out of wedlock is a disgrace to God." She rolled her eyes and took a deep breath.

"I don't get anything from the military because Cliff and I were never married, and his parents refuse to help because Cliff never mentioned me, and well, we don't know if she is his. Cliff doesn't have blue eyes." She dropped her eyes to the mug.

My heart hurt for the girl in front of me. Of course, there were welfare programs she could join, but she had one last thread to pull, and that was Brooks. Of course, he would have made that promise, and damn it if I didn't love him more because of it.

"Brooks will be landing soon. Follow me." I smiled softly, gesturing for her to follow me to the study.

We stood facing the wall of photos in Brooks' study. Cailey had more tears as she ran her finger down one of the men in the photos. *That must be Cliff.* Why didn't Brooks tell me about them? Why didn't he go to the funeral?

"You can stay here until we figure something out. We will help you," I said. She turned to face me and paused, looking at me for a second before wrapping her free arm around my neck. Brooklyn twisted her hands in my hair, causing me to smile and think about the little baby in my belly.

↟ ↟ ↟

Cailey and I were on the couch, Brooklyn fast asleep in her arms, when Brooks' car tripped the alert.

"He's home," I said, getting up to meet him at the door. She stayed put on the couch. Her raincoat and backpack were still on the entry floor, so I picked them up and placed them in the closet above the tray. I used the mop to wipe away the rain and put it back in the closet just in time for Brooks to open the door.

"Hey, baby!" Brooks said, sweeping me up into his arms and spinning me. I melted into him and pressed my lips to his, allowing his minty tongue to sweep in. I let out a small moan and then remembered we had an audience. I pulled away, and he let me slide back to my feet.

"Brooks," I paused. What should I say? Your ex-girlfriend/ex-date is here? "Eh, Cailey is here." I finished. Brooks' eyes widened as he set his bags down and grabbed my hand.

"Sorry, Em. I should have told you about everyone. The guys and

Cailey." His voice was no more than a whisper. I shook my head. He had handled Parker and Grey with such grace and kindness. He deserved the same.

"She's great. I think we all need to sit and talk, though." I leaned back into him and wrapped my arms around him, inhaling my favorite scent. "C'mon." I pulled back and retook his hand as we walked into the living room.

"Hey, baby D!" Cailey chuckled. "Ooh, look at you with your fancy outfit and beard. Who are you, and what have you done with my Brooks?" she teased. *Her Brooks? Baby D?* Jealousy tore through me, leaving me feeling queasy once again. Brooks half smiled and squeezed my hand but kept his eyes focused on her.

"Hey, CC. Who's baby did you kidnap?" he laughed.

She rolled her eyes, grinning like her savior was finally here to rescue her. "She's mine, you dumbass. Meet Brooklyn Catherine."

I didn't realize how hard I was gripping Brooks' hand until he went to sit and ended up yanking me down with him.

"What are you doing here, Cailey?" he asked, his tone more serious than a few seconds ago.

"Well, that, my bearded friend, starts with another question. Why didn't you come?" She was drilling her eyes into him with intensity. They were familiar with each other and had nicknames and a past I wasn't a part of. Heck, I didn't even know about her until an hour ago.

Brooks sighed, running his hand through his hair. "I'm sorry. I should have, but I have been so busy here with taking over the company and -"

"And getting engaged? Congrats, by the way," she snapped, cutting him off. This was not the same girl that was so sweet sitting with me before he came home. This girl was sassy and a little too comfortable with my fiance.

"It's not like that. I wanted to come." I gripped his bicep, laying my head against his shoulder, and felt a little tension release from him on his exhale. "I don't know why Cay. There isn't a good excuse, and I'm sorry. Colton texted me the day it happened. I was getting ready for our engagement party and just shoved it into a box to deal with later. Colton texted me again about the funeral. Emily was sick, and I didn't want to leave her. I'm sorry. I wanted to be there for you guys. I did."

Cailey had tears streaming down her face, and guilt ripped through me. I had been too sick to notice that he had lost another person. I was the reason he didn't go.

"I'm sorry, B," I said, my own tears now brimming. Brooks turned to face me and brushed away a tear.

"It's okay, sweetie. We can talk about it later."

I nodded and settled into the cushions behind me. I was searching my brain to think back to the engagement party. Brooks had been tense and a little off when we were getting ready, but we were so busy with last-minute details that I didn't pause to ask if he was okay, and he never said anything. Why?

"I promised Cliff I would take care of you, and I will follow through with that. I'm sorry it has taken me so long. Tomorrow, we can get you a place anywhere you want. I'm assuming things didn't work out with your parents?"

She shook her head. "Nope." The p popped as she said it. "They're still the same old, judgemental people proclaiming I am tarnishing their name and the Latter-Day Saints."

Brooks sighed. "Where do you want to go?"

Cailey shrugged, causing Brooklyn to stir.

"Are you willing to go to Seattle? We can get you a job and daycare. I'm there often, so I can easily check in on you."

Cailey wiped away another tear. "Yeah. Seattle. That's fine. Thanks."

"I said she could stay here with us until we figured it out," I said. Brooks looked back at me, and his features softened into a small smile. He brought our linked hands to his mouth and kissed my knuckles.

"I will get you a place first thing tomorrow. I'll take care of rent for the first year and pay for daycare until you can get on your feet. I'll also find an opening at Caston to place you." Brooks turned on his business voice. "We can talk tomorrow about jobs. For now, I think I need to talk to Emily."

He stood and took me with him.

"Hold on, B," I whispered, then turned to Cailey. "Did you have anything else other than the one bag? There's a room in the basement where most of our guests stay. You will be comfortable and have your own bathroom. There's a little kitchenette down there, too, if you need to keep bottles in it."

"Thank you, Emily. It's just the one bag. Would you mind showing me? I need to put her down, and I'd like to get out of these wet clothes."

"Of course." I released Brooks' hand and led the way to the basement.

"Here." I pushed open the bedroom door, revealing the king-size bed on the low, wooden platform against the dark green wall. I flipped the switch on for the soft lighting and made my way to the mounted wooden headboard and nightstand to grab the remote. "This operates the blinds. The bathroom is just on the other side of the door, and the closet is behind that door. You can hang anything up, and I can throw anything in the wash."

She cut me off again with another hug. "Thank you, Emily. Really. I'm sorry for all of this."

Tears pricked the back of my eyes again. "I'm glad you're here. Well, I will let you get settled. Let me know if you need anything. The fridge upstairs is stocked. The one down here has drinks." I turned to go, pulling out of her hug. "Oh, and one more thing. I just wanted to say I'm sorry. Brooks didn't come to the funeral because that was the week I found out I was pregnant. I was sick, like really sick, and he had to take me to the doctor." I shuffled my weight. "I'm sorry."

When she said nothing, I looked back up at her brown eyes. "It's not your fault, and it doesn't matter now. Thanks again."She turned and laid baby Brooklyn down on the bed. I dipped out quietly, not looking back.

Brooks was pacing upstairs in our bedroom. I closed the door softly and fell against it.

"Why didn't you tell me?" I asked, crossing my arms over my chest.

"I should have. I don't know why. I haven't talked about any of them because there was so much tension around that time of our lives. Telling you that I had friends and a whole life that wasn't just sad all the time made me feel guilty." He dragged his hands through his hair. "I missed you so damn much, and I was like half a person without you, but Cailey and Cliff and Colton and Jerome, Davis, Trent, and Mark. They were my Sara and Parker. Cliff, Davis, Colton, and I were all sent to Osan. Mark is still in Texas, I think. Jerome is in Colorado, and Trent is in Hawaii."

"Why didn't you tell me about her? She may not love you like I do, but she does love you."

"No, that's just how she is with all the guys. We were like her brothers she never had."

"Except you," I said. There was no judgment or irritation in my voice.

Brooks paused his pacing. His eyes darted out the window to the storm and then back to me. "It was one time, Em."

"One time, what Brooks?" my voice hitched.

"I didn't sleep with her. I took her on a date once. Things got a little handsy during a drunken kiss, and that was it. After that, I told her about you. She said she couldn't wait to meet you - the girl who had captured my heart."

I exhaled a long breath and crossed the room to him. I hated the tension between us that she had brought. Knowing she knew what his lips felt like wasn't exactly helping anything, but I couldn't be a hypocrite. I placed my hands on Brooks' chest and kissed his shirt. His arms wrapped around me and pulled me down onto our bed, where we snuggled up into each other.

"She will be gone tomorrow. I don't want her to stay here. I'll find a place tonight and leave first thing in the morning."

I ran my hand down the buttons of his shirt and then flipped over so that I was straddling him. "Baby D?" I laughed.

"The guys used to claim I had a baby face. Baby Devonshire, or Baby D for short." He smirked.

"I think," I started unbuttoning his shirt to expose his chest, running my palms down the warm, stretched skin. I bent down, planted another kiss on his sternum, and sat up again. He went hard under me. "I think I want to hear more of these stories." I bent down and ran my tongue along the valley of exposed abs. "Can't you have Michaelson deal with the apartment or have anyone else do it?" I kissed the v of his left hip and then moved to the right. "You just got home." My voice was husky and laced with need.

Brooks gripped my blouse and yanked me up to meet his mouth with mine. "Maybe," he said between kisses. "Now," he pulled away, trailing kisses along my neck. "Let me show you how much I missed you."

Chapter Forty-Five

Cailey was sitting at the counter when I came downstairs. Brooks was still asleep from his late-night apartment shopping. I was wearing his t-shirt and a pair of satin sleep shorts, my favorite fuzzy slippers, and my hair pulled into a topknot. Cailey's eyes darted away from me as I stepped into the kitchen to make tea.

"Good morning," I said with my back to her.

"Morning," she cleared her throat. I hope you don't mind. I made myself a cup of coffee. I had to watch a YouTube video to figure it out," she chuckled in disbelief.

"Sorry." I turned to face her. "Brooks and I both have a thing for fancy tech. He found this coffee machine and had to have it."

"Is Brooks awake?" she asked before taking another sip.

"No, he was up late. Where's Brooklyn?"

"Asleep." She held up the baby monitor in her hands. "How far along are you?"

"Umm..." I blew a loose strand of hair. "Twelve weeks, I think."

She slurped her next sip of coffee. "Wow. Wedding and a baby. He worked quickly."

"Excuse me?" I set my tea down with a loud clunk. My brows furrowed as I looked at my overly comfortable house guest.

"I didn't mean to be rude." She shifted on the stool and peered at me with a confident stare. "It's just he's been back, what, a few months? I've known him for years, and he was always so quiet and vigilant. The Brooks I know would have been more careful. It took a lot for someone to get him to slip into bed with them."

I wanted to reach across the table and slap the smirk off her face. I wasn't sure if her comment was meant to comfort me or rock the boat while I stood on the plank, blindfolded and balancing on one foot, but either way, I didn't like it.

This stranger would not come into my home and pretend to know the man that I have loved the entirety of my life better than I do. And she is especially not going to comment about how or who Brooks has climbed into bed with in the past or present. How dare she. I took a steady breath.

"Well, I have known him practically my whole life, and he's just making up for lost time." I gave a half-shrug and met her gaze, hoping to come off unbothered instead of territorial like I felt. "We should have been married already. We have a looong history together," I reminded her as I matched her cocky smirk. The claws were officially out, and I was flooded with a wave of satisfaction as I watched her falter.

"Then why didn't he marry you before he left?" The simplicity of the question shouldn't hurt as much as it did, but I refused to give her the satisfaction of seeing my pain.

"Look, Cailey, I don't know what your deal is, but frankly, it's none of your damn business." My patience was gone, and it was time to remind her whose house she was in, even if I had to kick her and her baby out of here. I may have promised her she could stay, but that was yesterday before she thought I was the interloper here. "Neither of us has to explain ourselves or our relationship to you or anyone else. We will be married in three weeks, and everything that happened in the past won't matter. He chose me. Get over it."

She dropped her head back and laughed. "Emily, don't get all crazy. I'm not pining after your boyfriend."

"Fiance," I corrected. I bit down a little too hard on the inside of my cheek, filling my mouth with the taste of copper. My anger was a living and tangible thing, but so was my jealousy. She had poked at my insecurities and hurts in just a few sentences. I needed to find a way to escape before angry tears poured down my cheeks.

"Fiance, whatever. I was just making the point that he's moving fast. You two didn't waste any time." Her voice clung to the "any" in an irritating way, or maybe it was the pregnancy hormones. It didn't matter; it was grating on my nerves. "What Brooks and I had was nothing more than a few passionate makeout sessions and a run between first and second."

She took a sip of her coffee while maintaining eye contact. Brooks said it was just a kiss, but I wouldn't put it past her to stretch the truth. "It stopped there, and I was fine with that. I don't like men who are in love with other women. I have more self-respect than that."

"So, what is your point exactly?" I snapped.

"Nothing. It was an observation. You hardly know each other." She shrugged.

"We know each other just fine. Hell of a lot more than you do."

"Except you don't." She slammed her coffee mug down onto the counter as she stood. "He didn't even tell you about me or Cliff or anyone. We were his friends. We partied together. We took trips together. He had a whole life without you," she argued.

"Enough," Brooks barked as he rounded the corner. "Emily is my fiance, soon-to-be wife. You can either treat her with respect or get the hell out." Brooks came to stand next to me, placing a protective arm around my waist. The touch alone soothed some of the fiery anger and hurt. "I don't know what your problem is, Cailey, but I will not allow you to treat her like she's some gold-digging whore. Got it?" I winced at his words as he moved toward the coffee machine. With his back to her, Cailey rolled her eyes as she sat back at the counter, once again taking a sip of her coffee.

"I didn't say anything other than the truth. You leave Osan, show up back in the States, and are engaged with a baby on the way in a matter of months. I'm just surprised." She put her hands up, feigning innocence. "Are we getting out of here or what?" she asked.

"I'm not going anywhere." Brooks shifted, leaning against the counter and folding his arms across his chest. "I found you a place. I have a driver coming in a few hours to take you and Brooklyn up to Seattle. One of our assistants, Tasha, will meet you at the apartment with your key. She's currently stocking it with groceries and all the necessities you and Brooklyn will need. She has a daughter, too, so I thought she would be a good fit to help.

"She will give you a prepaid card with some money. It has $1,500 on it, and I will refill it every two weeks for the next six months until you settle in. After Tasha gets you into the apartment, you have a meeting with our HR department to talk about jobs. There is a daycare around the corner that several of our employees use. I will pay the bill as promised for the next year.

"Your apartment has two bedrooms downtown near Pikes Place and the aquarium. It's an easy walking distance to get around. I will check in with you once a month, more if needed." I was shocked to hear him talk to her. His arms flexed, causing his shirt to tighten around his biceps and lift slightly to expose his inked arms. I should be focusing on the problem at hand - Cailey, but I couldn't pull my eyes away. Bossy Brooks was hot.

"Now that I have found you a place to stay, I expect you to treat my soon-to-be wife with the same respect you would show me, actually more. I don't care what history you think we may or may not have that somehow trumps hers with me, but you are mistaken. Don't push it, Cailey, I am not in the mood to handle your mood swings. Are you on your meds?"

I wanted to applaud his little speech, but I was taken aback by the mention of meds.

"I ran out," she muttered, looking down at the baby monitor in her hands and avoiding his gaze.

"Shit." He set his cup down, running a hand through his hair. "How long?"

"A couple of weeks." Setting the baby monitor down, she reached for her coffee like it was her salvation.

"I will have Tasha schedule you an appointment. I want you back on your meds by tomorrow, do you understand? That's how this works. If I'm going to take care of you, that includes your damn health. You know what happened last time."

"It's not like last time. I'll get on them. Calm down." Her hands slammed down into the counter, causing me to jump.

"CC, I'm serious. If you work for me, you're on meds. I won't put up with it." His voice was stern and a little high-handed while talking to a so-called friend. He had never spoken to me like that, and honestly, it made me uncomfortable for her, even if I still wanted to scratch her eyes out.

"Got it, Dad. Sheesh. Don't get your boxers in a twist." A noise came from the baby monitor on the counter, and she moved to check it. A moment later, Brooklyn's cries echoed through the kitchen, and Cailey rose from her seat.

"Cailey, I mean it," Brooks said, glaring at her. She held up her hands and was about to leave the kitchen, but she turned. "Sorry, Emily," she said with the fakest smile ever. Her tone was mocking, but she was gone before I could get a word in.

"You okay?" Brooks asked, embracing my head between his palms and bringing his coffee-tasting mouth to mine. I may have let my jealousy get the best of me because I decided to let that kiss turn into a fit of passion. Brooks and I were both panting when she returned. I smiled, pulling away.

"Just fine," I whispered into his ear. His hips were still firmly planted against me, hiding his erection from her.

Clearly amused and fully aware of my intentions, he leaned in to whisper in my ear. "Well played." He kissed my temple before leaving the kitchen without a glance toward Cailey and Brooklyn, taking his heat and desire upstairs.

I glanced at Cailey, offered a bitchy smile, then left the kitchen to go attend to my fiancé's desires.

↟ ↟ ↟

I settled into the sofa beside Brooks, who was deep in thought, reading through emails on his phone. The scowl across his face had me worried about Caston.

"Are you okay?" I asked. His hand brushed up my legs, which were pulled up into my chest.

"Yeah," he sighed. "It's fine."

"Nope. Don't do that. We have enough unsaid things between us. No more. You tell me everything, and I do the same. That's how this works," I said, repeating his words from earlier.

He chuckled, lifting his eyes to me. "Fine. Caston finances, we've found the pattern we were looking for, but we still don't know who or what is happening. I have to call in an independent team to help with this. If someone in the company is shuffling the money, we can't let them know that we are onto them."

"Okay, so what do we know? Shouldn't you talk to our attorneys?"

"Not yet. I don't know anything. It's just a gut feeling, and I'm not ready to blow this into something it's not. I hope I'm wrong, but several invoices don't add up with Kildaire, and we're missing over a million dollars." He ran his hands through his hair.

"Did Cailey get settled in?" I asked, chewing on my bottom lip.

"Yeah. Em, I am sor-"

"Eh." I held up my hand to stop him. We had already gone through this several times today since she left. "No more. I just want to make sure she made it okay."

"She did. Tasha texted me earlier, and Carol in HR has her set up to interview with Lacie and Tom Douglas tomorrow."

"Tom? I didn't know he was still there."

"He is. He's retiring soon. Possibly next year. He wanted to wait to see us take over the company." He paused. "Cailey is bi-polar. She's on meds that help to stabilize her moods, but most of the time, she is fine. When she got off her meds right before Osan, she trashed the bar where she worked in a fit of rage. Cops were called, and she was put on a 72-hour hold while they got her back on her meds."

"You didn't have to tell me. I trust you."

"I did, actually. You were nothing but patient with her, and you didn't deserve to be treated that way. She really is a nice person, but her swings leave a hell of a mess in their wake."

"Okay." I smiled, feeling reassured, and leaned onto his arm. "Thanks for being such an amazing, caring, supportive, handsome sex-god of a fiancé," I giggled.

"You, Ms. Barlow," he said, standing up and throwing me over his shoulder, "need a good, long orgasm from your sex-god fiancé."

I squealed when he pinched my bottom, ascending the stairs.

↟ ↟ ↟

The sun was making its way over the horizon when I awoke with a start to find a note on Brooks' pillow.

Went for a run. Be back soon with a chai from Lift.

Love you.

Brooks had been so busy with work and managing the deals for the new hotels opening in Europe that it felt like we were constantly in passing. We finally settled upon a wedding date, though, August 27th. Which was just a little over two weeks away. We still had so much to do before then.

With us in Seattle next week for meetings, I felt like we were in a time crunch. We still needed to finalize all the wedding music, food, and honeymoon excursions within the next week. I jumped out of bed and headed for the closet to change. I wanted a yoga session before Brooks returned with my chai.

My new adjusted yoga routine felt good on my tired muscles. The music playing over the speakers helped to calm me while I worked out the stress of all the newness in my life.

"Hey baby," Brooks said as he pushed the doors to the pool deck open.

"Hey, love," I said, wrapping my arms around him for a morning kiss. The taste of black coffee lingered on his tongue.

"Here's your chai. I'm so sorry, but I am running late and have a meeting in twenty. I ran into your friend Nayla at Lift, but she wouldn't let me leave."

"Nayla? What did she want?" A pang of unwarranted jealousy flared through me.

"I guess she's looking for a job in Seattle. I gave her Carol's number."

The last time Nayla talked to Brooks, she was overly flirtatious and insinuated that Brooks and I were like brother and sister. Ugh, he should have ignored her. I pulled Brooks in for another passionate kiss. At least I am the one who gets to kiss these lips. He sighed as he pulled away from me.

"I really need to go, and you're making me hard," he said, glancing down and chuckling to himself.

I giggled. "Sorry, go take a cold shower. I love you." Pushing him toward the doors.

He shot me a quick grin that warmed me from the inside out before disappearing back into the house.

↟ ↟ ↟

Brooks and I lay on the couch that evening, engrossed in our books. It had been a while since we had read together. I had picked up a new book last week while running errands. *Nurture* by Erica Chidi was the most recommended book, according to Natalie, who had inquired around at work for me.

Before opening the book, I had never even heard of a doula. The idea of home births frightened me, and since we didn't have a birthing center, a hospital birth was my only option. Despite my apprehensions, I found myself fascinated by this whole world of birthing that I knew so little about. I was surprised at how clueless I felt being pregnant and not understanding what my body needed or how to help a baby have a stress-free entrance into the world.

By the time we settled down to read, I was already halfway through the book, having struggled to put it down over the past few days. I leaned back against Brooks and yawned.

"You tired?"

"No, I'm good," I replied through my yawn.

"Okay," he chuckled. His hand gently stroked my arm as he read *Start With Why* by Simon Sinek. I had already read that book in college, and it had been worth the effort. I glanced back at my own book but suddenly lost interest in the words on the page.

"Hey, B?"

"Yeah?"

"What should we name our baby?"

He chuckled again, wrapping a warm arm around my chest. "I don't know, Em. We don't even know if it's a girl or boy."

"Can we talk about names?" I turned to plead with him. He rolled his eyes and bookmarked his page.

"Okay."

I tossed my book to the table and looked back at him.

"Okay, so if it's a girl?" I asked with way too much excitement since I was still exhausted. We spent a few minutes throwing out random names, but none of them felt right.

"I like Olivia. I like the idea of naming her after your mom," Brooks said. My chest squeezed, and I felt the tiny prick of tears in my eyes.

"Okay, so boy names," I said, pushing back the emotions threatening to ruin this moment.

Brooks's phone started ringing on the coffee table.

"Hold that thought, Em. I need to take this."

I nodded and moved out from between his legs.

"Brooks," he said instead of hello. "Okay, hold on. I need to get to my computer."

He pulled the phone away. "Sorry, baby." He stood and disappeared into the study.

Chapter Forty-Six

Brooks' watch buzzed against my arm, pulling me from a wonderful dream. I yawned as I slapped his wrist, trying to shut it off.

He groaned, "Come on, the car will be here in an hour. It's time to go." He rolled over onto his stomach, lifting my shirt. "Good morning, sweet baby. Tell Mommy to get up. Just one kick." His voice was sleepy and deep, settling between my thighs.

I giggled, ignoring the instant ache and need from him. "It will be a while before I start feeling the baby kick."

He groaned again before kissing my stomach. I reluctantly opened my eyes, squinting down at Brooks.

"Let's go, sleepy head. We have a flight to catch." His lips pressed into my stomach again.

"I just need a little more sleep," I yawned, pulling the covers over us and burying him in the sheets. He pushed up onto his knees, taking the sheet with him.

"Uh-uh."

I was not going to win this fight just by sheer strength. Plus, he was right. There was a flight to catch. If I was still tired, I could nap on the plane.

"Fine," I teased, jumping out of bed and running for the shower. I pulled my hair into a topknot before stepping into the steaming water. Like clockwork, Brooks appeared at the shower door. I held onto it so he wouldn't open it. Another failed attempt since it swung open with ease, almost taking me with it.

"No," I giggled, reaching for the soap before he could grab me. His arms wrapped around me and pulled me back into him playfully. "We have less than an hour to be ready, remember?" I responded breathlessly as I wiggled, trying to break free from him.

"I can be quick," he smiled, caressing my body. His hard length was pressed into my back.

"No time," I teased, knowing that this would be my third failed attempt for the morning. I was off to a great start, clearly. I squeezed some soap into my hand, but Brooks pulled the bottle away, spilling some on the ground. All I could do was laugh; at least this felt like normal for us again.

I rolled my eyes before rubbing the soap into his chest, across his shoulders, and down his inked arms. He squeezed what felt like half the bottle onto my shoulders before dropping the now nearly empty bottle to the floor. The soap felt like silk as it dripped down both sides of my shoulders. Brooks took the opportunity to kiss me while his hands ran up and down my body, spreading the soap around. The scent of bergamot and vetiver filled the air.

"B," I whispered, pulling away from his mouth. "I love you and want you, but can we do this later?" Guilt washed over me. I felt like I had been shutting him down a lot lately.

It made no sense. How could I want and need him so innately while feeling scared that I would get sick if he came near me right now? I groaned and buried my face in my hands while letting water wash over me.

Brooks assured me everything was okay and we'd have time later, but guilt still gnawed at me. I just had to trust that this was only temporary.

↟ ↟ ↟

Downstairs, the car was waiting for us. Brooks had filled our to-go mugs and already had the luggage in the car as I came rushing down the stairs.

"Good morning, Mr. and Mrs. Devonshire," the driver said as he opened our door. I glanced over at Brooks and grinned. *Mrs. Devonshire.* I love it. I guess Brooks failed to mention we weren't married yet. I pulled my lips in, fighting a small laugh as I slid across the bench. Once the door was closed, Brooks leaned in close, reaching around me to secure my seat belt for me.

"Mrs. Devonshire," he whispered into my ear as his seatbelt clicked. His hand settled on my thigh as he moved his fingers, trailing circles higher and higher on the inside of my thigh.

"Stop," I mouthed playfully, trying not to giggle at his touch.

"I'm just warming you up for tonight, *future* Mrs. Devonshire." He winked, letting his pinky brush across my panties. I let out a soft moan as I looked out the window. I could feel the heat in my cheeks. My heart pounded while a swarm of butterflies took flight in my stomach. His fingers brushed my panties again, making me pull in a sharp breath of air. Brooks chuckled beside me before pulling his hand away.

My eyes returned to his before I whispered, "You enjoy this too much." He nodded slightly, eyeing me up and down with promises for later.

↟ ↟ ↟

Tate was waiting at the stairs when we pulled up to the plane. The driver jumped out to help unload our bags while I grabbed my purse and headed for the plane.

"Great to see you again, Tate." I smiled.

"Miss Barlow, Mr. Devonshire." He nodded.

I sat in my usual seat, expecting Brooks to sit beside me. He opted for the seat in front of me again. As we went wheels up, Brooks' hands were in mine, and I focused on my breathing, hoping my nausea wouldn't kick in. Thankfully, there were no issues.

As we continued climbing, I thought about a trip I had taken with Sara and Parker during my junior year of college. We flew to Albuquerque for the Hot Air Balloon Festival. It was so fun and almost magical. I had never experienced anything quite like it. I sat in the middle seat, and both Parker and Sara held my hands as we lifted into the sky. It was a quiet, simple gesture they both gave me.

"Can I get you anything to drink?" Deborah whispered over my shoulder. My eyes shot open to see her smiling over me. "Do we have sparkling water?"

"Yes, ma'am. Mr Devonshire?"

"I'm good," Brooks mumbled, glancing up at her and then back to his phone. He was clearly enjoying whatever he was reading. *That was rude.*

I nodded to Deborah before she disappeared behind me again.

"Hey." I kicked his knee to get his attention.

"Ow, what?" he laughed, looking up.

"What are you doing? That was rude."

"Sorry." He began to laugh again. "Connor and Michaelson are organizing my bachelor party this weekend."

I raised my eyebrows and looked back out the window. *Please, no strippers, no crazy, wild party. No girls.*

Brooks unbuckled and knelt in front of me, pulling my arms off my chest, clearly reading my mind.

"Em, don't worry. It's Connor, first of all. And second, we are just going to go fishing and wakeboarding. Michaelson is getting a houseboat for us." I exhaled a breath I didn't know I was holding. Of course, their version of a bachelor weekend would include fish and boating instead of girls and parties.

"Okay," I sighed. He kissed my inner thigh before sitting back in his chair. I rolled my eyes as he smirked.

↟ ↟ ↟

The flight was quick and easy as we touched down in Seattle. Diane was waiting for us with a car as the plane stopped. I hadn't seen her in person since the funeral, and we had only been on a few Zoom calls. I hadn't noticed how old she was starting to look. Zoom didn't do justice. It made me wonder what my parents would look like if they were this old.

Her hair was pulled back into a tight bun, and gray streaks now highlighted her dull brown hair. She was wearing a black fitted suit with black pumps.

"Hey, Diane, you didn't have to come get us," Brooks greeted her as we stepped off the last step.

"Hi." I waved.

"Wow, Emily, you look so much like your mom. It's been too long since I last saw you in person. And, yes, I did. Mostly for Emily." She gave Brooks a quick smile before approaching me. It was fun to see how comfortable they were with each other.

"Yeah, I was just thinking the same thing. Well, about the last time I saw you, which was at...the funeral."

"Yes, it was. Wow, you are so beautiful. Your mom would be so proud of you. Your parents would be so proud of you both." She glanced back and forth at us.

My heart swelled with appreciation. Most people didn't know our parents; if they did, they avoided talking about them. I was thankful she still talked about them.

"Well, let's get going," she said, waving us toward the car. "We have a busy week planned for you both. We have your room ready over at the hotel. You guys are staying at Vincent this week. Hope that is okay. I reserved the penthouse suite, so you will have plenty of room to relax after work. We just remodeled the whole hotel last year."

I felt giddy as we made our way over to the black Mercedes AMG. Being here for work made me feel closer to my parents. I could remember being a kid coming on trips with them. They were always greeted by someone who would rattle off details about work, lodging, and anything relevant to that trip. Diane continued to talk while our luggage was brought to the car. I rested my head against Brooks' arm and exhaled.

"Glad you're here," Brooks whispered into my ear as the car pulled forward away from the plane. His fingers intertwined with mine, and his thumb softly caressed mine.

"So, are you ready for the wedding?" Diane asked from the front passenger seat.

I glanced first at Brooks and then over to her.

"Yeah, almost," I said softly, resting my head on my hand. I yawned before smiling at her and back out the window.

It was a thirty-minute drive through traffic up the 5 from the airport to Vincent Hotel, one of our stand-alone boutique hotels in downtown Seattle. Caston headquarters was just two blocks away, making it the perfect hotel to house any of our guests coming into town. The driver pulled up to the hotel and stepped out to unload our bags. Brooks and I slid out the opposite side, along with Diane.

"I will see you guys in the office in about an hour. Get settled, and let us know if you need anything." She smiled before getting back into the car.

This was my first time at Vincent Hotel. The hotel was shaded by the giant skyscrapers surrounding it. A bellman stood behind a tall, dark walnut desk just below a glass canopy. The building was only five stories tall, with large blocks of white stone serving as its cornerstones. The front doors were quite tall and featured waterfall glass set between more dark walnut planks.

The air was much cooler than I expected as it flowed between the buildings. I clung to Brooks' side while the driver unloaded the last bag. The bellman glanced up from his desk and quickly rushed over to Diane as if he were in trouble. Diane spoke to him briefly before he turned to us, his face as red as a can of tomato sauce.

"I can get this for you, Mr. Devonshire." He gulped nervously. "I will have them brought up to your room right away."

"Thank you," Brooks replied before wrapping his arm around me and guiding me into the lobby.

Chapter Forty-Seven

"Welcome to The Vincent," the doorman welcomed us. The lobby was much grander than I had expected for a boutique hotel. It was spacious and tall, with a delightful combination of vanilla and eucalyptus filling the air.

The front desk was adorned with a modern rustic plank that ran horizontally across the front, resembling the side of a boat from this angle. The floors featured a soft gray tile, and a large chandelier hung from the ceiling above, cascading like a waterfall of lights. Brooks continued to pull me along until we stood face to face with the petite blonde behind the desk.

"Name, please," she said. I smiled to myself, knowing she had no idea who she was speaking to. I liked that she didn't. I preferred that our employees treated us like everyone else. Yes, we owned the company they worked for, but we were just two individuals—not deserving of their praise.

Our parents also disliked the attention. Whenever they stayed at our hotel chains, they remained out of sight and avoided bothering the employees except to compliment them on their excellent job. Our company has consistently been rated as one of the best workplaces, and I planned to keep it that way.

"Brooks Devonshire," he replied without a single hint in his voice. The girl nodded, looking up the reservation.

"Oh, Mr. Devonshire." The manager stood from her desk off to the side and raced over to us. "I've got this, Michelle. I'm so sorry, Mr. Devonshire." I cringed and tried not to fault the manager.

Brooks' hand raised to stop her apology. "No worries at all." The manager continued around the desk nervously.

"I knew your parents but haven't seen you since you were a kid. I'm so sorry."

"No, please." He chuckled before turning to me. "This is my fiancé, Emily Barlow."

Her eyes grew as she took me in. "Nice to meet you both. I knew both of your parents. It's so nice to see you again. I was excited when I heard you would both be staying here. I didn't know you would be engaged, so I made two gift baskets."

"That's so sweet. Thank you." I felt bad. I could tell how nervous she was.

"Right, okay, let me take you to your room." She grabbed her keys off the desk and ushered us to the small elevator to the right.

"This elevator is exclusive for penthouse guests." The doors opened, and we all stepped inside the mirror-covered elevator. Barbara hit the round 5 button and scanned the keycard hanging around her neck.

Brooks looked down and smiled at me before placing a kiss on my forehead.

"Love you," he whispered.

My head rested on his side, but I could feel Barabara's eyes bouncing back and forth between us. Was it weird for her that we were together if she knew us as kids? The elevator dinged, and the doors opened into the penthouse. Barbara stepped out ahead of us.

"Mr. Keani is our in-house butler who serves this room. He can get you whatever you like. Your key cards are on the table; you must scan them to access the elevator. Let us know if there is anything else you need."

"Thank you," I replied, leaning my head back onto Brooks' chest. Barbara nodded and returned to the elevator.

I glanced around the room as I moved away from Brooks. The walls were entirely made of glass, offering a view of the city and the surrounding buildings. In the corner to my left was a baby grand piano, while to my right was a large light oak table positioned just outside the kitchen and what appeared to be a butler's door.

Directly in front of me was the living area, furnished with soft gray and ivory sofas arranged atop an oversized rug. A light wood coffee table held a large vase filled with orchids and greenery. Above, a modern block-style chandelier hung from the ceiling, casting a gentle glow throughout the space.

"Hello, Mr. Devonshire, Miss Barlow, I am Keani." The butler appeared from the door.

"Hello." Brooks shook his hand. "This is my fiancé, Emily." I smiled up at the tall Samoan gentleman, who had a kind smile and warm eyes. His hair was pitch black and pulled back into a tight bun. Beneath his white collar, I noticed tattoos peeking out.

"We have a full kitchen, so whatever you need, please do not hesitate to ask. We are here to serve. Mr. Layton will be here this evening to work through the night in case a need arises. Otherwise, we will stay out of your way and only appear around meal times. If you need anything, a doorbell is located in the rooms and out here next to the door. Before I leave, do either of you have any allergies, and can I get you anything to eat or drink?"

"No allergies," Brooks started. "Em? Are you hungry or need anything to drink before we head over?"

"Yes, can I grab a bagel with cream cheese, fruit, and possibly a London Fog?"

"Yes, ma'am. And for you, sir?"

"I'm good. Thank you."

He nodded before disappearing. Brooks pulled out his phone and sat down on the couch.

"Are you okay?" I asked, noticing the stress on his face. He assured me it was just work stuff and left me to look around. We had to leave in twenty minutes to make it to our meeting on time.

Brooks refocused on his cell phone as I decided to explore down the hall. To my surprise, the hallway was longer than I had anticipated. Soft artwork adorned the walls, illuminated by picture lights above each piece.

The hallway led to a bathroom nearest the living area, while the next room featured a TV lounge with comfortable chairs. Directly across from it was a private office space. At the end of the hall, another corridor branched off in both directions. I chose to go right and soon found myself in what appeared to be the master bedroom.

The dark walnut floors created a striking contrast against the soft ivory walls, complemented by large floor-to-ceiling windows and mirrors. A delicate white curtain was pulled back, revealing a balcony. The ceiling was fitted with several soft lights and a modern geometric chandelier.

The spacious king-sized bed was positioned against the wall between two floor-to-ceiling mirrors, and the charcoal-tufted headboard towered higher than usual. The bedding was soft white, accented with navy blue and taupe pillows, and a large taupe blanket draped across the bed.

To the left of the bedroom, there was a bathroom and a closet. The closet doors matched the dark walnut of the floor, arranged in horizontal slats. The bathroom featured gray tiles and stone walls. Uplights lined the shower floor, and a large freestanding tub was set in front of a window that offered a stunning view of the city.

"Want a bath later?" Brooks whispered into my ear as his arms wrapped around me. I gasped at his sudden appearance, and my heart beat excitedly. I hadn't heard him sneak up on me. I nodded, calming my heart to a normal rhythm. His hands grazed the skin on my arms as he brushed down from my shoulders to my stomach. His hands rested on the almost tiniest of bumps, *or maybe it was just bloating*. I sighed, resting against him. His touch was intoxicating, always throwing me off.

"You are making me want to crawl in bed with you for a nap, and we need to go," I laughed.

"Are you sure you want a nap? Nothing else?" he whispered just above my ear. His fingers slowly traced the curve of my hip.

"B," I moaned.

"I know." His hot breath tickled my neck.

"You know what? That we have work or that you are driving me crazy?"

"Both." He dropped his arms and pulled away. "Your bagel is ready." I rolled my eyes and smiled, turning to him.

"Let's go, Miss Barlow. We can't be late for your first meeting." He smirked back playfully.

Once inside the elevator, I remembered how Diane had looked at me in the car.

"Hey B, does anyone know that I am pregnant?"

"No. Why?"

"I don't know. I feel like Diane just looked at me like she knew."

"I didn't tell her, so if she does, she must have a sixth sense."

I laughed just as the door to the lobby opened. Brooks and I hurried across the lobby; we only had thirty minutes left until our meeting started. Outside, the city was loud and chaotic, creating a striking contrast to the hotel interior, which was filled with soft music and relaxing scents.

"Can we get you a car, Mr. Devonshire?" the bellman asked.

"No, thank you. We will walk." Brooks nodded before pulling me along. His computer bag was draped over his shoulder, along with mine. I held my purse tight on the opposite arm as we crossed the street to the next block.

It felt strange being down here. Brooks and I had grown up in this area, but it was rare for us to visit downtown unless we were with our parents on the way to Caston. I generally avoided downtown; city life wasn't for me. I much preferred open spaces and fresh air.

I glanced around at the bustling city blocks, the passing cars that seemed to be angry at every stop, and the tall skyscrapers shimmering in the sunlight.

"Have you not been down here?" Brooks asked, confused.

"Yes, I have. A few times before you came. I just went straight to the office in a car. I spent most of my day in the office and went straight back home."

My stomach was full of butterflies as we walked into Caston together. Brooks' arm was draped over me.

"Brooks, Emily!" Michaelson's voice boomed through the lobby.

"Hey, man!" Brooks slapped his shoulder as he leaned in for a hug.

"Emily," Michaelson said with a smile. "How are you feeling?" he whispered, cupping his hands around his mouth. He looked ridiculous.

"Just fine," I chuckled.

"Well, good. Glad to hear it. You had Brooks worried." He slapped Brooks' stomach, causing Brooks to bend over and start coughing. I couldn't help but laugh. They were like teenage boys all over again.

"Well, let's go upstairs before we get yelled at." Michaelson winked. I laughed as I walked past Brooks and Michaelson toward the elevator.

"You ready for this weekend?" Michaelson asked with a goofy smile once the elevator doors closed.

"Yeah, man. It will be fun. Thanks for coming down."

"Heck yeah. A whole weekend on the water, I wouldn't miss it."

For once, I felt like the third wheel with Brooks. He and Michaelson shared a deep friendship that I hadn't really been a part of, and I hadn't had many opportunities to spend time with both of them like this. Still, I was glad he had Michaelson. Brooks needed someone he could trust and confide in. Plus, I knew that Michaelson cared about me and would never do anything to put Brooks in a compromising situation.

The elevator door opened on the top floor. To the left was a glass conference room, and to the right was a reception desk. Straight ahead was Brooks' new office—our parents' old office—and just down the hall to the left were a few smaller offices for Michaelson and my new assistant.

The rest of the executive team was located on the floor below, known as the "fun" floor. Our parents believed that work shouldn't be everything in life. This value was important to them, and they truly embodied it. The executive level featured a fully stocked kitchen, a recreational room with a pool table, a ping-pong table, and a large TV with a sofa.

On the fifth floor, there was another recreational room for the rest of the staff. It was double the size of the executives' room and even included a gaming room and a popcorn machine. The basement housed a gym and showers for the employees, and the cafeteria resembled a full-service restaurant, offering a rotating menu tailored to each day of the week.

Our parents believed that happy, well-rested employees worked more efficiently than those who spent all day bored at their desks. They wanted their employees to enjoy their work and take breaks as needed. Their approach showed that employees were happier, completed tasks more quickly, and took on greater responsibility.

Brooks was still talking to Michaelson when he opened the large frosted glass door to our office. I smiled as I glanced around the room; I hadn't been in here since I was little. After our parents passed away, Allen Palmer stepped in as CEO to run Caston until Brooks and I were ready. A few months ago, Brooks took over, and with Allen planning to retire in Arizona next month, the handoff would finally be complete.

As I looked around the room, I felt a little disappointed by how empty it seemed. It all needed updating: new sofas, a rug, a coffee table, and plenty of plants. Maybe some art, too, along with a cozy sitting area in the corner bathed in sunlight.

"Yeah, see you down there," Brooks said to Michaelson, grabbing the remote from the desk to open the blinds. I sighed as Michaelson left the room, and Brooks and I were finally alone.

"Can I order some furniture for in here? I feel like it echoes," I said, sitting on the desk.

"You can do whatever you want," Brooks responded, grabbing my face between his palms to kiss me. "You look good on this desk," he teased.

"Brooks Devonshire," I gasped, pretending to be shocked.

He chuckled. "I just meant I'm glad you're here. This suits you. It wouldn't be the same without you." He smiled bashfully. "I mean..." His hands dropped to my thighs as he reached up my skirt. "You do look good in other ways too."

I let my legs fall open, flashing him as I watched his expression change.

"Emily Claire, you naughty girl. You will have to pay for that later," he chuckled, tugging my hips closer to him.

"I look forward to it," I whispered. Every part of me wanted him to take me right here to the desk, but we had a meeting any minute, and I wasn't fully sure if the doors were locked or whether there were any cameras. I looked at Brooks and pulled my bottom lip between my teeth. My eyes conveyed precisely what I wanted. Brooks' fingers brushed lightly on my panties as he leaned forward to whisper in my ear.

"There's a camera over my shoulder, Em. Otherwise..."

"Otherwise, what, Mr. Devonshire?" He cleared his throat, and his breathing changed. I could tell I was torturing him.

"I would bend you over the desk and find that sweet spot that makes you scream." I couldn't help but laugh as I slammed my legs together.

"Well, that would be highly inappropriate. This is a professional work environment." He smiled wryly before pulling away from me, putting some distance between us. Just then, Diane appeared, knocking on the glass door as she walked in. Brooks and I both cleared our throats, and he stood tall to face her. I blushed five shades of red.

"Five minutes, guys."

"Yep, see you down there," Brooks replied, pretending she didn't just walk in on us.

As she left the room, I let out a small giggle. "That was close."

"Too close. C'mon." He reached for my hand, helping me off the desk before he readjusted himself in his pants. "I need to start locking the door."

"You okay there?" I asked, looking down to his not-so-hidden erection.

He grunted. "All good."

As we approached the doors, Brooks grabbed my arm and pulled me back to him. It took me by surprise, pulling a small gasp from me. His hand slipped under my hair, gently drawing me closer as his lips softly brushed against mine in a barely-there kiss.

"I love you so much, I'm so glad you're here." His breath brushed against my lips. I pulled myself up on his shirt, pulling myself to his lips again.

"I love you. Now..." I whispered, "Let's go."

Chapter Forty-Eight

We spent the entire afternoon in meetings, most of which we attended together. This was my first opportunity to meet my staff in person, and Brooks was able to connect with everyone and learn about their work experiences. I was invited to several Kildaire meetings and asked to assist our design team when I had the time.

I found myself enthusiastically discussing the hotel interior designs. After about thirty minutes of sharing my ideas and what I would love to see in our hotels, the principal designer, Melanie, asked if I would be interested in collaborating with her further. I couldn't refuse this opportunity.

Brooks handled the tech meetings without me, which gave me a chance to catch up with my staff and discuss our plans to convert two abandoned buildings into shelters for families in low-income neighborhoods in the greater Seattle area.

Eventually, I wanted to explore the idea of building permanent housing in impoverished countries, but I realized that was a much larger undertaking than I was prepared for. By the end of the day, Brooks and I exchanged brief conversations as I waited in our office for him to finish his last meeting about a new fintech company they were reviewing.

I glanced at my phone and noticed I had twenty-three new messages, all from Sara and Natalie. Just then, Brooks walked through the door.

"How was your day?" I asked, noticing how tired he looked.

"Good. Yours?" he replied.

"Good. Lots to do," I said, returning my focus to my phone as another message came in.

Sara: Just no dancing on tables. She almost fell last time.

What? I chuckled as I opened the rest of the text thread.

"What's so funny?" Brooks asked, curious.

"It seems that Michaelson talked to Natalie about this weekend, and now she and Sara have planned an entire weekend in Portland."

"How do you feel about that?" he asked.

"I'll go," I said with a smile, setting my phone down. "I'll be fine. You don't need to worry about me."

"Em, I don't mind if you go. I just want to make sure you're comfortable being out of town by yourself." I felt a little nervous about my nausea returning, but it had been weeks since I last experienced it. Plus, Brooks had become increasingly overprotective of his family.

"Natalie will be with me, so I'll be fine," I assured him. He nodded, then stretched back in his chair and closed his eyes. Just then, Michaelson knocked before popping his head in.

"Hey, are you guys down to grab dinner?" Brooks looked at me, clearly waiting for my response.

"That sounds great," I said as I stood up and grabbed my purse.

"There's a place just around the corner that's amazing. It's called Aerlume. Have you been there?"

"No," Brooks replied, standing up to adjust his shirt.

"Me neither," I added.

"Great! I'll meet you both downstairs. I'll call ahead and get us a table."

↟ ↟ ↟

The room was buzzing as we approached the hostess stand.

"Table for Caston," Michaelson announced, his voice rising above the crowd. The restaurant was beautiful, with a back wall made entirely of windows overlooking Elliott Bay. The space was beautiful and hints of delicious food permeated the air making me hungry. As we navigated the space and headed out to the patio, the hostess passed us three menus.

"Your waiter will be over shortly," she said before leaving us.

"So, tell me, what are some funny memories you have of Brooks from school?" I asked. Brooks rolled his eyes and rested his head on his hand, bracing himself.

"Our boy Brooks, the troublemaker." Michaelson grinned, looking as if he was about to share some insider secrets.

"You two are not allowed to be friends," Brooks chuckled.

"So?" I urged Michaelson to share more.

"Okay, so it's the night before finals, and Brooks climbs out the window, wearing nothing but his boxers, socks, and a robe, and makes his way to the roof of our boarding house. Out of nowhere, he pulls out a cigar, completely unashamed, and lights it up. I was just sitting there, amazed that he even knew how to light one. After a few minutes of thinking he was hot stuff, he starts coughing uncontrollably and almost falls off the roof."

I glanced back at Brooks, who was hiding behind his menu.

"So after he stopped coughing, he joined us in prank-calling professors."

"Wait, were you drunk? Was he drunk?" I glanced between them both.

Brooks shook his head, and Michaelson laughed. "It's still up for debate."

"I was not drunk," Brooks said.

"Dude, you had like two shots in Mason's room."

"Two. I was not drunk off of two shots," Brooks shot back playfully.

Oh my god. He was drunk and on a roof.

"Em, there wasn't much trouble we could get into. That place is insane," Brooks laughed, looking over at me.

"Okay, so get this," Michaelson starts again. "The next morning, he woke up early to reset the sprinkler timer. As everyone walked into the last day of finals, the sprinklers unexpectedly turned on, soaking everyone. It was complete mayhem!"

That definitely sounded like something Brooks would do. I laughed with them before settling into my chair, eager to hear more stories. Conversation flowed so easily with him, which made it clear why he and Brooks were friends. I could see the similarities between him and Connor.

↟ ↟ ↟

I leaned against Brooks' chest as we sat in the bubble-filled tub. The lights were off, allowing the city lights to create a picturesque backdrop. His hands gently caressed my stomach. Thank you, God, if you exist, for this life. Thank you for my fiancé, thank you for my baby, and thank you for Caston. I felt overwhelmed with gratitude as I relaxed in the water, the scent of lavender filling the air.

"Brooks, do you believe in God?" I asked, my eyes falling closed.

"Um, I don't know. I mean, I guess there is a higher power, and I would like to believe there is a heaven, but I don't know. Do you?"

"I don't know. I mean, I would like to believe there is."

"Why? Do you want to baptize our baby or something?"

"I don't know. I haven't thought about it. I was just thinking about how thankful I am for you, our baby, and our life. So if there is a God, I am thankful for all the goodness."

"Yeah," he sighed. "Me too."

I crawled into bed wearing one of his undershirts, expecting him to join me. Instead, he pulled up the covers and dimmed the lights before leaving the room. Piano notes filtered into the room moments later. As tired as I was, I would never miss the chance to hear him perform. I traded the warm, cozy bed for the beautiful but uncomfortable sofa.

The music sounded so sad—was it the melody, or was it my mood? I wasn't used to hearing him play freely like this since he moved in. With the demands of work, travel, and me, it had become rare for him to spend time at the piano. Yet, I could feel the emotion in the music resonating within my soul. Something must have been troubling him.

I closed my eyes and let the music wash over me, feeling its depths before the melody rose with a hint of hope and then fell again. I wondered if he had a piano at school or in the military. I yawned for what felt like the millionth time and finally let exhaustion pull me under, surrendering to the sound of his melody.

↟ ↟ ↟

Tuesday felt much like Monday, filled with back-to-back meetings, and Brooks and I found ourselves heading in different directions. When I realized we would be working closely together, I had hoped we would spend more time together. However, starting this new department has actually pulled me away from him and the company's main focus. Still, I cherished the fleeting moments when he would pull me close to kiss me or place his hands on my stomach to greet our little blessing.

The final meeting of the day was with Katelyn Liu, a journalist from the Seattle Times, who was writing a piece about Brooks and me stepping into our parents' roles. Her long, ebony hair flowed gracefully as she sat on the sofa across from us. Brooks had his ankle propped up on his knee, with his right arm draped around me, drawing me close to his side.

"So, let's start with a rundown of the article. Your parents created quite the empire from scratch. Brooks, your dad was in foster care and aged out of the system. He was a self-made man. Your parents moved here from Perth when you were a baby, and they moved in across from the Barlows. That is how they became friends, correct?"

"Correct. It wasn't until they socialized at the Seattle's Children's Hospital fundraiser in 2003 that they became closer," Brooks replied.

"Emily, your parents were already in real estate and had amassed a small empire. When the Devonshires became investors in a larger commercial property, they started dreaming up Caston. Within a decade, Caston became a huge empire of Kildaire hotels, boutique hotels scattered in larger cities across the east and west coasts, and a large real-estate portfolio. Now, Brooks, you want to get into the technology sector. What prompted the move?"

"Business is doing great, and Caston has been doing well since our parents passed. With technology becoming our future's main focus and priority, it's smart business. Real estate has always been a great investment, and with the travel industry holding steady as one of the largest industries, with just over a trillion in revenue and a little over 2% of the GDP, it's also one of the largest contributors to jobs. Looking at the tech industry, they accounted for 9.3% of the GDP and are quickly becoming the largest contributor to our economy."

"We have it on good authority that you just signed a deal with Paradigm Wallet. A tech startup that plans to disrupt the current market with its revolutionary ideas concerning crypto and blockchain technology. Many people aren't willing to invest in the world of cryptocurrencies. Why would you take a risk like that as your first purchase?"

Brooks stirred uncomfortably next to me.

"No comment. Matters of the purchase have still not been finalized. Please remit any information you have on the deal until it becomes a matter of public knowledge."

She tsked and set her pen down.

"Okay, let's take a break about Caston. Many people are

interested to know about your relationship. You both grew up as friends, attended the same private school, and then, Brooks, you went to Brighton. We all want to know, how did Brooks propose? And how do you expect to work together?"

I nudged Brooks' thigh. "Our engagement happened over a weekend in Sonoma..." I told her about our romantic weekend and all the places we visited and stayed. When it came time to talk about how we would manage Caston together, we both bounced back and forth, mentioning our parents' teamwork as inspiration and the values of Caston being a family company.

The interview wrapped thirty minutes later with a promise to keep Paradigm's purchase out of the article for now if we promised they could be the first to print the article about the purchase. After she left, I said my goodbyes and headed for the elevators.

"Emily." Paul stepped into the elevators with me. Paul Woodman, our CFO, was a hefty man with salt-and-pepper hair. He had been at Caston almost as long as the company had existed.

"Paul, nice to see you." I smiled, looking up from my phone for a moment. He pressed the button for the fourth floor and settled in next to me.

"I heard you were in town. It seems like you and Brooks have gotten everything you wanted." His voice was polite, but it had an edge to it.

A cold chill filled the air, but I brushed it off. Paul had been nothing but encouraging since our parents died. When I graduated college, he even sent a fruit basket.

"Our parents must be putting in a good word for us with the man upstairs," I tried to joke. His fake smile flashed at me just as the elevator dinged.

"See you around." He stepped off the elevator, leaving a chill that washed over me once again. Somewhere in my body, an alarm was screaming, "Danger! Danger!" But I chose to ignore it. I took the elevator down to the lobby, convincing myself that Paul was just having an off day.

↟ ↟ ↟

The penthouse living room was darker today due to heavy cloud cover and pouring rain, but something about Seattle's rain storms brought a sense of peace and comfort; it felt familiar. I settled into the living room and joined the Zoom call.

"Hey, Evie!" I said with a grin.

"Emily, how are you?" Our wedding planner, Evie, was a young brunette with pink-rimmed glasses. She wore yoga pants and a comfy sweater, and her hair was pulled into a messy topknot. I was a little jealous of how comfortable she looked.

"Good. Brooks and I are in Seattle right now for work. There's a crazy storm outside, so let me know if I need to put my AirPods in."

"No, the sound is fine. So tell me, how are you feeling about the wedding, how are you feeling about the baby? What are some stressors you have right now?"

Did she truly want to know the truth? I was experiencing a whirlwind of emotions, most of which had my stomach in knots. I had to keep reminding myself that weddings were meant to be fun. They were fun! I just needed to channel my anxious energy into excitement.

"Well, baby is good. We just had another ultrasound, and everything looks great. I am finally in my second trimester, so I have a lot more energy and feel excited about the wedding now. As far as stressors go, I would really just like to finalize some things today and know exactly what needs to be done," I replied.

"Okay, so we will go through step-by-step with all the vendors, and once they join, we will have a clearer picture."

"Another thing, Brooks and I haven't even thought about a first dance song. I think because we are doing the reception at home, it just never occurred to me to pick one."

"Do you have a list of songs you like, or do you need help?"

"I think we both have songs we like, but the lyrics don't fit. Perfect by Ed Sheeran is up there, All of Me by John Legend, Love

Me Like You Do by Ellie Goulding, and even Grow Old With Me by Tom Odell."

"Well, those are all great. Have you thought about the music you want to walk into the reception with or down the aisle? We could still use the music and just remove the lyrics."

"I really like Turning Page by Sleeping At Last to walk down the aisle, too. I know, insert eye-roll because of Twilight." I laughed. "I like the flow and tempo, though. For the reception entrance, maybe whatever song we don't pick as the First Dance song?"

"Yeah, totally. Why don't you work with Brooks tonight and see if you can't figure that out? Email me by the end of the week with whatever you choose."

"Sounds good."

"Oh, it looks like Natalie and the photographer are in the waiting room. I will let them in, and we can get started, okay?"

↟ ↟ ↟

Brooks returned earlier than I had anticipated. He didn't seem as tired as he had the day before, which was great since we needed to talk about wedding songs. I was sitting at the piano, hoping to play the songs we'd discuss. When he saw me, he smirked.

"Whatcha doin' love?"

"Trying to figure out a first dance song." I slid my hand across the keys and laughed.

He slid his hands into his pockets as he approached me. A warm sensation filled me as I admired him. He wore navy slacks that highlighted the blue in his eyes, paired with a crisp white button-down shirt, a brown leather belt, and shiny oxfords. His sleeves were rolled up to his elbows, revealing his muscular arms—arms that felt like home.

"Well," he paused. "Did you learn to play while I was gone, or do you want me to play them for you?"

I laughed again. "Yes, some magical fairy dropped by and gave me the savant ability to play."

"Well then, let's hear it." I rolled my eyes and slapped my hands down on the keys, sending an awful noise through the room. He laughed with me.

"Okay, okay, please stop before I lose my hearing. Scoot over." I slid across the bench to the end as he sat beside me. I dropped my head onto his shoulder.

"What should I play?"

"Well, I need you to play just the music to Turning Page and possibly the music to Grow Old With Me."

"Grab my phone out of my bag. I have a music app I can use to pull up the music sheet."

He played both beautifully as I melted into his side. Each second made me fall for him more.

"Any others?" he whispered.

"No. We just need a first dance song. What do you think about Perfect, All of Me, or Love Me Like You Do?"

"Not Love Me Like You Do. Too fast." He stood from the bench, taking my hand. "C'mon," he said softly and smiled. "Dance with me."

A wide grin spread across my face as I stood up and took his hand. I placed my phone on the piano and hit play. Brooks was an excellent dancer who could do much more than just sway or waltz. I didn't want a choreographed dance, but I also didn't want to simply sway on the dance floor; there would be plenty of songs for that. Brooks' arms were firm against my back as the two songs came to an end, and his mouth hovered at my ear.

"Can I tell you what I think?"

I nodded.

"I think I like them both."

I laughed, pulling away from him.

"You're no help."

"Well, I think they're both great. I love you. So much." His voice changed, becoming more serious and deeper. I was turning into a pool of emotions with the look he was giving. Pure love.

"I love you," I replied, fighting back the surge of emotions dancing in my chest. In moments like this, when we allowed the chaos to fade away, we were left with a deep sense of gratitude and appreciation for each other. If I lingered on those emotions too long, I would end up crying, so instead, I leaned in for a soft kiss. "I love you, Brooks Caston Devonshire, always and forever."

Like most of our interactions, it didn't stop there. Before I knew it, I found myself lying on my back on the daybed chaise near the piano. My phone continued to rotate through songs as his lips traveled across my body while his hands gently undressed me. We took our time, savoring each moment to truly connect with one another, pushing past mere passion and desire into a deeper love and connection that came when we made love and united our souls as one.

Chapter Forty-Nine

I was surprised at how quickly Wednesday came and went. It was the last full day of meetings, and we were supposed to catch up on emails and projects that needed our attention for the rest of the week.

I woke up to the sunrise early Thursday morning, shocked to be awake so early. When Brooks woke up, he was ravenous for my body, pleasuring me in all sorts of ways imaginable, starting with his tongue.

By the time we ordered breakfast, we both needed fuel and hydration to make it through the rest of the day. I was thankful we had no meetings because, by the time we were ready for work, it was already nearing ten. My body was exhausted, but desire was a hairpin trigger away.

Unfortunately, work called, which meant I had to stuff down all the replays that continued like a loop in my mind, working me up into a hot mess.

The view from our top-floor office provided a glimpse of Elliott Bay. I watched a ferry pass by and thought about our parents when the door opened.

"Hey, beautiful, want to go grab lunch?" Brooks stepped into our office.

"Yes, I'm starving. The bagel and eggs were clearly not enough." I smiled, holding back my laughter.

"Michaelson wants to join. Is that okay?"

"Yeah, of course." I stood, grabbed my bag, and followed him out.

Michaelson joined us in the elevator, excitedly sharing all the details about the houseboat he had rented for the bachelor weekend. When the doors opened to the lobby, he headed to the reception desk for something while Brooks and I made our way across the space. A familiar voice called out to us from behind just before we left.

"Brooks!"

We both turned to see Nayla Freeman, the flirtatious teenager I had met in my cycling class months ago. What was she doing here, and why had she called for him? I glanced up at Brooks, who seemed just as confused as I was.

"I don't know," he mouthed, guessing my question.

"Hi, Nayla." I smiled politely as she approached us. Her eyes were quick to our interlaced hands and then up to Brooks.

"Hi, Emily, I didn't expect to see you here." She focused on Brooks, "So I got a job here."

He nodded. "Great. Congrats." I could feel my anger and frustration with her rising. Why does she always show up, and what is her obsession with my fiancé? I squeezed Brooks' hand and placed my left hand on his bicep to make my ring visible. Immature, I know, but she just couldn't seem to take a hint.

"Great news!" I said. Her attention went straight to my ring. *Finally,* "Brooks and I are getting married next weekend. We are having a small reception if you'd like to swing by." Brooks squeezed my hand.

She let out a fake giggle, clearly annoyed. "Well, thanks, but I can't make it."

Michaelson stood at our side. "Ready?"

Brooks looked at him. "Yeah. Let's go."

I looked to Michaelson, then to Brooks, and back to Nayla.

"Well, have a good day. Congrats on the job," I said, turning for the door.

"Wait," she said before we could leave. "Do you work here?"

The three of us chuckled. "She owns Caston, remember?" Brooks grinned at me.

Nayla's face turned down. "Oh, I didn't realize."

Didn't realize what? That you couldn't hit on my fiance at my company?

"Well, it was great seeing you." I smirked before turning for the door.

Once I was outside, I felt grateful for the fresh air. Wow, I had never wanted to hit someone so much in my life—except maybe Cailey. What was it with those two girls and my fiancé? Brooks and Michaelson laughed as I let out an exaggerated sigh.

"What was that?" Michaelson asked.

"She keeps trying to hit on Brooks and won't take a hint is what it was," I growled.

"Babe, she's not hitting on me," Brooks said.

I rolled my eyes. *Yes, she is.*

"I mean, she did seem pretty upset to find out Emily owned Caston," Michaelson offered up.

"Exactly, thank you," I replied, feeling sassy.

"Well, you have nothing to worry about. I'm never here, and when I am, I'm in meetings. Plus, Michaelson can help field her."

"I got you, Em." Michaelson nodded as if this was some cool bro-code tactic.

"Whatever, just please, make sure she stays clear of me too, or else I might just find a reason to fire her so I don't knock her out."

"Aggressive," Brooks teased.

"I don't know why, but she just hits every single nerve of mine. I have never felt the urge to hit someone until she decided to flirt with you in our house."

"Damn," Michaelson responded. Brooks and I both looked at him and laughed.

"Can we please change the subject? I've spent enough of my day thinking about that self-absorbed teen flirt."

Brooks and Michaelson both chuckled but agreed and continued with more conversation about their weekend plans.

↟ ↟ ↟

"I need to pack for this weekend. Connor will be here at three thirty to pick us up." Brooks opened the door to our house.

"Mind if I just chill on the deck and answer emails until he gets here?" Michaelson asked me.

"Yeah, of course. The fridge is full if you are hungry." I followed Brooks up the stairs to our bedroom before falling onto our bed. I closed my eyes and rubbed my hands softly around my stomach.

"Hey, you okay?" Brooks asked as he lifted his bag onto the bed.

"Mm-hmm. Just tired," I yawned.

Brooks' lips were on my stomach before I opened my eyes. "Be good for mommy this weekend while daddy is away." I smiled. I would never tire of seeing him like this.

"What time will Sara and Natalie be here?" he asked, resuming packing his bag.

"I think at four. It's a two-hour drive to the hotel, and we want to be there by dinner time."

Brooks finished loading his bag and slid onto the bed beside me, pulling me into his chest. I inhaled the soft hints of his amber cologne.

"I'm going to miss you," I muttered into his chest.

"I will miss you too. It's two days."

"I know," I sighed. "I don't know why, but I am just feeling super clingy right now."

"Well," he whispered, "I won't move until I have to go."

"Okay. Michaelson is fine, right?" I teased.

"He is fine."

"What time is it?"

"2:34."

"Take a nap with me then."

Brooks kissed my forehead and wrapped his other arm over me, cradling my head until I fell asleep.

We both woke to the sound of his phone buzzing against the duvet. Brooks pulled his arm out from under me and stood beside the bed.

"Connor will be here in ten," he said sleepily. He ran a hand through his perfectly coiffed hair, only messing it up slightly.

"'Kay," I groaned, sitting up. "I need to pack," I yawned.

"Want me to grab your suitcase or weekender?"

"Mm...maybe the suitcase so I don't have to carry it." Brooks left for the closet and returned with my bag.

"I'll pack when you leave. Thank you." I kissed Brooks before we both turned for the door to head back downstairs where Michaelson was waiting.

↟ ↟ ↟

"Hey, Connie," I squealed as I opened the door, throwing my arms around him.

"Mils," he said, spinning me and setting me back on my feet with a smile.

"Ready to go?" He looked up at Brooks and Michaelson, who joined me at the entry.

"Yeah, man. Thanks for coming." Brooks lifted his bag and wakeboard to head out to Connor's jeep.

"See you later, Emily!" Michaelson whooped as he followed Brooks out the door. "Promise we will return him in one piece."

"Thanks for that," I chuckled. Brooks and Connor tied down the board, and Connor and Michaelson loaded in. Brooks returned to the door.

"Miss you already," he whispered against my lips. His hands were tight against my body as he slightly lifted me up the door frame. I tugged him further into me while he kissed me deeply.

"Okay, lovebirds, time to go," Connor yelled from the car, making me blush.

"Okay, go. Miss you and love you."

"Text me when you get to the hotel tonight." He planted one last kiss on my cheek before running to the car.

"Have fun." I waved.

Brooks jumped into the passenger seat, and I could hear Michaelson tease Brooks, "Ready to say goodbye to your last weekend of freedom."

"Michaelson, she has had my heart for as long as I can remember. When have I ever been free?" Was it possible to swoon over your fiancé? Connor laughed as he backed up.

"Bye, Millie," Connor yelled before heading down the driveway. I waited until the jeep was far enough down the driveway and out of sight before I closed the door. Okay. Time to pack.

↟ ↟ ↟

Natalie knocked once and opened the door.

"Hey, mama." She grinned, wrapping her arms around me. "You're glowing," she cooed.

"Well, thank you." I tightened my shirt around my stomach to show off my almost baby bump.

"Well, it's almost there," she chuckled. "You ready? Sara just pulled in at the same time I did. Which car did you want to take?"

"Mind if I drive?"

The girls loaded up my car with bags and snacks while I made sure the house was locked up.

Natalie connected her phone to my Bluetooth and pulled up a playlist on her phone. "Ready?" she asked as Girls Just Wanna Have Fun played over the speakers.

"So, did you figure out your first dance song?" Natalie asked, waving her hand out the window, catching the currents of the air.

"I did."

"Well?" Sara asked from the backseat.

"We decided on," I paused for suspense. "All of Me. It just has a special memory attached to it."

"Yay! I love that one," Natalie squealed.

"What was the other option?" Sara asked.

"Perfect by Ed Sheeran."

She smacked my shoulder. "Oh, c'mon, that one is perfect for you guys. Pun intended."

We all laughed. "I know, it was a hard choice, honestly. There are so many good songs, but it really just came down to the memories attached to the songs."

"Okay, what memory have you both tied to All of Me?"

"Just a special date night," I responded, keeping my eyes trained on the road. A night of romance and bubble baths.

"Right," Natalie teased, looking back at her hand lifting in the wind as I blushed.

"Ooh, do tell," Sara plead.

"I do not kiss and tell." I playfully raised my nose.

"Since when?" she laughed.

"She never spills any details about Brooks. Always so private." Natalie winked at me.

"All I will say is that Brooks and I cannot keep our hands off each other." They both laughed as if it was ridiculous.

"You think?" Sara gestured to my stomach.

"Yeah, yeah." I rolled my eyes, turning up the music.

Chapter Fifty

The drive to Portland was filled with laughter and a lot of off-key singing. As we pulled into the Sentinel Hotel, I gasped at its beauty. I pulled up under the glass canopy and stepped out handing the key card to my Tesla to the valet. The girls were already unloading onto a cart when I came around the corner.

"Eeek," I squealed, wrapping my arms around their shoulders as we walked into the lobby. "I have been wanting to come here with Brooks. I met with our design team for our new chain and was telling them about this hotel. The library, the "Room at the End of the Hall", the whole vibe is just so cool."

"It's so chic and cute," Sara murmured, glancing around the lobby.

"Welcome to Sentinel," a young lady about our age said. Her long auburn hair wrapped around her arms and shoulders like a curtain.

"Hi, we are checking in for Natalie Spencer," Natalie replied.

The lobby of the Sentinel Hotel was a mixture of old and new. The hotel itself was a historical marker with a bold, white terra-cotta exterior. The interior had black and white tiled floors, Persian rugs, and leather sofas. It was like hipster meets roaring twenties.

"Okay, Ms Spencer. I show two rooms for you. The Bridgetown Suite and a Terrace Suite?" the receptionist asked.

We finished checking in, downloading their app, and finding our rooms on the fifth floor. The girls gave me the Terrace Suite so I could sleep in if I wanted.

I opened the door to my room, excited to take it all in. The oversized gray headboard caught my attention first. The king bed was covered in plenty of white pillows with a soft gray and green plaid blanket draped at the foot. The walls were a pretty dark green against the bright white curtains. The carpet was a light charcoal herringbone. I walked to the balcony door and opened it.

The terrace overlooked the city of Portland and housed a small sofa and two chairs on either side of the gas fire pit. The sun was lower in the sky, casting a golden glow on the city. I pulled my phone out and snapped a photo, texting it to Brooks.

Emily: Made it!

Brooks called instead of texting back, asking about my drive and reminding me he may or may not have service when they get to the lake. He promised to text me before bed if he had service, and we said our goodbyes.

I made a quick table reservation for the restaurant downstairs on the app, then grabbed my toiletry bag to touch up my makeup. I had just started on my mascara when there was a loud, playful banging on the door. *Geeze Sara.*

"Ooh, look at your room!" Sara pushed the door open and stepped in.

"I have something for you." Natalie lifted a small box up.

I chuckled, turning back to her. "What is that?"

"Just open it." She smiled, handing it over to me. I slid the lid off, revealing a white sash with Bride scripted in gold letters. *Aww.*

"Thanks, Natalie." I hugged her.

"Okay, well, we have an hour. Do you guys want to head down and just sit at the bar, or do you want to explore with me?"

"The bar, duh." Sara toyed with her hair.

"Well, it's technically a wine lounge," I corrected myself.

"Even better." Sara laughed, heading for the door.

↟ ↟ ↟

After dinner, the girls brought their wine back up to my room. I had a fun mocktail the bar made for me. Natalie ran to her room and returned with another box. We all gathered around the fire pit.

"Emily," she said, handing me a large white tote bag filled with tissue paper. It was heavier than I expected. Big sage-green letters spelling out BRIDE sat across the front.

"This one's for you, Sara," she said, lifting another bag from the box. It was a soft pink and had BRIDE TRIBE across the front.

"Thank you, Natalie." I stood, giving her a tight squeeze before falling back in my seat.

"Well, go on and open it."

Inside were several items: heart-shaped sunglasses logoed with our titles, a stainless steel tumbler etched with the same pairing, and a makeup bag filled with lip balm, lotion, gum, confetti bombs, and a sleep mask.

"These are amazing. Thank you. Did you get one for yourself?"

"Of course." She grinned, lifting out another tote. The title also read BRIDE TRIBE instead of Maid of Honor. Natalie was humble and knew that there was a chance Sara would be hurt, so she made sure to always treat her like an equal.

We sat around the fire, talking for the next two hours. The air was cool, but thankfully, the rain was holding off. Natalie shared more about her family and her new nephew, Jaxson. Her brother-in-law, Houston, had apparently passed out in the delivery room. We all had a good laugh about that.

Sara told us about her family's annual Christmas trip. This year, they were spending it in Connecticut. It was almost ten when my phone rang through as a FaceTime call. Brooks' face popped up on the screen.

"That's our cue," Natalie teased, grabbing the box and tote. Sara followed her. "Night Emily." And then they were gone.

The screen was still black when I turned back to my phone.

"Can you hear me?" I asked.

"Yes, sorry," he responded. A light turned on, and I could see his face. "We have service."

We talked for a few minutes about the boat they rented and dinner, and I made sure he knew how much I missed him. I felt like a stage-five clinger, but I couldn't help it.

"What are you wearing?" His eyebrows pulled together. I looked down and realized the sash was still draped across my chest.

"It's my bride sash." I giggled, lifting it up to the camera.

"Your what?"

"It's a sash that says Bride. I have to wear it all weekend. Normally, people buy you drinks, and you get free stuff. I'm sure Sara will gladly accept any and all drinks that come my way." I pulled out the heart sunglasses and slipped them onto my face. "I even have a pair of these." Pursing my lips into a kiss.

"Mm...I love those lips," he said. I chuckled and put the glasses and sash on the table before heading inside and curling up on the sofa.

"How's my baby?"

"Great. Happy. Fed. Being smothered in love."

"Perfect. I don't like being this far from you guys, especially since you aren't home."

"I know. We will be okay," I yawned.

↟ ↟ ↟

"Welcome to Knot Springs."

"Thanks!" Sara smiled. "We have a reservation under Harrison for the bride-to-be."

"Great! Let me see. Okay, I have you ladies doing the springs, massages, facials, and our signature foot rub?"

"Yes. That's correct."

"Perfect. Okay, you ladies will start with a 90-minute session in our hot springs. We have a board that recommends how to alternate between the pools, the sauna, and the steam room. You can choose whatever method you like. We also have a cold plunge pool - great for relaxing the muscles and clearing your mind. After that, our therapists will come and get you and bring you to the massage rooms. I have here that Emily is getting a prenatal massage and Sara and Natalie are getting hot stones?"

"Yes," Sara responded.

"Okay, so after your massage, you will go to our foot soak room, and the therapist will do your foot rubs, then, to finish up, you guys are more than welcome to head back to the springs or head to the locker rooms to rinse off.

"We do ask that before you enter the springs, you first shower. There is a locker room just down this hall. Please make sure to rinse off any deodorants or lotions. We do ask that you wear swim clothes as well. There are robes located in the lockers. Feel free to slip those on with slippers or sandals, and you can head out."

Natalie and I followed Sara down the damp hallway to the locker rooms. After a quick shower, we dressed in our swimsuits and covered up with big charcoal robes with the Knot Springs logo embroidered on the shoulder.

We went shopping this morning, upon my request, so we could get matching suits. The spring water had a chance of ruining our suits, so I wanted to pay for them. We found a local boutique that had the suit in five colors. It was a one-shoulder bandeau top with a thong bottom.

Natalie wore the suit in dark green, which brought out the color of her hair and eyes. It was lower than the usual suits she wore to cover the scars of her old pump. She looked so hot in it that even she agreed. Sara wore it in dusty blue, contrasting her strawberry-blonde hair and freckled skin. I opted for the white to go with my Bride heart sunnies.

We started with the exfoliation shower inside the spring room before heading to the tepidarium pool. The pool was warm, relaxing, and empty. After soaking for about ten minutes, Sara and Natalie jumped into the hot pool for a few minutes before daring to plunge into the cold plunge. I couldn't help but laugh as they both squealed and ran for the hot pool again.

"Oh god, that hurt," Sara laughed.

"Feel better?" I asked, smiling, enjoying their happiness.

"No, not really."

Natalie returned to my pool, fighting back the urge to start laughing.

"That was cold but not as cold as the last plunge pool I went to."

"What pool was that?"

"Durango Hot Springs in Colorado. That place is epic. It's all outdoors, and they have like twenty or more pools with varying temperatures. I was there last winter with my sister. There was snow everywhere, and it was about twenty degrees out. You can go from pool to pool. Some are super hot, like 112 degrees hot, and then you jump into the cold plunge, which is like 50 degrees. It's insane."

"No. Hard pass," Sara groaned as she climbed in behind us.

We spent a few more hours getting pampered before heading out for a light snack before our dinner reservations. It was nice to have girl time and catch up with Sara.

She told me about her brother getting a job with the Coast Guard in Florida, and her grandparents were planning a family reunion for next summer at their ranch in Idaho.

Natalie opened up about her blooming relationship with Michaelson, and the three of us settled into dreaming about our futures and what they looked like. One thing was for sure - I wanted all my people together if possible.

Chapter Fifty-One

Dinner was terrific, and I was ready to head back to the hotel and crash.

"We're going out," Sara sang as we walked to the car.

"What? Where?" I groaned playfully as she swung our connected hands around, spinning me in the parking lot.

"Just follow my directions."

We made several turns while Sara called out directions from the passenger seat refusing to connect it to my car. We had the windows down and sang along to one of Natalie's playlists she had created for the weekend.

We pulled up outside of a warehouse looking building where a line formed around the building and loud music came from inside.

"Clubbing?" I asked, already shaking my head.

"Oh come on, it will be fun. We haven't been clubbing since finals," Sara pleaded.

"Wrong. I went with Natalie and two, I distinctly remember telling you I wouldn't go with you again." I closed my eyes and fought to keep the smile from my face. I wasn't going to win. Sara always got what she wanted.

"You're coming in. This is your last weekend as a single lady. Let's go dance before I lose you forever to Brooks," she whined.

"Come on Em. I don't want to party hard either, but we love dancing, and she's right. You're going to be a wife and a mom and..." Natalie started.

"Okay, okay." I cut Natalie off. "Brooks is going to kill me." I pulled over and parked the car.

We showed our ID's and danced our way inside. The pop-EDM had everyone dancing or rocking to the beat. We paused just short of the dance floor and took another selfie before I texted it to Brooks.

Emily: Wish you were here.

On the dance floor, everyone congratulated me and offered to buy me drinks, which I happily declined. The music was perfect, and Sara and I felt like we had returned to our college years as we danced together.

As the song changed, the lights dimmed, and colored lights danced across the walls. My inner dancer took over as I swayed my hips to the beat. Sara dropped to her knees beside me, twerking on the floor.

This caught the attention of a man who had been lurking near the edge of the dance floor, nursing a scotch for the past twenty minutes. When he tried to reach for Sara, she hip-bumped him and then turned, pushing him away. He sneered at her and then moved on to find someone else to dance with. We all laughed at the encounter.

Dancing felt incredible. After college, I had given it all up. My loneliness had worsened, and I couldn't find a reason to dance, I couldn't connect with the music. That felt like a different lifetime ago.

Now, I felt the music in my bones. I felt it in my soul, connecting with it in a way I thought was lost forever. As emotion flooded my senses, I lost myself in the moment, uncaring about how I looked. I dropped, spun, and felt the beat like a caress. We were sweaty and tired by the time we decided to call it a night. Just then, a text from Brooks came through.

B <3: Be careful, please.

B <3: Have fun.

B <3: Don't accept drinks from anyone.

I laughed. *He's so cute when he's protective.*

Emily: We are just about ready to leave.

Emily: No drinks. We have water in the car.

Emily: I love you.

B<3: Love you.

B<3: Text me when you are back in your room safely.

Emily: I will :) <3

"Ready?" Natalie asked.

"Yes, please! I'm so hot." I was soaked head to toe in sweat, and my bra clung to me like we were hiking through a rainstorm.

"Me too," Sara yelled. We laughed and made our way through the crowded dance floor and outside. The cool air felt like a welcome caress, refreshing our bodies and drying our skin.

During the entire drive back to the hotel, we all kept grins plastered on our faces.

↟ ↟ ↟

The phone trilled once before Brooks answered.

"Back in your room safely?"

"Yes," I laughed. Natalie and Sara were on their way back in their pajamas for a movie night.

"Did you have fun?"

"Actually yes. It's been a long time since I danced like that. I'm glad Sara didn't tell me where we were going."

"Ah, yes, leave it to Sara," Brooks teased. What he intended to say, but was too kind to express, was to leave it to the wild child. Brooks was never really Sara's biggest fan, even though she always wanted to be everyone's favorite. She had a knack for being the center of attention—loud and, at times, quite obnoxious—but she was still my friend. Beneath her wild exterior, she had a fierce loyalty and a heart of gold.

"What are you doing?" I asked putting the phone on speaker so that I could get ready for the girls to come back.

"Just hanging in the hot tub. Probably going to head to bed here in a bit. We have an early morning."

"Why?"

"Connor needs to get back to work. He works tomorrow night."

Brooks and I talked for a few more minutes before hanging up for the night. I missed him and wished I could just hug him for even a second.

After a quick shower, I was dressed in my favorite pajamas and Sara and Natalie were already huddled up on my bed with Bride Wars queued up. I crawled between them and settled in. Sara was flat on her back with her feet on the headboard which made me giggle.

"Are you ready?" Sara asked, grabbing my hand and squeezing.

"For?" I laughed.

"To be Mrs. Devonshire?" she gulped. "I just don't want you hurt, Em. Are you sure?"

I was so sure. Nothing made sense without Brooks. The ache in my chest every time we were apart, the breathless feeling every time I saw him, or the warmth I felt wrapped in his arms confirmed it was and always has been him.

"The surest I have ever been," I confirmed with confidence. Her eyes met mine, and her smile caused them to soften. "I can't explain it, but we were made for each other, like two pieces of a puzzle. The way he kisses me, the way he holds me, the way he smiles and looks at me, only me. He's funny and romantic, he listens, he makes love to me like he can never get enough. There's this way he speaks to me, whether he's whispering in my ear or into the dark night. The sound of his whisper speaks to my soul like he knows how to speak directly to it." I was smiling like an idiot with tears in my eyes. "He's every dream I have ever had."

"Okay," she whispered, kissing my hand. Natalie hooked her arm through mine and rested her head on my shoulder.

"You guys are great together. I want a love like you guys have," she sighed. I turned to look at her.

"You will. If not from Michaelson, then someone else," I assured her.

We never started the movie. We spent the next two hours talking, laughing, and crying. It was the perfect end to a girls' weekend. Before they left the room, we promised to meet for brunch.

↟ ↟ ↟

I groaned rolling over to the light filtering in through the curtains. *Too early*. I yawned before sliding out of bed to prop open the door to the terrace. The air was still cool and smelled like the sweet flowers. I crawled back into bed, resting my hand on my stomach.

"We get to see daddy today," I said. The bird song from outside filled the room. My phone buzzed on the nightstand.

Natalie: Sara is still sleeping. We asked for a late checkout. See you in a few hours I guess lol.

Emily: I can get up and meet you downstairs for coffee?

Natalie: No! I'm going back to bed too. You should too. Are you still in bed?

Emily: Yes. Why? Lol.

Natalie: Just hoping you slept in. 'Kay text you later.

She is acting so weird. I laughed, dropping my phone to my side. My hotel door opened, startling me. As I rolled over to see who it was, Brooks appeared with a large bouquet in his hand. My heart melted at the sight of him making me weepy.

"Sorry love didn't mean to startle you," he said, making his way to me.

"Brooks, what are you doing here?" I asked, reaching for him. Tears filled my eyes, and the desire to be in his arms took over. Brooks slid into bed next to me as I rolled myself on top of him, burying my face in his neck.

"I missed you and didn't want to wait until this afternoon to see you." I nodded, kissing his neck and making my way to his mouth as I straddled him. His hands slid around my waist, holding me to him.

"I missed you, please don't ever leave again." Both of us were panting between each new lip lock. Brooks' tongue softly brushed my bottom lip leaving my mouth feeling cool and minty. My fingers wrapped into his hair as my body longed for him.

"Mmm..." Brooks moaned, pushing me away. "If we don't stop, I won't be able to stop." I pulled my lip in considering my options.

"Where are Connor and Michaelson?"

"They are in the lobby grabbing breakfast with Natalie and Sara." Brooks chuckled watching my expression as I realized everyone was in on it. I shook my head with a goofy smile.

"Of course they are. Not sleeping in, I guess." Brooks laughed, shaking his head no.

"Connor is driving them back so we have the whole day to ourselves."

"Really?"

"Yes. Since you brought your car, which ended up working out perfectly, I figured you could show me around the hotel, we could grab breakfast and head home whenever you want."

Well then... I smashed my lips back into his as I began to tug off his shirt.

Chapter Fifty-Two

We were curled up on the deck sofa, surrounded by our friends, but I was too focused on Brooks' fingers tracing hearts on my bare thigh, inching closer and closer to the promised land. Internally, I had never been more scared and more excited.

Tomorrow, I would become his wife—a dream I once lost but thankfully rediscovered. How did we get here? It felt so surreal.

Michaelson and Natalie were curled up on the sofa across from us while Connor and Sara sat in the chairs on either end, avoiding each other like the plague. I couldn't help but chuckle at how childlike they acted around one another.

After our girl talk in Portland, we learned that Connor and Sara practically hated each other. They first met when he came to the University of Washington to visit for a day. Apparently, Sara annoyed him to no end, and he made a snide comment about her being "too much." Since then, she had hated him.

Despite their rivalry, they laughed and shared old stories about school and work. It was perfect, and it allowed Brooks and me to remain in our little bubble while his lips trailed soft kisses up my neck, igniting my whole body.

That was until Sara interrupted.

"Okay, okay, we know you like each other a lot. Enough of that."

Brooks pulled away slightly, still keeping one hand on my upper thigh and the other resting over my belly.

"You get used to it," Connor chuckled. Everyone else joined in, including us. "You should have seen them growing up," Connor continued. "They always had their hands on each other, whether they were in the water or playing in the mud." He groaned while Brooks dropped his head back.

"Not this," Brooks whispered playfully to me. "It was a mud fight," he corrected, finally tearing his gaze away with an eye-roll directed at Connor.

"Don't think you had any of us fooled," Connor said with a smile, throwing a wink my way.

"Ooh, do tell," Sara urged.

"What happened with the mud fight?" Michaelson asked. Brooks chuckled as I covered my eyes, wondering if they could see the heat rising in my cheeks at the memories of Brooks' hands on me.

"It was raining, and as you all know, Emily loves the rain. She was quite convincing when she was younger. One afternoon, during a downpour, she managed to coax us outside, away from our video games." Brooks' eyes met mine with a mischievous gleam that told me he remembered it well, too.

Brooks jumped in to share the story. "We were playing soccer when she slipped and fell into a huge puddle. She was laughing the entire time, and when I reached down to help her up, she pulled me down into the mud with her. She happily rolled around in the mud while painting me at the same time. That's it—nothing more to tell." He looked back at our friends and shrugged.

"Nah, he's leaving out the part where she was wearing one of those little half-shirts that girls wear," he added. He lifted his shirt and motioned toward his abs for demonstration, earning a chuckle from all of us.

"Emily was not bashful about showing off her body, and add to it, she was a dancer, so she was used to being, um, less clothed," he coughed out.

"Connor, are you slut shaming my girl?" Brooks asked, raising his brow in Connor's direction.

"You're making me sound so promiscuous," I scoffed. I was always aware of what I was doing—dressing in outfits that revealed a bit more skin whenever Brooks was around. However, I would never admit it. Connor definitely didn't need to point that out.

"She was always dressed classy, but her parents didn't approve of those tight-belly shirts. Better?" He gestured with his hand and went on. "Anyway, now she's covered in mud, and so is Brooks. She's lying on top of him, laughing as she continues to paint his face with mud, drawing hearts on his cheek. Meanwhile, his hands are up her shirt, copping a feel with his pants growing under her. They both frequently forgot I was there," Connor complained, rolling his eyes.

Brooks laughed harder. "I mean," he said with a shrug.

I slapped Brooks on the arm and glared in Connor's direction. "Connor, could you just wipe some of those memories away?" My cheeks burned with humiliation, even though I knew it was all in good fun.

"It was one of the only times we pushed the boundaries. I was still a teenage boy with raging hormones and a super hot girlfriend," Brooks explained, giving me a once-over.

Michaelson laughed. "You guys are ridiculous. So straight-edge."

Connor guffawed, tossing his head back as he and Brooks recalled the memory.

"Okay, new topic, please," I suggested. Natalie raised her eyebrow playfully at me. Her smirk indicated that this kind of joking was normal among friends, but it didn't lessen the embarrassment warming my cheeks.

The conversation picked up again, and I turned my attention to my almost-husband.

"I get to change my name tomorrow," I whispered, lacing, unlacing, and relacing our fingers together.

"Mrs. Devonshire," he murmured against my lips as he leaned in for more, his fingers gently lifting my chin as he deepened the kiss.

"Well, I think we should head up to bed. Don't you agree, Emily?" Natalie asked.

I dropped my head back and groaned. This all felt silly. Brooks and I had been sleeping in the same bed for almost half a year, and now, on the night of our wedding, we were supposed to sleep in separate beds. I tried to argue that he could leave in the morning and get ready elsewhere, but Natalie and Sara would hear nothing of it.

"Okay, c'mon." Natalie reached for my hand. Brooks gave me a wry smile as he shifted away, and I pouted. Natalie shook her hand, pretending to be impatient.

"Fine." I laughed, sliding out from under the blanket. I grabbed her hand and stood up to follow her inside.

"Don't leave without kissing me goodbye," I whispered to Brooks before heading in.

Upstairs, the girls' dresses hung in the loft, already steamed and ready for the next day. Tomorrow, a styling team will be here to do hair, makeup, and nails.

I felt like a wreck as we crossed the loft. A mix of nerves and excitement twisted in my stomach, making me feel nauseous. I had to keep reminding myself that it was just pre-wedding jitters.

Natalie pulled me into my bedroom to show me the new pajamas she had picked out—a white silk short set with "Devonshire" printed on the back. I couldn't contain my grin as I hugged the soft material to my chest and threw my arms around my best friend.

"I love these! You're the best. I love you so much," I exclaimed.

Warmth spread across my cheeks. I truly loved Natalie; she had gone from being a stranger to my closest friend in such a short time.

"Well, try them on and kiss Brooks goodnight before they leave. I told Michaelson he had to wait," she replied.

"Always a step ahead." I grinned, clutching the pajama set and heading into my closet.

Excited to show Brooks my new pajamas, I ran downstairs but stopped short of the deck when I heard them talking. I knew I shouldn't eavesdrop, but my curiosity got the better of me, so I held my breath and quietly listened, worried about making a noise.

"Bro, you're going to be a married man and a Dad," Connor whooped.

"I know. Crazy," Brooks agreed, shaking his head in disbelief.

"You ready for that?" Michaelson asked more seriously.

"Yeah, I think so," Brooks responded. "I mean, I am happy and excited. I just wish Emily and I had some more time to ourselves. Like, for the first time ever, we can just be together, have sex whenever, vacation whenever, eat ice cream for dinner, but once the baby comes, that will change."

"Yeah," Michaelson said, nodding.

"Well, have as much sex as possible before the baby comes," Connor teased.

Brooks laughed. "Yeah, done."

I slid the door back open and crossed the deck to Brooks to model my new shirt for him.

"I love it." He smiled, pulling me into his lap, and kissed the back of my shoulder, where his last name was etched across the fabric. Our last name.

"I love you. I can't wait to marry you," he muttered into the fabric.

I slid off his lap to face him. "I love you, too and don't be late. I'm counting the minutes." He gave me another panty, melting grin before pulling me in for another kiss.

"Okay, promise. See you tomorrow, Miss Barlow." I scrunched my nose. *Barlow?* Tomorrow would be the last day I would be a

Barlow. Realization felt like a sucker punch to the gut. I was the last of the Barlow name.

I pasted on a smile, trying to hide my sudden change in disposition. I hated the idea of hyphenating my last name. I had never wanted that. I only ever wanted to be Emily Devonshire. Still, I couldn't help but feel this was another thing, another hurdle, another reminder that they weren't here.

"Goodnight, my love." I stood up and kissed his cheek before disappearing inside. I wiped away the tears as they began to fall down my cheeks. I promised myself I wouldn't cry or be sad. Tomorrow will be the happiest day of my life, just like they would want.

After convincing Sara and Natalie that I was tired and that wedding jitters were getting the best of me, I pulled my journal from the closet and sat down on the bed.

Mama,

Tomorrow is the day! It's finally here. I really miss you, Dad, Carrie, and James. Throughout this week, I have thought about what it would be like if you were all here. I can almost picture the chaos. I might have rolled my eyes at the parties, shopping, and the never-ending marriage advice, but I would have listened to every detail nonetheless.

Tonight would have been perfect. A last-minute fancy dinner, you and Carrie showering me with love, meeting my girlfriends who would adore you, and we would have danced and sung at the top of our lungs. We probably would have cried a lot, too. It's the little things I miss the most: the adoration on your faces when I put on my new pajamas tonight and the last-minute late-night pep talk to remind me that life is hard, but Brooks and I will always find a way to work it out. I can picture Dad fighting back tears as he said goodnight to his daughter, Emily Barlow, one last time.

I realized tonight that I am the last of the Barlows, and it hurts. I was so focused on my name becoming Devonshire that I never stopped to think about what it means to truly be the last Barlow. With both of you gone, it feels as though I'm erasing an entire line of my family with the final swoop of my signature. There are no surviving Barlows left to share this burden with me, and the weight of it is overwhelming. It's just really hard and unexpected.

It brings up so many questions that I never got answered. For instance, why didn't you and Daddy have more kids? Did you want more? Was Daddy disappointed not having a son? Was he happy with just having a daughter? I know it may seem silly, and I understand he loved me more than I could ever imagine, but I will never have answers to these questions, and I will never feel the love and reassurance to remind me that's not the case.

Wherever you are, I hope you know how grateful I am for both of you and that I had the privilege of being your daughter. I hope you will be with us tomorrow, celebrating together, and that you are proud of us.

Always and forever your little girl,
xo-Emily

↟ ↟ ↟

I pried my eyes open, wincing at the bright morning light, and found Natalie standing over me with the remote. "Time to wake up, my beautiful bride." Her voice was sing-songy and filled with joy.

I groaned, stretching my arms over my head. "It's too early, and I hardly slept at all last night."

"It's just wedding jitters. Come on, it's time to shower, and I'll bring you your tea. Everyone will be here in an hour." She clapped her hands together in excitement.

It was hard not to match her positive energy, so I returned her smile and rolled out of bed. "Okay, wedding day."

"Yes! In just a few short hours, you will be hitched to your dreamy fiancé."

"Dreamy fiancé?" I asked, raising an eyebrow at her.

"Don't act like he's not! Brooks needs to teach a Boyfriend 101 class."

I rolled my eyes. "Alright, I'll take that tea now." She nodded and stepped out of the room. I grabbed my cell phone and typed a quick text to Brooks before she returned.

I wasn't sure what the rules were today, other than staying out of sight of Brooks until I walked down the aisle, but I had no doubt that Natalie wouldn't hesitate to hide my phone if she knew I was already texting him.

Emily: See you at the altar in 5 hours.

x your blushing and anxious bride

B<3: Don't be late.

x your very excited and pacing "almost" husband.

After a long, exfoliating shower, I made my way downstairs to where Natalie and Sara were sitting on the kitchen island, which was covered with food, drinks, and an array of hair and makeup products. The music was blasting from the speakers.

"Taylor Swift?" I asked.

"What wedding day is complete without her?" Sara grinned before turning back to her phone.

Sara began singing along to "Romeo and Juliet," replacing the names with Brooks and mine. We all joined in, humming as I filled my plate with food.

Suddenly, my phone buzzed, alerting me to some cars passing through the gate.

"They're here!" I squealed.

We spent most of the morning surrounded by hairspray, makeup, nail polish, and laughter. In between getting ready, we took turns dancing and selecting the next song. Throughout the morning, I oscillated between waves of complete joy and feelings of overwhelming nervousness. It didn't make sense; I had longed for this moment, and now that it was here, I felt sweaty and anxious, with my heart racing.

Just then, Natalie left the kitchen and reappeared, her excitement palpable.

"Time for the dress!" she cheered.

↟ ↟ ↟

I let out a dreamy sigh as we arrived at the venue. The GlassHouse looked magical in the fading light. At this time of day, the forest had a soft glow, and the green trees, along with the dark brown, damp bark and soil, made it feel like a fairytale.

"Deep breaths, Emily. He's waiting for you," Natalie whispered, squeezing my hand. I could sense every emotion, ready to break free, but I focused on just one. Natalie lifted my train as I stepped out into the rocky parking area.

"Okay." I forced a smile, burying all my emotions. "Let's go."

Chapter Fifty-Three

I sat down on the white velvet couch in the waiting area, focusing on calming my breath. Sara peeked out the window, watching as the few people on the guest list began to arrive. The Cumberlands, the Isaacs, our childhood staff members, some executives from Caston who flew down on the jet, and a few friends from Hope. I thought my heart would beat out of my chest, so I stood up briskly to pace the room.

"Hey, it's okay. Almost there," Natalie reassured me, rubbing circles on my back.

Her gentle touch broke free the dam of tears I'd been holding back. My mother should have been here, quieting my anxious thoughts and offering comfort.

"I want my mom and dad. I feel like I can't breathe," I gasped, suddenly feeling like the lace bodice was constricting my lungs.

"You are breathing," Natalie reminded me, her voice tender and soothing. "Emily, look at me. Your parents are here, okay? They are so proud of you, and I'm sure they are rejoicing. Carrie can't wait, remember?"

I nodded, trying to steady my tears. "I know."

"Just focus on Brooks, okay? You get to marry your best friend, and he's so excited. When we go in there, keep your eyes on him, alright?"

I nodded again, the panic in my chest slowly subsiding to a dull ache. The familiar ache that has never left since I lost them. We lost them.

"That's right, deep breaths."

The door swung open, and Connor appeared with a wide, goofy smile that comforted the sad little girl inside of me. I exhaled softly, trying to summon a smile for him.

"Wow, Em, you look amazing. Brooks is going to cry when he sees you," he said.

"Eh," Sara replied, poking her head back into the room. "I bet five bucks that he won't."

"Either way, he's waiting until the wedding march begins to cry or not," Natalie declared, handing me the bouquet. The scent of the eucalyptus leaves enveloped my senses, calming my remaining nerves. It was intoxicating as I brought the bouquet to my nose and inhaled deeply.

The stems of the thick bouquet were wrapped in soft ivory lace fabric featuring mauve roses, eucalyptus, olive branches, blush peonies, and baby's breath. It was gorgeous—more perfect than I could have imagined. Taking another steadying breath, Natalie wiped away a stray tear.

Okay, I am ready. Brooks is waiting for me at the end of the aisle.

I looked around at everyone and beamed a genuine smile, all worries tucked away for now. "Ready."

As we entered the glass chapel, everything felt like it was in slow motion. The cobblestone floors reflected the dancing light from the pillar candles that lined the aisles. Twinkling lights draped across the glass ceiling, surrounded by a canopy of trees above. At the front, where Brooks stood, there was an arbor adorned with the same flowers as my bouquet.

My Brooks—my best friend, my partner, and the father of my

child. I looked up at Connor and squeezed his arm. He grinned back at me with a reassuring smile. At that moment, I realized Connor was a brother to Brooks and me. He was always there, encouraging us, having fun, and providing steady, healthy support. I stifled the overwhelming emotions and looked down the aisle at my groom.

His beaming smile warmed the entire room, adoration shining clearly in his eyes. My dress swooshed as we made our way down the aisle, and small praises from the crowd could be heard over the quiet music.

I focused solely on him. Each step felt like coming home, each second deserved to be remembered and etched into my mind, our memories, our story. I noticed Natalie and Sara dabbing at their eyes in my peripheral vision, but my attention remained fixed on him—Brooks. It felt as if every moment of our lives had led us to this point.

As we neared him, tears pooled in his eyes, mirroring my own. We paused in front of Brooks, and I turned back to Connor.

"Thank you," I whispered, barely audible. My heart was lodged in my throat, and I tried to suppress the emotions so I wouldn't ruin my makeup.

"Love you, Emily," he whispered, kissing the back of my hand and placing it in Brooks'.

The pastor began speaking, but I heard nothing. I was trying to capture every moment as a memory: how Brooks's eyes expressed how much he loved me, how they appeared grayish-blue in this light, the creases at the corners, and the perfect swoop of his hair, cut and faded just right.

His beard was so short that it allowed me to see his whole face. I could see the pulse on his neck beating steadily. His lips were a perfect pink—soft and inviting. I wanted to kiss them.

"Your vows, Brooks," the pastor said, interrupting my thoughts.

I glanced at the pastor and then back to Brooks, whose hands reluctantly left mine to grab the book from Michaelson.

"Emily," his voice broke. He cleared his throat, took a deep breath, and began again. "For twenty years, I have waited for this moment. I have loved you from the first moment I saw you. Every moment we've shared—filled with laughter, tears, and a mix of good and bad memories—has created a home in my heart for you. The tears and heartbreak only shook the unstable foundation, allowing us to rebuild something more solid, more eternal."

He paused again, fighting back tears as he sucked in a sharp breath. My heart felt like it was in free fall, floating lazily through the air, but I knew he would catch it. He would catch me. "I promise to love you always, without reservation. I promise to be a source of comfort and strength for you in happy times and hard times. I offer you my body and my soul for connection, comfort, and protection. I want to grow old with you, to laugh with you, to cry with you, and to always be yours forever. I love you completely, madly." He offered me a watery smile, his eyes glistening with tears, and I felt my bones melt into putty.

I dabbed away my own tears with the tissue Natalie handed me.

"My turn," I laughed through my tears. I can do this. "Brooks," I inhaled deeply. "You complete me in ways I never thought possible. From the first 'I love you,' my heart has always belonged to you and only you. You have always been my best friend, my biggest cheerleader, and my home." I paused to catch my breath. The vow book in my hand was shaking from my trembling grip. "You were there to catch me when I fell, to nurse me back to health, and to share in all of my joys and sorrows." My voice broke as I fought back a sob and continued.

"I have waited what feels like my whole life to share your last name. I promise to be a faithful partner, to honor and respect you, to support you in all that you do, and to celebrate life with you. I promise to love you unconditionally every day. I want to create a home with you that is filled with laughter, kindness, and service to one another. No matter what comes our way, I promise to always choose you. You are my always and forever, Brooks Caston. A lifetime will never be long enough with you. I love you forever." I sighed, relieved that I managed not to blow snot bubbles.

Brooks nodded, gently brushing away my tears as his hands cupped my cheeks. He leaned his forehead against mine, and we took a moment to calm our emotions.

"The rings," Michaelson said, handing them to Brooks.

The rest of the ceremony felt like a song playing in my head as he slid the delicate wedding band onto my finger. His warm hand steadied mine as the cool gold band slipped down my finger. My hand trembled again as I slid Brooks' black Tungsten band onto his finger. I smiled to myself, reminding myself to show him the engraving later in private. Our hands mirrored the overflow of nervous energy we both felt, but at least we were united in our overwhelming emotions.

"You may now kiss your bride."

Brooks' hands slid across my bare back, pulling me closer to him as I grasped his lapels. He was my home now. His lips caressed mine, soothing every vibrant nerve in my body that had been anticipating this moment.

The kiss held a deeper meaning and purpose as our lips danced together. Forever and always—we now belonged to each other. Through better and worse, we would always be together. In sickness and in health, we would serve one another. The crowd's cheers and applause grew louder, and Brooks smiled against my lips.

"I love you," I whispered, pulling my lips back for one final soft kiss.

I turned to face the crowd for the first time since entering the GlassHouse. Mr. Gordon, Mr. Michaels, and Ms. Hutchins were seated in the front row. Our friends and executive team—Diane, Ethan, our COO, Rebecca, and a few others—were all present. Mr. Whitney, Jared, and Audrey were also there. Brooks' house staff, Beck Davis and Jack Carter sat near Grey Stanley, who smiled and clapped for us as we were introduced as Mr. and Mrs. Devonshire. Brooks squeezed my hand before gently tugging me back down the aisle.

Outside, we raced to the suite, eager to steal a quick moment for ourselves.

"You look so beautiful," Brooks whispered as I hugged him tightly, unwilling to let go. I took a deep breath of his amber cologne, burying my nose into his neck and letting its familiar scent calm my racing heart and settle my nerves.

We stood silently, wrapped in each other's arms for long minutes, savoring the moment. He cupped the back of my neck with one hand, holding me close, while his other hand rested on my hip.

We didn't need words to express how we felt. I could sense the last of the walls I had built around my heart crumbling, freeing me from the darkness I had cast it into. All the compartments of my heart were now reserved for my forever with Brooks, just as they always had been, but with more trust and honest vulnerability than ever before. He was mine, and I was his.

I exhaled a soft whimper as his arms tightened around me. I wasn't ready to break free from this embrace.

Michaelson knocked on the door before he ducked his head in. "Hey, love birds. It's time to go." We sighed in unison before pulling apart.

"I love you, Mrs. Devonshire," he smiled softly, brushing a curl back.

"I love you, husband," I reminded him, with a beaming grin.

Brooks opened the door to see Natalie hovering behind Michaelson.

"Sorry, Em, the photographer needs us for photos before we head back to the house."

"Okay," I sighed again happily. We'd have all the time in the world now that we were finally Mr. & Mrs. Devonshire.

↟ ↟ ↟

Brooks and I had the converted Sprinter van to ourselves on the way back to Pacific Coves. My dress felt like an obstacle course that

Brooks had to navigate to get closer to me. I giggled as he lifted and pushed the skirt out of the way. The rest of the wedding party took Brooks' car back to the house and planned to be in the studio for a while, giving us some time alone.

During the ride home, Brooks' lips hardly left mine, except for the occasional smiles, giggles, and "I love yous."

As the van pulled up to the house, Brooks stepped out first and lifted me into his arms to carry me across the threshold. My cheeks hurt from the permanent, love-struck grin on my face. He took me straight to our bedroom, finally setting me down. The vendors were all downstairs, busy putting the final touches on the ceremony.

I lay back on the bed, watching Brooks remove his coat and gracefully lay down on top of me. The familiar weight of his body and the warmth of him had me moaning effortlessly as he peppered kisses up the side of my neck.

"B," I moaned. "I have to change."

"In a minute," he whispered against my neck.

My body was ignited with desire and a pulsing anticipation.

I could feel his chest against my breasts as his mouth claimed every bare surface in soft kisses. My body welcomed and urged him forward, clinging to him with each heated kiss.

"Okay, let's get you out of this thing," he said, his tone both reassuring and playful. He climbed to his feet, the fabric of his well-fitted black suit stretching snugly across his broad shoulders and muscular frame. I couldn't help but pause for a moment, admiring my husband. The way the soft fabric hugged his physique emphasized every defined muscle, making him look effortlessly handsome.

Brooks chuckled softly as he moved closer, searching for the concealed zipper of my dress. "I can't find it," he said, leaning closer to inspect my gown.

"It's down here," I replied, pointing towards the base of the lace bodice that topped my silk tulle skirt. With a gentle movement, I tried to reach for the zipper, the delicate fabric brushing against my fingertips.

"Here." I finally found it, my fingers latching onto the cool metal of the zipper hidden among the layers of lace. Impatiently, I tugged at it, eager to get out of the dress.

Brooks caught my hand, stopping me from yanking it down. "What are you doing?" I questioned, a mix of confusion and curiosity in my voice.

"Admiring you," he replied, his voice a deep, soft caress that sent a flutter of excitement through me. He spun me gently in his arms, his gaze lingering on me as if he were committing every detail to memory.

"Just once more before I take it off," he said with a playful glint in his eye, tapping his finger to his temple, as though he were taking mental notes. A rush of warmth flushed through me, and I felt my cheeks heat up in response.

Brooks' fingers softly traced the intricate lace that adorned my chest, moving with deliberate slowness. His hands followed the curves of the lace down each sleeve, taking in the delicate texture and design that wrapped beautifully around my arms.

He retraced his path, his touch becoming more intimate as his hands glided along my bare back, feeling the soft, bare skin beneath the lace. He lingered at the top of the bodice, as if savoring the moment before we exchanged the elegance of my dress for the closeness that awaited us.

It reminded me of the first night we had sex. Taking each other in, slow and steady. His lips pressed against my shoulder softly as he found my zipper again and loosened my dress. I shuddered in his arms, my skin tingling to life.

Once the zipper was free, he gently guided the lace from my shoulders and down my arms until it pooled on the floor at my feet. I was left standing there in my white lace panties and white pumps.

Brooks' hands were on my waist before I could finish setting it down. His body pressed into my back as his firm hands slid up my curves, wrapping his arms around me.

"I'm not going to start anything I can't finish," he whispered into my neck.

"What?"

"I want to enjoy my wife slowly, not rushed." He wrapped me in his arms while I turned in his arms to face him. His eyes focused on mine. "Let's get you redressed, Mrs. Devonshire, before I change my mind."

I melted a little more. "Okay."

↟ ↟ ↟

"Mmm..." Brooks slid his hand down the top of my spaghetti strap a-line dress. It resembled my wedding dress with a lace, backless bodice that flowed into a tulle court train skirt. "I like this one too."

He had traded out his tux for navy slacks, a clean white dress shirt, and a new pair of wingtips. He looked like he stepped out of an issue of Tom Ford.

"Hey," I giggled, slapping away his hands, which were palming my breasts through the material. I was half a second away from being so turned on that he would have to do something about it before I agreed to see anyone.

"Sorry, I can't help myself. Your boobs look so sexy and tempting in this dress." He pulled his hands back in mock offense. "It makes me admire you and want to do inappropriate things all at the same time."

I laughed. "Well, thank you for letting me know. I can change into a more modest dress that hides everything."

"No, no, please don't do that." His voice was huskier than seconds ago. "I like your dresses. Everyone can look, but only I get to touch." He had a devious smile as he planted a kiss on my shoulder, maintaining eye contact with me in the mirror.

I groaned and pulled away from him again to finish pinning back my blonde hair. I loved the extensions I had put in for the ceremony, and it made me realize how much I missed my long waves.

Hopefully, the prenatal vitamins would help my hair grow faster. I placed a palm on each side of my stomach, hoping to sense something from our sweet baby—something that would tell me they were just as happy as I was, as we were at that moment.

"You are the most beautiful bride." Brooks snapped a photo of me in the mirror. I blushed again.

"Thank you, B."

"Dance with me." He set his phone down and extended his hand toward me. I turned to him, placing my hand in his and leaning into his warm embrace. I couldn't help but smile as we swayed gently to the soft, quiet music that drifted upstairs from the party below. I could hear the arrival of guests and the band playing cocktail music downstairs. Brooks's hand moved to my stomach.

"How are you feeling?"

"I am feeling great. Excited to see our baby again when we get back."

"How many weeks? Fifteen?"

"Sixteen."

Brooks stopped dancing and released me, kneeling in front of me and kissing my stomach.

"Mommy looks really beautiful, and she's all mine until you get here. I love you, baby."

"Our baby loves you too," I whispered.

"Time to go," Natalie exclaimed as she entered the bathroom. "Oh God, I am so sorry. I should have knocked." Her cheeks flamed a dark shade of pink as she covered her eyes with one hand.

Brooks stood and took my hand. "Natalie, it's okay," he said. "Thank you for today. You look really pretty."

Natalie smiled. "Thanks, Brooks." She paused. "Okay, ready? They are going to announce you guys so just wait on the bottom step."

↟ ↟ ↟

The reception was everything I could have dreamed of. Our home was perfect for this seaside party. We opened the doors to the deck and pushed the furniture to the sides, allowing the guests to flow easily in and out. The pool deck was covered with an acrylic dance floor, and the band played downstairs, enticing the guests to the dance floor. Servers moved through the crowd, weaving in and out to deliver drinks and hors d'oeuvres.

"Hey, you two!" Connor exclaimed as he walked up to us.

"It's time for your first dance!" Natalie squealed.

Chapter Fifty-Four

I looked up at Brooks, excited to have this memory and milestone. Our first dance was a mixture of dancing, swaying, and Brooks charading out the lyrics. I closed my eyes and let the music wash over me. I could feel the warmth of Brooks' hand on my back and the gentle pressure of his chest against me as we swayed to the music.

I had never felt more at peace and in love than I did at this moment. My eyes met with Brooks, and he smiled back at me, making my heart skip a beat. All of this felt surreal. The wedding, the baby, all of it. It was like a dream that I hoped to never wake from.

"Did you see the engraving on your band?" I asked, my head resting on his chest as we swayed to the last notes of the song.

"I did." He wrapped his arms around me tighter. "My whole heart."

"My whole heart is yours, Brooks." He brushed his fingers under my chin, tilting my head back, and then his lips crashed down on mine.

When the music finished, Brooks pulled back and grabbed a glass of champagne from the nearest passing tray.

"A toast to my bride, Emily. You are and always have been my best friend. Every day, I wake up loving you more than the day before, which seems impossible, but somehow it's true. Thank you for saying yes to me. Thank you for loving me. I love you."

I dropped my head onto his chest while the crowd clinked their glasses together. The music changed, and our guests filled the dance floor and the deck.

"Congratulations, you two!" Mr. Michaels said, with Mr. Gordon by his side.

"Thank you for coming," I replied, offering them a genuine smile as I wrapped my arms around their necks.

"Thank you," Brooks said, shaking their hands once I released them.

"I always hoped you guys would work things out. I know your parents would be extremely proud of you both, and so are we. Despite your obstacles, you tackled them head-on and built a spectacular life together.

"Emily, I know your dad would want me to say this on his behalf: you will forever be his baby girl, no matter what. And Brooks, your dad would be proud of the man you've become; he would probably give a loud speech about it. I can hear it now: 'I couldn't be prouder of my son, and I know he is going to take care of our daughter Emily.'" Mr. Gordon had quite a theatrical flair. Brooks and I both laughed, picturing James's booming voice as he ensured everyone knew how proud he was. I looked up at Brooks, and he nodded softly at me.

"Uh, Mr. Gordon, Mr. Michaels, thank you again. It really means a lot to us that you could both be here. Also, we haven't shared the news yet, but..." I wrapped my hands around my stomach. "We are expecting."

Their faces lit up with unexplainable joy.

"Well, we won't say anything, but..." they hugged us in turns. "Your moms would be over the moon," Mr. Michaels said.

"I know," I replied, offering them a watery smile. "They really would. They would have loved all of this."

"Well, we won't take up any more time," Mr. Michaels said, hugging me again.

"Congrats, my sweet girl," Mr. Gordon said with a kiss on my cheek. *My sweet girl.* It warmed my heart. Today, my eyes were truly opened to my family.

It wasn't our parents, but the sibling in Connor, the "other" parents and grandparents we had in our staff and executive team, and our friends who rallied around us to be there. We weren't alone. How did I never see it before? A flare of anger at myself flashed through me. This whole time, I had believed I was alone.

↟ ↟ ↟

It was late when the last song ended, and the crowd had dwindled to nothing. The staff and vendors were cleaning up when Brooks came out to the deck and wrapped a blanket around me. I was just saying my goodbyes to Sara and Connor, who had been bickering until I arrived. Once I showed up, they both had been on their best behavior.

Natalie planned to stay a bit longer with Michaelson down in the studio. I couldn't help but smile, knowing they were getting closer to becoming an official couple. She had talked to him, and I assumed it went well, but I hadn't had a chance to confirm that yet.

"Ready for bed?" Brooks' voice was soft in my hair.

"Yes," I replied, leaning into his chest.

Brooks swooped me into his arms as we waved goodbye to our friends.

"Brooks!" I laughed as he almost dropped me halfway through the living room.

"Sorry, this blanket." He chuckled, setting me on my feet.

"C'mon, before we head up, I have a wedding present."

"What?" I asked, taking his hand.

He pulled me into the glass room off the study and sat on the piano bench. In the dim light, I could see the softness in his face, the way the moonlight illuminated his white shirt, and the outline of his well-built silhouette. I sat down on the bench next to him. He inhaled deeply and began to play a beautiful melody. His fingers danced over the keys as if by magic.

Tears started streaming down my face before I fully understood my emotions. We had made it. The keys echoed emotional highs and lows, twists and turns. My soul responded to the unspoken feelings. The song slowed, and he finished with a gentle kiss on my head.

"Wow," I exclaimed, wiping away a tear. "Thank you. I love it." I leaned into him.

"I wrote it when I was in Osan. I don't know why, but it came to me one day. I was thinking about you and how much I loved you."

I was at a loss for words, so I leaned in closer to kiss him. His breath lingered on my lips. "Let's go upstairs," he whispered.

I dropped the blanket, and he lifted me into his arms again. This time, my legs and arms wrapped around him like I was a clingy child as he carried me up the stairs. He closed our bedroom door with his foot as he gently set me on the bed. I was unwilling to let go and held him close to me for a minute.

"Are you tired?" he asked into my neck.

I released him, allowing our faces to meet. My hand gently stroked his cheek.

"Husband, you can keep me up all night if you want," I yawned.

He laughed, turning his lips to kiss my palm. "Okay."

He left for the closet, returning with one of his shirts and some tissue. He began shutting off all the lights except the single lamp on his nightstand, which he dimmed. He pulled me off the bed and helped me out of my dress.

"I want you to make love to me," I whispered as my dress hit the floor. His lips were on mine before I could process his movement, and we were in the bed a second later.

Strong hands were moving around my body, caressing and teasing. His tongue slid against mine, and the only thing separating me from his erection was the thin cloth of his boxer briefs. As my hands pulled at his back, I reminded myself to go slow. I pushed against his shoulder, rolling us so that I was on top.

My breasts were swollen with need as they brushed against his chest, and my core ached, needing to be filled. Brooks pulled my breast into his mouth, sucking, tasting, biting. Meanwhile, I rocked my hips along his length. His mouth came off with a pop before he was sucking the other one into his mouth.

"Brooks," I panted. His mouth released my perky nipple, moving along my chest and collarbone, licking and kissing his way back to my mouth. "I just need you in me," I whispered. With one hand stabilizing me, he used his other to pull down his waistband enough so he could kick them off. With his hands on my hips, fingers gripping into the skin, he readjusted me until I was sliding down onto his length.

He sat up, wrapping his arms around me while my legs wrapped around his back. Together, we lifted and rocked, our mouths never leaving each other. It was soft, slow, and a final severed piece of our connection healed. Marriage, the final promise of forever.

It was late at night, or perhaps early in the morning, by the time we finally fell asleep. After our second round, we ended up downstairs for a late-night snack and some hydration, which led to another round in the kitchen before heading to bed. We were then woken up around three o'clock for yet another round—by that point, we had lost count of our orgasms.

Chapter Fifty-Five

His arm was hot and heavy, draped over me as I woke up. The light was barely peeking above the horizon, but I felt nauseous and really needed to pee *again*. I slowly slid out from under him and tiptoed to the bathroom. My stomach was cramping as I sat down. Maybe we overdid it? Last night had been a never-ending saga of pleasure and romance on many surfaces of our room and bathroom.

I grabbed my stomach and tried to calm my breathing. I remembered Dr. Williams told me to expect mild discomfort from the stretching ligaments. Maybe that was what I was feeling. I closed the lid of the toilet and returned to the sink to wash my hands before taking a nausea pill. Crawling back into bed beside Brooks, I hoped I could get more sleep before we needed to get up.

Brooks wrapped his arms around me, pulling me into his chest. He felt so warm. I tucked my cold feet around his legs and tried not to giggle.

"You're freezing," he muttered in surprise.

"Sorry, I didn't mean to wake you," I whispered, stifling another giggle.

"What time is it?" he asked sleepily.

"Shh... go back to sleep. It's too early," I replied, closing my eyes and burying my face into his chest. I really needed this nausea to go away.

When we woke up an hour later, I realized there was no time for more sleep. I had procrastinated on packing for our honeymoon, and since our jet was leaving around noon, we had a long flight ahead of us. Reluctantly, I walked to the closet, plopping down on the floor to pull my suitcase out from behind my winter coats. The cramping had eased, and thanks to the nausea pill, I was actually feeling hungry.

I opened my swimsuit drawer and dumped all its contents into my suitcase. After that, I packed all the essentials: lacy lingerie, plenty of comfortable and sexy undergarments, and way more summer dresses than I would need. I tossed in several pairs of sandals and wedges, my beach hat and bag, and a few comfy outfits. Lastly, I grabbed my makeup bag and returned to my vanity to fill it.

As I sat there, I noticed the cramping returning. I caught a glimpse of the slight bump in my reflection. It honestly looked more like I had just eaten a large meal rather than being pregnant. I exhaled as I finished organizing my toiletries.

At that moment, Brooks entered the bathroom with a cup of warm tea in his hands.

"Good morning, wife." He smiled, setting the cup down in front of me. "Are these ready to go?" he asked, lifting my suitcase off the closet floor.

"Yeah, I just need to add this." I handed him the toiletry bag. "All that's left is my purse. Did you pack your phone charger, or should I grab it?"

"I got it. I'll take this downstairs."

I returned to the mirror and brushed my teeth and hair before slipping into my comfy joggers and crop top. I looked around the room to make sure I had everything. Before heading downstairs, I shoved my hairbrush, toothbrush, and charger into my bag. "Ready!"

↟ ↟ ↟

"Whose plane is this?" I asked as we boarded the larger jet.

"It's Xpansion's. They are letting us borrow it as a wedding gift." Brooks kissed my hair before tossing his computer bag on one of the leather chairs.

"They let us borrow their jet?" I chuckled. Who does that?

"Yeah, they thought we would be more comfortable. It has a bedroom, so we can sleep during the flight. It's a twenty-five-hour trip." Right. A whole day on a plane.

"This is beautiful," I said, astonished. Six large reclining chairs faced each other, with tables in between. Behind them were two large sofas facing each other, each with a coffee table. Just beyond them was a wall separating what appeared to be a bedroom.

"This is insane, B!" I spun around, taking it all in. I headed straight to the bedroom. A queen bed was on one side of the plane, and a couch and dresser on the other. Between the living room and bedroom was a bathroom with a small shower. *Some wedding present.*

"Do you like it?" he asked, meeting me in the bathroom.

"I have so many questions," I replied. "How did this happen, and why?"

"Well, I just mentioned that we were heading to the Maldives for our honeymoon after we signed all the contracts for Europe. The next day, the CEO called me and offered us the jet. I accepted because I thought you'd be more comfortable than if we took ours."

"Much more comfortable." Loud slamming came from outside, and I knew that the crew had finished with fueling.

↟ ↟ ↟

After we were in the air, a stewardess appeared from the front. Brooks and I were seated on the couch. I was lying down with my head on his lap, reading *All The Light We Cannot See*, Leah's newest recommendation. She and I both shared a love for books.

"Can I get you anything to drink or eat?" she asked warmly.

"Do you have iced tea?" I replied.

"Yes. Would you like anything to eat?"

"What options do you have?" I inquired.

"We have salads, sandwiches, and charcuterie boards. I can also pull some items from the freezer," she answered.

"No, I'll go with a salad, please." I looked up at Brooks.

"I'll take water and whatever sandwich you have. Thank you."

She nodded and left us. He sighed, lost in his book, *Money for Nothing*, by Thomas Levenson.

"How long is the flight to Tokyo?" I asked.

"I think eleven hours. We should be there about midnight or four pm in Tokyo."

"I hate time change. It's so confusing," I grumbled.

"Well, the Maldives are only twelve hours ahead. We are traveling through the future back in time."

I laughed. "Right. Thank you for the clarification."

He chuckled, returning to his book.

Does that even make sense? Japan is almost a day ahead in the future, but Maldives is only twelve hours, so we're back in time. Oh, never mind. I went back to my book.

The flight to Tokyo was long, and I was mildly uncomfortable. I tossed and turned in bed, trying to sleep, but I had no such luck. Finally, Brooks joined me in bed pretty late, and I was able to get a few hours of sleep before we landed. It was afternoon in Tokyo when I yawned, stepping off the plane to get some fresh air.

"Halfway," Brooks whispered into my ear, wrapping his arms around me. "Did you get some sleep?"

"A little," I sighed, relaxing into him. "I will probably nap here a little bit after we eat breakfast or lunch."

"I'm going to shower."

"You smell good to me." I turned to kiss him. He smelled faintly of his amber cologne, sweat, and Brooks. His scent alone made me feel warm and fuzzy.

"It's just the pheromones," he chuckled.

After his shower and some brunch, he came to check on me. We had been in the air for over an hour. No matter how much I tried, I was not going to sleep right now. He slid into bed beside me, sliding his hand across my stomach. "How's my baby?"

"Just fine." I smiled. "I have an idea." I giggled.

"What?"

I slid off the bed and closed the door. I crawled back up on top of Brooks and began to lift his shirt over his head. He chuckled.

"What will I do with you?" he smiled, lifting my shirt over my head.

As he slid into me, I gasped quietly at how he filled me and then some.

"Shh..." he chuckled.

"I am," I argued. *Or at least trying*. "Welcome to the mile-high club." I grinned. Brooks rolled his eyes, and his hands dropped to my hips. I dropped my head to shoulder, and we came together, flying over the clouds.

↟ ↟ ↟

When I woke up, it was night again. *This time zone change is killing me.* I glanced at my watch. It was three in the morning at home. I opened the bedroom door to see Brooks on the couch with his laptop. I yawned as I made my way over to him.

"Hi, sleepy head." He looked up from his computer.

"Where are we, or how much longer is the flight?" I groaned.

"I think we have about seven hours to go. I was going to head to bed here in a few."

"Okay." I slid down onto the couch next to him. "What are you working on?"

"Just sending some last-minute emails before we land. Then I promise I'm all yours." He kissed my cheek. "You should eat something."

"Did you eat?"

"Yeah. I just had some sushi."

I scrunched my face in disgust. Sushi sounded awful.

We glanced around for the call button and found one on the end table. After picking at my chicken salad, we crawled into bed together. Sleep was much easier this time, with Brooks' body heat comforting me.

We landed in Malé after what felt like an eternity. I had never spent an entire day on an airplane before, and I was thankful for the upgraded jet. As the door opened, the humid air hit me like a wall.

I stepped out into the fresh, beachy atmosphere, with Brooks following closely behind. I noticed a white BMW with a chauffeur waiting for us. For the first time since yesterday, I realized that my cramps had disappeared.

"Emily. C'mon, he's going to take us to the marina." Brooks approached me.

"The marina?"

"We have to get there by boat." I smiled and nodded. Brooks had decided to keep most of our honeymoon a surprise, but I knew we were staying in the Maldives; I just didn't know the specific location. We planned to be here for twenty days before returning home, just in time for him to return to Seattle.

I slid into the backseat of the BMW, smiling first at our driver, who looked completely out of place in his full black suit. Brooks climbed in beside me after our luggage was loaded into the trunk.

The drive to the marina was only a few minutes from the airport, making the need for a driver feel completely unnecessary—an Uber would have sufficed. I stepped out and saw a white speedboat waiting for us. Brooks and the driver unloaded the luggage from the car onto the boat, and I followed Brooks down the boardwalk.

"Welcome," the captain greeted us.

"Hi," I waved back as I climbed aboard. I sat at the front of the boat, soaking it all in. I was thankful that Brooks and I had been able to sleep during the last leg of our trip. The sun felt wonderful on my skin, and the warm, humid air washed away all my anxiety and stress. The water lapped quietly against the boat as I leaned back and enjoyed the sunshine.

"Are you okay?" Brooks asked, sitting down next to me.

"Yeah," I sighed. "Perfect."

He kissed my cheek and wrapped his arm around behind me. *Thank you, God, if you exist. Thank you for this life.* I leaned into his shoulder just as the boat pulled out of the marina and onto the open sea.

The boat slowed as we approached a gorgeous, modern-style home hovering above the water.

"Wow. Is this where we are staying?" I asked.

"Yep. Michaelson knows the owner. They let me rent it from them while we are here."

I was speechless. The two-story home, constructed of glass and wood beams, featured a large pool that seemed to hover over the ocean. Walls opened up to the sea on all sides. The boat circled the house once before pulling up alongside the deck.

Three staff members greeted us as we arrived. They smiled and placed a beautiful lei around my neck. "Welcome to the Maldives! We can take your bags. Please, step inside; we have drinks and refreshments for you."

"Thank you," Brooks replied, taking my hand to guide me inside. As we approached what appeared to be the front entrance, I could see straight through the house to the back, which opened up to the crystal-clear turquoise water and the light blue pool.

"This feels like a dream," I sighed. Upon entering the house, a man was waiting for us with drinks and a fruit plate.

"Wow. Thank you. What is this?" Brooks asked as he picked up the glasses.

"It's a coconut drink. No alcohol. No alcohol in the Maldives."

"Thank you." I smiled, taking my glass from Brooks. It was cold and very coconutty but so good. I turned about the room, taking it all in. To the left, across the living room, was a bedroom, and just past our server to the right was another outdoor living space with stairs that headed up. The kitchen was just behind the stairs.

"How many bedrooms, B?"

"One. Upstairs is a dining room and rooftop lounge area."

"Can we get changed and go in the pool?"

"Yeah, whatever you want."

The three staff members who greeted us entered the house with our luggage and carried it into the bedroom. The lady who welcomed us stopped in front of us.

"I am Rana, your head of house during your stay. We will take care of all your meals while you are here and are available twenty-four hours a day. We stay in the villa just on the beach, so if you need anything, please allow us a few minutes to get here."

"Okay. Thank you. I am Emily Bar...Devonshire." I shook her hand.

"Brooks." He shook her hand next.

"Well, I will let you two get settled. The fridges are stocked with drinks, snacks, and light foods. The cook should be here around five to make dinner. I just need to make sure before I leave. Do either of you have any allergies or food aversions?"

"She's pregnant, so no raw fish, lunch meats, the usual."

"Okay, and Emily, how do you feel about fish if it's grilled?"

"That's fine," I responded, leaning against Brooks' bicep and wrapping my hand in his.

"I will work on a menu for your time here, and we can look it over tonight."

"That sounds great. Thank you."

Rana nodded and left with the rest of the staff. For the first time in twenty-four hours, we were alone. I skipped to the bedroom and dressed in my swimsuit as fast as possible. I couldn't wait to get into the ocean.

Chapter Fifty-Six

"Hey, Em," Brooks whispered beside me sleepily.

"Hmm?" I groaned, burying my face into the overstuffed pillow. It was too early for whatever he needed.

"You awake?"

"Now I am," I mumbled. It was still dark outside, and the exhaustion from the time change was heavy in my bones. I had always hated jet lag.

Brooks reached over, sliding me back until I was cradled in his warm embrace. He wasted no time, moving his mouth along the column of my neck while his hand caressed down my curves, waking up every nerve ending as he went.

"I'm awake now," I chuckled sleepily. "I don't feel very good, though, and I am exhausted. Maybe later?"

Brooks paused and let out a small groan before kissing my cheek. "Yeah, sorry, love. Get some sleep."

I could feel Brooks tossing and turning beside me all night. I was also somewhat uncomfortable because of the heat. By the middle of the night, we had both shed our clothes and were sleeping under a light cotton sheet.

I was startled awake when the curtains in our room suddenly flew open. What on earth? I slowly peeled my eyes open, trying to focus.

Rana appeared as a blurry image." Your breakfast is ready out on the deck."

"Okay, thank you." I felt the heat of embarrassment creep up my neck and cheeks when I remembered our lack of clothing. I scrambled for the linen duvet, pulling it up higher and tucking it under my arms.

"Emily, I doubt this is the worst she's seen," Brooks chuckled, his voice deep and raspy with sleep. His hands found me, pulling me back into him as he all but smothered me under his huge body.

I fought back a playfully snarky comment.

"Good morning, husband. How did you sleep?" I asked instead.

"Not fantastic, but I'll live." He sighed as his erection grew against me. I turned, hiking a leg over his hip and rocking until he slid into me with a sigh of relief. He filled me so perfectly that I couldn't help but moan.

"Baby, you feel so warm," he groaned.

"Do I?" I teased, rocking my hips back and forth. His fingers worked their magic while I rode out my first orgasm on him. A few minutes later, we came together, melting into each other before he dropped to the side, bringing me with him until I was sprawled out across his sweat-slicked skin.

"Love you," he whispered, kissing the top of my head. A different kind of warmth spread through me, making my heart melt into a puddle of mush.

"I love you. Now let's go, I'm hungry."

↟ ↟ ↟

Our first week together flew by all too quickly. We spent nearly every day in the crystal-clear turquoise water or enjoying activities on the water. Our evenings were filled with intimacy, whether snuggled in bed, lounging on the couch, or relaxing on the pool chairs, cherishing every moment together.

I felt grateful for a break from work and for his undivided attention during those days. For the first time in months, I noticed he looked more relaxed. His face appeared at ease throughout the day, and instead of running his hands through his hair, they remained on me.

By the time we returned home, I would be seventeen weeks along, and my anatomy scan was scheduled for the day after our return. Knowing we were almost halfway to becoming parents made this special time together even more meaningful.

During one of our explorations of the island, we stumbled upon the cutest coffee shop nestled among the trees, with branches intertwined on the roof in the shape of a manta ray. This giant manta's mouth served as the coffee shop's entrance. That's where we spent our morning.

"I will take an iced Earl Gray with oat milk, please."

"Just a black coffee," Brooks followed up with.

Brooks and I sat at one of their tables, sipping on our drinks as a cool breeze swept through, rustling the trees above and filling the air with salt.

"What do you want to do tomorrow?" he asked before taking another sip of his coffee. The sun suited him well. He had a dark tan that made his white linen shirt stand out. His blue eyes appeared lighter here, reflecting the shade of the sky instead of the dark, stormy blue they had at home. I couldn't help but be completely entranced, getting lost in their new hue.

Tilting my face toward the sun and closing my eyes, I could have sworn I felt vitamin D soaking into my skin.

"What about taking a catamaran out? Or wave runners?" I said sweetly, hoping to convince him.

"Em, no. I don't want you getting hurt. We can do the catamaran, though. Let's walk down to the pier and find out."

"Okay." I winced as pain shot through my uterus and stomach, almost sending me to the floor. I gripped the edge of my chair, closing my eyes to focus on the pain and get ahold of it.

"Hey, you okay?" Brooks asked, concerned, reaching across to me.

"Ouch. No. It hurts," I groaned. Panic seized my breath as the crippling pain kept coming, wave after wave.

"What can I do?" Brooks was now at my side.

"Take me back to the house, please. I need to lay down," I grunted out.

Brooks lifted me into his arms and all but ran to the boat.

"Please, hurry back," he frantically told the captain.

The boat was back at the house in ten minutes, but it might as well have been an eternity. The pain had sent me into my mind, focusing solely on breathing and containing the pain.

"Do you have a doctor?" Brooks asked, taking me into his arms again. I cried, grabbing my stomach. All I could do was pray that our baby would be okay. He or she had to be.

↟ ↟ ↟

The doctor leaned over me, checking my vitals once more. "She needs to rest. I've given her some pain medication that should help her sleep. Please return home to see her doctor as soon as you can." I was drifting in and out of consciousness, trying to focus on his words. Home? Then I heard Brooks' voice.

"Can you get the plane ready?" The rest of the conversation was a blur as I concentrated on my breathing and managing my stress levels. Everything would be okay once we were back home.

Brooks hovered over me. "Emily," he said softly. "Hey, baby, I'm taking you home."

"B, I'm scared," I cried, fear choking my throat and making it hard to talk, swallow, or breathe.

"I know, sweetie. The plane is being fueled as we speak, and our luggage is already loaded. I'm going to carry you, okay?"

"Brooks," I began, tears welling in my eyes, "is our baby okay?"

"The doctor said he heard a heartbeat, but you are having some contractions, so we just need you to rest and get you home okay."

I nodded, leaning into his chest as he lifted me off the bed.

"I'm sorry," I muttered.

"For what?"

"For ending our honeymoon early."

"Baby, no. I am only worried about you and our baby. If you want, we can come back in the future, but for now, let's just get back to Oregon."

↟ ↟ ↟

I woke up somewhere between the Maldives and Tokyo. It took me a moment to get familiar with my surroundings. The last thing I remembered was being loaded into the car. I rolled over to look for Brooks, and he was fast asleep on the couch next to the bed.

"Hey, B," I whispered. He inhaled deeply and opened his eyes.

"Hey, how are you feeling?" he asked as he leaned forward to focus on me.

"Not great, honestly. But I'm starving and thirsty. Can you get me something?" I replied.

"Okay." Brooks stood up and left the room to look for the stewardess.

A few minutes later, he returned with a tray of crackers, fruit, and granola. He also opened a bottle of water and handed it to me. The pain medication was wearing off, and I began to feel the contractions again. Brooks grabbed the bottle of medication from his bag and read the label.

"Sorry, Em. You can't take these for another hour," he said.

"It's okay," I whispered, concentrating on my breathing. Tears tracked down my temples as I squeezed my eyes shut. Something was wrong. There's no possible way this pain was normal, right?

Brooks crawled into bed beside me, resting his head on mine as he held me.

"I'm so scared. What if something is wrong?"

"I know," he replied gently, cradling my head against his chest. "I don't know what is going on, but no matter what, we will get through this, okay? I will be right here." Exhaustion was winning out. Between the pain and the worry, I could barely keep my eyes open.

"Em, sweetie, you need to eat okay?"

I nodded and, after a minute, rolled back over to take a few bites of my meal before curling up next to him again.

We were both startled awake as we touched down in Tokyo. I finally felt some relief, and the pain had shifted to more of a dull ache. I sat up in bed and reached for the water just as Brooks opened his eyes.

After breakfast, I lay on the couch reading the rest of my book while Brooks sat next to me on his computer. Everything felt almost normal for the rest of the day, and I regretted leaving the glittering waters behind. We could have been aboard the catamaran, spending the afternoon swimming in the warm sea. I finished my book and turned on a movie, but it wasn't long before I fell asleep again.

↟ ↟ ↟

"Welcome home. The weather is forty-eight degrees, and local time is 2:04 a.m." The pilot's voice was loud over the speakers, jolting me awake. Brooks had moved me back to the bed sometime during the flight, and he was asleep beside me. The ache in my chest expanded as I took in the purple patches under his eyes. He woke by the time we touched down.

"I am going to get the car loaded," he said, mussing his hair.

"Okay, I am just going to use the bathroom." I winced again, grabbing my stomach as pain radiated through me. *Dang*. I thought this was past me. As I sat down on the toilet, I saw fresh blood in my underwear, and my whole world spun.

Oh no, no, no. I looked down into the toilet, seeing the swirls of purple and red. *No, please. Please, please. I can't lose my baby.* I began sobbing, too scared to stand up or move, but I knew in my heart - nothing good could come of this.

Chapter Fifty-Seven

The door swung open, startling me from my delirious, painful haze. Brooks looked as though the very life had been squeezed out of him. His face was ashen with with wide eyes and trembling lips.

"Oh my god, Emily!" he exclaimed, shaking slightly as he fumbled for his phone. Before I could even mutter the words that I needed to get to the ER, he was already dialing 911. The world around me blurred as though every moment stretched out in slow motion while also racing by in an unsettling rush. Each heartbeat echoed in my ears.

The paramedics arrived minutes later, their sirens growing closer as they met us out on the tarmac. I gripped Brooks' hand tightly, terrified for our baby. What if we lost our baby? I couldn't lose another person. The fear settled on my chest heavily.

With steady hands, the paramedics boarded the plane, carefully helping me from the confines of the bathroom, and gently lifted me onto a stretcher as they loaded me into the back of the ambulance.

"Brooks," I sobbed, reaching for him. He grasped my hand as he yelled back to the driver to take our bags to the house. Once inside the ambulance, the sirens turned on rushing us toward the hospital. Brooks' forehead rested against our joined hands while the paramedic checked my vitals. The warmth of his touch and the sound of his whisper, "You're okay. You're both going to be okay." were the only things keeping me tethered to the earth.

"Twenty-four-year-old female, one hundred twenty-seven pounds, seventeen weeks pregnant, heavy bleeding, possible placenta rupture." I closed my eyes. *In and out, in and out.* "Starting an IV, blood type is O-negative. Blood pressure is stable, no signs of hemorrhaging." One paramedic was talking into a radio while another was retaking my blood pressure.

A wave of nausea rolled through me before another sharp stab of pain. I pinched my eyes closed and focused on my breathing and the strength of Brooks' hand. *Mommy, please, don't let my baby die,* I prayed silently. The ambulance doors opened, and I was quickly rushed through the doors into the ER.

"Okay, Emily, tell me what's going on." A team of nurses began hooking me up to machines and removing my clothes. When I reached for my voice, I found no air, I had no ability to get the words past the lump in my throat and the heavy pressure in my chest. Why was this happening?

"I have been having pain. The bleeding that just started," I stuttered out in between gasps.

Brooks stepped in to clarify what I couldn't. "We were on our honeymoon in the Maldives. Two days ago, she started having severe cramping. We saw a doctor there who said she was having contractions, but he could hear the baby's heartbeat. He suggested she rest and we get home as soon as possible." He raked his free hand through his messy hair. "She did fine on the plane and slept most of the way here. But when we landed about thirty minutes ago, she started bleeding."

I squeezed his hand a little tighter, thanking him for his strength because it felt like I was spiraling head first into nothingness.

"Okay, let's get an ultrasound and see what's happening." The doctor squirted cold gel onto my stomach. Everything about this was the opposite of my previous ultrasounds. It was always in a dark room with large screens and warm gel. The tech was always smiling and excited to scan the baby.

This time, it was rushed and cold, and I was surrounded by strangers whose faces all masked a look of sadness that shone through their eyes. The wand crossed my stomach several times as we looked for our sweet little baby. The room fell silent around us, and a long, hopeful moment passed. Where there should have been a flickering heart, it was dark, our baby completely still, and there was no colorful blood flow.

"Umm," the doctor cleared his throat. "I am sorry, Mr. and Mrs. Devonshire." The doctor said no more. He didn't need to. I knew what the agonizing look on his face meant because the thick, pungent cloud of dread had been lingering in the back of my mind for what felt like hours.

This wasn't real though. We've had enough loss between us both in such a short time. The universe wouldn't do this to us. Our parents - our guardian angels wouldn't allow this to happen to us.

I turned to Brooks', expecting him to give me a reassuring smile, a shake of his head, denying this absurd discovery but his lip quivered and I knew I wasn't imagining this after all. This was real. This was really happening. We were losing our baby. My world came crashing down on me, crushing me beneath the rubble and blocking out every bit of light.

"What? No!" I cried, even though the sound was thousands of miles away. "No, please." Brooks held me as I screamed, begging with anyone and everyone. "Please, check again. Please."

"Mrs. Devonshire, I'm sorry. We're going to transfer you upstairs to labor and delivery. Your doctor will meet you upstairs to explain more." He excused himself hastily, leaving me clinging to Brooks.

"No," I sobbed. "Our baby can't die. It's not fair. I can't lose anyone else. No." Brooks squeezed me as my body trembled against his, my breath coming out in heavy gasps.

"Okay, Emily, we are going to take you upstairs now. Dr. Williams is on her way in." The nurse said softly as she lifted the bed rails. Brooks released me and my hands fell over my face. *I can't do this. I can't do this. I don't want to do this. I hate you, God. If you exist, I hate you.*

↟ ↟ ↟

There was a soft knock, and Dr. Williams appeared beside another lady. She was short, young, with copper hair pulled back.

"Hi, Emily," Dr. Williams whispered solemnly.

I stared back blankly, unable to fake a smile or even a simple hello. I didn't care if I came off rude because nothing mattered.

"I am so sorry for your loss." She squeezed my hand. *My loss.* What a stupid phrase. If there was anything left of me to shatter, it would crumble at the reminder, but I was already in pieces and there was nothing left of me to break. "This is Kenna. She is our bereavement nurse, and she will be here to talk to you and walk you through some things. First, though, I just want to talk to you both about how today will look.

"A nurse will come in shortly to start you on Pitocin. You're already dilated so I don't think it will take much. An epidural is an option if you would like one. Once we deliver your baby, you will be allowed to keep him, or her, in here with you while you recover if you would like. I do want to stress that your baby will not look like a baby, so I want you to be prepared for that."

Tears kept flowing down my face as if I were a fountain. An endless stream.

"What do you mean we can keep the baby in here?" Brooks asked, sounding as broken as I felt. His eyes were just as swollen and red, his face completely flushed.

"There's a program offered through the hospital. A bassinet, or cold cot, as we call it, can be brought in. This allows you some time to say your goodbyes."

I nodded silently. I was just numb. The whole thing felt surreal, like I was living a different reality, and my mind was trying to process and make sense of everything. The doctor gave me a tight smile and moved to leave.

"What did I do wrong?" I croaked out, finally finding my voice. Brooks looked at me, his handsome face contorting with agony. He squeezed my hand, probably trying to reassure me that this wasn't my fault but only a medical professional could be the judge of that and I had to know, even if it might kill me.

Dr. Williams placed her hand on my shoulder. "Emily, I'm sorry, but after looking over everything, we believe you have what's called an incompetent cervix. There was nothing you could have done differently. Now that we know you have this, for future pregnancies, we will have to monitor you closely and probably do a combination of bed rest and surgery. We can talk about that later, though."

Incompetent. Broken. My fault. That's all I heard. My body failed my baby. Why wasn't I warned ahead of time? Why did it take my baby dying to figure it out?

"What do we do after the baby is born and we leave?" Brooks asked.

"Your baby will be released to the hospital morgue. Once you have made arrangements with a funeral home, the hospital will release your baby to them for proper burial or cremation."

I began sobbing again. My baby is going to a cold morgue. I was positive I wouldn't survive this time. How much loss could one person take? Why did God hate me, us, so much?

The counselor sat with us as the nurse started the pitocin. We talked about what to expect and what services the hospital offered, like having a grief photographer come and take photos. We could try to get footprints and handprints, and our baby would be wrapped in a knit cocoon.

I stared at the green waffle blanket that was draped across me. It was uncomfortable, too light-weight. You would think that hospital blankets would be more comforting. Then again, bodily fluids. The hum of the lights was grating, and the occasional pressure from the blood pressure monitor made me want to yank it off.

But then again, what did it matter?

Was it possible to die of a broken heart? I wasn't ready for this. I wasn't ready for my baby either, but I was determined to be a good mom. I was planning our future around this little life inside of me, and now, it was all gone.

All the dreams of a nursery, the baby clothes, and breastfeeding are just gone. *I am broken. My broken body failed my baby. I killed my baby.*

"Um," my voice broke. "Will I have breastmilk?" I continued staring at the blanket as if it could offer up the answers of the universe.

"You shouldn't. Not this early."

I nodded. So essentially, when I leave this hospital, I will have no evidence that our baby ever existed. Tears continued leaking down my cheeks softly, and somehow, my heart continued to beat.

↟ ↟ ↟

"Emily?"

I turned my head in the direction of my name. I had been zoning out all day. This couldn't be my reality, yet here I was.

"How's your pain?" Dr. Williams asked, hovering over her laptop.

I stared back at her blankly and shrugged. I was confident that nothing could hurt me worse than my heart already being torn from my chest.

"What did I do wrong? I've been taking my prenatal vitamins, and I have been doing light exercise."

"Nothing. We will do more exams once the baby is delivered, okay?"

Brooks' arm tightened around my shoulders as he pulled me to his chest.

There was another knock on the door while Dr. Williams and a nurse were working with the Pitocin machine. I had been on Pitocin for two hours already, and nothing was happening.

"Hey, Emily." Natalie peeked her head in. She was holding a vase of flowers as she hesitantly entered the room. White tulips. I had seen too many white flowers in my life. White and yellow because that's what they tell you to buy someone who's grieving. I used to like white flowers, but now they remind me of cold stone, soggy grass, and goodbyes.

"I am so, so sorry. I wasn't sure what you would need or want, so I had your driver load your bags into my car. I also pulled some items from your closet, like your pajamas and stuff, so you won't be in these gowns afterward.

"Thanks, Natalie," Brooks responded while I just sat there.

"Brooks, I'm sorry I didn't know what to grab. I have your bag, so I just grabbed some jeans and plain shirts from the drawer. I didn't want to go through your stuff."

"No worries. Thanks you," he replied weakly.

"I will be in the ER today, so if you need anything, let me know."

"Okay," I nodded softly. She left the room, leaving our bags in the corner by the sofa and the flowers on the end table. I looked outside, noticing the light filtering through the sea of gray clouds. I usually loved the weather of the Pacific Northwest, but today, I hated it. Or maybe I had just lost all the color in my life.

After another thirty minutes, the Pitocin was kicking in, and my contractions were closer together. Brooks rubbed small circles on my back while I sat on the edge of the bed, squeezing the railing for dear life and breathing through waves of nausea and severe cramps.

"I don't think I can do this!" I sobbed.

"Em, you can do this. You are so strong, baby." He jumped off the bed and ran to the hall to find a nurse.

He returned with a nurse and Dr. Williams came jogging closely behind.

"Okay, Emily. Let's see where you are. Can you lay down, please?"

Dr. Williams did a quick cervical check.

"Okay, she's ready." She nodded to a nurse.

Brooks returned to my side.

"No, no. I can't. I can't do this." My heart raced, and I grabbed the sheets, fighting against the contractions and the pain.

Brooks kissed my temple. "I love you. You can do this."

"It hurts. I don't want to do this. Please, don't make me do this." I screamed out in pain. My whole body contracted uncomfortably, and I wished I could be elsewhere.

Two more nurses raced around the room while I focused on the green blanket again. The bed was pulled apart, and my legs lifted into stirrups.

"Emily, I need you to stay with me, okay? Focus on your breathing, honey," Dr. Williams replied.

"Emily, you can do this. I'm right here. You're so strong," Brooks whispered, brushing the sweat-soaked hair from my face.

"No," I cried out with the next contraction. My body was betraying me again. My baby wasn't ready to leave my body. It was too soon.

"Emily, I need you to push with the next contraction, okay?"

I groaned deeply with the next contraction, pushing even though I begged my body not to. It felt so natural as if I had always known what to do.

"One more," Dr. Williams encouraged. Again, I pushed, squeezing Brooks' hand like I was trying to break it in half.

A release of pressure came quickly as Dr. Williams stood, wrapping our baby in a blanket the size of a hand towel, and handing him or her off to a nurse. The cord was cut, and the baby was taken to the other side of the room.

I had watched enough movies to know this is when you hear the baby cry. Except there was no cry. It was silent. The silence was deafening, so unnerving. I turned my head into Brooks and sobbed again. I was cold, my stomach was flat, and the only thing I felt was a slight pop when the baby came.

"Emily, we need to deliver your placenta. I am going to gently massage, and when I say push, I just need one more push, okay? Then we are done."

"Okay," I nodded, except it wasn't my voice. Some other part of me was in control now.

"Okay, here we go. Last strong push."

Another long and draining push as I felt another release of pressure. *And just like that, it is over.*

"You did great, Emily. We will clean him up, and then you can hold him, okay?"

"It's a boy?" I asked through my tears before looking up at Brooks, whose eyes matched mine.

"We have a son." I smiled before reality came crashing back in that he was gone, that he would never cry, that he would never be. I held onto Brooks, my only source of gravity, my sole reason for living.

"We do," he cried.

Chapter Fifty-Eight

After the nurses left the room and I was cleaned up, they handed me a small swaddle. Instinctively, I cradled it to my chest. Looking down at my sweet baby boy wrapped in the blanket, no bigger than my hand, I whispered, "Hi, baby," running my finger along the swaddle. I was too scared to touch him. Tears splashed silently onto the swaddle from both Brooks and me as we admired our son.

He looked so alien yet so beautiful. His skin was translucent, and his eyes were sealed shut. We could count all ten fingers and ten toes. He was perfect.

"I'm so sorry, my sweet boy. I'm sorry. I love you so much. I wanted you so much," I sobbed.

"How about Liam James?" Brooks' voice broke.

I looked up at him and saw my own pain reflecting in his features, our pain. Our world had shattered once again. How many times would we have to lose our loved ones? How many times would Brooks and I find ourselves in this situation? I felt so angry, yet I was too broken to truly feel it.

“It’s perfect,” I said softly, smiling as I leaned my head on his shoulder.

“Liam, this is your daddy.” I leaned down to kiss his tiny forehead before passing him to Brooks.

Brooks held the small bundle that was our son in his hands and began to sob, his shoulders shaking as he held our tiny miracle. He hadn’t cried this hard even after our parents had died. I looped my arms around him and held him while he embraced our little boy.

The following day, Dr. Williams returned. She explained that everything looked normal and it was just my cervix. I wasn’t sure if that made me feel better or worse. She then told us that the staff would be back to take Liam down to the morgue. I knew my time with him was limited, and I had to soak in every second, no matter how exhausted I was.

Brooks and I took turns studying our baby's small face. I wished we could see his eye color, probably blue like ours. We talked to him about his grandparents and hoped he was already in their arms.

At that moment, I realized I wanted to believe in God and heaven, even though I was angry, and angry wasn’t even a strong enough word. I wanted my baby and my parents to be together in a safe and beautiful place. I didn't want them to just not exist or to be lost forever. *I'm sorry, God. Please keep my baby safe and let him know I love him. Please allow my parents to be with him.*

Our bereavement nurse came into the room, signaling that it was time.

“I am sorry, Mr. and Mrs. Devonshire. We need to take him now.”

“I’m not ready. Just a few more minutes,” I pleaded, holding him closer.

"Our hospital policy states that he needs to leave now." I felt a surge of frustration and wanted to shout in her face about the policy. I didn’t care about the hospital rules; I just wanted more time with my son—more time to memorize everything about him, more time to hold him close, more time before it would be goodbye.

"No, please," I begged. "Just a few more minutes."

"I thought we had 48 hours? That's what it says online," Brooks interrupted.

"Not in your situation. With a full-term stillborn, yes. In this case, your son is not developed enough to keep him here. His skin can't handle this. Please, Mr. and Mrs. Devonshire, we need to take him." I could feel him slipping from my hands. I knew I wasn't going to win this.

"Emily, honey, I know. It's time though." She sat at my feet, reaching for him.

I looked up at Brooks, who appeared as helpless as I felt. He nodded in agreement. I turned back to Kenna and slowly and reluctantly passed Liam to her. She gently placed him in the cot, and the nursing team wheeled him out of the room. A wave of anger and sorrow washed over me, followed by fear. He would be cold. He would be alone. I should be with him.

↟ ↟ ↟

The next day, I was released from the hospital. Brooks and I began making arrangements to fly him to Seattle to be buried alongside our parents. As we entered our home, my legs gave out beneath me, and I collapsed onto the floor in a puddle of tears and sorrow.

The weight of everything felt overwhelming. I despised being away from him; I needed Liam and would never hold him again. Brooks lifted me off the floor and carried me to bed, where he crawled in beside me. I slept for hours at a time, alternating between sleeping and staring blankly at the ceiling. Time held no meaning. Life had no meaning.

The following days were a blur as we chose Liam's white coffin, which was barely larger than a shoebox. We managed to convince the cemetery to let us bury Liam between our parents, especially since he was so small. Brooks and I spent hours looking at different headstones, finally settling on one that would fit perfectly between our parents'.

Natalie and Monica brought over a stack of black dresses from various shops for me to try on, while Michaelson and Connor brought several black dress shirts for Brooks. The house was filled with people, low whispers, and the heavy weight of grief. We were never truly alone, yet in every other way, we felt isolated.

On the morning of the funeral, I wasn't sure if I could even muster the strength to get dressed. I was grateful that Natalie and Brooks were there to help me. Natalie pulled my hair back into a low chignon and draped my mom's pearl necklace around my neck. It eerily reminded me of my wedding day, being dressed and doted on. How could the worst day of my life remind me of one of the happiest days of my life? I felt the darkness pulling at me as if the wind had been knocked out of me permanently. I was numb and struggled to see any meaning in it all. Everything felt so confusing.

When we boarded the jet, Connor and Sarah were already there, their eyes swollen and voices hushed. I moved to the back of the plane, taking a single seat behind the sofa. Everyone watched me, but no one dared to speak. Brooks followed me silently, sitting on the sofa nearby and reaching for my hand. Shortly after, the pilots boarded the plane.

Liam's tiny casket was unloaded into a car after we arrived in Seattle. We navigated the long, winding roads through Lake View Cemetery to our parents' plots. I hadn't been here in almost two years, and now I was here to bury another family member—this time, my baby.

Like the unexpected breaking of a dam, emotions flooded through me, sending panic and fear coursing through my body. My breathing became erratic, and my heart pounded in my chest. I felt like I was being suffocated by my own pain.

"I can't. Please stop the car. I need to breathe. Stop the car!" I shouted, leaping from the door before the driver had come to a complete stop. Strong arms caught me from behind before I stumbled to the ground.

"Hey, Em, shh. It's okay, it's okay," Brooks murmured, rocking me gently.

"Emily, look at me. You are okay. It's just a panic attack. Just breathe. Remember—in and out," Natalie said from her crouched position beside us.

Rationally, I knew I would survive this, but deep down, I realized I didn't want to. I also knew I didn't want to leave Brooks, even though that feeling was buried far beneath the surface, under layers and layers of dark, tormenting anguish. At that moment, all I could think about was wanting to be with my baby.

I sobbed through my panic attack, desperately begging for relief—relief from all the pain, not just the attack.

"I want my baby. I don't want to be here. Please," I cried, draping my body over Brooks. I felt ashamed to admit my vulnerability in front of him and the others. Brooks cried with me, cradling me in his arms.

"Emily, it's okay to be sad. This isn't fair. I know. You and Brooks have so much life to live together. Just hold onto that, okay?" Natalie whispered.

"I don't want to. Please. I can't breathe. I don't want to be here."

Our friends hovered nearby, silently watching me fall apart.

"Emily, I need you to be honest with me. Are you having suicidal thoughts? Do you want to hurt yourself?" Natalie asked in a hushed voice so that no one besides the three of us could hear.

"No," I sobbed. It was true. I wasn't having those thoughts, but I couldn't find the words to explain that I just didn't want to be here. "I don't want to kill myself. I just need the pain to stop. I need everyone to stop dying on me." There. That was the truth. Everyone just died on me.

"Em, please don't leave me. We will get through this together," Brooks said, his voice breaking.

I reached up, wrapping my arms around his neck and pulling our bodies together while I sat in his lap. "I just want our baby. Our family."

"I know." He hugged me as if I were slipping away. Was I? I had never felt this before. I had never experienced the nothingness that consumed me.

"I won't leave you. I promise," I whispered, hot tears soaking the collar of his shirt. I wasn't sure if I was saying it just for him or myself. I finally had him. He was still here. That had to count for something.

He nodded and turned his face into mine as he cried softly. "I can't live without you. Please, baby. Just live, stay. I promise to be here for you."

"I know." My tears slowed along with my breathing. "I won't leave you." I meant it. He needed me as much as I needed him. I knew it was irrational, the thoughts I was having. I knew I would never actually wish for death, but death had never seemed so peaceful, had never called to me as it did now.

Eternal bliss with my son and our parents didn't seem so bad, but it wasn't my time to join them. I had a husband whom I loved more than anyone else. I would fight for him, even if I wouldn't fight for myself. Somehow, I would find the strength to ensure that this feeling never surfaced again. My breathing evened out as I shifted off his lap, allowing Natalie to help me to my feet while Connor reached for Brooks.

"I'm sorry. I'm sorry to all of you." I glanced back at Connor and Sara, both with tears streaming down their faces, before I buried myself into Brooks' side and whispered to him, "I love you so much. I am so, so sorry for scaring you. I promise."

"I love you, Em. So much." He kissed my head, lingering as if he were fighting against the thought that I might just disappear.

"Let's go bury our son."

We were joined by Diane and Mr. Gordon. Mr. Michaels had been invited, but he was away for work. The service was short, but the amount of love that surrounded us by our family and friends was endless. As the small white casket was lowered into the ground and covered, I felt an odd sense of relief.

Although everything else felt confusing, at least he wouldn't be alone in the graveyard; he was positioned between my mom and Carrie.

That afternoon, we flew back to Pacific Coves, and I returned to my place in bed. *It's over. He's gone.* I was no longer a mom.

↟ ↟ ↟

In the weeks that followed, I felt lost and buried under the rubble of my own grief. The only times I got out of bed were to use the bathroom or when Brooks forced me into the shower. Each day felt the same: the weight, the darkness, the overwhelming pull that kept me buried, and the silent scream for help.

I knew I wasn't keeping my promise to him, my promise to live, but I just couldn't find the will to return back to the simple, mundane life that I had before becoming a mother-to-be. Not yet. Maybe never. Maybe I was a liar. Maybe I was broken beyond repair. But that was a problem to solve another day.

I watched the clouds drift across the sky while hugging the blankets, holding on to them for dear life. Brooks was in the doorway of our room with Natalie, whispering about something. Probably me. They were probably discussing sending me to the psych ward, and who could blame them?

I should have cared, but I didn't. Doing so would have required an effort I simply didn't have. It would have meant feeling something other than the dread and emptiness that crowded my chest and abdomen.

"She hasn't been out of bed in several days," Brooks whispered softly as if I couldn't hear him.

"Okay, I will talk to her," Natalie replied. "She may need some help. Postpartum depression is a tough battle to fight, especially on top of grieving a child." She then quietly made her way over to me.

"Emily, we need to get you out of bed, okay? Brooks is going to take you to see Dr. Williams. We need to get you some help."

Deep down, I felt another crack in my heart, a silent aftershock following a devastating earthquake. Still, it wasn't enough to shake the darkness loose that crowded every corner of my soul. A slow, quiet tear leaked from my eye, pooling on the bridge of my nose.

"It hurts," I muttered, feeling the strong pull of sleep.

Brooks' arm wrapped over me and pulled me into him. He was warm, *always so warm.*

"We are going to help, baby. I won't let you go," he whispered.

Natalie's slender hand squeezed mine.

"Time to get up, Emily. I will get you clothes and go make you lunch."

She stood, leaving me. Brooks followed, turning on the shower. Once she was out of the room, per our new normal, Brooks helped me undress, but this time, he did too and followed me into the shower. I leaned against his hard, toned body, using him as my crutch, my lifeline.

"I've got you," he whispered. I believed him. He was like a lighthouse in this dark storm. I could see the light, and I wanted to reach out for him, but the waves were too big and too dark. A tsunami of pain kept threatening to finish me off. My body ached for him, for the lifesaving connection between us. But would a life preserver be enough for a storm this big? *You have to fight. Remember - for him.*

↟ ↟ ↟

A soft, sad melody drifted upstairs from the study. I hadn't heard him play since our wedding night, and back then, it had been full of hope and love; now, it felt a lot like heartbreak. I followed the music and quietly slipped onto the chaise, hugging the pillow as I watched, listened.

He played a few chords and then stopped, the pattern repeated several times. The longer I watched him, really looked at him, I noticed his pale skin, the dark circles under his eyes, and the bright blue of his irises, now dulled to a dim, grayish hue. There was a heavy, invisible weight to the way he held himself. His own storm had been weathering him down, stealing the light from his eyes.

Another crack formed in my heart. *How does it still beat?* Seeing him like this, not knowing how long he had looked like this, and alone while I let myself drown in my own agony made it clear to me that I had to do better. I didn't know how, but I knew I needed to. He was carrying it all: work, me, Liam.

With wobbly steps, I finally reached him and threw my arms around his shoulders from behind, holding my husband close. The music stopped, and his hands grasped me as he broke down. Tears he had been holding onto so tightly that it was strangling the life out of him, racked his body as he finally unraveled his grief. *God, help him.*

"I'm sorry. I didn't mean to leave you alone in this," I whispered, my tears spilling down my dry cheeks. I didn't understand how I still had enough tears to cry.

His sobs gradually slowed to heavy breathing before he looked up and wiped his eyes. His palm ran along my thigh before gliding back to my hip, pulling me to straddle him on the bench.

"I miss you, Em. I need you. I can't do this without you."

"I know." I felt ashamed. He was right; I had promised. "It's just been so dark." More tears streamed down my face silently. "I couldn't find my way to you. I couldn't get out. I never meant to hurt you or scare you. I just hurt so much inside, and I didn't know how to stop breaking. How to hold the pieces together, even though I wanted to, for you."

"This is the most we've talked about it, you know?" His voice was soft, not judgmental or angry, just gentle. *It* referring to my postpartum depression and my grief.

"I'm sorry. I keep breaking. Everything hurts, and I'm just so tired. Can you help me find the number for that grief counselor?"

He nodded, and I felt some tension release from his chest. "We will get through this."

We sat on the piano bench until it became uncomfortable, and we were forced to move. We opted for our usual spot on the sofa on the deck. It was cold, but the rain had stopped for now.

Brooks and I wrapped ourselves in a blanket with a roaring fire beside us as we talked for the first time in weeks. We discussed Liam, our grief, our hopes, everything and nothing. The more we talked, the more we healed.

I missed Liam and my old self, but it was time to embrace this new chapter in my life. Just like before, when our parents' happy chapter ended and a new one was born out of pain, this situation was no different. It marked another painful ending and beginning. However, if the last chapter was any indication, Brooks and I would be okay. We would find each other again, and the pain would eventually subside.

Chapter Fifty-Nine

Another week passed while Brooks and I found a new, healthier routine that helped. It started with something simple and obtainable - me getting out of bed every day and getting dressed. It was something small and manageable, but I started to feel alive again just by checking off a task at the beginning of each day.

There was still so much work that I knew I still needed to do with a therapist, but wearing clothes, showering, and taking walks… made me feel just a little more myself.

Brooks had been there every day, ready for whatever I needed, whether that was someone to walk quietly with on the beach or there when the pain felt unbearable and my knees gave out.

During my first appointment with my grief therapist, Dr. Shavani, Brooks attended the session, per her recommendation, so she could get a feel of where I was at and what kind of support I had. She thought it would be best to start on medication temporarily, she reminded me, just so I could help calm my nervous system down and level out.

And for the first time since losing Liam, I felt like there was a future I could live for, hope for.

I finished toweling off my hair and headed downstairs, only to find Brooks hunched over on the couch with his face buried in his palms.

"Hey, B. Are you okay?" I asked.

"I will be. How are you today?" He looked up and offered a small smile, his eyes trailing my body, clearly satisfied that I had already showered and dressed for the day all on my own. Baby steps.

"Okay." He sighed, his shoulders drooping as he met my gaze.

"Em, baby, I'm so sorry, but I have to go to Seattle. I have put it off for as long as possible, but I have to go." My stomach flipped and the rest of his explanation was barely audible through the ringing in my ears. "Just a few days. You can come with me. We can stay at Vincent again or wherever you want. Or we can stay with Michaelson if you don't want to be around anyone."

A bus must have hit me and backed up to run me over because all the wind was knocked out of me with a traumatic force. *I can't get on a plane. I can't.*

"I have to stay." My voice cracked as I fought through the wave of fear that had me chilled to the bone.

Brooks stood to face me. "Sorry, sweetie," he sighed.

My eyes closed, fighting off tears. *Be strong.* "I'll be okay. Maybe Natalie can come over."

"I will be gone three days. Four max."

"When do you need to leave?" I gulped down the words. *Strong. Brave.*

"I need to leave this afternoon, or in the morning at the latest. Do you want me to stay here tonight?"

I shook my head sliding onto the couch and pulling a pillow into my lap.

"I will text Natalie for you. Let me grab you breakfast." He gripped my shoulders again, plastering on a smile that didn't touch his eyes, likely mirroring my own tight smile. He hurried past me to the kitchen and I deflated as my armor adjusted to the brief solitude.

When I purchased this house, I never considered the need to live in Seattle. I never planned on being with Brooks or returning to Caston. I never anticipated dealing with a long commute.

But this home was a world away from everything I had left behind. Now, more than anything, I wished it were in Seattle so my husband wouldn't have to say goodbye for days at a time, especially when I needed him the most.

I knew I should go with him, but I couldn't bring myself to board a plane right now. I lost Liam on a flight, and I buried him while flying with his remains. It felt too soon, and it was too much to bear. So, no, Seattle wasn't in the cards for me - not now or anytime soon.

Brooks had been my rock, especially over the past few weeks, but now I needed to hold myself together. I had to fight to stay strong and avoid spiraling again. I couldn't go back to that emptiness—back to feeling completely numb.

It would only be three days, but three days felt like an eternity right now. My husband needed to be in Seattle, and I knew he wouldn't go unless it was absolutely necessary.

I closed my eyes and fell into a suspended state of healing and protection. I could feel waves of panic washing over me, but as Dr. Shavani had taught me, I breathed through it, reminding myself that I wasn't dying.

Brooks' hand wrapped around my arm, jolting me back to reality in my living room. "Em?"

Great. Now, my body was trembling. Panic attacks had become more frequent these days, and I hadn't yet learned how to return to reality effectively.

I found Brooks looking at me, struggling with an internal battle. I knew how I looked, but he needed me to be okay, and as much as I wanted to be, I was far from it.

He handed me a tray, carrying an omelet with toast, tea, and medication and then sat down next to me as I stared at the white pill, adjusting the wooden tray over my lap.

"It's okay to need it right now," he said in a hushed voice. "It doesn't make you weak, Em."

But I didn't want to need it. Still, if I was going to survive his departure, I needed to accept taking the medication. I exhaled and popped one into my mouth, sipping it down with my tea.

Dr. Williams had prescribed me Ativan for moments like this. With that, I closed my eyes momentarily, allowing my body to relax.

Leaning forward, I lifted the tray, setting it on the coffee table in front of me, and laid down. I would eat later. I settled into the cushions, my eyes still tightly closed and felt the warmth of a blanket being pulled over me.

I had lost track of time during my nap when I heard the front door open and Natalie's voice as she talked to Brooks somewhere in the house.

A twinge of guilt washed over me, knowing that my husband was about to leave while I had spent the entire morning asleep. At least I was feeling something now, right?

"Emily! How are you?" Natalie sat on the back of the couch, bending over to rub my shoulder.

I briefly smiled and reached up for her hand, taking it in mine. I watched her glance back to Brooks across the room.

"I'm doing okay," I mumbled. I wasn't sure who I was trying to convince, them or myself. Brooks came and sat beside me, pulling me into his chest.

"I gotta go, Em," he sighed. His lips were pressed into my hair before I could respond. Silent tears splashed down on my cheeks.

"I will be okay. Hurry home. I miss you already." I offered him a pathetic smile.

"I love you," he whispered, looking deeply into my eyes. His thumb brushed a tear away.

After he left, I curled back into the pillow. I just needed to hold on for three days.

"Okay, no, you don't," Natalie said, pulling my arms back up.

↟ ↟ ↟

A storm had blown in overnight, and the wind and rain were angrily slapping against the windows, waking me earlier than I would have preferred. I reached for the remote to open the blinds in my room, allowing the dim light to filter through.

The ominous dark blue and gray clouds left me feeling unsettled. Maybe I just needed more sleep.

Fear crept in, reminding me that the impending doom and darkness would return. Somehow, the laughter and joy of the past few days kept me from the edge, but I was terrified of falling deeper, especially with him out of town. Today, I had an appointment with Dr. Shavani, which reminded me to use my "tools."

I focused on grounding myself. Three things I hear: the waves crashing angrily against the rocks, the wind producing a soft howl, and the rain hitting the windows like small pellets.

Three things I feel: the pillowcase soft against my cheek, the warm and heavy blankets, and my hair tickling my face.

Three things I smell: Brooks' cologne lingering in the air, the dried sweat on my skin, and the stale air in the room.

Three things I see: dark shadows dancing across the wall, dust collecting on the vent, and the framed light on the bathroom floor from the shower wall. *In and out.*

Chapter Sixty

With each ring on the other line, I could feel the fear dissipating. I wanted, no needed, to talk to Brooks, to hear his voice.

"Hey, Em," he answered in a groggy voice.

"Sorry for waking you. I just wanted to hear your voice."

"No, it's okay. I'm glad you called."

"I'm scared." Saying it out loud made it feel more real, but I needed him, and I didn't want to disappear inside myself again.

"Scared of what?"

So I told him. I voiced all my fears. I told him how I felt trapped beneath a blanket of darkness, except now, I wanted out. I didn't want to stay there.

"Baby, I wish I was there to hug you and tell you it will all be okay."

"I know. Me too. I miss you. I love you."

"I love you. It's all going to be okay. We will make it through this."

I was silent as the tears fell heavily on the sheets. "Can you," my voice broke. "Can you go lay some flowers down?"

"I can, yeah. Are you sure you don't want to go with me? We can drive if flying is too much." My heart ached to be near him. It was like a clawing in my chest, the need to be wherever he was.

"Yeah, okay."

"Okay, what?"

"I want to visit my baby. I want to go to Seattle when you get home."

"We can come up when I get back."

I squeezed the pillow tighter. "You get home tomorrow?"

"Yes. I'm sorry it took longer."

"You need to work. I'm doing okay. I promise. I just really want to hug you right now."

The sound that came from Brooks was a mixture of a cry and a hopeful chuckle. "I really want to hug you too. Tomorrow."

We fell silent, content with just having the knowledge that we had some type of connection, even if it was through the phone. Listening to the sound of his breathing through the phone was comforting. I closed my eyes and tried to envision him lying in bed beside me. It made me feel stronger and braver. I knew he wouldn't let me fail. It wasn't until Brooks' voice broke the silence that I realized I had started to drift back to sleep.

"Em, sweetie, I'm going to let you go. Get some sleep. I'll call you later."

"Okay," I yawned. "Love you, B."

"Love you, Em." The phone clicked, and the screen brightened. I flipped it over, closed my eyes once again, and drifted into a state of safety.

↟ ↟ ↟

"Emily, you are doing great," Dr Shavani encouraged.

"I don't feel great," I muttered.

"Healing is a journey. There are a lot of moving parts and lots of emotions. I want you to work on journaling this week as much or as little as you want, but at least once daily. I want you to name your emotions, then identify where they are coming from. For example, I am angry because..."

"It's hard to feel anything, though."

"It might be the medication, but Emily, I believe you also need to recognize the emotions you are suppressing. This is a defense mechanism. You've created a shield to protect yourself, but by doing so, you've also excluded the good things, like love, hope, and happiness. To heal, you must also allow those difficult emotions in, step by step. They just need to be processed—likely multiple times—before you begin to feel better."

"I'm so scared," I whispered, tears falling silently on my cheeks.

"Sweet girl, you are strong. You just told me that you want to find your way out of this situation. You want to walk toward the light." Her hands reached up toward this imaginary light, a metaphor for a place of hope and joy. "You have a fight in you, and you need to believe in yourself. Look around you—Brooks would never let anything happen to you. Natalie is taking care of your every need. You have friends and a wonderful staff who are all cheering for you and praying for you. You have a big, strong safety net, okay?"

I nodded.

"Okay, so remember to journal. Even if you only allow yourself to feel one emotion this week. I want you to tell me all about it next week."

"Okay."

Dr. Shavani got up from the couch and grabbed her purse from the coffee table.

"You can do this, Emily."

I looked up at her and smiled unconvincingly.

"Okay, see you next week."

The storm raged loudly outside as I watched in awe at the white-capped waves. The water was a dark blue, almost black today, with white froth stretching as far as I could see, propelled by the wind. It mirrored my mind—unstable, dark, and scary.

I took a deep breath, letting my thoughts drift to Liam, wrapped in the blue crocheted blanket in the hospital. *This isn't fair. I want my baby.*

Unknowingly, I gripped my stomach where Liam should still be. A long, painful groan escaped my lips before the sobbing took over. How was I supposed to handle this? He was so perfect and so small.

I wished I had known what he would look like. Would he have my blonde hair or Brooks' dark locks? Would he have Brooks' smile, or my nose? The vice around my chest tightened even more and a sob lodged in my throat.

"Hey, hey, it's okay. I've got you," Natalie said, wrapping her arms around me.

I could feel myself shaking against her.

"Shhh. Shhhh. It's okay, Em. It's okay."

After a few minutes of uncontrolled sobbing, I allowed myself to name it, but it didn't soften the sharp ache in my chest. This was just another wave of grief. God, I missed him so much.

When I calmed down, I told Natalie about my appointment and the journaling assignment. She thought it was an excellent idea.

"It hurts too much. I don't know how I should journal. I don't want to."

"That emotion right there. Start there." Natalie smiled softly, lifting my chin. I offered her a watery smile back.

"Oh, it's okay, Em. I promise this will get easier."

My phone buzzed around on the coffee table. Natalie grabbed it with her free hand, the other still wrapped around me. One day, she would be a great mom.

"It's Brooks," she said, handing me the phone.

I took a deep breath, trying to hold back more tears. Natalie answered the phone before it went to voicemail and hit the speaker button. I was doing so well this morning, and I didn't want to scare him.

"Hey, Brooks, it's Natalie."

"Hey, Natalie. Is Emily okay?"

"Yeah, she's sitting right here. We're having a moment. Dr. Shavani left about twenty minutes ago."

I took a deep breath before briefing Brooks with my appointment details, my journaling assignment, and my thoughts about Liam. Brooks and Natalie just sat listening as I cried. I wasn't even sure if I was making any sense, but I must have.

"It will hurt, Emily, but do you remember how much it hurt after we left the hospital after the accident? That hurt, too. You survived that. Alone. You can survive this, too. You are strong, sweetie."

"It's not fair, everyone dies." I was a blubbering mess. Natalie squeezed me tighter, fighting back her own tears.

"Baby, that's not true. I'm here. Natalie is here. You aren't alone. You are right, though. It isn't fair." The room was silent until my crying slowed.

"I'll be home tomorrow. I'm sorry I'm not there." I nodded like he could see me.

"She's okay," Natalie responded. "I'm going to make some tea, and we are going to go downstairs and watch Pride and Prejudice, maybe some Bridgerton," she laughed to herself.

So we did. Crawling into the warm blankets, we watched Pride & Prejudice - the Keira Knightley one because it was my favorite, before starting Bridgerton over at season one.

↟ ↟ ↟

It was almost dinner time when Natalie's phone buzzed in her lap. We had been binging Bridgerton all day. She mumbled something into the phone before jumping off the couch and leaving the room. She motioned back to me to keep watching. It wasn't like me to watch this much TV, but these past few days, it had been the only thing keeping my thoughts away. After a few minutes, she returned, curling up beside me.

"Who was that?" I asked curious as to why she suddenly disappeared.

"Just work." She slid in beside me, resting her head on my shoulder.

As the credits rolled for the episode, I sat up, feeling a turn in my stomach.

"You okay?" Natalie asked in an oddly nervous voice.

"Yeah, fine. Just hungry. I think I am going to go upstairs."

"I'll come with you. I'm starving. What do you want?" She was acting weird, like she was flustered about something.

"Okay." I stood, letting the blankets fall back onto the couch. I reached the stairs before her and headed for the kitchen.

"This storm is crazy," Natalie said, following behind me.

"Yeah. Are you sure you're okay?"

"Fine. Sorry. Just thinking about a patient at work." *That must have been the phone call.* Guilt hit me like a sucker-punch. Natalie had taken the week off to be with me. A week of hard-earned vacation and a week away from a job she loved.

"What do you want?" Natalie smiled, brushing past me into the kitchen.

Chapter Sixty-One

The mattress shifted as I felt an added warmth in my bed and the scent of Brooks' cologne.

"Brooks?" I groaned quietly, trying to get my eyes to adjust. *Why is he home?* The last thing I remembered was watching Bridgerton with Natalie. How did I miss a whole day?

"Shh, go back to sleep, it's okay." His voice was soft and tender as he pulled the blankets around me.

"What day is it? When did you get home?"

"It's still Wednesday. I came home tonight. It's late, baby, go to sleep."

"Are you okay?" I asked, adjusting to the light. Brooks looked over at Natalie, who closed the door and left us. I sat up, leaning into him, breathing all of him in, and feeling the warmth and strength of his chest and arms wrap around me.

"Em," he whispered into my hair. That's when I noticed the trembling, the tension in his body, and the shaking in his voice. I pulled away to look at him and saw something—was it remorse?

"Honey, I had to come home because something happened at

work." My eyebrows knitted together, worried about what he would say next. What could have happened that would have sent my husband home this late at night?

"First, I want to promise you that nothing happened between us. I need you to listen to everything before you say anything, okay?"My stomach plummeted. Nothing good ever came after those words.

"B, you're scaring me. What happened?"

"She's gone. From Caston, everything. Cailey," he paused, squeezing his eyes shut. Cailey what? Anger pulsed in my veins in an instant, consuming me completely.

"Cailey, what, Brooks?" I asked, my tone low and growling. He ran a hand through his hair before meeting my gaze again.

"I was working alone in the office tonight after everyone had left for the day. She came in with some papers - I don't even know what they were. She..." He paused as if the next words were too painful to say aloud.

"She put her hands on my chest and said she wanted to take away the pain I was feeling. I was facing my computer with my back to her when she slid her hands down my chest. I stood up immediately, trying to get away from her, but she stepped closer and tried to kiss me. She had undone the buttons of her dress, so she was standing in her underwear. I pushed her back, but she threw her arms around me, crying and wrapping herself around me. She begged me to let her take away my pain."

Tears and anger streamed down both our faces. It felt like a dam that had been holding back for years had finally broken free. I was overwhelmed by anger, regret, and every other emotion flooding my soul faster than I could process.

"I pushed her away, grabbed my stuff, and left. I jumped on the jet and got here as fast as I could. Baby, I'm so sorry," he said.

Anger clouded my vision, not towards him, but at Cailey. I knew she would be trouble; I was aware of her feelings for him, even if she had denied it. But to try to kiss my husband at work? I clenched my fists, feeling the sting of my nails digging into my palms. I knew him well enough to sense that he was consumed with guilt, even when he had done nothing wrong. Taking a few deep breaths and giving myself time to choose my words, I set aside my anger because, right now, he needed me.

"Are you okay?" I asked, looking up at him through my tears. My fingers interlaced with his, and I felt clarity for the first time in weeks.

"I'm so sorry," he muttered, still fully dressed, sliding under the sheets beside me. I curled against his chest, feeling the warmth of his skin under my palm as I rested it above his heart.

"Where is she?" I asked, my anger teetering on the edge. I had to tread carefully; I didn't want it to come out on Brooks.

"I don't know. Michaelson called security. They had her escorted out the last time I heard. Nayla helped her get into my office. She'll be fired in the morning. I don't want this drama at work."

I nodded slightly, clinging to Brooks' shirt. Cailey had been working as an administrative assistant at Caston, and I assumed that's how she met Nayla. Brooks checked in on Cailey a few times to ensure she and Brooklyn were doing okay. I hadn't heard anything about Cailey since she tried getting Brooks to come to her house. He had denied her request and told her she needed to find friends. My rage simmered just below the surface, and if I didn't do something soon, I would explode.

Using my weight, I pressed his shoulder down and rolled over on top of him, burying my lips into his. My fingers wrapped into his hair, and I allowed myself to drop my guard. I wanted to feel all of him. I wanted to want all of him. His grip tightened around my waist, pulling me close. His need for me to be closer was obvious.

I tugged at his shirt, and he let it slide free. His hands slid up my shirt, or rather *his* shirt that I was wearing, and pulled it over my head, exposing my sports bra.

My breasts grazed his chest, and I relaxed against him, so exhausted from this hurricane of emotions, especially after having them muted for so long. As badly as I wanted him, my body seemed to fight against me. I was so damned tired, and as my fury and jealousy had dissipated, it left me drained, which wasn't hard these days but had become an even bigger task now that I was trying to work through my emotions one at a time. Our kiss slowed, and Brooks slid out from under me.

"I'm so sorry," I sighed, fighting back tears. I felt exhausted, and my mind was clouded. I wanted to reassure him, not just with my words, but with my body. I just couldn't muster up the energy that was required to do so.

"It's okay. I love you. Just go back to sleep," he reassured me. He kissed me again, gently pulling my neck down for a deeper kiss before tucking the blankets around me.

↟ ↟ ↟

Beautiful sunlight filled our bedroom—the kind of light that only appears after a terrible storm. My eyes were heavy, my head rested on Brooks' chest, and his arm was wrapped around me. For the first time in a while, I felt safe and whole.

But just as quickly as the calmness settled over me, memories of everything that had happened the night before flooded back, bringing with them the gripping pain and anger. Cailey. I needed to steady myself before Brooks woke up. After a few minutes of trying to sit still, I realized I needed to use the restroom and possibly go for a run to exert some of the negative energy surrounding our little safe haven. I hadn't been on a run in weeks, and now that the thought crossed my mind, my muscles practically buzzed with the need to flee from reality. As I attempted to carefully roll over, he pulled me back.

"No," he whispered. "Stay." His sleepy voice did something sweet to my insides, stealing all of my motivation to get out of the house and replacing it with the desire to pick up where we left off last night.

I couldn't help but smile. It beamed out of me as if the clouds had parted. It felt wonderful. I nestled closer, bringing my face inches away from his. He always looked so peaceful when he slept.

His dark, long lashes rested against his flushed cheeks. I caressed his jawline with my thumb, my fingers brushing over his short, trimmed beard. He looked so tired, not just from coming to bed early this morning but from something deeper. Grief. Worry. Anxiety. He was like me in that way - unable to be okay unless we were okay and unable to focus on his own healing until he was confident that I was moving in a positive direction as well.

Without thought, my mouth moved to his face, and I kissed away the streaks of purple beneath his eyes and moved down his jaw until my lips found the soft pillows of his lips. He sighed, pressing his lips against mine while keeping his eyes closed.

"Brooks Caston Devonshire, I love you more than anything. I'm sorry," I whispered against his lips.

His eyes slowly squinted open as he tried to focus on me.

"I love you." His gaze searched my face like he was trying to read my soul.

Heat rushed through me, and my need to touch and feel him consumed me. One minute, the kiss was soft, meant to be an antidote to his pain. The next, it was frantic, like my racing heart, as my hands moved, discovering and rediscovering the hard lines of his body. My hips rocked forward with a moan, causing him to pull away.

He laid back down, brushing my hair from my face while he looked at me. Really looked at me. It was like he was looking at my soul, unpacking everything beneath the surface. He tugged me back to his chest, brushing a hand down my spine while he yawned.

"Maybe later, okay?" I sat up as his eyes fluttered closed, and I knew he was headed back to sleep. I rolled off of him, feeling the crash of surging hormones on top of being denied. I couldn't deny that it hurt. I shut the door and left him to sleep longer.

Natalie was sitting on the couch downstairs with her bags packed next to the door.

"Good morning, sleepyhead," she whispered from across the room.

"Did you..." I hesitated. "Did you hear about Cailey?" Saying her name felt like another punch to the gut, and I could feel an infuriating heat rising in my limbs.

Natalie's big brown eyes looked back at me with sympathy. Of course, she knew. Brooks would have had to tell her why he arrived home late the night before.

"He called last night," she replied reluctantly.

"What?"

"Brooks called while we were watching Bridgerton. It wasn't work. Please don't hate me. He asked me not to tell you because he wanted to tell you himself, and I hated every second of keeping it from you."

I knew that she would never agree to lie, and Brooks would never have asked her to if it weren't as important as this.

"Don't worry, I won't hold it against you," I said softly with a small grimace. I sat down beside her, pulling my knees to my chest. Everything felt so different. The dark shadows of my grief were replaced by the surreal reality that a friend of his had tried to kiss him after she had told me she wasn't interested. It was as if the whole scenario had popped my grief bubble, reminding me that there was still life beyond it.

"I am really mad at her." I tugged at a strand of loose hair, twirling the ends in the sunlight. "Like really mad. In what universe did she think Brooks would kiss her back? Also, why now? As if life wasn't hard enough, she thought she'd just slip in. And Nayla. She was my friend. Kind of."

Natalie's hand moved to my hand, which was still resting on my shin.

"I don't know, Emily, but you have every right to be mad. Are you," she paused. "Mad at Brooks?"

"No, not really." I grabbed the remote for the fireplace, turning it on before resting back against the pillows of the couch.

"Not really?" she asked.

"Not about Cailey." All I wanted to do was run back upstairs and snuggle up with Brooks and start the morning over.

"Then about what?"

I sighed. It was stupid and probably all in my head. Plus, even if it wasn't, who could blame him? I wasn't exactly doing anything to deserve that level of attraction.

"He wouldn't have sex with me."

"What?" she shrieked before covering her mouth with her hand and glancing upstairs. Okay, maybe having jealous sex wasn't a good idea.

"I don't know. Last night, I was overwhelmed and tired," I shrugged. "And I started taking my clothes off, but then I was just exhausted, and he seemed to agree." Natalie nodded, still perplexed but urging me on. "Then this morning...I tried again, and he just went back to sleep."

Natalie pursed her lips before speaking.

"Brooks is tired. He isn't shutting you down. I'm sure it hurts to put yourself out there, but I will play devil's advocate for a second." She gave me a tight smile that looked more like a grimace. "Emily, he's been in a dark place too. He's grieving Liam, and you, and the life you had and the future you were supposed to have had. He has had to be strong for you, not that I think he regrets it. But now all this stuff with Cailey." She waved a hand in the air, sweeping the notion away. "I'm sure you guys will work it out, but it's probably a good thing nothing happened. You don't want your sex life to be medication."

Ouch. She was right, though. I didn't want our reconnection to be born out of jealousy, and certainly not obligation.

"You have a point." I picked at a loose thread on the sofa.

"Keep trying. You guys will work through it, and I am sure, soon enough, you guys will be back to being all over each other." She blushed before downing the rest of her coffee. "I'm going to go. It sounds like you have a lot of people who need to talk to him. And you two should probably talk some more. Also, don't forget to journal." She stood, taking the mug with her to the kitchen. "At least you have something to journal about now." Her disbelief came out in a laugh. I rolled my eyes. *How perfect.* Fury, jealousy, and violation were my first emotions that I would be journaling about.

I walked her to the door, and as she gave me one last squeeze. It was the kind of hug that lingered long after she had left, a hug that felt similar to a warm blanket. I nodded and my lips curved up into a half smile as she pulled away and stepped out the front door.

I filled up a cup of coffee for Brooks before gathering what was left of my dignity and heading upstairs. We needed to talk about last night and get ahead of this with our legal team and HR. I hated waking him up, but we didn't have the time to put this off, especially if we wanted to avoid a lawsuit. He may have not been at fault in the matter, but unfortunately, working late hours and being the head of our company may not work in our favor. I slid into the sheets next to him and laid my head on his chest. His cologne still lingered in the air, tethering me back to him.

"B, we need to talk." He exhaled, pulling himself out of sleep. His hand ran down my hair, tracing a tickling line down my back.

"Yeah," he replied.

Once he was more awake, I slid off his chest, allowing him to sit up. He grabbed the cup of hot coffee and began sipping it while I turned to face him. I had so much to say, but I had no idea how to start.

"I'm sorry," he said, dropping his free hand into my lap, squeezing my thigh gently.

"You stole my line," I chuckled. "It wasn't your fault."

"I just keep thinking about all our interactions, and if somewhere along the way I—"

"No," I interrupted. "We all could see it. She's hurting, and you're taking care of her. She was just waiting for an opportunity to push the boundaries. That's not on you, even if I mentally predicted it weeks ago." I looked down at our interlaced fingers. "I'm sorry, B.

I'm sorry for my depression, sorry that you've been left to sort your own stuff out, sorry for so many things. I could keep listing them out, but most of all, I'm sorry if it seemed like I believed my grief was bigger than yours."

There it was, an ugly truth that I hadn't even realized was there until now. I looked up, my eyes meeting his bloodshot blue ones.

"I forgive you," he whispered, kissing the back of my hand. "We will get through this."

Chapter Sixty-Two

"B, we need to go! We're going to be late!" As I looped my earring, I glanced at the clock and saw that the time was quickly approaching six o'clock. Brooks emerged from the closet, rolling up the cuff of his shirt. Damn. Every time I saw him dressed like this, it still took my breath away. I inhaled dramatically, trying to focus as I let my gaze finish raking over him. "Wow," I said breathlessly. I cleared my throat, searching for my voice. "You look handsome."

Brooks grinned at me before moving to his other cuff as he pressed his shoulder into the door frame. His teeth bit into his bottom lip while his eyes slowly devoured me. I wasn't prepared for the rush of heat between my legs. He hadn't looked at me like this since our wedding. I stepped forward from the sink, and like gravity, my body moved to his warm embrace.

"You sure you are up for tonight?" He buried his face in my neck, kissing the skin just below my ear causing me to arch against him.

"Brooks, I'm good. Promise. Now, please, kiss me." He paused, reading the honesty in my eyes before he slanted his lips over mine with hunger and gentleness all in one. How was it possible to feel both at the same time?

Brooks still hadn't touched me since he returned from Seattle two weeks ago. It wasn't for lack of trying, either. Maybe tonight would be the night. His hand wrapped in my hair, pulling my hair back to expose my neck while his lips moved to the now-exposed stretch of skin.

"I want you," I moaned. His lips pressed firmly once more into the spot below my ear before lifting away.

"Time to go." He smirked, brushing past me.

My hormones growled within me, sexual frustration building in my core, but he was right. We were going to be late. I turned and followed him out the door and into the car.

The rain poured steadily tonight, and the sound of drops hitting the pavement created a rhythmic melody that filled the air. A storm system had lingered for days, casting a gloomy atmosphere over the city. Thankfully, my drive to the restaurant was short. A certain dread came with navigating slick, reflective roads during such weather.

As I pulled into a parking spot at the back of the lot, I took a moment to appreciate the dim glow of the restaurant's neon sign through the sheets of rain. I locked the doors of my car and, without a second thought, quickly climbed onto his lap, a sense of warmth breaking through the chill of the storm outside.

"Whoa, Em, what are you doing?"

My need for him was like a live wire inside me - and it was officially at its bursting point. I was so overwhelmed with desire and uncertainty that I didn't know how to describe what I needed or wanted.

"Please," I whimpered, unbuttoning his pants.

"We are in a parking lot, and they are waiting on us."

"Please, B. I need this more than I need to breathe. I need you deep inside of me. Please," I begged.

He cursed my name before shoving my panties aside and feeling my soaked core. He groaned, moving his hands to grip the globes of my ass, rocking me forward. My lips met his with a small moan, and I let our mouths do the talking. All the pain of the past few months and my love for my husband poured into that kiss.

He fumbled with his zipper as I continued my gentle assault with my tongue, but as he lifted his hips, releasing his erection, I pulled away, delighted to see him bounce free, his erection standing tall. All prior worries of him not wanting me, or not finding me attractive anymore, withered away as he used his fingers to pull my panties to the side once again and thrust into me in one motion.

My reaction was more of a cry than a moan. I pulled away from the kiss to hold his head to my chest while my fingers wrapped into his hair. I took the opportunity to soak in every glorious inch of him inside of me, clenching his length as my muscles contracted around him as a loud groan fell from his lips. My hips rocked forward, grinding my clit against him.

"Don't," he hissed. "I'm going to come so fast, baby. Just give me a second." I was already there, though, racing toward my edge and ready to jump. I covered his lips with mine once again and rocked forward as he lifted my hips, only to slam into me, and I tumbled over the cliff head first after a few short breaths. The freefall was spectacular and mind-blowing as I came around him. Brooks groaned loudly as he guided me up and down his length, slamming into me over and over until he met me on the downfall before lifting me off of him, and pouring into his hand.

It was both shocking and devastating. Not once had he denied me the feeling of him emptying his release inside of me - until now. Hopefully, it was just because we were moments away from walking into dinner. After grabbing a few tissues to clean up, he pulled me back against his chest, and we both sat in silence, trying to ground ourselves. My heart was still pounding, heavy with the overload of the heady orgasm I'd just experienced for the first time in weeks, and the whiplash that I felt watching Brooks nudge me to the side to fill his empty hand. Hot tears brimmed, blurring my vision before cascading down my cheeks as I sobbed into his shoulder.

His free arm wrapped around me, alternately playing with my hair and drawing random patterns on my dress.

"Shh... baby. What's wrong?" His voice was calm and soothing.

"I... I just love you so much. I've missed you. I need you more than air. I want to crawl into you and stay there. I... I don't know. I just love you, Brooks. So much that it's scary."

He chuckled softly and placed a small, chaste kiss on my shoulder.

"I know, baby. I know what you mean. I love you too." He paused and inhaled deeply. "We need to get inside, and I need to get cleaned up."

I nodded and pried myself away, shifting back to my own seat to fix my makeup. I stepped out into the cold and sprayed some body spray to hopefully mask the smell of sex that lingered on us. His arm wrapped around me, pulling me close as we crossed the parking lot into Providence, an upscale seafood restaurant that had just opened in town.

When we stepped into the cozy atmosphere, I spotted Lily and Henry waiting for us. Brooks excused himself to head to the bathroom while the server seated us in a booth in the corner where we could have a private conversation.

Lily was stunning. Her long dark hair fell in loose curls down to her mid-back framing her face beautifully. Her hazel, almond-shaped eyes were soft and welcoming, and her smile radiated pure joy. There was an undeniable aura of kindness surrounding her, and I instantly felt a desire to connect with her. She seemed like someone you could easily be friends with.

When Brooks returned from freshening up, he and Henry quickly dove into conversation, sharing stories and laughs. They had met at the boat show, and Brooks had been eager to learn more about new neighbors, though i'm not sure the term applies given that their home was still half a mile down the road. Their newly acquired home was nestled amid the towering trees of the forest and opposite side of the road, complete with a creek that meandered through their backyard.

Lily, thought initially somewhat reserved and shy, began to open open up when prompted. She shared her vision for the updates she dreamed of making to their home, describing her ideas for landscaping and how she wanted to transform the backyard into a more welcoming space for guest. I could see her passion shining through as she spoke, especially when she mentioned her part-tie job as a preschool teacher.

My arm linked through Brooks while his sturdy hand rested on my thigh. It was almost high enough to be a tease and sat just at the hem of my dress. It was distracting, even if he had my toes curling only an hour ago. My heart raced when he brushed back my skirt to draw shapes on my inner thigh.

"Emily?"

"Huh? What?" I looked up to find Henry staring at me, seeming concerned. I shifted in my chair uncomfortably, silently hoping I hadn't zoned out long enough to embarrass myself.

"How are you feeling?" Henry asked, looking at me with curiosity. Brooks clenched the fabric of my dress, clearly nervous about the topic. My stomach sank and a pang of guilt hit my chest like a lighting bolt. I glanced at Brooks who appeared nonchalant if you didn't know him, but the tiny wrinkle between his brows, the firm set of his jaw, and the way his fingers fisted the hem of my skirt told me he was worried. Did my husband really think I couldn't keep it together at a nice dinner with new friends?

Of course he isn't sure how I'll respond, I scolded myself internally. I'm the one who put that doubt in his brain after days on end that I wasn't even able to pull myself out of bed.

I needed to show him that I was getting better, that I am better. I'm grieving in the right way now and healing.

"Eh, okay. Thanks," I replied, feeling a tightness in my chest.

Slowly, I exhaled, aware that Brooks was watching me from the corner of my eye. "Better every day." I managed a reassuring smile.

"How did the closing go?" Brooks asked, taking a sip of his beer, changing the subject.

I squeezed his hand under the table and met Lily's gaze. She looked confused, her brows pulled together. Maybe Henry forgot to tell her. Brooks had told me that he let it slip one day while they were chatting outside. It wasn't a huge secret, but something like that can scare people away. Grief does funny things to people, especially when it isn't theirs.

Thankfully, dinner ended early, and I was spared from any other awkward questions about my miscarriage and recovery. While standing outside the restaurant, saying our goodbyes, Brooks and Henry continued to chat, but Lily grasped my hands, surprising me, and turning me away from their animated conversation.

"I'm so sorry," Lily began. "I didn't know. I thought you were sick."

"I know, it's okay," I replied, giving her a small smile. She gave my hands a slight squeeze, before dropping them to dab at the tears welling in her eyes.

"Henry and I have been trying to have a baby for over a year, but we've been unsuccessful," she admitted.

"Oh, Lily, I'm so sorry to hear that."

"We just started seeing another specialist. We haven't told anyone. It's not really dinner conversation." She chuckled nervously, but I could see the pain in her eyes. She was being vulnerable with me, probably to make up for bringing up Liam. "So far, they haven't found anything. I'm not sure if that's comforting or not. I'm grateful for our health, but it would be nice to have an answer or a solution."

"I can only imagine how difficult that must be for you."

I stood next to my new friend as she explained the various tests and options they had been given. It came pouring out of her as if she was relieved to finally share her story. She had carried that pain mostly alone, aside from Henry. She briefly mentioned a strained relationship with both of their families, and I was grateful to be here with her to share this burden.

↟ ↟ ↟

The trees in Pacific Coves had finally shed all their leaves, and each day was cooler than the last. Working from home provided the structure and routine that I desperately needed. During my extended absence, my team compiled a list of various charities and organizations they believed would be a good fit for Caston and the direction that I was aiming for taking us to the next level of helping our community.

They also collaborated with Paul, our CFO, to determine a suitable percentage of profits to be donated to those charities. On my first day back, the team took a moment to celebrate virtually before we got straight to work. I didn't expect to feel so alive and relieved about coming back to work, but with them welcoming me back with open arms, I felt right back at home. We set a goal to finalize our final charity selections before the new year arrived.

After reviewing the extensive list, we settled on five: Alex's Lemonade Stand, which funds research for childhood cancer treatments; Peer Seattle, which offers support and community for those dealing with addiction, mental health issues, and/or HIV/AIDS; Buddy Baer in Berlin, our new location for the next chain, which works locally and internationally to promote peace and tolerance while giving back to support children; The Fisher House Foundation, which assists our troops and veterans; and finally, I couldn't pass up the opportunity to partner with an organization called Operation Underground Railroad, a nonprofit dedicated to rescuing children from human trafficking.

The strategy for the next year was to closely monitor these charities and assess whether Caston's donations were having a genuine impact. If necessary, we would adjust our approach. We had turned down many other worthy charities, such as those supporting individuals with life-limiting diagnoses and assisting underprivileged children in Seattle. With my grief still fresh, I felt the need to give and channel my emotions into something meaningful.

I was intensely focused on work when Brooks' voice interrupted my concentration.

"Hey, Em?" he said, standing against the wall near the door. I had been answering emails while relaxing on the chaise lounge in the glass room, lost in thought and unaware that he had slipped in. I looked up to see his eyebrows furrowed in concern.

"Yeah? Are you okay?" Brooks knelt beside me, pulling me into his arms. I snuggled into his warmth and felt my whole body relax.

"Sorry, love, but I need to fly to Vancouver next week, and I'll probably stop in Seattle for a day before coming home."

"Why?" I groaned. The constant back-and-forth travel was becoming exhausting.

"They found a new location in Scotland, and I have to meet with everyone face-to-face to get the ball rolling."

"Can't they come to Seattle instead?"

"We've been trying to get them to come, but they have a big meeting the next day." I tightened my grip around his neck, taking another deep breath of his heady scent. His arms tightened around me too. I wished I could just pause time and keep him right here with me, wrapped in each other's embrace.

"What if you moved your meeting up by a day?" I asked with my face still buried into the crook of his neck.

"That would mean I would need to leave here in two days."

I could feel his tension radiating through me. I was still struggling the last time he left, and then Caylie happened. I knew he wouldn't be leaving me if he didn't have too. Plus, this was the sacrifice for moving away from Seattle. I shifted back, letting my hands fall to his shoulders while I looked into the depths of his cobalt eyes.

"Brooks, I will be okay. Move the meeting, fly to Seattle, and then hurry home to me."

He ducked his head, pressing his forehead to mine. "Emily

Devonshire, I love you and miss you already. Are you sure you will be okay?"

Nibbling on my lip, I fought back the urge to joke that I didn't want anyone else kissing him, but I held it back, knowing we weren't in joke territory yet. Maybe we never would be.

"I will absolutely be okay." I kissed him before dropping my arms and returning to my laptop. However, Brooks quickly wrapped his hands around my waist before I could take more than three steps away. He pulled me back to his chest, his breaths coming in short, shallow pants.

"I wasn't finished." He smiled into my cheek while his hand slid down into my jeans, cupping me and awakening me in one move.

"Mr. Devonshire," I gasped. "How inappropriate of you." I arched my back, bringing my hips up higher before dropping my hips back to him and grinding into his erection.

"I want to do more inappropriate things than this, Mrs. Devonshire." He plunged his fingers into me. My legs almost gave out with the shock. I was still recovering when he pulled me back into the study and bent me over his leather couch, showing me how much I would miss him while he was away.

Chapter Sixty-Three

It was freezing when I stepped out onto the deck, confused about why Brooks was leaning over the railing with his coffee. It was barely six-thirty in the morning, and the sun was still low, just beginning its ascent over the trees. The shaded gray skies and the roaring, angry ocean ahead reminded me of the winter storm warning. The wind tossed strands of my hair across my face, the sharp chill of the wind biting my skin and sending a shiver of chills down my spine. I pulled my arms further into my sweater and wrapped them around my chest, trying to hold on to as much heat as possible.

"Why are you out here?" I practically yelled above the sound of the incoming storm.

Brooks, dressed in joggers and a silver windbreaker, seemed unmoved and frozen in place until he finally exhaled and glanced down at me, pulling me into him. His lips pressed against the top of my head.

"Couldn't sleep," he sighed.

"So, you're standing out in the storm?"

"No," he chuckled. "I went for a run earlier and then did some calisthenics. I just finished my workout and stepped out to cool off." My mind momentarily flashed to an image of him downstairs in the gym, doing a pull-up with his bare torso exposed and muscles flexing, stretching his tattoos. Mmm, that would have been a sight.

"Why couldn't you sleep?"

"I just can't help but think I missed the signs." He ran a hand through his hair and sighed, leaning over the rail again. Of course, he would think my miscarriage was his fault. It tore a fresh wound into my healing heart. "I messed up bringing you home. I don't know, I'm just trying to process it all." He gripped the railing tightly with one hand. "Selfishly, I want everything to go back to how it was. I want my son. I want a happy, healthy wife. I want to erase the trauma and sadness and return to our happy place."

"B," I fought back tears. I felt the same way, but there was no use dwelling on the past. I had to keep moving forward. "Dr. Williams said it wasn't our fault. We couldn't have known." I reached up, cupping his cheek in my palm and bringing our bodies flush. He relaxed under my touch. "I'm sorry if I made you think things aren't getting better with me internally. I'm really trying. I'm doing the work and even though I'm not doing backflips every time something goes my way, I'm on the right track to being happy again. I am happy most days."

I gave him a tight smile, swallowing hard. "But then there are things that remind me of Liam, or of my pregnancy, and I want to collapse under the pain of it." Gripping his hands tightly and interlacing our fingers, I blinked up at him through my tears. "Do you know how I'm able to keep it together?" I paused and he shook his head, his messy hair falling over his forehead.

"Because I have you. You're my anchor, Brooks. You keep me grounded and safe. You give me everything." His jaw twitched and turned his gaze back to the sea. My words seemed to fall flat at his feet and I tried not to take it personally. Dropping his hands, I wrapped my arms around his waist, holding him tightly like he had done so many times for me.

After a few beats, he squeezed me back and pressed a kiss to my forehead. "I love you," he murmured. "C'mon, let's get you inside." His tone changed, and we turned for the door, still wrapped in each other.

The fireplace roared to life, and I slipped under a blanket while Brooks refilled his coffee and poured me a cup of tea, returning with both. He lifted the blanket and slipped in, pulling me onto his lap. My body relaxed as it warmed against his familiar embrace. Sometimes, touch was better at communication than our words.

↟ ↟ ↟

When I rolled over and felt the cold spot in the bed, I knew he was already gone. A twinge of guilt and sadness passed through me. I wanted to say goodbye, but he was gone again before I was awake.

I pulled my phone from the nightstand. He would be landing in Seattle any minute if he didn't already, and that means I should be getting a text or call.

I couldn't wait around, though. I could feel the draw to stay in bed and pout, especially with the nasty storm outside that had arrived midday, which meant I had to get moving before I caved in. I changed into some workout clothes and headed down to the gym. A morning spin session would be the right thing to pull me from this funk.

As I settled into a nice, even pace, Brooks called. *Of Course.* I paused the music blaring in the background and answered the call.

"Hey, babe. Did you land safely?"

"Yep. Rough ride, though. You sound winded."

"On the bike."

"Ah, good. Well, I will let you go."

"Wait, you didn't say goodbye. Brooks, you know I hate that." Annoyance prickled at the back of my neck, and I pedaled harder.

"I know I couldn't wake you, but I did kiss you goodbye. You moaned in your sleep, too, when I did." I softened under his playful tone.

"I am sure I did. Those warm lips are my favorite."

Brooks chuckled. "Okay, and on that note, I need to go before I regret not waking you up to give you a proper goodbye."

"I will play nice just this once, but you owe me."

"Love you, baby," he chuckled again, and I could all but see the smile plastered across his face.

"I love you. Be safe. Call me tonight."

The phone clicked, and the music returned, blaring through the speakers.

↟ ↟ ↟

Mrs. Hall passed me on the stairs as I was coming down from the shower, and I was glad to see her smiling face. She had taken a few weeks off to be with family after hearing that her dad had passed away.

When I reached the door, ready to head out for a nice cup of tea, the doorbell rang. I quickly opened it, wondering who could be here this early in the morning and brave enough to venture out in the storm. I hadn't ordered anything new, and Brooks hadn't mentioned whether he had.

"Surprise!" they yelled. My heart jumped, and I stepped back, shocked to see my friends standing there - Natalie, Sara, Monica, and Leah.

"What are you guys doing here?" I asked.

"Brooks." Natalie rolled her eyes before pulling me in for a quick hug.

"Wait, what?" I replied, still processing the surprise.

"Ugh, your perfect husband called us to see if we wanted to keep you company while he was out of town," Sara said, exaggerating her eye roll. "You know he is making every other guy look worthless, right? He should stop this!"

We all laughed. He had done it again—somehow surprised me and arranged everything in his absence. I was okay with him being gone, but I think he was still holding on to the idea that I would somehow slip back into the depression that consumed me weeks ago.

I propped the door open with a permanent smile as they filled the entryway with their beautiful presence and bags.

"Where do you want us?" Natalie asked, glancing up the stairs before looking back at me. "We're staying until Saturday morning."

"Don't you all have work?" I asked, still in shock. How were they here, and how did they all manage to have time off?

"Divine intervention or something because we all had these two days off." Monica shrugged before leaning in for a quick hug.

"Well, I'll be checking my email, but otherwise, yes, I'm off," Leah chimed in.

"Alright. Natalie and Sara, you can take your usual rooms, and Monica and Leah can choose any of the rooms downstairs."

After they settled in, we gathered back in the living room.

"So, we have a packed schedule for the next two days. We have hair appointments in forty minutes," Natalie announced, dropping onto the couch and pulling a pillow into her lap.

"What?" I couldn't help but smile, feeling the ache in my cheeks. It had been a long time since I had smiled this much for this long.

"We can grab breakfast on the way," Sara chimed in. "I'm starving."

"How did you guys pull this off? Brooks told me on Monday that he needed to head out of town."

"Yeah, well, he texted me that afternoon, and I let everyone know. We all wanted to spend some time with you." Natalie shrugged as if adjusting their schedules was no big deal. But it was—a huge deal. I didn't deserve them, my husband included.

"Brooks," I sighed, focusing my gaze on my left hand. The oval diamond on a dainty gold band served as my engagement ring, reminding me of the day Brooks proposed paired with the diamond encrusted band that he gave me on our wedding day, when he officially became mine, made me feel warm and fuzzy. I thought after knowing each other for so long that he'd eventually stop surprising me, but I was so wrong.

"That boy would give you the entire universe if he could," Sara quipped. She wasn't wrong. His love for me, his dedication to us, is what makes me strong. My heart swelled, warming my chest again.

"So what, now you don't hate him?" I teased. Sara had never been a fan of Brooks, however she didn't officially hate him, but she certainly didn't trust him. I hoped that after everything he and I had been through would eventually bring her into rooting for us instead of waiting for the other shoe to drop.

"What? Hate? Nah, that's not in my vocabulary. Actually, maybe it is." She shivered. "I hate Connor. Ugh." I laughed and rolled my eyes. I could never understand how two bubbly people could dislike each other so much.

"Alright, time to go." Monica was eager to get moving.

When we reached the front door and bundled ourselves into our coats, I opened the door to see a black SUV with Ryan inside.

"Oh, yeah." Leah leaned over my shoulder. "He thought it would be safer if Ryan drove us around in the rain."

As I made my way to the SUV, another disbelieving chuckle escaped my lips. Brooks was definitely a little over the top but absolutely perfect.

"Hi, Ryan!" I smiled, leaning in for a hug. I had missed his cheerful face.

↟ ↟ ↟

After a long day filled with hair appointments, board games, and a round of Never Have I Ever, we sat on the sofa to watch movies. I was bundled up under a blanket with Sara when my phone rang.

All four of them glanced at me, and I didn't need to check the screen to see who it was. I jumped over the back of the couch, signaling for them to keep watching and not to pause the movie.

"Hey, honey," I said into the phone.

"There's my girl. How was your day?" His voice wrapped around me like a comforting blanket, and I longed to bury myself in him. It was too bad he was several hours away.

"You know, I got a lecture from Sara about how you're making the dating scene pretty terrible."

He chuckled. "You deserve the best."

"I don't think that's true. I don't deserve anything, but thank you nonetheless. It was a great surprise, and we had a really fun day."

"Good."

"How was your meeting?"

"Same old, same old. Just business. The new location looks like it will be better than the original."

"That's great to hear."

"Yeah. If you're up for it, we can fly out to check it out in January or February for the groundbreaking once we get the permits."

"I guess we'll see." I settled into the leather sofa in the study, and the memory of being bent over the edge earlier in the week flashed through my mind. "I miss you."

"I miss you too. Anyway, I'm going to let you get back to your friends. I need to shower and head out to grab dinner with Michaelson. I'll call you tomorrow."

"Okay. Love you. Sleep well."

"Love you."

I held the phone against my chest as I returned to the girls.

"Do you ever fight?" Monica asked, sounding almost offended by my happiness.

"Yes," I told her simply, deliberately not going into further details. She rolled her eyes and I ignored the skeptical brow she shot my way before starting the movie. What did it matter anyway? We had enough stuff going on in our life. I brushed off the annoyance and felt the tension leave my body when she wrapped an arm around me apologetically.

Chapter Sixty-Four

The next day, there was a significant break in the rain, and we seized the opportunity to go hiking. Before we left, Mrs. Hall prepared our lunches to go. Since the trailhead was close to Lily's new house, I invited her to join us. I really liked her so I was glad that she was able to join us on such short notice.

Dressed in leggings, windbreakers, beanies, and hiking boots, we hit the trail just before nine. Ryan was hesitant, knowing we would be out of cell service, but I convinced him we would be okay with such a large group. Natalie was also a nurse, so I assured him we would be okay if anything went wrong. He let out a long sigh, realizing he had lost the argument.

As we ventured deeper into the forest, the damp earth filled my senses. The loud crashing of the waves faded until it was no longer a sound but a salty, briny scent that permeated the air. The forest floor was tranquil, occasionally interrupted by large drops of rain that had pooled on the canopy above, dripping onto the wet soil with a loud plop. It had been months since I last went hiking, and being out here with the girls felt healing.

We walked in comfortable silence, enjoying each other's

company without the need for conversation. Occasionally, Sara or Monica would crack a joke, or someone would hum a tune, and soon, they would sing the lyrics at the top of their lungs. They were wild and fun, making the experience even better.

Leah and Lily lingered behind, occasionally exchanging small talk about Pacific Coves and their jobs. Natalie stayed close to me, as always. I reached for her hand, and we walked together, holding hands for a while until we faced a section of the trail that required us to climb over a large boulder.

In the stillness of the early afternoon and the quiet of the forest, I felt a sense of clarity and recognized the strides I had made in my own healing. I wasn't whole yet, but I was on the right track and I could appreciate where I was. Outside the confines of my home, which had become both a sanctuary and a prison, I found myself able to breathe deeply, process my grief, and allow myself to mourn for my old self. Dr. Shavani had been impressed with my breakthrough after the Caylie incident. Now, it was time to begin tackling individual issues.

This week, I was supposed to work on forgiving myself and Brooks. Although I didn't blame him, it was essential to sift through all my emotions and ensure that I held no grudges or anger toward his response, or even the sex we had leading up to the miscarriage, which I questioned for its role in the situation.

I gripped the straps of my backpack and whispered to myself that I was forgiven. It felt ridiculous to say that, even though I had been told countless times that it wasn't my fault. Deep down, I knew I was still blaming myself.

"Oh, wow!" Sara exclaimed as she took off. For the first time in twenty minutes, I realized that I had muted my senses while lost in thought. The sound of the ocean roared ahead, and as the canopy cleared, a lighter gray sky emerged.

"Wow," Lily gasped. I looked up and jumped onto the boulder to join them. We had reached the peak, which overlooked the town of Pacific Coves and the ocean beyond.

A small sigh escaped my lips as my body released some of its grief and heaviness. Natalie wrapped her arms around mine, resting her chin on my shoulder. Her brown hair lightly tickled my cheek in the wind.

After admiring the view for much longer than we had expected, we settled into a circle on the surrounding boulders and fallen logs.

"We're all falling, and we need a place to hide. A safe place somewhere in the woods we can start a fire. All we know is what will be our home.

We will stay 'til the break of dawn," Sara smiled, singing out, knocking her shoulder into me, knowing full well I knew the rest of the song.

Together, we sang, "The cold night takes us to a place to escape the chill. Tucked up somewhere in the woods on a hill. Wake up feeling the cold in between our toes. Is there a way back? Nobody knows. And we leave it all behind. Can't you see we need some time? And we all sit around the fire, we feel a little warmer now."

We both laughed, hitting the pitch completely wrong.

"What song is that?" Lily asked.

"The Woods by Hollow Coves." Sara grinned, twisting a branch in her hand.

"I wish we had a bonfire right now," Leah sighed, tugging her windbreaker sleeves over her hands and curling in on herself.

"Time to go?" I asked, looking at Leah. She was almost to the point of shivering.

"Definitely," she grumbled between her chattering teeth.

The hike down was much louder as we took turns picking songs and seeing how many of us knew the lyrics. We sang everything from Lewis Capaldi to The Eagles and Ben Folds, transforming our group into a walking ensemble.

Thankfully, the rain had stayed away for the rest of the day, allowing us to enjoy a chilly fall evening on the deck. Both fireplaces were roaring, and we wrapped ourselves in too many blankets while sipping wine and hot drinks.

We laughed and playfully bumped into each other as Monica animatedly recounted the story of her high school crush asking her to the spring fling and how epically it had failed, starting with her getting her period.

Our laughter filled the air when the glass door suddenly slid open. We all gasped and shrieked in unison before realizing it was Brooks.

Without thinking, I leaped from the back of the couch and landed in his arms. He handed the large bouquet he held to Michaelson, who chuckled at my reaction. I pressed my lips into Brooks' neck and took a deep breath, inhaling his scent as I tried to steady my racing heartbeat with his. Too soon, he released me, and I slid back to the ground.

"How are you home?" I asked, my heart quickening again.

"Meetings ended early, so I thought I would come home and surprise you," he replied, dropping his hands to my waist and pulling me in for a welcome-home kiss. I felt everyone's eyes on my back, causing a rush of heat to rise up my spine to my cheeks.

"What are you guys doing out here?" he asked, stepping back from me. "It's freezing."

"Just talking about our high school crushes." Monica smiled. "Of course, nothing has changed for Emily," she teased.

Brooks' eyes danced back to me. "Forever, my girl." The girls all awed in unison. "Oh, ladies, this is Michaelson. He's a co-worker and a friend. Michaelson, the girls. Their husbands graciously let us borrow them."

Michaelson nodded, blushing as he noticed the girls all eyeing him like a piece of candy. "Eh, I am going to head down and shower. See you tomorrow," he said, turning to Brooks. He paused, twisting in Natalie's direction. "Tallie, will I see you later?"

"Sure, I will be down in a bit." She blushed and quickly looked away. My eyes bounced between her and Michaelson and then back to her again. Oh my God, no way! *They are actually a thing and he has a freaking nickname for her!* I felt like dancing and singing—I was bursting with joy—but I didn't want to make a scene and embarrass them both. The deck fell quiet as everyone else began to take notice.

"Nice to meet you all." He waved before disappearing back inside. Brooks' hands were still on my waist, cradling me.

"Oooh, that boy's accent is cute," Monica teased, looking over at Natalie, who was ready to bury her face in the pillow.

"I'm going to steal Emily for a few minutes if that's okay with you?" Brooks asked the girls.

"Of course!" Leah responded. All the girls were beaming, trying to hide their giggles. I couldn't help but chuckle to myself. We were all acting like a bunch of schoolgirls.

As we passed the kitchen, I noticed the flowers that Brooks had brought lying on the counter, they were beautiful.

Upstairs, Brooks softly closed the door before pressing his whole body into me and wrapping his hands around my thighs as he lifted me off the ground and onto our bed.

"Well, hello," I purred. Brooks' lips trailed down my jaw and onto my neck, softly and slowly working their way down to the collar of my shirt. My heart galloped, and heat warmed my inner thighs.

I pulled his chin back to my mouth, and we got lost in a tangle of tongues, worshiping lips, and a few drawn-out moans. He bit down on my bottom lip, dragging his teeth across it and igniting my soul. My fingers wrapped into his shirt, pulling him closer.

He tasted so good, and the mint from his gum lingered in his mouth, cooling mine. His cologne blanketed my senses, turning everything into one big craving to be connected deeply with my husband. I would never have enough of him.

Brooks pulled away and stood hovering above me, my back still pressed into the bed while my chest rose and fell as I gasped for air.

"Where are you going?" I tried to gulp down the fiery desire. His fingers wrapped in mine as he gently lifted me to a sitting position and placed his lips on my forehead.

"Your friends are downstairs waiting for you."

"I don't think I can return to them like this," I admitted.

"Well then, make the night end soon and come and find me. I can take care of that."

"How will you take care of it?"

He chuckled, moving his mouth to my ear while his hand slipped into the waistband of my leggings. His fingers played with the top of my panties while he whispered, "By making you come over and over again until your whole body goes limp."

The sound that escaped my lips was something between a moan and a giggle. "So not fair." I shook my head.

He freed his hand and stepped back so I could slide off the bed.

"I'll see you soon, Mrs. Devonshire." His gaze heated as his eyes devoured me. I smirked before leaving the room, all hot and restless. *Time for bed, everyone.*

Chapter Sixty-Five

Another hour had passed before we finally found a spot to break up all the giggles and head to bed. I let out a sigh as I shut our bedroom door and I dropped back against it, trying to release all the burning desire I had repressed the past hour. Brooks was sitting in bed reading. His black boxer briefs and a pair of blue-light glasses were the only clothing he donned and any willpower I had scrounged up went right out the window..

He glanced up from his phone, smirking at me, and then returned to reading. My heart fluttered again as my eyes trailed down from his shoulders, across the mountain range of his stomach, and down to those briefs that fit like a glove.

I slipped into the closet and found his favorite black lace panties of mine and a white belly shirt that fit tight, exposing the peaks of my nipples through the material. As I walked back through the bathroom, I stopped to brush my teeth and fix my chaotic hair.

He still hadn't looked up by the time I crawled in next to him. I slapped the phone out of his hand playfully, only half pretending to be jealous of his attention. Impatient, I rolled over, straddling him, making sure my breasts were front and center of his gaze.

"Pay attention to me," I pouted.

"Whoa, yes, Mrs. Devonshire." His response was said and felt as his bulge grew under me. His thumbs grazed the skin between my shirt and panties, leaving a trail of fire in their wake. Brooks brought our mouths together in a mind-numbing kiss. Nothing outside of the kiss mattered aside from the desperation to get closer.

"How much did you miss me?" I panted into his lips. Brooks' mouth met the sensitive skin on my neck, working his way to my collarbone then to my breast. He sucked one hard pebble into his mouth through my top, flicking his tongue against my nipple before sucking on it long and hard, all while groping my other breast, careful not to leave it left out of the fun. *Oh god.* My head dropped back, allowing for more access to this ecstasy. By the time he paid the same attention to my other nipple, I was head over heels in a Brooks driven frenzy.

"Brooks," I begged, tugging at his waistband. In one swift move, I was beside him while we both tore at our remaining articles of clothing. Eagerly, I moved to straddle him, ready to calm the aching pulse throbbing in my core. My body sank down his length and I gasped as his shaft stretched me until he was nestled in my warmth and I was fully seated on him.

Feeling the pleasure of him deep inside of me, filling me in so many ways, had me lightheaded. My head dropped back and I moaned loudly as he cursed before he found my nipple again. My arms wrapped around his head, feeding him more of my breast.

"Maybe I should leave more," he teased, using his thumb to find the sensitive bundle of nerves and sending me racing to the edge.

"Brooks," I cried, grinding against him. He cupped his other hand over my mouth while bucking his hips from beneath, driving deeper into me and rubbing me until my muscles spasmed around him as ripple after ripple of bliss rolled over me, leaving me gasping for air. As I fell back to earth, my body still trembling from the after shock, he released my mouth, replacing his hand with his lips.

"My turn," he whispered against my lips. He flipped me over to my hands and knees and took control of my body like it was his job. I fisted my hands into the comforter, my voice muffled in a stack of pillows, I chanted his name over and over, encouraging him to fill me with everything he had. His thrusts became sloppy as he grew inside of me before unleashing his orgasm deep within me. Satisfaction rolled through me and I wiggled my hips, causing him to shudder from sensitivity. His body wrapped around mine limply as he collapsed on his side, pulling me down with him.

"You, my love," He kissed my shoulder. "need to be quiet. Natalie and Sara might hear you."

"Natalie is with Michaelson, and Sara can deal with it," I responded breathlessly, brushing sweaty hair out of my face.

"I miss you," I sighed, feeling more content and hopeful than I had since before the miscarriage. He brushed back my hair, kissing the top of my head as his chest rose and fell. "I've missed you. And I don't mean while you were gone. I miss this. I miss us," I murmured, my lips pressed into his side.

"I've missed this, too. I feel like this fills in the gaps of all the things I want to say but can't find the words for."

"Yeah, I know what you mean," I yawned. Brooks pulled the blankets up higher over me.

"Goodnight, my love."

"Thanks for coming home early," I whispered, closing my eyes.

↟ ↟ ↟

Natalie stayed back after the girls left.

"So," I paused for dramatic effect. "Do spill." I hadn't stopped thinking about the two of them, hoping my suspicions about their relationship was correct.

Natalie blushed, dropping her head back. "He kissed me at your wedding. We've been talking a lot and want to try this long-distance thing."

"Oh, my god! Yay! That's amazing, Natalie."

She was not joining in my dancing. "I don't know," she huffed. "I really like him, but he's so far away, and we both love our jobs. Plus, he told me his parents want him to marry an English snob. Did you know his uncle is an earl or lord of something?" She was now whisper shouting.

"You will figure it out. Look, if he wanted to be in England, he would be. Plus, I don't think titles matter that much now. Just take it slow. See where it goes." I squealed again, pulling her in for a hug. "I am happy for you! Are you happy?"

"I am, yes, but it's so intimidating. *He's* intimidating."

"Why?"

"Because he's so good-looking and confident. He comes from a freaking wealthy British family. Like what? Who am I? A nurse from a small town in Oregon who went to public school, drives a Subaru, and lives in a small townhome. My parents are middle-class Americans, and we have never even been to England. I know nothing about how he was raised, and nothing to understand his culture."

"Is that a problem? So what? Okay, so his family is rich." I shrugged. "You are an amazing human being. You're so kind and fun and have a heart of gold. Anyone would be lucky to marry you." She made a face that relayed a sarcastic "thanks." I laughed it off. "Have you guys...?"

"No, not yet." Pink crept up her neck as she coughed and took another sip.

I nodded and pulled her in for a hug.

"It will all work out," I assured her.

We both laughed, earning curious stares from Brooks and Michaelson as they joined us in the kitchen. Brooks wrapped his arm around me, pulling me in while I watched Natalie and Michaelson exchange a glance that I knew too well. They were falling for each other - *hard.*

Chapter Sixty-Six

Michaelson spent the weekend and the early part of the week in Pacific Coves. Most days were spent working with Brooks, and Natalie would come over after work. We would either all have dinner together, or they would disappear into the studio for the night.

It was enjoyable to watch our best friends become a couple. Natalie and I listened to Michaelson share stories about growing up in a wealthy British family and the very traditional mindset that came with it. To spare Natalie's feelings, he avoided the topic of marriage.

Last week, when the girls were over, we discussed my idea of reviving my parents' tradition of hosting a New Year's party on January 6th or the nearest weekend. Although they had no religious background, January 6th is an important holiday in the Eastern Orthodox Church, known as Theophany or Epiphany. It was initially Carrie's idea, and everyone embraced it.

I remember it being fun to celebrate on a different date, as this usually meant that people weren't too busy. It felt like our own special holiday.

We planned to meet today to finalize some details since the date was quickly approaching. We considered various themes, such as a Roaring Twenties theme, a champagne theme, a glow party, and a masquerade.

After getting input from Michaelson and Brooks, we settled on "A Night Under the Stars." I needed to contact the local planetarium and museum to see if we could hold the event there.

We also agreed to go shopping for dresses together. Once the party planning was complete, we relaxed on the deck with wine while the men—including Leah, Monica, and Lily's husbands—grilled and watched a soccer match.

Dinner was loud and chaotic, yet perfectly perfect. Brooks and I exchanged a knowing smile as everyone spoke over one another while passing dishes around. We had found a family here.

↟ ↟ ↟

Thanksgiving Day arrived, and Brooks and I decided to host a last-minute Friendsgiving. Although most of our friends had left Pacific Coves to return home, we wanted friends like Michaelson, Henry, and Lily to have a place to celebrate, and it kept us from dwelling on the family members that we were missing this time of year.

Unfortunately, Natalie had gone to Bend, Sara was in Vancouver, and Connor was in Seattle. Before Brooks and I got back together, I used to spend the holidays with Sara and her family and once with Parker in Nashville.

"Brooks, what did you do for the holidays last year?" I asked while we set the table.

"I was in Osan. The guys and I just played soccer. Some meals were prepared for us. It was pretty lame. For Christmas, the guys decorated our barracks and we got drunk. Total single guy Christmas."

"I'm sorry," I said as I set out wine glasses. I don't know if I would ever stop feeling guilty about breaking up with him, especially knowing he didn't want to. In one decision, I wrecked both of us. Sure he had decided to enlist, but I dealt us the final blow. If we had stayed together, maybe he would have come home and married me, or we could have figured out the long-distance thing.

"What about you?" he asked, pulling me from my thoughts.

"Last Thanksgiving, I spent the entire day packing up my house in Seattle."

"What about Christmas?" he asked.

"Er, well, last Christmas," I paused. I hated spending the holidays without Brooks but never spent them alone. Last year was the first time I did, but I met Grey. "I spent time with Grey. I met him on Christmas. He didn't fly home for the holidays and didn't want to be in San Francisco, so we both ended up alone at a diner and started talking."

"That's how you met?" he snorted, seeming amused over my admission.

"Yep," I clucked my tongue. "His family kinda sucks," I said, passing by him to pull the chilled wine from the fridge. Brooks wrapped his hands around my waist, settling his chin on my shoulder.

"Should we have invited him tonight?" His breath tickled my ear as I leaned into him.

A smile spread across my face. Brooks never failed to surprise me. This wonderful husband of mine was willing to invite my almost-ex to dinner.

"Um, I don't know. It's fine," I replied.

"Call him, Emily. I can handle sitting across the table from the man who fell in love with my gorgeous wife. He couldn't help it."

I chuckled before reaching for my phone. "Are you sure?"

"Yes. Call him."

After a quick call to Grey, I discovered he was alone at home. He was avoiding his parents until Christmas and planned to head back to San Francisco next week, so he planned to spend the holiday alone on the couch watching football.

"Well, he's coming. He leaves next week."

"Okay then. I'll set the table for one more."

I groaned nervously before turning to the oven to check on the turkey.

↟ ↟ ↟

We were all seated at the table, Brooks' hand wrapped in mine as we shared stories. Each year without our parents was becoming more manageable, but this year was the first time I didn't feel alone. I looked around the table, feeling grateful for the family of friends we were creating, and yes, that even included Grey.

Grey had brought a bottle of scotch for Brooks as a peace offering, although none was needed. Michaelson sat across from me at the table, next to Brooks, and kept making small talk with Grey, who sat beside him. They were getting along well.

Lily sat beside me and shared that they had found a new infertility specialist in Portland. She seemed hopeful. I glanced over at Brooks as he leaned back in his chair. He squeezed my hand softly, and we shared the same feelings of gratitude for this life.

Grey talked more about his parents. They were hosting a New Year's party in Connecticut, complete with a big, expensive ball. The room would be filled with everyone who's anyone on the East Coast, along with those wealthy enough to fund his father's campaign. Grey repeatedly expressed how much he despised politics and how uncomfortable he felt at those events.

We finished the evening with pie and coffee in the living room. Michaelson began to open up more about his "future bride" situation. His sisters were expected to marry into the elite social class in London, and Michaelson was already on thin ice for moving to the States. His parents hadn't stopped calling to ask how long this "charade" of his would last.

They had tried multiple times to persuade him to date some young women from their extensive circle of friends, whom they believed would be suitable matches for him. Thankfully, Michaelson did not agree, especially for Natalie's sake. He was more interested in living a normal life with a girl he loved rather than marrying for money. By the end of the night, I was convinced that he and Natalie would make a perfect couple if only his parents weren't in the way.

↟ ↟ ↟

Another week passed, and it was finally time for our trip to Southport to dress shop. With Christmas just a few weeks away, it was the perfect opportunity. Monica had called ahead to several boutiques to inform them we were coming, as we were a large group. We rented another Sprinter van—Sara's idea—to drive us around for the weekend. It was definitely better than taking two cars.

The drive to Southport only took about thirty minutes. However, Sara and Monica still played DJ for the entire trip, insisting we needed some tunes to set the tone for the weekend. Taylor Swift dominated the playlist, and we all danced and sang along.

After checking into our hotel, we headed straight to our first shop. Our goal was to find dresses for all six of us before returning to Pacific Coves.

Southport had always felt magical, but this time, it was as if we had landed inside a Christmas movie set. The city square, with its old brick buildings and charming shops, was adorned with twinkling lights strung across the streets. Each tree was beautifully lit with delicate lights, and every store displayed varying sizes of evergreens decorated with precision in their window. The pier also had decorations, which created a striking contrast with the ocean backdrop.

We entered Chloe's Formal Wear, and the scent of frosted cookie candles hit me, causing me to scrunch my nose. I disliked the smell of fake, unnatural fragrances. In a sing-song voice, Monica approached the counter and told the lady that we were the group she was expecting. She led us to the dressing rooms, where a whole rack of dresses in various sizes had already been pulled for us.

After briefly browsing through the smalls, I sat on the sofa and waited as most of my friends disappeared into the row of fitting rooms. Sara stayed back with me, equally unimpressed by the selection of dresses.

I was nervously picking at my sweater when she grabbed my hands.

"What's up?" she asked.

"Just having a moment. I don't know why," I sighed, frustrated that grief seemed to show up unannounced and ruin the mood.

"Well," she said, wrapping her arm around me and scooting in closer, "I think that's bound to happen. It's only been a few months, Em." Those few months felt like an eternity without him.

"Yeah, I know. I'm always so shocked when it comes back. Grief just slams into me like a huge wave without any warning."

"What caused this wave?" she asked gently.

"One of the shops on the way over was a baby clothing boutique with cute Christmas outfits in the display window. I don't know; it made me miss Liam."

She didn't say anything in response. Instead, she tugged at my shoulder, so I laid my head on her shoulder. We sat silently until the girls reappeared to show off their dresses and grab more from the rack.

Monica had fallen in love with a navy satin off-shoulder gown that featured a small train and a high slit. Natalie also found a dress — a dark green sequined velvet number with an extremely short hemline and an open back. She looked like a piece of candy, and I knew I'd have to tease her about it later.

They put their gowns on hold while we walked to the next store, Willow + Grace, one of my favorite shops. The owner, Melinda, greeted us at the door, offered us champagne, and escorted us back to the open dressing room area. It had large mirrors, six dressing rooms, and a spacious sofa in the center of the room in front of a platform.

Thankfully, the wave of grief I had been feeling had passed, and I was ready to be present again. Melinda knew my preferred style of gowns and had already lined them up in my dressing room. Everyone else took turns browsing through the two racks of gowns Melinda had pulled, and one by one, we all disappeared into the dressing rooms to try them on.

Sara and I found our gowns right away. Sara fell in love with a eucalyptus-colored gown that had a rose-gold chiffon overlay, a deep V-neck, and a thigh-high slit. She paired it with some white sparkly heels to complete the look. When I stepped out in my chosen gown, their expressions confirmed it was the right choice.

"You have to buy that dress," Leah said.

"Emily, Brooks won't be able to keep his hands off you all night," Natalie teased.

"Actually, on second thought, she's right. Don't get it. You two have enough problems with that," Monica chimed in, and we all laughed.

"You look beautiful, Emily," Lily said, raising her champagne glass to me.

I turned to the mirrors and admired the gown. They were right; this was the one. It wasn't flashy, and it wasn't immodest. My hands ran down the satin fabric, and I smiled. Perfect.

Chapter Sixty-Seven

We entered the loud café and found a large table at the back.

"I'll be right back!" I yelled over my shoulder as I pulled my cell phone from my bag.

"Hey, beautiful," Brooks answered.

"Hey, B." His voice tugged at my heart and reminded me of my sadness about Liam.

"Are you okay, sweetie?"

"Yeah, I'm okay. I just had a moment earlier—Christmas baby clothes," I sighed.

"Ah, I see. Are you sure you're okay? I can come get you if you need to come home."

"I think I'm fine. It was just a moment. We had a lot of fun shopping, actually. We've all found our dresses, well, except for Leah. We have a few more shops to check out."

"I'm glad you're having fun. The guys are all going to be here around five tonight. Michaelson is really excited."

I chuckled at the thought of Michaelson playing poker. "Is he any good?"

"Probably too good. It's almost unfair to the other guys."

"Is Connor able to make it?"

"Yes, actually. He's staying downstairs for the weekend. Hope that's okay."

"Of course! I just wanted to call and say hi. I miss you." I rolled my eyes - it had only been four hours, and here I was, missing my other half.

"I miss you too, Em. I love you. Call me tonight, okay? I promise I will answer."

When I returned, the girls were already placing their drink orders, so I ordered some hot tea. Without Brooks' warm body next to me, I felt like I had a constant chill. I sat down beside Natalie and nudged her, ready to tease her about her very short dress, which I was certain was influenced by Michaelson.

"So, that dress," I said, waggling my eyebrows.

"Too short?" she grimaced, looking away.

"Oh no, he will like it. Just make sure to shave."

She chuckled and pushed against my shoulder. That was the end of that. She knew exactly what I meant.

After lunch, we decided to window shop a bit to work off our meal before heading to the next dress shop. I took them on a guided marina tour, sharing stories about sailing, yachts, and my parents' engagement. When we got back to the town square, we entered Vintage Affairs, and the heat and smell of pine enveloped me, surrounding my senses like a warm blanket.

"Wow," I giggled, glancing over at Sara. Sara had lived with me long enough to know how sensitive I was to scents. Still, I was utterly captivated by earthy, natural aromas. They were my favorite.

"It smells amazing," she laughed.

Leah found her dress almost immediately. A mannequin was dressed in the reddish-copper sequin gown. It had one shoulder and a high slit, a common theme of all of our dresses, it seemed.

↟ ↟ ↟

"I think I'm going to turn in," I yawned.

The girls all booed. "It's not even 9:30," Monica teased.

"I know. I'm sorry. Have fun without me!" I insisted.

Once I closed the bedroom door behind me, I broke down into a puddle of tears. The exhaustion was overwhelming, and a part of me felt guilty for having so much fun, for laughing as if Liam never existed.

Natalie and Sara must have sensed something was wrong because they slipped into the room behind me. They were silent as they helped me off the floor and onto the bed. They curled up on either side of me, rubbing my back and holding my hands.

How did they know? I hadn't even realized it myself—at least not until my knees hit the floor. Just ten minutes earlier, I had been oblivious to the wave of emotion that struck me. As we lay there quietly, Lily slipped into the room.

"I'm sorry. I didn't mean to interrupt. I just wanted to check on Emily," she whispered bashfully.

"She's okay," Natalie replied softly, motioning for Lily to join us on the bed.

I was glad Lily was there. She understood—kind of. I wiped away my tears and reached for Lily's hand.

"I'm sorry, guys. I didn't mean to be a downer."

"No, no, it's okay," Lily responded gently.

"I am terrified that I am forgetting him and moving on," I said, tears streaming down my face. "I feel guilty for smiling and laughing as if I should be thinking about him all the time."

"Hey, Em, that's completely normal, okay? Dr. Shavani would tell you the same thing. Liam wouldn't want you to spend your life feeling sad all the time." Natalie wrapped her arms around me, spooning me, which made me feel so loved.

"I know," I whispered, releasing a deep sigh.

Lily and Sara exchanged glances. They didn't know what to say, but they stayed silent, allowing me to cry. Their presence alone was the support I needed.

"We plan to see him during Christmas week." I shifted until I was partially sitting up and I sniffled, swiping a tear from my cheek. "We're going to bring flowers for our moms and leave Liam a teddy bear."

Sara rested her head on my chest and hugged me tightly.

"It's hard—it's so hard knowing that our parents and our child are gone. Brooks cries in his sleep sometimes, and I don't think he's ever done that before, at least not since the funeral."

"Men just take longer to process things," Lily whispered.

"He feels guilty for taking me to the Maldives," I admitted, chewing on my bottom lip. I still hated that he blamed himself, even if I knew self loathing was something we both silently struggled with.

"He knows it wasn't his fault. It was nobody's fault, right?" Natalie asked.

"Yeah, he knows." I took a deep breath.

We could hear the laughter of Leah and Monica outside the room.

"You guys should go back out there. I'll be okay," I said.

"I don't think so!" Sara replied, her voice sassy as she pulled back the covers and crawled into bed next to me.

Sara patted the bed beside her, inviting Lily to join us under the covers.

"I love you guys." I gave them a watery smile, wiping away more tears.

"I know what you need," Natalie said as she sat up. She jumped to her feet and grabbed my phone, which was ringing as she jumped back into bed. She FaceTimed Brooks.

"Hey, Natalie," Brooks said curiously when he picked up the call.

"Hey, Brooks." She shifted the camera to focus on me. My head rested on her shoulder, and Sara and Lily leaned in behind me.

"Hey, honey, are you okay?"

"I'm good," I whispered. Just seeing him helped soothe the ache.

"We're just having a good cry about Liam," Sara chimed in.

"Ah, I see. I miss him too, Emily. All day, every day. I'm still happy to come and get you." The guys laughed loudly in the background.

"No, I'm okay. I'm going to let you go," I said encouragingly. "Go have fun!"

"Are you sure?" Brooks asked hesitantly.

"Yeah, go. I love you!" I forced a smile and hoped I didn't look like a raccoon.

"I love you. See you tomorrow, okay?"

"Feeling better?" Natalie asked as she set my phone on the nightstand.

"Better," I sighed, scooting back down to the pillow and closing my eyes. The girls all curled in close, and Lily turned off the light.

↟ ↟ ↟

"I'm glad you're home," Brooks whispered, kissing my forehead as I hugged him. He wasn't wearing any cologne yet and was still in his joggers. I inhaled his masculine and intoxicating scent while I nuzzled against his chest.

"Me too," I said, exhaling. Brooks didn't pull away; instead, we stayed in our hug in the entryway as he continued talking.

"Michaelson and Connor bonded over sharing stories about my adolescent rebellion," he chuckled.

"Is Connor still here?" I asked.

"Yeah, he's downstairs."

"Natalie is in the studio with Michaelson," I replied before releasing him to look into his eyes. I reached up and pulled him down for a kiss, savoring the warmth of his lips. After a few breathless moments, Brooks kissed me several times, making me laugh.

"I want to go talk to Connor. Do you want to come down with me?" I asked.

"No, I have a few things I need to finish up. Let him know we can do lunch in town before he leaves."

I nodded and headed downstairs where I found Connor watching a Hawks game.

"Hey, Millie," he said with a boyish grin, patting the couch beside him. I sat and rested my head against his shoulder. He smelled like the ocean. After a few minutes, I decided to confront him about his reaction from months ago. Sure, it didn't matter anymore, but it still gnawed at me. It was so strange, and honestly, the whole interaction still left me confused.

"Connie..." I began. "Can you tell me the full story of what happened between you and Brooks? I'm still so confused. He mentioned something about a party with girls, but that's all I know."

Connor paused the TV and turned to look at me. "That's basically it," he replied, swallowing hard.

"Are you sure?"

"Where is this coming from?" he asked, taking my hand in his.

After Brooks left during high school, Connor and I drifted apart, and I feel like there's a part of my life that I didn't share with him. He was always just as important to me, and I hate that we were torn apart, just like Brooks and I were.

"I just feel like this is the one thing that feels unsettled. It doesn't matter, but I want clarity. I mean, your reactions toward each other were so intense."

He chuckled lightly. "Guys can be like that sometimes. Look, it was nothing major. I was angry at him for hurting you. I was upset that he wasn't coming home and even more pissed that he was acting like a playboy while you were crying in your dorm." He shifted to face me. "Cailey and some other girl, Ashley, were drunk and giving him lap dances. I'm sure he's told you everything you need to know, but I hated seeing you like that so I couldn't just stand by anymore. So when I found out he was back here, yeah, it pissed me the hell off. I didn't expect you both to still love each other. I'm sorry."

The mention of Cailey's name had my blood boiling. I wanted to hunt her down and slap her. "Yeah, he has," I sighed, resigning to let it go "And I forgive you. Thanks for always looking out for me." He ruffled my hair, earning himself a punch to his stomach. He chuckled and pulled me to his chest for a hug.

"Hit play. I'll watch the game with you, and then Brooks wants to go to lunch."

"It's just a rerun from Thursday night."

"I don't care." I smiled and settled in beside him. Connor kissed the top of my head and then hit play. "Oh, and one more thing," I paused. "Why do you hate Sara?"

Connor laughed. "I told you, she is Satan's spawn. That girl wouldn't recognize a compliment even if it hit her in the face."

I swatted his arm and decided to leave it at that. I realized there was no fixing the situation. I would just have to find someone else for my chosen brother.

Chapter Sixty-Eight

I shifted my weight on the blue linen sofa and glanced at the clock. Ten more minutes to wait. The window in front of me revealed sleet pouring down, sending a shiver down my spine.

I looked back down at my nails and rubbed over the soft polish, feeling overwhelmed at the thought of getting onto the airplane.

"Emily, do you remember what we discussed during our last session? You can do this. The fear of it is often bigger than the actual event," Dr. Shavani said as she uncrossed her legs and recrossed them on the opposite side.

"I remember, and I know. I just start to feel like I can't breathe, and my heart starts to race, and I feel my whole body just shut down and this need to run," I replied, rubbing the polish on my nails harder and harder.

"Take baby steps. You can do this. Take your time, but I promise you will be okay once you've done it. You'll feel so much lighter. Stronger."

She was right. It was probably all in my head. Next week, we were flying to visit Liam and our parents, and every time I thought about getting on that plane, I froze. I physically felt as if I couldn't do it. It was irrational on many levels, but even acknowledging that didn't help eliminate any of the worry seeded in my gut. Maybe I wasn't ready. Maybe it was too soon. I wanted to visit my baby, but I just didn't know how to make myself get on the plane.

I joked with Brooks about getting knocked out until we arrived. He didn't appreciate my dark humor. I sighed and glanced over at the elderly woman sitting in her oversized chair in the corner of the room.

Her deep creases and wrinkles were comforting, reminding me of her experience and expertise. I trusted her. Her graying hair was pulled back in a loose chignon at the nape of her neck, and her shawl, in different shades of deep red and dark yellow, draped loosely over her shoulders like a blanket.

"I can do this." I smiled at her. "I can do this, even if I have a panic attack, I will survive." I stood up and grabbed my leather bag from the table next to me.

"Call me if you need anything before then. I'll see you in two weeks," she replied, closing her laptop.

"Thank you, Dr. Shavani. I hope you have a great Christmas."

"You too. Tell Brooks I said Merry Christmas."

As I jogged down the stairs from her office, an invisible weight that had been sitting in my chest lifted. All the courage I had felt in her office moments before seemed to dissipate with every step I took away from her. *I can do this.* It's just a plane.

I pushed the large glass door open and stepped out into the freezing cold. The rush of cold air hit me, clearing away my anxiety, and just like that, I felt ready for the day, feeling ready to tackle whatever the day had for me.

I was meeting Sara in Southport to go Christmas shopping. Brooks had offered to go with me, but I told him to stay home since I needed to get his watch engraved.

It was a forty-minute drive to Southport, and with the weather, people forgot how to drive. The road was slick with water, and the temperature outside was plummeting, leaving a chill in the air. My heater was on full blast as I listened to my latest audio book about fae and dragons. As I drove into Southport, my spirits lifted. I loved Christmas time and the magic of the season.

Everyone seemed cheerful with big smiles, offering greetings as they passed, and there was a general feeling of joy in the air. The stores were decorated and with the weather, it felt cozy. I parked in one of the empty spots in front of a row of boutique shops, where I planned to buy gifts for all my friends, and I texted Sara to let her know I had arrived a few minutes early.

While waiting for her response, I pulled my foot up onto the seat and started searching for hotels in Greece. Brooks had been bringing up the idea of us going to Scotland for the groundbreaking ceremony of Kildaire, and we had briefly discussed traveling across Europe since our honeymoon had been cut short. I know I would enjoy taking that trip if I could overcome my fear of flying.

Greece has always been at the top of my list of destinations abroad. The warm, blue waters, delicious Mediterranean food, and rich history make it seem like the perfect getaway. I leaned back against the headrest, closed my eyes, and envisioned myself flying. *I can do this. I will do this. I will be okay. Germany, Italy, Greece.*

Just then, a knock on my window startled me. I opened my eyes to see Sara's face against the glass, her little body dancing back and forth, trying to stay warm with her coat pulled tightly around her face. I laughed as I shut off my car and grabbed my coat and bag before joining her outside.

"Ready?" She sounded giddy.

"Yep! Which store first?"

↟ ↟ ↟

I opened the garage door with an arm full of gift bags.

"B, I'm home!"

"I'm in the kitchen," he replied.

As I walked into the kitchen, with bags still dangling from my arms, I noticed that the living room and kitchen were filled with pillar candles, and he was cooking. I took a moment to admire the thoughtful arrangement of everything before turning my attention back to him.

"Wow," I gasped, setting the bags on the floor beside the table.

"Here," Brooks said, handing me a glass of Pinot Grigio before sliding into the barstool.

"Where is all this coming from?" I asked, still taken aback.

"It's been a while since I've cooked you a meal," he said, offering me a big smile.

I took a sip of my wine, then got up and hugged him. I walked around the island to where he stood at the stove, wrapping my arms around him and resting my cheek against his shoulder. I could feel his body relax as his hand softly rested on mine, which was sitting on his chest.

"How was shopping?" he asked.

"Good. I got everything I needed. How was your day?" I replied.

"Good. I played the piano, caught up on some reading, and sent the staff home early so I could be alone with you."

My heart leaped as I pressed my lips into his back. "I love you," I said into his shirt.

↟ ↟ ↟

After dinner, Brooks and I sat on bar stools facing each other, discussing my session with Dr. Shavani. Once again, Brooks assured me he would be by my side the entire time. His hands played with mine as he spoke, and his voice was almost a whisper. The light from the taper candles danced in the dimly lit room.

"Dance with me," he said, standing up and pulling my hands with him.

I didn't hesitate, resting my head on his shoulder as we swayed gracefully back and forth. Our bodies moved together as one to the soft music playing over the speakers. The darkness of the room enveloped us, creating a sense of intimacy and connection. With each sway, an unspoken understanding between us felt palpable. We would always have each other.

The steady rhythm of his heartbeat made me want to cry. I didn't know why. I just knew that it did. Tears of joy, gratitude, peace, and love welled up inside me. He gave me everything and more. His jaw rested against my temple as he whispered, "I love you, Emily Claire."

I pulled back, leaving the warm embrace and safety of his arms to look at him. His eyes met mine in a silent exchange of understanding. Before we could say anything, he leaned in and kissed me softly, slowly, and reverently.

The taste of his wine still lingered in his mouth. His lips molded against mine, moving slowly as if he had all the time in the world. His hands moved under my hair to the top of my neck and tenderly embraced my head.

His tongue occasionally reached out to slowly slide against my lip or into my mouth. The house could have been burning to the ground around us, and I wouldn't even have noticed. I had a singular thought that consumed every one of my senses- my love and appreciation for my husband.

I wasn't aware of how much time had elapsed as we lay on the floor next to the fire in each other's embrace, our mouths still passing unspoken conversations back and forth. We took turns undressing each other slowly.

Like that first night, we studied each other's bodies before returning our mouths for more. The small, quiet moans, the occasional gasp of air, and the soft music were the only sounds filling the dark, candlelit room. I would have made it last forever if I could have.

Staying wrapped in his arms, I rolled off him and lay on the blanket beside him. I buried my face into his side, inhaled his scent, and closed my eyes. Relaxation and peace consumed me, and I wanted nothing more than to fall asleep right here on the floor beneath the fireplace next to him.

He chuckled lightly, breaking the perfect stillness.

"What's so funny?" I whispered.

"Do you remember that Christmas before everything?" *Everything*. Our codeword for the accident and death of our parents. Life before and life after were so distinctly different.

"Our last Christmas with them?"

"Yeah. Do you remember walking down the hallway to my room that night?"

I still had no idea where he was going with this. "No? Which night?"

"I think it was like two days before Christmas. You had come over to watch Christmas movies, and we had both fallen asleep on the couch? It was late. I woke you up, and instead of going home, you came into my bedroom with me to hang out."

"Okay. Yeah, I remember, but why?"

He just started laughing again.

"Brooks, why?"

"I can't believe you don't remember. We were lying in my bed talking about what we wanted to do for spring break, and then we heard them. My parents. In their bedroom."

My face blushed as I recalled the memory. It was the only time we had ever heard either of our parents in the bedroom.

"They thought we were still asleep on the couch." I smiled.

Brooks rolled over so that our noses were almost touching, and I could feel his breath on my face. "That night, you told me you didn't understand why people moaned like that."

I grimaced in embarrassment. "I did, didn't I? Well, now I know." Every sensation in my body was on high alert. His mouth was soft as he pressed his lips back into mine. Every hair on my body stood on end even though we were enveloped in the warmth of the fireplace. His fingers slowly traced up and down the side of my hip.

"I could stay like this forever," I whispered against his mouth. He nodded softly before rolling me over and laying on top of me. My hands were pinned above my head by his sturdy hand while the other brushed my cheek.

"Ready for round two?"

↟ ↟ ↟

I was humming along to Jaymes Young as I walked into our bedroom. Mrs. Hall had just returned from shopping, and the entire staff was here today, pulling out the few boxes of Christmas decorations that Brooks and I had saved from our childhood.

I was excited to start decorating, but first, we needed a tree. Our original plan was to order one, but we decided to try a real tree this year. We found a tree farm not too far from home where we could cut down our own. We hoped to start a new tradition: a yearly tree-cutting adventure, coming home to decorate while enjoying hot cocoa and Christmas music.

I saw Brooks leaning over his sink as I walked into the bathroom to shower and get ready. He was quiet and didn't even look up when I entered the room. I instantly knew what was bothering him. The white box of pregnancy tests was sitting on the counter between our sinks.

I had asked Mrs. Hall to pick them up after a scare this month. I was only two days late, but that was enough to make me anxious. We hadn't talked about having another baby, or about babies at all, for that matter. How could I reassure him not to worry when I was concerned enough to have the tests in the house?

"B," I said as I walked toward him. When I reached for his arm, he yanked it away.

"Don't," he said, his voice stern.

"Please, don't act like this." My heart sank.

"Emily, it's time for you to call Dr. Williams and get on birth control. I can't deal with this right now."

"Deal with what? You know how I feel about birth control."

His hands raked through his hair, messing up his perfect wave.

"Fine, but this will change things." He stormed out of the bathroom, and I followed him into the bedroom.

"Change what exactly?" My voice cracked as tears began to fall. This wasn't the reaction I was expecting. I thought he might be afraid or a little upset but not angry.

He turned to face me, tears in his eyes but also an anger I wasn't used to seeing directed at me. I had witnessed his anger before, usually regarding other people, but never aimed at me.

"Condoms, pulling out, no more spontaneous anything. And remember, you decided this, not me."

"Brooks, that isn't fair."

"Emily, I can't—and I won't—watch you almost die again. We lost our son, and I lost a part of you too. I can't go through that again. So if you won't get on birth control, then..." He sighed and sat on the bed.

I wanted to reach out to him, to hold him, but I knew he would only pull away again. The distance between us felt like a growing canyon. My legs felt weak, and my heart raced as I processed what he said. Fear bubbled in my stomach, and my breath barely supported my voice as I tried to respond.

"Brooks, do you not want any more kids?"

He stood up and walked out, murmuring, "Not right now." The worry etched on his face sparked a mix of curiosity and concern within me about the emotions he was grappling with.

I slid down the wall to the floor and pulled my knees in. Maybe it was foolish to assume that Brooks would be okay with having another baby. I wasn't ready by any means, but the idea of getting pregnant and having another child wasn't so bad.

Even with the morning sickness and the loss of Liam, I still had the desire to be a mother. I wanted to hold a baby in my arms and look at that little miracle—a perfect, tiny being that would be a combination of Brooks and me. We would be creating a family, and that is something to celebrate.

It felt like that dream was distant right now, and I didn't even know how to talk to him about it. The only thing that had changed was a box of pregnancy tests on the counter.

I wiped my tears on my sleeve and pushed off the ground. We needed to be at the tree farm in an hour, and I still needed to shower. For now, I had to push the whole argument and the idea of a family out of my mind. I didn't want the tradition Brooks and I were starting to be tainted with bad memories and negativity.

Chapter Sixty-Nine

After giving Brooks a few minutes to sit with his emotions, I decided to skip my shower and get ready. We needed to talk about how he was feeling. I wasn't sure if we could address the entire issue today, but we had to start opening that area of communication.

Clearly, he had strong feelings I wasn't even aware of. As I turned off the bathroom lights, I grabbed a sweater for Brooks before heading down to join him in the study.

I knocked lightly on the doorframe to get his attention. He was sitting on the sofa, sipping a glass of scotch. When he looked up at me, I could see the fight in him had faded. His eyes were no longer filled with fiery anger but rather with remorse. He waved me over, and I crossed the room, kneeling in front of him and placing his sweater on the arm of the sofa. I took his hands and whispered the most sincere apology I could muster.

"I'm sorry." I kissed his hands gently.

One of his hands slipped out of mine as he reached up to brush my cheek with his thumb.

"I'm sorry, Em. I shouldn't have treated you like that. You didn't deserve it. I broke my promise."

I cupped my hand over his, pausing to gather my thoughts so I didn't say something I would regret. I wanted to say it was okay, but deep down, I knew it wasn't. He was usually so good at communicating, always so patient and attentive. This side of him was unsettling and I hoped I never experienced it again.

"Please, don't do that again. It's okay to be upset, but don't make ultimatums."

He nodded.

"Brooks, we need to talk about all of this, but for now, we have to go."

He leaned forward, kissing my forehead before standing up with his sweater in hand.

"Okay." His voice was soft. He took my hand in his, and we walked out of the study toward the garage together.

↟ ↟ ↟

The crisp air bit at my cheeks as we stepped out into the gravel parking lot. The sound of crunching stones filled the silence around us. I zipped up my vest and tugged my beanie down, seeking warmth against the chill, before walking around the car to take Brooks' hand. I could still feel the tension from our earlier fight lingering between us, but I was determined to push past it and enjoy our afternoon together.

We approached the small green shed that functioned as their office, its weathered paint and creaky door giving it a rustic charm. After checking in for our reservation and signing a few waivers, we were allowed into the lot. The scent of pine filled the air as we entered. Brooks selected an ax and a bow saw from the tool shed. With a renewed sense of purpose, we strolled down the first row of towering trees, their branches swaying gently in the breeze.

As we strolled through the first row of trees, I was amazed at how different they all seemed when side-by-side. They varied in size and thickness, some slender and delicate, while others more robust and sturdy. Despite their beauty, none felt right for what I was looking for. Eager to find our tree, we moved to the second row.

"Well, this one looks nice," I said, pausing in front of a larger spruce tree.

"No, not really. The base has a curve in it, so it won't sit right in the water. See down here?" He pointed to where the trunk veered left slightly. "Let's keep looking."

I couldn't help but smile. Was he really turning into a lumberjack, scrutinizing the curvature of the trunk? I tried to turn away to hide my smile, but he pulled back on my hand until I spun to face him.

"What?" he asked.

"Nothing," I said, though my smile only widened.

He rolled his eyes and let go of my hand. I grabbed it again with an exaggerated motion.

"Where did you learn about trees?" I asked as I began to walk again.

"My dad."

"What? When?" I was sure my expression reflected a mix of shock and confusion.

"Pretty much every Christmas, Em."

"Every Christmas?"

"Who do you think picked out our Christmas tree every year?"

As a child, I was amused by the contrast in holiday traditions between our two families. The Devonshires had always embraced the charm of a genuine tree, its fragrant pine needles and rich, earthy aroma wafting through their home. My parents, however, loved their opulent, flocked tree with its false snowy branches. To replace the lack of aroma, my mother always had an assortment of pine-scented candles. Carrie always boasted about the unmistakable difference in pine scents.

Their friendly rivalry kept the rest of us laughing through the holiday season. Though it was never a genuine competition, a sense of playful tension filled the air. Who would decorate their tree with the most dazzling decorations? Who could complete their shopping first? In the end, no one was ever declared a winner, and every playful exchange ended in lighthearted banter and infectious laughter. Our mothers weaved a joyful and festive spirit into the air every year. With their absence, the holidays had never felt so dull.

"I guess I always assumed someone just brought it to your house. I don't remember you ever mentioning that you picked it out yourselves."

"Yep," he muttered, studying another tree.

I couldn't help but smile to myself as I watched him. Despite all the time we had spent together, countless mysteries still surrounded him—fragments of his life that remained unknown to me. His fingers grazed over the rough, thick branches, while I observed him. He circled the massive tree, lost in thought.

The wind picked up, carrying with it the scent of the trees mingled with the aroma of the damp soil. I took a deep breath, feeling the cool air settle around me while the clouds above hinted at an impending storm. I closed my eyes, longing for snow.

Snow in Oregon, particularly along the coast, was rare. If we were fortunate, we might receive an inch or two, enough to transform the landscape into a winter wonderland. I dreamed of watching snowflakes drifting down, carpeting the ground, and nestling among the deep emerald hues of the towering trees, turning our town into a set from a Christmas movie. Just as I opened my eyes, I caught Brooks looking over at me, his expression curious, as if he sensed my unspoken wish.

"You okay?" he asked.

"Never better." It was true. I was being reborn *again.* I would survive this, and I had Brooks by my side this time.

"This tree looks good," he said, moving toward me.

"Okay."

"Do you like it or want to keep looking?" he chuckled.

"I like it."

"Alright then." He grabbed the ax and began hitting at the base of the tree.

↟ ↟ ↟

At home, lunch was ready, and the staff had gone for the day. The Christmas boxes, labeled from years ago, sat stacked in the living room.

"Well, should I start opening boxes?" I asked, crossing the room to the first stack.

"Yeah, I think they should all be labeled with what's inside," he replied, taking another bite of his lunch.

Sure enough, all the boxes from the Devonshire's home were accurately labeled. I moved the boxes around the room, organizing them into towering stacks. Brooks and I had decided to hire a company for our outdoor light installations but chose to handle the interior decorating ourselves. I wanted our kids to experience the same joy we had while decorating our trees growing up.

However, as I reflected on our earlier argument, my stomach soured. When would Brooks feel ready to move forward? It felt like we were on two different pages, and I didn't know how to discuss it with him. It hurt to feel shut out by him. I sighed as I lifted the last box off the ground and set it on top of the pile of random house decor.

If I was still pregnant with Liam, my belly would be large and swollen, a sign of the life growing within me. We would be busy decorating the nursery, filling it with soft blankets and tiny clothes, painting and laughing, and enjoying the last few weeks of just the two of us while we awaited his arrival.

This Christmas would have been filled with joy and excitement. Instead, I felt a deep void in my chest, a painful reminder of his absence that seemed to linger in every corner of our home and my soul.

Without thinking, driven by a motherly instinct still within me, I gently placed my hand over my flat stomach, imagining where he should be sleeping, growing. I couldn't help but hold onto the hope that another little life would be growing there one day, bringing warmth back to our lives.

Silent tears began to fall as I started opening boxes, trying to push aside the deep ache of grief that, without warning, consumed me. Little wet splatters of tears dampened the edges of the cardboard as I searched through the box to see what was inside.

Brooks wrapped his strong arms around me as I felt my knees buckle beneath me, bringing us both to the floor. Tears streamed down my cheeks, disappearing into his shirt as he held me, creating an intimate cocoon of safety and love.

I would never understand how quickly joy was overcome by sorrow, and yet, I still held onto the hope that one day, we would create our own little family.

The sensation of Brooks' heartbeat against mine provided a steady rhythm that anchored me, allowing me to come back from the edge of darkness.

"It's okay, baby," Brooks whispered into my hair.

"I miss him. I hate this. It isn't fair." My body shuddered, expelling the grief.

"I know, I do too. We will be there in a few days with him."

"I want him in my arms, not buried in the cold ground."

"Me too."

After several minutes of sobbing, I felt the suffocating weight lift, and was replaced with a flicker of hope.

"Brooks, I know we planned to discuss this later, but I need to be honest with you. I want to be a mom," I said, my voice trembling with raw emotion. I could feel the tension ripple through his body beneath me.

"I know you do," he replied softly, his eyes reflecting understanding and hesitation. "I want kids, Em, but maybe we should wait a year...or some time, at least. I'm just getting you back." A year? That felt almost unbearable, like an eternity. But perhaps this was the fresh start we desperately needed. We had transitioned from being newly reunited to learning about an unexpected pregnancy and then married all in a matter of months.

However, the thought of birth control sent a wave of unease churning in my stomach. It wasn't just the fact it prevented me from having a baby. It was the fluctuating emotions, the hormones, all of it. Yet, if that's what I needed to maintain the spontaneity and intimacy in my marriage, I would endure it. I was desperate for a chance to return to what we had together.

"Okay," I sighed, burying my face into his warm chest and inhaling his scent. His amber cologne mixed with pine and the smell of rain. "I can start birth control."

He nodded thoughtfully, his brow furrowing. "We can talk about it after Christmas. For now, are you okay?" he asked with a gentle voice.

I pulled away, meeting his gaze, and noticing the worry etched on his handsome face. A mixture of emotions swept through me, but I nodded.

"Come on," he said, rising to his feet and pulling me with him. "What's in this box?"

As he gestured toward the large cardboard box beside the tree, the tension that lingered between us began to dissolve. I felt a sense of gratitude wash over me as I watched the playful grin return to Brooks' lips. Together, we started pulling out the colorful decorations of our childhood. Cheerful Santas, renditions of Rudolph, and so many miniature trees.

At that moment, I was reminded of one of the things I cherished most about our relationship. We could navigate difficult conversation one moment and transition into laughter and playfulness the next. It was a beautiful balance that we brought to our marriage.

We weren't finished talking about it, but it was enough to feel settled until we were both ready. We shared laughs about different memories and created a pile of donations consisting of all the decorations we both disliked. Among them were the Grinch babies, which Carrie thought were adorable but that we both found a bit creepy.

My parents always had this weird stack of snowmen set out front of the house. It looked more like snowmen bent over each other with weird faces that made us think of weird sex positions, even when we were younger.

Brooks and I had created several art pieces as kids that our mothers felt compelled to keep, even though they were quite ugly and resembled smushed-faced creatures.

By the time we finally began decorating the tree, it was almost dinnertime. We decided to use the Devonshire family ornaments. I had always thought the contrast of the deep green tree against the vibrant gold and red ornaments was beautiful. I first threaded the various ribbons through the tree before adding the lights and ornaments.

After what felt like an hour, we stepped back to admire our work. I wrapped my arms around Brooks and smiled up at the decorated tree.

"Our first Christmas together as a married couple. As Mr. and Mrs. Devonshire," I said. He kissed the top of my head just as I heard his stomach growl.

"Time to eat?" I laughed.

"Yeah."

Mrs. Hall had prepared dinner before she left for the day and had left it in the oven for us. As I plated the food, Brooks opened a bottle of wine, and we sat at the table.

"So, I was looking at hotels in Greece," I said, still looking at my plate and stabbing the chunk of beef.

"Really? So do you want to go then?" His voice was hopeful, but I could tell he was trying to remain calm.

"I do, actually. I was thinking that after the groundbreaking ceremony, we could country hop—see Germany, the UK, Italy, Greece."

Brooks' face was beaming with joy. He still hadn't taken a single bite of his dinner.

"What? Why are you looking at me like that?" I laughed, taking a sip of my wine.

"I'm just really happy. Finally, I get to travel with you and spoil you. I want to take you everywhere."

My eyes rolled, cutting him off. "I just want to have fun with you. Then maybe," I took another sip for courage, "Maybe we can talk about babies when we get back?"

"Okay, deal." He lifted his wine glass to his lips and paused. "We can talk about it, but that doesn't mean I will be ready to try again. But we can talk."

I nodded and sipped again. That was the best I could hope for.

Chapter Seventy

I had barely slept, but my alarm was blaring, cutting through the quiet darkness of the room. I turned slightly, feeling the warmth of Brooks' body beside me.

He was still fast asleep as his chest rose and fell gently as he held me. With a sigh of frustration, I rolled over, struggling to reach my phone. My arm stretched awkwardly, fumbling for it on the nightstand. I grasped it, and the bright light pierced the room, causing me to squint and shield my eyes.

December 22 | 6:01 | Weather: Overcast
High: 54° Low: 43°

I sighed and nestled back into Brooks' chest, closing my eyes. Today, we were going to see Liam. Last night, I had packed a bag at midnight, including a teddy bear lovey from one of the shops in Southport.

I also added some twinkle lights to a lantern to bring along. Showing up empty-handed didn't feel right, but what do you bring to your baby's grave? I settled on those two items and set them beside the plants we were taking - some poinsettias, snowdrops, and two small pine trees still in their buckets.

Brooks' watch buzzed softly against my back, a reminder we couldn't hide from today. He pressed the button to silence it, inhaling deeply as he did. Brooks leaned down and pressed his warm lips against my forehead, a simple act that made me feel gooey inside despite my growing anxiety over the day ahead.

We both felt the heavy weight of the day, but his touch communicated a promise to remain by my side through it all.

As I lay there, a lump formed in my throat, a tangible mix of anxiety and sadness brewing within me, waiting for the moment it might overflow. The emotional weight of everything we were about to face hung in the air between us.

"It's time to get ready, my love," he said, his voice barely audible.

I didn't move, I didn't want to.

"Come on, Em. Let's get dressed and grab coffee and food on our way out. How about Lulu's?"

I sighed, "Okay. Let's go." I kissed his chest and rolled out of his arms.

I reached for my black sweater dress, slipped it on over my black tights, and grabbed my over-the-knee black boots.

At our parents' funeral, I hated wearing black, but now I understand its significance. Black reflected my feelings - empty, broken, devoid of happiness.

Brooks was finishing brushing his teeth when I stepped out of the closet. The atmosphere in the room was thick with apprehension, a silent acknowledgment of the heavy emotions looming over us. He offered a half-smile that barely reached his eyes. As he stepped closer, he gently pulled me in for a kiss - one that held both comfort and an unspoken promise of support amidst our shared sorrow.

"Ready?"

I nodded.

"You drive." He grabbed our coats from the mudroom and helped me into mine.

"Me?"

"Yeah. We do this at your pace."

I looked down at my hands, at the same polish I rubbed incessantly in Dr. Shavani's office.

"Okay," I nodded. "Thanks, B."

When we pulled into Lulu's, I struggled to breathe as my chest felt constricted. We ordered our drinks and two Nova Lox bagels to go. I knew every second that ticked by until we took off would only make things more challenging.

I exhaled deeply and pushed the door open to the parking lot. Brooks was behind me, holding the bag of food and our drinks in a small carrier. *It's just a plane ride, one hour in the air. You'll get to be near your baby. You can do this.* I slipped into the driver's seat and gripped the steering wheel tightly.

"Are you okay, Em?"

I shook my head. "No. No, I'm not. Nothing about this is natural or okay. Nothing about visiting your parents and your child in a graveyard, talking to their headstones - none of that is okay." A deep ache filled my chest. I wanted nothing more than to be rescued from this painful reality. I wished I could close my eyes only to open them again in a world where this was all just a nightmare. But that illusion held no weight, as this was my truth, my reality. This was the only way I could spend time with my parents and my baby: out in the cold, surrounded by headstones, overlooking a serene lake, the stillness of the place accentuated by painful memories.

"I know, baby," Brooks said softly, his voice thick with empathy. "I wish I could take away all of your pain. I wish there was something - anything - I could have done to save him. I'm here with you, and I'll be here...always.

"Life has dealt us some shit cards, and while I don't understand why this happened, I know we can face it together. We will face it together." He wrapped his strong arms around me, pulling me into a warm embrace that felt like a lifeline and I clung to him tightly. He was my anchor in this storm.

After a moment, I pulled back and gazed up at him, looking for comfort in his eyes, but I found my own pain and emotions mirrored back at me. But in our shared pain, I also felt a surge of gratitude. I was thankful to have someone I loved standing beside me, someone who understood my sorrow and had walked the same path of loss.

"Yeah. I'll be okay. Let's go," I sighed heavily, the weight of my emotions still pressing down on me but manageable with his presence. With a deep breath, I backed out of the gravel lot, steering the car onto the road that would take us to the airport.

↟ ↟ ↟

A heavy fog enveloped the plane as we arrived, much like the cloud of worry surrounding my thoughts. Tate came over to assist Brooks with the plants. I stood beside the car, gazing up at the jet—our jet. This was not the same plane where I lost my son. Everything about this jet was different from the one we were on that day: the bathroom, the layout, the staff.

I had created so many good memories on this jet. It took me to Seattle for our first official date. It brought us to Sonoma for our engagement, that beautiful weekend in wine country. It has become a means for us to travel back and forth for work.

With renewed hope, I wrapped my arms around my chest and headed for the stairs. This was just a plane and my means of transportation to see my baby. Brooks was by my side as I reached the base of the stairs and looked up into the soft, welcoming light of the cabin. One step at a time, and soon, we would be on our way to Liam.

My longing to be near him again grew with every passing second. As broken and complicated as it was, I wanted to be there. I wanted to lay on his grave and tell him that I loved him.

Step by step, I walked up the stairs, gaining speed as I got closer to the cabin until the warm air from the heater enveloped me. I sat down in my usual chair and closed my eyes. This wasn't as difficult as I had anticipated. Dr. Shavani was right; it was more a matter of my mindset. Brooks sat across from me, positioned to look at me. I smiled back at him and retrieved my tea from the carrier.

"I'm okay. Really. I just want to get this over with so I can visit my son," I assured him.

He returned my smile and leaned forward to kiss me. "Okay. We're almost ready to go."

At that moment, Tate stepped into the cabin and moved toward the front. A minute later, the door closed, and Tate's voice came through the speaker, informing us that we were cleared for takeoff.

Brooks held my hand as I watched the runway speed past before fading into the fog. My stomach flipped, as usual, as we lifted into the air. After taking another sip of my tea, I let go of Brooks' hand and settled back in my seat. I was surprised by how easy this was, especially considering the fear and anxiety that had consumed me before. Once we reached cruising altitude, Brooks lifted the table between us and took out our bagels.

↟ ↟ ↟

The air in Seattle had a bite to it that I didn't anticipate, creeping into my bones and sending a shiver down my spine. The ground was sodden, the result of the relentless rain from the night before.

As Brooks and I ambled up the hill toward Liam's grave, I could feel the hell of my boot sink into the mud with each step, adding to the heaviness I felt.

A blanket of fog lay over the cemetery, making the reality of death seem more palpable. The eeriness only amplifying the quiet. The whole place was devoid of life aside from the movement of the trees, their leaves trembling gently in the breeze.

Brooks' thumb rubbed rhythmically across the back of my hand, a soothing gesture against the almost white-knuckled grip I maintained in his hold. My heart thudded in my chest, its rapid beat neither a result of fear nor anxiety but rather an urgent need to reach my son and sit with him again. I would have broken into a desperate sprint to reach him if I were convinced that my presence could somehow revive him.

Yet this visit felt different from the last time I had stood in this final resting place. With each step, I cataloged my surroundings, noting how the once pristine headstones had faded under years of weathering, some sinking into the earth at various angles.

Row after row of stone markers testifying to lives once lived, all belonging to someone beloved, echoed stories of joy and pain left in their wake. Every engraved name was a reminder of the person that had left a mark on their families, friends, and those they touched in their lives. Grief hovered in the air surrounding those we mourned.

I could see the profound appeal of embracing a faith, especially if it offered comfort in the belief that our loved ones had found peace in their death.

As we made our way to Liam's grave, I couldn't help but notice how the earth was in the process of reclaiming several of the older headstones and monuments around us. It was a stark contrast to Liam's grave whose headstone was still so clean and so small. The grass was new where it had regrown over the hole that was dug during his burial.

We stood together in silence, facing the beautiful white granite headstone that had recently been placed, adorned with a small angel baby lying across the top. Its delicate wings stretched out on either side, and it cradled a teddy bear in its arm. I reluctantly released my grip on Brooks' hand and reached out to touch the angel, running my fingers along its smooth, cool surface, tracing the contours of its wings, the tiny fingers, and all ten toes.

At that moment, I wished more than anything to know what Liam would have looked like. I wanted to know what color his hair would have been, his eyes, to know the sound of his laughter echoing through our home.

As the reality of my grief crashed over me like a wave, my knees buckled, sending me to the soaked grass as moisture seeped into my tights. The biting winter breeze cut through my coat like a knife, a harsh reminder of the emptiness gnawing at my heart. *Gosh, I miss you so much.*

Overwhelmed, I fell forward onto my hands, gripping the blades of grass, and leaned in to kiss the cold stone. It was undeniably beautiful and sad. A reminder of the baby that should have been born into a world and embraced in the arms of his parents. My fingers brushed gently across the inscription -

Liam James Devonshire.
Our beautiful baby boy
gone too soon, forever loved.
September 8, 2022

The white monument dedicated to our son was nothing short of heartbreaking. The pillar rested on two small platforms, with a branch extending across them, all crafted from the same white stone. Surrounding the inscription was a large circular wreath that mirrored the pattern of the branch.

It was a stark contrast with our parents' headstones, which were positioned on either side. Their headstones were made of black granite, several feet wide, and if Liam's monument wasn't situated in between, the two would form a sloping shape like the bottom half of a sphere, completing each other.

Large planters adorned both sides of their headstones and they were identical except for the names and dates. They exuded a commanding presence, a testament to the lives they commemorated. Now, that once comforting sphere was disrupted by Liam's headstone.

Brooks dropped his puffer coat onto the ground and sat beside me. I shifted closer to him, eager for the warmth he always provided. Our tears flowed silently, a reflection of our shared grief. Each tear, slow and heavy with heartache.

I was content to stay exactly where I was. I leaned my head against Brooks' shoulder, seeking both comfort and connection, as we gazed out over the lake in the distance. This would be the closest we would ever come to being a whole family again.

All five members of our family rested beneath the earth, taken from us too soon. I felt a wave of solace as we clung tightly to each other.

Is this what reality was like for all parents who've endured losing their babies? Sitting in heavy silence on patches of grass, facing a cold stone that only bore a name and date. Could there ever be peace or happiness, or would it always be a reminder of shattered hopes and dreams? Would it forever echo sorrow and reminders of death?

The pain of losing our parents was a different kind of heartache. Over time, I gradually learned to live with the grief, to carry it with me. But would losing Liam feel the same? Deep down, in the quietest parts of my soul, I knew it wouldn't.

We all live with the knowledge that one day, we will have to say goodbye to our parents. It's an inevitable farewell that we all expect. We certainly never anticipated saying goodbye so soon, but losing a child? Burying a baby that didn't even have a chance at life? That is a weight no parent should endure. Ever.

As the sun crept across the sky behind the thick blanket of clouds, we found the strength to return to the car. After placing the small trees beside our parents' headstones and leaving the lantern and lovey for Liam, I lost it.

Each tear that fell seemed to soften the sharp pain of my heartache, soothing the cracks that had formed. Brooks and I shivered from the chill in the air. The weight of our grief felt unbearable, but we carried it together. It was nearing one in the afternoon and we desperately needed warmth and food before heading home, back to the reality that felt so broken without Liam.

A deep sense of finality washed over me as I closed the car door. I glanced up the hill one last time, the weight of my heart so palpable. "Bye, Mama and Daddy, Carrie and James. Please take care of our boy," I whispered softly. We are the parents of an angel baby and will only ever have the opportunity to carry him with us in our hearts.

Chapter Seventy-One

It was Christmas Eve, and despite the difficult journey to Seattle, we felt a tangible sense of excitement in the air. We both realized how much we needed a mood booster before attending Cumberland's Christmas party tonight. Leah and Peter had decided to throw their very first Christmas Eve party, embracing the idea that it would be a great reason for all of us to gather together. After all, most of us didn't have family coming into town.

The morning light poured through the kitchen window, illuminating the holiday decorations around the room. Brooks and I had woken with playful moods. Laughter bubbled between us as we nudged each other, racing down the stairs, racing to see who could reach the kitchen first. The stakes were nothing less than breakfast: fluffy pancakes oozing with warm syrup or hearty omelets filled with colorful, vibrant vegetables.

My heart raced with the thrill of the small contest, but as we burst into the kitchen, I was surprised that Brooks wanted the pancakes since he typically favored savory over sweet. His enthusiasm was contagious with his high from his win. The warmth of the kitchen, the aroma of coffee brewing in the background, and the anticipation of our first Christmas as a married couple made it feel like the perfect start to Christmas Eve.

"I win!" he exclaimed, making me buckle over with laughter.

"You cheated," I chuckled.

"Well, I would have won, but I didn't want to knock you down the stairs."

I rolled my eyes. "Fine, you win, but I get to choose the music."

Brooks smiled as he began pulling the ingredients from the butler's pantry.

"Hey Siri, play Pentatonix Christmas."

Brooks didn't say anything, but his chuckle and the way he shook his head repeatedly signaled that he knew nothing had changed. Pentatonix has always been my favorite band to play Christmas carols. No other album or group came close to capturing the same feeling. To me, they exuded the joy of the carols like no one else.

While Brooks worked on the pancakes, I started the coffee and my tea before plopping down on the counter beside him.

"So, what are you wearing tonight?" he asked, his eyes intent on the measuring spoons as he carefully measured the ingredients. I glanced at him, noticing his concentration and smiling at how cute he looked. He glanced back at me, his brows lifting, reminding me of his question about tonight's attire.

"Ugh, don't remind me. I hate ugly sweater parties," I groaned. I could never understand why people loved ugly sweaters; it seemed like a silly theme, and people paid way too much money for sweaters with sexual innuendos illustrated through reindeer or naughty Santas.

"I don't know; it might be fun," he replied, pouring the milk into the stand mixer.

"What are you wearing?" I asked, playfully throwing a kitchen towel in his direction. He caught it in the air with one hand and gave me a lopsided grin.

"I found one of my dad's old sweaters in a box of his clothes. It's pretty ugly, and I thought, why not?"

"Can't I just wear a dress?" I pouted.

"Emily, you should participate. Our friends have shown us nothing but support. It's time for us to show up for them - in ugly sweaters," he joked.

"Fine, I will find the ugliest sweater in my closet. No promises on it actually being ugly," I sighed.

Brooks looked up and shook his head before wiping some of the batter across my lips. I smirked and tried reaching for the batter, but he pulled it away before I could get to it. With one hand holding the bowl out away from me, he pulled himself in between my thighs with his other. I licked the batter off my lips. His mouth parted just inches from mine.

"That was nasty. Pancake batter is gross before it's cooked," I giggled.

"You missed some." His voice was soft as his tongue gently glided to the side of my mouth.

"Brooks Devonshire," I gulped. "You need to be careful, or we won't get breakfast."

He paused, considering my offer before pulling away and turning toward the stove.

"Fine," I quipped, sliding off the counter to fill our mugs. "Have it your way."

He chuckled, igniting the stove. I slid his cup of coffee beside him and kissed his bicep before returning to the island and sat at one of the barstools.

Once the pancakes were finished and plated, Brooks and I sat down at the table. It felt unusually formal. We typically ate at the island, on the couch, or outside on the deck. The table was reserved for when guests were over.

We both ate in silence, but I could sense that Brooks was on the edge of his seat, as if he was waiting for something. He kept glancing at me, watching with amusement as I took each bite. With only two bites left on my plate, I dropped my fork.

"Are you going to tell me what's up?" I asked playfully.

"When you are done." The corners of his mouth twitched upwards.

"I'm done." I slid my plate away from me and leaned back, bringing my fingers to my mouth to suck off the syrup that had managed to find its way up my fork.

He turned his chair out and stood, taking the plates to the sink, and I could see that he was tenting in his pants.

My body was aroused before he returned to the table with the syrup. I couldn't fight the grin that crossed my face. The last time we had used food for foreplay was during our engagement weekend, and it had been spectacular in every way.

"That's messy," I teased.

"Good thing there are showers," he responded, setting the syrup down on the table.

He pulled me out of the chair with a little too much strength and straight into his muscular chest. His mouth rested on the space below my ear, and his hands gripped my butt and lifted me to the table.

The anticipation of what was to come was almost too much, and I knew that I would most likely have several orgasms in my future. Just feeling him pressed into me with his breath hot on my neck and his strong hands now on my waist, I was marching toward a peak.

"Brooks." My breath was heavy on his bare chest as I lifted his shirt off.

He was slowly working his mouth along my collarbone and couldn't be interrupted clearly because he didn't respond. I began sliding my hands into the waistband of his joggers, but he stopped me with his hand and continued onto the other side of my neck.

"You are driving me crazy."

"I know," he murmured, still moving at a snail's pace.

I leaned back onto my palms and closed my eyes, trying to calm down.

After his mouth finished its descent and ascent to the opposite ear, he whispered for me to lay back on the table. Of course, I followed his instructions without a single hesitation.

"Good girl," he whispered, sending goosebumps all over my body. Dear God. He was going to give me a heart attack.

My hips protruded out of the pink and white striped shorts, and my shirt sat loosely just above, showing enough skin that his mouth rested on the curve of my hip while he worked to slowly unbutton my top. His hands were heavy and warm on my skin as he slid them back down to my waistband. While he worked to pull my shorts and panties off, I pulled my shirt off, tossing it across the kitchen.

"I want to taste every inch of you," he said before sliding his tongue up my inner thigh.

"Mmm," I moaned in agreement. I was already panting and arching my back, trying to fight against the absolute need for him to be in me. To feel his warm length pulsing in me. He paused just short of my slit and grabbed the syrup.

"Ready?" he asked with a naughty grin.

I nodded. I'd be ready for anything as long as it ended with him inside of me.

The syrup was warm and sticky but managed to make every inch of my skin tingle like it never had, making my whole body an erogenous zone. He set the syrup near my head and leaned down for a powerful kiss filled with passion, love, yearning, and promises.

His tongue slid past my bottom lip and jumped to my chest, where he began his magical work of sending me to the stars. He claimed every inch of bare skin, and in the wet, sticky trail, my skin burned with the need for him.

"I need you. I can't," I moaned, rubbing my thighs together. At this point, anything would send me off. A single touch, a single lick, it didn't matter. I was ready.

"Not yet." He bit my side before continuing south. "Always so anxious," he teased.

My breath was rapid, and I was sure that I was going to die under the pressure if it wasn't released soon.

"It's your fault," I laughed breathlessly. His nose was dragging along my belly button.

"Please," I cried out.

"I will, baby - just give me a minute." His tongue had just finished on my left leg and was now working up my right. I gripped the table on either side and pulled my legs up and open. I was ready for whatever he was willing to give. His tongue found my core, licking languid strokes and sucking my clit into his mouth. My legs trembled as I neared my orgasm. Alternating between sucking and licking, I finally found my release, clamping my legs around his head, holding him in place.

His fingers found my entrance and stroked me through my aftershocks, sending me into another fast and powerful orgasm. I fell back onto the table as his mouth worked its way up my sensitive body. I needed him. I needed to feel every inch of him.

He pulled me toward the edge of the table again and pulled me into his arms so we were flush with my sticky breasts against his bare chest. We fumbled to get his joggers off, but he kicked them away once they hit the floor. With a single, deep thrust, I clamped down around him and cried his name out.

"That's right," he groaned, still thrusting in and out. I locked my ankles behind him and rested back on my elbows, watching him. The way his muscles rippled with every thrust, the look of love and lust written so clearly in his cobalt eyes, and the way his lips parted.

The orgasm that rocked through me was so sudden that I hadn't even felt the warmth until I was burning white hot and collapsing around him, arching my back as I moaned my way through it.

As my vision cleared, I focused on him. His eyes were watching me with so much love and so much joy. His warm hands were resting on my thighs as he pulled me toward him with every thrust that sent me away again.

I sat up, kissing him deeply before trailing my lips down his jaw and across his salty skin.

"I love you so much." My tongue darted out, licking some syrup off his chest. I could tell he was preparing me for a second orgasm. "I love every inch of you."

"I love you too. Now turn over," he whispered into my ear.

I did what he asked without hesitation. My legs were already jello, but he held me up with one arm draped around me as my chest was pressed down onto the table. His free hand pulled my scrunchie out of my hair, letting it fall so he could wrap his hand in it while he pulled back as he raced into me. I could feel him lengthening in me.

"Come on, Emily. I won't last with you like this."

His hand on my waist dipped between my legs and sent me once again. Glorious warmth started low in my belly and spread rapidly. Colors blurred as my vision turned dark. He found his own release, and somewhere in the blackness, we both collapsed onto the table in a pile of skin, syrup, and sweat. Our hearts were galloping and our chests expanded for more air for several minutes before either of us moved.

"You should definitely make pancakes more often. I really like pancakes," I laughed.

He chuckled, carefully sliding away from me. "Omelets aren't as exciting."

As I lifted off the table, I couldn't help but laugh at the sticky residue in the shape of me across the dark wood.

"Well then, time for a shower."

I left my clothes and walked upstairs with Brooks right behind me, taking in the view. He let out a small groan. Once in our room, he threw the towels into the warmer before joining me in the hot water.

When the shower door closed behind him, he was already claiming my mouth, pushing me against the cold tile in the shower. I rested my head back and let the warmth, heat, and fire consume me.

↟ ↟ ↟

When I woke up to the house shaking from the thunder outside, I noticed that Brooks was still fast asleep beside me. His dark lashes rested against his cheeks, his lips were slightly parted, and he looked a lot like the boy I fell in love with so many years ago.

I fell back onto the pillow, groaning. It was too early to be awake. Brooks and I had stumbled in late from the Cumberlands party. We had both only had one drink, but we were so exhausted that we left a trail of clothing across our bedroom floor.

Peter and Leah hosted a wild party, and it felt like everyone in town was crammed into their home, which wasn't designed to hold large gatherings. Still, it was fun. We learned that the Cumberlands loved drinking games and loud music.

Throughout the night, Brooks and I were pulled in separate directions multiple times, but I finally made him promise to stick by my side. That lasted at least until Peter goaded him into a dance-off to "Brick House" and "Tricky." Leah and I, of course, captured the whole thing on video. I'm sure it will be the talk of the town.

Brooks rolled over, slinging his arm over me and pulling me to his chest. I rested my head against his warm body.

"Merry Christmas, Em," he mumbled, his voice still thick with sleep.

"Merry Christmas, B."

I wasn't ready to move or wake up, but I was perfectly okay to just lay here with him. Every Christmas since our parents died has been tinged with unspoken sadness lingering in the air and in our hearts. A constant reminder of how alone I was. Even when Brooks was in school in England, he couldn't visit for the holidays. His uncle made sure he remained there.

When I was in high school, my staff would make a big deal out of breakfast. They had all picked out gifts for me and presented them like my parents had. While their efforts always made me smile, I knew deep down Christmas would never be the same. I also felt guilty they didn't have anything better to do because of me.

In College, I felt a glimmer of joy with Parker. We had spent a Christmas in Nashville together, and during our senior year, we decided to stay home, inviting friends over for dinner that filled the house with laughter and love.

As I inhaled Brooks's singular scent, a profound sense of

gratitude washed over me. This Christmas was so different from the last in every way. Brooks leaned over me, brushing his lips against mine in a gentle kiss.

"Do you want coffee or tea this morning?" he asked, his voice laced with sleep and his mouth close to mine.

"Coffee sounds good," I replied, a smile spreading across my face as I leaned in for another kiss. With a playful grin, Brooks rolled out of bed and made his way to the closet, pulling on clothes before disappearing downstairs. I took a moment to enjoy the warmth of our bed and the lingering taste of his mouth before I followed him a few minutes later.

Chapter Seventy-Two

There was a rich aroma in the air from Brooks' coffee when I came downstairs. I found him in the kitchen preparing my coffee, smiling and humming a tune.

"Merry Christmas, beautiful," he said. I wished I could hold onto the way his grin lit up the whole room.

"So," he started, taking my hands in his and planting soft kisses on my knuckles, "what do you want to do today?"

I smiled, feeling love radiate from him.

"I'm thinking a classic Barlow-Devonshire Christmas."

He chuckled, "What's that?"

"Aside from the over-the-top breakfast, I was thinking of gifts first, then A Charlie Brown Christmas, followed by It's A Wonderful Life. Board games tonight?"

"Sounds perfect," he responded with excitement twinkling in his eyes. He raised his steaming mug to his lips while he slid mine toward me.

While Brooks busied himself preparing breakfast, I set the mood, turning on the fireplace and selecting a Christmas music playlist. We cozied up on the couch to eat instead of the table.

"What did you do for Christmas after we broke up?" I asked, shoving a piece of avocado toast into my mouth. I moaned as my tastebuds exploded with the creamy and crunchy texture, earning myself a grin from Brooks.

"That was during my time in Texas. I was stuck on base, so we tried to make the best of it. The guys played some Christmas music, shot a few pool games, and went to the gym. Pretty much nothing worth mentioning." He shrugged. "What about you?"

I let out a small laugh. "Honestly, I spent the entire day in bed watching Christmas movies in my pajamas. I only left the dorms to use the restroom. I ate some leftovers from the fridge and a bowl of cereal for dinner," I snorted before taking another bite.

"Wow, Em, that's tragic," he said with a mocking expression of sympathy. We both burst out laughing.

"Do you remember that Christmas our parents took us to Colorado?" I asked, trying to change the subject. Part of me wished I didn't have such a negative gut reaction to thinking about the years we spent apart, but I just wasn't ready to address that yet.

"The year we got snowed in at that big cabin?" he replied.

"That's the one. There was so much snow and presents everywhere."

"That place was so cool."

"That Christmas, you got me ice skates," I said, turning to face him, my grin widening.

"I hoped you would learn to skate with me, but you hit your head on the ice. Your mom was freaking out." He winced at the memory. My mother was definitely one of those helicopter parents.

"At least I got to spend the rest of the day with you, bringing me hot cocoa with tons of marshmallows. You always took the best care of me. You still do."

"That's because I love you," he replied, punctuating each word with a gentle kiss. "Always have. Always will."

"Which Christmas was your favorite?" I asked before taking another gulp of warm coffee.

"Our last Christmas."

I nodded, knowing he was referring to the one when our families were still whole. "It was a good one."

"Olivia and my mom were so tired of being cold," Brooks chuckled with a smile spreading across his face at the memory.

That last Christmas with our parents, we spent on a big, beautiful yacht in the turquoise waters of the Bahamas, hoping to avoid the nasty winter weather back home. The yacht had been decked out with twinkling lights and tinsel, and we spent the week in swimsuits and Santa hats instead of winter coats and gloves.

Brooks was stung by a jellyfish that trip and it fell on me to care for him. I was so scared to get back in the water after that that I vowed I would never dive again.

Brooks was unrelenting and would hear nothing of it. So sporting his red, welted sting and all, he grabbed his mask and jumped in after winking at me and waited for me to follow. I did, of course, just as I always had and always would. Brooks had a way of convincing me to do just about anything.

Our moms had spent months planning the trip, trying to convince our dads to agree. Both of our fathers had dreamed of skiing the Alps and having a white Christmas. In the end, our mothers' determination and persuasion won out.

Eventually, the idea of spending Christmas on the ocean and fishing for an entire week started to sound appealing. We had spent so much time on the water sailing that the prospect of swaying gently on the sea in a yacht and soaking up the sun felt like an exciting adventure. On Christmas Eve, we settled into a cozy spot on the boat to watch our favorite movies, complete with hot cocoa topped with whipped cream.

Brooks and I were in our awkward teenage years but found it impossible not to flirt or keep our hands to ourselves for longer than five minutes. Every stolen glance and shared laugh only fueled our love for one another. Meanwhile, our dads spent the whole trip cracking jokes and being playful. Their laughter echoed through the entire boat. For being our last Christmas with everyone alive, it was perfect.

"Are you ready to open gifts?" Brooks asked, breaking me out of my reverie. He stood up and grabbed one of the small presents from under the tree, handing it to me with a lopsided grin. I took my time opening the box. Inside the gold wrapping was a jewelry box containing a delicate necklace.

"It's beautiful," I murmured, running my fingers along the chain.

"The pearl comes from my mother's favorite necklace, which your mom gave her one year for her birthday. The charm is Liam's birthstone."

A lump lodged in my throat as I pinched the sapphire between my fingers and traced the pearl.

"Brooks, thank you," I said, my eyes brimming with tears. I threw my free arm over his shoulder and kissed him deeply, a single tear escaping and wedging itself between our cheeks. He smiled against my lips and gently wiped away my tears.

"Love you," he whispered. As he helped me fasten the necklace, I felt a surge of gratitude. It was a beautiful combination of our mothers and our son. Only Brooks could have come up with something so meaningful. I sighed, thankful that he understood me so well and knew exactly what would mean the most to me.

"My turn," I said, setting the box on the coffee table.

I returned from the tree with a shoebox-sized present wrapped in glittering green tree paper. It felt heavy as I placed it on his lap.

"What's this?" His voice was filled with excitement.

I held back a gleeful smile as I watched him open the box. Inside was a navy sweater wrapped around another small box. Brooks admired the sweater before reaching for the smaller box. When he opened it, he found a pocket watch beautifully engraved with the words, "Tout mon cœur, Toute mon âme."

"What does it mean?" he asked, a hint of uncertainty in his voice. "My French is a little rusty."

"It means, 'my whole heart, my whole soul,'" I whispered.

Brooks flipped the watch back and forth, deep in thought. Both of our dads had owned pocket watches. It all started as a joke from our moms because our fathers were always running late. Despite having expensive watch collections, they claimed it was because they never looked at the time. After that day, though, they always had the pocket watches tucked away and carried on their persons. The pocket watches were one of the few belongings recovered after the crash. We buried them with our fathers.

"It's perfect," he croaked, his eyes welling with tears. He quickly looked away, tightening his jaw to regain control of his emotions. As he turned the watch over in his hand, tracing the intricate details with his thumb, he attempted to lift the box to place it on the table. However, he soon realized something heavy remained inside. I laughed when he glanced at the box, puzzled.

"What's in this thing?"

"You'll see," I replied, grinning.

He lifted the bottom of the box, revealing a stack of old notebooks. As he pulled them out, the box fell to the floor. Brooks began flipping through the pages, and I added, "These are our dads' old notebooks about Caston, sailing, and their random thoughts. They're mostly my dad's, but somehow your dad's got mixed up in there too."

He looked back at me, curiosity shining in his eyes.

"Where did you find these? I've never seen them before."

"They were in my dad's desk when we started packing and selling everything. Well, Gordon found them."

"These are so cool. Thanks, love."

After exchanging a few more gifts, we cleaned up and headed downstairs to watch our movies.

"This was more entertaining as a kid," Brooks groaned.

I threw a pillow at him. "Hey, it's a classic!"

"Okay, but still boring."

Brooks' fingers tickled my side, causing me to giggle.

"Stop!" I wheezed.

"Uh-uh." He pushed me down on the sofa, pinning me beneath him, tickling me until I was completely out of breath, and begging him to let me breathe. His hands rested on either side of my face while my chest heaved, trying to catch my breath. His blue eyes sparkled with a genuine smile as he looked down at me.

"You..." I gasped, "I will make you pay..." I took another breath, "for that."

He just continued to grin at me and shook his head.

"I don't think so," he chuckled.

His tone was light and playful, but the look in his eyes ignited something low in my core. The air became hot and heavy between us, and our moment of silliness was gone in a flash. His mouth devoured me before I had fully regained my breath.

Every nerve ending was on high alert as his hands moved down my sides, squeezing every inch as they descended. His body weight pressed me further into the sofa, and I locked my legs behind him, pulling him closer.

Forty minutes later, our coffee was cold, and our clothes were hanging on every piece of furniture, including our new tree, while Charlie Brown's Christmas credits rolled.

"Are you hungry?" he asked, running his hands through his hair.

"No, I'm still full from the cookies," I replied, feeling content to just lay wrapped in his arms for the rest of the day.

"How about a workout to burn it all off?" he suggested.

I groaned at the thought of exercising but eventually stood up anyway. He remained seated under a pile of blankets. "Race you!" I chuckled before darting up the stairs, making it to our room just before he did.

"You get ten extra burpees for that little routine," Brooks laughed as he lifted my shirt over my head.

We changed into our workout clothes; I chose my black Lulu shorts and sports bra, while Brooks opted for my favorite joggers of his. They fit him in such a way that I couldn't help but pause and admire. I'd never been particularly into guys' butts, but those joggers made me reconsider my priorities.

Brooks turned on heavier rock music and led our warm-up before moving to chin-ups on the power rack. While he showed off, I focused on doing squats with our Tonal.

"Quit checking me out and get to work," he playfully barked.

"I can't help it," I replied, doing another squat. "Have you seen your backside lately?"

"Emily, I swear to God, get moving," he chuckled.

As he started to slow down, I knocked out another squat.

"Ooh, I like it when you get bossy," I said, grinning at him.

He chuckled again and jumped down from the station. After drying himself off with a towel, he approached me while I obediently did my squats. On my last set, he playfully whipped the towel against my backside. It stung, but all I could do was laugh.

"Your turn on the bar. Let's go," he ordered.

Reluctantly, I jumped for the chin-up bar while Brooks spotted me.

"I'm going to die. I can't do this," I complained as I struggled through my first repetition.

"Yes, you can. Ten! Let's go. Don't give up," he encouraged.

I managed to do two more.

"No, really, I'm weak. I haven't done these in a long time," I said.

"You can do it, baby. No talking. Just power through. Keep your core tight."

I nodded and did another five. I thought I was going to fall. My arms shook, and sweat rolled down my back in thick beads.

"Two more, Em. Don't think, just do."

I nodded and powered through the last two. His arms came up around me on the last one and brought me down.

"Good girl," he whispered, then bit my ear playfully. "Push-ups, let's get 'em done."

Something about the way he commanded but also encouraged had me dropping to my knees even though I was positive he was trying to kill me. He knelt beside me, and together, we counted them out. I dropped off at twenty-two and rolled to my back. Brooks didn't hesitate a beat before hovering over me, still pumping his out.

Each time he hit the bottom, he would place a kiss on my face and then back up. Each time he brought his body down on mine, my hips rocked forward, causing him to laugh through each number he called out.

"I think we should practice this in the bedroom," I teased. Brooks' smile just widened as he stayed focused. Once he was done with his ridiculous one hundred and forty-three push-ups, I was a wet mess, not just from the sweat from our bodies.

"You owe me ten burpees," he said between breaths. He took a long sip of water, his eyes never leaving mine. I was still lying on the floor, trying to calm my arousal. "C'mon, Em," he goaded.

"Ugh, fine." I stood and turned so that my butt was just inches from him. I bent over nice and slow to "retie" my shoe. It was laced perfectly, but a little tease wouldn't hurt him.

"Nice try." He slapped my butt. "Do the burpees and finish the workout. Tonight, we can play." He took another sip of his water.

"Fine." I stepped forward and did my best ten burpees with some flair at the end. I turned toward him, placed a kiss on his chest, and then made sure to rub my stomach across his front. He inhaled sharply.

"Take a breather, then start your sets on deadbugs," he said before returning to the power rack.

I sat on the mat, catching my breath while Brooks moved onto his chest. The way his muscles flexed, the deep valleys between muscles, and his perfectly tan skin with inked arms had a permanent warmth settling low in my tummy. I decided then and there that weekly workout sessions together needed to be foreplay.

"Emily," he begged, his eyes meeting mine.

"Oh, right. Sorry." I shrugged and laid back, and got to work on my core.

After an intense hour of sweat and nearly tears, we both found ourselves in the sauna. I lay across the wooden bench while Brooks sat beside me, his thigh resting near my head. His eyes were closed, and his breathing was steady. We remained inside for twenty minutes before I crawled out, quite literally. The infrared sauna was conveniently installed next to the bathroom, featuring a steam shower.

Brooks chuckled as I collapsed onto the cool wooden floor. I was exhausted and ready to crawl into a cold bath, but Brooks had other plans. He lifted me into his arms, my jello legs wrapped around his waist, and carried me upstairs.

How he still had the strength to carry me up two levels was beyond me, but I was ready for it. Just when I thought he was going to strip me bare and do something about his exquisite erection, he slapped my butt and told me to shower quickly because he was taking me to George's.

Thirty-eight minutes later, we pulled into the parking lot of a little diner. It was clad in stainless steel and neon lights, featuring a red sign that read "George's Diner" above the front door.

"How have I never seen this before?" Brooks asked as he got out of the car. "You could probably see it from space."

"So dramatic," I teased, though he was right. The neon lights made it stand out against the dark night.

As we entered the dining room, I was reminded of last year. The same black-and-white checkered tiles and red leather booths with white Formica tables greeted us. A thick red stripe lined the ceiling, and a white beadboard ran halfway up the walls. Above the beadboard were random photos and maps of Pacific Coves, depicting the town's early days when it was still being settled. Everything was a tribute to the 1950s.

"Please, take a seat anywhere. We'll be right with you," an elderly man said over his shoulder while delivering plates of burgers and fries to a family in the far corner of the restaurant.

"Do you think that's George?" Brooks asked as we made our way to the open booth on our right.

"Shh..." I giggled. "What if he hears you?"

I settled into the worn, comfy leather seat and noticed that Brooks had chosen to sit beside me instead of taking the bench across from me. It struck me that exactly one year ago, I was sitting next to Brooks in the same restaurant where I had sat across from Grey, convincing myself that I needed to move on.

"What's good here?" Brooks asked as he glanced at the extensive menu.

"The burgers," replied an elderly man who had appeared at our table. "Are you from around here?" he inquired.

"Yes, we are newlyweds. It's our first time here," Brooks responded. It was his first time; I had spent six hours here the previous year.

"Many years," the man smiled. "I am George, the owner."

Brooks's face lit up as he shook the man's hand while I pretended to study the menu to hide my laughter.

"We'll take two burgers, fries, and your best milkshake to share," Brooks ordered.

I set my menu down and looked at him with a big, goofy smile, feeling like we were two teenagers again sharing a shake. George hurried away with our menus.

"Merry Christmas, Em," Brooks said as he pulled me to his side and kissed the top of my head.

Chapter Seventy-Three

The days between Christmas and our New Year's party were hectic. Brooks had left the day after Christmas to handle a sudden work emergency in Seattle, which he was vague about, but he promised he would be home by the end of the week.

I knew he and Michaelson were gathering more information about the missing funds and considering hiring private companies to conduct an investigation. For the moment, everything was still very hush-hush. I decided to let him worry about the missing funds while I focused on our upcoming party.

The girls and I had been busy finalizing the guest count, which had climbed to over a hundred. The locals seemed excited, and we loved the opportunity to give back to our community by hosting the event. Our dresses were hanging in the upstairs guest room, hemmed and steamed, and all that remained was our final meeting with the museum event planner, Lucy.

With a busy day ahead, I slipped on my running shoes and started my favorite playlist. The weather was clear and calming, birds sang beautifully in the treetops, and the ocean roared its soothing melody. I ran to the edge of town and back, keeping the run short so I would have enough time to get ready.

At home, I rushed through my shower and got ready. When I ran downstairs, Mrs. Hall was making breakfast for me. I ate quickly and sipped my tea before calling Brooks when I got in the car.

"Good morning, beautiful," he answered, his voice warm and comforting.

"Good morning, my love. How's Seattle today?" I asked, wanting to hear more and missing him so much.

"Crisp and lonely."

I laughed lightly. "Well, I miss you too. I'm on my way to meet with Lucy."

"Right. Well, I promise I'll be home on Wednesday," he reassured me.

"You better be," I teased with a smile.

He chuckled softly this time. "Oh, and Michaelson is going to fly home with me. He said he can hire a car to take him back to Seattle."

"Or Natalie could take him." Did I have ulterior motives? Yes, I did because I wanted my best friend and his best friend to fall happily in love. Playing matchmaker was becoming my favorite pastime. If I could pair off Natalie and Michaelson and Sara and Connor—who cares if they hate each other?—then life would be perfect.

After saying my goodbyes to Brooks, which still made my heart ache, I pulled into a parking spot just a few minutes later and jumped out with my bag in hand. Lucy was waiting for me at the door. She was dressed in a burnt orange suit with black pumps, looking amazing against her dark, carob skin. Her big, round, brown eyes were bright, especially compared to mine, which were probably shadowed by dark circles from nights of tossing and turning.

"Emily, how are you?" She reached her arms out to me and air-kissed my cheek.

"I'm well, thanks! How was your Christmas?" I asked.

"It was wonderful! Our daughters woke us up at the crack of dawn, begging to open presents. They were so adorable we couldn't say no."

I felt a twinge of jealousy. Brooks and I hadn't talked about kids since we were decorating for Christmas, and while I knew he had given me a timeline, it still stung. I wasn't in any rush to get pregnant, but putting a halt to what we had both envisioned for so long was painful in more ways than one. It also made our intimate moments feel slightly less romantic, knowing we weren't on the same page and wondering what he would do.

"Brooks and I used to do that to our parents when we were kids. It drove them nuts in the best way possible. Is anyone else here yet?" I asked, changing subjects.

"No, not yet," she said. "While we wait, maybe we can do a quick walkthrough?"

"Sure."

↟ ↟ ↟

The day had finally arrived. I was finishing the last few sips of my London Fog from Lulu's when Brooks walked in. The deep v of his hips was even more pronounced today, and his joggers hung a little lower than usual. I nearly chewed off my lip as he strode toward me, his body pumped from his workout and his dark hair tousled in a sexy-but I didn't have to try mess.

"Morning, love," he greeted.

"Good morning," I replied, nearly choking on the last sip of my tea. He kissed the top of my head and turned toward the coffee maker.

"What time are you meeting the girls at the salon?" he asked.

"In about thirty minutes."

He nodded at me before returning to pack the coffee grounds.

"What are you doing today?" I asked, raising an eyebrow slightly.

"I figured I would get some more work done."

"Brooks." My hands slid around him as I pressed my lips to his shoulder, feeling his muscles tighten ever so slightly beneath my touch. The throbbing ache between my legs intensified as my palms glided over the warm skin stretched over his muscles.

"Baby, I thought you needed to go?" His voice was husky as he turned to face me, a smug smile dancing on his lips.

"I have a few minutes," I said in a husky voice.

"More than enough time." He grinned against my parted lips before dropping to his knees to pull down my leggings. His lips were soft on my inner thigh as he worked his way back to my mouth, stopping to kiss, nip, or lick, leaving my whole body on fire and ready for him.

He pulled his pants down to expose his length, which was rock hard and dripping with excitement for me. I swiped my thumb over the swollen head, stealing his arousal to sample for myself. He watched as I licked the pad of my thumb and moaned.

Matching my greediness, he lifted me and pulled my legs around his waist before my back slammed into the wall. At the same time, he shoved into me with a force that told me he was going for a gold medal.

My head fell to the side as I took every inch of him, stretching to accommodate him.

"Look at me," he said, tilting my chin up.

I opened my eyes and found his a deep blue, hooded with pleasure. Somehow, that made everything more intimate, more pleasurable. It felt like my heart was trying to jump out of my chest and into his.

"Tell me what you want, Em," he grunted with another thrust that had my back sliding against the wall.

"I...I want you to come with me. Don't pull out, please." My voice was nothing more than a broken whisper. "It's not...my window."

"I'll come with you, baby."

I nodded and closed my eyes again, unable to focus. He set a punishing rhythm with his thrusts, and his mouth moved along my neck, sucking and licking, careful not to leave a mark.

I needed this. I needed him inside of me, over me, everywhere, all at once. Brooks was the very air I breathed, the blood running through my veins. I would never have enough of him. With a few more grunts, moans, and thrusts, I was barely holding on by a thread.

"Let go," he demanded. His voice was gruff as the wave of ecstasy rolled through me and left me crying out as I clamped down around him. At the same time, I felt him pulsing in me as he hit my wall harder and harder as he grew. I could never tire of this feeling. Feeling so completely lost in each other.

My name fell from his full lips as he emptied himself inside of me, and his body shuddered through the last few strokes of our combined orgasms.

He pulled back and looked at me with so much love that I wanted to cry, just from all the emotions constantly swarming inside me. He gripped my head and planted another long kiss on my forehead.

"See you later, beautiful," he said, his voice warm and teasing.

"I love you. I love you. I love you," I chanted, not ready to leave our little bubble.

"I love you too, baby." His eyes sparkled with affection. I paused, and the corner of my mouth rose in a playful smile.

"What?" he asked, grazing my bottom lip with his thumb, sending a shiver down my spine.

"You said too. You never say too," I pointed out with a teasing lilt.

He rolled his eyes. "Fine, I love you." His emphasis on the "*you*" was exaggerated, and I couldn't help but chuckle as I readjusted my clothes. I left him standing in the kitchen, the sound of his laughter trailing after me.

I was a few minutes late to the salon, and the girls were already there.

"Wow, how good was it?" Monica teased, a knowing smirk on her face.

"I don't know what you're talking about, Gossip McGee," I responded, trying to suppress my smile.

"Oh, come on," Natalie chimed in, crossing the room with a smirk of her own, "It's all over your face."

I rolled my eyes in faux annoyance. "I don't know what you guys are talking about," I lied as I hugged Natalie, hoping to distract them from the truth.

"Liar," Leah chimed, still studying hairstyles on her phone.

"Who's a liar?" asked Jenny, one of the stylists, as she came to the sitting area to bring us back.

"Just Emily. She got laid this morning and won't admit it," Monica said in mock indignation as she walked toward the salon chairs.

"I mean, she's not wrong. You do look..." Jenny paused, eyeing me up and down. "Well ridden?" She laughed.

"You guys are awful. All of you," I replied, pointing around the room at each grinning face staring back at me.

"It's just that your sex life is exciting, and ours... isn't," Leah said, her voice piping up from behind me.

"Well, make it exciting," I groaned, sinking into the plush chair in front of Aleksandr, my stylist. He towered over me with his tall, lean frame and blonde hair that fell in messily over his forehead.

His know-it-all attitude was obvious as he assessed my hair with an arched eyebrow. He was always dressed in all black and sported a collection of faded band t-shirts. His arms were covered in tattoos, adding to the edgy vibe he exuded. I wondered how he managed to seem so effortlessly cool while I felt utterly mundane in comparison.

"My sex life is fine, thank you," he responded, tossing my hair over my shoulder so he could snap the cape around my neck.

"Mine too," Morgan chimed in, another stylist who had four kids and a rocking body.

"See," I teased Leah.

"A few pointers would be nice," Monica inquired from Jenny's seat.

"I don't know. How about ripping your clothes off as a subtle way to tell him to pay attention? Or, if you're comfortable, just talk about what you want. Make a game of it. Also, don't be afraid to just have sex wherever, whenever. The spontaneous interactions are so much more fun and exciting."

"My dog likes to watch. I can't do that." Megan, the other stylist, shuddered.

"I'm with you," Aleksandr whispered into my ear before grabbing a brush and running it through my hair. A full-body shudder rippled down my spine.

"New topic. Did you guys hear that Ashton, the new barista at Lulu's, just had a screaming match with her abusive ex in the coffee shop? Vasyl called the cops, and I guess there's a restraining order against him now. Chloe was telling me all about it last night at Patrick's," Megan began to gossip. I rolled my eyes and closed them, enjoying the feeling of Aleksandr brushing my hair. This small town was full of gossip, and I hoped my sex life wouldn't become part of it.

Patrick's, the local bar, was the center of the gossip wheel, though this salon was probably a close second. These girls thrived on the gossip of others, while Aleksandr, my beautiful Russian, just smiled and laughed at it all, always staying quiet. He once told me he wasn't one to kiss and tell. This was after Brooks arrived, and the town was in full-blown gossip mode about the new arrival and me dumping Grey, their self-proclaimed "most eligible bachelor."

The rumors spread quickly, and a few of them made me laugh. One claimed that Brooks and Grey had gotten into a fistfight in my living room, declaring Brooks the winner. Another suggested that Grey kissed me, prompting Brooks to declare his love for me. There were several others, including one about me leaving Grey high and dry and another about Brooks being Grey's estranged brother.

Eventually, the town moved on to more exciting topics, such as Morgan expecting another baby and Chloe getting into trouble with the law for breaking into the local library in the middle of the night just to read in peace. Despite the multitude of stories circulating, none resembled the actual truth.

The latest gossip was about the town's mayor, Sheena Girardi, who had a child while still in high school and gave her up for adoption. Her daughter, Keegan, recently showed up in town to introduce herself. Keegan is married to a man named Henry Delton III, who comes from a family that helped build half of a wealthy city on the East Coast and vacations at Martha's Vineyard. Mrs. Girardi felt humiliated by the revelation, but now they are trying to build a relationship, and her husband has forgiven her for keeping this secret.

By the time Aleksandr finished styling my hair, Natalie, Leah, and Monica were just wrapping up. The salon closed early so they could attend the party with their significant others.

When we arrived back at my house, Sara was already inside with Brooks and Connor. Michaelson had just arrived as well, while Natalie disappeared with him.

"Hey, B!" I called out as I stepped through the front door.

"Upstairs," Sara replied with a smile, crossing the room to hug me. Seeing her filled me with a familiar sense of longing.

"Hey, we missed you at the salon," I said, wrapping my arms around her neck. She smelled like sunshine - if that's even a thing.

"I know. Connor was taking forever to finish his work," she replied, letting out a long groan.

"Wait, you two rode together and didn't kill each other?" I asked, surprised.

"Daddy Lucifer needed his fiery chariot for another event," Connor interjected as he crossed the room to greet me.

Sara shot him a glare while I struggled to stifle a giggle at the daggers she seemed to be aiming at him.

"My car is currently in the shop for a tune-up," she said, glancing back at me with a hint of frustration. "Dad wouldn't let me borrow his, and since I can't rent a car yet, I was left with no choice but to take this alternative." She turned to Connor, a playful smirk on her face. "Conman." With a playful swing of her arm, she gave him a light slap in the stomach, surprising and making him gasp for air.

"You're the worst! I should have pushed you out of the car," he retorted, still catching his breath.

"Believe me, it might have been safer than riding with you in that 'death trap' and enduring the smell of the trench," she shot back with a laugh.

"You're welcome for the ride and your safe arrival, Princess of Darkness," he said, chuckling as he took a theatrical bow. She shot him a mock glare. "Make sure Daddy Lucy teaches you to shoot fireballs later!" he called out as he walked away, flipping her hair over her head with playful mischief. Their banter was filled with good-natured fun, brightening the mood for everyone around.

I bit my lips to suppress the grin spreading across my face and raised my eyebrows. Something had shifted between Sara and Connor. It was an unusual pairing: Sara, my eternal hype-girl, the party girl often loud and obnoxious, and Connor, our sweet, stable, and funny friend. He could help calm her down.

Sara rolled her eyes and shooed him away after he gave me a quick hug. Or not.

"Gosh, he smells like rotting seaweed and brine. He's the absolute worst human! I seriously don't understand how you can be friends with that asshat," she exclaimed.

I snorted. Her passion for disliking him could easily be converted into passionate love, not that I wanted to point that out. You know, the fine line between love and hate and all that.

"Sara, he's a surfer; I think he smells like the ocean. He's not the worst, either. I love him. I told you once, but I'll say it again—he's a package deal when it comes to me."

"Yeah, eww. You're lucky I love you enough to put up with that half-human," she replied.

I rolled my eyes and turned back to hold the door open for the rest of the girls, who were piling in with their make-up bags and accessories. While Sara chatted with the others, I ran upstairs.

Brooks was pacing back and forth in the bedroom. When I entered, he looked up and pointed to the earbud. I ducked out quietly, but Brooks yanked the door open and pulled me back inside. The door shut softly behind me before he pinned me against it with his hips. His hands found their way under my shirt and softly brushed over my curves.

"I don't care what the contract says. Fix it," he barked. I pinched my lips together, trying to hide the smile that threatened to take over my face. Being pinned between a bossy Brooks and the door had my mind racing down a dirty path, and my body was all too eager to wish into fruition.

"No. Call Danny back and tell him we need him there with the whole team first thing in the morning, or we will have our lawyers kindly remind him what his job is."

Brooks tapped the mute button and buried his tongue into my mouth without warning. My arms swept up and around his neck, pulling him closer.

"How was your day?" he asked with a warm smile on his face despite the argument he was having on the phone.

"Really good. Yours?"

I was met with a finger to my lips, silencing me.

"Tell Danny he has two hours to decide. I want it in writing. Call me back." Brooks hung up the phone with an exaggerated sigh, burying his face in my neck.

"Are you okay?" I asked, genuinely concerned.

"Remind me why we took this on. I hate being a grumpy boss, but sometimes it seems necessary."

I couldn't help but chuckle. "B, you're doing great. They just need a tough leader. You can be one person at work and come home and be your soft, romantic self with me."

"Soft? That's not exactly what I was going for. I prefer 'handsome, irresistible, and protective.' Soft? No," he said with a teasing glint before he tickled me.

"Okay, okay. Not soft. Definitely handsome, completely irresistible, and always protective. You know you make me feel safe."

He dragged his nose along my neck, pushing his hips into me further, enveloping me in his warmth.

"I need to go get ready," I said breathlessly. "I'm going to leave this room before I end up naked and begging for round two," I said, trying my hardest to push thoughts of him pressing me against the door while he buried himself in me.

"My little temptress," he groaned. I rolled my eyes and slid out from under him, prying the door open like the room was on fire.

"See ya." I winked.

Brooks stepped out of the master bedroom with a joyful expression, quickly approaching me for a kiss. He greeted the girls with a smile, then leaned in to whisper something inappropriate in my ear before heading downstairs to join Connor and Michaelson.

↟ ↟ ↟

I was genuinely amazed at how the quirky Pacific Coves Library and Astronomy Center had transformed into a beautiful event space. In the center of the room, a makeshift dance floor had been set up, adorned with twinkling lights that sprawled overhead. A strobe light cast various colors onto the dance floor while the DJ played music nearby. Overhead, several screens displayed the night sky.

Cocktail tables lined both sides of the room, decorated with tall centerpieces and cascading white florals draping over champagne-colored linens. The servers were dressed in black uniforms with white aprons and carried acrylic trays. I turned to Lucy, who seemed pleased with how everything had come together.

"Wow, Lucy. Thank you," I said.

"Of course! Thanks for letting us host you all," she replied.

I glanced back at Brooks, who was mingling with the guys in the corner near the bar. Just past the bar was the outdoor patio area, which had also been transformed into a cozy sitting area with more twinkling lights. There was soft furniture instead of the usual wrought iron tables and chairs, creating a welcoming atmosphere.

I slipped my arm around Brooks' back to remind him that we needed to get ready to open the doors and greet our guests—who happened to be half the town. Brooks excused himself, and together, we made our way to the front doors where Lucy was waiting. A line had already formed outside, and our guests were eager to enter. I nodded to Lucy, and she opened the doors.

Chapter Seventy-Four

Brooks and I spent the next thirty minutes welcoming our guests, friends, and coworkers, all dressed in gowns and tuxedos. The DJ had already gotten a group on the dance floor, and the chatter and excitement in the room were palpable. I could feel the energy and low buzz resonate through my entire body.

This was probably the most exciting event that had taken place in our little town. The last significant event was Sapphire's opening last year. Wow—was it really a year ago? Well, not quite, but close enough.

My mind drifted back to when I stood outside Sapphire, crying because talking to Brooks had overwhelmed my heart. After all these years, my heart still only beats for him.

Once the last couple arrived, Brooks finally took my hand. Together, we made our way to the front of the dance floor to officially welcome everyone and share information about the donations we collected for Alex's Lemonade Stand.

After our brief introduction, I was excited to dance with my handsome husband, who looked sharp in his black tuxedo and mauve bow tie, perfectly matching my dress. Brooks took my hand and twirled me to the center as we stepped onto the dance floor.

My heart swelled as he pressed his lips to my forehead and held me close. Life had been difficult, but I knew things would get better. They had to. Brooks and I deserved a happy future, and I was determined to fight for it.

Songs came and went, and my husband never took his eyes off me. When the music picked up, he spun me out of his arms, and when it slowed down, he pulled me back to his chest, where we swayed softly to the tune.

By the time we came up for air, my blonde hair was sticking to my face and chest, and my skin felt like it was boiling.

"C'mon," he said, taking my hand. "Let's get some food for you." He led me through the side door to a patio area that had been set up. The server came by and dropped off a few plates of different foods for us.

Michaelson and Natalie were already on the patio, and Natalie was sitting in his lap, his tongue deep in her mouth. The door slammed shut, startling them apart. They turned in unison to see Brooks and me smiling back at them.

"Shut up," Natalie said, her cheeks flushing a deep shade of pink.

"I didn't say anything," I replied, casually taking a seat on the opposite sofa, trying to lighten the mood.

"Nice, man," Brooks teased with a playful grin as he plopped down next to me and draped his arm around my shoulders, pulling me into him.

Michaelson shrugged nonchalantly, glancing at Natalie with a smirk, while she playfully slapped his chest.

"So, uh," I cleared my throat, trying to gather my thoughts, "how long has this been a thing?"

"Officially?" Natalie asked, glancing at Michaelson as if asking his thoughts on the matter.

"A couple of weeks," Michaelson replied, his eyes lighting up as he shot an amused glance at Natalie.

"A couple of weeks?" Brooks echoed, raising an eyebrow in surprise.

"Yeah, after we got back from Southport," Natalie admitted.

I looked at Brooks and laughed, resting my head on his chest. I inhaled the scent of his amber cologne and allowed his warmth and relaxation to wash over me. How had she kept it a secret all this time? It didn't matter; I was happy for them both.

Sara and Connor drifted out, taking seats as far apart as possible while still participating in the conversation.

It was just past eight when we decided to stop mingling and head back to the dance floor. We swayed to a slower song by Jaymes Young, which had replaced The Lumineers.

"How about Greece in April?" Brooks whispered in my ear.

"I think that sounds amazing. Can we island-hop?" I replied.

"Of course. We can start planning tomorrow if you want."

I nodded and squeezed Brooks tighter. "I think our parents would be happy for us."

"Yeah, me too." His mouth descended to mine, his tongue tracing the outline of my lips.

A loud commotion from the other side of the dance floor caught our attention, pulling us apart and drawing us toward the source of the disturbance as the crowd gasped and parted. A group of police officers and FBI agents were making their way into the room. Brooks stepped forward to ask them what was happening as the officers split into two groups. To the right, Paul Woodman, our CFO, was being thrown against a table and arrested.

My head spun as I tried to comprehend what was happening. We were at a party, and they were arresting Paul? Why?

"Paul Woodman, you are under arrest for embezzlement and tax fraud involving Caston funds. You have the right to remain silent and the right to an attorney. If you cannot afford an attorney, one will be appointed to you."

The words hit me like a punch to the gut as I searched for Brooks.

No, they had to be mistaken. But then I remembered Brooks mentioning that something had been off with the invoices—something Paul would have had full access to.

Oh my god, had Paul been stealing from our company all along, and we had no idea? It didn't make sense. He had been part of Caston for as long as I could remember.

The music stopped abruptly, and our guests began to whisper among themselves. It felt like a scene from a terrible movie, where the record scratches and whispers fill the silence. My heart raced as I found Brooks in the crowd and clung to him, trying to ground myself.

"What the hell is this about?" Brooks stepped into the whirlwind of activity in the center of the room, his presence commanding attention. An agent acknowledged Brooks with a nod, and two others approached us.

"Brooks Devonshire, you are under arrest for allegedly aiding in the embezzlement by your CFO'," one agent announced. Another agent forcefully separated us, and it felt like a physical blow to my heart.

My stomach flipped, bile raced up my throat, and my legs wobbled beneath me, threatening to give out. I glanced over at Brooks whose expression mirrored my own fear and heartbreak.

"I didn't do anything!" he protested, but I knew it was meant to reassure me. Needing to hold him, I lunged towards him, but another agent stepped in front of me, blocking my path. I struggled against her grip, my pleas filling the air as I fought to reach Brooks. All I wanted was to tell him that everything would be okay.

"You have the right to an attorney..." the agents continued, their words fading into the background as my world spun around me. Deep down, I knew Brooks was innocent, and yet here he was, being treated like a criminal in front of our entire community.

Just then, Natalie grabbed my arm from behind, steadying me gently. "It's okay," she whispered. Michaelson appeared beside her, his face stern but concerned. I shook my head defiantly, determined to break free once more. Just then, Connor wrapped his arm around me, holding me close as I pleaded for him to let me go.

"We'll get it sorted, Brooks. I'll call our legal team," Michaelson said, interrupting me. "Shit," he whispered, grinding his molars. The agents turned their attention to Michaelson.

"Are you Michaelson Hughes, his chief of staff?" one agent asked.

"Yes," Michaelson replied.

"Please come with us for questioning," another agent said. They didn't handcuff him, but they surrounded him, making it clear that he had no choice but to comply. The fight drained out of me, and I sagged in Connor's arms.

"He'll be okay, Mils. Calm down, or they'll arrest you, too," Connor said against my ear so no one but me could hear him.

"We have to do something," I cried, my voice breaking under the weight of panic.

"Emily, baby, it's okay. We'll get this sorted out," Brooks said, his tone meant to be calming, but the fear etched across his face betrayed him. Confusion swirled in my mind like a storm, the urgent thoughts racing through me as I desperately thought of a way to help him.

The agents had already escorted Paul out of the venue, and now Brooks was being pushed forward, handcuffed like a criminal. Michaelson followed close behind him. I felt Natalie squeeze my hand tightly, steadying me. Connor released my hand but stayed close by my side.

Suddenly, Thomas Clark, our Vice President, emerged from the crowd, his expression serious as he rushed toward us. Leaning in, he whispered urgently for us to follow him. Without hesitation, Natalie and I followed him and Connor promised that he would handle the guests and keep the event running smoothly. Not that there was a real chance of that happening. We'd soon be the biggest source of gossip.

As we navigated through the crowd, I stumbled a bit, feeling disoriented and sick. I was practically being tugged along by Natalie.

Each step toward the door felt weighed down with uncertainty and fear. How could this night have ended so badly? Everything had been perfect until the FBI showed up and arrested Brooks. They arrested my husband. This couldn't be real. It felt like a nightmare I couldn't wake from.

Chapter Seventy-Five

Tears tracked silently down my cheeks as Thomas drove Natalie and I back to my house. The sky was black and the cloud cover hid the moon and stars. Funny how the weather and sky always seemed to mimic my emotions.

Brooks was surely innocent, right? I mean he had told me about the missing funds. He had been working late and been looking into other companies. But why would Paul steal the money? He had worked at Caston for so long. He was one of the highest paid employees.

I didn't know much about business law and legal proceedings, but the FBI couldn't just arrest someone without plausible cause. Or could they? A bone-deep chill settled in and my fear for my husband seized my breath. What if Brooks went to prison? I'd lose him too. Vomit burned my throat but I managed to swallow it down.

Natalie wrapped an arm around me and I noticed fresh tears welling her eyes. Why did tonight have to go to hell?

"He's innocent. Brooks wouldn't steal money from our company," I murmured. I wasn't sure who I was talking to. I was just stating that reality. Maybe it was an accident or maybe he signed off on something he shouldn't have.

He was a brand new CEO of a multi-billion dollar corporation, and yes, the board and executive team had been working with him during the hand-off, but maybe he messed up unknowingly. Why would he steal from our company? We had more money than we knew what to do with. Doubt filled my mind, like a little devil on my shoulder whispering *but what if.*

Deep down I knew Brooks wouldn't have done this - at least not on purpose. He was the one looking into this, not causing it. My mind kept swirling with possibilities of both his innocence and accusations that I knew he was innocent of.

Thomas pulled up to our gate and I gave him the code before we drove through the trees and up the winding drive to the house. The home I shared with my husband who wasn't here right now because he was just arrested. Where had they taken him? I seriously lacked knowledge in this area. Was he behind bars? Were they taking his photo in front of those white poster things? Would I be able to talk to him?

"How long will they keep Brooks?" I asked. "He has to come home right? Innocent until proven guilty and all that." Natalie shrugged and we got out of the car and I punched in the code robotically on the front door, letting the three of us in.

My cell phone kept pinging with text messages, but I ignored them all.

"I'll make a call to the rest of the board," Thomas said, slipping away into the kitchen while Natalie and I went upstairs.

"I'm sure it will get cleared up and it's just a big misunderstanding," Natalie said with a slight grimace. We both changed into leggings and sweaters and pulling our hair into top knots.

I paced my bedroom thinking about everything Brooks had told me over the past few months. Surely there was evidence somewhere.

I didn't know what I was looking for but surely he had kept files. Just then, there was a knock on the door downstairs, and I called out to Thomas that I would get it.

Several FBI agents were at the door and pushed their way in, asking me to give them access to Brooks' work computer and any Caston documents we kept in our home. Thomas met me at the door, asking for a warrant and they shoved it in his face. They also took my computer, telling me I'd get it back when they were done going through it. My hope for finding evidence to help Brooks went to nothing.

Another car pulled up and more of the Caston executive team got out, walking up the steps.

"Emily, Weston is on his way right now," Diane said.

One of the agents blocked their entrance.

"I'm sorry. I will need all of you to come in for questioning before I can let you in," the agent said. Diane reared back, looking to the other three members of our team.

"Very well," she huffed. The agent held out a hand, motioning for them to get into the black SUV that was still running. The agents I had let into the house came out from the study with our computers and files in plastic bags. I backed away from the door, feeling too small and lacking all confidence. I owned this company and it was being torn to shreds and I had no idea what to do about it.

"Mrs. Devonshire, I would recommend you stay here. You will be brought in soon, I'm sure." The agent blocking the door left without a backward glance and the three SUVs that were in the driveway, disappeared with only their red tail lights illuminating their retreat.

I closed the door, finding Thomas and Natalie there with coffees in hand.

"Let's talk," Thomas said.

↟ ↟ ↟

"Emily, what has Brooks told you about those financial

documents?" Ethan Chapman, our COO, was pacing back and forth behind the couch. His gray suit was wrinkled and his tie was hanging loosely around his neck.

They had all been cleared and questioned over the past two hours and now were sitting in my living room. All I could hope for was that they knew what they were doing because I sure as hell didn't.

"I don't know. I don't remember. He just mentioned that the Kildaire invoices didn't add up. Something about money going missing." I groaned, frustrated with myself. I should have asked more questions. I should have pushed him to let me in. "He said he was looking into it." *Unless he didn't want you to know.* I wanted to punch myself every time a thought like that swept through my mind.

"Weston just called, agents will be here in five minutes. Emily, you need to go with them. Looks like it will be a long night," Diane huffed, accepting another cup of coffee from Mrs. Hall.

"He's innocent. I know he is," I said, my voice broke but I needed to push through this. How could I be in charge of this company if I wasn't willing to fight for it. If I couldn't face the hardship placed in front of me. I sucked in a sharp breath and pulled myself together. "What do I need to do?" I asked.

"We will get things sorted out. It's going to take some time though, so for now, just tell them everything you know," Ethan said. "Weston will meet you there."

There was a loud pounding on the door from the FBI agents. Mrs. Hall let them in and several officers filled the room.

"Mrs. Devonshire, we need you to come with us." One of the female officers gestured with one hand.

"Yep," I said, refusing to give them the satisfaction of seeing me break. I grabbed my coat from the closet and slipped into my favorite pair of Sambas. I clenched my fists together, feeling the bite of my nails in my palms as I left my house.

Ethan, Diane, Andrea, and Rebecca all remained in my living room discussing how to get ahead of the publicity and discussing our stocks tanking. Dan Ford, our Chief Sales Officer, had already been brought in, up in Seattle, along with Jake Newman, our CTO. I knew the news was already all over town and online, despite the fact I had been ignoring my phone.

Instead of the Pacific Coves Police Station, we were brought to an older office building just on the edge of town. It looked like they had created a makeshift FBI office. I was ushered down the hall to an open door. Inside, Weston and Brooks were standing with another officer.

I broke into a sprint and leaped into his arms. He caught me, holding my vibrating body to his chest while I buried my face in his neck. He was okay. He was here and he was okay. Maybe if I said it enough, I would believe it. I was crying before the agent that brought me in, was at our side.

"Mrs. Devonshire, please, let's go."

"Emily, you need to go with them. Tell them everything. We have nothing to hide," Brooks said, kissing me despite the watery mess on my face. I had exactly one second to examine him. The tightness around his eyes, his messy hair from hands being run through it, the way his smile fell flat.

"Mrs. Devonshire," Weston started.

I pulled away from Brooks and Weston was holding out an arm, waiting for me to follow the agent. I was ushered into a smaller office with bright lights and a faux wood desk. A layer of dust had settled on the surface of the desk.

"Mrs. Devonshire, mind if I call you Emily?"

I shook my head, biting down on my cheek and willing away the tears that threatened to make an appearance. *It's a mistake. He will be okay.* I kept repeating it over and over, almost willing it into existence. My palms had dark red crescent indents from my nails, but I continued to push them further into my palm, using the physical pain to hold my emotional pain at bay.

"Okay, Emily. I'm Agent Cruze. Agent Dessen will be joining us here in a minute."

The door opened just as she finished the sentence and a tall, stoic man walked in.

"Agent Dessen, I was just talking about you. Okay, let's get started. Emily, please take a seat."

Agent Dessen set a stack of papers on the table in front of me, sending dust up into the air.

"So, tell me about Caston," Agent Cruze started.

I was in the room being questioned for over forty minutes. Everything from why I refused to initially step into a role at Caston, what Brooks was doing before he came home to Seattle, and even why I took an extended absence a few months ago. I was angry they were dragging my personal life into this, but I did as I was told. I told them everything I knew and more.

When I left the small office, I was still fighting the urge to cry. I did not want to let them see me break so I held strong. I was exhausted and confused and all I wanted was to curl up in bed with Brooks. My stomach soured, which was beginning to feel like a permanent state. Would Brooks even be coming home tonight?

The agents had several invoices with Brooks' signature on them that Paul had Brooks sign off on. There was clear evidence that Paul had been embezzling Caston funds for the past two and a half years. Now they just needed to figure out if Brooks was an accomplice or not.

It seemed to me that he was guilty until proven innocent. Not the other way around.

None of it added up. The offshore bank account, the fact that Brooks wasn't even at Caston two years ago, and yet, the evidence looked damning as hell. I couldn't believe Paul would do this.

I walked back into the main room alongside Weston, only to find it empty. Brooks was nowhere to be seen. Agent Cruze placed her hand on my back and ushered me back out into the parking lot.

"Mr. Devonshire is at home," she started as she pulled out of the parking lot. "There is an agent assigned to you both. You cannot leave town. For now, I wouldn't talk to anybody at Caston except for your lawyers." She kept talking but I tuned her out as I watched our little town pass by through the windows.

When I got home, Agent Cruze dropped me at the door where another agent was waiting. The agent assigned to me was Agent Rachel Booker. She was a younger lady, maybe mid-thirties, with dark brown hair. She had light, almond skin, and a soft smile.

"Mrs. Devonshire," she said, pushing me through the front door. Another agent was inside Agent Carter, who was assigned to Brooks. Brooks met me at the door and pulled me into his arms. I collapsed into him and sobbed.

"Shhh...it's okay baby. It's okay," he whispered. It was only when I took a few deep breaths that I noticed our living room was full of our friends. Sara, Conner, Michaelson, Natalie, and Grey Stanley. What was he doing here?

I stepped out of Brooks' arms and wiped my face. Brooks took my hand and together we walked into the living room. Michaelson was also assigned an agent. I felt like I was living out some dumb reality TV show. This wasn't my life. This didn't happen in real life.

Brooks and Michaelson filled me in about Kildaire and how they had seen a pattern for the past few months and were ready to present the evidence to Chris and Weston but were waiting until after the holidays.

Paul was being taken back to Seattle and was awaiting trial. The rest of the team were also being taken back to Seattle and not allowed to return to work until they were each cleared officially.

"I called my dad," Grey finally spoke. "He's going to make some calls tomorrow."

"Thank you," I said, forcing a small smile. I knew it took a lot for Grey to call his dad. They didn't exactly have a great relationship. I was so cold and tired as I sat beside Brooks. There was quiet chatter in the room but I wasn't paying attention to any of it.

"Let's go to bed, Em." Brooks stood, reaching for my hand.

I nodded, accepting his hand and allowing him to pull me into his side, into his familiar warmth and amber scent.

"Goodnight guys," Brooks said as he ushered me back to the stairs.

"Wait, are they staying?" I asked.

"Grey is heading to his condo. Natalie and Michaelson are staying in the studio and Sara and Connor will be here."

I nodded and wrapped my arms around Brooks' waist. Both agents nodded as we passed them.

I crawled into bed still wearing my leggings and sweater. Brooks crawled in beside me after undressing and pulled me into him. I settled into his warmth and fell asleep after a few deep breaths.

↟ ↟ ↟

I woke in a panic in a dark room. I was soaked in sweat and my heart was racing. I turned to see Brooks' side of the bed empty. I jumped out of bed and checked the bathroom. Then I was taking the stairs down to the study quicker than I ever had after looking over the railing in the loft to see the living room empty.

Agents Carter and Booker were nowhere to be seen. I opened the study door and found Brooks sitting on the Chesterfield with a glass of scotch in his hands. My breathing was still coming in and out heavily. Brooks waived for me to come sit with him. I crawled into his lap and wrapped my arms around his neck.

He was tense and smelled of more than one glass of Macallan. His arm pulled me into his chest as he sat back. I rested my head on his shoulder. The room was dark aside from the moonlight coming in through the glass room. The shadows on his face made every tense muscle even more defined.

"I love you," I whispered. Brooks relaxed beneath me.

"I love you. It's going to be okay, Em. Promise." I nodded and with that, I felt my own body relax. I believed him. No matter what, I knew Brooks was going to be by my side, and together we could walk through fire.

"I really need that vacation now," I chuckled despite the

unending waves of nausea and the bone-deep ache in my soul. Somewhere in the back of my mind, I knew this wasn't over, but I was too tired to deal with it right now. I just needed a moment's reprieve in my husband's arms.

He shot me a genuine smile. "Me too."

Chapter Seventy-Six

Brooks

After ensuring Emily was comfortably settled back in bed, her arms wrapped around a fluffy pillow as she nestled back into the sheets, I quietly slipped out of the room. The air was crisp as I stepped onto the deck, the faint chill of the early morning wrapping around me. Dawn was still a couple of hours away, but sleep felt like a distant memory, slipping further away no matter how hard I tried to grasp onto it.

At times, my life resembled an obstacle course—each day presenting a new challenge to navigate, and I couldn't shake the overwhelming fatigue that settled deep in my bones. Yet, I reminded myself that this latest trial was just another hurdle we would face together. *We* because I thought of Emily and I as a team, two halves of a whole, and I found solace in our combined strength.

I pulled on a heavy coat and walked over to the fireplace, feeling the reassuring warmth of the flames flickering to life as I lit it. I stood near the glass railing, peering into the darkness that enveloped the ocean, the rough waves crashing energetically against the cliffs below, though I couldn't see them clearly. It was hard to believe that when I had arrived here last year, I could never have imagined the tumultuous yet beautiful whirlwind our lives would become. We had experienced our share of lows, heartbreak, and uncertainty, but those were consistently outweighed by the exhilarating highs.

This view—this breathtaking spot—was what had captivated me from that very first night. I had instinctively known I would need a place where I could find peace, somewhere quiet to think and breathe, away from the chaos of life. I could vividly recall that first night standing on the deck below, my heart racing as I took Emily's hand in mine, hoping she would forgive me for the mistakes I had made. I desperately wished she would give us another chance to mend what had been broken.

My phone had been filled with countless photos of her that had kept me company over the years we were apart—images that held moments of joy and tenderness—along with a treasure trove of memories that played on repeat in my mind. Yet, nothing compared to the reality of having her by my side. The most unforgettable moment was when, without a second of hesitation, she had leaped into my arms as she opened her door. The warmth of her body against mine felt like an embrace of home, grounding and so damn familiar. To me, she was home—my sanctuary, my anchor, the other half of my soul.

At that moment, I had made a conscious effort to absorb every detail about her, mentally taking note of the subtle changes that had occurred over the years we were apart. She had transformed into a beautiful woman, not that I didn't find her breathtaking before. I had found myself captivated by the soft curve of her smile, the way her bright blue eyes sparkled more when she spoke about something that made her happy, and the way she kept blushing. I watched the way her nose scrunched up when laughter escaped her and then there was the sweet, almost instinctual gesture of her tucking her hair behind her ear whenever she felt shy or vulnerable, a simple action that reminded me of the many tender moments we shared.

My experience in the Air Force had provided many lessons, but nothing had struck me more powerfully than the realization that nothing and no one would ever fill the void in my heart—except for her. She was it for me—my everything. She always had been, and I knew in my core that she always would be. No matter where life took us, there would always be her, standing at the center of my world.

A flicker of light from the studio below caught my attention. Glancing down at my watch, I noted that it was only 3:50 in the morning. I took the stairs leading down. As I approached the deck below, I saw Michaelson looking up from the path that led away from the studio, his expression drained.

"Can't sleep?" I asked, breaking the silence that hung in the air. He shook his head, hands shoved deep into his pockets, his shoulders drooping slightly as if the weight of the world rested upon them.

"Not surprised you're up," he mumbled, his eyes darting uncertainly. The quiet stretch of night enveloped us as we contemplated our surroundings, and before long, Agent Carter emerged from the basement door, his demeanor suggesting he was equally exhausted.

"Are we allowed to walk?" Michaelson inquired, directing his question towards Agent Carter. He nodded in agreement, trailing behind us with an air of disinterest, his face drawn and fatigue evident.

"Natalie asleep?" I asked, trying to steer the conversation toward something lighter. Nothing productive would come of discussing work at these hours. Michaelson nodded, his expression shifting as if he was lost in thought. "Do you want to talk about what's going on with you two?"

He let out a low groan, dragging his palms down his face in frustration. "I'm so screwed. Seriously, how do you do this? How did you manage it all back then? I thought you were completely insane in school—always rushing back to the dorms and spending all your free time on the phone with her. God, I thought you were so whipped."

"And now?" I chuckled softly, feeling a surge of warmth as nostalgia washed over me. The wind chilled our faces, refreshing and invigorating us as we strolled along the quiet, dark beach. It felt familiar—Michaelson and I discussing girls, just like we always used to, navigating the complexities of love and life together once more.

"I get it," he groaned, again. "I like her man, and it's scary as shit. I don't know how it happened so fast. We were just hanging out, and she's fun, and caring, and there's just so much depth to her, unlike all the other girls I've dated and slept with. I haven't even slept with her and I feel like I want to just follow her around like a puppy dog. What happened to me?"

I didn't respond, instead, I let out a soft chuckle, kicking up a spray of sand as I continued my walk along the dark beach. The roar of the ocean was much louder down here, each wave crashing against the shore resonating in my chest. In the dim light of the moon, I could see the tide ebbing and flowing rhythmically.

"It's going to be okay," Michaelson finally said, breaking the heavy silence that had settled between us. We had walked for several minutes, lost in our thoughts, but now his voice cut through the chill in the air. "We'll figure it out together. You better not even think about stepping down. It's going to work out. You have the entire company behind you."

I swallowed hard, trying to push down the lump that had formed in my throat, and raked a hand through my hair in frustration. I desperately wanted to believe him—hell, I had been telling myself the same thing for weeks—but the fear weighed heavily on me. I missed my parents constantly, each day a reminder of their absence, but tonight, more than ever, I craved my father's guidance. I would have given anything to hear his commanding voice cutting through my doubts or to feel his strong arms wrap around me in a comforting embrace.

My father had always been open with his affection, and I considered myself fortunate to have known just how deeply he loved me. I found myself longing for the familiar earthy and spicy scent that was inseparable from his presence. It lingered in my memory as vividly as his infectious laughter. God what I wouldn't give to hear it once more.

My father would have known exactly what to say to calm my racing thoughts—what steps to take to ensure everything turned out alright. The fear of messing it all up haunted me, compounded by the terrifying thought of ending up in prison and losing the company they all had worked so hard to build. I had been in my position for less than a year and I was already messing up.

Eventually, after what felt like an eternity on the beach, Michaelson and I succumbed to the cold biting at our skin. We trudged back home, our breath escaping in misty puffs, and once safely indoors, we boiled a pot of coffee—a welcome warmth in our chilled hands. We poured a cup for Agent Carter, who had been waiting in the living room, and settled down to watch the sunrise.

As the first light of dawn broke over the horizon, the sky transformed, gradually shifting from a deep, somber gray to a muted blue. The soft hues painted the world anew, a symbol of hope amidst the uncertainty.

Tomorrow had arrived, and with it came the promise of a fresh start. It was time to get to work.

Acknowledgments

It's a late summer day, and I'm sitting in my office, having just submitted my last chapter. Throughout the house, my kids are arguing and making me laugh. They start school in a few days and are ready - they've said so themselves.

Getting here is an unbelievable time in my life. Never in a million years did I ever imagine writing a book. I didn't grow up loving books, and I especially knew nothing about writing them. Aside from my love of the Twilight Series and Harry Potter, I didn't read much. This book was born from a literal dream about Brooks and Emily. I woke up early one morning, before the rest of the house was awake, and just started writing. I didn't want to forget about them.

I had dreamed of a handsome man walking up the driveway to his long-lost love. They were clearly in love but hesitant about their feelings. I don't remember much else of the dream, and version one of me recounting it makes me laugh. Brooks and Emily were not named Brooks and Emily. They lived in Seattle, not Oregon, and the military wasn't the reason he was gone.

Still, those first ten chapters became the groundwork for this book. I shared it with some close friends, who encouraged me to look into publishing. I didn't know the first thing about it, but I knew someone who did. I called my Grandma right away and began asking questions. She has several published novels and has been writing most of her life. I owe a tremendous amount of gratitude to her. She answered all of my questions, telling me what steps I needed to take, and pushing me to look into a critique partner. She has been an invaluable source of encouragement and help.

I want to thank my critique partners who didn't hold back on an agonizing number of critiques. My book is so much better because of you all—especially Samantha Brown. Sam, thank you from the bottom of my heart for all your hard work and long hours spent helping bring my vision to life and helping it all make sense. As a first-time writer and author, my work was a disaster.

Thank you to other authors who encouraged me along the way. I'm looking at you especially, Tisa Matthews and Tricia. The authors in my small local writer's group, the ones who helped me learn about self-publishing, and the ladies in all the online writer's groups who, along the way, let me chew their ears off while working through scenes.

I owe a bunch of thanks to my friends and family who have been there, cheering me on, asking where I am at, and checking in every once in a while to make sure I was okay. I have learned so much along the way, and whew...writing a book isn't for the faint of heart. Erin + Blake, Paige, Miles - I see you!

I also want to thank my beta readers, Stephanie and Hope, for falling in love with my book and helping me gain the confidence I needed to keep going. Sending a book to Beta readers is scary. To have someone read it all the way through and give feedback—yikes! Stephanie, girl, you read it faster than I could get the chapters uploaded.

Asa, thank you for answering all of my T1d questions. I know a few may have made you uncomfortable, but you surprised me by going above and beyond to give me all the information I could possibly need about Natalie and her blooming relationship with Michaelson (hint, hint).

Daniel, my go-to for all Air Force, Special Ops, and random military questions! Your sarcastic answers were a delight, lol. But really, thank you for all your help.

William, thank you for being my on-demand lawyer and

answering all my questions about embezzlement, the FBI, legal proceedings, what this kind of scenario would look like, and how it would play out. I definitely could only have thrown in this plot twist with your help.

Thank you to Hollow Coves - Matt & Ryan, your team, Michael, and the girls at Secretly Group, who helped me get the rights to use your lyrics in my book. Hollow Coves' songs not only gave life to so much of this book, but they also helped me through my grief and some of the darkest moments of my life. Chapter sixty-four would not feel right without it!

Last but definitely not least, I want to thank my husband and my kids. This book is only possible because of them. For encouraging me in those early months when this was all for fun, then again when we lost our son at fifteen weeks pregnant. In the grief that followed. And again, when I decided to finish this book and let Emily's healing become my own. There were so many long days and late nights, many weekends where I holed up to write. On rainy days, they would either hand deliver me tea and let me disappear into my office or send me away to a coffee shop to write.

To my husband, thank you, my love, for all that you have done and continue to do to support all of my dreams and help make them a reality.

I also want to say a huge thank you to all of you who are reading this. I hope you have fallen in love with the Devonshires and Pacific Coves as much as I have. Book two is on the way. We'll get to see some fun destinations and drama and get all the answers to Brooks' and Caston's embezzlement in book two!